Photo: Andrew Barrett

Robin Dermond Horspool, F.R.S.A. comes from a literary and artistic Yorkshire family – his father, Maurice Horspool, businessman, dramatist and broadcaster; his grandfather Robert Horspool, artist, writer and poet.

Robin has lived and worked in Yorkshire, London, Sussex, and France.

As a practising artist, writer and lecturer, his previous publications, illustrated by him, include *The House Of Powolny – Life and Death of a Hull Restaurant; Boyle A Quart Of Cream –* 18th century country house life through food, and *Avenues Of Pleasure –* a nostalgic account of his formative years and their environment. Like Siegfried Sassoon, he is happy in his craving to revisit the past and give the modern world the slip.

Robin and his artist wife Rose live in a converted chapel in a Yorkshire Wolds village where they run their own arts business.

THE MOULD OF TIME

Robin Dermond Horspool

The Mould Of Time

*To Fiona
with all good wishes*

Robin Dermond Horspool

AUSTIN & MACAULEY

Rochester 10 · VI · 12.

Copyright © R o b i n   D e r m o n d   H o r s p o o l

The right of Robin Dermond Horspool to be identified as author of this work has been asserted by him in accordance with section 77 and 78 of the Copyright, Designs and Patents Act 1988.

All rights reserved. No part of this publication may be reproduced, stored in a retrieval system, or transmitted in any form or by any means, electronic, mechanical, photocopying, recording, or otherwise, without the prior permission of the publishers.

Any person who commits any unauthorized act in relation to this publication may be liable to criminal prosecution and civil claims for damages.

All characters in this publication are fictitious and any resemblance to real persons, living or dead, is purely coincidental.

A CIP catalogue record for this title is
available from the British Library.

ISBN 978 1 84963 035 1

www.austinmacauley.com

First Published (2011)
Austin & Macauley Publishers Ltd.
25 Canada Square
Canary Wharf
London
E14 5LB

Printed & Bound in Great Britain

DEDICATION

To the memory of
Madeleine and Maurice, my parents,
to whose loving encouragement and support
I shall always be indebted.

ACKNOWLEDGEMENTS

My thanks are due to Mr Charles Dickens for first firing my literary enthusiasm while I was still at school and kick-starting my love of imagination, language and story-telling.

Grateful thanks also go to Annette, Kim and Kat and their team at Austin & Macauley Ltd, for the consideration and patience they have brought to the publication process.

Lastly, but by no means least, it is a joy to share my endeavours and projects with my wife Rose; she, as ever, is an invaluable support throughout all creative and emotional stages; it has been a particular pleasure to have *The Mould of Time* enhanced by her cover design.

Contents

Editor's Note 15

Principal Characters 19

Uncle Louis's Prologue – 1882 23

Expectations of a Great Lady 60

Tableau I 60
II 78
III 105
IV 161

Entr'acte 186

Tableau V 191
VI 233
VII 249
VIII 275
IX 333
X 356

Uncle Louis's Postscript –1882 370

EDITOR'S NOTE

Back in the mould of time, a branch of my mother's sprawling Greek ancestors settled in France where the name became localised as du Monde. From there, the Hugenot persuasion came to Spitalfields, London, in the reign of James II and continued to expand, the name becoming anglicised to Dermond during the reign of William IV.

The journalist Louis Xavier Dermond, my Victorian Great-great Uncle, has been remembered in the family chiefly for his connection with the popular novelist Charles Dickens; but also attached to him was the intriguing belief of an infatuation with an influential older woman. This naturally endeared him to me as, from an early age, I have always been one to appreciate the more unorthodox aspects of human nature which probably says a good deal about me. On his death in August, 1883, Great-great Uncle Louis's box of literary effects was inherited by his eldest nephew living in Australia. What then happened to it has not been ascertained, but sometime after 1904, the box was deposited in the vaults of the London bank Coutts and Co. in the Strand, remaining hidden until coming to light during extensive alterations and rebuilding in the 1970s. The recent death of a distant cousin who claimed it at the time caused the box to become mine.

How thankful I was that Uncle Louis's papers had survived, passing through the hands of time to me, striking a chord in my appreciation of his experiences and achievements. Amongst them were a few letters, not in his hand, and a number of sinister drawings of a woman in a white dress burning to death; also some of Queen Marie Antoinette of France being guillotined in 1793.

A red folder caught my interest – a prologue and postscript encasing a saga of love, passion and heartbreak, mystery and deception, hatred and murder; the downright bizarre too, but the whole tempered with a sympathy for every aspect of the human condition. It also confirmed that Uncle Louis's infatuation had been true.

It has been my pleasure to edit this work and present it in contemporary terms whilst keen to preserve that flavour of individuality and period which marks Louis's style – a testament to the order and chaos of life which I have entitled *THE MOULD OF TIME*.

Robin Dermond Horspool
England and France
2007

Principal Characters

PROLOGUE

Louis Xavier Dermond	Victorian journalist
Charles Xavier	Louis's father
Adelaide	Louis's mother
Charles and Henri	Louis's brothers
Miss Primlie	Louis's governess
Mrs Estella Eldon	wealthy charitable widow
Charles Dickens	popular novelist

FRANCE

Emil du Monde	doctor practicing in Versailles
Amelia	his wife, *nee* Pocket. Estelle's aunt
Amelia, Emil-Louis, Antoine	their children
Dr Philippe Curtius	founder of the Wax Museum, Paris
Marie Grosholtz	his niece and adopted daughter
Madame Grosholtz	Marie's mother
Louis XVI	King of France
Marie Antoinette	Queen of France
Madame Royale	their daughter
Louis-Charles	their son, later *Dauphin*
Madame Elisabeth	the King's sister

ENGLAND – KENT

Mrs Comfrey	housekeeper at Satis House
Mr Comfrey	brewery manager at Satis
Mr Brand	brewery under-manager
Mrs Hall	later housekeeper at Satis
Augustus Havisham	wealthy brewer of Satis House

Estelle	his daughter
Arthur	his son, Estelle's half-brother
Hugh	groom at Satis House
Dr Sawley	Havisham family Physician
Zilla	Estelle's personal maid

ENGLAND – LONDON

George Compeyson	Magistrate of Rookwell Park
Victoire	his wife, *nee* de Bayonne
Alexander	their son
Adolphus Fawn	Alexander's school friend
Jaggers and Son	lawyers of Little Britain
Septimus Sharps	lawyer of Holborn
Abel Magwitch	rough villain
The Cap'n	landlord of The Bargee Joe
Peg-leg Jem and Old Croak	cardsharps at The Bargee Joe
Daniel Pocket	historian. Estelle's uncle by marriage
Caroline	his wife, Estelle's aunt
Sarah, Matthew, Camilla	their children

ENGLAND – BRENTFORD

Mr Gravely	local physician
Sally	lives a tTudor Cottage
Mrs Wormold	housekeeper at Tudor Cotage

POSTSCRIPT

Etienne du Monde	Louis Xavier's uncle, his father's elder brother

LOUIS XAVIER'S PROLOGUE

The LONDON PICTORIAL INTELLIGENCER
Est. 1830

January 31st 1882

'FRIEND OF POOR' BURNS TO DEATH

Our subscribers will be grieved to learn, through these columns, of the tragic demise of Mrs Estella Eldon, for many of her seventy-four years patroness of several Charitable and Philanthropic concerns. Her worthy efforts on behalf of the poor and underprivileged of our Metropolis, Lambeth in particular, will sorely be missed.

As a young heiress, Mrs Eldon, the only adopted daughter of the wealthy but eccentric Miss Estelle Havisham, late of Satis House, Kent, whose death in fiery circumstances we chronicled in the first edition of this publication 52 years ago, was frequently to be seen in London's fashionable circles, where her many suitors hoped to claim her hand.

Mrs Eldon's first union was with Bentley Drummle, Esq., of Somersetshire, and after his death consequent upon a riding accident, she married Edward Eldon, a doctor with a modest practice in Shropshire. Their union was cut cruelly short by a mortal disease contracted from one of his patients.

Her subsequent return to the diversions of her London circle was both agreeable and necessary. Then began the Charity work for which Mr Eldon became justly renowned and loved…

Loved. Yes indeed; I can vouch for that from my heart. I find it hard to believe that the object of my love is no longer sharing this earth with me – that she has slipped the bonds of earthly time and left me to slip mine alone, which I am surely doing. I doubt I shall see my forty-fifth birthday. But before my time runs out I must continue trying to come to terms with this report in front of me.

Our publication has been proud, on many occasions, to put before its faithful public accounts of her many occupations, not to mention writings on social matters. It is therefore with increased pain for it to relate the circumstances of her expiration, particularly as it occurred just prior to Christmas last – that most robust and charitable season.

The foul perpetrator was a German Tree erected for the delight of 155 widows and orphans at a Yuletide Refection in the New Cut Bethel, Lambeth. From amongst the green boughs, sparkling decorations and lighted wax tapers, Mrs Eldon's generous hand was engaged upon untying one of the many pretty gifts. The spectre of her mother-by-adoption must have loomed in many minds as the fatal flame caught the befrilled wrist and flared the length of Mrs Eldon's arm to engulf her shoulders and head.

Amidst outbursts of screaming, the hapless woman was extinguished by swift action and an assortment of fabrics. A doctor was quickly in attendance but pronounced her dead immediately, her heart unable to sustain so severe a shock. Readers of these pages may well remember the demise of her mother-by-adoption, Miss Havisham, who also burned to death after a red hot ember fell from the grate into the folds of her dress as she sat at her own fireside.

We can do little but stand aghast. It seems a double pain that neither of Mrs Eldon's unions was blessed with children to whom we may convey our heartfelt condolences. To the members of her many Associations and Organisations therefore – not least the tenants of her properties in both London and Kent – we extend the certainty that through our columns, hearts will be united in tribute to the fount of much goodness so frightfully taken from us...

I cannot continue reading. Time is a bringer of companions – a taker-away also. The only companion time has left me now is death. With Mrs Eldon's passing, nothing stands between him and me. He and I, Louis Xavier Dermond of Kensington, are hourly becoming closer acquainted. He already passes me hand to hand along the lonely road of no return. As spring hangs out her perfumes along our mortal way, the heavy vapours of silence begin to thread my nostrils and the mould of time grows dankly across my reputation.

But before the closure of all that I am, let me pass back along the bridge of time just once again – to my first realisation that a certain Mrs Eldon had significance in our family. She had inherited from Miss Havisham, her mother-by-adoption, the crumbling brick Manor House in Kent called Satis, where her girlhood had been spent. After years of neglect it was in a bad way and Mrs Eldon decided to demolish it in order to develop the land. In 1845 – on my fifth birthday actually – my father took on the tenancy of one of the newly completed villas built on the site. Our family being its first inhabitants meant there were a number of problems to cope with. A lengthy spate of communications with Mrs Eldon ensued regarding repairs, maintenance and finance. From what I heard my father say I formed the opinion, concurrent with learning a poem by Shelley and discovering a folio containing engravings of an antique land, that Mrs Eldon was a statuesque edifice about as endearing as the sand-locked Ozymandias himself, King of Kings. I was not sure, however, that *I* wanted to look on her works and despair.

Look on her I eventually did, though – one day when I was nearly 11. She had expressed, so I was told, a desire to meet me on the strength of my talent for story-writing, a hobby of mine. It was with some apprehension, therefore, that I accompanied my father up to London, dressed in my best and most uncomfortable outfit. The house to which I was conducted might have been Ozymandias's Palace, so smitten was it with architecture: of stone balls ponderously balanced on thin necks, pilasters supporting nothing, balustrades protecting nothing. Compared with the flashing uncluttered glory of The Crystal Palace across the way, her dwelling appealed to me as much as the schoolroom back at our villa after the bother of Miss Primlie's efforts. The Great Exhibition, to which my father had taken me that morning, had been much more my idea of pleasure. Even as we stood on Mrs Eldon's steps, Papa tugging at the important bell-pull, I longed to mingle again with the summer crowds in the park and explore the stalls fizzing with ginger beer, piled hairily with coconuts, over-burdened with pyramids of oranges… listen to flower-sellers and bird-catchers hawking their wares… disentangle cries of 'twopence a-pound grapes!' from 'Yarmouth bloaters – three a penny…!'

Silence. The maid shut the door firmly behind us. The stairs up which we were led us seemed to rise for ever – I thought what it must be like to ascend the scaffold. I know now that Mrs Eldon would have been in her mid-forties but she looked younger, there being neither line nor wrinkle to confuse her pale, grave beauty – a beauty I did not think it possible for a human to possess. But there was a detached intensity about it which further held my attention; for young as I was, it occurred to me how sad her eyes were – almost empty. None of life's fervour lustred there. Her manner appeared as chilly and stiff as her black jet jewellery cut in a thousand facets, their polish scintillating sharply about her like constellations of cold stars as she rustled towards us in heavy dusk-blue silk, her full skirts seeming to encase her as a shroud-like bee hive. I was overawed; and whether my Ozymandias addressed any words to me I would be hard-pressed to say for certain.

I do remember the maid bringing in a tray of red, blue and gold tea things. And cake. A glass of milk for me also. I thought how well Mrs Eldon's face and the whiteness of the liquid complimented one another. I was content to apply my lips to the creamy surface whilst observing her over the rim of my glass – large and decorated, on a stem. Her air of remoteness fascinated me – I have no idea even now as to what she and my father discussed. It obviously bore no relevance to me and my story-writing was not mentioned once. However, I felt a certain security in being part of their time together whilst remaining apart from their direct concern. The impact of this first encounter has never dimmed; nor has it lost the sense of occasion I felt from the moment I entered her profound presence. I have never forgotten how I would have liked to say or do something to cheer her – to make her laugh even. I sensed she never laughed but wished that I, Louis Xavier, could have been the one to break the spell.

It was in somewhat more dramatic circumstances that our second meeting took place the following year. You could almost say I 'dropped in' on Mrs Eldon.

Satis House, the original Elizabethan property, including a good-sized brew-house, had itself been developed on much earlier foundations, some of which were believed to be Roman. But I don't think even my father, pessimistic as he was about much in life, quite expected an earthquake suddenly to open up our wash-house floor in the March of 1852. Down went a fair portion of the domestic quarters, part of the villa's side wall, section of garden with summerhouse and my pet geese Albert and Victoria. I clambered into the crevasse and dug about for their poor flattened bodies until my father laid down the law.

This was not, however, before I had taken the chance of observing that the collapse had occurred into a sort of brick vault – damp, dirty and well below garden level. Papa said that judging by the strata layers at the brink, extra earth had been brought in to make up levels. This, and not an earthquake, was responsible for the catastrophe. A palisade was built round the pit and the villa's side wall shorn up with baulks of timber which to my mind must have come from some earthless man o'war.

My father, convinced that the rest of the property was poised to disappear at any moment made hasty arrangements for the family and servants to evacuate. The modest country house near Tunbridge Wells recently purchased was still undergoing renovation so I was hustled with my two brothers and Miss Primlie (if only she and the schoolroom had gone down!) to the purlieus of Connaught Square near Hyde Park, my paternal grandparents being conveniently in France visiting relations.

Mrs Eldon arrived suddenly one evening – an unexpected procedure as I knew Papa was in the habit of calling on her, and in the afternoon too. Her appearance was the culmination of an altogether tantalising period for me – I had become increasingly aware of an undercurrent of excitement which the family tried to suppress when ever I was at large. My brothers, always revelling in their seniority, had doubtless sworn the parental oath of secrecy for they, too, were at pains to keep me in ignorance.

I had been put to bed in one of the top rooms at the front of the house when I heard a vehicle draw up in the Square outside. I hurried to the window and recognised Mrs Eldon as she alighted, in a red dress on this occasion, from one of the little pony carriages she herself liked to drive. I hastened to the staircase and peered down the shaft of landings and banisters as she was ushered across the black and white tiled hallway into the library.

Fascination goaded my desperation. On the garden side of the library projected a new conservatory – what to my mind was my grandparents' own miniature Crystal Palace. The roof looked approachable by the latticework of creepers locked against the wall. In spite of the chilly air I clambered in my nightshirt out of the lower landing window onto the ribs of the conservatory roof where I observed that the glass doors were closed onto the little garden. Like a cat with not many lives left I crouched on the lead flashing where the frame joined the wall, frustrated by the poor level of conversational volume and lack of clear sight through the jungle of tubs and greenery. Suddenly my brothers appeared through the back gateway to the mews lane carrying between them a wooden container – circular like a bandbox bound with metal straps. Charles and Henri were too intent, thank goodness, on conveying their load safely to think of raising their eyes. Further intrigued as the bandbox was taken into the library, I over-reached my luck, for as I secured myself more firmly to the creepers with one hand, at the same time trying to lean out more over the glass for a better view, my feet slipped on the flashing. With creepers popping off the wall, I lumbered onto the panes like a blind man on ice, my enthusiasm for silence breaking as did the glass; a gratifying yell accompanied my descent amidst a tinkling shower onto the tubbed and potted unfortunates beneath. It took me no time to realise I was not dead and to thrust my head out of the flattened chaos. I was not prepared for what I saw: a half-circle of perplexion, crimson-clad Mrs Eldon in the centre, the bandbox open before her. In her hands – a human head.

I think I yelled a second time. I may even have settled again into the long-suffering vegetation. I was numbly aware of being carried in strong arms upstairs and of waking from fighting the vision I retained of the impassive head severed at the neck, eyes open but glassy – staring – a full display of hair nicely arranged in an old fashioned style under a circlet of faded flowers. Somehow I confused this ghostly image with a blood-soaked Mrs Eldon, so that when she came to see me once I was safe in bed, my cuts and bruises dealt with, I froze against my will into the white sheets. I do not remember her words, but they were kindly meant I know, though all I wished for was a bath of milk in which to submerge until she was gone. Which did I fear the most – the face of death, her face of life or my father's living wrath?

I had hoped that given time he might forget what I had done. Perhaps he could be persuaded I had been sleep-walking. Despite my eventual beating, I like to believe that my family were really rather relieved I had not been killed; and once I recovered I expected my curiosity concerning the head to be satisfied, if only as a reward for not dying. But when it became obvious this was not to be, I decided it was up to me to take the initiative. By the time I had turned my grandparents' house up-side-down I concluded that Mrs Eldon must have taken the bandbox with her and decided I was not prepared to have suffered all my recent indignities to no avail.

I walked briskly round to the re-sited and rebuilt Marble Arch, crossed Hyde Park, the site of the dismantled Crystal Palace near Rotten Row, and so to the architectural house I easily recognised beyond. The maid's surprised look amused me but resolutely I made my request to see Mrs Eldon. It was only while she went on her errand that I considered my lack of preparation, my unsuitable appearance, grubby hands – and fingers beautifully tipped with black-crescented nails. The maid returned to conduct me once more up into that deep-piled hush. Today there was a gentleman in the drawing room also. He stood by the window eyeing me with what seemed amused interest. I would have said he was about my Papa's age, with a noble forehead and luxuriant brown hair beginning to turn a wiry grey. But it was to his eyes that mine were instantly attracted. What eyes they were! They fairly *beamed* – were almost liquid with a kind of joyous gusto likely to overflow at any moment. What eyes – what a face – to behold on entering a room! Compared with Mrs Eldon's marble perfection his features positively ran with keenness and good cheer; his smile, like the lighting up of a beacon, clean knocked all I wanted to say from my mind.

'Ah, Master Louis,' said Mrs Eldon, holding out her polished hand to me, 'how very good to see you again and none the worse for wear. You have some communication from your father?'

'Er – no, ma'am,' I stammered, as I felt the effect of Mrs Eldon's beauty once again work upon me. 'I wanted to see you on my own...' My spluttering voice guttered like an empty lamp. The gentleman by the window stepped towards me with spirit and placed a hand on my shoulder.

'Perhaps his crashing descent from the higher regions has severed his vocal chords?' I looked at him in puzzlement as he raised his arm skywards. How much did he know of my *faux-pas?* 'Mrs Eldon has told me about your coming down with a bang. She knows how I relish a good story. I hope you didn't damage the plants too much. They would, I'm sure, prefer the gentle rain from heaven.' Completely at a loss I stared at him. 'I have a boy about your age,' he continued, going from me. 'Always up to mischief is Walter. I have other boys at home just like him – *so* many boys – the house is *alive* with boys. There are some girls too, I believe – I must ask their mother.'

Mrs Eldon kindly rescued me from my inarticulate dilemma. 'Mr Dickens is a busy man and feels the burden of his children acutely. You are no burden to your parents I trust, Master Louis?' I well understood that she also referred to the burden I had recently been on various panes of glass.

'I try not to be, Mrs Eldon,' I replied as honestly as I knew how.

'Of course you do,' said Mr Dickens. 'They all do. At least, that's what they all *say* they do, which to them is the same thing.' He sat in an armchair (or perhaps it would be truer to say he arranged himself in its padded comfort) – I found it difficult not to become caught up in his vivacity and verve.

'May I ask,' said Mrs Eldon, 'the reason for your visit? Is there something I can do for you?'

Thus invited, and encouraged by Mr Dickens's dominating good will, I took a deep breath to support my returning courage. 'I hope you won't think me impertinent, ma'am, but the other night when…'

'When you fell from grace?' suggested Mr Dickens.

'When I – yes… well, I couldn't help noticing you had somebody else's head. Cut off. With hair on. At the neck. I just wondered whose it was, that's all. And where it came from. And why you've got it and if I could have a look, please?' Mr Dickens, exchanging glances with Mrs Eldon, threw back his head to emit a deep mahogany laugh. Mrs Eldon almost smiled and dabbed her nose with a lace handkerchief.

'What an inquiring young fellow,' said Mr Dickens, wiping tears from his eyes. 'Enterprising too, wouldn't you say, ma'am? I could do with him on my magazine.'

'You are very sweet, Louis,' said Mrs Eldon, her beauty enhanced by her kind words. 'Yes, I can appreciate how intriguing the head must have looked from where you were. I am going to ask Mr Dickens if he would be so kind as to show it to you. He finds it rather more fascinating than I – the drama of it appeals to his theatrical nature, does it not Charles?'

A nagging notion of having seen this gentleman's features reproduced somewhere crystallised into the realisation that I was in the presence of none other than the genie who had bewitched me through a convalescence a while back with the delights of Mr Micawber, Mr Dick and David Copperfield, all firm friends of mine by now. I simply gaped in speechless admiration as Mr Dickens moved to the door like any ordinary man.

'My father says you are very clever, sir,' I said by way of compliment. 'He's read all your work. He says you certainly know what you're talking about.'

'I am much obliged,' said the author with a courteous little bow, opening the door. 'I have been accused of many things in my time but I shall value your Papa's opinion the most. I understand *you* like writing stories? If you care to accompany me I'll show you something which would make a good story.'

I think in that moment I would have accompanied to the edge of the world and beyond the creator of David Copperfield. He took my hand in his – firm and friendly – led me at a good pace along the landing, down the stairs and to a door at the far end of the hall. It opened into a sort of study, smaller than my father's, but immaculately ordered and neat, like Mrs Eldon herself. The desk was prettier than Papa's but just as crowded with candles, busts, ornaments and *objets d'art*. I immediately recognised the bandbox beside it; with excitement I watched Mr Dickens lift it onto a chair, raise the lid… take out the head. It did not horrify me as on first viewing. There was no blood; the skin colour was not drained and lifeless though it had more shine than usual. The face, though young and lovely, had a hard look about the features – the mouth formed a firm-set line across a strong jaw not dissimilar to Mrs Eldon's. Perhaps it was she when young. The fair hair, dressed carefully beneath the flowers and in a fine manner, was not of the modern fashion, being higher arranged with curls down the back of the neck.

'Who is she?' I asked. 'Is she dead? Where's the rest of her?'

'Woa, old boy!' steadied Mr Dickens as if I were a carthorse. 'One thing at a time. Now then. She is Mrs Eldon's mother-by-adoption, aged about fifteen. No, I don't know where the rest of her is – if there *is* a rest of her. No, she isn't dead because she has never been alive. In short, as Mr Micawber would say, this is a portrait model in wax. Miss Havisham, who adopted Mrs Eldon when she was a very small child, died about twenty years ago; but this piece of artistry was created long before that – before even *I* was born, and that's saying something.'

He could see, I think, that I was disappointed not to be staring actual death in the face after all my efforts. He smiled again, his whole countenance radiating fatherly benevolence and humour. 'An interesting creation, don't you think, Master Louis?'

'But what has it to do with my family?' I said. 'There seems to be some kind of mystery which nobody will tell me. I don't think that's fair.'

'Mysteries are exciting, aren't they? Wherever there are people there are mysteries. That's what makes people so fascinating. The facts are simple: this model was discovered in a vault beneath the villa your father rents from Mrs Eldon. Satis House, her old home with Miss Havisham, used to stand on the site so the head is legally her property. But where that mystery ends the next one begins: how did the head come to *be* in the vault, who made it and why? Are you still interested in mysteries?'

'It's incredible,' I said, spellbound. 'What a story it would make. Why don't you write it?'

'Do you know, Louis,' said Mr Dickens, 'that isn't a bad idea. I might just do that one day. I'm always on the lookout for good stories to tell. As a fellow writer I'm sure *you'll* find that's the case too.'

'Are you writing a story now, sir,' I asked boldly. Mr Dickens, treating me as an equal, made me feel glad to be alive.

'There is a little something on the go at present,' he said modestly, 'though I fear you'll find it somewhat heavier than David Copperfield's history. You'll have to wait until you're a trifle older in order to enjoy it, if enjoy is the right word – I'm afraid it's no fun at all – distinctly *bleak* in fact.'

Mrs Eldon entered with a letter which she handed to me. 'I have written to your father informing him that it was perfectly in order for you to visit me and for Mr Dickens and me to answer your questions.'

I thanked her, realising that I was expected to depart. It seemed that though I was too old to warrant a glass of milk I did not yet qualify for a cup of tea.

'I would suggest,' said Mr Dickens, coming into the hall with me, his hand back on my shoulder, 'that in future you do not creep about on roofs – you might have a nasty accident. The *bold* approach such as you have displayed today is better by far, take my word for it. May one inquire... what is your ambition when you're quite grown up?'

'I should like to write stories like *David Copperfield*,' I said, having given the prospect no thought whatsoever.

'I need people like you on *Household Words*,' said Mr Dickens. 'That is a weekly journal I conduct. We shall have to see what we can do in a few years' time. Meanwhile, keep writing and good luck, my boy.' He shook my hand cordially and I looked my last for that day on my new hero.

After running back to Connaught Square elated by my achievement, I was not prepared for my father's anger once I had delivered Mrs Eldon's letter. Commanded to follow him forthwith to the library, the scene of my former disgrace, I shifted uncomfortably on the red Turkey carpet.

'Do I understand by this letter,' he began in the measured tones I hated, 'that you actually took it upon yourself to call *unannounced* on Mrs Eldon – and in your present uncouth state?'

'Yes, Papa,' I murmured meekly, hiding my grubby hands behind my back. 'She was very nice to me.'

'Of course she was very nice! Mrs Eldon is a lady. That is why I feel disgraced by your behaviour. What do you think her opinion of our family is likely to be now? – that I should permit you to visit her in such a way and you looking no better than a common crossing-sweeper? We have a position in society, Louis, and you must learn how to behave in it. This is a sad reflection on the family name and I am exceedingly vexed. How *dare* you interfere in business that doesn't concern you. You have let this family down in front of one of the most excellent men of our time – a father with children of his own. I am ashamed of you.'

I wanted to explain to Papa that I was sure Mr Dickens had not viewed my visit so tragically, but I dared not interrupt the tirade from the other side of the desk.

'You obviously do not appreciate the enormity of your actions. You have the effrontery to ingratiate yourself on the time and generosity of these busy people...'

'Please, Papa,' I ventured, 'I'm very sorry if I've displeased you but I'm sure things aren't as bad as you think.'

'Oh, you are *sure*, are you? You are a better judge of the situation than I? It is a situation in which I should have been consulted first. On no account would I have allowed you to act so impulsively, particularly after what happened the other evening. I have no alternative but to beat you, then you will retire to bed.'

Like a martyr I allowed myself to undergo the indignity of bending over the desk, my hands on the sides, and receiving four humourless bombardments on my bare vulnerability. No amount of aggression, though, could beat out the undoubted success of my expedition nor pale the significance of having Mr Dickens for a friend.

Later, as I tried to hide my shame under the bedclothes, I felt a pressure on the bed as someone sat beside me. On emerging I saw it was Mama. My mind was still so full of Mrs Eldon that I found myself involuntarily comparing her sad beauty with the comfortable sweetness of my mother's.

'Louis, dear,' she said softly, pushing back the hair from my forehead. 'You are a big boy now to be beaten. Your Papa is as hurt as you.'

'I know I should have asked him first,' I said, subdued by contrition, 'but he would have said no and I *had* to find out about the head. If I hadn't already met Mrs Eldon I wouldn't have gone – I promise Mama.'

'I understand, my dear, and so does Papa, but he needed to reprimand you because you didn't ask his permission first. If this business had concerned you he would have informed you of it himself. Now, don't tell him I said so but he secretly admires your pluck.'

'I like Mr Dickens, Mama,' I announced. 'He's so warm and kind. Mrs Eldon is kind but she seems cold.'

'You should not say that, Louis,' said Mama, smoothing the counterpane. 'It is not for you to criticise. Mrs Eldon has not enjoyed a particularly happy life.'

'I'm not criticising,' I said. 'I'm just telling you what I think. Mr Dickens is famous, isn't he Mama?'

'Because he's a good and clever man. Your father has an extremely high regard for him. He does much work on behalf of the poor and uneducated, particularly children. Have you heard of Lord Ashley and Miss Coutts? They are all concerned with improvement and charity. Mr Dickens is at present working on behalf of impoverished writers and journalists by raising money through The Guild of Literature and Art. His books have done much to help society – point out its failings. His Journal…'

'*Household Words,*' I put in knowledgeably. 'He said he could do with me when I'm older. Can I go and work for Mr Dickens?'

'*Household Words* has a good reputation and is very popular,' said Mama with a laugh. 'I expect Mr Dickens was only trying to be nice to you. You'll be going to school soon – Miss Primlie has done all she can. After that will be the time to think about a profession. And now is the time for sleep. Papa will call on Mrs Eldon and put everything to rights. Good night, Louis darling.'

I was not aware that anything *needed* putting to rights. To my mind, Papa had enlarged the issue out of all proportion. It was hard sometimes being the youngest of the family.

A few days later I was summoned again to the library. I took hope from an aura of humanity that even my father, seated behind the desk, could not hide.

'You will be pleased to know that I have rectified matters with Mrs Eldon and cleared any misunderstanding. I think she appreciated my point of view. Understand that in future you will see her only if she or I choose, and until you are of age, accompanied by me. Is that clear?'

'Yes, Papa,' I answered meekly.

'I may say now that I admire the spirit in you that prompted you to act as you did – also the way you accepted punishment like a man. Mrs Eldon is of the same opinion and will therefore be pleased to receive you in the future. She also told me how impressed Mr Dickens was. You obviously remembered how to conduct yourself, despite your excitement. That I find particularly gratifying. It is a sign that you're growing up.'

There was no reply I could make as I was of the same opinion. Just as I thought I was due for release my father started again.

'There is another matter, Louis. Two years ago the inimitable Mr Dickens inaugurated an excellent journal called *Household Words* – here is the latest number. What you probably don't know is that it is fast becoming a training ground for aspiring young writers – many careers are being forged under his patronage. It seems he gave you to understand that there might be possibilities for you, based on his assessment of your aptitude. Mrs Eldon assured me that his was no empty statement. She suggested that if you wish to be considered in the future you continue to write your stories and improve your abilities. I may say that I should be extremely proud if any sons of mine entered the employment of Mr Dickens. So, in view of the satisfactory way this business has terminated, I am prepared to overlook what Mrs Eldon refers to as your *fall from grace*. But, Louis, consult me next time you want to be a hero.'

'You don't mind me writing stories, Papa?'

'Why should I, as long as you don't anger Miss Primlie by neglecting your education?'

'And you want me to improve?'

'Naturally. But why this inquisition?'

'Then will you tell me the story of Mrs Eldon's head, Papa? Did you know Miss... Amersham?'

'Havisham. No, Louis, I did not. I can see you're going to give me no peace until I tell you. The fact is, I'm afraid I can't, for a number of reasons, the first being that I don't know the story – not fully. And even if I did I could not divulge it without Mrs Eldon's consent – she might not want it known. Why not invent something – employ that fertile imagination of yours? Here, take *Household Words* and look through it... and this booklet too – it's the Inimitable Mr Dickens's new story.'

I thanked Papa and carried them away to see what 'little something' my idol had put his pen to – what poor misunderstood scrap of youth was again suffering under a harsh society? *Bleak House.* What sort of title was that? What did In Chancery mean? What was the Michaelmas Term and who was the Lord Chancellor? And what in the world did a forty-foot Megalosaurus look like? Through this fog of vocabulary I groped my way to the next paragraph. *Fog everywhere,* it began. Yes, I know, I told myself before I gave up the fog completely. It seemed to underline for me an all-pervading obscurity, not least concerning the waxen head, the vault beneath the villa and how they both came to be there.

* * *

As the year progressed, I prepared to follow my brothers to school. Though I continued to think about Mrs Eldon and Mr Dickens often, I did not see them again nor did my father make further reference to the prevailing mysteries. *Bleak House* turned out to be another mystery to me – one I abandoned trying to unravel each month, in spite of Miss Primlie's verbose attempts to help (and probably because of them). At least I learned what a Megalosaurus was, knowledge which I was sure would be of profound benefit to my future prospects.

We did not return to our rented villa before I departed for school. Though it had been repaired and the void made good, my father decided that our country house was now habitable enough so arranged for us to move there. He then secured from Mrs Eldon the lease on a property at Devonshire Terrace, Regent's Park – a terraced house next-door-but-one to that vacated the previous year by Mr Dickens in favour of Tavistock Square. It would have seemed an auspicious omen for our family and his to have been such close neighbours.

My scholastic progress was not one of academic fireworks. My abiding interest continued to be writing, an occupation I pursued at every available opportunity. I took my father's advice and invented a fantasy around the waxen head – pretty desperate stuff – which kept me awake for nights; some mawkish nonsense about a beautiful princess, closely resembling Mrs Eldon, locked up in a tower and how her wicked stepfather cut off her head to give as a memento to the handsome young knight busily hacking his way through the undergrowth. My work impressed me but not the classics master who confiscated it one morning as I refined it in preference to interminable declensions.

Early in 1857, the question of my future employment became my active concern. I wished to do something constructive with my life, unlike Papa who had a more accepting attitude to inherited wealth. I had not deflected from my desire to take up a literary career; nor had I forgotten for one moment the remark Mr Dickens had made to me in Mrs Eldon's drawing room about needing good people on his journal. Almost for that reason I had kept writing and to try and earn my living by it seemed the logical continuation. *Household Words* was now a household name, with a high standard of work appearing in its pages. I was only too aware of the quality required and endeavoured to improve mine accordingly. My father could do nothing but concede to my wishes, agreeing to obtain Mr Dickens's opinion by showing him the best of my output.

The Inimitable wrote to me saying that much of the work he was looking for tended to be of a freelance nature, which at this early stage would not provide me with a regular or adequate income; but would I be good enough to call at his offices on such and such a day at four o'clock? With trepidation and a tremendous amount of hope, Papa and I made our way to 16, Wellington Street, off the Strand, and the shambolic desk of the editor's cramped surroundings.

I was disturbed to find how five years had not treated Mr Dickens with respect. His hair, greying considerably, was scantier about his noble brow. But nothing could dim those eyes nor that face's sunny animation – not the lines beginning to fold into it nor the tufty moustache and whimsical beard he had encouraged for his amateur theatricals. My father was of the opinion he worked too hard. I learned afterwards that he had made a special effort to see me that month amongst a busy schedule of private acting projects, attending to matters concerning his recent purchase of a Georgian house and 120 acres of land at Gad's Hill in Kent, entertaining Hans Andersen there, dealing with *Household Words* matters and concluding his latest *magnum opus, Little Dorrit.*

He received me cordially with all his old gusto and interest. He had obviously considered my literary efforts carefully; also the practicalities of my future wish for more than simply casual employment. With Papa to oversee my interests, the outcome of our discussions was the suggestion that I replace a member who was leaving the magazine's small staff. The work would be of a general nature but with a first hand opportunity to learn the trade and be able also to contribute matter of my own, as well as dealing with the matter of others – under Mr Dickens's guidance. No one even breathed, it seemed, without Mr Dickens's guidance.

Once I had put my good fortune into its proper perspective and restrained myself from rushing up to the ball and cross on St Paul's to proclaim it to the shires, I set my mind to what now seemed the most important undertaking for the immediate future; establishing my literary worth in the form of a stalwart slice of serious prose. With examples in black and white crowding more and more household words onto the pages before me – Mrs Gaskell, Bulwer Lytton, Wilkie Collins, not to mention The Inimitable Himself – I felt I owed it to my talent and energy to join ranks as a willing sufferer from writers' cramp. I wanted to suffer as a slave to my art. I wanted to use again the idea of the waxen head and forget, as well as disown, the wretched princess in her bloody tower.

Whilst I was contemplating how best to rework the material into a more acceptable (and Dickensian) form, I received a letter addressed to me in an unknown hand. Imagine my surprise when it disclosed its contents signed by Mrs Eldon. Surprise is perhaps too mild a description – panic would be nearer the truth; for the impression she had made on me over five years previously had remained unaffected by the mould of time. I must admit to a quickening of my senses – a numbing at my knees – as I read that she requested me to call upon her the following Thursday afternoon at three o'clock precisely. My second solo visit. Oh dear – the world was expanding before me too rapidly. How ever would I be able to face her again without the bravado of extreme youth to protect me?

With a much groomed appearance worthy of my seventeen years and a pocket full of self-doubt, I arrived once more on her threshold, pondering on the mystery of why I should be there. My hand fairly shook on the bell-pull; my brain swirled with half-formed phrases and disintegrating remnants of everything I had ever known as her drawing room door swished closed behind me whilst her French clock chimed the hour. She greeted me pleasantly and bade me be seated. It was from across no swathe of milk but the gold rim of her red and blue Derby teacup at last that I found myself viewing her once more – and her attention was solely on *me*. The intervening years had placed on her features neither stain nor blemish. To my awakened appreciation she appeared to me even more beautiful than I remembered. My own self-consciousness deferred to her magic, my nerves relaxed to her unhurried manner, my senses tingled to the sound of her voice: gentle, deliberate, assured.

'So. Master Louis is become quite the young gentleman. An elegant example, if I may be permitted an opinion.'

I swallowed hard, embarrassed by her forthrightness; but flattered too, for instinct had already made me aware of a disarming honesty in her character and an unflagging attention to everything she believed significant. I considered myself fortunate to have gained her approbation – to be thought worthy of her attention. I attempted to construct the right reply but Mrs Eldon continued, 'Our mutual friend has fulfilled for you a sort of prophecy once made under this roof. He is a hard driver, not least of himself and will put your stamina to the test. Of that you may be sure.'

With these words she succeeded in reducing me to feeling about as juvenile as I had been at our first meeting.

'Before I continue, Master Louis, you must appreciate that I have not had an easy or necessarily joyful life. That is why I desire to do what I can for others – what else can an empty woman usefully do with her money and time? I admire direct, practical action – such as you displayed when seeking information about the waxen head of Miss Havisham. I happen to know from your father that your interest prompted you to construct a story round what you saw. What I wish to do now is tell the true story.'

I stared at her, almost mesmerised by the promise.

'I shall talk to you about my mother-by-adoption and of what I know of her history from the interminable hours – just her and me – alone before the hearths of the only two rooms she occupied in the whole of Satis House. You, for your part, shall document it in the most interesting and readable fashion you can. You would, I'm sure, have a ready outlet for your work in *Household Words*. I shall, though, insist on you carrying out this work for me in the strictest confidence and that on completion, the manuscript be submitted to me prior to its bid for publication – this weekly and monthly instalment writing as is currently in vogue is not to my taste. That is my proposition. Do you have any questions?'

She looked steadily at me for some moments, during which time her charm threatened to overwhelm my collected thoughts. All I could do was to ask her why she should have singled me out for the task.

'Yes,' she said, 'it must seem strange to you for a woman of my years to confide in a young man of yours; and I dare say there are those who think I should not.'

'Mr Dickens?' I enquired.

'Not Mr Dickens. He does not know of this arrangement between us, nor do I wish him to for the moment. I simply wish to have set down such information as I shall give you – without falsification. I am hopeful that it might perhaps blow the dust of misunderstanding from my adopted mother's name. In the course of my life I have unearthed many factors about myself and about Miss Havisham, even as that head of hers was unearthed beneath your father's villa. Some will be revealed to you as I understand them – facts from before you or I were born. I have long wanted to place things in their proper context concerning Miss Havisham's influence on me. She was an eccentric recluse, Miss Havisham, but not without good reason. Because of your interest you shall learn of that reason.'

'I feel honoured,' I faltered, 'that you feel you can entrust me with this project. What can I say? I'm still fascinated by the waxen head – actually I was preparing to work another story of my own around it but I'd rather work for you. May I ask where the head is at present? I should like to take another look – to inspire me...'

'I regret no,' said Mrs Eldon, not unkindly. 'If you wouldn't mind I should prefer you to retain that original curiosity and impression until your task is complete. Then I shall be more than delighted to arrange a viewing. I must also make it a condition that nothing is veiled under false names and unreal events. You will retain even my own, though it is certain your narrative will not need to include me. Estella Havisham, or Drummle, or Eldon, has quite another tale to tell, but not to you.'

'When will you want me to begin?' I ventured, still scarcely believing my good fortune. So Mrs Eldon was to be my patroness. I had not thought at that stage of whether I was to be paid for my labours. In fact I did not care – to share something of her life and be near her had greater value for me.

'If you will be so good as to dine with me here next Monday evening, arriving as near seven as is convenient, we may make a start. I shall inform you of each subsequent meeting at the conclusion of the preceding one. I trust those arrangements will be to your liking. A chance to put your learning of shorthand to some use, Master Louis?' A knowing smile indicated to her that I comprehended her meaning, for I knew also that in his days as a dashing young reporter, Mr Dickens had become legendary for penning the fastest shorthand in the business. I enjoyed the understood, unspoken admiration I shared with Mrs Eldon for my new employer, knowing it would be years before I had anything like the same mastery.

My father was delighted with the proposition though I had to admit that no fee had been discussed (to which he replied it would have been vulgar – he trusted Mrs Eldon's business head implicitly). And as a prelude to the following Monday he decided to treat me to some information – surely the best indication that I was a child no longer. It appeared that the Havisham family and ours had a tenuous connection through marriage; about 1775, Miss Havisham's Aunt Amelia had married Emil du Monde, a Versailles doctor. I knew nothing, at that stage, of family history, but this information caught my interest, particularly as I felt it strengthen my commitment to Mrs Eldon. Papa also told me that he himself was responsible for anglicising our name to Dermond when he married my mother in 1833.

Over dinner, on that longed-for Monday evening, I was able to tell Mrs Eldon what Papa had said – information she already knew, making it fitting, I thought, that I should be the one entrusted with Miss Havisham's history. There were other guests at the table though not Mr Dickens. Lord Ashley acted as host, but it was Mrs Eldon who once again claimed my interest and attention. She looked particularly stunning in sombre *décolletage* – a spawn of solemn sapphires winking like blue bubbles about her pearly skin. I had my manners to display. I was not fully happy until the ladies had adjourned to the drawing room and Mrs Eldon and I left the gentlemen to their port in the dining room. We settled in her neat study where a good fire shining in its marble surround doubled the warmth in my heart. I had taken pencils and paper with me, presenting a thoroughly business-like image as I sat in an armchair on one side of the fireplace, she on the other.

'I have pondered long on my mother-by-adoption,' she began softly. 'I have tried to reach the truth of what made her as she was when I was taken to live with her at Satis. I have amassed as much as I can – it is your job to piece the patches together as invisibly as possible. Unlike her life I want a smooth-flowing narrative that will not jar. Some of the work you will, of necessity, be obliged to research for yourself. But I shall advise and guide you when the time comes. My words to you concern

Miss Havisham directly. She was... what can I say...? an extraordinary phenomenon – tender, kind, passionate, violent. Cruel also, as I was later to discover for myself. She was born shortly before midnight on the last day of January, seventeen hundred and seventy-four, the eldest child and only daughter of Augustus Havisham, brewer of Satis House in Kent, and his wife Isabella. See – here is a miniature painted when she was seven or eight.'

I looked upon an angelic face framed with light curls beneath a wide-brimmed garden hat then in vogue.

'She was a lovely child – sunny, generous, considerate – the centre of her adoring father's attention, provider of all his joy, for her mother did not long survive her birth. Poor little girl – so many of her later troubles stemmed from this early loss and a surfeit of fatherly indulgence. The time came, you see, when she grew to expect it...'

My pencil skated across the pages, trying to capture not only Mrs Eldon's information but also turns of phrase – endearing sometimes as being rather singular and quaint. My shorthand was a considerable aid, I soon found, and would improve as my labour increased. That first evening, though, I learned of Miss Havisham's early life at Satis being for the most part uneventful; schooling at home under governesses interspersed with excursions about the country and to Bath and London. But for all her expensive tastes, her social expectancy, her enviable loveliness, she remained as a young child seemingly unaffected – an engaging personality commanding yet pleasant, proud yet sympathetic.

'But there were two people, as she grew older, who brought out the worst in her. Her Papa was one, with his money and lavish praise. The other was her younger half-brother whom she despised and was probably a little jealous of, though I doubt it she realised. Arthur and she had never been on the best of terms – I think they aggravated one another, but the older they grew the more marked became their antagonism. Life at Satis became increasingly strained – Arthur could become violent and his half-sister compensated by putting on a bravado which was often more cruel than intended. She loved her Papa and could not bear to see his patience tried so often. On the other hand, Arthur irritated her directly, goading her beyond endurance sometimes. She objected to his coming between her and her Papa. So there it was – the three of them together in an uneasy triangle… and her with little sense of humour and a quick temper.'

Mrs Eldon must have talked to me for well over an hour that evening before she felt it her duty to return to her guests. I joined them also, though my writing hand ached and my head suffered from the unaccustomed intensity. Thus far, Miss Havisham seemed a somewhat uninteresting but pleasant character – too rich to be exciting, too ordinary to be original, too sweet to be anything but nauseating. At each subsequent meeting throughout the following months and beyond Christmas, my professional enthusiasm increased to personal concentration. I had, in effect, two occupations, if I did not discount my duties on *Household Words*. These provided my regular income but it was Mrs Eldon who provided for my soul. I began to consider the interim between one meeting and the next as a necessary nuisance; I don't mean this to sound like disloyalty to Mr Dickens – working for him was the best thing I could be doing – he was always considerate to me though I was well aware of his more wrathful moments.

I secured comfortable lodgings in Albemarle Street which I came to regard as my private office, for it was here that I undertook the drudgery side of my work for Mrs Eldon in sorting out my notes, researching, annotating, enlarging. I was pleased to let it take over my existence, hardly venturing out to theatre, chop-house or walks about the neighbourhood, though periodically I would go down to Kent to see my family. Amongst the secrets I kept were my feelings for Mrs Eldon.

On Monday, 29th March, 1858, I received the intelligence that Mama had been unwell for two days. She and Papa had been dining out the previous Friday evening and had returned home in jocular mood. But during the night severe abdominal pains awakened her. The doctor appeared unable to settle on a single diagnosis – his various medications seemed only to aggravate. Mrs Eldon interposed by asking Sir James Clark, the Queen's Physician, to give a pronouncement on her condition. My father's opinion of Sir James, never high at the best of times, plummeted further when the 72 year-old Scotsman's considered opinion was that my mother was with child! – a freak of nature obviously familiar to the stupid man as Mama was nearer 50 than 40.

Despite his recommendation of fresh air and simple diet, (she could eat nothing) dearest Mama was dead by Good Friday; her *post mortem* revealed what we have now come to recognise as rupture of the appendix. This accounted for the agonies which accompanied her to the grave. I wonder if my distress at losing Mama, my youth's constant elixir of love, support and sympathy, in some way heightened my need for surrogate embodiments of comfort and assurance. Though thoughts of work, Miss Havisham and waxen heads were temporarily suspended, my increasing commitment to Mrs Eldon was not; she represented my only beacon of joy – the last centre of grace, beauty and hope my crippled spirit needed to regain its command over my life.

I had several meetings with her on my return to London but she did not press me to resume my task; I requested it, however, in order to deflect my grieving. To be in her company again was sufficient to ease my pain – her sympathetic presence became stay and prop on which my hours were balanced.

One evening I was more restless than usual. Though I felt wretched and depressed I had insisted on taking notes. At one stage Mrs Eldon poured me a brandy which I accepted gratefully. Instead of applying the glass to my lips though, I impetuously pressed them to her kind hand, not because it was brandy instead of milk but because I felt like a drowning man who needed to keep afloat.

'Oh, Mrs Eldon,' I sobbed desperately, 'I'm so unhappy. I can't go on like this.'

'The loss of a parent is a grievous time,' said Mrs Eldon calmly. 'It is to be hoped that the pain lessens with the years.'

'That's not what I mean. I loved Mama more than I can say but I feel the same for you... only in a different way. I've tried to keep it to myself all this time in spite of it making me ill. I can't explain – it hurts so – I don't know what I mean. Please don't be angry... I want to be with you... everywhere... always...'

Mrs Eldon placed her hands either side of my scalding cheeks and drew my face towards hers, implanting a most tender finger on my lips. She led me to the *chaise longue* and settled formally beside me, taking my hands in hers.

'My dear Louis,' she said warmly, looking into my eyes. 'You have paid me one of the greatest compliments of my life. Thank you, my darling boy.'

'I *love* you more than I can say,' I pursued recklessly. 'You make me feel *safe* and *worthwhile*. If I don't *marry* you I think I shall *die*.'

'Louis, Louis... how young you are – how *very* young, for all your grown-up clothes and worldly airs. What can you know of love?'

'I *know* I love *you*,' I replied fiercely. 'What else can it be? I loved you when we first met but I didn't know what it meant then. I *do* know *now* – it means *everything* to me.'

Mrs Eldon patted my hands. 'Now listen, Louis – listen carefully – I want to talk to you as a man... you will be one soon and a fine one too. You know that Miss Havisham adopted me when I was about two years of age? She adopted me to grow up and learn how to break men's hearts as hers had been broken. For her sake I married my first husband. Bentley Drummle was rich and hateful and after his death and hers I married again. Edward was poor and I learned to love him as Miss Havisham's teaching gradually lost its power. For the first time in my life I felt neither fear nor shame. I was free. I had barely reconciled that freedom when my Edward died.' She paused to take a deep breath, as if trying to cushion some inner pain. 'But before all this – in the days when I was your age and younger – I became acquainted with a boy who Miss Havisham put in my way in order that I should be cruel. He was a common blacksmith's boy and I was then too proud to be kind to him. For my sake he made himself into a gentleman but I remained proud and we were lost to one another. We continued friends apart until he became too proud to accept my charity. Therein lies a separate story that forms no substance of your work for me. It may be told one day, if only to save others from a fate like mine.'

I continued to follow her every expression.

'All my life I have been surrounded by sycophants – admirers – flatterers. With the exception of Mr Dickens, three only have been sincere and honest: Pip the blacksmith's boy was the first; my dear Edward was the second; and you, I think, are the third. Oh yes, lovely Louis, I have seen you to be honest for longer than you realise – honest to yourself – honest to me – which is why I know you love me in your way. But I also am honest and must tell you I shall never remarry.'

The thumping of my heart seemed intent on knocking me off my seat. How very unsubtle I must have been for her to read me so easily – see so clearly into my heart.

'Perhaps you know that I have no children... no family. My social work is my family I suppose. To me you have been the son I never enjoyed and I love you for it – no, no, let me say what I have to. I *do* love you, dearest Louis; I love your mind, your character, your personality. I love your serious face, your impetuousness, your honest determination. I love your youth and *naivete*. I have the capacity for loving you completely. But you have to understand that I revere above all the love I felt for my Edward and despise above all the hurt I did the blacksmith's boy. I love you too much to risk putting those to the test at your expense. I don't want to hurt you – our ages and outlooks are so different. I couldn't bear not living up to your expectations.'

The heat of the fire threatened to scorch my confusion. I moved away to the centre of the room saying, '*How* could you hurt me? What do ages and outlooks matter? I love you *because* of them. You are everything I want of life…'

Sounds welled in my throat which I thought were more words but unmanly frustrated sobs blurted out instead as I stood helpless before her. She came to me with comfort in her arms as I cried like the child she never had.

'I'm sorry,' I said, becoming calmer as she led me back to where my brandy still awaited me. 'I'm better now. My father would say I've lost my manners talking to you as I've done. I've made a fool of myself. I think I must go.'

'But you will return.' Her voice again gave no hint of emotion. 'I need you to remain my amanuensis.'

'If that is all,' I said, straightening, 'perhaps it would be better if I didn't. I have to think of our family name in Society and not spoil yours.'

'Ah,' she said, nodding, 'the family name. That sounds like your father speaking. But does the family name bar you from expressing honest feelings? Emotions? I hope not. If everyone thought of the family name what *would* become of human relationships? Too much repression and hypocrisy festers because of the family name – and Society. It is too easy to become shut in with our private complexities and that is not wholesome. It destroyed Miss Havisham as it nearly did me. You must help me to tell the story.'

Once back at my lodgings I found myself slightly dizzy – from shock I supposed. But shock at what? When I objectively reviewed my recent role as a suitor I could not pretend I was shocked at rejection. Mrs Eldon made sense. But in no way was I ashamed of having declared my feelings, adolescent as they appeared – they were just as valid and I believed in them. My only fear was that I had caused undue distress to an obviously sensitive and complex woman. I wrote to her asking forgiveness for my outburst and when it would be convenient professionally to resume my commission. Her reply set the date and time, making no reference to the rest of my letter.

Our resumption was not as strained as I had anticipated. The air was clear between us and I was glad of the understanding rounding the edges of our association, restoring my confidence, nourishing my soul. I thrived again on the extra work I did for her at Albemarle Street throughout that summer's exceptional heat and on into 1859, constructing my narrative, dividing my time between Westminster, Kensington and Kent, my shorthand improving, my longhand deteriorating and my midnight oil running dry. At last, on 6th May I delivered into Mrs Eldon's hand the completed fair copy.

I find the mixed sentiments I felt difficult to express. I imagined giving birth entailed as much pain and sweat as I had endured during my labour. What anguish! What elation! What inexpressible relief at a safe outcome! Mrs Eldon had impressed on me that I was not to document a history such as Mr Carlyle or Lord Macaulay might do. Mine was to be a living, breathing unravelling with my own life-force coursing its passages. Experiencing what I felt for Mrs Eldon had greatly enhanced my understanding. And now my task was all but over, a new sense assailed me – bereavement. It was natural, I suppose, particularly as I began feeling low and depressed during the weeks of waiting for a verdict. I even began to wonder if I had offended her by what I had presented.

At last I received one of her notes asking me to call.

My doubts and loneliness evaporated as she greeted me affectionately and asked me to sit. I noticed my manuscript closed on the table by her chair.

'So many claims on my time, Louis dear – please understand and forgive my delay.'

'I have so wanted to see you often,' I said earnestly, forgetting my inner resolve. 'I've tried not to but it's difficult.'

'You will always be welcome here,' said Mrs Eldon. 'You know that. We have a special bond, you and I. Here it is – our joint literary venture. My belief that you were the correct choice has been amply borne out. You have captured the essence of my interpretation and clothed the essential bones with a new but appropriate flesh. I would like it to remain as it is. It is most thorough – I do admire your approach – you are a born storyteller. Thank you for what you have done – you shall receive remuneration and, of course, I shall claim nothing from any additional benefit from it you may enjoy hereon. I only hope it will help to further you career.'

'Thank you,' I said gratefully, not daring to say again what I truly felt. 'I've done my best for you – I'm happy to know you're pleased with my work. Something bothers me, though. You've made no attempt to withhold names or incidents nor have you let me use any form of writers' licence to preserve anonymity or reputation. Surely, with the standing you have in Society, an advertisement of your private matters could harm all you represent.'

'Dear Louis – sensitive to the last. But the story does not concern me. And besides – truth exists whether harmful or not. We cannot alter it without being *un*truthful. Those who wish to use the truth against me are not of the company I wish to attract. There is too much sham in Society as it is. I am not insisting on the tale's publication nor would I finance it through the press – it must run on its own merits to find its market. Either way I consider that I shall lose nothing by it and possibly gain more;

already I have my release, you see, and you have your story.' She leaned towards me and kissed my cheek.

'Now that your writing is finished I can throw further light on the waxen head, which I'm sure will interest you. Since you last saw it here it has been in the Wax Museum at The Bazaar, Portman Square. Joseph Tussaud delivered it for you here today at my request. From the content of my story you know how it came to be made. Monsieur Tussaud has verified it as his mother's work – a particularly fine example, he says, of her pre-revolutionary period. Interesting as all this may be from an historical point of view, I find the model distinctly macabre. Not for that reason but because I appreciate your long fascination for it, I propose it as a gift to you in part recognition of your services. If you don't wish to accept please feel at liberty to say – I shall not be offended – and Monsieur Tussaud will be pleased to add it to his collection.'

There would have been a time, I expect, when the offer would have seemed the ultimate accolade, but now it seemed to have about it the cast of finality – a waxen seal on our association.

'I don't know what to say,' I said, truthfully.

'Place your feelings into your work, Louis, as I do mine. That way, no idea, no experience is wasted. You are lucky – you are a creative artist. I am not. You have charge over your soul – others have charge over mine.'

'*You* have charge over mine,' I said, before I could check myself.

'You are still young with the world to conquer. Take every experience in your stride – use it – learn by it.'

'Is that all I have been to you?' I asked. 'An experience?'

'Louis, that is cruel, my dear...'

'Don't call me my dear unless you mean it.'

'My *very* dear Louis... what do you want me to say? That I understand? For I do understand, you must believe me. You have always been dear to me and will remain so. I know I have been fortunate enough to receive your affection – your love – and hope I always shall. And if you love *me* as I believe you do, you will try not to confuse dreams with reality...'

I hardly listened to the rest of her homily, sensible and reasoned as it was. I think I was admitting for certain that I had reached my journey's end. Even the thought of being a famous author did nothing to revive me. What was the point in anything without Mrs Eldon? I almost wished she hated me.

I had promised, however, that I would give her a personal fair copy of the original manuscript before I talked with Mr Dickens about its publication. I bound it in a blue sugar-paper cover of my own design and bearing the title *Expectations of A Great Lady,* was thus able, in due course and with due composure, to present it as a compliment to her trusting me with so many secrets.

In the meantime, I had joined the staff of a large London newspaper with offices in Holborn; and it was from there that I went one evening with a copy of my original manuscript to see Mr Dickens at Wellington Street. Since I had left *Household Words,* he had broken with his current publishers and re-adopted Chapman and Hall, his previous, now in Piccadilly. He had also closed *Household Words* and begun a new periodical, *All The Year Round,* with an office a few doors away from his old one. This had been in April when *A Tale Of Two Cities* had launched the first number. Wilkie Collins's mystery *The Woman In White* was due to follow in November; dared I hope that *Expectations Of A Great Lady* would succeed it?

Here I was, at last able to put my work into Mr Dickens's hands and await his sanction. *The Woman In White* was well into its fourth number when he wrote to me in his usual loose, inky style, saying that he had been intrigued by my efforts and was full of admiration for what I had undertaken. He had discussed the matter with Mrs Eldon but was somewhat concerned at present about the lack of veiled identity in the characters, even though they were all now dead. He had always to be aware, he said, of not offending his public. He wrote that though he based many of his characters on people he knew or had known, he always took great pains not to make their origins obvious. He also felt that the period of my chronicle was too close to his own two cities tale. As my mist of depression increased, he intimated that he was committed to follow Collins's story with Charles Lever's *A Hard Day's Ride* and that when it got off to 'a jogging start' he would consider my offering.

The *Ride,* once it began, limped rather than jogged. The Inimitable naturally became concerned about the slackening sales of his young periodical. It was decided that the *Ride* would have to be hastily terminated. I was then informed that under no circumstances could the further risk be taken of presenting a new, unproven unknown. Indeed, The Inimitable would dash to the rescue with something of his own. My manuscript, he requested, should remain with him on the understanding that he would let me know if and when its serialisation would be contemplated. I heard nothing more from him but continued to purchase my copies of *All The Year Round.*

On 1st December, 1860, a new story by Charles Dickens appeared in its pages. It began with Pip, a blacksmith's boy, shivering with fright in a marshland churchyard whilst pounced on by an escaped convict. The title of the work struck a dissonance in my heart with its almost conscious economy – *Great Expectations.* With the introduction of a haughty miss named Estella by the end of the fifth number, I was convinced that I was reading about the young Mrs Eldon; but a history that had not been imparted to me.

It seemed pointless to speculate further on my fortune. Everything appeared as clear as if in a show of lightning. My narrative and Mr Dickens's compounded one continuous history – mine centring around Miss Havisham's development, his around Mrs Eldon. Or should I now refer to her as Estella? Had she taken him also into her confidence, running two stories side-by-side? What sort of woman was this, who of her own admission, not only held no store by the anonymity of false names and unreal events, but could countenance so personal a life story being published in her own lifetime? How much was, in fact true? How much had Mr Dickens, like me, had to research or invent in order to weave a gripping narrative? It was clear to me, however, that Estella had no intention of enlightening my professional curiosity, leaving me to imagine what I pleased.

I little doubted *Great Expectations* would be a winner all the way. I was already enthralled by the cool, clear style of its telling – the best thing he had done since *A Christmas Carol* and the early chapters of *Copperfield,* though I understand his friend Bulwer Lytton persuaded him to change his original less happy ending, where Estella and Pip remained friends apart, for the published version which allowed them to marry. In view of what he had told me about the importance of veiling the identity of characters, I felt a little hurt that he had chosen not to follow this stricture whilst damning my work because of it. But who was I to compete with such a titan? – novelist, editor, amateur actor, public speaker, reader and entertainer, charitable wizard, walker with commoners and lords by the handful. My roseate dreams of fame and influence were as moonshine before the glare of this God.

In August, 1861, I bought the 3 volumes of the newly published masterpiece for thirty-one shillings and sixpence.

* * *

More than 20 years have elapsed since then. I have those volumes still, as I have my original manuscript for Mrs Eldon. It has never been published. I am now about to re-read it. When I have done so, I shall complete this memoir then encase her story and mine in a red cover. Meanwhile I turn back the faded blue of my original and see my name on the title page. Above it the word *Expectations*. Time moulds us to meet expectations; this is no less true of characters and events in a book or the writer who casts them. I feel no bitterness that mine have come to naught. I am glad to have understood that with the first breath we draw, or page we turn, which I am about to do now, we possess nothing *but* expectations…

EXPECTATIONS OF A GREAT LADY
A CHRONICLE IN TEN TABLEAUX

by
Louis Xavier Dermond

TABLEAU I
Versailles, December, 1788.

The Sun-King's palace glittered like a fairytale. It glittered so much, in fact, that the very sun *le Roi Soleil* had modelled himself on seemed to be paying wintry homage to the colossal pile. All day it had crept obsequiously along the *Avenue de Paris*, flashing humbler windows and masonry until it fawned on the southern and western flanks of the royal *Chateau* lording it over its artificial plateau on what had once been natural marsh land. It sprawled gluttonously behind its gilded gates and railings, its contrived lakes and fountains, controlled courts and gardens commanding the outlook on all points of the compass as if ready to devour the very position it occupied.

For one hundred and six years, since the removal of France's vortex of power from Paris to this provincial swamp, Louis XIV's machinery of Absolute Monarchy had clocked unchanging time through changing times – through progressive thought – through a new social awareness. The control of France he had once imposed gradually took on an ugly distortion, like the eventual pox-ridden carcass of his grandson, Louis XV, rotting alive and black amidst the stench of his costly bedding.

To the *Chateau's* august inhabitants, not least the four thousand servants amongst the soaring sheen and polish, the current season of Christmas hopefully brought some light relief at the end of what had been a troubled year. Louis XVI's inherited absolutism reflected in his myriad of mirrors moored in harbours of marquetry, parquetry, tapestry, *ormolu* and marble was finding the outside swell of public opinion disturbing – free-thinking ideas in others' minds at odds with his long-established autocratic inheritance.

The slurry of discontent had recently increased throughout his almost fifteen years of easy-going enthronement, at his divine side his light-hearted, heavy-breasted helpmate. The unconventional Queen Marie Antoinette was said to spend with ease and aplomb the nation's finance – hers now by rights of birth and marriage. The Court, as out-dated as its knowledge of the modern world and its people, closed round them like a neglected wound; its deference to *l'etiquette,* tiresome to Her Majesty at the best of times, seemed relevant no more. The *Chateau's* kitchens and cellars might well be stocked with bread, meat and wine, but half of Paris was hungry; well may there be an army of menials to pick and brush the dust from every gilded scroll in the *Galerie des Glaces* but half of Paris was unemployed; a bedroom the size of a parade ground might well accommodate the sleep of a King but half of Paris was homeless. Well might the Queen be suspected of having paid one-million-six-hundred thousand *livres* for a diamond necklace when her adopted country was already in debt to a sparkling twelve-hundred and fifty-million, but well over half of Paris was angry. The Queen of Pleasure was rapidly becoming the Queen of Disquiet. Well may she seek consolation in the Arcadian groves and grottoes about *le Petit Trianon;* well may the King prefer his lathe, clocks and hunting. Life beyond the *Chateau* windows may well appear in good health.

To doctor Emil du Monde's way of thinking, it mattered little whether the Royal Family were Christmasing at Versailles or Marly, St Cloud, Rambouillet or the inhospitable Tuileries in Paris. He was more concerned over how much longer this mild, good-natured King, his Queen and children, his two brothers and sister, Madame Elisabeth, could remain unaffected by an unquiet nation. Emil, after forty-five years of optimism, was now inclined to believe that reputations stood to be lost, not gained, through being too openly sympathetic to the crown.

That was his sentiment in Versailles. It was also the sentiment in Paris, according to his city friend and *confidante* from student days, Philippe Curtius. Both men sat by Emil's library fire in his cosily shuttered residence on the Boulevard de la Reine. The sun had sloped serenely from the horizon, leaving a frigid wind to bite the frozen ruts. With an emptying decanter between them and the rest of their families affably social in the *salon* across the hallway, the two doctors rolled up the old year with an exchange of backward and forward issues.

Philippe adjusted his white wig tied behind with an elegant bow. 'Discount what I say if you wish, Emil,' he said, his chubby – humoured features becoming serious, 'but I foresee an upset of some magnitude before the new year is out if the Director of Finance can't tighten the purse-strings somehow and the States General legislate more fairly when they meet in May.' He raised a warning finger. 'This country will be on its knees if not, and God knows how people will react.'

Emil nodded and sighed, his well-formed features expressing concern. His older friend had every reason to speak so feelingly about the economic and political climate – he had much to lose if this growing fashion for equality got out of hand. Philippe found wealth and fame weighty enough, but royal patronage, too, had heaped his measure though he had not deliberately sought such benefits. Once a doctor of moderate means, he had been content with his practice in Berne, tending his patients and, being a bachelor, having plenty of time to indulge in his hobby of wax modelling. This had arisen out of a need to produce wax limbs as teaching aids at the hospital. He had revelled in a natural ability, and after venturing first into portraiture then complete figures dressed and life-size, he became something of a celebrity. The Prince de Ponti had overloaded the scales by providing him with patronage and a Paris studio; with the opening of his Wax Museum in the Rue St. Honore, followed by a palatial mansion with studio and new museum in the more fashionable Boulevard du Temple, Philippe's future was assured, medicine put aside.

How the populace adored seeing their social models chronicled in wax. The *tableau* depicting the Royal Family at dinner back in 1775, soon after the Coronation, had been an instant success, Marie Antoinette's likeness still talked about to this day, together with the friendship and enthusiasm she and her family had so readily supplied the museum.

'My friend,' said Emil, honestly, 'I think I am rather glad to be still but a humble practitioner. I am quite content with my thirty-thousand *livres* a year. I don't envy you your position and fortune in these troubled times. I am concerned for your niece too. What is to happen to her?'

'I have persuaded Marie to give up her position at Court,' said Philippe. 'The King's sister will have to look elsewhere for a companion and secretary. If things become more difficult, and it looks as though they might, the Court will be the first to suffer. I don't want Marie to be in the firing-line, if you take my meaning.'

'She'll be sad at leaving Madame Elisabeth,' observed Emil. 'She's been at Court a long time I think.'

'Ten years,' said Philippe, draining his glass. 'I sometimes find it hard to believe she's now twenty-seven – I'm inclined to regard her as still a child I'm afraid.'

'And what has she to say at leaving? As you say she is no longer a child.'

'I expect I shall always look upon her as a child – a dear child – who's taken the place of the daughter I never had. She is all I have now – all my museum has. She must not be lost to either of us. Besides, it's unhealthy that she should stay at court too long. She needs to know the world more, particularly if the writing *is* on the wall.'

'Does she share your alarmist views on the future, I wonder?' laughed Emil, passing the decanter. 'I too fear for the future but can't help wondering if you're being slightly over-dramatic…'

'*Mon Dieu!* I am not. If you were in Paris – as informed as I am – you would not be so complacent. I am no fool – our Royalist sympathies are well known – that makes our museum's future uncertain. Marie is my niece, that is true, but don't forget she is also my adopted daughter. I have pledged to love and protect her at all costs, also her mother, my sister. They have brought me more happiness than I can ever express.' He leaned across the table and placed a hand on Emil's cuff. 'The Royal Family Dinner Tableau – that was Marie's idea, you realise? She knew what the public wanted. She has a keen business head, and nimble fingers. I am resolved she will never founder amongst the shipwrecks of others. If the King and Queen continue along their present course they may soon have to account for their existence – the Queen is far from popular. Do you know what they call her? *L'Autrichienne* – the Austrian Bitch – *Madame Deficit*. Can you imagine such discourtesy? It is as though she is being held responsible for the problems of the entire system. It's too ridiculous. She and the King are poorly advised. If there *is* to be a revolt – think me lunatic if you wish – I intend to be prepared for it. And if you accept the advice of an old friend, I would seriously consider getting your wife's niece back to England as soon as possible. France will be no place for an English flower like Estelle when things get out of hand.'

'Estelle will be as broken-hearted at parting from Marie as Marie will from Madame Elisabeth,' reflected Emil, sadly. 'They have become such good friends and she's been here barely a year. Her papa would so like her education completing and besides, Marie is such a good influence; Estelle is a dear but needs to mix more with others and think less of herself.' He topped up his glass. 'I'm sorry if I don't seem to share your pessimism, dear friend. I suppose it's the result of being a moderate. So, until the violence you appear to believe inevitable, I wish to propose a New Year toast – a personal toast: *Vive le Roi. Vive la Reine. Vive la France!*'

As the warm red wine engorged his gullet, Philippe could not help but associate its passage with that of blood springing at the surgeon's knife; Emil, though, was content at present to savour its true consistency and flavour, calmly enjoying his optimism a little longer.

* * *

In the du Monde's pretty and pastel *salon,* the twice widowed Madame Grosholtz, Philippe's sister, rested from her incessant talking. She never tired of relating how her seven sons by her first marriage had become men of the world. All her hopes now centred on her only daughter Marie. Since brother Philippe had offered them both a home after her second husband's death, she had watched Marie's development with increasingly proud pleasure. Out of the rather *jejeune* seventeen-year-old who had gone to Court had grown a shrewd, sensible woman, short in stature but well endowed with common sense and no fear of hard work. She balanced an amicable compromise between her employment at the royal *Chateau* and her duties at her Uncle-Papa's wax museum, the *Cabinet de Cire,* in the Boulevard du Temple. Her artistic and business acumen were unquestionable, giving her determined jaw, sharp features and hawk-like eyes an intense and searching quality.

For nearly ten years she had been enjoying the benefits of her two worlds – the crisp focus of Paris and the shimmer of Court life as she instructed Madame Elisabeth, three years her junior, in the art of wax modelling. She thought it not at all peculiar that her secretarial and companionable duties to the

King's sister should include assisting her religious and charitable mistress to pursue her pious fervour; she knew well that wax models of poor folks' affected limbs were commonly offered up, together with prayers, in the belief they would help recovery. Marie herself had modelled from life, from death, from her own inborn talent, since becoming part of Uncle Philippe's household after her real father's death. She was happy to share her talent and knowledge with anyone who showed interest, particularly her gracious royal mistress with the rose and lily complexion.

Yes, her daughter had done well for herself. The Widow Grosholtz smiled with satisfaction. Beside her on the settee, Emil's wife Amelia tried to think of something stimulating to say. Having nothing of a specialised nature in common, both ladies were frankly bored with one another and had reverted to discussing children.

'*Ah, oui,*' continued Madame. 'I must confess to feeling flattered by the affectionate friendship that has developed between my daughter and Madame Elisabeth. But then, Marie always knows how to behave. I taught her so. Such a good example. Mark you, I would hardly concede that Marie is beautiful – she is too clever for looks.' The widow surveyed her daughter across the room. 'Her nose is too big and her eyes too dark and piercing. *Non, non,* Madame du Monde, be honest. Marie herself is under no allusion.'

Amelia nodded non-committedly, trying to swallow a yawn as she glanced at where her niece Estelle sat with Marie in the corner by the *clavecin*. Though Estelle was nearly fifteen her looks were infinitely more refined and attractive than Marie's, there was no doubt. Her open English complexion remained unsmirched by nearly 12 months away from the bracing air of her native Kent. Compliments on the glazed attraction of her eyes, even white teeth and fair luxuriant hair had become one of the requisites of life to which she was now accustomed and even expected; nor was she at pains to disguise the firmness of her delicate mouth set above a determined chin. Both, along with her general demeanour, presented effortless reminders of authority it might be regarded as folly to challenge. Amelia likened Estelle to the graceful but frivolous Rococo clock on her mantelpiece, whose crafted charm and light-hearted outward appearance concealed complex workings driven by a tightly coiled spring.

Amelia's own children, playing on the floral carpet, were slightly younger than their cousin. They had not enjoyed that special *rapport* which had developed between Estelle and Marie. The two young ladies, dressed in the gentle colours and cut of the latest fashion, seemed rooted intently in their quietude, Estelle's hand between Marie's.

'You must not feel sad on my account, *ma cherie,*' said Marie kindly. '*I* am not sad. I love Madame Elisabeth it is true, but I love Uncle-Papa more. If he desires me to leave Versailles then I am happy to do as he asks and my Mistress is so understanding. He becomes dreadfully tired sometimes – I need to do more to help him. Mama has enough to do looking after the house. Why should you be sad for me working at what I enjoy best? Could it be, I wonder, that you will miss my association with the Court? It is glamorous, is it not? – and I know how you like glamour.' She raised Estelle's chin with an enquiring index finger. '*Oui* – as I thought. But you will visit me in Paris and I you here.'

'I should like that very much,' replied Estelle, letting Marie dab her tears with her lace handkerchief. 'You have been so good to me – much nicer than those cousins down there. I don't think they like me though I've tried to make them.'

'Estelle,' said Marie more purposefully, 'I want to say something to you and I want you to listen. You are young – you are pretty – you have your life before you. You also have a great deal to learn – *non, non,* don't interrupt – I'm telling you this because I love you and want you to do well with your life. Listen to others, Estelle. *Think* of others – you can when you want to. Never be too proud to take advice – believe me I know this to be true. As you get older you'll find being a woman in a world of men has many difficulties, if one is to be truly happy; and isn't that what we really want of life?'

'I know you're right, Marie,' Estelle replied, smiling. 'I do want to be liked, you know that. I shall try and do as you say – you make it sound so easy but sometimes, with some people, it's so difficult.'

'That is the challenge. That is what tests us and makes us want to win…'

'Marie. Estelle,' Madame Grosholtz called and beckoned. 'Come over here my angels. You have been closeted in that corner quite half-an-hour and looking oh so serious! Marie, entertain us on the keyboard, *cher coeur* – that tinkly tune of Herr Mozart's the Queen plays. Such a pretty composer, do you not agree, Madame du Monde.' Amelia smiled politely. 'There is a story, don't you know, that at Schonbrunn, the young *maestro* aged all of six proposed to Her Majesty aged all of seven. *Charmante, n'est pas?*'

Estelle's aunt continued to conceal her boredom behind her smile. She had a headache, too, but bore it nobly. She often had a headache – an aggravation she attributed to being an alien living in her husband's country. And the candles on the side-table dripped so onto the polish.

* * *

By the beginning of February, 1789, Marie had bade her sorrowful *adieus* to Madame Elisabeth and the Court. Her rooms next to Madame's suite in the north wing were closed up. The farewell presents she had acquired, including some rather splendid furniture, were already at the Boulevard du Temple awaiting her arrival.

The bare trees and ice-stopped fountains that had been part of her second home for nearly a third of her life were touching to her heart in their colourless, petrified state. Madame Elisabeth's private but modest haven at Montreuil on the outskirts of Versailles was similarly frozen. That both must surge and blossom again was certain but Marie felt that somehow it would not be so easy for the puppets of the *ancien regime* to do the same.

But they had been good to her and she would miss them in spite of having her much-loved work in Paris to occupy her. How thankful she was that through her time at Court, she had been able to preserve a private world of her own – separate from the veneer of ritual and deportment that the Queen disliked. It would have been too easy to become complacent. Royal Patronage was one thing but self-awareness and fulfilment quite another.

As she sat in the *cabriolet* brushing away the inevitable tears of self-indulgence she despised so, her thoughts turned increasingly to positive improvements to be carried out at the Boulevard du Temple as well as the second exhibition at the *Palais Royale*. The Director General of Finance, Monsieur Necker, must be persuaded to sit for his model; also the Duc de Orleans, a known sympathiser with the Parisian masses. If Curtius's *Cabinet de Cire* was to survive, Marie knew it was up to her to keep her mind open, her tongue still and her fingers busy.

By way of diverting her emotions as the *Chateau* receded behind her, she directed the *cabriolet* to take her to the du Monde residence. Amelia, as usual, seemed rather pre-occupied; she had somehow translated Marie's leaving of Court as heralding the end of the world. To make matters worse, Estelle was in a mood. Amelia watched her run to Marie and snuggle her face close amongst her furry winter wraps.

'Uncle Emil has just told me I am to go home,' she sobbed, tears blobbing into the softness like melting snow. 'He says Papa has demanded it. It is too cruel and so soon after my birthday. Don't let them make me go like they did you.'

'Sit down Estelle,' said Marie patiently, catching a hopeless sort of gesture from Amelia. 'Stop crying and listen to me – I said listen. We talked at Christmas about this. I do not like to part from my friends but Uncle-Papa wishes it. It is prudent. Because I love and respect him I do not complain. You have a real Papa to love and respect.'

'But it was intended I should stay longer – *I want* to stay because everyone's kind and I don't have everything spoiled by my half-brother. I'd rather die than go back to Arthur just now.'

'That is not fair, Estelle,' said Marie, angrily. 'How can you upset us all whose only concern is your happiness and well-being?' Amelia had to smile to herself – Marie was no fool when it came to handling Estelle who had stopped crying in sheer surprise at hearing a voice raised against her. 'There are good reasons for all this – my family and yours are trying to safeguard our future safety because they love us. The sooner you understand that the better.'

'Are we in danger? I don't understand.'

'Nor is there need for you to,' replied Marie calmly. 'Just accept that there are others older and wiser than you. Don't spoil all the happiness and good that has been achieved during you stay or I shall be much upset.'

Emotional blackmail, thought Amelia, *but it is working.*

'You're right, Marie,' announced Estelle, straightening. 'Of course I don't want to upset you. I'll do as you say and make the best of it.' Her set little mouth softened – hurt points of light no longer flashed her eyes.

What a prickly specimen this English rose, thought Marie. *In fact, quite a hothouse of thorns and thistles.* She studied Estelle's perfect features with the artist's critical eye. 'I have a suggestion to make. What would you say to a parting gift? A portrait model in wax.'

'Of the Queen?' said Estelle, her natural charm restored. 'I'd love a portrait of Queen Antoinette. Then I could look at her all day long and pretend I...'

'*Not* of Her Majesty – of Yourself. Your *own* model for everyone to admire. Who knows... you might be mistaken for the Queen – in England.'

'Would I be put on show in your museum next to the Queen and King?'

'I meant it more as a present for you – *un petit cadeau* to take home – a souvenir.'

'How lovely of you,' considered Estelle with a small frown. 'I shall wear my pink gown with the muslin *fichu* – that will compliment my complexion, *n'est pas, Marie?*'

'*Absolument,*' Marie replied, knowing that was what Estelle wanted to hear, 'but I shan't be making all of you, so it doesn't matter what you wear. Now, *attends, si tu plait*. I will send for you to Paris very soon – it will be within the next few days as your father seems anxious to have you home with all speed.'

'Fancy!' exclaimed Estelle, strutting round the room holding out her skirts at both sides. 'I am to be chronicled by the hands that were responsible for The King and Queen of France.' She caught her breath as she realised the enormity of her luck. She relived again the sight of Their Majesties emerging into the spectacular *Galerie des Glaces* – the Queen's tall dignity florid with fashion and *finesse,* the King's rounded features filled out with amiability and good will as they acknowledged the bowing obedience of their Court. As Estelle's hand held Marie's tightly she had almost fainted from forgetting to breathe as Her Majesty's fair being, more awesome in her gorgeous pride than an entirety of Emperors, swept the banks of her subjects like an obliging breeze unfurling a fleet of sails. Was this wondrous force with the oval face, blue eyes and clear skin the woman who tired easily of etiquette and sought repose in a make-believe world of charm and rustic peace: the contrived naturalism of *le hameau* near her adored garden pavilion *Petit Trianon?* Were those diamond-dressed fingers the ones that led her pet cows by silken ribbons across carefully brushed meadows? Was that political and interfering mind so often discussed the one that attended to the dairy-splashed milk into gold-rimmed Sevres pails?

'Do you remember last year, Marie, when you took me to see the royal models in your show? How handsome they were, specially the Queen. I wish to be like her when I grow up. I wish I were her daughter instead of Madame Royale.'

'To my mind,' said Marie, 'Madame Royale is not as fortunate as you imagine. She is not free. Neither is the Queen. You are. So am I. Freedom is worth life itself.'

'Oh, I shall be free,' said Estelle, 'for I'll have lots of servants like Papa – and money – and friends. They'll all be mine one day because our family is one of the richest in Kent – in England – and I am the eldest child.'

Marie moved towards the door without a reply. 'I'll leave now. We'll talk further when we meet in a few days' time – twenty, Boulevard du Temple – pink gown!'

* * *

Estelle had never before encountered such studio premises. The entire space had become subservient to nothing but the production of models. In varying states of incompleteness they crowded each area in each room like some bizarre slaughterhouse; it seemed perfectly in order to palm a waxen hand onto the mantelpiece to keep vases and candlesticks company, or to prop headless torsos in a corner against a long-case clock. Wax heads, limbs, curls of hair, feathers, jewels, lengths of fabric crowded upon Estelle's curiosity – nothing escaped her scrutiny, from the plaster of Paris, modelling clay, lumps of beeswax, moulds, crucibles, stoves, paints, to tray on tray of glass eyes, all pair-matched and staring. Each room further overflowed, as would a theatre scenery-store, with mirrors, pictures, chandeliers, furniture, *bric-a-brac,* to say nothing of painted panels, screens and a multitude of assorted pillars, pedestals and *torcheres.* She became a race of endless questions as she swished up a bouquet of purple ostrich plumes here to hold them to her *coiffure a la Reine,* or swirled a length of royal blue velvet there to encase her slender body before a gilt mirror. Marie had difficulty in persuading her sitter to come to rest on a high stool before her modelling table.

Once composed to her satisfaction, Marie was able to contemplate the features she had become so familiar with. Today, however, they were nothing more than arrangement of basic geometric shapes, though she was careful not to let Estelle know that. Why is it, she asked herself, that all her sitters must pose in the manner most unnatural to them? Here is Estelle, no different from the others, flagstaff-straight as if she has a scratch of holly down her back.

'You *are* allowed to breathe, Estelle,' she suggested. 'I intend this should be a *life*-model.' Covering her own frock with an over-worked apron on which she wiped her fingers now and again, Marie began poking, prodding and pinching at a large lump of clay humped on the revolving stand before her. Immersed and happy in her work, she continually leapt forward brandishing a pair of callipers before an alarmed Estelle with which to measure the width of her forehead, length of her nose or distance between left ear and right nostril. With intense concentration, eyes and fingers darting all ways at once, Marie organised the clay into some semblance of life-sized recognition, preferring the challenge of the creative process to that of merely taking a cast of Estelle's actual features. That was a technique better reserved for the dead.

'You will give me a long neck, won't you, Marie?' Estelle pleaded. 'I have always wanted a long neck – like Queen Antoinette. It shows off my head to better advantage.'

Marie paid no attention to such engaging vanity, following only the dictates of her instinct and expertise. While she worked she talked, as Estelle directed, of her half-brothers, all fine handsome soldiers; of how her mother had married again after her first husband's death; of how her second husband had also died, resulting in her and Marie becoming part of Doctor Curtius's household. 'My Uncle-Papa allowed me to make my first model when I was seventeen – a portrait of Voltaire. In my life at home and at Court I have been extremely lucky. You have a half-brother, do you not? Is he like you to look at?'

'Indeed no,' said Estelle, with naive disdain. 'He looks nothing like anything. We'd all prefer to forget he exists, but he does so there it is. Being only my half-brother he doesn't signify much. And he's one year younger than me. Papa's always having to smack him because he's disobedient.'

'Mon dieu,' said Marie, in mock alarm, 'he sounds a problem.'

'If you promise to keep it a secret I'll tell you why – Papa won't mind because you're foreign. After my real mother died – she was Aunt Amelia's sister – my father got the cook with child then secretly married her. She became my step-mother and that's where Arthur came from. She died a year after that... well, wouldn't you if you'd given birth to a monster like Arthur? That's what Papa says and I agree. He calls him The Whelp. He has to be shut in a cupboard sometimes because he becomes noisy and throws things about. None of his tutors stay very long as they get frightened and want paying extra. I've tried to be nice to him but I don't think he likes me. Papa doesn't like him so I feel I shouldn't...'

'I'm not sure you should talk so of your family,' said Marie, without pausing in her work. 'Are you sure this is all true?'

'I'm telling you what Papa told me. He thinks the world of me and I of him, even though he *is* fat. He calls me his Bright Star – my name means 'star' in Latin you know, though mine's the French version I'm glad to say. Once, when he was *really* angry with Arthur he threw some books at him – screamed he wished he'd never been born – that he wasn't fit to be his son. I once had two real brothers but they died – Papa said my mother was useless at producing boys but he was glad she produced me as he liked girls. He married the cook to make her respectable but she gave him a useless boy – he said he wanted another useful girl. He hugged me in a very pressing way and got very loud and I ran away into the garden… I thought he'd been drinking too much of his own beer… I wonder what it would be like to drown Arthur in one of those barrels, like an unwanted cat…'

The only way Marie could halt Estelle's catalogue of drama was to call for a rest so she could flit round the room from costume jewellery to gold brocade as she imagined herself any number of fine ladies. It really was amazing – almost alarming – what she considered suitable conversation – if she was capable of considering.

Once Marie had completed the modelling of the clay head, she could only describe what was involved in converting it into a wax portrait over the next few days. Estelle listened attentively as she explained that a plaster mould would be made in two halves round the clay model, taken apart when set, then reassembled ready to receive the molten wax. The clay head would then be broken up as it had served its purpose. Once the mould was full of wax, a thick crust would be allowed to form, the remaining wax poured out from the middle thus rendering the casting hollow. When the wax had cooled and solidified, the mould would be taken apart again, the casting removed and prepared to have its glass eyes fixed in position from the inside. Eyebrows, eye lashes and the head of hair would be inserted strand by strand before the entire model was carefully and accurately tinted with water colour mixed with a little gum. Marie made notes of her sitter's complexion, hair colour and texture. As she selected the correct pair of eyes, she said that she probably could not complete the model for Estelle's departure for England but promised to send it as soon as was practical.

When Uncle Emil came to collect her in his *chaise,* she bid Marie an affectionate and grateful farewell, distraught at the thought of losing the secure attention of one who seemed like the elder sister she had never enjoyed.

Her father arrived at the Boulevard de la Reine within the week and flourished himself into the du Monde household. Amelia regarded her brother-in-law with some discomfiture. His height, his hefty bearing, his increased weight always had her reaching for her *sal volatile;* the constriction of woody hair about his features, also, and the way his bushy eyebrows almost joined across the top of his nose, giving the impression of a perpetual frown. How, she never ceased to wonder, could he have been responsible for such an attractive daughter? Poor Isabella's inexplicable choice of brash and moneyed ostentation had, at the time, left many minds aghast. But then, Isabella's knowledge of the world was limited.

True to her family name of Pocket she could be said to have virtually lived in one. Indeed, there was more than a hint of miracle-working about the fact that she had married at all, let alone mothered a daughter and two dead sons in her short married life. To the sentiment 'poor Isabella' ought now to be added 'poor Estelle', thanks to her Papa. All the good achieved during her stay would soon be ruined back in that old, mouldy house beside that odorous brewery.

Mr Havisham bullied himself into one of Amelia's refined, gilded chairs, placing great strain on its structure. He further threatened its collapse by commanding his dear Estelle to perch on his knee. He was much more suited to his sturdy Kentish Manor House, cluttered with bulbous oak and resilient Elizabethan panelling.

'I'm glad to be having my Bright Star at home again,' he exuded, in jocular mood, clenching his wine glass as if it were a tankard of ale. 'The house has been so empty with only the servants and Arthur. I was going to bring The Whelp with me but his behaviour worsened. Glad to get away from him and that's a fact.' As he drew the wine aggressively into his mouth and swallowed, Amelia was convinced she could hear its agonised rush to his stomach where it gurgled like a swilling barrel vat. Too bad Emil was not at home yet to soften the atmosphere. Already Mr Havisham had launched into a monologue of all that was wrong with France, all that was wrong with England and what ought to be done with both.

His stay lasted a slow three days. After his departure with Estelle, Amelia took to her bed with a handful of headaches. His generous promise of another visit when the climate of the times became more temperate proved too much; once the curtains were drawn tightly round her bed, Augustus's voice still gruffing in her every fibre, she doubted very much if she would live to enjoy temperate times.

TABLEAU II
1789

Once aboard the unrefined Dover Packet where Mr Havisham appeared less conspicuous, Estelle was not sure whether she was pleased or not to be sailing home. At the time of parting from Marie, the prospect of the return seemed the hardest blow fate could strike, made worse by not fully understanding the reasons for the decision. Whilst butting through the grey channel-choppings, her thoughts had returned to the sights and sounds of Versailles and Paris, the interest and attention, the new *accoutrements,* the *cadeaux* trunked in the ship's creaking hold. Only the waxen head remained to become one of her possessions. The journey gave her ample opportunity to regale her father with all she had seen, done and been complimented upon – her father patted her cheeks with his fleshy hands and interspersed her continual animation with damp kisses.

As their carriage passed through the town to Satis House, she sat upright on the upholstery and glanced with an air of distinction out of the windows. Her Queenly wave came naturally as she passed the good folk going about their business. They noted the return of the 'brewer up-town's daughter' – how adult she looked – a fine young lady. She leaned forward to catch a glimpse of the red brick mansion as the coach turned in at the gate to the front courtyard.

The February sun, the same which inflamed the *Chateau* at Versailles with added splendour, spread its radiance on her homecoming. The many bright windows twinkled their response; the chimney stacks with smoking pots reaching into the sky like countless fingers stretching for more space, told of the many wide hearths within ablaze with welcome. A high, enclosing wall shut the house off from the public roadway beyond – not even the sounds of industry from the brewery complex adjoining the side appreciably disturbed the tranquillity as Estelle alighted at Satis's impressive portico. The pageant that had been France for a twelvemonth seemed strangely distant as she trod the familiar steps into the darkly panelled hall. The servants, assembled to curtsey their greetings, were headed by the housekeeper, Mrs Comfrey, her kindly face and firm hands redolent of honest labour.

'Welcome home, Miss Estelle,' she said, placing her motherly features close to her cheek and imparting a deferential kiss. 'Welcome back, sir. I trust you had a satisfactory journey?'

'Only satisfactory, Mrs Comfrey, thank you,' Mr Havisham grunted, divesting himself of his cloak into a steward's dutiful arms. Estelle smiled to notice how the little servant girls were surreptitiously coveting her French bonnet and cape; her personal maid Zilla took charge of them with no less admiration. Estelle could not resist turning just once to display the effect of her *a la mode* outfit underneath, imagining herself Queen Antoinette benefiting her public.

'And Arthur,' said Mr Havisham, bluntly, looking round the crowded hall. 'Is his tutor with him? They are not here to greet my daughter.'

Mrs Comfrey clapped her hands sharply, turning to the servants. 'Quickly now! About your business.' Except for Zilla they scurried away like birds before a cat. 'A word, sir,' she said more quietly, drawing her master aside. 'We've had such troubles with Master Arthur since you went away. Mr Caston has gone, sir – left in the night without a word, poor young man.'

'Into the library, Mrs Comfrey, if you please. Where is Master Arthur at present, may one ask? In the game-larder I hope hanging by his neck from a meat-hook?'

'He's... in his cupboard, sir. We didn't know what else to do with him...'

Estelle lifted her hem, and leaving Zilla to attend to her duties, rushed up the stairs to the first landing. She ran along the corridor, past her own dressing room, to another staircase at the far end. Up she hurried onto the landing above and along the gloomy passage to where a devil-black cupboard, built with the ornate thoroughness of a Tudor war-ship, pompously dominated the space. She tapped on its warped doors.

'Arthur,' she called, sweetly, 'Arthur, dear boy? Are you at home?'

'Who's that?' a hoarse, muffled voice demanded.

'The Queen of France.'

'Tell her to go away.'

'That is no way to address Her Majesty,' Estelle scolded laughingly as she shook her finger at the cracked woodwork. 'She has travelled all this way to see her brother dear, only to find he is a prisoner in his little ease. It cannot be her fault if the Bastille holds all that is dearest in the world to her.'

'Get the key and let me out,' pleaded Arthur, banging on the doors.

'I shall let you out only so you may admire my new dress. I shall let you see how pretty and sophisticated your half-sister has become.' She withdrew from inside a large blue and white lidded jar a brass key which she turned in the lock with both hands before standing quickly back – a prudent move as out clattered a dishevelled tumble of boyhood.

Though younger than Estelle, in his present state he could easily have passed as one of the older knaves of Newgate. A plum-ripe bruise down the left side of what was otherwise a pleasing face lent startling effect to his shock of fair hair and bleary eyes blinded by the passage's poor light. Even Estelle was alarmed to see it, wincing as she sensed Arthur's pain. She went to help him as he picked himself up off the matting to hunch in front of her, his breeches wet with distress.

'Arthur,' she whispered, incredulously, 'what has happened? Let me see your face. Shall I bathe it?'

'Estelle! Estelle!' called her father, entering the passage at a great pace. 'Take care!'

'Get away from me!' yelled Arthur, running to the door giving access to the roof. It was locked. As Mr Havisham caught up with him he cowered, begging to be left alone. Mr Havisham dragged him backwards by the hair and slammed him shut in the cupboard, pocketing the key.

'Are you unharmed, my Bright Star?' he asked anxiously as a cannonade of blows and curses hammered the doors. He kissed her forehead. 'You were in too much of a hurry for safety.' He gave the cupboard an almighty kick. 'You will stay in there as long as you have to, now *shut up!* you little monster.'

'Monster!' added Estelle for good measure. 'You will await the Queen's pleasure!' She and her father laughed as they departed leaving Arthur's sobbing threatening to turn hysterical. But Estelle was shaken; Arthur had never before seemed so broken – the sight of him had sent a wave of panic through her. What *had* he been up to this time to warrant such extreme neglect?

'Come and see what your Papa has bought you, my pet,' said Mr Havisham, encasing her hand in his. He led her out of the house and across the yard to the stables.

'It's a white horse!' she exclaimed, even before they reached them. 'I know it is. How clever you are, Papa.'

'Where have you put Miss Estelle's animal, Hugh?' he asked of the young groom sweeping down the length of cobbles.

'End stall, sir,' said Hugh, indicating. 'Welcome home, Miss Estelle.'

'Why, thank you, Hugh,' replied Estelle, graciously. Her acknowledgement dissolved into a lingering glance; my, how the lad had grown during her absence – how his limbs had strengthened, filling out his clothing with new power characterised by an attractive face framed by long corn-coloured hair tied behind with a black ribbon. He turned from her, his dark eyes nervously averted as hers momentarily surveyed the shape of his mouth, cheek and jaw as if assessing their suitability.

With an effort she attended to the horses peacefully blinking at her as she passed their stalls. She smiled as she thought of charging powerfully across the marsh roads east of Satis to the long line of the very sea itself, twenty miles distant.

'Oh, Papa,' she cried, as she reached the end stall. 'It's tiny. I can't ride *that!*'

'This will suit you better at the moment,' said Mr Havisham, patting the pony's neck. 'I shall buy you a full-sized steed when you're old enough.'

Estelle turned with a swish of her dress. '*I am* old enough. Everyone would laugh at me on this.' She ran down the stables almost knocking the lovely Hugh into his pile of sweepings.

The air struck cold; the day was closing in; but Estelle felt hot and disappointed; humiliated, too, in front of the groom. What did Papa know about riding, anyway? He rode like a barrel rolling in a dray. Apprenticed at fourteen into his father's brewery, what need had he of French or music or drawing? An ability to dance the minuet was not likely to increase the quality of his beer. She would have a proper mount or nothing.

Skirting the communicating lane to the brewery and rattle of work leaping the wall as if to be free, she passed through a side-gate into the garden. Behind her rose the vast rear pile of Satis House. Beside it stood the brewery with its manager's three-storied house, a clock on its wall; before her, the prospect of box trees, lawns, walks and flowerbeds awaiting spring as were the greenhouses and forcing frames in the neat kitchen garden. She perched on a stone bench and surveyed the dusky estate. It had never signified until now how much the manager's house windows overlooked the garden. It seemed an intrusion which could be rectified by thicker, darker planting. The garden, too, needed modernising attractively. Though the Manor House was old-fashioned, its grounds need not also be dull.

Satis. It meant 'enough'. Owner and inhabitant were supposed to lack for nothing. Queen Elizabeth had lacked for nothing when staying once under its roof. 'Satis,' had been the royal reply when asked to assess arrangements for her comfort. Much as Estelle loved the old house, however, she was beginning to find its arrangements far from Satis. She had no one particularly to talk to, nothing particularly to do, no where particularly to go.

An impulsive idea occurred to her. She returned quickly to the house, impatient to reach her dressing room where Zilla was unpacking her trunks.

'I am going to have a party,' she announced, 'a Reception. My father is bound to say yes. Would you like to attend?'

'Oh, my, Miss Estelle,' said Zilla, drawing in breath. 'What a spectacle. 'I'm afraid I wouldn't fit in with what fine company there'd be, my goodness.'

'That's true,' agreed Estelle. 'Besides, you'll have duties. Never mind – I expect there'll be something for you with the other servants. Come on – don't stand there with your mouth open catching flies – I want you to see what I've brought from France.'

Estelle's apartment was as handsome as any at Satis, with its patterned plaster ceiling and liberal scattering of interesting but out-dated furniture. It was well lighted by wax candles in forests of graceful sconces branching from the panelling. A virile fire, framed by stalwart chimneypiece, cheered the chilly atmosphere. A door beside it, leading to her bedroom, stood ajar. Behind the mullions, curtained by thick burgundy brocade, the cold lurk of night stood little chance of tainting the close-snug luxury.

Estelle sat before a framed mirror propped up on a shabby table in the room's centre. As she surveyed her reflection, she wished this makeshift dressing table were as refined and attractive as Aunt Amelia's in her Versailles *boudoir*.

'Stop unpacking, Zilla,' she said. irritably, 'you're causing draughts. Come and redress my hair. Travelling has set me all *deshabille*. That is a French word. It means untidy. I shall be using some of them from now on but don't worry – I will explain them. Please get out my pink striped dress. Madame du Monde bought it for me in Paris. I shall wear if for dinner tonight when I discuss my Reception with Papa.'

She was pleased to see only two places set at the long, polished table in the dining room. Arthur was obviously to remain incarcerated until repentant or dead. She liked having her father to herself – that was when he was in his best mood. As she took her place he was already slicing into the joint of beef before him as if it was Arthur's backside. As the servants moved with quiet efficiency Estelle realised again that she had never cared for the dining room. Its heaviness, even in the daytime, was further encouraged by ranks of inhibiting family portraits glaring with assorted degrees of censure at the amount of food one impaled on one's fork; at whether mouthfuls were being chewed thoroughly; at whether one was speaking with one's mouth full. Indeed – was what one had to say, in fact, absolutely necessary?

She decided then and there that a singularly disapproving old maid opposite her place would have to go. Until then she directed that her place setting be reassembled next to her father under the benevolent gaze of a bewigged old Hogarthian who had obviously enjoyed the good life, judging by lobster-pink cheeks and jowls. Estelle had fallen for the airy French rooms with their pastel colourings and light furniture; she had delighted in crystal and gilt and gorgeousness – how much this black hole would be improved by polished mirrors replacing these death-blank faces eyeing her every chew and swallow. A pair of modern crystal chandeliers would worthily oust the heavy brass contraption snaking its dripping candles over the fruit *epergne*.

'Papa, I would love my rooms redecorating if possible. They are too gloomy even when the sun is in. I need light and air with lots of gold and red. Those are the colours at Versailles. If I am to be home for any length of time they ought to be done. I know my birthday was last month but they could be a late present.'

'Your pony was your late present,' said Mr Havisham, filling a tankard with beer from a pottery flagon. 'I'm grieved you don't like it – it cost me good money.'

'I'm sorry, Papa, but I'd rather have modem rooms. Please say yes. And to giving a party – a Reception – so I can meet people here again. I get quite lonely sometimes and France was full of activity and interest.'

'We can't have you lonely, my Bright Star,' said Mr Havisham, almost emptying a silver *entree* dish of vegetables offered him.

'I promise to shine if you say yes,' Estelle affirmed, playfully.

'Then I'd better have your rooms done, my dear. Do you think your adoring Papa would refuse? I shall probably set Arthur to do them. It's time he shook down to something useful and he comes cheap.'

'Please, no, not Arthur. I want them doing properly. And what *has* he been up to whilst I've been away? He has a beautiful bruise on his face.'

'He insulted Mr Caston. Quite rightly he destroyed some drawings Arthur had done when he was supposed to be working on his Latin. He wasn't afraid to keep Arthur out of mischief by working him hard and beating him harder. He was the best tutor we've had here. Mrs Comfrey tells me things got out of hand while I was away – she had to call assistance from the brewery. I tell you – I'm getting that boy off my hands as soon as possible. It's time boys of his own age beat hell out of him and sense into him.'

'Is he going to London?'

'Too close by half,' said her father, drinking and sleeving his mouth. 'I want somewhere farther afield. I've been looking at Yorkshire. Reports are favourable concerning that God-forsaken part of the world. And not expensive either – twenty guineas *per annum* and no vacations.' He lowered his voice. 'What would you say to being free of Arthur?'

He did not expect her to put her cutlery down with a frown and say, 'I don't think he ought to be sent so far. Think what he'd miss in the way of a happy family life. I know he can't help being naughty but not to let him ever come home – that seems too cruel. Besides, we'd be lost without one another.'

'Estelle,' he replied incredulously, 'you never cease to amaze me. I thought you would be delighted. He doesn't deserve your concern. It's in his blood, I'm afraid – poor stock.' He exchanged a knowing glance thus avoiding being too explicit in front of the remaining servants. 'I will accompany you after this meal to the top landing and you may release him.' He fumbled and produced the key. 'After all, you have not been together for a whole year. Just keep him out of my way until he's ready to leave for school. Alright, my dear, *not* Yorkshire – I must arrange something else.'

'And my Reception? I would like it while Arthur is still here – it will be his special treat before going to fight the world.'

After dinner her father retired to the library having been persuaded that she did not need protection from the little urchin. Taking a candle, she collected some slices of meat and a wedge of cheese in a napkin which she opened on the floor in front of the now silent cupboard. Putting some cheese in her mouth she blew the fumes through the join between the doors.

'Arthur?' she breathed, 'can you smell me? I've some lovely things out here for you. If you're good now I'll let you out.'

'I don't believe you,' whimpered Arthur's still voice. 'I want to die.'

'What a smell *that* would make!' Estelle exclaimed, 'for I don't suppose anyone would come and clear you up. You'd rot away in a *black sticky smear.*'

'Please let me out.' Arthur started to cry. As she opened the door he stared at her as if she were a stranger. Tears had marked clean channels through the dirt on his face; he was obviously in some discomfort from his clothes having absorbed the natural expressions of his stress. He crawled out but showed no interest in the food. Estelle helped him down to the lower landing, opening a door facing hers and lighting the candles from the one she carried. The room was an exact architectural replica of hers, only the doors, windows and chimneypiece were placed in the opposite positions. The lack of warmth and animation, however, were no replicas, a fire not having been kindled in the rusty grate – the mixed jumble of surrounding furniture, books and boyish paraphernalia struck chill and unwelcoming.

'Shall I look at that bruise?' she offered, sympathetically, checking there was cold water in the bedroom jug. He sat on the bed and let her bathe it, looking almost grateful for her care.

'Did someone throw a blackberry pie at you?'

'Papa hit me,' confessed Arthur. 'You know he did because he's told you.'

'That's what comes of being a bad boy,' said Estelle, simply. 'You even made your tutor leave. You'll never learn anything if your tutors keep leaving and Mr Caston was nice, if I remember rightly.'

'He was horrible. Papa told him never to let me out of his sight. He was always pulling my hair if I didn't learn – and my private parts. He thumped me too.'

'I expect it was for your own good. None of us want you to turn out like your mother.'

'Don't talk about my mother like that,' said Arthur, almost fiercely. 'She would never have been as unkind as you.'

Estelle laughed. 'She was a cook – a common cook. It was my father who was not unkind. By marrying beneath him you were born respectable. You ought to be grateful you're allowed to live here as one of the family. Good gracious – how cold it is in here.'

'Estelle,' said Arthur quietly, getting into bed, 'why are you sometimes so nasty to me? Do you hate me that much?'

'Hate you?' queried Estelle, wide-eyed. 'I don't hate you. I *pity* you – that is *quite* different. I wish you were more like me then we'd get on better. But there it is – you're not, so we have to put up with it.' She looked at her half-brother, his spare body and bleached face; she found it impossible to imagine that in a few years he could have the capacity to resemble Hugh the groom.

'To show I don't hate you,' she resumed, 'I shall invite you to my Reception. Papa says I may have one because I am newly returned from abroad. I hope nobody will laugh at your face.'

'Nobody will laugh because I won't be there.' He lay down under his coverings and stared at the wall. 'I would only spoil it and embarrass you in front of all the people Papa will force to attend.'

'I'm sorry you feel like that. I thought it would be a treat before you go.'

'Go?' said Arthur scrambling up, 'go where?'

'Hasn't Papa told you? Oh dear, I hope I haven't spoken out of turn. I thought you knew you were going to school.'

Arthur sank back. 'I don't believe you. 'You're playing games again.'

'Would I play games with you, dear brother? It's the truth. But before you start being beastly to me again, let me tell you that Papa was all for packing you off to Yorkshire, I think the place was, but I persuaded him that was a bit extreme so he's agreed to let you stay in civilisation at least. See what nice things

I do for you. And if you like, I'll also let you have pony Papa gave me. He's going to buy me a grown-up horse.'

'I don't want it,' said Arthur, retreating into his crumpled comfort. 'Please go away... I'm tired.'

'Good night, dear little brother,' she said, thrusting an icy hand under his bedclothes and giving his sparse bottom a friendly pinch as he flinched. 'Pleasant dreams.' Humming a French song she closed the bedroom door, went through the other room and across the landing to her own fireside.

One of her favourite pastimes was to sit or kneel on the floor beside the hearth looking for pictures in the flames. As if visions of the future powered the glowing tunnels between the coals, she felt drawn to penetrating the truth of her coming inheritance – an expectation which would enable her to transform Satis into the most splendid mansion in the neighbourhood; personally to oversee her manager and employees in the brewery, the tenants of her many properties in the town and in London. She would pay frequent visits to Versailles and Paris – perhaps even achieve the ambition of having her full-length wax portrait placed in the perpetual company of the King and Queen of France.

A new sensation suffused her consciousness as she stared – the response of living flesh beneath her touch. Despite Arthur's lack of substance, he had felt oddly pleasant. Though impossible to compare with Hugh, a certain mysterious daring attached itself to Arthur and the interest he might provide as a way of alleviating a certain *ennui*.

* * *

Reception indeed! The housekeeper snorted at the thought as she directed its preparations. Surely, thought Mrs Comfrey, the invitations have been sent out at rather short notice? But then again, things at Satis are never done conventionally. What would the mistress have thought? Mrs Havisham had given up trying very early on. Was it really fifteen years ago this month since she had died? She had survived Miss Estelle's birth by only a few hours. Had she ever wondered about the Master and the cook? Mrs Comfrey was convinced that had the wretched woman not died after Master Arthur was born, Mr Havisham would have schemed to get rid of her, embarrassment as she was, presumptuous upstart. Mrs Comfrey had taken it much amiss that she should have been dictated to by nothing more than a glorified fellow servant elevated through indiscretion. If Mrs Comfrey's husband had not been manager of the brewery, with a secure income and dwelling, she would have sought a position elsewhere. But Mr Havisham's money was as good as anyone's, and there had been Miss Estelle to consider – if only for the sake of her dead mother.

Mrs Comfrey had been Mrs Havisham's personal maid long before the marriage to the wealthy brewer of Satis. She had been as sorry as her mistress to leave the family home in Somerset for their new residence in Kent. She remembered Mrs Havisham's Papa with affection; Mr Thomas Pocket, in common with all his family, had been kind and gracious. It had been rumoured that though he had understandably been in favour of Isabella, his eldest daughter, marrying into money, he had found it difficult to come to terms with Augustus Havisham's age and eccentricity. When Miss Amelia's turn came, on the other hand, she appeared destined to live abroad. A worthy man, Doctor Emil. What did it matter if, compared with Mr Havisham, he was as poor as a blunt lancet?

The housekeeper had often counted her own blessings. Since marrying Mr Pocket's steward, she had enjoyed a settled if childless union, contented with her lot and prudent enough, over the years, to keep her opinions to herself. And, my goodness, what opinions: how Estelle and Arthur were being brought up; how poorly Arthur was understood and how shabbily treated; how Mr Havisham drank too much and was too fat in both figure and self-esteem. It would be no bad thing for Master Arthur to go to school – away from the closed-in atmosphere where it seemed even the sun found difficulty in penetrating the warren of deep-set passages, stairways and closets.

As Mrs Comfrey busied herself between entrance hall, dining room, library, parlour and drawing room where the music was to play, she could not admit to feeling particularly elated by the prospect of the house being invaded by humanity at large, the majority of which promised to be recruited, complete with wives, from the brewery and tenancies – since Mrs Havisham's death, many acquaintances had retired into the background. Mrs Comfrey was only thankful she could escape to her house and husband across the brewery yard – but even there she was not immune, for the clock on the wall never failed to remind her of duty's inexorability circling the weeks, months, years.

That morning Estelle had been in ecstasies on entering her *boudoir,* as she now called her dressing room. A mystified excitement filled her awakening as she beheld a large, shrouded object placed where her old dressing table had stood the night before. Zilla seemed to have some secret about her tiresome giggling which she kept girlishly trying to smother with her apron.

'Belated birthday greetings my little Bright Star!' effused her father with hearty bounce. 'I am impatient to see the effect of my *new* present on my angel. Better than a pony, I'll wager. Come now – unveil it and mind if it bites! I took the wagon to London to collect it specially.'

Estelle approached the sheeted hump, cautiously lifting the hem. Having ascertained that no gruesome creature lurked beneath she drew off the covering.

'Oh!' she exclaimed in genuine wonderment. 'It's beautiful!' Before her stood the neatest, most stylish French dressing table with gilt-framed looking-glass to which were attached, on either side, two scrolling pairs of candleholders. Light sprigged muslin hangings pinioned by dimpled cherubs cavorting about the frame's apex, draped down each side to meet the gatherings of fine-spun fabric round the table's belly and legs. Her silver brushes, silver-topped jars, candlesticks, gold and enamel *etui* and silver dishes authoritatively dominated the space before the mirror as if proud of this new home worthy of their quality.

'It's adorable, Papa.' She sat before the mirror, her eyes shining, on the arm of her old chair. 'It's a fine lady's dressing-table – just right – and I am the fine lady.' She glanced at her reflection. 'Now you'll *have* to redecorate my rooms – all French – something Queen Antoinette would approve. And I need a chair to match – this one's so shabby. I shall dress before this mirror tonight for my Reception. Come, Zilla, you can brush my hair now – I am quite awake. Has the pony gone yet, Papa? If not I should like Arthur to have it. The poor boy is not to be here much longer.'

Mr Havisham remained where he was by the door for a moment longer, admiring the image Estelle created, seated in her flowing housecoat before the mirror of truth reflecting her proud beauty; such an image, he thought, as would enhance her wedding day when she would prepare herself for her fortunate bridegroom before the same silvering. He blew her a kiss.

The only person who looked in on Arthur that day was Mrs Comfrey. Her motherly instinct would not let her abandon him, in spite of her many other duties. But even she could not tempt him to glass of warm milk or biscuit. She nearly shed tears on his behalf to have to leave him in solitude, seeing nothing of the preparations for the evening: the acres of white table linen spread like moonlight on the sea; the piles of gilt-edged apple-green crockery; forests of silver candelabra amidst meadows of savouries and desserts; extra servants got in from the town dovetailing with one another under Mrs Comfrey's hard-pressed but efficient ministrations; the lighting of extra candles – arrangements of extra chairs; the fixing open of all doors to all party rooms in extra swings of abundance. Arthur heard the muffled happenings reverberating up to his room, up the bed legs, through the mattress, along the very fibres of bedding to his ears. But he was content to lie in his isolation – happy to expire, even... anything to save him the bother of growing up. Deepening dusk calmed further until candle-bearing Estelle, busy in the curl and cut of fashion, entered to ask him nicely to get up and dress for the Reception was about to commence.

'If you told me I was not allowed to attend,' he mumbled, 'you know I would want to. You know I *don't* want to which is why you want me to.'

Estelle was almost too hurt to know how to reply. 'How mean you are,' she said suddenly, boxing his ears with unfashionable inelegance. 'Stay here then and fester then for all I care.' As she hurried out in a flurry of chiffon and silk her father met her on the landing. It was plain to see by his ruddy complexion that he had been sampling the liquid refreshment – it was lubricating his beaming affability which he wielded with as much delicacy as a terrier with a rat whilst he told her the guests were arriving. Though out of sorts with Arthur, she immediately composed herself and descended the staircase where she stood proudly to receive on the bottom step in her crisp green-striped satin robe and French *fichu;* her beribboned toque she supported as if it were a crown.

The multitude, encased in their best and even new clothing, shuffled past in humble discomfiture, offering their greetings with a social smile. Pleased as Estelle tried to be to see them, she could not move Arthur's behaviour from her mind and it coloured her outlook on the evening, even to such details as Mr Hollingberry's waistcoat which appeared at least three sizes too large. Mrs Parsons's garments looked to be twenty years out-of-date, but still a good deal younger than their occupant. There were the Misses Wishton – elegant, but without their own coachman. She remained on her dais until her sense of duty, and her father's promptings, propelled her forward *a la Antoinette* as the fiddler from The Blue Boar and his friends began coaxing melodies from their instruments in an attempt to encourage animation. But the populace remained ill at ease, as if unfamiliar with one another in such affluent surroundings. An air of mixed misfortune prevailed, hampering the atmosphere like a badly managed disaster. Estelle addressed her nearest neighbour in desperation.

'Such a delightful gown, Mrs Parsons. You must be extremely fond of it having kept it so long.' Mrs Parsons smiled uncertainly, sipping at her cup of punch. 'So curious to see such clothing these days. Ah, Mr Haspole. How was last year's hop harvest? While I was lately on the Continent, I was able to behold that the French had enjoyed a particularly fine crop. Tell me, for I am most anxious to know, how does the English market compare with across the Channel?'

'Well, Miss Estelle,' began the hapless employee, clearing his throat uneasily, 'I...'

'Ladies and gentlemen!' Mr Havisham's spirited voice crowded an easy hush as heads turned towards the staircase. 'My daughter and I are overjoyed to welcome you all to Satis House this evening – don't be afraid to ask for anything you want – there are plenty of servants to do as you say and no expense has been spared on anyone's account so feel free to make the most of it. As you are all aware, my daughter has been abroad for some time, but has returned glad to see you all and eager that you'll benefit from her friendship. She takes a great interest, as indeed I do myself, in the people I have working for the Havishams and is the first to thank you for being received here tonight where so many of you are not used to this kind of event before. So I shall be pleased if you will raise your glasses and drink to the good health and wealth of my Bright Star, Miss Estelle Havisham, God bless her.'

God's blessing, as it trickled from mouth to mouth, was soon submerged and awkwardly swallowed.

'And now,' continued Mr Havisham, raising his eyebrows like a couple of fluffy drawbridges, 'thanking you I'm sure. I am pleased to announce the magnificence of the repast you will find provided at no mean expense from which you are heartily invited to help yourselves, for it can't be often you're allowed to regale yourselves to such a degree, so don't hold back and feel you'll be judged by how much you eat and drink. Thank you.' He pushed his way through corporate inhibition towards his daughter. 'My Bright Star! I take your hands and kiss them. Are you having a splendid time? Have I told you how you look in green stripes?'

'You, Papa, are inebriated.' Estelle pulled her hands away. 'It's so upsetting... and tonight of all nights...'

'Inebriated only with your success, my love,' smiled her father, swaying slightly.

'What shall you do about Arthur? He won't come down and join us. I don't want him to get away with defying me.'

'You leave Arthur to me. When I've filled my belly I'll be in a fit state to settle him.'

The dining room had been set out, on Estelle's orders, with large tables of food for a *buffet*. Those guests with full plates drifted back into the hall and other rooms. The punch and ale, as they began to suffuse the collective bloodstreams, had helped to imbue the gathering with a little more life. Even slivers of laughter could be detected. Miss Charlotte Wishton, forbidden by her sister to decline the evening, graced a seat at the foot of the stairs whilst conversing with Miss Pinfold whose father leased from Mr Havisham, the haberdasher's premises in the High Street. They had just commenced discussion, *sotto-voce,* on Estelle's green-striped superiority, when their attention was diverted by a yellow liquid splashing onto Charlotte's plate from above. Thinking someone had spilled a drink Charlotte glanced up. Screaming, she leaped from her place, catapulting her food over her neighbours as she saw the naked figure of a boy standing at the edge of the landing responding to nature's call between the banisters. Miss Wishton's solo became a chorus as the steaming torrent, now in full flood, slashed an ever-widening embrace, scattering its stained recipients.

'Leave him to me!' bellowed Mr Havisham, bounding into the hall, his eyes narrowing as he beheld his son hosing down his scattering audience. Arthur turned on his heel and ran along the corridor, past his room, to the staircase at the end, skipping nimbly up with his father close behind hurling insults. He ran back along the top passage, past his cupboard and down the stairs that joined the landing at the front. His very nudity seemed a protection against capture as he descended to the body of the party. His father, panting and cursing down after him instigated Arthur's zig-zag course into the dining room where he kept his father and anyone else at bay with volleys of bread rolls and fruit. Nearby stewards, attempting to disarm him, lost their quarry as it dived under the tables dislodging cloths and arrangements. His father, a horse-whip springing in his hand like a snake smelling blood, dived amongst the *debris* and pulled a now hysterical Arthur out by an ankle. He lashed the whip across his bare buttocks. 'You want to join the party, do you? We'll see how much you enjoy it now you *are* here!'

He demanded that Hugh the groom and other young assistants drag him over the chaos into the hall amidst a scarified silence and thrust his arms through the carved banister posts to secure him by pulling until his ribcage locked against the knobbly woodwork. He flayed the whip across Arthur's thin back, cutting crimson rivulets shoulder to thigh.

'No, no!' called several voices, but it was Mr Comfrey who pushed forward and stayed Mr Havisham's arm, nearly collecting the next cut himself.

'For the love of God, Sir, what are you about? You'll kill the lad.'

'What of it?' demanded Mr Havisham, crashing his dark eyebrows together. 'I'll thank you to mind your own business!'

'This is murder – you must not do it.'

'*Must* not?' shouted Mr Havisham, unsure of whether to be more angry with his son or his manager. 'I can do as I please with him, as I can with you. None of you know what I have to put up with on account of this whelp. Call himself a Havisham! Don't tell me…'

'Father! Touch him again and I shall summon the Magistrate. Soldiers if necessary.'

Mr Havisham slumped round. 'Estelle? What the devil…'

'Release him, Hugh,' commanded Estelle coming forward. Arthur almost collapsed into her arms as she was assisted to carry him upstairs. Her father stared disbelievingly after them amidst surrounding surprise, but composed himself enough to apologise for the comedy and invite everyone to continue enjoying themselves. He took the first opportunity to shamble away with a bottle of brandy to the privacy of his brewery office.

Mrs Comfrey took charge of the situation, with her husband's help. But one guest wishing to depart was the signal for a general exodus; before long only a handful of retainers remained. Her heart was heavy as she considered the evening a failure despite so much hard work. Fancy the Master going for the boy like that and fancy Miss Estelle going against her Papa – an event of some import in the Havisham annals.

Estelle had directed Arthur to be lain gently on his bed. She simply looked at him too confused for words, her anger as unpredictable as an unguarded fire.

He lay back and smiled cheekily. 'Did you like my present? I saved it for you specially. Now you really *are* famous, for I don't suppose anyone will talk about anything else for a very long time.'

'I think,' said Estelle, selecting her words carefully, 'that I would be quite happy to dip you in tallow, shut you in your cupboard and set it alight. When Papa has finished with you, that option will seem like paradise.'

'You can do what you like. It doesn't matter to me any more. I wouldn't mind being dead if it meant you were hung, drawn and quartered with your bits pecked out by the crows at the roadside.'

Disappointment and frustration powered her fists onto Arthur in a frenzy of movement which he tried to avoid and repay, a maelstrom of shouts and unsheathed language bringing the servants running in at the door as furniture overturned. As they screamed, 'fetch the Master!', Estelle clutched at a clump of Arthur's hair, pulling it out with such force that blood clung to its roots – she would probably have clubbed him with a heavy candlestick rolling on the floor amongst their fight had her father not crashed in with his blunderbuss.

'Stop it! *Stop it! Both of you!*' he bellowed, spraying the air with brandy-charged saliva. He turned the muzzle on his children. 'Estelle, let him be! Go to your room! Leave him to me!'

Trembling and tearful she rushed out slamming the door behind her. Zilla, who waited with concern, was sent away for the night. As Estelle slumped in her arm chair beside her fire, she noticed blood on her dress and saw that she still held Arthur's hair. She pitched it hurriedly into the blue, frost-bitten flames, watching it smoke with an evil darkness before hissing into nothingness. From across the corridor echoed fierce beatings and screamings, a vibrating door-slam, the jangle of keys then footsteps diminishing into silence. She remained shivering where she was; not even the friendly memory of a smiling Hugh, almost unfamiliar but no less attractive in his best attire, dispelled her fright and depression as it melted into the soothing salve of sleep. Zilla, finding her in the morning curled and cramped by the dead fire, helped her into bed where she slept a good part of the day; her father had resorted to the bottle. When she ventured downstairs for dinner she saw that all signs of the previous evening's revelry had been removed. Her father, a little vague with brandy, sat in his place and spoke to her as if he was continuing an existing conversation... 'locked in his room... that's where he'll stay till he goes to school... you won't need to see him before then if you wish.'

'That would be sad,' said Estelle, equally quietly. 'I should like to speed him on his way. Who knows when I may see him again, poor deranged mooncalf. Life won't seem the same without him.' She now knew that after further discussion he was not to be sent, after all, to the fastness of Yorkshire but to a worthy establishment in the Midlands with an academic credibility which would add intellectual pressure to physical. This, perhaps, would be emphasised by his arriving after the start of term, the result, Estelle and her father considered, of his own difficulties. His trunk was packed and in two days' time he was to accompany his father on the coach to The Cross Keys, Cheapside, in the City, in order to take his place on the north-bound coach round at The Saracen's Head, Snow Hill.

He was still locked up when a substantial wooden container – a bandbox bound with brass straps – was delivered into the hall at Satis. Estelle immediately recognised Marie's handwriting and ordered the package to be undone without delay. This was the moment she had been awaiting so keenly since her return. Once the lid was detached she would have nobody but herself disengage the contents from its masterly packing, a work of art in itself. The perfection of the waxen head emerged unaffected by its long journey from Paris. Estelle placed her likeness on the hall table, confronting herself with mixed emotions. She was particularly impressed by the matched pair of eyes and attractive coif of bright artificial flowers. Her only disappointment was that the model's neck was not as swan-like as she had hoped. But then, Marie created only what she truthfully saw.

Estelle sent to the brewery for her father. His fulsome praise fizzed as unreserved as hers. He considered the head excellent in both feature and colouring. Estelle was pleased to be able to explain how it had been made, as if she were the expert, particularly when the servants were bidden to view and voice favourable opinions. Only one of them enthused slightly wide of the mark – an ancient laundress rather hard-of-hearing – who declared the model an unmistakable likeness of the late Mrs Havisham... the living image in fact! She was soon returned to her stains in the wash-house. Estelle took two letters from the box, passing the one in Aunt Amelia's handwriting to her father.

'Don't tell Arthur about this model,' she said, going upstairs with Marie's letter. 'He'll find out about it in due time.' A servant followed with the head, depositing it on the dressing table. Estelle sat in her armchair by the fire and unfolded the note.

Here, as promised, is the portrait, complete in all details and delivered with affection as it leaves my studio. It is fragile so must be treated carefully. I am interested in your comments, cherie, yet you do not write since your return to England. Your aunt also has concerns for you and is asking me to enclose her letter to your Papa.

I am sad to report Paris is unsettled at the moment and our dear Royals not enjoying favour. Also, le petit Dauphin is not well – he can hardly walk now. Thank God he has a younger brother to take his place should the worst occur. Already the Queen has lost one little daughter, Madame Sophie Beatrix.

You remember that terrible hailstorm here last July when windows were broken and many villages damaged? Uncle-Papa tells me it ruined the harvest so much that bread prices have risen alarmingly – we may have to pay as much as fourteen sous a loaf by the summer – a bleak prospect when placed against our national bankruptcy. Your Aunt Amelia is worried more than most as she does not fully understand the complexities of the situation though the good doctor tries his best to explain.

Please write if you can spare the time. You know how I dislike writing letters so forgive the shortness of this — I have much work to see to also. Being busy distracts the mind from problems, I find. I am wanting to know your criticisms of the model — the patron must always be contented. I value the likeness, particularly en profile. What do you do in England in cold weather? If only Spring would bring a settlement to all our problems.

Affectionately yours,

Marie

I must write, Estelle told herself sternly. I shall when Arthur is packed off and I can think clearly again. In the meantime I must show him my model, but at the best time for him to appreciate its artistry and drama. Smiling to herself she rang her bell and awaited Zilla's attendance.

'We're going to have fun,' she said, as Zilla knocked and entered. 'I have a particular fancy for diversion — to see some play. You will assist me but tell no one. Is that understood? Draw up that stool and *attendez-vous* — that means pay attention you.' Zilla sat submissively at her mistress's feet, interspersing Estelle's monologue with sentiments such as, 'oh no, Miss, I couldn't,' and 'Lawd save us, what if the Master found out?' But both girls relished the guilty sense of humour and were of one mind at the end of the transaction.

The morning of Arthur's departure arrived as surely as another day of sunless chill. He was released early from his immurement. It was five-thirty — the London coach departed from The Blue Boar at seven, to arrive at Cheapside about noon. His trunk was corded; he had breakfasted and appeared to have no particular regrets at leaving. It seemed a good omen that Estelle had not stirred herself on his behalf.

'Master Arthur,' said Zilla, coming down the stairs to him as Mrs Comfrey organised his muffling-up, 'Miss Estelle requests you to step into her *boudoir* as she wishes particular to see you, prior to your journey, expressly.'

Mrs Comfrey stared at Zilla. Where in the world had she picked up such a speech? 'Be quick then, Master Arthur – you know your Papa doesn't like being kept waiting.'

Zilla took Arthur's hand and led him upstairs to Estelle's darkened room. 'Miss Estelle has a present she wants for certain to leave with you. It's there – in the bedroom – through you go.'

At the doorway he stood and stared. Round the bed at regular intervals were placed candles from both rooms; in the bed lay the silent, straight figure of Estelle, hair gracefully arranged under a coif of flowers, eyes glassily staring at the ceiling, waxy mouth closed. He felt his breath surge upwards into a stifled scream even as Zilla guided him to the bedside with a fond smile. 'Now she looks as she says you've often wished, the dear Mistress. Lovely, isn't she?'

'Oh God,' he managed to say. 'What's the matter with her? She's not dead?'

'This is the Death Trap,' breathed a voice behind him, 'and this is the shroud to put you in.' He turned in alarm. Coming towards him from behind the door he saw Estelle – white-faced, white-gowned, white-handed – shaking a folded white sheet at him. 'Let me dress you for your death, little brother. This is your shroud. See? Is it not a pretty thing? As pretty as your sister?'

Arthur stared dumbfoundedly at the living image then the dead, his mouth opening and closing, wordless.

'No, no, no,' he uttered at last. 'Get away from me... who ever you are. You're mad... leave me alone!' He tore the quilt from the bed and rushing with it towards the white spectre, threw it on her as he fled the room, nearly colliding with his father when he reached the corridor.

'What the hell are you doing, Arthur? We'll miss the coach if we don't get a move on – the gig's been waiting ten minutes. Have you finished your goodbyes to your sister?' He saw that his son, with moist eyes, was unable to get his words out for trembling. 'I'm glad to see you registering *some* emotion at leaving us. Perhaps when you're at school you'll reflect on how fortunate you are in your home. When you return for a holiday, if you behave yourself, perhaps you'll appreciate your advantages. Come on now, lad, time is not with us.'

As the sounds of departure faded, Estelle and Zilla tried hilariously to suppress their shrill mirth.

'Did you see his face?' laughed Estelle, the more controlled. 'He thought he saw a ghost. He won't forget *that* in a hurry.'

'Lawks, Miss,' spluttered Zilla into her apron, 'I never did see such a performance. What ever you'll think of next I'm sure I don't know.'

'I'm not much of your opinion,' said Estelle curtly, suddenly tired of the charade. 'I want to go back to bed awhile – make it ready and clear up the room – I will take charge of my model.'

Later that day she wandered along the corridor and up the stairs to the top passage. The house felt somehow incomplete without Arthur's sequestered presence. It was an unfamiliar experience. It seemed unnatural not to address a few select words to his cupboard as she passed. His room, too, was neutral ground – grey, gloomy, shabby, untidy. As far as she could ascertain, only some of his scant wardrobe had been bundled off to school with him – a handful of books too – that appeared all. The dressing room and bedroom were littered with the disturbance of continual habitation. As she drifted round she thought what a fine bonfire it would all make; and these rooms would do up most handsomely – the view onto the garden was particularly attractive on this side of the house: *le Petit Trianon, par example.*

Some half-buried drawings on the window seat caught her wandering attention. She extracted them from the clutter of cushions, books and other papers. Arthur had a vivid imagination and some ability for drawing, particularly caricature, as Estelle knew his tutors had discovered to their cost – many a formal piece of work had the adornment of corpses hanging from trees, monsters consuming human sacrifices and damsels burning on funerary pyres. Estelle immediately recognised herself amongst them, dressed in her green-striped Reception dress and a broad-brimmed French hat. Tied to a stake, she begged for mercy from Arthur as the flames closed in. Another showed her hanging from a beam in the brewery, hooded monk-like beings brandishing blazing torches with which they goaded her.

Sickened, and releasing a prickle of tears, she glanced at the largest drawing – one that made her bite her lip in disbelief. It was drawn with more precision than the rest. There, quite plainly, was her unmistakable figure sitting in her armchair by her fireplace and dressed in some sort of fantastic outfit reminiscent of a bridal gown mixed with her draped dressing table. A large piece of glowing coal appeared to have fallen out of the grate, causing a swirl of flame to sear her side, to tower as tall as herself above her mask of agony. Behind her stretched a long table set as if for a banquet. Countless numbers of faded, hooded apparitions, Arthur amongst them, regaled themselves, raising their goblets to cheer her as she burned.

Faint with shock she scooped the drawings together in crackling frenzy and hurried them to her room where she ripped them to fragments. She stabbed them into her fire, poking... poking... fiercely until they were ash.

TABLEAU III
1789

Had Estelle persevered in corresponding with Marie on a deeper level, she might have acquired a greater insight into events developing the other side of the channel. Had she persevered in her drawing, music and dancing, she might have acquired a greater insight into self-expression through the graceful arts. But she had never been encouraged to look to the higher issues of mankind; though there was the potential, it had never successfully been drawn out, except, perhaps, for during her year in France under Marie's influence. But try as she might, her letters to Estelle did not spark the deeper responses she had hoped for, even when she wrote of how the May sun wreathed the bed of the eight year-old *Dauphin* dying of rickets in front of his helpless parents; of how it illuminated the 1,200 or so members constituting the States General, meeting in the white and gold Hall of Lesser Pleasures at Versailles in an attempt to diffuse a political and economic crisis; of how Uncle-Papa saw the shadows continue to fall across the monarchy, as by June 23rd, the old States General became the new National Assembly; of how its growing authority weakened the monarchy's; of how His Majesty, fearing disturbances, supplemented the Paris garrison of 15,000 police and 5,000 troops with a further 16 regiments – not a soldier too many when the first shudder of Parisian unrest began with looting at a military prison; of how it was now a positive advantage to be seen to be sympathetic to the populace and its concept of liberty and equality.

Marie, as fearful of inactivity at the Boulevard du Temple as she was of increasing activity in the streets of the capital, made sure she kept herself well informed, though having decided that events were now way beyond Estelle's comprehension. The evenings of home-bound ease with Uncle-Papa, Mama, sometimes Doctor Emil, provided ample opportunities for discussion and consideration of several options of necessary action should the need for self-preservation manifest itself. The only certainty at present was Marie's refusal to close the *Cabinet de Cire* – education through art could be a powerful factor for the general good – the public expected to be kept up-to date with personalities and their roles in current events; the Wax Museum must never for one moment be allowed to fall behind the times and appear biased.

But in the peace of Kent and around Satis, the orchards and hop fields unclosed in unbothered fragrance. The same sun that had penetrated the Hall of Lesser Pleasures and its deliberations slipped its radiance down the Havisham garden glowing in kept colourings. Box trees and hedges put out fresh green limbs from the dark; vines, melons and cucumbers, glass-framed in protective entities swelled with sap and vitality; doves and fantails fluttered about rooftops and their white barrel house on a pole in the brewery yard, the promise of high summer flashing from white wing to wing.

Likewise in the red brick reaches of Chelsea, up by the Thames, other pigeons cooed about their freedom in quiet gardens sweetened by flowers tended by caring hands. Daniel Pocket's were amongst those. He loved his flowers – they made him smile. But today his brow was as furrowed as newly dug earth. He sat on the circular rustic seat built round the trunk of his weeping willow, in his hand a letter from his sister Amelia at Versailles. She wrote of troubles in Paris and the prevalent atmosphere of impending disaster. Husband Emil, true to du Monde inquisitiveness, was ever punctilious in obtaining the latest information and he and his friend Philippe Curtius could be relied upon. She admitted to not being completely *au fait* with what they told her but was sure Daniel would know all about it anyway so did not feel the need to attempt an explanation.

He sighed. Amelia had not changed. She remained as vague as always – as vague as their sister Isabella, whisked away over fifteen years ago to a vague life and vaguer death in that dreary Kentish tomb near the marshes. Then again, saddled to a man like Havisham, death might seem the kinder option. He returned to his sister's letter. She had added a postscript giving details of the States General's meeting in Versailles, knowing of her brother's interest in politics – it told him little other than that the town had been fortified with numberless kilos of extra provisions and that new latrines had been dug and disinfected with floods of vinegar... Daniel burst out laughing. Did she actually consider he would find such knowledge relevant? Poor Amelia – she was almost engaging in her incompetence. How ever did Emil manage? Her headaches must try his patience and pharmacopoeia to extremes.

His expression changed quickly as he remembered something more pressing than problems and pillage in Paris – the imminent visit of his niece Estelle. That ugly brute Havisham had written to tell him that now the weather was proving more favourable to his wishes, he desired his daughter to become further acquainted with the social arts and graces in the company of her dear aunt, uncle and cousins in the good air of Chelsea, which meant he would not be obliged to open up the house in Brook Street, Mayfair. Instead he would be willing to reimburse the Pocket exchequer for any financial deficiency Estelle might incur – he fully realised that men of books and letters such as her Uncle Daniel could not hope to enjoy the pecuniary stability of a businessman such as himself. His daughter, however, had said that she was prepared to make allowances and looked forward to benefiting from her visit as much as her hosts.

A wily man, Havisham, thought Daniel. He knows that however much he insults me I will yet oblige him for the love I bore Estelle's mother. What does *he* know of brotherly affection – an only son who loves only himself and his only daughter? But that did not alter the fact that Estelle resembled Isabella in many ways; to Daniel she was the closest tangible reminder of his happy childhood at home with his sisters. Not having seen Estelle for some time he was curious to know whether the pleasant side of her nature was further developed.

Her cousins, who had always been jealous of her, were miserable at the prospect of her invasion; miserable with their parents for allowing *that Havisham man* to dictate to them; miserable with one another for being miserable. Thirteen year-old Matthew, his elder sister Sarah and younger sister Camilla retained unaffectionate memories of previous associations. Matthew was particularly dull in Estelle's eyes because he had inherited his father's virtue and plain honesty; Sarah, equal to Estelle in self-esteem, was too much of a rival ever to be a friend; Camilla did not count as she suffered from her mother's family failing of headaches, as made fashionable by her Aunt Amelia. They much preferred their cousin Arthur – he was good fun, especially with his funny drawings. What a pity he was at school – perhaps he could come during a holiday. Arthur was daring, too... he thought nothing of swimming as nature intended!

'There's no doubt,' the children heard their father say to their mother, 'that Havisham's money will be useful. If he offers it and means it I shall not refuse it out of false pride. We must do what we can to make Estelle's visit enjoyable – for all of us. We know she can be a little madam but that's not altogether her fault. Deep down somewhere she's good-hearted. Let's see if we encourage more of it to surface.'

Caroline nodded with a smile as she completed her flower arrangement by the window. She, too, loved the garden and was as fair as any of the blooms she and Daniel so thoroughly tended.

'Besides,' he continued, 'I am anxious to have first-hand news of France, though I know it's been nearly six months since she was there. It'll be something, though.' He turned a warning countenance upon his children. 'What ever your natural inclinations, my dears, remember – Estelle is also a Pocket. I forbid you – absolutely forbid you – to disgrace us in front of our guest with bad behaviour. If it'll help, try and forget she's a Havisham.'

'Yes, Papa,' came the downcast, three-fold reply.

'Couldn't we,' wheedled Sarah, in what she imagined was her most winsome manner, 'put just one *tiny* cockroach in her bed – *ever* so tiny?'

Daniel shook his head. 'Nothing worthwhile is achieved by demeaning yourself to the lowest common denominator.'

'We don't understand your big words, Papa,' said Matthew seriously, 'but we promise to be as good as we can despite Estelle's a Havisham. All I hope is that she smells a flower and there's a bee in it and it goes up her nose and stings her.' He could tell by his father's ineffectual attempt to mask a smile that he, too, might be gratified by the possibility.

A show of baggage accompanied Estelle's arrival the following day. The children greeted her with a gush of welcoming affection which would have spelled insincerity to the better adjusted. She received it in a courtly manner, however, administering hers likewise. 'I have much to tell you of my time in France.'

'We want to hear all your news, dear child,' said Uncle Daniel, 'particularly concerning Versailles and your aunt and uncle. But all in good time. Matthew, take your sisters and cousin into the garden – let her see the river and inhale the flowers. Remember instructions.'

'What instructions?' inquired Estelle, following him outside.

'About falling in,' said Matthew, pointedly, 'or being pushed.'

This was not going to be easy – Estelle had grown up so and she knew it. Papa was right about self-control. But could it survive ten days?

'...London looked smaller than I remembered,' she was saying, gazing down-river. Sarah glowered at a tree trunk – Camilla prepared to retreat into an ailment. 'I'm glad you live out here where the river doesn't smell so. I wish your house had been large enough to accommodate my maid...I don't know what I'll do without Zilla.'

'We like it here,' said Matthew, his hackles already rising. Sarah, he noted, had that evil glint in her eye. 'Papa says it's more healthy than Westminster – or Mayfair. If he *does* go into Parliament he says we shan't be moving.'

'Fancy someone who writes books going into Parliament,' laughed Estelle, favouring the daisy-spangled grass with her feet. 'And such dull books at that, with no pictures. Who wants to know what happened years and years ago? It's all done and finished with.'

'That's an unkind thing you've said about Papa,' retorted Matthew heatedly, quite forgetting his promise. 'I'm not going to let you get away with it – Camilla, don't interrupt – he's very clever... cleverer than yours, and kinder.'

'That's right, Matthew,' encouraged Sarah, nodding eagerly, 'you tell her.'

'I'm *older* than you, Matthew Pocket, so I know *more* than you.' Estelle tossed aside her loose ringlets. 'You seem to forget – I have lived in France, so I *ought* to.'

'What do you know about France?' demanded Matthew, so like his father in times of seriousness. 'Papa has explained it all to us – it's all happening because of people like you.'

'If by that remark you mean the King and Queen, then it simply proves how little you really know. You've not been to France – I have a friend there called Marie and she knows the King and Queen well. I have seen them and you haven't. They're a good deal more exciting than the mad, pig-faced farmer on *our* throne...' She stopped abruptly. She had not meant to become so volatile. She found it too easy when trying to prove herself.

'Papa! Mama!' Camilla ran indoors. 'Matthew and Estelle are fighting! He's going to drown her! I'm going to be sick!'

Disbelievingly, Daniel hurried out after her into the garden.

'Papa,' announced Matthew, taking his hand, 'Estelle has been insulting you and King George and I don't like her and she makes Camilla sick and neither does Sarah.' Camilla, prompted by his sentiments, leaned threateningly over some undeserving flowers.

'To the nursery, Camilla,' Daniel ordered. 'You have obviously had too much sun. Take her up, Sarah, and tell Annie to put her to bed.' He watched them depart before turning on his son. 'I am disappointed, Matthew. You have no call to argue with your guest. Apologise at once – take that smile off your face, Estelle, you forget yourself. It was uncalled-for of you to provoke your host – I hope this is not the example you set at your Aunt Amelia's – do *not* turn your back on me, young lady! I have not finished with you yet.'

In amazement Estelle stopped in her tracks. Her uncle went to her and placed his hands on her shoulders. 'My dear... we are a peaceful household here. Please try to appreciate that – look on us as friends with whom you needn't feel you have to be on show. We accept people for what they are and certainly have no wish to challenge for the sake of it. We want good feeling on all sides.' He looked back with meaning at Matthew.

'I'm sorry, Estelle,' said her cousin, pleasantly. 'Please let's try and be friends.' There was something of a pause during which she did not look round.

'I, too, am sorry,' she said softly.

Daniel hugged her as she tried to suppress some noisy sobs. 'There, it's all over now and forgotten. Dry your eyes. Matthew will take you indoors and show you your room then come and join us when you feel ready.'

After Matthew returned from his errand he received a stern talking-to from his father, rather Parliamentary in reasoning and delivery, which impressed him for reasons his father had not intended.

Without letting her emotions run too wild over dinner that evening, Estelle managed to give an account of the waxen head, her year in France, her association with Marie Grosholtz, the glory that was the Queen and Court at Versailles. By the end of the meal she fairly beamed with benevolence.

She wrote three letters home to her father during her visit but in trying to dwell on the more pleasant aspects, felt it unnecessary to mention the altercation in her Uncle Daniel's garden:

...The Pocket family are doing their best to provide me with an enjoyable stay but it proves rather tedious sometimes as they talk about things which I don't always understand, even when it's about France. Cousin Matthew seems to know more than me though he's younger. Sarah ignores me completely and I her. It is best that way. Camilla is a constant pain in the neck – I've not known a day pass without her drooping like an unironed ruffle.

We were taken to see a collection of pictures at Somerset Palace by the river where I met one of Uncle's friends, Sir Roseberry Topping, who was most civil to me. The Royal Academy of Painters was putting on a show but it was so hot and busy that I inherited one of Camilla's headaches. The walls were so crowded with pictures up to the ceiling that it was difficult to see above half way but there were some lovely things on show, many of which I would love to have at Satis. I must confess, I am rather taken by the notion of having my portrait painted by Mr Romney, a pretty passable painter I should say...

Uncle has been anxious for me to experience a Spa, my never having visited Bath or Tunbridge Wells. We visited some wells owned by a Mr Sadler – all so diverting. There was a pantomime in the playhouse and lots of avenues and groves in a park with lakes and trees full of lanterns. We could sit out on benches at tables and eat cold chops and ham pasties. The wine was not as good as at Satis I am pleased to relate, and had no effect on me whatsoever – you would have hated it. I became quite giddy enough simply watching the rope-walkers and ballet dancers and some extremely skilful balancing tricks. A strong man performed amazing feats wearing only a leopard skin and stick-on whiskers.

I wish particularly to see the Royal Family and compare them with the French, but Uncle said they do not like going about much as the King is far happier in his library talking to Mr Boswell, who ever he is. The King is much better at the moment – he has not been mad for some time. He just tinkers with clocks and likes digging. King Louis likes clocks too, and locks – perhaps they should work together.

We did, however, promenade in St James's Park, so I was able to approve of the Queen's House which is at one end. I thought it would be like le Petit Trianon but it is much less private and quite old-fashioned behind railings and a courtyard from which there is a nice view of London. I think that is the best feature. When the front door is open, Uncle says, you can see straight into the hall which is full of pillars and has wonderful painted ceiling…

Of an evening, Chelsea is full of all kinds of strangers who have perambulated along the river bank from Westminster and the City, even actually crossed the river. They come from miles around on family excursions, all covered with dust, to what is called The Bun House where they purchase – a bun! It is considered a great delicacy but having tasted it I am not sure why.

I confess I shall be a little sorry to leave here, where there is so much industry and busyness and where everything is active and alive. I have met some fascinating and influential society – Uncle Daniel introduced me to Sir Weely Springs and Sir Kirby Gryndalythe. I savoured the attentions of the young rakish Sir Goredale Scar, but certainly not those of the ageing fusty Sir Melton Bottom. The Pockets have been most agreeable and made my stay most enjoyable, even my cousins who have been trying with their manners...

On the eve of her departure for Satis on 12th July, Uncle Daniel requested her to join him in his study. The strain of having her had lessened considerably as her gratitude had become more evident. They talked over a number of issues, not least her stay, and whether she would wish to return the following year. Above the mantelpiece hung a triple portrait of Daniel with his two sisters. It had been commissioned from Mr Devis as a present from Daniel's father to his mother shortly before Isabella's marriage. Isabella; there she was in all her beauty. Estelle contemplated her mother, knowing that she had inherited some of that beauty. Uncle Daniel's pleasant features had enlarged only, preserving a lucky, youthful look; Aunt Amelia's too, though paler in reality than the artist had suggested. The Pockets certainly possessed a natural elegance not bestowed on the Havishams.

'I wish I'd known Mama,' she said wistfully. 'I love Papa of course, but I sometimes wish he wasn't the only one.'

'He isn't the only one, Estelle,' said her Uncle candidly. 'You also love yourself.'

'Yes,' she considered, not angrily, 'but that is not the same.'

'Quite different,' Daniel agreed. 'Self-love often gets in the way of self-improvement.'

'I hope you're not going to lecture me, Uncle Daniel,' said Estelle with almost a twinkle. 'I don't want to leave Chelsea with a bad impression.'

'Nor does Chelsea want you to. But mention of your dear Mama leads me to say that I naturally have an interest in her only child. You know I speak my mind when I have to and now is as good a time as any. I am pleased to be able to say that I shall miss you when you are gone. I mean that as a compliment. I have been delighted in your change for the better and hope you will take it and use it to help others. Arthur, for instance...'

'Arthur is a bad boy.'

'Hear me out, Estelle. I have no doubt Arthur is the very devil incarnate, but there are reasons. Consider his situation. He has none of your advantages. I know you don't love him, nor, sadly, does your Papa. But at least be kind to him – grant him a little humanity.'

'Believe me, Uncle Daniel,' said Estelle earnestly, 'Arthur won't *let* me love him. I've tried but he seems to repel it. He repels everything you say and do. Papa has given up. That's why he sent him to school. You need to be a saint to cope with Arthur and I don't know how to be.'

'I did suggest humanity,' reminded Uncle Daniel. 'Nobody, how ever repellent, can be beyond deserving that, surely? What I'm trying to say, my dear Estelle, is that it's no sacrifice to put others first. It's clear your Papa loves you and puts you above everything. That is not your fault, don't misunderstand me. I simply wish you to think of those less fortunate than yourself.'

'My good friend Marie said similar things when we parted at Versailles,' replied Estelle in subdued tones. 'I've been trying to do as she suggested and make people like me – I really have...'

'But you can't *make* people like you. You have to trust that they will because of the qualities they enjoy in you.'

'When I was in France and while I've been here I can understand what you mean, Uncle Daniel. But when I'm at home with Papa and Arthur it hardly makes the same sense. It's not my fault we have money. Why should I feel guilty about it? Grandfather worked hard to build up the brewery and Papa is rich because of it.'

Daniel left his chair. 'It isn't about money, Estelle. There are riches of other kinds just as valuable. You must see that. One day you might understand what I mean when I say I hope money will not spoil life for you.'

'I shan't be mean with my money if that's what worries you. I shall put it to use and help people with it. I shall have parties at Satis and make people laugh and enjoy themselves. I shall transform Satis into a place to be talked of and you will be proud of me. Papa calls me his Bright Star, you know – well, I intend to carry that brightness deep into the next century.'

'What makes you so certain *you* will inherit Satis?'

'I shall inherit Satis because I'm Papa's daughter.'

'But Arthur is his son.'

Estelle pulled a puzzled face. 'Arthur can't inherit Satis. He's younger than me. He's a dolt, besides. Papa would never waste it on him – he'd ruin us in a fortnight.'

'Alright, my dear. As long as you are sure.'

'But it's *understood* I'll have Satis. Papa's always told me so.'

'As I say, Estelle, as long as you're sure.'

Once she had returned to her room to finish packing, her Uncle's words rolled in her mind like empty casks. How sure *was* she? She had spent so much of her life assuming she was an heiress that when it came to hard facts she could not say for certain *what* she was sure of. She needed to know the contents of Papa's will. He had made a will, she supposed. But suppose not? Of one thing she *was* sure – the need to find out… and a good deal more besides.

With these thoughts uppermost she was taken by Uncle Daniel's hired boy to London to meet the Dover coach the following day.

'I will predict,' said Daniel, as the crunch of wheels receded, 'that within a dozen years her life will not have fulfilled her expectations. If only she could acquire a basic understanding of human nature. Affluent as her father may be, he cannot supply her with *that* particular bag of riches.'

'If only he could supply *himself*,' added Caroline. 'Estelle is very young still. The trouble is she wants to be thought a lady too soon. But Matthew and the girls have done their best, bless them. He has been the perfect gentleman.'

'Now, my dear, we must turn our attention to the worsening conditions in France,' said Daniel, taking her hand. 'I'd like to know more from Amelia than just the latest sanitary arrangements.'

'Dearest, write to her – invite her... all of them... to come here. How we would house them I don't know, but we'd find a way. Think how pleasant it would be for us all to be together. The children have never met their French cousins. Write today, my love – Amelia would be so grateful and I'm sure it would constitute a headache less... for *her!*'

* * *

During her stay, Estelle had received one letter from her father containing mostly generalities. The most exciting news concerned her rooms which he assured her had been redecorated exactly to her specifications – the soft pastel shades of blue and green favoured by Queen Antoinette, with plenty of gilding and ornament. She was impatient to see them, gratified also to see that her father had driven personally to collect her from the Cross Keys, despite the Sunday being hot and oppressive. He had expressed no intention of collecting her from Chelsea nor personally thanking his brother-in-law for accommodating her – a note would do in the future.

'I feel I should warn you,' he said, when Estelle had completed narrating her experiences somewhere between Chalk and Gadshill, 'that your brother is at home.'

'He's still alive then?' said Estelle in mock surprise. 'School and work have not exactly broken his spirit?'

'On the contrary. His master's speak favourably of his efforts. The discipline is obviously doing him good. He should have gone away years ago. No, My Bright Star, nothing is broken but his leg; it seems his mind is still full of nightmares; one night running away from a ghost waving a shroud at him he fell down some stairs. But he won't tell me anything – I've only his friend's account.'

'Friend?' queried Estelle with a small laugh. 'Arthur has a friend?'

'You shall meet him at Satis, my sweet one – he's keeping Arthur company for a while.'

Another brat, thought Estelle, frowning. *And two Arthurs are worse than one. But everyone says I must be kind so I'll try. School may have humanised him a little so it will be easier.*

Once she had inspected and enthused over her luxurious rooms she went along to Arthur's quarters; full of new resolve she knocked politely before opening the door. Her half-brother reclined in a wing chair, his leg resting on a nest of cushions. A young man sat beside him but arose as she entered, putting down the book he had been reading to the invalid. She was unprepared for this example of manners combined with youthful beauty and refinement which presented itself in the seedy room. He appeared about Arthur's age – perhaps a little older, but next to his friend's mousiness seemed to possess a glossy, deep-eyed maturity expressed in a strong, almost classical face framed by richly curling hair. Estelle particularly noted his neat, finely composed body – taller than Arthur's and nearly as developed as Hugh the groom's.

'This is my half-sister,' said Arthur joylessly, indicating her entrance as if she were a burden every individual should carry. 'This is Alexander.'

'*Enchante, Madmoiselle.*' The elegant young man smoothly took her finger tips and brushed them with his lips as if she were a Queen. '*J'espere que vous avez bonne sante.*'

Was there some mistake? A friend of Arthur's as refined as this? She pitched her brain into groping for some kind of months' old store of vocabulary. 'Er... *pardonnez moi, Alexandre... je ne comprend pas... vous etes Francais?*'

'No, Miss Estelle – just educated.' Alexander laughed. 'But you have been to France?'

'Quite right,' she asserted, regaining some of her English composure. 'I became involved with the Court at Versailles and had my likeness modelled by Marie Grosholtz of the *Cabinet de Cire* in Paris. She was instructor to the King's sister, you know. Come to my *boudoir* and you shall see it – in the company of my personal maid, of course.'

'*Naturellement,*' said Alexander, smiling.

'How delightful to hear French spoken again at Satis,' continued Estelle. 'I used to be the only one so I was obliged to discontinue...'

'What she means is she can't be bothered to work it out,' Arthur interposed. 'It's too much effort when you've no brain.'

'You should know, little monster,' scorned Estelle. 'Hell's too mild for anyone who produces such drawings as *I* found after you'd gone.'

'I'd be happy there if it meant I'd see you burning in agony too. Please finish the story, Alexander.'

'Later,' decided his friend. 'I am intrigued by what your sister has been saying. She has something to show me. *Apres vous, Madmoi...* I mean, after you, Miss Estelle. A French name is it not?'

'My Grandmother was called Ernestine and my mother Isabella, so Papa put them together and christened me Estella. But I never liked it – too hard. I prefer the French so much more... Estelle means 'bright star' you realise?'

'Perfectly,' he said, opening her boudoir door for her.

'Wait here a moment, Alexander. I'll tell you when you're to come in.' She closed the door behind her. Arthur called him from across the corridor.

'You mustn't be selfish,' chided Alexander, coming to the doorway. 'I won't abandon you, dear boy, but you can't expect me to remain imprisoned here *all* day.'

'Remember what I said about her. You're *my* friend. I need you with *me*.'

'I have to be polite to the ladies,' Alexander explained, coming to Arthur. 'I'd much prefer to be with you. You're right — she *is* rather proud, isn't she?'

'I told you. That's what I've had to put up with all my life. She never used to be this bad but now you try everything you like to please her and sooner or later she wears you down.' He caught sight of Zilla in the doorway.

"Scuse me, Master Arthur, but Miss Estelle...' She blushed as she glanced at Alexander's enchanting eyes. 'Er... would Mister Alexander be pleased to step this way, please...'

He found Estelle attending to the flowers in the waxen model's hair. It stood on a table, the bandbox on the floor; Zilla continued unpacking her mistress's luggage, happy to take as long as possible while Alexander was nearby.

'Zilla and I played a trick on Arthur with this model the morning he left for school,' said Estelle, no less affected by Alexander's proximity. 'She powdered me white and I pretended to be a ghost with a shroud. It was very silly but immense fun. Arthur and I always have fun. I put the head in my bed and made a body of pillows under the covers. Poor Arthur thought he was seeing things — the living dead — the dead living... he didn't know what to believe.'

'And he's had nightmares about it ever since,' said Alexander simply. 'They can be extremely noisy. I have to sleep in his bed sometimes to reassure him. The night I was in someone else's he fell and broke his leg.'

Estelle looked askance. 'You sleep in his bed? With him in it? It's a wonder you haven't caught some horrible disease.'

'At school it's quite normal,' said Alexander, as she placed her model on the bureau, 'specially with us older boys. Some beds have six or more of us in them. Arthur has one to himself because of his nightmares. Then he wets it. He gets laughed at for that as well. But at least he's not locked up. That happens here he tells me.'

'Papa has to lock him in a cupboard. Come on – I'll show you.' She prized Alexander away from Zilla's fascination up to the top passage.

'So this is it,' Alexander shuddered. 'How dark and gloomy it is up here. I didn't believe him at first. My father has never locked *me* up – never beaten me even.'

'I expect you are too good for that,' admired Estelle. 'Come out onto the roof – I want you to see the view. It's all right – it's very safe.' She led the way up the flight of wooden steps, through a beamed loft, then to a trapdoor hinging back to a bright sky and sun-baked tiles covering a wide area between chimney stacks and parapets. Directly beneath spread the front courtyard, rear garden, brewery complex with its white pigeon house on its pole, the Comfreys' house with wall clock and lane separating it all from the main house. The high wall encircling the entire property forbade passing glances from the exterior world except through the decorative iron gates set between their sturdy stone posts. The nearby town with its chubby masses of castle and cathedral seemed to submit to this high-placed viewing, Satis House being set on a lordly incline at the town's edge.

'My father owns all this,' Estelle explained, as if Alexander were a prospective purchaser. As if extolling the virtues of Versailles, she embraced the view with an over-generous sweep of her arm towards the distant river and marshes. 'Also those fields over there. He has property in the town and in London and I have an Uncle in Chelsea.'

'My father,' said Alexander, by way of balancing the scales, 'owns a large house in the country surrounded by a beautiful park. Papa is almost like the Squire. We have another in St James's Square which we let from time to time for extra income. My Mama likes town life but Papa does not. Mama is French – she can trace descent from King Henry of Navarre. She is very beautiful... I am supposed to resemble her.'

'How long have you been at school?' asked Estelle quickly, wishing not to be obliged to divulge her purely English parentage.

'Papa sent me when I was ten after finishing with tutors. Though I hated it at first and missed Mama terribly, I took the bad with the good, as Arthur is learning to do. I'm helping him, in fact. You don't mind, I hope? He looks to me for guidance.'

'All I hope is you have better luck than me. I can't do anything with him.' She turned to Alexander. 'Is there much bad – at school?'

'You would never believe me if I told you half of it. Such things are not for girls.'

'I shall hate you for ever if you *don't* tell me!' she flared. 'I'm *not* a girl any longer – I've seen the world and know all about people.'

'You want to imagine the bad happening to Arthur. Isn't that the truth of it? Come now, be honest.'

'Please Alexander – I don't know what a school is like – I simply want to picture my brother enjoying his daily routine. I shan't let you leave until you've told me.' She sat carefully on the warm roof with her back against a chimney stack. Alexander settled beside her with a distinct lack of reluctance.

'We're left to ourselves a great deal more than is good for us. The masters have many duties so they can't keep an eye on us all the time – there are prefects, like me, to do that. We are allowed to beat the younger boys if we need to keep order. Our opinions we keep to ourselves.'

'I don't keep opinions to myself.'

'You would if you saw someone being fixed to a desk-top by a penknife through his hand.'

'I wouldn't. I'd tell someone.'

'That would be regarded as sneaking,' said Alexander. 'That is the worst crime of all. What ever happens – how ever awful – you are expected to keep your honour and not sneak. If you have any sense you put up with anything and everything like a man.'

'Has Arthur any sense?'

'You mean is Arthur suffering?' He smiled to himself. 'Let's say he's learning. He's seen a friend hung upside-down by his toes from a beam and scorched in front of an open fire. Why? Because the victim complained to his tutor that a prefect – not me – had got him out of bed to stand him for half an hour in a butt if icy water.'

'That sounds a bit silly,' said Estelle, scornfully. 'He must have been very naughty to need such punishment.'

'Do you know what he'd done that was so naughty? Accidentally forgotten to latch the prefect's study window properly. Another boy was shut face-downwards in a trunk filled with sawdust because he refused to fag for a particular prefect he was afraid of. I could show you a scratch or two but I've survived so far and it's not done me much harm.'

'Why can't you tell your Papa if you can't tell your tutors? My Papa would never let any thing like that happen to me.'

'The trouble is that some of our fathers probably went through the same sort of things when they were at school in the belief that it helped them to prosper, so naturally they want it for their sons. We're all in it together – it is the system and we accept it. Sharing each other's secrets is a help – you don't feel so alone.'

'Do you share Arthur's secrets?'

'He shares them with me. They are quite safe... like his appearance at a certain Reception clad only in his lack of modesty...'

'That's enough. I don't wish to be reminded. I can never forgive him for that. There's some compensation in thinking of the poor boy going through such initiations into the world of grown-ups such as you've been telling me.'

'The *poor boy* is well able to look after himself, make no mistake. I would say he even seems to enjoy it sometimes. He told me once that when he bullies others he imagines they are his sister.'

'What a strange thing to say,' commented Estelle, with a forced little laugh. 'Did he *really* say that?'

'On my honour as a gentleman,' said Alexander, hand on his heart.

'What other secrets does Arthur share with you?'

'If I told you they wouldn't be secrets. He has many. He trusts me because I am older.'

'I'm sure half his secrets are fantasies. He has lots of those. I expect he'll also have told you a lot of untruths about me. I've often told him I would like to be his friend but somehow he doesn't believe me.'

'He likes to do as I say,' said Alexander, getting up and going to the parapet. 'We have a deal, Arthur and me; in exchange for obedience he enjoys my friendship and patronage. I protect him, so to speak – he says it compensates for the years of misery endured in this house. And he's good at lessons – quick to learn. His French is noticeably better than yours – don't look so offended – it is true. But then, you haven't the benefit of my tutoring.' He knelt before her. 'Miss Estelle, I am telling you all this in confidence, you understand. Arthur would be more than a little upset if he thought I was betraying him.'

'And are you?'

'I don't regard it as such. I think everyone should be able to speak their mind.'

If Estelle had been blessed, at that moment, with powers of seeing into Alexander's mind, she would have perceived that he was reticent to speak openly of what was in it, intending to veil that side of his school life in which he excelled: his sense of cultivated authority up to which he encouraged the younger, more impressionable boys to look. She remained unaware that his engaging, persuasive manner disguised a deep-seated need to control people and events connected with him in order to compensate for a basic insecurity. Explanation for this would be hard to find by an outside observer, coming, as Alexander did, from a loving family: doting Mama and sisters who spoiled him on either hand: a father, whose warm, caring nature perhaps too readily expected his only son to be similarly possessed. It was certain that the family had no concept of their idol's reliance on those school-fellows who conformed to his way of thinking – particularly concerning money; what had begun as light-hearted forages into the commanding world of sharing, lending, borrowing, accounting, winning and losing, had developed into a code for living in which Alexander determined he would never, at any price, be the loser.

'So,' he continued, 'I have no intention of betraying Arthur. And if you like me, you'll keep what I say to yourself.'

'I *do* like you,' said Estelle sincerely, 'even though you *are* Arthur's friend.'

'But do you *know* me?' Alexander warned, going back to the parapet. 'If you did you mightn't like me.'

'Stop fishing for praise,' said Estelle playfully, going to him. 'I like what I know, but you puzzle me.'

'Then you're getting to know me a little. But if you *really* knew me, you'd realise I'm not Arthur's friend at all. Does that puzzle you even more?'

Estelle frowned. 'What you say doesn't make sense.' The blinding heat bounding up from the roof threatened to make her head swim.

'It will in time – trust me,' came the reply. 'That is all you have to do. It's *our* secret. I dislike being questioned…'

'But Alex…'

'If *we* are to be friends you must let yourself be persuaded to more my way of thinking – as long as you don't change in every other way, like Daphne.'

'Daphne?' said Estelle, by now thoroughly bewildered. 'Is she your sister?'

'Daphne, as every educated person will tell you, was a beautiful nymph, daughter of a river-god. She ran away from Apollo when he tried to befriend her, begging her father to save her. He changed her into a laurel tree so that Apollo wouldn't recognise her.'

'Good gracious,' said Estelle. 'Do you see yourself as Apollo then? And I the beautiful nymph? Did Apollo dig her up and plant her in his garden?'

'He declared that from then-on, laurel was his favourite and that prizes for outstanding achievement should be wreaths made from its foliage.'

'I see,' said Estelle, none the wiser. This Alexander, friend yet not friend of Arthur, was something of an enigma.

'Now,' he concluded, leaving the parapet, 'I promised I would finish reading to the invalid. He likes stories too – and illustrating them. I'd hate him to think I'd abandoned him. *Adieu,* for the present. I've enjoyed our little talk but I always keep my promises.'

Leaving a bemused Estelle he found his way back to Arthur's room.

'Where've you been?' he demanded from his chair. 'You've been away ages. I want to get back into bed. What's Estelle been saying? I know you'll have talked about me.'

'So many questions,' said Alexander, bending to let Arthur slip his arm round the back of his neck. Though only a lad he was strong for his age, well able to transfer his burden easily to the bed. 'I've asked you before not always to question me – it sets me on edge. If you value my friendship you must do as I say.'

'Sorry,' said Arthur as Alexander tucked him in and arranged his nightshirt more closely round his chest. 'But now Estelle's around again I can't help feeling suspicious. She's always had a way of getting what she wants and I don't want you to like her more than me.' He took hold of Alexander's wrist. 'I want you to stay *my* friend. You're the only one I've ever had.'

Alexander took his hand. 'Yes, I *am* your friend,' he promised, 'so you don't need to keep challenging me.' Gently, he brushed Arthur's forehead with his lips 'There. Does that prove it? Depend on me and let me take care of you, as I do myself. You get yourself better and leave the Lady Estelle to me.'

* * *

In her boudoir that evening, Estelle sat at her bureau, a blank sheet of notepaper before her. The heat from the roof seemed to have branded Alexander into her mind – as she took up her quill she heard his beguiling voice, saw his sweet seriousness of expression on a face with which any Greek sculptor would have been pleased to crown the perfect torso. She felt a strange warmth – separate from the aggressive glare of afternoon – a warmth which pervaded her inner being, making her restless in her chair. His maturity had obviously something to do with his aristocratic upbringing. Fancy being able to claim ancestry back to Henry of Navarre. Perhaps the family owned a *chateau*. She had enquired about his mother's family name over dinner – Marie may know of it:

I must apologise, dearest Marie, for the lengthy delay in writing to you, but since my return life has been overcrowded with activity and my time severely curtailed.

Since your model arrived it has been the chief talking point of the neighbourhood and I am overjoyed with it. Everyone thinks it most elegant and cleverly constructed, they cannot think how you did it. But I am able to enlighten them and they say they have never encountered anything like it.

Arthur, who I told you about, was supposed to have been sent to school but is at home at present with a broken leg due to his carelessness. He has a school friend here with him – Alexander (what a beautiful portrait you could do of him!) who has a French mother who comes from the wealthy family de Bayonne. Are they known to you?

I have lately been in London staying with my Aunt Caroline Pocket and cousins. I was taken to many fashionable places where I fulfilled a number of engagements. I was delighted to wear my new French dresses which were much admired. My Uncle Daniel is hoping to go into Parliament as he is most particular about doing good. I have not forgotten what you said about me doing good and try my best also.

My Uncle is also worried about Aunt Amelia. Is the tiresome business in your country over yet? I am so longing to return. I gave Papa her letter you sent with the portrait but he has not spoken to me about it. I have started taking an interest in the news now as our papers are becoming more informative of what is happening abroad. Papa favours The Times – though it costs only four pence it is not bad for all that. He says it is outlandish that commoners should presume to take the law into their own hands.

You will be delighted to know that my rooms here have been much improved with redecoration – all the dark old-fashioned panelling is painted pale green, blue and white, the Queen's favourites, with mouldings picked out in gold. I am going to have a new carpet and curtains, also a crystal chandelier to complete the ensemble which now includes a fine lady's dressing table…

Alexander remained at Satis for nearly three weeks. The splendid weather continued, and though Arthur insisted on cooping himself up in his rooms, Alexander made no attempt to stay continually in his company. He was keen to be out and about the town, the garden, the brewery; he spent some time, not unnoticed by Estelle, in the stables showing friendship to the horses – and Hugh. How attractive the two lads looked together. She could foresee what a splendid specimen Alexander was destined to become once he had matured to Hugh's physical level. She delighted in the way his forearms began to absorb the sun's deepening action – the way the push of tiny, downy hairs lustred like strands of gilt gossamer. He was well aware of her partiality and saw no reason to deny her sight nor sense.

'Do I strike you as daring?' he remarked impulsively one day, recumbent on the lawn in full glare, the open front of his fine shirt revealing a persuasive amount of chest. He glanced at her as she protected her complexion under a fringed parasol.

'You know very well you do,' she said, 'otherwise you wouldn't ask. I don't *have* to be out here with you – unaccompanied – if I don't choose.'

'I don't alarm you then? I alarm Arthur sometimes.'

'You do? How do you alarm him? I didn't think that's what friends were for.'

'I alarm him by not always doing or saying what he expects. Some friends need alarming – it makes them think. Arthur needs to do a lot of thinking and I want to help him. Friends learn from one-another – Arthur has learned a lot from me already and I from him. Partners in crime, you might say.'

'Crime's all he's good at. I'd hardly have thought he needed any help.'

'My attention to Arthur doesn't make you jealous then?' Alexander suggested.

'Not in the slightest,' she affirmed, with a shrug. 'Don't be idiotic – who in their right mind would be jealous of Arthur?'

'If you *were* jealous, I would hate to have to get Arthur to help me teach you a lesson…'

'Alexander!' Estelle threw down her parasol. 'How could you let me think you'd stoop to such a low trick? I would have to get Papa to send you away...'

Alexander laughed. 'Ah, but you see, you won't. I fascinate you because you don't know what to make of me. I keep you guessing – first one thing, then another. Mama says I'm a chameleon. That can be very useful sometimes.'

Estelle stared at him. Was it his unpredictability which intrigued her, charmed her, excited her? Of course she begrudged Arthur a share of his charisma. Of course she was jealous. Something must be done.

While she rested in preparation for the evening, Alexander took the opportunity to be with Arthur again. He was finding her continual attention somewhat wearisome – the invalid's company seemed vastly more refreshing. But Arthur was out of sorts. He had grown discontented with being closeted so long in his own fellowship, increasingly uneasy over his friend's absences, restless at the circling hours of drawing, reading, sleeping; the intricacies of the plaster ceiling lay on his eyes and brain like a cage. His chief delight was to be able to take most of his meals *tête-à-tête* with Alexander instead of having to endure the formal constriction of the dining room. At his insistence, Alexander had purloined several small flagons of beer decanted from the barrels in the wine cellar, and secreted them in Arthur's care. Having acquired a taste for alcohol at school he was anxious not to let slip his ability to sustain a good pint or two. He could drink level with Alexander any day and here he was handing him a tankard with a good head.

'Better brew than at school,' approved Alexander. 'I hope your Pa doesn't miss a drop.'

'If he does he'll think it's the men. This does my leg good – I don't feel the pain. What's the latest on Estelle's prattling? Is she about to wade over to France and sort out its troubles single-handedly?'

'I think she has greater concerns nearer home to want to get her dainty little feet wet,' said Alexander, mopping his lips.

Arthur looked puzzled. 'What do you mean?'

'What is my information worth, I wonder?'

'As my friend you should tell me as a matter of course.'

'I never do anything as a matter of course, Arthur. You should know that by now. I have some tremendously interesting information to divulge...' The servant entered after knocking and served the boys' meal at the round table. Alexander remained silent until they were alone again. 'I think, however, it will cost you this time.' He attacked his chicken with relish.

'Cost me how? I've no money – you know I haven't, and I won't get any till Papa dies. He doesn't look like doing that for a long time.'

'Your sister seems to think *she* is to inherit everything,' pondered Alexander, pointedly. 'Anyway, that's what I infer from what she's told me. Interesting information, eh?'

'I know she'll try and stop me having my rightful share,' said Arthur, 'I just know it. She may be the elder but I am the son of the house. She and Papa will cook up some way of serving me right – I know them of old.'

'Which brings me back to Estelle's concerns nearer home,' said Alexander, simply. 'I have a proposition. Interested?'

'What do you mean?'

'Has your father made a will?'

'A will?'

'Yes, Arthur, a *Will*. Has he or hasn't he?'

'How should I know? Papa never tells me anything. Why?'

'So that I can help you, dear boy – put in a good word for you. For a consideration, of course... two considerations. First, you leave all the arrangements to me – absolutely and without question. Secondly, that you sign a note promising to pay me, as soon you inherit, one hundred pounds for my trouble. And if I can't work it for you then you owe me nothing. What do you say?'

Arthur surveyed the chicken going cold on his plate. 'It's too fantastic... how will it work? How did you get the idea?'

'Did I say no questions?' said Alexander, as if he were chiding a disobedient puppy. 'Just make the decision – be assertive – agree.'

'But...'

'I can't do anything if you're going to question me the whole time. What a lot you have to learn, my dear Arthur.'

'Please don't patronise me,' said Arthur, kindly. 'You sound like Estelle.'

'Then don't dally and do as I say. If I'm willing to do this for the sake of our friendship then the least you can do for it is accept, otherwise I shall think you don't want my friendship. Besides, wouldn't you *like* me to get one over on Estelle in money matters – the only thing she cares about?'

'Alex...'

'Come then. Look – here's paper and ink. This is what I'm writing – listen:

I promise to pay Alexander Francois de Bayonne Compeyson the sum of £100 out of my inheritance, such as it may be, within six months of my father's decease, in grateful recognition of services rendered in friendship.

Signed,

Here, Arthur, put your name to it. Quickly. The servants will be in soon to clear away and you've hardly touched your chicken.'

Hesitatingly, Arthur took the quill from Alexander. 'I don't know... it seems an awful lot of money...'

'You're buying the services of a Gentleman, I would remind you, and his word. Of course, if they're not worth that much, then...' He watched his friend stab the quill resolutely into the ink and scrawl his signature. 'And the date, Arthur – it's more professional that way – the twenty-first of July.' Arthur added 1789 of his own volition. 'I will keep this now and destroy it when you fulfil your contract, when ever that may be. Let's drink to it and get back to the table – business transactions always sharpen my appetite.'

Arthur prodded his food for some time, barely attending to what Alexander was telling him about fading away for want of food. 'I want to ask you a question,' he said at length. 'If you'll answer this one I promise not to ask any others.'

'Very well,' said Alexander, patiently.

'You... and Estelle... you are not in league, are you? Don't be angry, please – just tell me – I promise not to mind – I only want to know where I stand.' He watched his friend leave the table and wander to the window, wishing he had not asked such an insulting question. 'I don't think you are,' he added quickly, 'but I want to know – from *you.*'

'I thought we understood one another better than this,' said Alexander, returning to his chair, shaking his head. 'What more can I do to prove myself to you? I know a good investment when I see it. That brewery out there could be a goldmine – all yours if you run it properly. New blood – that's what it needs, and progressive ideas. You could be just the lad and I'd like to help you.'

'I wouldn't know how to begin,' replied Arthur. 'Papa's never let me be any part of it.'

'We're talking of the future, Arthur. You've years to learn – to join in and find your way through. I can help you, if only you'll let me.'

Arthur's anxious face relaxed a little, tears softening his eyes. 'I'd be much happier about it if you *did* help me.'

Alexander took the outstretched hand, holding it momentarily. 'Now I shall tell you something else, then you can decide whether I'm in league with the Queen of Pride. Your nightmares – who's always in them?'

'She is, of course. They wouldn't be nightmares if she wasn't.'

'Have you ever thought about what you saw in her room the day you left school – how it was done?'

'It was a trick – it must have been – something to do with the wax head. But I'm certainly not going to ask her – that's what she wants me to do.'

'It was a trick, certainly, and a pretty mean one, I should say. She told me about it. She and Zilla planned it deliberately to scare you. She's had her likeness modelled by a friend in France – waxworks are all the rage in Paris at present. She keeps it in her boudoir like some hunting trophy. It's an excellent likeness I have to say.'

'I don't want to see it. I'd smash it to bits. I wish I could have seen her face when she found my drawings. She likes to sit by her fire a lot – they were of her burning to death. I knew she'd come nosing in here so I left them as a parting gift. I hope they gave *her* nightmares.'

'Be guided by me,' assured Alexander, confidentially, 'and we'll *both* give her nightmares...' A throttled sort of sob halted him. He closed up to Arthur, enfolding his heated body, patting his back comfortingly. 'There. Don't get in a state.'

'Alexander... I'm sorry... I've never had anyone to help me before... anyone I can trust... I've always been on my own. It's hard to get used to something different...'

'I'm sure it must be,' agreed his friend, 'but you have me now and I want you to stop being the underdog to Estelle. There are ways, trust me.'

At bedtime, after the house had grown silent to the breathless summer heat, Alexander sat up on top of his counterpane. He had not been to sleep but had lain in his nightshirt listening to the night sounds scaling the wall to the casement sill as if looking for a place in which to be quiet. The midsummer moon crinkled its blue beauty through the lattice, brightening his woken schemes. He climbed lightly off the bed, and lighting a candle, took Arthur's promissory note from the table. Making his stealthy way to Arthur's dressing room, he opened out the note and dipping the quill in the inkpot, deftly converted the figure 1 into a 4. He smiled as he read back to himself: *I promise to pay... £400...* He blew on the result to hasten its drying as he thought, briefly but gloriously, of adding a third naught before coming down on the side of expediency.

Refolding his note and preparing to steal away, a noise the other side of Arthur's bedroom door made him extinguish his candle and dart into the deep shadows between an old-fashioned cupboard and the chimney breast.

Arthur shuffled into the dressing room on his crutches but moving with a certain amount of ease, even dispensing with one, leaning it against the cupboard before lighting a candle. Taking it up in its brass holder he went to Estelle's boudoir which he entered with extreme caution.

Not for a moment did Alexander's eyes slacken. He monitored Arthur's reappearance holding the waxen head under his arm. It was a marvel the way he coped with his burden, crutch, candlestick and awkwardness as he descended the stairs. Like an inquisitive ghost Alexander trailed him across the hallway, down the long service passage off which, at intervals, other lengths and hollows blackened into nothingness, indicating untold regions plunging and bisecting the bowels of the house.

By the time Arthur had reached the top of the narrow stone stairway, he had done away with his crutch altogether. With slow efficiency he made his way down to the damp floor, his candle illumining a pillared, brick-vaulted basement extensive in low-humped gloom and disuse, believed to be of Roman origin. He deposited the model amongst some dirt in a far corner.

'Julius Caesar can haunt it,' he muttered, as he re-climbed the steps. 'They can haunt each other.'

Alexander, his amazement at its fullest, watched the invalid retrace his tracks, collect his crutch and return, slightly breathless, to his room. When the door had closed and all was still, he went to Estelle's, turning the handle stealthily – a shame to leave so fragile and pretty a head unprotected in the dust of ages; Arthur would surely have included the band-box had he been able – besides, a friend's duty was to serve...

Estelle's shock prostrated her. The servants became jumpy under suspicion – Zilla was accused of damaging the head and hiding the evidence – Mr Havisham's frustrated anger did nothing to elicit confessions. Arthur had legitimate cause to be mystified by the band-box – but though his natural inclination was to boast of his night's exploits to Alexander, some instinct made him keep his own counsel.

Alexander faced inquiry with equal innocence; he even ventured to help by suggesting that Miss Estelle herself might have inadvertently mislaid it. He soon learned that the Havishams had no sense of humour. By way of making amends he paid her a formal visit out of courtesy. He found her seated in her chair before her looking-glass, disconsolately fingering some jewellery – a compensatory present from her Papa; but its sparkle did nothing to dispel the misery hanging like marsh-mist about her boudoir.

'There's sure to be some simple explanation,' he said calmly. 'It can't be far. I expect it'll turn up while Arthur's away.'

'Away?' Estelle's voice caught the blaze of her diamonds. 'Where away?'

'He's coming home with me. Your father hasn't informed you? Mama and Papa are happy for him to convalesce at Rookwell Park. We shall go riding and he'll be better in no time.'

Estelle threw down her brooch. 'I was *not* told. Why has this been arranged behind my back?'

'I think your father has other things on his mind...'

'Don't presume to think what's in my father's mind! I don't think Arthur's well enough to go.'

'What you mean is you think you ought to go instead.'

Estelle faltered. 'Well, supposing I do? I'm too upset at present to remain here.'

'You can come.'

'Not with Arthur. I must be on my own. But I expect you'd rather have Arthur.'

'Arthur and I are friends.'

'And are we not? Why have I spent so much time with you?'

'That was different.'

'How different? I don't think you like me now – that's how different.'

'Estelle...'

'Don't talk to me!' As Alexander made abruptly for the door, Estelle left her chair in a flurry and called, 'Please don't be angry with me.' She followed him across the corridor into Arthur's room. 'I'm sorry, Alexander. I'm upset. I didn't mean what I said.' She tried to hold his wrist but he shook it away with a show of unexpected strength, causing her to stumble back against the old-fashioned cupboard. In a succession of thuds it jolted down an amount of heavy books from the top, dislodging with them some empty pottery flagons which crashed in smithereens on the floor around her.

Startled, she stared at the split bindings and scattered shards. 'I might have known! Arthur's an alcoholic now. Wait till Papa finds out – he thinks its Hugh.' She turned to the door as Alexander slammed it shut.

'Don't tell him,' he whispered hurriedly, 'and you can come to Rookwell alone.'

'Promise?'

'Promise!'

Arthur appeared in his bedroom doorway as the dressing room door opened violently, nearly knocking Alexander off balance.

'What *ever* was that terrible banging?' demanded Mrs Comfrey, marching in. 'We thought Master Arthur's bed had collapsed.' A handful of men servants peered round the door.

'It's all right, Mrs Comfrey,' stammered Estelle, moving as if to hide the mess on the floor with her skirts, 'there's no cause for alarm...' But the housekeeper was too quick for her.

'Oh, *isn't* there, Miss?' she replied, picking up some pieces. 'Not when my husband's held responsible? I recognise this pottery, don't think I don't. Dear me, no... there'll be no cause for alarm when this little matter's cleared up good and proper...' She left the room clutching her spoils, including a handle, as if they were plunder from a Pharoah's tomb.

The offenders remained in individual states of reaction: Arthur almost ready to cry, Estelle warm with impatience, Alexander in cool control.

'It wasn't my fault,' blurted Arthur. 'I didn't do the stealing – I can't leave my room. I'm not going to sneak.'

'There's no need to,' said Estelle quickly. 'Just keep quiet and do as I say – that's if you want me to help you.'

'*Help* me? *You?*'

'If you won't make a fuss about me going to Rookwell instead of you, I'll take responsibility for your crime.'

'But it's all arranged,' Arthur began. 'I'm so looking forward to it.'

'Quick, stupid, yes or no – here comes Papa.'

'Oh...' Frustrated tears started glistening.

Mr Havisham banged into the room with a rowdy, 'How *dare* you!'

Estelle placed a restraining hand on his arm. 'Papa, Papa... you're being too hasty. Arthur isn't to blame. How can he be? He can't leave his room.' Mr Havisham turned his red face upon his daughter thinking he had misheard. 'Dearest Papa. I'm so *very* sorry but I'm afraid this is all my fault completely. Arthur is in no way responsible. Sit down and hear me out. I wished to help the boys enjoy their time together so I obtained some beer for them. I know now it was wrong to do so without your permission and am truly sorry... it slipped my memory. Can you forgive me? I was trying to be a good host on your behalf – make you proud of me. They told me they drank it at school so I wanted them to feel at home.'

Arthur and Alexander watched her performance in amazement. She even ran to a few tears when she lamented that she had not realised innocent people would be blamed. 'Please apologise to Mr Comfrey and I didn't mean for Hugh to get into trouble – he's one of the soberest of our workers.'

'Estelle,' said her father, offering his open arms, 'don't do this to me, please – I can't bear to see you distressed. You meant it for the best, I dare say, but it was wrong of you. It's Arthur who should feel badly... allowing you to set such an example before our young guest. What can Alexander be thinking of us?'

'Please don't be hard on him, Sir,' said the young guest. 'If he's to be punished then I ought to be also. Could it be that he gives up his visit to my home for the moment? Could Miss Estelle be allowed to take his place?'

'Please say yes, Papa. It would be like being back at Versailles. I shall be able to take Zilla this time.'

'You meant the beer kindly, which was thoughtful of you, My Bright Star. Of course you may go – you'll practise your French with Madame Compeyson and when you return we must speak about plans I have for your future... an establishment in London... a companion...'

The lads watched them leave the room. Arthur, his crutches still propping him up like an unsafe building, mastered his emotions. 'I don't know how it is,' he said slowly as Alexander helped settle him in his chair, 'that whatever I have, or am going to have, Estelle manages to take it from me. I shall never have anything as long as there is an Estelle.'

'And *I* don't know how it is,' said Alexander slowly, 'that someone who needs helping to his chair can get himself up and down staircases by candlelight without breaking wax models, let alone his other leg.'

Arthur looked at him spiritlessly without attempting surprised innocence. 'You know!'

'I saw. I just happened to be thirsty and was coming to your room to see if you were awake enough to join me in *une demi-tasse de biere.* I saw everything. I thought I'd better follow in case you had another accident – I could see you were still asleep.'

'I was wide awake,' disputed Arthur emphatically. 'She thinks she can trick me with a shroud – well, one trick deserves another.'

'Before you ask me, Arthur, let me tell you I shan't be telling Estelle. Did you think I might?'

'I don't know what to think. But I didn't take the box.'

'I believe you. *I* did. Now do you see whose side I'm on? It seemed a pity not to finish the job properly.'

'I couldn't carry it,' confessed Arthur happily. 'My leg hurt too much to go back for it.'

'Remember the conditions of our friendship and nothing more need be said. It would be a tragedy, wouldn't it, if the chaps at school found out the truth of what your mother really was? And I don't think my family would much approve of our friendship then, do you?'

'My mother? I think you can be very heartless when you want to be, Alexander.'

'Not heartless, *mon ami,*' said his friend, leaning forward and touching the side of his cheek, 'only practical – that's all.'

* * *

As soon as Zilla received the information that she would accompany her mistress to Rookwell Park, she flung up her hands in excitement and began so flapping that Estelle had to check her with stern words. Satisfied that she could then safely be left to her duties, Estelle turned her attention to another concern on her mind and made for the stable block.

After being told where Hugh was working, she walked across the cobbled yard acknowledging nods of deference from the men and lads going about their hostelry duties. Lifting her hem delicately above her ankles she carefully skirted their scatters of brooms and buckets, straw and sweepings, until she stepped out of the sunshine into the relative gloom of the stable with its line of stalled steeds nodding contentedly as she drifted by until she saw Hugh at the far end. He was stripped to the waist in the heat, rubbing the flanks of her father's black stallion Diabolus with handfuls of hay. Flies and insects droned and flitted at every movement; the air bustled and buzzed with warm aromas, brewery sounds, activity from the coach house. Her senses were heightened, even to the cut and glare of shadows angling the building complex outside.

She continued watching the young man, unwilling to shorten her enjoyment of such lovely shoulders and curve of back. His fair hair, glossy in the webs of light from dusty windows, hung looser than usual, caressing his shoulder blades like tender fingers. She flexed her own as her eyes took in the tightness of his breeches while he half-knelt to see to one of the horse's legs. She found herself breathing rather short but heavily, even though she was the one standing still. What a creditable specimen of subtle strength – of graceful purpose – moved before her. Instinctively she knew him to be as fine a master of his craft as might be wished for; for he could be trusted to the correct rubbing of stirrups, sponging of bridles, adjusting of girths, safe bedding down of a neat flank. Nor was he a mean hand, neither, at coaxing a timid foal, soothing a fretful filly or controlling a regular kicker. His intense eyes turned to hers as he sensed her presence. He scrambled up dutifully, touching his forelock.

'Ah, Hugh,' she said, stepping forward, 'there you are. I feel I must see you personally regarding the missing beer.' As he straightened before her she found her attention to words wandering. His agreeable face reminded her of the statue of the dying Gaul in the park at Versailles.

'Miss Estelle?'

'The beer, Hugh – yes, I owe you an apology. You see, I completely omitted to inform the Master that I had borrowed some for the little house-party Master Arthur and I gave for our guest from Rookwell Park. He comes here to talk to you from time to time, I believe. I had no notion that this small omission on my part would in any way affect you. The Master now knows the true state of affairs and you have nothing more to worry about. Please accept my sincere apologies.'

'That's all right, Miss,' replied Hugh good-naturedly, rubbing a bead of sweat from the end of his nose. 'Accidents happen. I knew as I wasn't guilty – that's what most matters.'

'Yes, but you wouldn't have wanted to lose your employment here without a character, would you? It can happen to anyone at any time, you know. But, of course, you would never go against any of our wishes, including mine.'

'Not as I'd know I would, Miss.' He shifted awkwardly, his hands on his hips. 'Leastways not as I'd want.'

'Of course not, Hugh,' she agreed. She could see that he found the directness of her manner and gaze slightly disconcerting as he stood waiting for her to go. He felt his sweat cooling on his flushed flesh, running down his neck and torso in tepid rivulets. She watched its course, not least to where, reaching the cliff-edge of his nipples, it splashed over the edge. The remembrance of also having seen Alexander's chest revealed by his open shirt in the garden sent an extra current through her... she leaned forward to Hugh's cheek, her lips roughened by his stubble as she formed a spontaneous kiss.

'That,' she said, as she drew back from the galvanised groom, 'is to prove you won't lose your employment – if you continue to humour my wishes. Good day, Hugh, and thank you.'

His reply was unintelligible.

As she returned to her room she was conscious of no other kiss having given her such a pleasing sensation before – such a sense of purpose: not Papa's, her Uncle's and Aunt's – certainly not Arthur's. Not even Marie's. As far as the young aristocrat with the smooth tongue was concerned, how different would *he* be from the diversion on offer in the stable department? Perhaps the forthcoming visit to his home might present an opportunity to find out.

* * *

Her idea of what a Country House should be had manifested itself in her first sight of Rookwell Park. As Alexander's parents were at pains to explain over her first dinner with them, they had employed that eminent Scotsman, Mr Robert Adam, the most sought-after architect and designer, to give the original heavy Baroque house a lighter, more Neo-Classical air. There were enough mirrors and crystal chandeliers to satisfy even her – and to compliment Mrs Compeyson's French furniture also, a collection amongst which Estelle felt immediately at home; some of it adorned the suite of sunny rooms she had been designated overlooking the Park. Zilla seemed to have settled in well with the household servants – she found the atmosphere less daunting than at Satis, also delighting, as was her simple way, in 'all them polished things and smelly flowers' As Estelle wrote in her first letter home to Papa:

Alexander's father is a Magistrate and extremely particular. He goes out riding every day, even in bad weather. He demands much of his horses as he does of people, and everyone has to 'jump-to' to please him. He is inclined to be handsome though he looks as if he does not sleep enough – not at night anyway. He is often out then and comes back for breakfast.

Alexander's mother is absolutely beautiful – almost as much as Queen Antoinette. She is very, very French and has such an engaging manner in her English speech though her French is excellent. She has never heard of Aunt Amelia though she does know of Marie's Wax Museum. I am still devastated about my model's disappearance and hope you are doing all you can to find it.

Alexander is thought of highly at home. He inherits his looks from his Mama who has high ambitions for him. He and I continue to get on well together and have certainly created some interest in the neighbourhood. All eyes turned my way when I entered the family pew in church last Sunday. They can never have seen French clothes on one so young before, I suppose. Adelaide and Emeline, his sisters, spoil him unmercifully. They are quite pretty but inclined to loll about. I converse with them though they have not half my dress sense...

Yes, Alexander's gentlemanly treatment of her made it easy for her to behave the perfect lady. She delighted in his conversation, occasional dry humour and the bother he went to concerning her comfort and well-being. Thoughts of Hugh she kept firmly under control but found herself forming comparisons between the two young men, leaving her wondering what it would be like to touch Alexander's white teeth with her tongue; something about his elegant bearing, though, deterred her from making the first move despite many opportunities.

During his stay at Satis he had displayed a relaxed attitude which, in the tranquil surroundings of his own home, encouraged a familiarity which relaxed her too. Though he did not exactly remove his shirt when they were in the sun together, she was left in no doubt as to the qualities of his body, even if they were not as developed through labour as Hugh's. But what she saw pleased her, his attraction lessening her guard against showing her ankles on occasions or by surreptitiously monitoring what she sometimes detected shaping the front of his breeches. Was it, she could not help wondering, anything like Arthur's? Obnoxious as her half-brother was, she was forced to concede that he had, at least, one manly attribute.

For all his attention to Estelle, Alexander, with his customary efficiency, still found the time and opportunity secretly to write and dispatch a letter to Arthur:

I am so sad not to have you here at Rookwell – you would have savoured every moment, as would I. There is so much to see and do. Your leg will probably remain delicate all your life and stop you doing many of the things possible had you been normal. Papa had a cousin who fell off a horse and broke his leg but it did not mend properly and he limped for ever.

It is unfortunate that your condition makes it now ill-advised for you to accompany me on The Grand Tour which Papa has promised in a very few years' time as part of my education. I had hoped that you would be my companion – just think how many drawings you would have been able to do as well as see great art works. But I realise it would be too much to expect you to clamber comfortably over Roman ruins in Italy or the Acropolis in Athens; even to contemplate the recent excavations at Pompeii near Naples – and what a disaster if you slipped into a Venetian canal. Your incapacity would spoil it for others so I might ask Papa if Estelle may be included in the party instead, then at least you will be able to listen to her marvellous accounts.

I have your promissory note safely locked away and feel sure that there is no need to remind you of how it has purchased my help and discretion in all things.

I hope this letter cheers you up, old lad. You will be happy to know that everyone marvels at your sister's taste and beauty and that my Mama and sisters have taken her to their hearts. How you would have relished their kind and loving attentions, knowing how deprived your life has been. You might sample them one day when you are better – if you remain my dutiful friend in all things.

Yours, with a loving hug,

Alexander.

* * *

Absence, goes the old adage, makes the heart grow fonder; and had not Estelle been completely absorbed by the success of her visit, she might have settled sooner to writing a second letter to her father. As it was it took one from him to encourage her to open the *ormolu* inkwell on her writing desk again, but not before she had read her father's news several times through:

It was a joy to receive your letter, My Bright Star, and know you are being accommodated in such agreeable style. Your hosts appear fine people and it is good you like them.

What a state, though, we have been in since your departure – all on account of Arthur, of course. That boy will be the death of me, you see if he isn't. I'm beginning to wonder if he's seriously wrong in the head, for after you'd gone he began his antics by refusing food and staying in bed and moping. He would tell me nothing, even when threatened with a thrashing – he became just about uncontrollable – Mrs Comfrey declared she was frightened to go near him, and you know how she stands no nonsense. Your brother is obviously malingering as he's as strong as an ox but not as useful.

This is not the worst, My Sweet, though I blame myself a good deal for what happened next – I should have put him under lock and key sooner. He received a letter one day – I don't know who from – but it did something to him – he sort of 'snapped', if you understand me. He got himself out into the tool-house, I ask you, back upstairs to the top passage with an axe in broad daylight and set-to demolishing his prison cupboard to splinters. Not content with that he then set fire to the evidence where it lay. Burkin, one of the gardeners, gave the alarm, seeing smoke and flames billowing from the top corner of the house.

All hands from the brewery and helpers from the town worked like demons with water-chains and were able to bring the blaze under control before it got a hold in the roof and we were done for. Your rooms though, my dear, are safe – be assured of that – not a mark or drop of water, which is as well seeing how much I spent on them.

I'm convinced Arthur intended to have our lives though he swears this is not so. He said he just wanted to burn the letter he got.

He's calm again now as I think he frightened himself with what he did. After I'd beaten him I felt a sudden sharp pain in my chest – it stabbed right through me but was soon mended. I expect it was my dyspepsia – you know how the wind troubles me so. But I felt more cheered after I'd opened a third bottle of port wine. Arthur is now shut in the basement thinking over the error of his ways and can stay there, for all I care, till he goes to school again or Bedlam, where he rightfully belongs I think.

I have been putting more thought to your having an establishment in London and also taking advantage of the trouble in France, regarding your Aunt Amelia. Matters seem to be getting worse – The Paris mob attacked a medieval prison-fortress in the east *of the city on the 14th of this month and released its prisoners after murdering the Governor. I know what I'd do with these troublemakers if I were King – cut off their heads and stick 'em on pikes somewhere public as in olden times – London Bridge was always full. Anyway, should your Aunt Amelia decide to leave this shocking business for a while, I would offer her the house in Brook Street, with a pair of servants and you and Zilla to join them. You could be of great service to one-another in this as it would relieve your Uncle Daniel of trying to make ends meet if she went to him at Chelsea.*

Think this over while you're away – we'll talk further on your return. I am afraid to report that the disappearance of your waxen head remains a mystery – Arthur swears on the bible it's nothing to do with him – I don't know, I'm sure.

Your affectionate Papa.

*Rookwell Park,
Hampshire.*

Dearest Papa,

Your letter arrived safely and brought me much pleasure in spite of your news. I was alarmed to read of your stabbing pains. Is it your heart? You must not hesitate to send for Dr. Sawley and not over-indulge in port and pork.

Poor old Satis. What will Arthur get up to next? Is he not the absolute limit? I wonder from whom his letter was? Certainly not from me and Alexander has not even thought about him, he tells me. Who else does Arthur know? I am so relieved you and my rooms are safe after his criminal act.

Your proposition regarding Brook Street sounds excellent. Perhaps if Aunt Amelia will not come, Marie might be glad to, especially if you make it worth her while. I quite see I cannot return to France at present so will have to put up with London instead. Perhaps you would write to Marie – her address is on a piece of paper in the Sevres box with ormolu mounts on my bureau. Alexander's parents were talking the other day about this prison-fortress you mentioned; his Mother is tremendously upset as she has just received the news that one of her nephews was killed defending it. She says, like you, it is a shocking business, or as she expresses it, quel horreur! She worries about her relations who are all important people with masses of fine houses in and around Paris. There are many in the south, too.

I have many diversions here and am feeling well on them, but of course, dear Papa, I look forward to the time when we can be together again.

Avec l'amour,

Estelle.

She placed a firm full-stop after her signature and sucked the end of her quill... *a sudden sharp pain in my chest...* It had not been the first, to her knowledge. She did not like to think of her father in pain, partly because it brought home to her the as-yet unfulfilled obsession, thanks to Uncle Daniel's chat in Chelsea, of finding out the contents of his will – if it indeed existed. Somehow, when she returned home, she must tackle him about it. In the meantime, Alexander awaited her pleasure.

* * *

While letters, secret or otherwise, were passing between Rookwell Park and Satis House, Aunt Amelia in Versailles was committing some of her headaches to paper and having them dispatched across the channel to Chelsea. To Daniel they bore all the hallmarks of a mind under siege:

...Your invitation to bring my family to your dear house is more than kind. You know there is nothing I would wish for us more than to rest in the flowery peace of your garden down by the river and talk of the old days at home with dearest Mama and Papa. Alas, Emil is so extremely busy that he cannot possibly leave, nor I without him, and I would worry myself sick about him on his own at this time. The King has apparently organised nearing thirty-thousand troops in and around Paris to act firmly with the mob if necessary. Every day there are fresh disturbances.

Though Emil says we are in a volcanic situation he remains calm in a way I wish I could, what with our peace of mind and that of our friends being eroded round us. Emil says the devil of it all is MONEY (or the lack of it) and that France will drain dry before new life is pumped back, which sounds as if it ought to make sense but I am not sure how. So as Emil is so much better at expressing what I only half understand I am asking him to conclude this letter from your loving but sorely-tried sister,

Amelia du Monde

Mon cher Daniel – your interest in politics will make good sense of our situation in my poor country – a situation, can you believe, that is challenging the authority of our hard-pressed King. We wait, as you say in England, with our hearts up our throats, to see what His Majesty will do. He seems unable to make up his mind and all the while propaganda and insurrection plague Paris with increasing ferment. The King will not go there and take responsibility but rides off hunting. I fear with each new kill he is allowing more and more of the blood of his ancestors to wash his throne away from under him in the direction of the people. If they have it they will surely tear it to pieces like a pack of his own hounds – Camille Desmoulins, a stammering young barrister from Picardy, advocates, quite publicly, that positive action be taken against a tyrannical King and his Government!

I have to say that I think some of this has been fuelled by the fairly recent unfortunate fiasco of the Queen's supposed purchase of a costly diamond necklace. It turned out, however, to be part of a vindictive invention by an unscrupulous family bearing personal grievances against the Royal Family. But the public believe what suits them when it suits them and the Queen happens to be a convenient scapegoat.

On Sunday, July 12th, a general uprising plundered gunsmiths' shops, ammunition and military arsenals. Barricades were set up in the streets and on the 14th, fourteen-thousand or more people converged on the fortress of the Bastille, intending to destroy what they considered to be the prime symbol of monarchical tyranny. They set free its prisoners (amounting to all of 7). Governor de Launay, an old friend of my colleague Dr. Philippe Curtius, was 'arrested' (if that is the correct word) where he stood. His crime? – defending that which he is paid 60.000 livres to defend in the interests of public peace!! Phillipe, with tears on his face, told me how the situation soon got out of hand – how the mob hustled this gentle and most humane of Governors away in his grey frock-coat to the Hotel de Ville. There they molested him by the hair with swords and spittle and obscenities *until a cook by the name of Denot levered off his head with a butcher's knife. They stuck it on a pikestaff with a notice denouncing him as a disloyal and TREACHEROUS enemy of the people, mon Dieu!*

Only the other day a friend of mine was waiting for a carriage under the arcade of the Palais Royal when a noisy procession appeared, dragging a naked corpse along the cobbles and waving aloft a head on a pike. It was an old man of seventy-five whose so-called 'crime' was accepting a post in the Ministry. The crowd exhibited this unbelievable sight to his son-in-law who they then butchered likewise! And they were not the only sufferers – with savage triumph the mob waves every section of freshly butchered anatomy about the streets as if they are banners of victory paraded on the Champs de Mars. I tell you, the very buildings are starting to run with blood.

I fear, mon cher Daniel, that this must mark the start of something too monstrous for the human mind to contemplate. There can be no going back now. The people have their head (forgive the unintentional pun) – others could well follow (heads, not puns). It is up to us to keep level heads and some sense of perspective. I never thought, six months ago, when Dr. Curtius and I began earnestly discussing the Nation's problems, that such a state as this would become fact. We must add a new word to our parlance – not revolt but Revolution. That evil young Desmoulins, brandishes the word like some sword of liberty while he calls for equality of rights and also an end to authority!!!!!!!!

Can you conceive the impossibility of such ideals? We may as well be back in the jungle. All Paris has gone mad and France is rapidly following suit, soon to be drowned in a commodity I am quite at home with in my profession – BLOOD. It is as if it exists now only to be shed, particularly if it is blue...

Nausea punched Daniel. He forbade Caroline access to the information. He could barely see out of his study window for tears. What magnificent specimens the roses were this year. He watched them almost slumbering against the summerhouse wall where the sun lounged about their heavenly fragrance. Thank God for a stable English Parliament and accessible monarch prevented from Absolute Rule by a sound Democracy.

* * *

When Estelle returned to Satis in mid-August, having not taken much persuasion to prolong her stay a little, she found that her father, in desperation had packed Arthur early back to school. A generous sum of money had ensured that he would complete his holiday there. Mrs Comfrey had pleaded for his release from the basement, her heart saddened by his treatment. His one secret and comfortable thought had been the prospect of being able to break up Estelle's model if he had so wished; but his incarceration had given him the opportunity to reflect on the consequences; he knew, for certain, that Alexander would disapprove — may even have planned the model's use in one of his own future schemes. Any scheme directed against Estelle must not be jeopardised or Alexander would be upset and angry.

She, for her part, was disappointed he was not still at home. She had long anticipated the chance to upset him by extolling the glories of Rookwell. She turned instead to a letter which had been delivered two days before her arrival. She recognised Marie's assertive but awkward scrawl and was soon in her boudoir ready to enjoy her communication. Though she had received a clearer view of France's problems from Mrs Compeyson, she was unprepared for Marie's information:

Your Papa has kindly invited me to share a house with you in London. I have written to tell him I cannot. Though I should naturally like to be away from trouble at this time (many of our friends are leaving Paris — even France) I could not leave Uncle-

Papa and Mama alone at the Cabinet de Cire. It has to be kept open at all costs and we must be seen to work, keeping our collection up-to-date with events. He could not do that on his own as he is not as well as he was and Mama is totally hysterical at shooting in the streets and ready to believe her head will end up on a pike – and not a model of it either.

You cannot hopefully possess any notion of the mental torture we are at present living under. Our Royalist sympathies are well known as is our association with radicals and free-thinkers. But how long will it continue? Somewhere between the two we may yet find security. I am deliberately appearing to keep a calm head and open mind and am making a point of adding the newest leaders and agitators to our collection. We have not closed our doors once during all the turmoil.

July 12th will remain with me until I die – Sunday – a hot day – stifling – Paris alive with precautionary troops and unrest as if one of our own melting pots in the studio was about to over-boil. As we sat down to our midday meal with little appetite, listening to the unrest behind our windows, news reached us of the Director General of Finance's dismissal the day before – Monseur Necker's model was one of the most popular in our collection. Then came a thunderous banging on our doors and demands to open up (we did allow ourselves the luxury of closing on the Sabbath). Uncle-Papa himself, against Mama's entreaties, answered the summons, serviette in hand. He faced a deputation from Citizen Desmoulins, an agitator with a growing prestige, requisitioning our model of Necker in the name of the people. I had fearful visions that our entire collection would be commandeered in this fashion – our life's work taken from us – bankruptcy – as had happened to Madame Bertin, you remember, the Queen's dressmaker.

We afterwards learned that our model of Necker was paraded in an ever-swelling procession through the streets towards the empty Tuileries Palace (the King and Queen being still at Versailles) but was confronted in the Place Louis XV by a squadron of German cavalry led by the Prince de Lambesc – did I ever tell you I have a couple of half-brothers and an Uncle in the Guard? There was a running battle – many lives lost to sabres and pounding hooves. Our model we presumed smashed (the precious mould we would never relinquish!) but it was returned unharmed, such is the respect for Uncle-Papa thankfully. Duplessi-Bertaux has produced an engraving of the fracas in which our model is clearly visible.

We had hardly recovered from the impact of this when the Bastille was attacked with looted firearms – burned – demolished. One of its 7 prisoners was the Count de Lorga, an old man with long straggly hair and beard down to his knees. He had been shut up for 20 years. Uncle-Papa brought him home to live with us but he died within a few weeks, unable to come to terms with freedom, but not before I made a model of him – a sound piece of work, I think, if somewhat macabre. The fate of Governor de Launay and many others is too sensational and distressing to relate to you – suffice to say that the carnage will haunt my every moment for ever.

The King travelled to Paris three days later to a Civic Reception at the Hotel de Ville even while they were making paper-weights and doorstops as souvenirs from the Bastille being broken up by 1000 men under contract. He smiled – waved – nodded – in a most affable and unaffected way, promising that French blood will never be shed on his instruction. He went as far as to accept the new tricolour cockade of Bourbon white and Parisian red and blue as a mark of respect for the new people's order. How anyone can consider him an enemy of the people and a tyrant is inconceivable – he wishes to make peace with this new order without violence.

The real enemy is the sunny weather – it has brought a drought which is bound to have affected the crops – we can but pray for a good harvest to reduce the price of bread. There are those, I can well believe, that blame all this, too, on the King.

But we remain open for business as usual and keep our own counsel. We continue to attract good crowds and have opened another exhibition in the Palais Royal. We cannot help thinking that if the King and Queen came to live in Paris for a time, some of the tension would go and confidence would be restored. But you know how they hate the Tuileries so – it is old-fashioned and almost derelict and not particularly private – the Queen would pine for her beloved Trianon, but it would surely be a small temporary sacrifice for the good of the country.

Enough of trouble! Forgive me. I am better working my thoughts in clay and wax. I also do not know how much of our true news is printed in your newspapers – what can you think of it all? You have not had such things in your country since the time of King Charles the First, I think.

I am interested for you to tell me of your de Bayonne family. They are not known to me. I must confess that at present it is not wise to think you know anyone, for fear of putting trust in your enemy...

Estelle's mind still reeled from Marie's news in the staid peace of the dining room that evening.

'These last weeks have agreed with you, Bright Star,' approved her father, before completely disposing of his mouthful. 'You look prettier than ever – society is obviously your lifeline. You'll be a tremendous success in London I don't doubt – the envy of every assembly, ballroom and *soiree*. What gladness to your old Papa's heart.'

'I always want to live up to your expectations of me,' agreed Estelle. 'And talking of your heart, Papa, did you see Doctor Sawley as I bade you in my letter?'

'If you are living up to my expectations at this moment, my love,' replied Mr Havisham with a playful smile, 'then I should say what *really* concerns you is that I don't pop off without having made a will.' He laughed to see his daughter for once lost for a response.

'I don't like you laughing at me, Papa,' she reprimanded. 'How could you think of me so?'

'Because, my dear, *you* are a true *Havisham*. Come now. Isn't there some truth in what I say? There is as much truth in Sawley telling me to eat and drink less. I don't need *him* to tell me that.'

'My only concern,' said Estelle, ignoring his breaking of wind, 'is your health.'

'And my money!' He fortified himself at his tankard. 'You can't change your ways now, my little Miss. You have a name to live up to, so better not try.' He patted her hand and went on eating. 'If your only concern *is* my health, then you'll be pleased to know I'm fit enough to have made a will. And would you like to hear what's in it? I thought you might.' He cleared his throat as if about to make a public announcement. 'You are to receive an allowance of thirty pounds a year until you marry, after which – nothing.' He forced the slack muscles at the sides of his mouth not to pull his full lips into another smile as he perceived the thunder rolling across Estelle's face. 'Everything goes to Arthur – including the business. Hey-ho! My Bright Star is about to turn into a shooting star it seems. Can something be amiss, my dear?'

Estelle's cutlery had all but clattered onto her plate. She stared with vacant horror across the table and collective spikes of candle light.

'That is – impossible,' she breathed. 'Arthur is nothing... what has he ever done...' She felt a tide of hysterical outrage beginning to bear down on her sanity. Mr Havisham, for all his alcohol, quickly recognised the signs. Leaving the table he went behind her chair and placed his hands at the sides of her elegant shoulders.

'Am I not a *wicked* old Papa? I can see you're in no mood for farce, My Bright Star who works so hard to keep his favour.' Lingeringly he kissed the side of her neck and returned to his place. 'My – what a face to turn the beer cloudy. I thought you'd be *amused* at my *levity* – I was trying to make *light* of my money.'

'Never make light of money, Papa – you should know that. I don't understand you when you behave this way – I feel you don't love me.'

Mr Havisham sighed dramatically. 'Yes, I should have known better than to tempt you with my wit. You are quite right, my dear – money is *not* something to make light of. It is serious – deadly serious, as I know to my cost...'

'*Talk* to me about your *will*, Papa,' insisted Estelle. 'You *must* do now, after what you said.'

The weight of this demand made him nod heavily. 'And why not, indeed, seeing as you must have everything. Very well, my dear, *have* everything. Arthur'll only waste it, for as you so correctly observe, he's nothing. Your inheritance awaits *you*, my love. Isn't that what I've always promised?'

'Is that still your promise, Papa?'

'What I said about Arthur was an empty jest – a joke – nothing more.' Mr Havisham raised a greasy hand. 'On your mother's grave I swear it – signed, sealed and safe with Old Jaggers in London. I thought it best after my last attack – no humour there, *I* can tell you. Had me fair worried it did – and you away from home. Everything goes to you – money, house, brewery, stock, tenancies... you look unsure, sweet one.'

'Arthur was the joke?'

'Hasn't Arthur always been the joke? No, perhaps he hasn't. But you don't think I'm so completely failing, do you, that I would bequeath my legacy to your half-brother? He'd be bankrupt before he knew the time of day, just like those wretched French. Besides, what does he deserve? It's his fault I had to marry his mother.' Mr Havisham helped himself to another drink. 'Why do you smile?'

'Your wit, Papa. And your logic. Some of it appeals to me, but more than your attempt at humour just now. I don't understand that.' A conversation that had taken place between her and Alexander threaded her mind as she said, 'However, I'm not sure I want Arthur to have nothing. I should like you to leave him the brewery.'

'The *brewery?*' spluttered Mr Havisham at the mercy of a choking fit. 'You're as mad as he is. What could he possibly do with the brewery except drag it down into the dregs? He can't tell a hop from a dandelion.'

'Then he'll learn,' said Estelle simply. 'It'll do him good. Alexander said he's quite different at school – he works hard and is intelligent. I've been giving a lot of thought to this lately and Alexander's been helping me. Arthur should have some responsibility – a challenge.'

'I don't understand you, Estelle. One minute you're damning him to hell-fire and the next giving him a business and financial independence. It doesn't make sense. My plan was to provide an allowance for him to live elsewhere – separate from Satis. Then it's up to him but he'll have no claim on you. You will marry and live here as the Havishams have for two generations. Your grandfather built the brewery – it's yours by rights.'

'Papa, Papa,' soothed Estelle, placing her hands on his, 'you have taught me the value of money – Alexander says I understand it better than what's going on in the world. Money is power – it can achieve everything. You don't think I would let Arthur make a mess of the business, do you? Of course not. He would be persuaded long before to come to some arrangement – I would see that he remains indebted to me for his salvation. It would be my favour to him. He always has been indebted, though he may not realise it, and I like it that way. This is a much subtler way of dealing with Arthur than cutting him out completely.'

'I shall have to think about it. I hope he realises what a good, kind, thoughtful sister he has…'

'*Half*-sister. I can take care of Arthur. Don't underestimate me, Papa – you've taught me well.'

Mr Havisham noisily cleared the last of the sauces on his plate. 'I sometimes think, my dear, I've taught you *too* well – you learn too easily. I look at you and see how I used to be, but I was nowhere near as advanced at your age – you have a sensible head on those lovely young shoulders. I think you have matured tremendously since you became acquainted with Master Compeyson – *that* is a favour Arthur has done *you*.'

Estelle did not need her father to point that out. She herself felt a new confidence – the result of Alexander's attentions. He seemed in sympathy, too with her attitude to Arthur. It was good to have a true friend such as he – one whose breeding and education could be relied upon as if they were extensions of one's own.

'What I really want,' Mr Havisham continued, almost to himself, 'is to be spared long enough to see My Bright Star take her rightful place in Society... so irritating her friend Marie can't be persuaded to come to London... I asked Amelia but haven't heard from her yet... you'd think any normal people would be glad to get out of that mess... if I were King I'd have the army in... I ask you – hunting and carpentry...'

'Papa,' protested Estelle, frowning, 'I don't think you should talk of the French so – it doesn't seem right.'

'That *revolution* of theirs isn't right... devil be praised I got you out in the nick of time. There were riots in *London* about ten years back... you may remember hearing of some religious fanatic – Gordon was his name, I think – went round the place shrieking *NO Popery!*... burning Catholic churches... even attacked Newgate... not much success of course, and it wasn't a *quarter* the size of the Bastille... our Georgie had the gumption to use his troops until the rioters had had enough... *fire with fire*... that's the *only* way... set an *example*...' Mr Havisham's head, having grown heavier, now rested on his arm, his eyes closed.

I shall set an example, thought Estelle, as she left him to his snoring. *Believe me I shall – with Alexander's help.*

TABLEAU IV
1789

Arthur had been content to return early to school. Its peace and freedom were preferable to Satis House, even without Estelle. He imagined his leg to be healing with renewed enthusiasm and forced himself to increase his mobility daily. Though a random pocket of boys had remained behind for what ever reasons, he did not seek them out particularly but chose his own company in order to read or draw. He found it strange that he did not miss Alexander as much as he expected to. If he was honest with himself he had to admit to feeling loosened from oppression, now able to think clearly away from surrounding constraints; nor did he feel in any way threatened. But he knew only too well that once the block of boys were back in a few days, the fear, the bullying, the deceit would begin again, to be interspersed with Alexander's patronage.

Sitting in the shade of the great cedar he continued pencilling, with nasty precision, his pictorial memory of his basement days. But instead of Estelle's wax model invading his privacy, he portrayed the contorted and skeletal form of Estelle herself, in shredded finery, chained and manacled to the moist walls glistening as if with ready saliva at the feast of her misfortune. Arthur placed himself before her – a Giant enlarged with his own powers – turning a branding-iron in a volcanic brazier at his side. Fired with a passion for his abilities he set Satis alight, the flames not least about his cupboard from which another Estelle, blazing and screaming, clawed her escape. He gorged the pyre with misfortune: the errant mother he had never known, father, brewery – even Alexander; a confusion of maddened misery until his design swirled into a black, reeling labyrinth of stopped-up hopes and hollow fears.

Almost without a conscious awareness, he realised that here, in the neutrality of school on a sunny day, temporarily disentangled from pressure, his life belonged to no one but him – to make of it what he could – to embrace an existence which allowed him some breadth of vision – some worthwhile project to lift him onto a high plateau of enthusiasm and purpose. He would find his way to France and seek out his Aunt Amelia's family. What he would then do did not occur to him, nor did it matter – to arrive at Versailles was sufficient ambition. His French was fair, thanks to Alexander's ministrations, his drawing fairer. Though he could not swim, the channel was no deterrent to liberation on the other side.

About one hundred miles lay at present between him and the south coast – miles to be demolished by any means possible and without money. He waited until midnight, then displacing the rats and mice in the larder, filled a borrowed kerchief with bread, cheese, fruit and pies, stocks having been conveniently replenished against the school's return. Stuffing them in his pack which contained only his drawing implements, he slipped unchallenged from the main entrance to where the receiving country road, swooped by silent owls, met the open highway tracking south. No enquiring moonlight silvered his retreat, nor the moment he decided to ditch his crutch – in a symbolic gesture he hurled it as far as his strength would allow, gratified to hear it slash like a scimitar through undergrowth and clank in splinters against a tree. Hoping he had not upset some passing vole or hedgehog, he was quite content to trail his best through the dew-hushed landscape until his fumbling the face of a wet milestone informed him, as if he were a blind man, that Huntingdon lay 6 miles ahead.

Market Day, once the late summer daylight broadened, provided ample opportunity to test his expertise in building up resources; a food-basket temporarily unattended by two gossiping women; a pocket-book from an unsuspecting fellow by a cattle-pen which yielded its prosperous emptiness; but not so the money bag from a weather-beaten swain of pastoral appearance carelessly asleep outside an ale-house over his tankard. A coach journey to London, then the coast, became a realistic proposition as it musically disgorged its contents into his gratified palm.

Entering further into the spirit of his success, he desired a change of appearance. As he innocently meandered, he was able to slide from assorted stalls a pair of breeches more or less his size, loose shirt with frilly front, something that passed for a cloak and a wide-brimmed hat supporting a bent ostrich feather. By the time his cunning had transformed him beneath a hay wain, his attentive audience a scrimmage of dogs, he emerged with an attitude of shambling eccentricity to stand against the future, confident in defiant intent. The clerk at the coach office regarded him suspiciously – particularly when he produced the adequate fare – but as it seemed as authentic as any one else's, was disposed to sell him the last seat on top.

As he took his place he decided that a further journey to Brightelmstone would be preferable to making for Dover as that would necessitate a stop for a change of horses in the posting yard of The Blue Boar at his home town, the route perilously close to Satis and familiar regions about the Medway.

On his arrival in London, after a breezy journey through St Neots, Knebworth and Hatfield, he left the coach at Snow Hill and spent an equally breezy night crouched under his cloak in a draughty corner of St Paul's Churchyard, sleeping as best he could. In the morning, after breakfasting from his purloins, he found his way to the south coast coach office only to be told that the first available seats as yet unreserved were on The Red Prodigy, not departing until the day after tomorrow. Nothing daunted he was prepared to risk his leg standing a rougher passage as he struck out resolutely south across Westminster

Bridge with no crutch to cripple his chances. He rested on a seat for a time in one of the embracing stone embrasures interspersing the parapet; enchanted by the airy view of down-river reflections, St Paul's dome and City steeples bristling like towering quills ready to defend the metropolis from financial and commercial ruin, he sketched what he saw with relish as if drawing up the first document legalising his freedom.

As he later reached open fields, he found that though he had progressed carefully, his leg noticeably ached. By midday he came to a crossroads cornered by a small ale-house and market gardens set beside a timber-shaded pond. He rested on a handy log, dangling his feet in the water, the day being heavy and windless. If only he had not spurned the pony Estelle had offered earlier that year – he could have stolen to Satis under cover of darkness from where a journey to Dover would have been simple.

As if responding to his thoughts, the sound of approaching hooves attracted his attention. Turning to look up the dusty road, he saw a man on a black horse and smart boy about his age on a nicely proportioned chestnut stop at the ale-house door and dismount. The animals pawed the ground as their owners secured their reins to a tree and retired indoors. Arthur stared at the neat chestnut – ready saddled – just his size...

With his cloak flapping behind him like some apprentice Dick Turpin, he bent himself over his pounding steed until well away from the crossroads. He allowed the chestnut to find its own pace as it trotted through the afternoon towards shades of evening streaking weald and downland surrounding Ditchling Beacon's high-point. Arthur took his pony, which he had christened Sweet Chestnut, into a field and fed him apples and bread before leaving him tied to a hedge to crop the grass. A nearby haystack provided Arthur with a sound night's sleep until the first slants of sunlight edged across his tangle of dreams. Another cloudless day rejoiced in his chalky ascent to the Beacon's summit where contours of patchwork countryside below expanded in mellow, sun-filled acreage dissolving away to west, north and east into pale, ethereal mysteries of undisclosed shires.

Evening's dusk purpled his approaching destination. Sweet Chestnut ambled into Brightelmstone's cobbled huddle before the shingle and channel beyond. Amber lights from gaming rooms, ballrooms, public rooms, private rooms, encouraged Arthur's enthusiasm for his adventure as he crossed The Steyne, passing the bowed and pillared east front of the Prince of Wales's recently completed Marine Pavilion extended in new Classicism from the old farmhouse of former modesty. He inhaled the salty tang-sting of breezes whipping from the water – they overlaid his lips with tongue-tipped tastes of brine, pushing lustily into his lungs. He headed for a cosy batch of boats and fire-glow at the shoreline, leading Sweet Chestnut cautiously out over the shingle.

'I want to get to France!' he called, in a grown-up way, to the homely-looking men and lads spit-cooking fish over spirited fires. 'What should I do?'

'Try a boat,' suggested a voice, 'unless you can swim good.'

'I've a bad leg,' replied Arthur, covering that he could not, 'otherwise I'd try.'

Once the laughter had died down a shingly voice inquired, 'An' why should a young shaver like yourself be wantin' to skip over to France? You know they've troubles there.'

'That's why I have to go – my Aunt and Uncle are involved and I need to see them. I can pay if that's the problem.' He tugged his money-bag from his shirt.

'Let's see the colour of them shiners fust, son,' said a third voice, 'makin' no promises, mind.' Arthur's coins were counted between them.

'I'll do it for the price,' said the man with the shingly voice, 'an' the nag thrown in the deal.' He jerked his thumb at Sweet Chestnut.

'But I'll need him in France,' said Arthur, crestfallen. 'I've got to get to Versailles somehow…'

'On *that*? Never make Fauville, that won't. You from London, cully?'

'Yes,' said Arthur, defensively. 'What of it?'

'Nag's wore out, that's wot of it. Won't get to Christmas if you hammer it. Nobbut a youngster.'

'I'll take you for your money-bag, young man,' said a voice gentler than the rest, 'and you can keep your mount.' A kind-looking man got up and took the money from his comrades. 'Don't you listen to any o'them – can't tell a gentleman's mount from a workhorse. Sell it for meat they would, along with their grandmothers. You keep your animal, lad, I keep your purse and we sail with the tide. Rory's the name. Follow me with the bonny'un – we'll feed him and get him aboard. Jack! Jack!' A blazing torch appeared in the darkness ahead of them down the beach and a boy not much older than Arthur ran to the call. 'Two guests aboard, Jack – from London… so mind y'manners!'

Arthur followed the flaming brand to the bulk of a trim-masted vessel hauled up from the water and supported on baulks of timber to prevent her from keeling over. Once aboard he was surprised at her commodious size and comfort, delighting in the snug cabin fitted out in natural timbers smoothed and warm in the lantern glow. He was welcomed, not least, by a one-eyed terrier called Hawser whose devotion to him knew no bounds once bread, cheese and milk appeared on the table.

'I could live here for ever,' he murmured contentedly, relaxing visibly. 'What a grand life it'd be.'

'Aye,' agreed Rory, 'Jack an' I'd have none other. Right, son? Not even if you was to offer for me to be King of England. And as for King of France…!'

'Do you often go there?' asked Arthur, drinking his milk. 'It's a long way, isn't it?'

'With a fair wind, sixteen hours or so,' said Rory, cutting himself a corner of cheese. 'I'm there on business from time to time, never mind what. You're a welcome companion as I pleases m'self when I comes and goes. Mother Fortune's shining on you now, young spalpeen, also the sandman, by the looks o'your eyes. Get y'head down on Jack's bunk yonder and leave the rest to y'old mates.'

Arthur needed no second bidding. Hardly had he touched the pillow than he hit the ramparts of sleep with the force of a cannonball and remained embedded until bands of creaking sound surfaced him to a rocking motion. Excitedly he leapt down barefoot onto the scrubbed planking. Hawser did not seem particularly concerned about him this morning, barely opening his surviving eye as his young guest stroked his head before opening the hatch and going up onboard.

The breeze-boom in the straining sails claimed his attention from the expanse of shining sea about him. Not a tail of land guided his eye – not a seabird – beneath the ascendant sun; a ball of fiery magnetism pulling the plucky craft through hissing surf. At the stern stood Sweet Chestnut blinking patiently, tethered either side with steadying ropes. Arthur caressed his soft muzzle, glad to greet his friend.

'Good morning, you beautiful creature,' he said, patting the side of his neck. 'I don't know where we are, do you? Not much grazing out here, is there?' He smiled as Rory approached. 'Where are we, please?'

'Six hours out,' came the reply. 'We left you to sleep. T'was as pretty a dawn as ever you saw. Jack'll get you something to eat – it'll soon be noon, sleepy cove that y'are.'

During the lengthy afternoon, after Arthur and Jack had squatted on the deck to play knucklebones and Meg Merrilees, Rory took a nap and Jack the tiller. Arthur basked beside him, his face turned to the sun.

'How is it,' he said, 'if your father's a fisherman I haven't seen any tackle? I'd like to have a look at the nets and things.'

'We don't always be out fishing,' said Jack, with a twinkle, 'and this ain't a fishing trip.'

'But he said you were coming out on business,' said Arthur, puzzled.

'That we are. Not fishing business, though. My Pa's as slippery as a deckful of fillets when he has to be. Ever hear tell of Jarvis Brook?'

'No,' said Arthur, shrugging. 'Should I?'

'Jarvis Brook of Alfriston, up Sussex way, the greatest of 'em all. Across from France we sweeps to Cuckmere Haven, an' stand-to of a moonless night – 'darks' we call 'em – my Pa here in *Nightstar,* Ned Wanless in his lugger – Perry Bonniface, Josh Taylor – gentlemen all an' experts at outwitting the Preventives... tip 'em off to landing at one beach while we land at another! Some o'the gentlemen go over downland routes, but we mizzle up the Cuckmere itself, under the Preventives' very noses. We row right up to the church at Alfriston in Mister Brook's best tradition himself; one barrel – hundred barrels... it's all the same to us – an' baccy. There's none as can pin a thing on us – our nets be stacked below all neat an' my Pa's a-one at words. The night has eyes, he says, but we can outstare them anyways.'

'Smugglers,' Arthur whispered, wide-eyed. 'Gummy, wouldn't I like to join you! Wouldn't I just. And Sweet Chestnut. What excitement!'

'Don't tell Pa you know,' said Jack, finger to lips. 'He might be angered I've told you. So I shouldn't an' that's what. We be honest smugglers, or fisher-folk, which ever be asked.'

'Of course I shan't tell,' said Arthur. 'What a life. I'd join you if I could, only I must get to France straight away. Are you going to pick up a cargo now?'

'We shan't be wasting the journey an' that's for sure,' laughed Jack. 'Fecamp can always be counted on anytime.'

'Is he another smuggler?'

'My eye he ain't.' Jack gave Arthur a questioning grin. 'You're a rum go an' no mistake. Fecamp's where we're taking you. It's on the coast – near Etretat. Sweet Chestnut'll get you to Paris in no time, with a following breeze. It'll be dark when we beach so y'won't see the famous Monastery there – famous for its brandy liquor it is. That's why we go to Fecamp. *'Aim high'* is Mister Brook's motto an', well, y'can't aim higher than a Monastery on a hill, now can you? Luc an' Benoit have never let us down yet. Are you by way of speaking the language of them Frenchies, Arthur?'

'I learned French from my tutors and at school,' said Arthur with certain pride, 'and I had a friend who helped me – and I can draw.' He showed Jack his sketch of London from Westminster.

'My school's this,' said Jack, indicating the open world. 'There's more here than what's in books, and what there isn't don't be worth knowing. I can read a bit, write a bit an' count a lot, specially barrels and fish. What else I want I ask m'Pa. I've sharp eyes, good ears and a smell for danger – they'll get me by I'll bet m'last jimmy o'goblin.'

'I'll remember what you said,' promised Arthur. 'Perhaps I'll get as lucky as you.'

Darkness had enfolded the seascape before Rory told him the French coast was within reach. He extinguished all lamps but one. He coaxed the boat with diminishing sail until it moved with a tiny crunch onto dry land. Arthur had already been provided with food, had collected his drawing things and some old seafaring clothes Jack had out-grown should he need them later. Everything was bundled and secured onto Sweet Chestnut's saddle. Led down a plank from the ship's side the pony found his land-legs again while Arthur took an emotional and sorrowful farewell.

'Make for Rouen,' Rory advised. 'From there Paris won't be difficult, then Versailles which isn't far. But take it gently or you'll have a dead animal on your hands. Away with you now – there's work to be done. You watch these Frenchies... God's speed and good luck.' He shook Arthur's hand but found himself embraced – Jack also – seeing by the lantern light tears of gratitude in Arthur's eyes. They helped him into the saddle and watched him mount the cobbled causeway to become enshrouded in an unpredictable French night.

'A brave lad,' said Rory, holding Jack's shoulder. 'I wonder what's in store for him?'

Wishing he could have stayed amongst such compatibility to be a smuggler, Arthur jogged mechanically through the town deciding that he would sleep locally until dawn. Once out of Fecamp he sought a meadow, tethered Sweet Chestnut, made himself a nest of spare clothing in the lee of a wall and curled up like a dormouse.

A rumbling cart and snorting horse alerted him to the need for breakfast and an early start. Passing a milestone denoting that Rouen was 70 kilometres distant, he began his journey with a spirit of heart, body and mind which seemed to have inspired Sweet Chestnut too – he responded happily, though Arthur was a far from expert handler, having ridden a little whilst Estelle had been at Versailles, enabling him to avoid her laughing derision at his mistakes. He now felt able, for the first time, to contemplate how autumn had begun its surrounding command of summer instead of having to fix his eyes with steadfast apprehension on the road before him, as in England.

Further on, at Cleville, he dismounted to allow his backside its share of circulation. He felt surprisingly at ease and by the evening had reached the fertile, timbered environs of Caudebec en Caux, where directly ahead flashed a breadth of river. On enquiry, the first to test his linguistic powers, he was informed that it was the Seine and flowing from Paris which lay away to the left.

As his journey continued the next day, following as near as possible the river's course, he became conscious of Sweet Chestnut losing some drive – hanging his head – blowing in a coughing manner through his nostrils... his muzzle felt hot and hard, extruding a mattery substance which ran also from his eyes. That evening, at Duclair, Arthur was distraught; communication by voice and touch with the only living creature he had ever come to love being wholly inadequate for the fever of his concern. His behaviour caused interest – he was eventually told by the burly but gentle smith at the forge that Sweet Chestnut had developed pneumonia and would probably not live many more days. Broken-heartedly Arthur agreed to let him be led behind the smithy, shutting his ears with fierce hands to the pistol shot as he sobbed. Feeling no better than a murderer, he crept away to the cold river's autumnal edge, trying to drown his emotion in the slop and eddy of troubled water, the occasional falling leaf emulating the downward sensation in his heart.

His bundle on his back, his pouch savouring the money from the sale of Sweet Chestnut's *accoutrements,* he walked the 20 kilometres to Rouen the following day. Amongst the Cathedral's soaring tranquillity he considered his position. *The river flows from Paris,* the man at Caudebec had said. *So,* thought Arthur, *why not the river!* Inspection of the busy waterfront revealed a paradise of craft all shapes sizes, hues. A protracted search revealed just the nicest boy-sized shallop in bright canary, moored on a long rope behind a listless barge. *Alouette* scrolled graciously in red along the prow was enough for Arthur's yearning heart immediately to go out to this pretty yellow lark. The oars lying her length seemed to be waiting for his hands alone – how she would skim the water like her namesake in an azure sky.

Darkness's conspiratorial cover was an obvious ingredient for success, until which he was more than content to dangle his feet innocently in the water whilst sitting on the edge of a low jetty. He sketched what he saw on the opposite bank, attracting an interested crowd given to uttering sounds of French incredulity at the talent of one so young. He drew some of their faces – swift caricatures in a few deft lines.

Bad light and an aching hand eventually halted production. Had he known, as he ate some hurried morsels, that due to many watery windings Paris lay a further 200 kilometres, he might not have taken charge of his new pet so lightly. The presence of a black cat under the seat in the stern augured well though, particularly as it did not seem disposed to spring up with an affronted shriek from its curl of contentment – animals had a habit of taking to Arthur. Untying the rope he cast-off, deciding he would row to a nearby cove or creek and sleep in order to be fresh for daybreak.

For the next three weeks he delighted in how rapidly his thin, pale arms took on a healthy glow – he became convinced his muscles were developing visibly. But his delight was hard-earned, for there were times when he was near to tears at the slowness and tedium of his advancement, despite the ever-changing scenic stimulation. There were outbursts of rain; days when it was still too warm to labour; days when only labour kept him warm; and so many bends which looked like so many others. Some days he and the cat ran out of food; some days he purloined more; some days he learned from the cat and did nothing but rest.

Beyond the gardens at Chaillot, towards the middle of October, Arthur first sighted the towers and domes of Paris – the Tuileries, St Germain L'Auxerois, St Etienne du Mont, Notre Dame, les Invalides, the new Pantheon... all vied for prominence under the grey morning sky; indeed, there had been rain in the night with the promise of more to follow. As he sculled urgently beneath the Pont Royale laden with noisy, moving crowds, his second wind returned to inflate his somewhat dampened spirit. He must make for Notre Dame, an obvious focal point from which to orientate himself in more peaceful surroundings than here, where the disturbed air bustled with a calling and a chanting and a tramping of many feet. Intermediate rain spotted his attention as he approached the Pont Neuf, intending to shelter under its arches. Above him the area resounded with a denser throng — women mostly, by the look of it — shouting, cheering, waving sticks and pitchforks, pursuing some slow-moving purpose ahead jammed by more noise.

The cat, who until now had shown a marked indifference to events, viewed the overhead concourse with a feline apprehension which caused her to look desperately about for an easy escape route. Deciding that the Quai was within springing distance, she propelled herself off the seat before Arthur could restrain her. She missed firm claw-hold on her landing, slithering backwards into the water where Arthur interpreted her attempts at swimming as drowning. She being too far out to hoist to safety, he dared not leave the boat. It was the first time during his journey that the thought of being unable to swim distressed him.

A woman on the bridge swooped down headfirst, landing near the animal with a gargantuan splash which nearly swamped *Alouette*. She swam with sturdy strokes and after scooping up the cat deposited it back in the boat with remarkable energy. Arthur was not prepared for her expanse of bare arm thickly implanted with black hair, nor her rough, square jaw.

'Don't fret, *mon frere,*' gurgled a deep, husky voice from the bedraggled figure in the water, 'she'll live.'

Arthur's bemusement was completed by the tangle of dark hairs clearly visible through the water-transparent top of her red cotton dress. 'Are you a man?' he asked, hugely amused by the thought.

'Like many of us,' replied the stranger, indicating the bridges. 'It's necessary.'

'For what?'

'For Versailles – we've to reach the King – soldiers won't attack women. The King must give us bread – hear that drum? – we're to follow it...' With a few strokes the young stranger reached the Quai steps and tripped up them as best he could for sodden petticoats and ribald comments from friends.

Versailles! Urgently, Arthur rowed to an iron ring set into the stonework and secured *Alouette*. Snatching up the cat, dripping and subdued, he wrapped her in his cloak, stuffing the bundle inside his shirt with her green eyes and pink tongue protruding guardedly. Though the object of curiosity in his fancy dress during his travels, his blend into this motley congestion became seamless and perfect. He walked abreast of a real woman, her uncompromising expression as determined as her step, short clay pipe clamped between her remaining black teeth. Unattracted but curious, Arthur mazed his way amongst the throng: hundreds upon hundreds – all ages, shapes, sizes – laughing, cursing, spitting – marching, striding, lumbering – a ragged assortment surging along by the Hotel de Ville having liberally taken charge of all manner of agricultural tools and weapons. Back to the banks of the Seine they trooped, their numbers augmented by masses from across the Jardin de Tuileries, Place de Carousel and Quai de Louvre. Elated by the acquisition of arms adding to arrays of crowbars, scythes, pikestaffs and axes, they headed along the Cours la Reine in unbroken stream beneath rain abated to a spitting apology, as if temporarily demoralised by the sheer weight of numbers on the move beneath.

Drums tatted unerring pulses throughout the *melee*, almost obliterating the rage of restless feet and tongues as the unwieldy bulk reached the bridge at Sevres where the Guard from Paris under La Fayette, on his white charger, had taken up a watchful rear position, uncertain if intervention was advisable – it seemed a little churlish as this female representation was *en route* to the Chateau only to ask for bread. A good downpour would do the trick.

When it *did* arrive half way through the afternoon, the marchers simply hoisted their skirts over their heads without faltering in pace; children sought shelter as best they could or frolicked in the muddiest ruts and messiest puddles. Arthur's cloak, once it was a dripping rag, gave no service, nor did his once stout hat with its bent and sorry feather now peering down at him from over the edge of the braided brim. Not that he minded – he was much too charged with excited purpose as the vanguard surged along the uphill gradient until, in the early evening, it swept the two hefty bends curving into the tree-lined length of the Avenue de Paris, stretching with unbending accuracy towards its palatial target. Had this *really* filled part of Estelle's year in the town? What would she say now, Arthur wondered, to this rough crusade cluttering up its fashionable approaches? He felt glad he was here – a wave of something akin to triumph joined the chill in his bones.

Benefiting from returned strength to his leg, he had managed to retain his position amongst the front ranks, though his muscles ached and his knees sank like melting wax. Cold, wet, tired, hungry as he was, he could not deny his senses their full appreciation of their eventual close-view of magnificence, spread before him behind its gilded gates, the Chateau's bulk of daunting proportion intimidating his spirit into submission. All he wanted to do was stare and then draw – to block in the commanding east front with its two projecting wings on either side of the marble courtyard which created the equivalent of a gigantic central mouth about to bite a piece from its outlook.

The Guard unexpectedly opened one of the front gates a little, allowing the admittance of five or six women before shutting and locking it again. Arthur watched them being escorted across the vast main courtyard, to disappear eventually through a distant doorway at the side beyond another range of gates and railings. Time hung like a banner heavy with the sweat of battle. Somehow, camp fires were encouraged to spring up as groups began to bivouac and eat their scant provisions bought or plundered. The cat had become accustomed to its steamy nest in Arthur's clothing, showing no inclination to attend to any matter but relaxation, encouraging Arthur to seek out a place to do the same. The extensive gathering had formed into unsettled quietude, flickered by random camp fires in the departing daylight, as well as lights radiating from a number of Chateau windows. Arthur rung out what clothes he could, spreading his cloak beneath him on which he soon lost himself to slumber, the cat curled in his arms.

As a later cloudburst drenched him afresh, a kick in his ribs jolted him from diluted dreams with a start – also the cat from hers and his arms. She hared away into the small hours as Arthur sat up to find movement about him – he had just been tripped over by a man, judging by the ungainly sway of draperies. More people appeared, and amidst murmurings and pointings, seemed to be making for the right hand side of the Chateau. With the errant cat on his mind, he followed the movement, pulling his cloak round his shoulders whilst impulsively donning a white frilly cap removed from an obligingly heavy sleeper.

At a gate beside the great chapel, a small army of surprisingly unfeminine men waited for their numbers to be swelled by anyone who cared to join, no matter how they were dressed. The gate gaped open – a soldier lay motionless – someone had charge of his musket. Arthur followed the conspirators across the Cour des Princes, snatching such scraps of whispered intelligence as, 'open main gates', 'Queen's apartments', 'stick to Jourdan – he knows the way…'

They're surely not going to ask for bread at this time of night, thought Arthur.

Gunshots suddenly ricocheted round courts and corners – a drum rapped – a tattoo rasped through increasing roars of voices surfing like tidal waves at Arthur's ears as he merged into massed movement towards the left of the building where those at the front were already smashing into glass and woodwork with axes and pikes. Torches and soldiers everywhere; flashing weaponry; flailing limbs; faces white with terror turning crimson at the stroke of a blade.

'The Queen! To the Queen!' The universal cry rebounded on itself from metal to stone to brick, the polished multi-marbled staircase receiving clump and clatter of threatening footwear pounding towards defensive bodyguards bunched in front of the Guardroom doors where axes and mattocks hacked them to pieces, their heads rammed on pikestaffs in elevated triumph.

'Save the Queen!' screamed the last bodyguard through the closed doors behind him before musket butts ground his skull into the pretty white and gold carvings surrounding its panels. More muskets, hatchets, pikes; splintering assaults on fragile symmetry of decoration; the sickening strain of woodwork at every joint and hinge; the breakthrough into the Guardroom watched warily from the painted ceiling by Jupiter in his silver chariot; forward to the next set of locked doors into the Grand Couvert Antechamber, then to the Salon of the Queen's Gentlemen... and so to the doors of the Queen's bedroom itself.

Set upon with renewed venom they were left, moments later, a shambles of matchwood through which the masses poured, Arthur propelled with them. The sight of the chamber's opulent emptiness – the hurriedly vacated bed, the glowing embers in the grate – infuriated the leaders who lashed out at silken hangings and upholstery, slashing them to shreds, ransacking cabinets, shattering mirrors.

Arthur became pressed into a safe space between the marble fireplace and low gilded balustrade fencing off the overbearing bed from the rest of the vast chaos-filled chamber. Walls of near panic closed on him – he felt his healed leg take the strain. As he turned this way and that for escape, he noticed, the other side of the balustrade, a dark tell-tale crack, similar to one at Satis, round a concealed door in the silk-hung panelling on the left of the Queen's bed. Once over the balustrade he pushed to find it opened easily into a long, dim, narrow passage lit in the distance by some receding candles amongst moving people.

'Please!' he called in French. 'Help me! I'm lost!' He scraped after them past a series of intimate, open-doored *cabinets* as the people started round in alarm – three women in nightgowns frozen in momentary terror – the central figure tall, her noble face heavily framed by an aureole of fair, undressed hair swept from her temples, brushing her shoulders enclosed in a loose shawl. She carried what appeared to be a pair of stockings. As Arthur approached, one of the shorter women pushed the taller frantically through a door at the end. As the third followed he again called, 'please – I want to escape too!' The door crashed shut in his face, the lock turned against him; but not before his glimpse into the sumptuous *salon* beyond, where a stout, fleshly-faced gentleman in white wig stood between two frightened children staring anxiously at the women stumbling towards him.

The dark passage behind Arthur began filling with light and noise, his exit from the bedroom discovered. In panic he ran towards them as soldiers attempted to subdue the confusion. The late arrival of La Fayette, fresh from his slumbers on his brother-in-law's settee at the Hotel de Noailles, had not undermined his control and direction of bands of grenadiers driving the living back over the dead, through rooms scarred with terror, and down a staircase unrecognisable beneath its squelching lava of blood and limbs.

In the courtyard, under military authority, a corporate chant unfurled into roaring flags of sound: 'The Queen! The Queen!' From his vantage point pressed against a wall, Arthur obtained an acute angle view of the central balcony beneath the clock to which all faces were directed. After a while the three long arched windows reflecting the rising sun flashed on opening. Into a radiant dawn stepped the tall, noble lady from the passage, but now clad in a yellow-striped dressing gown, similar to one Estelle had brought back. At each hand she held the two children he had glimpsed: a girl about his age and a boy of five or six.

'No children!' demanded the multitude, whereupon they were obediently passed back indoors.

No golden arrows bolting along the Avenue de Paris could have found their mark more accurately than the sun's rays striking the Queen's high-placed pride as she stepped forward to face her flood of potential assassins. Not a sound disturbed the swift hush. She held her position – solitary – unguarded – above her new masters, a chilled breeze teasing her dishevelment but not her dignity. To Arthur it might have been Estelle up there above the *Cour de Marbre,* surveying a society outside her understanding.

Then, with infinite grace, as if before her own sort in the spangled glaze of the *Galerie des Glaces,* the Queen bowed her head and dropped into a perfect curtsey. For an instant she became an integral part of *le Roi Soleil's* golden sunbursts decorating the protective balcony rails of the *ancien regime.*

'*Vive la Reine!*' called some voices, confusingly at odds with previous moods. '*Vive le Roi!*'

The King breezed onto the balcony bringing with him La Fayette who promptly redoubled enthusiasm by gallantly kissing Her Majesty's hand. The King raised his languid arms to silence the repeated shouts of '*vive La Fayette! La Reine a Paris! Le Roi a Paris!*'

'My loyal friends... I shall be pleased to go with my dear wife and children to Paris – if such is your wish... and I trust all I hold most precious here to the love of my good and faithful subjects. Look after my poor Versailles... until I return.'

'*Vive le Roi!*' continued the mob, reluctant to be silenced by La Fayette after Their Majesties had retired, nor vacate the courtyards and return home. Too much expectancy thrilled the air for a moment of it to be wasted. Women and children fainted from hunger, their clothes still soaked about their fatigue; boredom encouraged skirmishes – but the waiting continued. Arthur dozed, waking once or twice at his own sneezes – he missed the cat's warmth, resolving to remain and search for him before seeking out his Aunt Amelia.

A general hustle of activity, overseen by the soldiers and encouraged by the watchful crowds, continued throughout the rest of the morning; roars of approval greeted the clattering appearance, some time after noon, of an impressive carriage drawn by six horses which then waited over an hour by the steps to Grand Entrance. The King appeared – beside him, the fair object of all mixed gazes and sentiments, her broad plumed hat insufficient to hide eyes smarting from confused tears – to shield a face so recently saddened by the eventual death of her eldest son, the *Dauphin*, and now perplexed with hurt pride as she helped the new little *Dauphin* and his sister into the satin-lined interior. She was followed by a younger lady, her features bearing a marked resemblance to the King's and wearing a jewelled crucifix; the King's brother also climbed in, to be followed by the governess. The National Guard escorted the royal cargo and its surrounding swarms out of the courtyard onto the miry Avenue de Paris – away from the Sun King's paradise beneath the westering sun.

From their windows the travellers found it impossible to ignore the trophies of conquest brandished at them: women waving pikes stuck with bread loaves and bodyguards' heads; women arm-in-arm with soldiers – drinking, smoking, singing, carousing, laughing – as if being escorted *en fête;* women astride cannon; behind them, carriages and carts from the King's stables piled with sacks of flour and food from the King's stores. The

Royal travellers sat well back, the Queen with the *Dauphin* on her knee, trying to ignore surrounding chants of, 'here is the baker, the baker's wife and the baker's boy... now we shall have bread...!'

Too drained to move, Arthur remained by the Chateau gates watching the nation's problems disappear; behind him a fresh sound punctuated the vacated air; the echoing of Chateau doors being banged and bolted – of window shutters clamping into place – of chain-links clanking through gates and railings. About the churned *Place* before him, miserable as an ill-used battlefield, stragglers meandered amongst the dead and those who soon would be – a child cried for its parent – a parent cried for its child – but no cat cried for its foster-parent. Tired and shivery as he felt, he retained the image of the white-faced Queen – what a fine picture *that* would make; but instead of her haughty features...Estelle's; and engraved beneath, QUEEN ESTELLE IN HER CARRIAGE, JEERED BY MOBS – HURT BY PRIDE. How well *her* head would grace a pike. His senses burned white as his knees refused to remain strong – his legs jellied into ground heaving up to meet him as he lost consciousness...

He was next aware of a blanket's tickle under his chin as reality began ebbing back, sight and sound, daylight and warmth reviving his sense of purpose. On either side an assortment of movement told him he was lying on the ground in an improvised infirmary.

'*Vous vous reveillez,*' said a gentle voice, a face appearing above him. '*Essayez manger un petit morceau.*' A young man stirred a small bowl and guided a spoonful of steaming broth to Arthur's lips. It tasted meaty and good, smoothing his tongue with a comfortable wash of flavour.

'What happened?' he asked dazedly, as its settling presence revived him a little,

'*Vous etes Anglais?*' The young man stared in surprise. 'How came you here?'

'I walked from Paris... with those people... I've come from England to find my Aunt... I don't feel quite well...'

'You are feverish. You have the luck to stay alive – there are many dead around.'

'I want to see my Aunt... Amelia du Monde.' Another sense of faintness gauzed him. 'You understand me?'

'*Absolutement, mon ami.* I am Doctor du Monde's assistant – he is treating others. Wait here please...' Much as Arthur would like to have waited, his consciousness would not allow it – he had again melted into that unknown region by the time his Uncle came to him...

He would have relished his transference to the Boulevard de la Reine and been amused by his Aunt's immediate headache on confronting not only Estelle's half-brother all the way from England, but also his bizarre dress-sense. As it was, by the time he began his certain recovery, his bedroom became almost as busy with visitors as one of Queen Antoinette's *Levees*. His cousins, excited at having the erring wastrel Estelle had described under their roof, found him not fitting her description in the least; due to his exploits and stamina, he even took on a hero-status worthy of having sailed single-handedly round the world. He begged his Uncle to allow him to remain at the Boulevard de la Reine – as unpaid servant if necessary... anything to spare him being sent back home.

'I feel bound to tell you, *mon cher* Arthur,' said Uncle Emil, taking the boy's hands between his own, 'that when you were so ill I felt it correct to write to your father. I have had no reply to that letter – he may not be receiving it with the way things are this present time. I shall not turn you out, *bon ami,* but you understand I would not be doing my duty if I had concealed you – my mind is clear. You are welcome to remain here as long as you desire... you could be of service to me in my work, if you wished.'

'But he knows where I am now,' replied Arthur, desperately. 'It's undone all I've gained by getting away. I just couldn't stay at home any more, or school. I must be on my own, Uncle Emil. I *can't* go back until I'm *ready*. I dread Papa coming here to find me... I need to be free...'

'So my countrymen say too,' agreed Uncle Emil, nodding. 'Perhaps now that they have their King and Queen where they want them, pray God they will take on what they want without more cruelty and carnage.'

The du Monde family were not alone in their apprehension regarding the events of 17th October. The town emanated an uneasy calm; knots of people gathered inquisitively at the Chateau's protective gates to stare across the empty cobbles. The Sun King's Palace no longer glittered like a fairytale but exhumed its dead weight over its artificial plateau like an unclaimed lump on a mortuary slab. Its fountains were still, its lakes and groves left to natural strangulation, its shuttered windows eyes blindfolded to reality and closed in on visions of departed glories. The descendants of those glories were now embarrassments, caged like curiosities under military surveillance in Catherine de Medici's inhospitable *Palais de Tuileries*. For what duration? To what end? How well the doctor knew that there could be no operation without blood; but how much would have to be sluiced away after removing the problem parts so the patient could live to dress again in his best regalia?

For the weeks that Arthur remained with the family, no word reached them from Satis. But years of distrust and doubt had trained Arthur not to be optimistic, despite the pleasures he derived from being in a well-ordered, loving household with cousins who liked him as much as they disliked his half-sister.

Amelia-Lucie showed him particular affection, but of the two boys it was Emil-Theo who became his natural companion in a way that highlighted Alexander's patronising and gaoler-like attitude. He did his best to enter into the easy attitude of the household without a troubled mind – to help his Uncle in the dispensary, his Aunt in the garden; he drew caricatures to amuse his cousins and enthralled them all with tales of how he left England to become entangled in the *melee* at the Chateau – the Queen's bedroom – the Queen herself, not five metres from him. Recalling her children sent shivers down his spine; the little *Dauphin* so frail but courageous – his elder sister so proud, like her mother, but equally courageous.

As time passed and nothing was heard from Satis, he grew increasingly uneasy instead of calmer, daily expecting his father to come plunging unheralded up the Boulevard de la Reine like an entire mob to drag him away, frail but not so courageous. His Uncle had also informed him that Estelle's friend, Marie Grosholtz, had expressed a desire to meet him. The thought of having to talk to her about Estelle and be questioned about himself preyed further on his heart and mind.

One morning, approaching Christmas, Uncle Emil sat and wept over the note discovered on Arthur's pillow:

I feel safer if I don't stay in your loving care any longer, much as I would love to. These last weeks have been the happiest of my life but I fear my father. He has an unpleasant habit of turning up at the wrong moment. I want to outdo him and Estelle for as long as I can...

Emil brushed his tears. How could so much fear and hate exist in the soul of one so young? Though he had been able to form some opinions on life at Satis House, it still seemed inconceivable that an attitude as naturally warm as Arthur's could become as threatened as a cornered dog.

...I feel well enough to stand on my own two feet now, thanks to your great kindness and loving attention, which I shall never

forget, my dear Aunt and Uncle. It has done me more good than I can say, or you will ever know, to have been with you all, but please do not try following me or find out where I might be – I don't know yet. I shall take care of myself. I want the sunshine such as you have given me. When I come of age perhaps I may be free to take charge of myself and come back to see you without being afraid of shadows.

Until then, be assured of thanks and gratitude to the du Monde family and my best kiss to Amelia-Lucie.

From Arthur,

With my love

ENTR'ACTE

For four further autumns the Chateau's royal park, never again to charm and refresh its doomed family, glowed with as much russet, amber and bronze gilding as the gardens of Satis House, the only difference being that the Mistress of Satis was in residence – when not in London. Her years from fifteen to nineteen supplied the stage for her to develop into the darling of society her father had hoped for. He had established her in Brook Street, Mayfair, under the constructive eye of Madame Pinon, a recent French *émigré* recommended to him by Alexander's mother.

In Estelle's prodigious position as representative of her father's fortune, her assertive beauty soon commanded and confused her many admirers as they confronted her innocent appeal, quick passion, dismissive disdain. She encouraged no shortage of seekers after her penetrating eyes, appealing hands, demanding heart. But only two of her admirers had any claim to her sincerity. One was Hugh the groom.

He had advanced from well-formed lad who perspired easily into an unimpaired young man whose perspiration, Estelle was astonished to realise, provided one of his attractions. He and the steeds he so affectionately tended seemed to represent something more basic and earthy not to be found in the lacquered drawing rooms of London. She would visit the stables on any pretext; dawdle about the horses whilst monitoring Hugh's industry; his stooping and lifting – his straightening – his tautened clothing round and across his moving energy – his sturdy neck brushed by plentiful summer-coloured hair. He was always polite to the Master's daughter, if always shy – he had no option, simple lad, particularly as she had as good as promised him instant dismissal if he did not let her kiss him... rest her hands on his shoulders before slipping them behind his neck... take his hand and place it round her waist... encourage his body to relax as she savoured his weight on her breasts and pressure of his thigh against hers. Heated as she might become, she retained her dignity, well aware of the effect she had on him but always leaving him to his own devices.

It was Alexander though, who represented higher, purer aspirations. With him Estelle felt equal – happy for him to make himself indispensable in so many little ways, his own personal beauty taking on a further *success d'estime* from hers, his silken manner creaming through his attendance as easily as his father's gold through his fingers. Though she had often dwelt on the idea, she had made no attempt, from the moment she had first stayed at Rookwell Park, to be as forward with him as with Hugh; nor had he with her. There existed a deeper, richer understanding between them which displayed itself quite adequately, at present, in an agreeable and respectful balance of personality.

Since leaving school and settling in town, not in St James's Square but at a house in Hanover Street, leased for him by his father, he had taken on the role of quite the fashionable young blade seen at all the best clubs, gaming houses, hunts and race-meetings. It was often his pleasure to escort Estelle to the opera, theatre or fashionable assembly, being in his turn as welcome a guest at Satis as she was at Rookwell when their London commitments permitted.

Her fondness for and dependence on Alexander became more sharply focused when the time arrived, in 1793, for him to fulfil his parents' wish for him to embark on The Grand Tour. Now twenty, he was considered mature enough to benefit from the glories of Italy and Greece. Though the continuing revolution in France was making some aspects of travelling difficult, money still had a reliable habit of opening many a door and paving many a path. His parents dispatched him with a suitable contemporary from schooldays, Adolphus Fawn, whose own parents hoped to see some of Alexander's polish freshen up their son's. Adolphus, like Arthur, had become one of Alexander's *protégés*, taking it as a compliment that he should have been sought out and selected to serve the assertive young master of Rookwell Park. Estelle had taken the prospect of non-inclusion in the excursion with surprisingly good grace out of respect for Mr and Mrs Compeyson; at one time Alexander had indeed considered her, with Zilla as companion. He then admitted to himself that spared her equality of manner and personality, his own prestige would remain securely unshadowed, particularly as Adolphus's lack of lustre was likely to enhance it.

His legacy to Estelle was a wanting heart. Throughout the twenty-three or so months he remained abroad, she increasingly faced the reality of missing him most painfully. She also considered the possibility that she might be in love with him, a notion she had no previous experience of in order to compare. She knew that her use of Hugh, however consoling she found his presence, was only superficial – in fact he made her more curious about Alexander... why he had not taken control of her... why she had not felt able to take control of him... why their familiarity had never spilled into that region which now began dominating her thoughts. She decided that her lack of progress was due to the fact that he mystified her on occasions – could be distant, as if holding back. It was then difficult to approach him on any level. She smiled to herself, though, accrediting this to his being the perfect gentleman and, like Hugh, engagingly shy of offending her.

It was as well, then, that it did not occur to her that this perfect gentleman on his travels might not always be attracted, perhaps, to the pure level of living she equated him with – that he and Adolphus might be the perfect match for one another when it came to the *bordellos* of Venice and Naples; that they might behave, in fact, like any pair of careless young men embracing the world and its temptations through the perfect anonymity of journeying. His letters back imparted only information he knew was safe and bound to impress; she felt cheered, too, by his protestations of affection and how much he missed her. Replying likewise, she filled her letters with diversions from Satis and Brook Street: her father's heart – the quality of Mrs Siddons's performance as Cordelia at the Theatre Royal, Hay-Market – a broken carriage-axle in St. James's Street – Mrs Comfrey's chilblains… drab information indeed compared with the colours, sounds and scents with which Alexander tinted his.

She also visited Uncle Daniel in Chelsea – he remained as concerned for her well-being and happiness as ever; but he made it clear that he understood why he was not particularly welcome at Satis. Since failing to get into Parliament in the 1790 Election, he knew he must rank as *persona non grata* to the Havishams by his inability now to represent their interests at Westminster – had they displayed the lack of sense and tact to ask him. The Pocket children kindled no new enthusiasm for their haughty cousin, though she made efforts to be friendly – Sarah's sour refuge had lost none of its strength; Camilla did not have the strength of a cheap emetic; Matthew, now seventeen, had found strength in seriousness bordering on the boring, particularly since becoming employed in a Counting House off Fetter Lane, where his financial and common sense eminently fitted him for dealing with money not his own.

During her sometimes more reflective moments, Estelle contemplated two other areas of her life which, through their unresolved nature, pulsed in her mind like the dripping pump in the brewery yard. Since 1789, she had received no word from Marie, though she had sent her one letter. And now, as if to bother matters further, France was at war with Prussia as well as Austria. Her Papa's views on the Revolution's fanatical developments, in answer to what was reported in The Times, left little unsaid. Madame Pinon had not been at pains to conceal her emotions, nor Alexander's mother. All were repelled by the execution, back in January, of King Louis, marking the birth of The Reign of Terror. The widowed Queen had become the talk of London circles. Estelle wept at the thought of her noble bearing, mouldering in black weeds, carrying the last waverings of a dying dynasty through her long imprisonment and trumped-up trial. Deprived now of her children and in a white gown like a waiting bride, the dung-cart came to the Conciergerie to take her to the guillotine where her head thudded into a basket, her cropped white hair riddled with crimson streamers.

The other matter difficult to resolve concerned Arthur. From the time of his abscondment, the only news of him had come from Uncle Emil – once in October of 1789 and once near Christmas saying that after his stay with them he had departed to an unknown destination. 'Hell, hopefully,' her father had remarked, ignoring her directive to reach for his hat and rush off post-haste to retrieve him. After her initial disagreement with his policy of non-intervention, she secretly felt glad he had vanished. With luck the Revolution had absorbed him, and the brewery, now his to inherit under the altered terms of her father's will, would simply join the rest she was destined to own: the land on which it stood, all lands adjoining, Satis House and contents, all revenues from local properties and three in London.

But however great her expectations, her greatest centred on Alexander's eventual return...

TABLEAU V
1795

The long-awaited letter from Rookwell Park announced Alexander's safe arrival and impatient desire to see her, if she would care to spend some time with him. Zilla, who rather admired James, one of the footmen there, became as excited as her mistress, the busy preparations punctuated by swirls of girlish glee shared with equal vigour until Estelle remembered her dignity in time to remind her maid of it. But they had enjoyed a friendly relationship for a good many years, Zilla being five years her senior. During her attendance as personal maid, a *rapport* had developed which allowed for a certain levity now and then. Her greatest asset was discretion; she understood the limits of familiarity and the requirement to comment only when her opinion was sought. She had not been impervious, neither, to her mistress's occasional preoccupation with the stables during Master Compeyson's absence, nor the rather breathless bloom of complexion her visits seemed to inspire. Though nothing was overtly referred to, Zilla's intuition led her to believe it might be caused by more than simply horse.

Her normally elegant mistress almost fell out of the carriage in her animation at seeing Alexander descending the portico steps to swirl her into an embrace she hardly dared believe was happening – an enclosure of safe haven, so different from Hugh's, confirming her love for this handsome, young dependant of good stock, a little taller and fuller in the figure for his time away, his healthy complexion advertising celestial suns branding Mediterranean and Aegean shores.

Her suite of rooms awaited, the Park from her windows shimmering with late summer abundance, great elms and chestnuts punctuating verdant swathes with deep craters of lengthening shadow.

'Have you missed me as much as I have you, I wonder?' she asked when Alexander came to see that she was settled.

'Of *course*,' he assured, kissing her again. 'Adolphus was an agreeable companion but really no substitute. One day I shall take you to Venice – to Delphi – the Acropolis beneath the moon – and show you what I think you ought to see.'

'Did you bring me anything back from these wonderful places, Alexander?'

'Would I be doing my duty if I didn't remember my enchanting Estelle?' he laughed. 'Not for one moment did I forget her. See. They await her possession.' He knelt beside the bed, Estelle watching his graceful black curls brush the back of his collar as he bent forward in reaching his arms underneath, his tensed back contoured against the fabric of his bottle green coat. 'What have we here? Why, two boxes – *cadeaux* – *regali*.'

Quick to undo the coloured twine on the first, she lifted the lid to reveal a lustrous glass urn-shaped vase with handles, gentle fluting twisting round its Classical shape like a delicate shell.

'From Murano,' boasted Alexander. 'Glass has been made there for centuries – the best in the world. I brought a chandelier for Mama.'

'It's beautiful,' admired Estelle. 'Just the right choice for me. How clever you are.' She stood it on the dressing table, admiring the light refracting through. 'We must fill it with flowers… it must always be filled with flowers.'

'And your second *regalo*,' reminded Alexander.

Estelle undid the flatter box, parted some soft papers to draw out an amount of exquisite pale pink silk embroidered with posies of flowers entwined with ribbons in delicate shades not unlike designs favoured by the late Queen of France. She could only sigh at its beauty. 'I shall have Mrs Needler make it up into my favourite dress!' She ran to Alexander and after hugging him again, kissed him full on the mouth.

'*A mia piccolo Estelle piacciono i suoi regali?*' he enquired, smiling thankfully.

'I do not like you speaking to me in Italian,' she complained, wishing he had taken the initiative to kiss her similarly. 'I don't understand it.'

'*Ma petite Estelle est elle tres heureuse avec ses cadeaux?*'

'*Mais oui, certainment. Elle est tres content.* Let's go into the garden now. I want to hear all about your travels – in English please – where you went, what you did, who you saw...'

She could not fail to have been impressed by what he selected to tell her, nor the manner of his telling: the blazon of art, the flourish of music, the parade of ruins, the flaunt of food and dash of wine – the lonely nights when all he thought about was her. She remained impressed, impressing Zilla that evening as she prepared her mistress for bed.

'Well, Miss, did you never hear nothing like it. Such fine places and all manner of things to see and do. Maybe that'll be your luck one day when you come back talking his Italian as well as how you do in the French.'

'Mister Alexander said he'd teach me if I'd like him to. But it may be that I won't need to learn Italian if he's always to be around.'

'Be around what?' said Zilla, turning down the bed.

'Around me, of course – around Satis. Really, Zilla, you can be slow sometimes. I may one day become Mrs Compeyson. You don't seem exactly jubilant for my happiness.'

'Oh, I *am* jubilant, Miss, really I am. I know you love him – beg pardon for speaking so bold – specially now he's come back... and the presents.' She brushed Estelle's loosened hair carefully before the dressing table mirror. 'Has he asked you yet?'

'*That* is an *impertinent* question, Zilla,' pointed Estelle at their reflection. If only she could have told her he had. 'I shall inform you of such an event at the appropriate time – *and* I shall expect more respect if Mister Alexander is to become Master of Satis when I become Mistress.'

'Yes, Miss – sorry, Miss.'

'Come now – don't sulk. Cheer up and tell me about James. Have I ever seen him? What does he look like… anything, for instance, like Hugh?'

'Oh, he's ever so nice, Miss… quiet… and quite funny when he's not serious – not that he's ever serious with me… er, in *that* way, I mean… you know, Miss…'

'I know, Zilla.'

'We just like each other, sort of, when we're with the other servants… we're always with the other servants…'

'Yes, all right – there's no need to harp on about the servants. I know you'll never let a man on his own touch you again after last time…' Zilla had stopped brushing, tears pricking her eyes. Estelle turned round in alarm.

'Zilla, Zilla – I thought you were over that. It was seven years ago.' She held her hand. 'Tom was dismissed from Satis – your child went to the Foundling Hospital.'

'Sorry, Miss,' sobbed Zilla, her face in her apron. 'It still hurts so… he'll be eight soon and I don't know what he looks like.'

Estelle enfolded her in her arms and patted her back. 'There, Zilla, I'm so sorry – I didn't mean to upset you – it just slipped out without a thought. You'll have to forgive me – it was a foolish thing to say. But that's all in the past and Papa was kind enough to keep you on… we like you, Zilla – you're a good servant and we'll always give you a character.' She gave her one of her French handkerchiefs.

'I'm fine now, Miss,' she snivelled into the lace. 'It came over me like it do sometimes.'

'I'm sure it must. Nobody forgets something of that sort.' She paused, with a little thoughtful frown. 'Zilla, I want to ask you something... a question... a serious question – woman to woman – and I require a straight answer, if you feel better. It's your advice I'm seeking, you understand... I *need* your advice because there's nobody else I can ask.'

'I'll do my best, Miss, but I don't know as I'm any good at advice.'

'Brave girl,' continued Estelle slowly. 'Tell me... when you went with Tom... what was it like?'

Zilla involuntarily sat on the bed. 'He said he loved me, but when I got pregnant he said he didn't...'

'No, Zilla, that is not what I meant. Here, have another handkerchief. What I mean is... how shall I put it...? what was it like with Tom *before* you became with child...? *in that way,* you understand? What did it *feel* like – down *there?* I need to know.'

Zilla stared at her Mistress's earnest face while she demonstrated the region as if it were a foreign country on a map. 'Oh, Miss,' she shrugged, 'I don't rightly know as which words to use.'

'Did you like it?'

'Aye, I have to say.'

'Was it comfortable?'

'Only at first it wasn't.'

'Were you with him more than once?'

'He had these things, see, he put on, which meant he could be with me when he wanted without getting me... in the family way – don't fret, Miss, I'm not going to cry again. I can tell you what you ask.'

'What things did he have, Zilla?'

'Like fingers of a glove they were... all separate... which he put on himself when he was good and ready in his state, like a sheath, sort of. He called it his armour. He said it would make him safe so I needn't worry about being with him like we were, so I didn't. Where he got them I don't know – it wasn't any of my business. Then there was this time – just once – when he was in his state without his armour... what could I do? I didn't think there'd be harm in it.'

'That was unfortunate, Zilla, and not your fault. Don't even think of it. I'd simply like to know if... I'll be honest with you... if it hurts – whether I'll like it. I don't want to be frightened. You *do* understand my reasons?'

'If you love someone like I thought I loved Tom there's nothing to be frightened of, Miss, truly there isn't. Anything else doesn't matter.'

'Yes, I see that, I think.' Already she was wondering if Alexander had knowledge of this armour and whether there was some way of her discovering whether or not she would be frightened.

* * *

Barely had she formed this resolve when a hot and dishevelled messenger from Satis requested to see her urgently. Her father, not quite forty-seven but weighing just over eighteen stone, had suffered his second mild heart attack followed shortly by a stroke whilst contemplating his well-stocked plate at the dining table. The gravity of his condition called for her immediate return for there was no telling how long he would last. Alexander threaded his offers of help and support when the situation had been assessed amongst flusters of hasty packing and the boarding of a carriage, loaned by the Compeysons, the following day. Estelle's distress – torn between wanting to be with Alexander and her father – did not make for a relaxed journey; but Zilla knew her mistress's moods well and was easy about conversing or remaining silent as requested.

Mr Havisham's bed had been brought down to the dining room where he had fallen, his partially paralysed mass made as comfortable as possible, notwithstanding being surrounded by the staring censure of ancestors whose removal from the walls he would have liked but could not request.

With this stilling influence poured over the house in glutinous silence, Estelle assumed responsibility in order to deflect her mind from the mixed emotions of her father's possible death and her resultant elevation to fortune. Much to Mrs Comfrey's discomfiture she asked her for a duplicate set of household keys. As her father lay dumb and staring, she made her presence felt in a hundred places where Mrs Comfrey's should have sufficed; she acquainted herself with every closet and drawer, linen cupboard, silver pantry, larder and wine cellar, dairy and wash-house; she familiarised herself with her father's every chest, box and trunk; she would have undermined Doctor Sawley's authority had she not been so grieved by the spectacle of her own flesh and blood, once so active and indulgent, bellying the bedclothes in that mountainous manner. There seemed so much to die, let alone decompose.

True to his word, Alexander placed himself at her disposal; the courteous way he declined to take charge, but was willing to help, endeared him to Satis's staff who were also grateful for the calming effect he usually achieved on their Mistress's volatile nature. But even *his* artistry was tried to the limit when she faced her first serious issue; the disappearance of certain small but valuable trinkets. Initially, she missed a gold and enamel *etui* from her dressing table. Mrs Comfrey brought similar losses to her notice: silver snuff boxes, wine coasters, a pin-tray, a George II lidded tankard – there was no accounting for them. In desperation, Estelle forthwith accused two housemaids she had never trusted – a third left of her own volition, unable further to endure Miss Havisham's unfounded suspicions, known below stairs to disturb even Mrs Comfrey's equilibrium.

Throughout the rest of the autumn the mystery remained unsolved, particularly as the disappearances continued. Alexander divided his time between Satis, Rookwell and London, attending, as he explained, 'to business and other matters,' leaving Estelle to care for her father with the help of a good woman from the town. Much as she would have relished some time at Brook Street, she preferred to instruct her father's lawyers, Jaggers and Son of Little Britain, in the City, to procure a suitable tenant. For the most part, a certain *ennui* pervaded her days; when Alexander was with her, at least she could listen to him affably imparting his theories about property development and business management, money-lending, improving his father's not always wise investments. He generously shared nursing duties, happy to sit for time at a stretch reading aloud to Mr Havisham, quite content to receive no conflict of opinion through the inactive mouth, though the ears and eyes remained quick.

Alexander preferred to sleep in Arthur's old rooms instead of the orthodox guest apartments; many a night tempted Estelle to visit him, but the enduring vision of her father downstairs in his private anonymity carried her natural instincts to the threshold of the tomb, robbing them of health and vigour. By the end of November, though still unable to speak, some easing of movement enabled him to be placed in a wheeled chair in order to sit him by the fire where he could at least stare more easily at what went on about him. Some of his bulk had wasted away, transforming him into a figure Estelle hardly recognised as his tears glazed his puckered face.

If Christmas had expected a rollicking welcome at Satis it was disappointed, particularly as Alexander felt obliged to celebrate it at Rookwell. For Estelle, one day passed much like another until he returned on New Year's Eve despite a sickening sky frothing snow. East winds, doing their best at huffing indoors to keep warm, caught at cavity and crevice with a vengeance – whipped at stone and brick – spiralled long chimney funnels to sparking hearths – bothered clustered candle flames – shuffled through ill-fitting doors, along shivering-matted floors to the very bed in the dining room where it lifted the pleated valance to inquire whether as much of Mr Havisham lay beneath the mattress as on top – a wasted effort on this occasion as he sat in his chair before a gusty fire with his daughter and possible son-in-law. Estelle wore her new gown made up from Alexander's present, its blush-pink complimenting the sapphire pendant she had received from him for Christmas. She was learning of the festivities at Rookwell when, after a tap on the door, Mrs Comfrey entered in some agitation.

'I'm so sorry to disturb you, Miss Estelle, but I wonder if you'd mind stepping into the hallway a moment.'

'It's cold out there. Can't what ever it is be dealt with in here?'

'I need to see you in private,' said Mrs Comfrey, inclining her head subtly towards Mr Havisham, 'if you wouldn't mind.'

Taking up her shawl, Estelle followed the housekeeper, closing the door after her. Alexander poked the fire, adjusted the blankets round Mr Havisham's legs, flicked through a half-read book – the grave old clock in the corner chimed nine-thirty... what could be keeping Estelle? He at last got up to find out. He left the door open as he saw her sitting on a hall chair, the colour drained from her face, Mrs Comfrey patting her hand as if to warm it.

'Mr Alexander,' she appealed, as he hurried to her in concern, 'I think she nearly fainted... it's bitter out here...' He knelt in front of her, rubbing her hands between his; her eyes seemed to find it difficult to focus on him – they strayed continually beyond his shoulders... to where Mrs Comfrey's point of vision appeared also to be centred. He looked round to the shadows where, with a slight cough, a slight, bearded figure flecked with snow emerged slightly from the direction of the servants' hall.

'Oh, my God,' he almost whispered in disbelief as the figure came into the circle of light.

'*You* were my God – once,' it said. 'Where's my Papa?'

'We thought you were dead,' said Alexander, composing himself rapidly, but holding onto Estelle – an action not unnoticed by the apparition.

'He's come home, sir,' said Mrs Comfrey, wiping her tears. 'I always knew he would, bless him. He's tired and hungry... we'll look after him downstairs... warm him up a bit, my lamb.' She was about to take charge when Estelle rose uncertainly from her seat and approaching her half-brother with open arms, enveloped him in a slow, generous hug.

Then she pulled away to deposit a resounding slap on his face. 'How *dare* you come back! After all this time!'

'I dare because I live here.'

'No you don't – you ran away ...'

'And now, as you say, I've come back...' Arthur was absorbing the view through the open doorway behind Estelle – the comfortable room – the pathetic figure by the fire.

'Papa?' He moved towards him uncertainly.

'You can't go in,' hastened Estelle, barring his way but Arthur ignored her.

'I told Master Arthur he was very ill,' offered Mrs Comfrey, as Estelle hurried to a protective position beside her father. Alexander stayed close to Arthur who touched Mr Havisham's shoulder.

'Father?'

'He can hear you and see you but that's all,' said Estelle. 'How *could* you come here at a time like this and upset him like the whelp you are – upset us all?'

'I need money,' said Arthur directly. 'Papa must give me some.'

'Papa can give you nothing. You must get it for yourself... as you've presumably been doing...'

'You don't understand, Estelle...' His plea ended in a small shock of coughing.

'I understand you've come back only because you want something. As it happens, your journey hasn't been wasted as you can start work when Papa dies because you'll have the brewery.'

'I don't want the brewery – I mean, not just the brewery. At least half the rest is mine... it's mine by rights...'

'Excuse me, dear boy,' said Estelle, with a tight smile, 'but a bastard *has* no rights.'

'I'm *not* a bastard!' Arthur faced his sister across their father's vulnerability.

'Quite right – you're not even a *proper* bastard.' She led him to another part of the room. 'I'll have you know it's thanks to me you're getting anything at all. Papa wanted me to have everything, but because I felt sorry for you and thought he was being unfair, Alexander and I managed to persuade him to leave you the business. You ought to be grateful... but I own the land it stands on.'

'So you can charge me a high rent, I suppose. Don't think I'm still a fool, Estelle Havisham. I've learned a good deal since being abroad... the best thing I ever did.' Mr Havisham, unable to join in the discussion, could only gaze at his children.

'You certainly are not the poor little Arthur of old – much more my equal now. We shall have to be on our guard, don't you think, Alexander, or we shall be taken advantage of...'

'Please, please,' pleaded Mrs Comfrey, putting a finger to her lips, 'do think of the Master...' Her voice faded as she observed a troubled difference in Mr Havisham's attitude then understood the gradual change relaxing his face. Arthur and Estelle followed her attention to where the eyes were becoming encased in unregistering distance. Mrs Comfrey felt his pulse then laid the wrist carefully back on his lap. 'Be so good as to send for Doctor Sawley, Madam,' she said with quiet efficiency.

Knowing the question was unnecessary, the Mistress of Satis said, 'Is he dead?' even as Mrs Comfrey closed his eyes. 'I hope you realise, Arthur, that this is your fault. Why can't you mind your own business? Until you arrived he was making some progress...'

'And deferring your inheritance. I can't believe you're sorry he's dead.'

Faced with a strong element of truth, Estelle could only push past him with a command that Alexander accompany her to the boudoir.

Arthur remained where he was – Mrs Comfrey's arm round him – as he took his own time in adjusting to the situation.

'Don't you fret, my lamb,' she assured, giving him a kiss, 'the poor Master wasn't long for this world, make no mistake. It was only a matter of time. I thank the Lord you at least saw him alive. Now, you come with me, there's a good lad, and get something warm inside you. That'll get your strength back.'

'First,' said Arthur, 'I will send for the doctor. That *is* my business.'

Once in the boudoir, Estelle sat disconsolately at her dressing table as if she needed her reflection to give her added support. 'Why, oh why did he have to come back?' she inquired of the world in general. 'Everything was going so well. Why does he have to spoil it after so long?'

'As he so rightly observed,' Alexander tried to reason, 'he lives here – he's every right to come back, no matter what the purpose.'

'I want to know where the whelp's been... what he's been doing... who he's seen... how he's survived – he looks like a Romany. Find out and tell me. And what are we going to do about the brewery? I can't live with him on the premises again – he upsets me too much. Look at me – and he's been here only two minutes. I can't think why I let you talk me into persuading Papa to let him have it. If I buy him out I'll have paid for something I could have had for nothing in the first place.'

'But don't you see, my dear, that this way Arthur will have no claim on you – he won't be able to say he should have had the business – he *will* have had it but voluntarily sold it because he can't *deal* with it. I can make sure he's grateful for your price selling him his freedom.'

'And the share of the estate he expects? What about that? He's not such an imbecile as to have *overlooked* that. He'll contest Papa's will – I know his devious mind.'

'Estelle, my dear.' Alexander idly toyed with the muslin hangings draping the looking glass. 'Are you *so* used to my assistance and efficiency that you have overlooked my involvement in this matter? Haven't I said before, leave Arthur to me? He trusted me once and will again – as must you.'

'I want to be free of him, Alexander. I want my life back. He shuts me in too much – I can't be myself.'

'That,' replied Alexander, moving towards the fire, 'will involve thought and time. I may have to enlist outside help. It could involve a price.'

'What sort of price?'

'I can't be specific at present. What price is it worth – to you?'

'Worth my love, I should have thought. I am somebody now. You have still to inherit.'

'An astute observation – by which I take it to mean that you'll relish purchasing my services from now on so you'll feel you're obtaining better value for your money – only in this case you're leaving the poor piper also to call the tune. Then again, my dear Lady of the Manor, I'm not sure whether I should come between brother and sister, however tenuous the connection.'

'How can you come between something that doesn't exist, Alexander? He's come back only to suit himself and brought his troubles with him, I shouldn't wonder. Well, he can have his due and no more. I can see he's set on complicating matters.'

'And I shall see he doesn't, my dear. I shall go and talk with him now – see what his intentions are. Be assured – your best interests are at my heart.'

'Thank you, Alexander. You are very good to me – I so appreciate it. I can rely on you without a worry. That boy gives me a headache.'

Alexander planted a kiss on the top of her head and held her shoulders momentarily before leaving the room. He sent word with a servant that when Master Arthur had finished his supper he was to join his old friend in the library, bringing with him two glasses and a full decanter of sherry wine. In the meantime, Doctor Sawley arrived from attending a patient at The Blue Boar. Alexander helped him wheel Mr Havisham to his bed in the dining room then lift him onto it, draping his diminished enormity with the quilt before closing the double doors and seeing the doctor out to make the necessary arrangements.

Arthur found Alexander musing before the library fire. He placed the drinks salver on a side table. He felt calmer now – was fed, refreshed and in a change of clothes Mrs Comfrey had found for him; he remained rather white, though, with tired rings round his eyes. He let Alexander come to him and lead him caringly to a comfortable chair by the warmth then pour a couple of glasses of the syrupy wine. His hand shook imperceptibly as he accepted it from Alexander's firm hold.

'I must apologise,' he began, sitting opposite Arthur. 'We were not expecting you – and what with Mr Havisham's condition and Miss Havisham naturally overwrought…'

'*Miss Havisham*? I don't understand you.'

'Forgive me. I refer, of course, to *Miss Estelle* – if you prefer.'

'I don't,' said Arthur tersely, ignoring Alexander's affability. 'I prefer only facts… and the fact is she will never be *Miss* Havisham to me, or *Miss* Estelle, or *Miss* anything. You obviously have more respect for her than I have and that's because you don't know her as I do.'

'Your rebellious nature hasn't diminished, I'm glad to see, my dear Arthur. I admire that.'

'And you're as mysterious as ever, I'm glad to see. I won't have to get to know you all over again. They said at The Blue Boar you spend a fair amount of time at this house.'

'Blue Boar?'

'The brandies warmed me up before I came here... I've not been well.'

'Since Mr Havisham's illness I've tried to be of assistance. I considered it my Christian duty. He died fearing you, Arthur. Did you realise that? Could you not see that in his eyes? I really do think you should feel just the slightest part responsible for his death.'

'I didn't know he was dying,' Arthur protested, slumping further in his chair. 'They said at The Blue Boar he was ill... but not dying. I've every right to see my Papa when I choose.'

'And he chose your moment of entry – what a coincidence. His heart simply couldn't take the strain.'

Arthur coughed a little. 'I didn't do it. You know I'd never meant to. But I didn't know who else to ask for money... I'm in a bad way, Alexander... you've not forgotten *your* promise to help me, have you?'

'I haven't forgotten,' Alexander assured, reaching across to touch his forearm. 'I promise to see you get what's coming to you.' He recharged Arthur's glass. 'A toast, *mon ami* – to our renewed friendship – long may it continue. It's good to see you back, dear boy. I am intrigued to know what your fortunes have been since we last met. Will you share them with me?'

Arthur leaned forward earnestly. 'I need a friend... a friend with money.'

'Most friends have money,' observed Alexander. 'That's why they *are* friends. *You* have money now – you're a man of property, if you work hard and don't fritter it away.'

'I need ready cash, otherwise I'm lost.'

Alexander laughed. 'Nobody worth anything is ever lost for need of ready cash. I never am and I need it frequently. I can't say I find it hard to come by. We'll have to see what we can do for you. Incidentally, how is your leg these days?'

'It hurts sometimes – but I *don't* walk with a limp... that was years ago. A lot has happened since those days.'

'Indeed it has,' Alexander agreed. 'I have seen the world – mixed with people of quality and importance. I am the possessor of a wholly inadequate allowance from my father and free to do precisely what I wish in London and elsewhere. True, I haven't my own horse and carriage, but Papa keeps me in a house in Hanover Street with enough to hire them when necessary. I am a soft touch for the odd guinea here and there I may tell you – strictly on a business basis, you understand. I can fence, shoot, play cards, dance, ride to hounds, hold my head up with Dukes and vagabonds – I'm as much at home at a *soiree* at Carlton House hob-nobbing with His Royal Highness as I am pouring gin down the gullet of some old crone in the hovels of St Giles.'

'You think yourself very fine,' reflected Arthur, as everything Alexander represented eddied back to him on the tide of their past association. 'You still have all the advantages... I've always envied you your looks, your manner... your elegant clothes...'

'I have Mama to thank for those. She, too, is beautiful, with impeccable taste. She *is* French after all.'

'I know you won't agree,' said Arthur, 'but for all the differences between us I think my life has been better than yours... what money I've had during these last six years I've earned, so I've felt no conscience over spending it on what I wanted.'

'How quaint,' queried Alexander with a quizzical smile. 'I've no conscience over spending *any* money whether I've earned it or not. I'm a gentleman, you see, not a tradesman... talking of whom – please inform me of your dealings after you disappeared. You've obviously earned yourself a fortune though returned a beggar. Come, dear friend, convince me.'

Whilst Arthur related how he had crossed the channel and worked his way to Paris, then Versailles, he remained unaware that Estelle's curiosity demanded that she press her ear to the door. She caught the words Uncle Emil – Revolution – The Directorate... until she wondered why she was reduced to eavesdropping in her own house. That would cause comment in the Servants' Hall! She sneaked into the room, closing the door softly behind her, remaining in unobtrusive shadow behind where Arthur sat.

'I didn't want to get involved in all their troubles... just to see if Aunt and Uncle were anything like Estelle and Papa. They weren't. They were so kind to me. And my cousins. I would love to have stayed but I couldn't – not when I thought Papa might come after me. I needed to be free. I went back to see them after the Revolution but they weren't there... the house was shut up... deserted.'

Visibly moved, he paused to drain his glass.

'I don't think your father intended chasing you half way across Europe,' said Alexander, filling his glass. 'It wouldn't have been worth it.'

'I don't expect you to understand – nor Estelle. She's like the Queen of France. I often wished I could see a howling mob tearing at the gates of Satis as they did at Versailles. I *saw* her, Alexander – I was there the day she was taken – bundled into a carriage with the rest of her family. None of her finery could save them. All she had was her pride. And how the crowds jeered – just as I should jeer Estelle. Suppose Satis burned down... I tried it once – do you know that?'

'You're drunk – you don't know what you're saying,' said Alexander, glancing uneasily in Estelle's direction. She sat on an upright chair – very straight – very pale.

'You think so? You think I'm inventing it, perhaps? How can I invent it when I get drunk to forget? And to kill the pain in my leg. Drink and my talent are all I have. They've kept me alive so far – and luck. Ask Desmoulins and Maillard… you can ask Colbert – Jourdan – Robespierre even… ask them all. How can you ask them…? they're all dead! They didn't have my luck. They didn't want to die but did… I wanted to die but didn't – that's the joke my life's become.'

'Arthur, Arthur.' Alexander tried placing a calming hand. 'Don't distress yourself…'

'Let me be!' Arthur shook him away. 'I want to tell you – I want you to understand – you're my friend. I lived in Paris… drew pictures for a living… and caricatures. Desmoulins was my employer for those – political cartoons – propaganda – the King and Queen sold the best. I did a magnificent one of her leaving Versailles – it was *my* best because I gave her Estelle's face. What do you think of that? Just imagine – Queen Estelle! My comrades didn't think much of it… said it wasn't like Her Majesty… but that's because they didn't know my mind. I knew better because I'd *seen* the Austrian and English Bitches for myself. My work got in anti-royalist papers and pamphlets. Desmoulins ran one and took my work. It was good to see it engraved and printed for sale… not that I received a fortune for them. Then I learned to engrave so I could do the work myself. That was much better – I'd work for anyone who'd pay me… buy me a drink… a decent meal…'

'How very fortunate,' said Alexander, feeling that perhaps Arthur's murky monologue had progressed far enough. 'Whilst you were scratting around in the Parisian gutters with your comrades, I was improving my education and social standing in Europe's cultural centres. It would take more than a revolution to impede *my* progress. Did you know that a buried Roman town has been discovered near Mount Vesuvius? All manner of things are being excavated – even people… well, their skeletons…'

Alexander's boasting did not have the desired effect of silencing Arthur, who seemed barely aware of his distant voice as he helped himself from the nearly empty decanter.

'I saw her die – the Queen of France. We all saw her... a big woman... white face... white gown... white cap... white hair chopped off, like her power. She looked as I imagined Estelle would look... proud – imperious – white. I did drawings of her on the scaffold, and then when her head had been severed. They were praised by no less an expert than Citizen David, Official Artist of the Revolution. He showed me a drawing *he'd* done of her riding in the tumbril to her death – a few lightning strokes and it was all there. He entrusted me to do a lot of copies for sale. He said I had talent. A great artist is Citizen David.'

Arthur remained rigidly in his seat, his pupils dilating, fear shivering about his face, his knuckles starting bony and pointed as he gripped the chair arm.

'Blood... there was so much blood... everywhere... spotting, gushing, gurgling at every crash of the blade – I can hear it now... can't you? Crash! Crash through flesh and gristle... then the cheering. See the white bloodless faces in baskets... more and more of them... endless... in lines... like ghosts come to plague me – all these Estelles advancing with shrouds to smother me in and she the White Queen of them all...' He began moving violently, waving his arms before him as though warding off unseen threats. 'Every head on a pike was Estelle's... I wanted her head... I wanted to smash her white head into the blood... into the pit of quicklime... to kill the white... to...' He caught sight of Estelle rising from her chair, her face white with fright as she hurried into Alexander's arms.

'No! No!' called Arthur. 'Don't let her touch me...!' He toppled forwards to the floor grasping at empty air, shaking his head from side to side as guttural breaths heaved him about the hearthrug.

'What in God's name's the matter with him?' whined Estelle, close to hysterics. 'It's like some kind of fit. Stop him, Alexander!'

'Leave him to me,' said Alexander, saving the slender drinks table from overturning. 'You shouldn't have come in.'

'I *had* to know what he said.'

'I hope you're satisfied. Go and wait for me. I'll deal with Arthur – I'm used to dealing with Arthur.'

Her looking-glass showed her a face as pale and apprehensive as the Queen's. Estelle knew that sleepless nights awaited her – as when she had first learned of her lovely Queen's fate. Damn Arthur for imprinting her own image onto the catastrophe – for casting *her* with the dead and headless. Damn him for bringing her a New Year as welcome as a spiteful ailment.

'Arthur's asleep now,' said Alexander, bringing Estelle a glass of brandy. 'We've made him comfortable by the fire.'

'I hope a log falls out and burns him to death – no, I don't mean that – what a terrible thing to say… but what with Papa and now this I don't know if I shall go mad or worse. Is Arthur mad? He looks it.'

'After what he sounds to have been through, poor lad, he probably is – a little. But then, there is no cure for the bottle either.'

'Bottle? What bottle?'

'Why, any bottle, as long as it contains alcohol.'

'But he had only a sherry or two.'

'He was at The Blue Boar before coming here, downing brandy as if life depended on it. Getting up some Dutch courage, if you ask me. Doctor Sawley observed him in there too, with some concern. He'll be back to see him tomorrow. His experiences in France are bound to have disturbed him, and no mistake. He drinks to forget the pains of life.'

'Then we must see he's not kept short of pains.'

'You wish to finish what the Revolution started?'

'If it means a swifter end to the brewery deal and his departure, then yes.'

'Subtlety and persuasion, *Estelle, ma cherie,*' warned Alexander, pointing his index finger upwards as if to impale the philosophy of his suggestion. 'You have agreed to trust me.' He kissed her on the forehead as he wished her good night and a Happy New Year.

He then returned to check on Arthur, prostrate on the library hearthrug, his face set in uneasy peace, his breathing in uneasy rhythm. He adjusted the blanket covering him and brushed his hair from over his brow with a caring hand. 'Just as you used to sleep at school,' he whispered. 'We've come a long way since then, you and I. Sleep well, dear boy.'

* * *

For the next few days, whilst arrangements were put in hand for Mr Havisham's funeral, Arthur remained at Satis, too disturbed and exhausted to be either a help or hindrance. Alexander allowed him to inhabit his old rooms while he adjourned to the guest suite. Doctor Sawley, not unduly worried, advised complete rest and a light diet.

There was much to see to; a notice of death for the newspapers; attention to callers who wished to pay their respects – the Misses Wishton, amongst others, were not alone in remarking how much more concerned Miss Havisham seemed about having to receive them in funereal clothes than her misfortune at having lost 'the best of fathers and kindest of employers'. The one feature she and Arthur had in common was that neither wished to view their father once he was prepared and suitably shrouded in his satin-lined box. He lay in the centre of the dining room, cornered by four stands supporting candlesticks spiked with tapers as thick as a man's fist on loan from the cold stone church by the marshes.

'When *I'm* dead,' remarked Estelle, with a shudder, 'I hope *I* shan't be laid out in the dining room to be stared at. Those portraits are bad enough while I'm alive. I should hate people to see me looking like some sort of ghastly waxwork at a fair. I don't want to be equated with the laying out of a meal.'

The Pocket family put up at The Blue Boar as an invitation to stay at Satis did not materialise – not that they would have preferred it if it had. They gathered, along with the other mourners on that ragged January day in 1796, like spare autumn leaves in the forecourt of Miss Havisham's house, where the continuing snow-flurries from a pewter sky accompanied them and the draped hearse out of the gateway. Instead of keeping the other ladies company at the house, Estelle, black in her carriage with Alexander, accompanied the *cortege*. It passed out onto the lone and level marshes, the wind shivering in from the distant sea across a wilderness of dykes, gates and mounds; it rattled branches of elders and pollards planted in stilted serries to screen the church with its squat tower and slender spire; it moaned and whipped the overgrown churchyard huddling low and grass-bound as though trying to tie itself together in order not be blown away. A number of tenants and townspeople waited amongst the lichened gravestones in the corner section where generations of Havisham dust mingled beneath lurching, ostentatious monuments.

As Arthur, cold and tired as he was from his self-appointed walk with the Pockets, approached the freshly dug chasm, he could not help but rejoice in the realisation that one pain less in his life was passing beneath that coffin lid. But his eyes then unfocused from its pall of snow to a darkly-cloaked figure beyond, black against the white horizon, his face partly obscured by a broad-brimmed hat.

Arthur felt his heart miss a beat and turned his back in an attempt to concentrate on the priest committing ashes to ashes, dust to dust...

Alexander noticed. So Arthur knew the young stranger too, did he? Why else should he nervously keep looking round to see if he remained? After the burial he watched Arthur trying to brush off the stranger's attentions before asking for space in Estelle's carriage to return to Satis. He remained silent, as did Estelle and Alexander; on arrival he immediately consumed a quantity of brandy whilst remaining in his outdoor clothes awkwardly in front of the library fire. He refused, point blank, to enter the dining room, even though it had been restored to its former state and brightly set out with refreshments for those who cared to indulge; Estelle preferred to retire to her rooms leaving Alexander and Mrs Comfrey to deputise; Arthur also, if he was sober enough. But as he entered the empty library and made to close the door, he heard Uncle Daniel asking after his whereabouts and was almost inclined to bring him into the library when he heard another voice asking for Master Arthur – a gruff voice which, had there been a key in the lock, would surely have made him turn it firmly. As it was he had barely time to think what to do when Mrs Comfrey swished in with the message that a person in the hall wanted particular to see him in private. She almost sat down in astonishment as she saw him make a sudden move for the casement, unfasten it and almost vault out into the wintry afternoon. Her first thought as she shut it was that he would catch his death-of-cold without an extra greatcoat.

'Thank you, Mrs Comfrey,' said Alexander, appearing with the stranger. 'I shall deal with this. Close the door, please, and see we are not disturbed.'

Though aged about five and twenty, the stranger's appearance indicated that he had frequently been at the butt-end of life's tougher moments, doing nothing to enhance his rough clothing or gaunt, weathered face, pitted like yesterday's gruel.

'I shall attend to you on Mr Havisham's behalf,' said Alexander with bluff graciousness. 'He is at present indisposed and unable to see you.'

'I should think he 'ain't able,' replied the visitor. 'By the looks on him I reckon he's none too particular pleased to see sich as I. Fancy finding you hereabouts, Sir. Wot a small world, to be sure. Mind, it's wot you'd expec', you being a fine gent an' getting about an' all.'

'Forget we have ever met before,' said Alexander, pointing. 'I'm not asking you – I'm telling you. Come now, what have you to do with Mr Havisham?'

'May a mere warmint make so bold as to put his mouth to the word – *money?*' inquired the man, raising his eyebrows.

'You want money?'

'My money – yes – wot I lent the young gen'leman in London.'

'Sit down,' said Alexander, indicating a chair and sitting himself opposite. 'I require to know more. I was not aware the gentleman had been in London – you do not have to be close with me – I have his every confidence. I am his business advisor, to be precise.'

'Well sir, to speak plain. I am, as you well know, wot you might term a gambling man – that amongst many others of my talents – Old Abel'll turn his hand to anything should his palm be crossed to his satisfaction. In The Happy Hangman it wos, hard b'Newgate. Your client Mister Havisham – him an' me – we fell to talking over a couple o'glasses. Tells me who he is, he does, as if I should have knowed – an' as how he's fresh returned from France with a small fortune as has somehow gone through his fingers. That were his very words – "gone through me fingers like chalk dust". Now, Sir, you being a man o'the world'll see how I reco'nises a kindly chance of benefiting a fellow creetur by sharing wot benefits had come my way through some agreeable hands of cards, him promising to pay within the fortnight, y'see. Since not hearing nothing from that day to this an' coming across the name Havisham in the papers, I takes a gamble in getting m'self here, never expecting to be bumping into my gambling partner from Epsom, of all things, though now I comes to think on it, why shouldn't I, him being another gen'leman an' all.'

'I'll thank you to keep your voice down,' said Alexander, resting his elbows on his chair arm and placing his fingertips together. 'And have you received what you're owed.'

'Not a farthing,' said the man, with a sharp kind of sigh. 'On my mother's bible I woul'n't have come a bothering if it weren't the money I owes another urgent which I'll be a gonner if I don't cough up.'

'To speak plainly, Mister – I don't think I quite caught…'

'Ah,' said the man opposite, rubbing his rough chin and staring hard at his interviewer, 'your mem'ry ain't as bad as all that, I'll wager. The name's the same as last time, which is more than can be said for *some* individu'ls round these parts I could be naming.'

'I can't possibly conduct business without knowing the names of the parties,' said Alexander, deftly turning aside the observation. 'My memory is neither better nor worse than I require.'

'Well then Sir,' said the man, 'if I wos you, I'd require it to cast itself back to Epsom Racecourse of last year an' the exact minute you wos interduced to Mister Abel, or Mister Magwitch – they'se one an' the same to hiself.'

'Well then, Mr Abel,' resumed Alexander smoothly, 'or Mr Magwitch – to make my point clear: my client is not, at present, in any position to recompense you for your generosity. However, I shall see you are not kept wanting – debt can be the very devil.'

'The devil it can, Sir. When I has the money you'll not hear another squeak from me – not on that score, though I'm hopeful we'll share more pleasant hands o'cards when it suits.'

'I am extremely pleased to hear it,' said Alexander, with a condescending smile. 'I shall hold you to the bargain. What is the sum required? Accurately, mind.'

'Would a mere hundred an' fifty be considered accurate?' ventured Mr Abel.

'Is that the sum loaned to my client?'

'Not a sixpence more. I am accurate in that, Sir.'

'Then that is what you shall receive, with sixpence more for your accuracy. *And* your discretion, Mr Abel. Is that understood? I would like to think you are still the fellow I took you for last year.'

'Now it's you wot's accurate, Sir,' asserted Mr Abel, touching his forelock in light-hearted respect. 'But go agin me – anyone – an' if they don't value their life I'll have it, if driven – that I will… put a prize scar on that han'some face o' yourn I would even.'

'I don't doubt,' replied Alexander sincerely. 'Remind me never to be on the receiving end of your temper. You've always had the look of Newgate about you – you're pretty familiar with its inner architecture, I'll be bound.'

'Could lead you through with me eyes out for a shilling,' Mr Abel boasted.

'I'll keep my shilling, thank you,' returned Alexander, 'and you shall take this. My client cannot pay you and I don't intend to do so for him. This salver is worth a good deal more than your accurate price. Get for it what you will – the profit is yours – the value of silence.' He slid the silverware into Mr Abel's hands. 'Don't expect more to come your way in like manner – Mr Compeyson or Mr Fleece would find it distasteful to accuse Mr Abel or Mr Magwitch of theft. I can tell by your expression we understand one another.'

'In my eyes you'll always be Mister Compeyson, Gent.,' promised Mr Abel, muffling the salver within his cloak. 'You're as much a gent as our mutual acquaint'nce, Mr Fleece – the greetings o' th' season on you both, an' thanks kindly, Sirs, for your considerations. Wish there wos more like you.'

'If you will oblige me,' said Alexander, opening the window, 'you will leave by this route. Follow me.' He scrambled unceremoniously over the sill, followed equally gracelessly by his interviewee whom he conducted down a side passage and out into the lane beside the brewery yard, bidden thence to vanish with all speed and the warning that a return to Satis, no matter what the circumstances, would be at his peril.

As he tried calmly to return to the library through the lattice, he remained shaken by the visit. A chance meeting with a ruffian on a racecourse had no place here. Emerging into the hall from the library and marching through the waning guests, he took custody of a bottle and glasses on his way to Estelle's boudoir.

'Well,' he said, making himself comfortable before the fire, 'Arthur's really excelled himself this time.'

'In what way? The Garrison are after him?'

'That salver of your father's in the library – it's missing. Who else is likely to know anything about it? He's probably drinking away its value this very moment.'

'If I hear any more about Arthur,' said Estelle in measured tones, 'I think I shall be ill. It's up to you, Alexander. You said you'd deal with him. Subtlety and persuasion, you said. I'm leaving it to you. If it was up to me I'd have him committed to Newgate or Bedlam – even transported.'

'I shall need to go to London shortly,' said Alexander, unruffled. 'A number of matters await my attention – the question of Arthur is one of them.'

'At a time like this?' complained Estelle. 'I can't manage without you here. It'll be me that's committed to Bedlam, I'll tell you, if things go on like this much longer... forgive me, my dear, I'm overwrought – of course you must go to London if you have to. I shall look forward to your return. But do make it for my birthday.'

'Old Jaggers will need to come and see you...' A knock on the door interrupted him. Mrs Comfrey waited on the threshold.

'I think you ought to know, Madam, that a man's here from the Blue Boar – he's brought home Mister Arthur – he's not as well as he might be.'

'You mean he's drunk, Mrs Comfrey,' said Alexander, swiftly leaving the room. 'I'll deal with him. Where is he?'

'The hall, Sir. The guests have gone...' Estelle followed them both to where Arthur slumped in a chair.

'Where is it, you little thief?' she demanded, shaking his shoulder. 'It's no use pretending...'

Alexander moved her away. 'Leave him – he can't understand you. It'll have to wait until morning. Mrs Comfrey, get him to his room, if you please.' As two strong servants came forward at her direction, he turned to the man from The Blue Boar. 'Mr Havisham is far from well, as you can see. You are more than kind to have brought him back safely. Allow me to escort you to the gate.'

Once in the misty confines of the forecourt, Alexander lowered his voice. 'If, in the future, Mr Havisham should become similarly incapacitated, you will favour us by not deeming it necessary to deliver him again to our door like a cheap dispatch. Miss Havisham is adamant that he should be left to his own devices – no one need feel responsible for him. Should this occur again, you have the family's permission to see he's locked in the pound. She wishes this to be known at The Blue Boar – some pecuniary arrangement can be made by way of endorsement... you understand me, my good fellow?'

'Aye, Sir, that I do. I'll see the message is passed on. But he did seem awful queer like – talking about blood and not rightly able to stand.'

'Part of his condition, it is to be regretted,' said Alexander, sympathetically. 'One has to be realistic about such matters – what runs through a family for generations can't be got rid of at one stroke.' He closed the gates once the man was in the roadway. 'The Havishams are known for their generosity to those who oblige them. A very good night to you.'

It came as no surprise to be awakened from a light slumber, in the small hours, by unhealthy sounds emanating from Arthur's room nearby. As Alexander entered with his candle, the stench of vomit assailed his nostrils while he watched his friend's pale form lean out from a saturated bed to slop more of his rejection onto the carpet. Setting down his light on the washstand and pouring water from jug to bowl, he sponged Arthur's hot face and lips, placing another empty container beside him. Single-handedly he cleared the floor, changed his bedding and nightshirt; and in the morning, much to Estelle's *chagrin,* took personal charge. Under the terms of their agreement she felt powerless as she heard their muffled conversations behind Arthur's closed door. Not stooping to more eaves-dropping, she took herself off in search of other concerns in her impatience for Old Jaggers to set the seal on the legality of her expectations.

'...And she called me a thief,' said Arthur wanly, 'but I don't know what she meant.'

'Indeed,' said Alexander, shaking his head, 'it's a shame about the salver. I'll have to think what can be done. You were too unwell to know what you were about – that's your only excuse.'

'But I haven't taken any salver,' Arthur persisted. 'What would I want with a salver?'

'You mean you don't *remember* taking it,' corrected Alexander, helpfully. 'We must adhere to the facts. And the fact is, I'm afraid – I saw you.'

'You weren't in the library.'

'I saw you leave it as I brought the stranger in – a dramatic exit, if I recall correctly, by way of the window. You threw the salver out first then followed it.'

'That's not so,' pleaded Arthur. 'I left by the window – that *is* true – but not with any salver. Why should I? Where is it now?'

'Who knows what you get up to and why, my friend. You need time to grow well and adjust to being back in a normal life. You're confused – overwrought – upset… you're not always aware of your actions. It's perfectly understandable in the circumstances, you being the sensitive sort of person you are. But I'm sensitive too, which is why I've always said you can turn to me for help and protection.'

'Estelle went straight to her room,' pondered Arthur. 'Why did *she* accuse me when she couldn't have seen me?'

'She found it missing and immediately jumped to conclusions – you know how she does now and again. It was I who pleaded your case and defended you – she was all for having you hauled off to the castle prison. Arthur… how many times do I have to make it clear that I have your best interests at heart? I *know* your ways – I *know* your secrets – Mr Abel for instance…'

'He's not a secret. We met in London over cards.'

'He lent you money. That's a secret. I didn't know about it – that's another. That's what he came for. That's what upset you. Don't pretend with me, Arthur. Please. You should have told me. How can I help if you pretend?'

'He said he'd tear my heart and liver out if I didn't repay him in two weeks. I intended to repay him but couldn't… that's why I had to see Papa…'

'Your greatest mistake was to tell him your name, dear fellow – your *real* name. The first lesson to learn in transactions of that sort is anonymity. There are times when it's prudent to veil your true identity. You as good as invited him here.'

'I didn't mean to. How was I to know what sort of cur he was?'

'He seemed a decent sort of scoundrel to me,' assessed Alexander lightly.

'I was scared.'

'Scared?' Alexander laughed. 'You who've survived The Terror? – seen the end of The White Queen…?'

'Don't!' cried Arthur, clamping his hands to his ears. 'I don't want reminding… I want it to go away…'

'Your *debt*, Arthur, has gone away. I paid it. You owe Mr Abel nothing.'

Arthur reached out and held his hand. 'You mean it? Alexander, I don't know what to say. That is the act of a true friend. Thank you. One day I'll be in a position to repay you for your kindness.'

'In the not too distant future, I'm hoping. I, too, have financial commitments, as you can well understand. I think the original agreement was for six months. All we do is put the two sums together.'

'Two sums?' questioned Arthur, frowning. 'How two? There was only one to Mr Abel. What original agreement?'

'My dear boy, I do realise you must find all this most confusing after everything you've been through. You must have forgotten – just over six years ago – in this very room – when I agreed to guard your financial interests? In return you signed a promissory note to take effect on your father's death. Need I continue?'

'Oh, that,' said Arthur, stifling a cough. 'I remember now. It was on your first visit.'

'Well done,' said Alexander, patting his arm. 'Your mind is clearing admirably.'

'Sorry, Alexander. I'd genuinely forgotten about it. I'm sure you'll be able to have your two hundred and fifty pounds within the agreed time.'

'Two hundred and fifty isn't a very generous start,' Alexander replied. 'After all, you've enjoyed six years' interest which I have lost. I suppose it's a beginning, though I really think I ought to insist on the figure in full.'

'That *is* the figure in full, Alexander – two hundred and fifty pounds – a hundred and fifty for Mr Abel and a hundred for you.'

'Your memory, Arthur. I spoke too soon. You think I agreed to help you for a hundred? It can't be done, even though I must make allowances for your condition. See – it so happens I have your note with me. Let's look at it together. Here.' He lay the unfolded piece of paper on the bedding.

I promise to pay Alexander Francois de Bayonne Compeyson the sum of £400 out of my inheritance, such as it may be, within six months of my father's decease, in grateful recognition of services rendered in friendship.

Signed,

Arthur Havisham. 21st July, 1789

'You look unwell, my friend. Is anything wrong? That's right – pick it up and look at it carefully. I know we were only youngsters at the time – I daresay we would have been more professional about it now, both of us knowing what we do of the world and its ways.'

'Four hundred pounds,' murmured Arthur, letting it slip from his fingers. 'It was a hundred, surely – I *know* it was …'

'What an imagination,' said Alexander, taking the note and placing it refolded in his pocket. 'You artists certainly have no appreciation of value. You always *have* been prone to flights of fancy – but it's horrible, isn't it, to learn where fancy ends and reality begins.'

Arthur sank back on his pillows. 'I don't believe this. I would have remembered such a figure – I wouldn't have agreed to it even…'

'But you did agree and I'm afraid disbelief is no excuse. A bargain was struck and signed upon. I am willing to wait but you must be willing to pay. Have you forgotten the waxen head? I haven't. It's still there, you know – I've been down to make sure. I can't see Estelle being particularly pleased I've kept your secret so long, can you?'

'If you mean what I think you mean,' said Arthur, grimacing at his confused wording as much as his confused thoughts, 'then how can I believe you're my friend?'

'Have you forgotten how instrumental I was in securing you with the brewery in your father's will? Estelle, as you know, was warm for you getting nothing. Does that act of friendship and support not signify? Now here's another. I am prepared to waive the full five hundred and fifty. For the sake of old times I ask only five hundred. I can't say fairer than that, now can I?'

'And you still agree to help me with the brewery? I'd not have let myself be saddled with it otherwise. You said it could be a goldmine.'

'Help you with the brewery? I don't follow your train of thought.'

'When you were staying here... when my leg was broken... when you talked me into wanting the brewery... when you said you'd help me make a success of it... isn't that what the promissory note was about?'

'Indeed it was. So where's the confusion?'

'Helping me run the brewery – being its Manager. Isn't that what you meant?'

'*I?* Your *employee?* Are you *completely* deranged?'

'Don't look at me like that, Alexander. I thought you offered to make the brewery into a goldmine for me.'

'My poor deluded Arthur. I don't know where you get some of these wild flights of fancy from. You've promised to pay me for *obtaining* it, not for *working* in it. You must manage your own business – it's *you* who has to make it a goldmine. My role is purely advisory – when I'm free *to* advise. Here's some advice now. How do you know you're not being cheated right and left by those brawny rogues down there?'

'But Mr Comfrey...'

'What about him? How well do you know him?'

'I've known him all my life.'

'Is that long enough? Now that your father's dead, how do you know he isn't feathering his own nest at your expense? You have to watch people all the time, Arthur, or they'll fleece you for all they can get. You ought to be amongst them – asking questions – going through the books – showing you are master like you father and grandfather. Do you care nothing for the family name?'

'I don't know,' said Arthur miserably. 'I don't know what to think about anything. I don't know about running breweries – I don't *want* to know. All I want is to go on drawing and engraving – it's all I know... all I love.'

'Then you'll never have a goldmine,' said Alexander, sadly. 'On the other hand, you could do a lot worse than selling it.'

'Selling it? It's always belonged to the Havishams.'

'And would continue to – if you sold it *to* a Havisham.'

'Estelle, you mean?'

'I think you'll not find her hostile to the idea. Just think – you'd have a lump-sum to pay off your debts. Free at last – do exactly as you wish – a studio in London – in Paris even, when it sorts itself out.' He noted a glint of enthusiasm enliven Arthur's anxiety. 'Here again I can be of help to you. Look, let me see to having a valuer assess the place's potential – no harm in finding out what you're worth. I'll see you through the business transactions – I know Old Jaggers's reputation for efficiency. Come. What do you say?'

'How much will it cost me *this* time?'

'Not a silver threepence more, dear boy. It's all part of the same deal.'

Arthur put a hand to his forehead. 'I'd love to be free again... really free. But I don't know... there's so much to take in... I have to think... I want my fair share of Papa's estate – I've a right to it... oh, Alexander, please get me something to drink – my head hurts so ... I can hardly see...'

* * *

When Alexander was next free enough that day to spend some time with Estelle, he found her in no better sorts than earlier – in fact her mood had matured like a ripe blister as a result of an interview with her housekeeper. Mrs Comfrey, having taken advantage of Alexander's diversions in Arthur's room, availed herself of her mistress's undivided attention.

'Really, Madam, I simply must speak my mind. I don't know how much longer I can go on running your house in this way. Since Mr Havisham passed on things have got out-of-hand.'

'I have no complaints,' said Estelle. 'You would be the first to know if I had, Mrs Comfrey.'

'And that I should expect and be glad of it. But things, as they are at present, are not what I'm used to. To speak plain words – it's never been easy here but I've always done my best... my husband too... and busied myself with what concerns me. But it's got that my conscience stops me standing by much longer without speaking directly... about Mister Arthur...'

'Has Master Arthur put you up to this?'

'No, Madam, he hasn't... and please don't rank me as an interfering old woman but I've been with your family a long time and the Pockets beforetimes. I've watched you and Mister Arthur grow up as if you were my own and loved you the same as your poor dead Mama. It hurts most grievous to stand by and see how Mister Arthur is used so – he's hardly back and all the old times are starting again – and him not well – he's sick, Miss Estelle...'

'In his mind he's sick, Mrs Comfrey.'

'So much more the care and love he needs…'

'Forgive me, Mrs Comfrey, but that shows how little you understand matters – for all your years. He is the son of a common cook – a common cook who became Mistress of Satis. He was the bane of my father's life and now he's the bane of mine. He's never gone out of his way to make himself loveable.' *If such is the case*, thought Mrs Comfrey, *he has followed no better model, My Lady.* 'We all had to give deference to a Mistress who was a servant – you had to take orders from a servant no better than yourself'.'

'But is it right Mister Arthur should be made the scapegoat? – for that's what he is, Madam, and it's not right. I know it's not for me to have opinions but I can't stand by any more and see an injustice done.'

'Very commendable to be sure,' said Estelle, coolly. 'I wish I could view it in the same light. It amazes me, then, that you've been able to stand by for so long while such injustices were taking place.'

'For the sake of your dear Mama I could not abandon her children. She *was* a lady and no mistake – and so good to my husband and me. How could we seem disloyal by going elsewhere when she died? The brewery was doing well – we were thankful and grateful. But times have changed – what I could live with twenty years gone I can't now, in all truth. My husband and me… well, we've talked this over – he was all for coming to see you himself but I wouldn't let him. We've decided now is the time to retire – from your service – from anyone's – and live out our days thinking on the good times.' She came to a sudden halt, her heart beating fast, her cheeks flushed. *That's over*, she said to herself. *Now I can't be dismissed.*

'You?' said Estelle, momentarily lost for words. 'Retire? How shall you afford it?'

'We have savings – we've worked hard and spent sparingly. I'm sorry, Madam, it has come like this. I wanted to talk more friendly about it.'

Estelle regarded her from before the fire, completely unable to form a rational opinion on the situation. Why wasn't Alexander here to guide her? 'I think I don't understand any of this,' she admitted. 'You talk to me of being friendly when you are really being most *un*friendly, though I'm sure you don't intend to be. I look upon it as unfair that you should consider withdrawing your loyalty at a time when I most require it.'

'Never have I been accused of disloyalty,' said Mrs Comfrey, her eyes smarting with tears. 'Your family have always been my first and last concern – Mr Havisham would have vouched for that, and Mr Pocket.'

'Ah, those Pockets!'

'I am not what you want for this house any longer,' said Mrs Comfrey, with some force. 'You are not the light-hearted Miss Estelle of years ago – you're the Miss Estelle your Papa and Mr Compeyson have made you, so strike me dead if it isn't true. Them and money. And Mister Arthur's trapped between the two...' She gave a despairing gesture and made for the door but Estelle leaped across the room and flung herself between her housekeeper and her outstretched hand at the handle.

'How dare you speak to me as if I were a five-year-old! I am two and twenty at the end of this month and a woman of the world. As for your callous innuendos against Mr Compeyson – they are unforgivable. I demand an immediate apology.'

Mrs Comfrey looked Estelle directly in the eyes, her own regaining their dry composure. 'Madam, I apologise only when in the wrong.'

Estelle, her colour risen, tried to pull Mrs Comfrey from the doorway in uncoordinated confusion, but she stood her ground, the frustration and disappointment of years overcoming her natural discretion. She held her mistress's arm. 'Please take heed,

Miss Estelle, my dear – he'll ruin you if you let him – he doesn't fool me with his charm and looks – it's the heart that counts – you've such a lot to learn...' She watched Estelle draw away to the centre of the room, her hands pressed over her ears, her head shaking. Her first inclination was to embrace her as she had so often in those far-off innocent days – to provide calming assurance within those motherly arms. *Let Estelle consider my words*, she thought wisely but sadly, leaving her in peace.

It was thus Alexander heard Estelle's account. She felt aggrieved by his coolness towards Mrs Comfrey's treatment of her, not to mention her allegation against him. She was unprepared for his philosophy that it might be an advantage to have the Comfreys out of the way.

'Don't you see, he said, remarkably cheerful for someone whose charm, looks and heart were in question, 'Arthur will have to cope single-handedly with running the brewery – that will only strengthen his resolve to sell. I've already planted the seeds in his mind. We must nurture them. Forget the old beldame's rantings – it's time we found someone younger anyway.'

'It was awful. I've known her all my life. I said some cruel things to her – I don't know where they came from. She made me angry and now I've made her angry.'

'Oh,' said Alexander lightly, 'it's nothing an apology on either side won't cure. Women can be so quick with one another. Be nice to her while she's still here – it'll do no harm.'

'I could have done with you earlier, Alexander. How would I cope without your logic and sense?'

'You'd pay Old Jaggers. There's always someone somewhere to take someone's place. No one's indispensable.'

'If I told you I think you're indispensable,' pondered Estelle, with a wry smile, 'what would you consider me – condescending, impertinent or flattering?'

'I'd consider you honest, perceptive and just a little reckless. You're learning fast.'

'Now who's condescending?' said Estelle amusedly, tracing an unspecified pattern on his lapel.

'Not only I,' he replied, pressing her hand still beneath his and kissing her, 'otherwise I should have the sharp end of your tongue by now.'

'I have moods, sometimes... sick fancies... I don't mean to be unpleasant and never think I am until afterwards. But I feel full of life and warmth when you're about – you have always been Apollo to me, since our first talk on the roof here... but I oughtn't to tell you *too* much in case it changes you...'

'I shan't deflect you from saying anything nice about me, my beautiful nymph. No Daphne will ever change *me*. This Apollo hopes *she* will never change – should he catch her in the future.' He kissed her gently on the brow but she directed her mouth to his, holding it there in a long moment.

'Take me away,' she said, with intensity. 'Away from Satis. I want to go to Italy – to the sun – where you went. My nerves are in shreds. You can show me all the wonderful things you said I should see – I want to share them with you as you said we would one day.'

'We *will* go,' Alexander replied, 'just as soon as Old Jaggers has completed all the legalities and I am back from London having sorted Arthur out. Then we shall reward ourselves by celebrating your establishment as a Lady of Worth and Substance.'

'Make love to me there,' pleaded Estelle. 'I want you to love me – to seal our bond. Promise you will – under the Italian stars.'

'Of course, *la mia stella brillante* – if she wishes it. *L'Italia e il paese d'amore.*'

* * *

Old Jaggers arrived at Satis in his capacity as executor of Mr Havisham's will. He brought with him his son, Young Jaggers, a man of about Arthur's age. He attended, presumably, on the pretext of opening up experience beyond circumscribed bounds of office, courtroom, prison, condemned cell, prison, courtroom, office, hemmed in close huddle between Aldersgate, Newgate, Smithfield, St Bartholomew's and St Paul's. His eyebrows, like his father's, bristled down from his forehead as if to admire themselves in his watchful eyes. As he sat next to his father in the chilly dining room, Estelle felt unavoidably intimidated by the way he kept treating his teeth to the seemingly succulent side of his index finger – an affectation obviously developed for the court's benefit in order to prod at some cowering unfortunate boxed by dock, legal system and burly Jaggers method.

Estelle headed the table whilst the lawyer detailed a number of small bequests, realising that as major beneficiary she was, at last, legally confirmed.

Her expression did not escape Young Jaggers whose own usually caused the most innocent babe-in-arms to feel guilty about being born. She glanced at Arthur to see his reaction, if any, to Old Jaggers informing him he was to receive the brewery. Shorn now of his beard, more of his troubled mind was expressed by pale contours harbouring eyes which closed against periodic shots of coughing. All he said was, 'is that all?'

'The brewery is not without value,' bumbled Old Jaggers briskly. 'I merely state that it is not in the best of repair and is somewhat out-dated, but with a good degree of consolidated attention and modernisation is not beyond being made cost-effective and viable.'

With some relief, Alexander knew Arthur accepted what he was hearing as confirmation that the success of its future was too horrendous a responsibility for which to be accountable. It remained only a matter of formality to take charge of Arthur's destiny and have a bill of sale drawn up in Estelle's favour.

Mr and Mrs Comfrey's gratitude at being left a token of Mr Havisham's appreciation touched Estelle, particularly as she had made her peace with them but had been unsuccessful in changing their minds about retiring. No staff could remember a time when they had not been amongst them; and many were the exchanges of guesswork below stairs, when Mrs Comfrey was about her duties, as to the true reasons for their departure.

The evening before Alexander left for London, he sat on Arthur's bed wondering why he was making such an effort to communicate when his friend and client seemed so distant, a confused head exacerbating his general lethargy; it was only the thought that he would receive no opposition from him in this state that encouraged him to persevere – and the knowledge that he was successfully negotiating on Estelle's behalf.

'In the circumstances you are making the right decision,' he endorsed. 'It is what I would do in your circumstances. Business, whether a goldmine or not, is nothing but a worry and, to be honest, your health is bad for your worries.' Arthur had not argued with the valuer's assessment of £950; indeed, Alexander had persuaded him that it represented a major benefit for him if he considered the advantage it wielded over his half-sister, whereby she stood to shoulder the responsibility of ownership – the trusted reliance she would have to place on managers, advisors, bankers, stewards and honest workforce too. He was further at pains to point out that she, also, would receive no managerial help from him – he would act solely as her agent – in which capacity he was in possession of a letter from her to Old Jaggers authorising him to arrange the details of sale. It would entail Arthur's visit to his office at Little Britain, in the City, to append necessary signatures before he could consider himself free enough to quit Satis and embark, with his old school chum's help, on his second bid for freedom.

Once Alexander had departed, Estelle absorbed herself in ordering new curtains for the dining room and banishing the more self-righteous portraits. She made plans for dismantling Arthur's rooms, once he had gone for good, and after redecoration, planned for them to be a day-room with antechamber – admirable as they were with their choice outlooks over the gardens. Her boudoir opposite would remain the same, her dressing table enjoying its accustomed prominence. By the time Alexander returned she would very much be Mistress of Satis ready to embark on her Grand Tour.

TABLEAU VI
1796

Ceaselessly, day and night, the flotsam of humanity and Hungerford Market mingled in the warren of ramshackle terrain between Charing Cross and the Thames. Known as Porridge Island, it coagulated round St Martin-in-the-Fields, infusing the neighbourhood with crippled staircases crazing from rotting basement to rotten garret; vegetation rooting from illicit cracks in parapet and chimney stack like spreading fungi; needling bugs and lice trekking about their gritty territories; tunnelled alleys and courts overflowing with slippery filth; grimy rain overshooting leaking roofs to swill green-stained cobbles coursed by rats twitching nightly whiskers over sleeping children cornered in tangled rag-heaps.

From Whitehall to the White Tower, similar decaying locations inclined towards the all-receiving river slip-slopping about its mud, barges, creaking stanchions, shored-up walls; flimsy walkways willing to pitch the hapless down amongst bobbing boats and boxes, hawsers, offal, refuse and thin cats done with struggling but buoyed up by their own swelling gasses.

The Bargee Joe was a popular rendezvous, tottering on its groaning wharf at Old Hungerford Stairs. Mr Fleece wound his careful way through white mists closing about the groaning waterfront to catch in every throat, cloud every patched window inflamed like eyes rubbed raw by January's brutish knuckles. As he entered the tavern, he admitted enough mist with the swirl of his cloak to compete with its wood smoke, tobacco smoke, tallow smoke and circling sociability bustling its crooked beams and flagstones. Barely pausing to acknowledge recognition of his presence, he pushed through to a coop-like den secreted along a stunted passage, where he swept off his hat and dumped the bundle he carried onto the table. A tousled female of uncertain health but certain breasts appeared behind him, as if by magic, bearing a bottle of wine and a rummer.

'Thank you, Meg,' said Mr Fleece courteously, indicating the table. 'Is The Cap'n at large?'

'Cap'n's below deck, sir,' said Meg, advancing with swaying allure to set down her tray. Mr Fleece slid a pulling hand round her waist as she spluttered between giggles, 'will oi be getting' 'im for 'ee?'

'You will,' allowed Mr Fleece, warming his cold lips on the side of her neck. As soon as her hands found their way round his back he repelled them smoothly, his attention diverted to helping himself from the bottle.

'Mister Fleece, Sir!' The Cap'n entered, wiping his swarthy hands on a length of soiled cloth. That part of his face not filled with cunning was covered with a black eye-patch slung rakishly from somewhere above his left ear to somewhere below his right. 'A stranger to our 'umble 'ouse these days, if I may make so bold a hobservation.'

'I have been out of town,' replied Mr Fleece, undoing the bundle. 'Some complicated business. Out of town but not out of commission, you'll be pleased to know.'

The Cap'n, after bolting the door, slid up a chair as he watched Mr Fleece's practised fingers pulling at the string. 'So I was 'earin',' he said, his good eye rolling in its socket as if glad of its liberation. 'Wot 'ave we 'ere this time – a meas'ly di'mond or jus' the jules from the Tower?' Mr Fleece opened the wrapping and tipped a clink of trinkets onto the board.

'A few items I've been saving for you,' he said, 'knowing your disposition for small stuff.'

'Pretty,' said The Cap'n, with a gratified smile, examining a silver pin-tray. 'Nice quality – always rely on y'self for quality,

Sir. A reel pleasure to get rid, if y'takes mi meanin'. Now that's wot I calls a fine lady's piece.' He held up a gold and enamel *etui*, turning it this way and that before his singular optic. 'Called at Carlton 'Ouse on y'travels?'

'Not yet,' said Mr Fleece, taking back the *etui* before it mysteriously found its way into a handy pocket. 'Just as rich pickings to be had at a safer distance.'

'You be a hexample to us all,' said The Cap'n, admiringly. 'Gen'leman Fleece 'as the edge on us, I alway sez, and 'im good for a spot o'learnin' into th' bargin.'

'Well now,' said Mr Fleece, bundling up the glittering prizes, 'just you hand over forty-five guineas, then we'll get down to the real business of the night.'

'Forty-five's a bit steep, ain't it?' said The Cap'n, his eye coming to rest like a stopped marble. 'They's only fiddlin' an' small.'

'A drop in the Thames to you, I'd have thought,' remarked Mr Fleece calmly, his level gaze meeting the marble. 'I know you like to go through this ritual every time. And I have to go through reminding you that what I know of The Bargee Joe is a dangerous commodity to tamper with. Mr Adolphus is of the same opinion and we're both gentlemen of honour, as I'm sure I don't need to emphasise. So, to prove I'm a fair man of business, let's make it a round forty and no questions – not even requesting my absence while you visit the bank.'

He unlocked the door and stepped outside, knowing full-well, as he closed it, that the indecipherable nautical mutterings were but a prelude to The Cap'n moving the table, wrenching aside the threadbare matting and hoisting up his money box from its worm-eaten stronghold between the joists. Mr Fleece smiled to himself to know that had he asked only a twopenny jig for the trinkets, The Cap'n's indignation would have been equally as strong.

Pocketing his generous earnings on returning to the apparently innocent room, he demanded that now the sordid part of the visit was over, the rest of the time should be given over to remunerative pleasure. 'Who have you that can turn an honest card and hold his liquor with the best?'

'There's Peg-leg Jem,' said The Cap'n, 'an' Croak, th' schoolmaster, along wi' a cove of 'is not many months out o' Newgit. Stir the fire, will you, an' I'll conduct these worthies to your lordship's presence.'

Having been pleased to receive his high sum so easily, Mr Fleece saw no need, during The Cap'n's absence, to disturb the room's flooring. Instead, he fed the fire and set four serviceable chairs round the table, placing a candle in a bottle at its centre.

In clumped Peg-leg Jem, who claimed to have lost the majority of one limb to a greedy cannonball during an unspecified naval battle. In its place he usually sported a finely turned support; tonight, as he could not be bothered, the stump left him by an unspecified Admiral's surgeon ended at the finely tied tunnel of his blue striped trouser-leg which swung like a bell-pull as he jerked himself along on his wooden crutch. Croak the schoolmaster's lengths of greasy hair and green teeth projected farther into space than his beaked nose, helping his ill-fitting clothes cramping his sparsity to give him the appearance of a crow-scarer in tight circumstances.

The card sharps had with them an individual whom Mr Fleece instantly recognised as the man he had first met at Epsom. Fresh from Newgate, was he? He had kept that quiet during the interview at Satis. He went immediately to Mr Abel, and as he extended his hand in mock-welcome, crushed it warningly whilst hissing under his breath, *'we've never met.'*

'Fleece is the name,' he then announced, full-voice, his crushing contact converted into cordiality, 'an old partner of these gentlemen. Come – let's be seated. To which of us, I wonder, will Dame Fortune incline her cornucopia.'

'*Labor omnia vincit,* as the poet says,' said Croak, an intellectual smile revealing that those teeth trapped inside his mouth were as green as those escaping below his upper lip. 'Labour overcomes all difficulties,' he translated, helpfully. 'Latin.'

'An educated con,' said Mr Fleece, approvingly, 'our honourable man of letters – not unlike myself: Latin, French, English – *verbum sat sapienti* – one word is enough for the wise. Now, gentlemen, to the universal language of cards, if you please. Cap'n, another few bottles would not go amiss, nor a fourpenny double-Gloucester. My thoughts are in particular need of a little oiling, and Peg-leg's dealing arm here looks in need of double strength. Take the cost out of the five guineas I saved you.'

Mr Fleece and Mr Abel (or Magwitch – they were one and the same to him), sat opposite one another and throughout the night's proceedings conversed as total strangers about only the fall of the cards. The felon was no mean hand; he possessed a certain rough style which appealed to Mr Fleece, particularly when, at a crucial moment, he could produce the king of hearts as adeptly as Mr Fleece could produce his ace.

'*Palma non sine pulvere,* as the proverb says,' spittled Croak, the fruit of the vine having failed to drown his loquacity, 'a prize is not without dust. Quite a useful evening – for some.'

Once the night had fulfilled its potential by continuing Mr Fleece's ability somehow to maintain his pecuniary superiority, he departed with as much swirl and flourish as he had arrived, paying a link-boy to light him to Hanover Street, north of Piccadilly. As he turned from Conduit Street into Great George Street, leading up to Hanover Square, he could not deny the growing suspicion that he was being followed. He knew better than to look apprehensively back, marching resolutely along the right hand corner of the Square and into the quiet stretch of elegance where he knew his comfortable bed awaited him. Though the stewards and servants loaned from Rookwell did their best to keep the house warm and aired, it was a losing battle against the raw season – the chills of the small hours sliced into him as he slid the bolts on the front door quietly for fear of waking the small staff. As he consumed a last warming glass by the embers of the front parlour fire, it was no nearby shutter stirring in a draught nor blind man's stick on the paving stones outside that made him aware of a soft tapping which he traced to the front door. Arming himself with a pistol from the table drawer in the hall he stood beneath the fanlight and demanded to know, *sotto-voce* but authoritatively, who was there.

'You'd know better if you was to open this door,' rasped a voice unmistakably Mr Abel's or Mr Magwitch's. 'I'd have words with you, Sir, if you'd so oblige.' Silently, Mr Fleece drew back the bolts and ushered his gaming-mate into the parlour.

'Who gave you leave to stalk me here?' he said angrily, once the door was safely shut. 'I never allow my business connections freedom of this house. You should have arranged to see me in Brentford as normal. Were you followed?'

'You needn't be affeared,' he was reassured. 'Mr Abel ain't no fool when it comes to dodging them as goes for him.'

'Not so of late, it would seem, if your recent spell in Newgate is any indication of your ability.'

'That weren't no fault o' mine, so strike me dead if it were,' asserted Mr Abel, thumping his chest in the approximate vicinity of his heart. 'Blind Mick it wos who did for me.'

'Trust nobody in this life,' warned Mr Fleece, unstoppering the decanter. 'I've told you that before.'

'Ah, but now I *can* trust Blind Mick, y'see,' said Mr Abel, winking. 'He's not a lot o'bother at the bottom o' Puddle Creek. Drownded he did, Mr Fleece, an' drownded he stayed – even at low tide – not prevented, poor soul, from walking where the planks wos rottenest – straight through he went, stick an' all. They picked him up at Three Cranes – his stick shot London Bridge an' wos fished out at Billingsgate.'

'What do you want, Magwitch, or what ever you call yourself? I'm tired and want my bed. I'm also extremely vexed that you have lighted upon *my* separate identities – such as I've been at extremes to conceal. I can promise you that should you attempt to use this discovery to further your own ends, it won't be only Blind Mick at the bottom of Puddle Creek.'

Magwitch nodded in agreement. 'May me heart an' liver be tore out, roast an' ate if I do so much. You're a clever Gent, Mr Fleece – Mr Compeyson – they're one an' the same to me. You can count your secret safe wi' Abel Magwitch, a mere warmint wot's been in-jail an' out-a-jail as long as he can remember.'

'Here,' said Mr Fleece, handing him a glass of spirits, 'drink this and tell me why you're here – I want you gone before the servants stir.'

'I be here, Sir, on account o' your invitation at Epsom last fur to step this way, if you please. You've been uncommon good to your comrade an' pardner Magwitch an' you has his respec' fur it, as much as one tiger can another.'

'Have a care, Magwitch,' warned Mr Fleece, pointing his glass, 'you have been handsomely recompensed for keeping a closed mind and still tongue – and that salver paid a debt.'

An' sich they are, Sir – wild horses wi' gunpowder in their fodder wouldn't drag nothing from me – who'd be I to a'vertise Your Honour's skills at forging neither, or swindling, passing stolen banknotes with a coolness an' use o' brain as is the wonder of us lesser mortals? – you an' Mister 'Dolphus.'

'I don't need you to recite my catalogue of accomplishments,' said Mr Fleece modestly, sitting at the table. 'You could do well to take lessons from it – perhaps your visits to His Majesty's prisons would then be things of the past.'

'I'm of that opinion too, Sir,' Magwitch agreed, rubbing his chin, 'though it's a poor individual you sees before you wot's learn'd to write by a deserting soldier an' reading by a travelling fair; wot's left to thieve turnips by a tinker an's been thieving ever since – an' tramping an' a-begging, when he weren't doing a bit o' labouring or poaching. It wos me stomach wot did it – always complaining when it were empty, always wanting more when it were full. Leastways they feeds you in jail an' me stomach's got that it's none too partic'lar.'

'My heart bleeds for you,' Mr Fleece said. 'If I didn't know you better I'd be of the opinion you think the world owes you a living.'

'It were a good day that – when I were put in your way at the races. Mind, I don't say I wosn't cautious on first sight of Your Honour sitting among them tables with your fancy looks an' nimble fingers – a fine gent to behold. "That's him," sez the landlord who'd picked me out for you. "Him as is finely dressed in rings an' watch an' chain?" sez I. Sez him to you, "I think this is a man who might suit." An' you sez to me, "wot can you do?" "Eat an' drink," sez I, "if your Lordship'll find me the materials".'

'Stap me, Mr Magwitch, what a memory. I must confess I cannot match you there.'

'Ah, Mr Fleece – how could Abel Magwitch ever forget how he wos took a fancy to – how he wos give five shillings an' told to come back the next night, which he did, to be took on man an' pardner. Only…' Magwitch stopped to drain his glass with an appreciative noise. 'Only – pardner in wot? From that day to this, not a trick – no swindling, no forging – nothing to keep me off the old life wot got me committed to Kingston Jail before we took up. So then this visit, as you inquired, is to find out wot sort of traps you're setting for others to get caught in. Me fingers is a'twitching for want of real tricks and me stomach's as demanding as ever.'

'I'm afraid,' said Mr Fleece, refilling Magwitch's glass, 'that your stomach will have to go on demanding – for the present. But there *will* be tricks, I promise. I am currently engaged on a most delicate piece of business in which the slightest footfall could cost me dearly.'

'Is it permitted to be of an opinion to its nature? Would it, for instance, concern certain tricks in a certain old house ouside o' London? Would the first letter of a certain house take the form of a big S?'

'Why ask if you know?' said Mr Fleece, superciliously. 'I don't intend to play games – unless, of course, I win. And I have yet to play one I lose. You consider yourself my partner, and therefore the secrecy of our different affairs and methods are equally important. When I have work for you I shall inform you, so be prepared. Now, be off with you – no more begging devices at my front door. Remember – *verbum sat sapienti.*'

'Afore I do,' said Magwitch, putting down his glass, 'let me a last word. Young Mister Havisham – knowing him the both of us as we do in our ways – is he part of your delicate tricks, or has he your invalu'ble protection like when you gives me that han'some tray from him? For which I thanks you kindly, thank you.'

'He is not my partner as you are, if that's what you mean. I have known him from schooldays, as I have Mr Adolphus. I *do* have financial plans concerning him and he may become useful to us in what you call "our delicate tricks". Other than that I am not prepared to say at this moment. Be warned – outside our joint dealings we are strangers to one another – total and complete – Fleece or Compeyson, Abel or Magwitch, Adolphus or Fawn... perhaps Arthur or Havisham. If driven we look to ourselves. I want to know nothing, hear nothing, see nothing – other than what I dictate. Softly away with you now.'

In silence, Mr Fleece let him out into the anonymity of mysterious mists and himself into the muffled luxury of a feather-bolstered sleep.

* * *

While Alexander remained in London, Mr and Mrs Comfrey made a supreme effort to leave Satis with all possible speed having worked their notice. Mr Comfrey's brother had been approached with a view to overseeing the move of personal effects from the brewery house to his own hostelry premises at St George's turnpike, Southwark.

Their destination became a talking-point amongst the domestic staff – Hugh in particular wished to hear its details. With his limited knowledge and experience, he was unfamiliar with the concept of a bar across the road to ensure travellers paid a toll for the surface's upkeep; but he understood readily and lovingly the work involved with the horses – those tired after a long journey as well as those fresh and ready to be exchanged for the journey's continuation.

Miss Havisham proved dull and difficult without Mr Compeyson, the Comfreys found, and not disposed to celebrate her birthday – welcome news in the kitchens. No replacement housekeeper had yet been found and no manager appointed to the business. Estelle, seriously in two minds as to whether Arthur should forcibly be placed behind Mr Comfrey's desk, was on the point of chivvying him into action; he would, after all, have Brand, the under-manager, to support him. But his continued bouts of inebriation, headaches and impaired vision dictated that he remain unable, unaware, unsought, unwanted. Hugh, too, enjoyed some respite from his Mistress's interest – pleased to be freed of his unsure but firm responses to her attentions – glad to be warmly swathed in unconducive clothing and protected by belligerent weather keeping her at a distance.

Though a choked, rimy day in February, two covered wagons with a horse a-piece drew up in the brewery yard to receive such of the Comfrey's cupboards, crockery, tables and chairs as were not part of the Havisham hoard. Mrs Comfrey found an opportunity, during the disturbances, to slip unseen by Miss Havisham, into Satis House.

'Dear Master Arthur,' she said, as she closed his door and sat on his bed. 'It grieves me more than I can say to leave you here like this, my dear. But I don't know what is to be done. I've organised below stairs that the servants'll keep an eye on you for me – Zilla is a good girl, and discreet. Promise me, my lad, you'll come to me if ever you need help. I'll get word to you of my address when I have one – we hope to go into the country. Here – I've written where you can find me in Southwark till then. See – I'm putting it here – under your mattress – for safe keeping. Don't forget where it is. Zilla will help you. God bless you always, dearest boy.'

She hugged Arthur's remote form, the stretch of years striding away. 'Be on your guard,' she sobbed. 'There are those here who wish you ill. Be your own man again... you shouldn't have come back. Start afresh – there's evil here...'

Though Arthur hugged her in return, a lustreless distance glazed his dark-ringed eyes. Had he any notion of what was happening? She felt inclined to bundle him up with her household effects – could he be smuggled out rolled in a carpet? Perhaps Mr Pocket might be able to do something for him before it was too late. She barely took in the good wishes of the staff lined in the servants' hall, on their mistress's instruction, like bystanders at a public hanging. She cried a good deal on her way to Southwark, not least over the future of the two children on whom she had tendered her loving loyalty for so long.

Mr Comfrey, on the other hand, felt neither regret nor apprehension. His sympathies lay with the honest, simple men left to labour under increasing difficulties. Brand was a sound individual but could not be expected to cope single-handedly for long. Mr Comfrey refused to let himself feel slighted by not having been asked to consider postponing his retirement; though having been thanked for his services, he suspected that his employer somehow took it as a personal slight that he possessed no further wish to help enable the Havishams to grow richer. He put his arm round his unhappy wife. 'But Hannah... what can we do? They don't need us any more. Times change and so do people. We have to let them. We know we've done our best and that's what counts. But we can't alter what will be...'

As she listened to her husband's wisdom she silently disagreed; she could at least try. Her mind was made up. As soon as they were settled in Southwark she would do what she could...

* * *

She had not visited Chelsea since Master Matthew's christening twenty years previously, though she had last seen Mr and Mrs Pocket at Mr Havisham's funeral. She found it peacefully reassuring to sit again with Mr Daniel in his riverside paradise. Her adjustment to her new life south of the river had wearied her somewhat; but she derived new purpose from reminiscing over her early days when Daniel was a boy. My, how his children had grown – Matthew, having left the counting-house, was newly embarked on a hopeful career as Parliamentary reporter; Sarah, her disposition as sour as her apple pies, seemed content to remain housekeeping at home with Mama; and Camilla, though only seventeen, found herself in the market for a husband – lucky in her present attentions from a wan individual of indulgent manner: Mr Raymond was not in the least perturbed by the prospect of taking on a veritable Pandora's box of ailments with his intended.

Mrs Comfrey glanced again at Devis's pleasing triple portrait of the three young Pockets above the fireplace. It reminded her of Master Daniel's early-formed high principles; of Miss Isabella's beauty bestowed on Miss Estelle; reminded her, too, of Miss Amelia's alliance through marriage with a country from which no word had come since the Reign of Terror. 'Forgive me, Mr Daniel, for appearing here like this. My husband would be surely vexed if he knew I was troubling you with my worries. He let me see you on condition I didn't.'

'You are most welcome, Mrs Comfrey,' Daniel assured. 'Why, we regard you as one of the family. We shan't give you away, never fear!'

'Indeed not,' rejoined Mrs Pocket, threading her needle. 'We, too, have our worries over life at Satis House, but they are of no consequence as I'm sure we are now regarded as too poor to be anything but an embarrassment. Indeed, one might almost be led to believe that Mr Daniel's defeated hopes for Parliament were personal slights against his niece.'

'Now, my love, I should rather not consider the possible contents of Estelle's mind,' said Daniel. 'Poor Estelle – the improvement I so hoped for years ago seems not to have matured. Our concerns must remain nearer home, though. Sarah, for instance, Mrs Comfrey. In spite of all we've said to the contrary, she *will* have it that her Uncle Havisham left her a bequest…'

'All of us a bequest, in fact,' interposed Mrs Pocket again, stabbing her needle into her embroidery.

'…And that her cousin has, by devious scheming known only to Sarah, denied us of what is rightfully ours. I wrote to Mr Jaggers but showing her his reply hasn't convinced her. She even went as far as to accuse him and Estelle of conspiracy, though not to his face I'm glad to say. We really don't know what is to be done. And now your virtual dismissal. It's all too bad.'

'Matthew is particularly angry about it,' said Mrs Pocket, cutting her thread. 'Dear Matthew – he says he would most emphatically not accept a shilling-piece – least of all from Estelle or her father. He and Sarah have rather fallen out over it. Matthew can be as proud and resolute as Estelle, when he so wishes. It must run in the family.'

'He's all for marching off to Estelle and giving her a piece of his mind,' said Daniel. 'I've persuaded him, I think, not to waste time on making a fool of himself.'

Mrs Comfrey nodded in agreement. 'There seems such little opportunity, these days, to reason with her. I thought she might listen to me – she always has in the old days – but it's as if she's almost a different person from the one we used to know. She was lovely, once – such a dear. Of course, you know I blame that father of hers and now this beau she's got herself entangled with – playing with her affections – playing with her money as well, I shouldn't wonder – he's far too nice to be sincere. But it's Master Arthur's situation that makes my blood boil. He used to be such a sweet, giving little fellow – underneath he still is. You've only to look at him to see he needs love and care. It's sheer cruelty, that's what it is, after all he's been through – he's worse now than he was at the funeral. There are things going on behind his back – I know it. I fear for his safety, I really mean that.'

'Don't distress yourself, dear Mrs Comfrey,' said Mrs Pocket, sitting beside her to hold her hands. 'Daniel, is there anything we can do?'

'If so,' sighed her husband, 'then it's up to us to decide what. But you, Mrs Comfrey, must enjoy a well-earned rest and put the past behind you. You deserve that, you and Mr Comfrey, though you mustn't think for one moment we are not concerned...'

'You and your family have been our life, Sir. We've had no other. I've served the Pockets and then the Havishams as well as I know how, so I can't help the way I feel. There it is, plain and simple. But I shall try to do as you say – retire with the well-earned past resting behind me... it won't be easy, but that's no different to what it's been like these last few years.'

'What a shame you consider your days of service ended,' said Daniel, moved by her words. 'I know of at least three situations where you could ask a King's ransom – and get it – for the quality of your service.'

'Thank you kindly, Mr Daniel,' she replied, flattered though unconvinced, as she put a hand to her grey hair, 'but now it's come about natural like this, I'm not sorry to be attending to my own matters, for a change. Mr Comfrey and me we're with my brother-in-law at St George's turnpike in Southwark, you know, though we'll be looking about for our own place somewhere – all snug and friendly – with a bit of ground to grow flowers and keep a pig, perhaps, and a few chickens. Don't get me wrong – I'm in gratitude to those who believed in my work, your parents being my dearest time with you all and Miss Isabella.'

'And on behalf of my family,' said Daniel, giving her a comradely hug, 'I should like to thank you – both of you – for your joint loyalty and hard work. You will wait here a moment, if you please.' He left the room, returning in a short while with a small paper package tied with thin green ribbon. 'I don't need to tell you how grieved we are at the circumstances of your departure – I can only apologise for my niece and feel some shame on her behalf. If you want my considered opinion, you are well rid of Satis. If you forget *them,* please don't forget *us.* You are welcome here at any time; and if there's anything any of us can do for you, you have only to say.' As he placed a kiss softly on her cheek, he pressed the package softly into her hand.

After she had departed, Matthew, who took his role as senior family man next to his father extremely seriously, was not to be fobbed off with the explanation that Mrs Comfrey's visit had been purely social; she would not have come all the way to Chelsea simply to compare its cold climate with Southwark; nor would she have left Satis so abruptly without a logical explanation – his sisters, also, were beside themselves with curiosity. Backed by a mixture of feminine charm disguised as bullying, he managed to break his father's reserve. By the time he reached Arthur's involvement, Matthew's sense of fair play allowed him no respite.

'You should have let me go and tackle Cousin Estelle when I first asked you, Papa. Even *I* could see that all was not well. Give me your permission now – I want to try appealing to her conscience before it's too late.'

Daniel looked down at the buckles on his shoes then up at the three faces caught between their gilded swags. 'I cannot honestly say that I have ever *disliked* the idea of you polishing up your armour and dashing away on your white charger in defence of family honour.' He poured and offered his knight errant a glass of brandy. 'On the other hand, I'm not sure I should *approve* such a venture – you know how much comment Estelle and that Compeyson scoundrel engender. I'd prefer that our side of the family avoided any association with such adversity. Let us say that if I know your crusade is to take place without my knowledge, then how will I be able to prevent it? Do we understand one another, my son?'

'Thank you, Papa,' said Matthew gratefully, raising his glass.

Mrs Comfrey, arriving back at St. George's turnpike about the time Mr Daniel and Mr Matthew understood one another, had no difficulty convincing her husband of an innocent afternoon taking polite dishes of tay; of talking pleasantly of pressing flowers, the seasons and comparing the superficial virtues of Mrs Glasse's recipe for making Calves Head Pye in *The Compleat Housekeeper's Companion* over Mrs Smith's recipe in *The Accomplished Gentlewoman's Directory.* It was only when in the privacy of her bedroom, that she found herself faced with an emotional dilemma; untying the green ribbon of Mr Daniel's package, several banknotes fluttered onto the table.

TABLEAU VII
1796

Clattering over cobbles through a post-horn's brazen snarl, The Winchester Flyer, west-bound from London, delved round the corner of the archway into the yard of The Ferry and Flood Inn, Brentford. Once in the tap-room, Alexander Fleece dispelled his traveller's chill with a few warming glasses. Public transport was all very well, he reflected, but not quite suitable for an image such as his. Next time he would employ one of Miss Havisham's gigs, unless he could talk his father into providing him with one of his own – he must have a more discreet method of covering the area between the Upper Thames and the Medway. But his father seemed to be holding his money closer these days, with no explanation; much as Mr Fleece thrived on secrets, this had the potential of being one without an attraction.

These considerations foremost in his mind, he set off along the High Street, to a margin of older houses at the town's edge as yet by-passed by property developers. They stepped zanily up several stories from their thresholds, half-timbering joisted on half-timbering in half-crazed asymmetry, each busy-fronted projection bent on out-shooting its neighbour. At the door of one of the shorter properties, almost cowering as if afraid of being trodden into the ground by its taller guardians, Alexander fingered a key from his pocket and let himself in.

The remnants of a meal for two littered the gate-leg table beneath the fitful shine of a candle in a wooden barley sugar-twist holder. He added some firewood to the crumble of embers in the grate; as firelight began dancing about dark oak panelling and low-beamed ceiling he drew the skimpy curtains across the latticed twilight.

Attracted by some muffled creaking overhead he ascended the stairs as quietly as dry treads would allow, his candle flame unfurling lively shadows like black flags about the plaster walls. Stealthily, he lifted the latch to the room above the parlour where one frost-bitten tallow-dip in a flat candlestick did its best to distribute a little warming cheer as it outlined lumpy contents active beneath a patch work quilt on the bed. Discarded male attire carelessly jumbled with a woman's in various areas of the room. Whilst activity continued unabated, he moved to a low cupboard on which he set his light, unlocked it and took out one of three pistols, little caring whether it was loaded or not. Stepping towards the bed he sprang back the covering, his tautening temper snapping like a strained spring as he pointed his weighty firearm at the first feature in the firing line – a naked backside. Amidst a spread of flesh and mixed limbs, two faces appeared, shot with alarm. As Alexander cocked the flintlock, the young cove let out an abortive yell whilst jumping from his position, his own weighty weapon leaping rampantly to his defence and waving like a mooring post in a gale as he dived about the floor scooping up garments.

'You'll be on the receiving end next time,' threatened Alexander, clicking the trigger and watching the flint strike a spark in the empty pan. The visitor did not wait to give thanks for being spared but hastened to drag on his clothes whilst tumbling downstairs.

'Get up!' commanded Alexander, turning on the frightened woman half hiding behind a held wall of bedding. She took it with her as she modestly crept about the chamber retrieving her garments. 'And stop snivelling. I can't stand a wet woman.'

'Don't be hard on me, Alexander... you don't understand.'

'You follow me to the parlour, my girl, and tell me what it is I don't understand. Make haste.' He clumped down the stairs, flinging the pistol at the strange lad's head as he dashed, still half naked but no longer rampant, through the door into the street. Alexander locked it, picked up a dropped shoe and pitched it on the fire.

The girl joined him directly; she could have been pretty, in a weary sort of way, with dark tresses she had made some attempt to dress; her pale youthfulness, though, exaggerated the merest ghost of a bruise shadowing her left eye.

'Oh, Alexander.' She approached him, raising her face in a deliberate gesture of welcome. 'It's good to see you again...'

'Flattery won't work, Madam. 'Have you not learned by now?'

'But I love you...'

'As I've no doubt you said to that well-endowed jackanapes you were entertaining at my expense, to say nothing of the others. I hope they used that armour I gave you – we don't want any accidents, thank you very much.'

'I don't love him... none of them, I swear...'

'So I've heard – and half Brentford.'

'If only you didn't leave me here alone... for days on end... weeks... months even... you don't tell me what you're doing, where you're going, when you'll be back...' A hefty slap on the bruised side of her face silenced her backwards against the wall.

'You remain here, Madam Strumpet, because I pay you to. Let me remind you that yours is not to think what I'm doing or where I'm going or when I'll be back. I pay you not to think.'

'You can be cruel, Alexander,' said Sally bravely, pushing back her hair.

'There I would agree with you – cruel to return at such an inopportune moment. What a waste of a well-primed weapon! At bottom you're no better than a Drury Lane tally-woman. I sometimes think I should have left you in the alleys of Porridge Island.'

'And I often wish you had. There's life there – laughter – companions. There I wasn't lonely. Ned was rough, but at least he loved me – in his way.'

'He never beat you? Was that his way too?'

'No more than you. But he's not put a burn on my arm I'll take to the grave and that's a blessing.'

'Something to remember me by, my dear, when you go to the devil.'

'I loved Ned – really loved him. I loved him and you killed him.'

Alexander held her scarred arm tightly. 'That is your fault, not mine. You made me jealous. And he crossed me at his peril – thinking he could dip his greasy paw into my share of the pickings just once too often. But he'd reckoned without the vigilance of my trusty confederates. So he had to pay the price. Do I cheat, forge, steal only for myself? This cottage and you in it are part of the deal – the reward for silence. Or is that too subtle for you to remember? If I swing for Ned, then by God, I'll see the Newgate toll bell clangs for you too – and if it's drinks on the house at The Magpie and Stump in celebration, then my ghost'll be there joining in. Now, get me some liquor, Sal, and sit down. I have other matters to talk to you about before we go to bed.'

Sally disappeared into the small back kitchen, returning shortly with a jug of ale and two mugs.

'Incidentally,' said Alexander, satiating his thirst, 'who *was* your fine upstanding admirer? I didn't recognise any part of him.'

'Please, Alexander… he's only a boy – and lonely, like me.'

'Who?'

'I don't know – that is – I don't know his name. He helps out sometimes with the ferry across to Kew.'

For a time, Alexander seemed studiously to contemplate his drinking vessel, then the flames leaping the herringbone brick hearth. 'I have a task for you,' he said at last. 'I also have something for a good little girl who does as she's told and asks no questions.' He felt in his pocket, withdrawing a clenched hand. As he held it over her outstretched palm he let something warm and metallic drop into it. She became wide-eyed with delight as she beheld a delicate pair of fruit scissors fashioned in silver filigree grapes entwined with vine leaves. Alexander took it from her, holding it between finger and thumb before her face.

'Pretty, eh? Like you. Had an old Jew at The Bargee Joe offer me an excellent price the other day. "No," I said. "These are for a young lady who likes pretty things – when she can get 'em." You see, my dear, I do sometimes think of you when I'm away.'

'They really *are* for me!' exclaimed Sally, smoothing her dress as if suddenly aware of how ill-arranged she was to receive such munificence.

'If you behave and promise to do as I tell you, I think I can promise you *more* pretty things from now on – and people – and life... all that you profess to miss here, in fact.'

'And if I don't promise?' She took charge of the scissors.

'Have you ever considered,' reflected Alexander, retrieving the trinket, 'what a disgraceful number of rotten wharves and walkways there are between, let's say, Westminster and Wapping? Treacherous, they are, unless one knows the way about...'

'What must I do?'

'Your task is to become a housekeeper,' he replied brightly, pocketing the scissors. 'And I have the very place for you.'

'But I don't know anything about housekeeping.'

'You have a week in which to learn. Tomorrow I shall arrange with Mrs Barklea at The Ferry and Flood for you to become acquainted with essentials – she was once housekeeper to the Marquis of Swineflete, so mark her well. Then tomorrow-week you'll close up this place, bring the key and yourself to The Cross Keys, Wood Street, in the City, to be met at half-past-two in the afternoon by a private gig which'll take you into Kent. In the meantime I shall have prepared the Mistress of the house for your arrival by writing your character from your last employer who I've yet to invent. There is nothing to be anxious about – the housekeeper who's leaving will settle you into the routine. Should you require further guidance, I or Miss Havisham will instruct you.'

'You?' said Sally with some surprise.

'I am business advisor to Miss Havisham, and her personal advisor on a number of important matters relating to her estate, her father having recently deceased. If you do exactly as I tell you, you'll find your placement at Satis House highly *satis* – which in this instance will mean *satisfactory*. It is *vital* you obey my instructions to the letter of the law otherwise nothing will be *satis. Comprends-toi?*'

Sally nodded, quite familiar with occasional bursts of foreign superiority.

'Firstly, at Satis House and in comparable society, I am known under my professional name of Alexander Compeyson. Don't ask why. Just accept I am. From now on, that is the name by which you will address me at all times. And I know you *only* as the housekeeper I have engaged for Satis House. The name Fleece, by which I am known here, must be forgotten.'

'Two names? Why two?'

'Two names – two identities – one for business, one for pleasure. They must never mix nor become confused. My success, and consequently yours, depends on that.'

'I shan't forget.'

'Good girl. My second requirement is that whatever you may observe, hear or think you understand regarding Mr Compeyson's interactions with any member of the Havisham household, you must keep it to yourself. It is nothing more than part of the business I told you of. You must not discuss it with anyone – that includes Mr Compeyson and Mr Fleece – they are both to be trusted without question. From now on, you too, will have another identity. You are Mrs Ferry, a young widow recently in service until calamity befell you – I shall prepare your way, have no fear. I should never consider pushing you forward for this if I didn't think you capable. You've a good brain and can turn yourself out well when you make the effort. Why do you think I scooped you out of Porridge Island?'

Sally looked quizzically at Alexander in the dying firelight. 'What's your game?'

'The game of life, dear child – same as yours, only I hold all the trump cards. But rest assured – anyone who helps and obeys me is never denied a share of my winnings. Droll, am I not?' He tossed the scissors onto the table.

'Heartless,' corrected Sally, retrieving them.

'Heartless? He who brings you presents to prove he's no hard feelings against your lusty ferryman and his pole?' Alexander laughed. 'Come to bed and you'll be given more.'

'There's more heart,' reflected Sally, making an effort to stir herself, 'in the night wind blowing up-river from Traitors' Gate.'

* * *

Two days later Alexander returned to London, having organised matters to his satisfaction between Sally and Mrs Barklea. He made straight for the City, booked a seat on the next-day-but-one coach to Satis, then stepped over to the seedy little office of Mr Chiplock, his landlord's lawyer of Lincoln's Inn. Requesting pen and paper, he addressed a few lines to Mr Chiplock's client, Richard Byland, Esq., Snuggery Bower, Turnham Green, respectfully begging that he find enclosed by his tenant, Alexander Fleece, Esq., the sum of ten shillings, being the annual renewal rental on Tudor Cottage, High Street, Brentford. Having left the package in Mr Chiplock's obliging care pending transference to his client, Alexander called on Old Jaggers at *his* deedy office in Little Britain, squeezed like a large felon in a small dock. He delivered Miss Estelle Havisham's letter endorsing the bearer's verbal intelligence of her intent to purchase Satis House

Brewery from Mr Arthur Havisham for an agreed sum of nine hundred and fifty pounds, appointing Mr Alexander Compeyson of Hanover Street, London, and Rookwell Park, Hampshire, executor of her wishes. He informed the clerk – for father and son were attending to criminal business – that on receipt of Mr Jaggers's instructions, he would bring Mr Havisham to the office in order to effect the transaction.

The following afternoon, he went, on behalf of Arthur, whom he described as a gifted young *protégé* of his, to Humphrey the Printer and Publisher in New Bond Street. He prepared the way for a future introduction to James Gillray, the popular lampooner and political caricaturist whose viciously witty designs had been delighting the masses for the last twenty years. Successful in his mission, he then repaired, for the evening was glum and flat, to The Bargee Joe where he swiftly sought out The Cap'n, his empty back room and full bottle.

'There's twenty in that,' he said, placing a tempting leathern bag in line with his functional eye. 'Your trickery is required.'

'Fur ready money – anythin',' said The Cap'n, feeling its contents with loving fingers. 'Spin us th' yarn then.'

'I have an acquaintance – a Gentleman not unlike myself – who'll be coming to our wicked capital in due course. I shall want him taking care of.'

'Wharf, knife or rope?' said The Cap'n, nodding intelligently.

'It goes against my nature to disappoint you,' regretted Mr Fleece, 'but I really do mean *taking care of* – he will require a roof over his head, food, drink, a decent bed, company. You have access to all those. He is Mr Arthur and I want him looked after. He will have employment and can pay his way, but I trust to your dishonesty when it comes to settling up with you over any *minor* expenses which may be incurred. I shall be out of circulation for a time – possibly considerable – and have to thus leave him to the mercy of others. I can rely on you?'

'May I be keel'auled if you can't, Mr Fleece. This young Gent. not unlike y'self, Sir – does 'e, by any stretch o' th' cat-o'nine tails, be one of our sort?'

'He has the potential. He *could* be useful, but until I return from business abroad he must muckle through as best he can, then we shall see. Early associations have given me a liking for him and I want him treating kindly and with respect – I direct you and your associates to *equate* him with me, otherwise you'll have to *reckon* with me. Another old school friend of mine will be with him also, to introduce him to our London ways. Mr Adolphus has some of my characteristics but not my intellectual cunning.'

The next morning, after a cardless but constructive evening's business discussions with The Cap'n and his land-crew, he boarded the coach at the Cross Keys, Cheapside, in good time. He hoped to secure one of the corner seats by the window, where he could inflict himself upon the padded and buttoned right-angle in order to patronise more easily the view without and passengers within. As he settled himself, he noticed a well-muffled individual approaching whom he recognised but could not place. The rather pale young gentleman clambered to the top of the coach where he braced himself against cold weathering as the braying horn heralded its trundling out under the archway. With cracks of iron-shod hooves and wheels on cobbles, it left the criss-crossing activity of crowds and vehicles chuntering like muffled secrets beneath St Paul's black blister bubbling amongst fuming chimneys choking City towers and needle spires.

Throughout the journey and changes of horses, Alexander tried to recall where he had seen the young outsider before; it was only when he heard him address a few remarks to a fellow companion on arrival at The Blue Boar that he recognised him as one of Estelle's cousins who had attended the funeral. What the devil brought him to this vicinity? Alexander hurried on to Satis before being noticed.

Estelle's delight at having him back, and the security she regained from his presence, soon evaporated any criticism she may have harboured over his absence and lack of comprehensive communication – she put her lips eagerly in the way of his whilst his arms dutifully encircled her.

'Have any of your relatives paid you a visit during my absence?' he asked.

'If you mean those impoverished Pockets, then all I can say is they have more sense than I gave them credit for in keeping away – they obviously know better than to come sponging here.'

'You overestimate your pale cousin,' said Alexander. 'He's presently at The Blue Boar – we travelled down on the same coach, but he was herded up top with the rest of the cattle. Be on your guard for an assault on your doorbell.'

'I shall have him admitted,' assured Estelle, 'in order to have him ejected. Until then you must come to the library – I want to hear what you've been doing in London – I feel the lack of society at the moment – I quite yearn to circulate once more. Is Arthur and the brewery taken care of?'

'Most successfully. There's only the paperwork concerning him to be attended to. I have also, with your leave, taken it upon myself to interview several suitable candidates for the position of housekeeper. I have found one who will suit admirably – a young widow by the name of Ferry – energetic and industrious… slightly raw, perhaps, but that'll diminish under Satis's influence, I've no doubt. She'll arrive before the week's out. Mrs Comfrey must be organised to instruct her before departing.'

'I fear that's not possible. I had no powers to detain her. It seems strange without her after all these years. Brand is managing the brewery at present, and not unsuccessfully.'

'No matter,' said Alexander thoughtfully. 'It can still be done.'

'Alexander.' Estelle hugged him. 'It's wonderful of you to take such trouble on my behalf – it lessens my burden. This house is more like a tomb at present – all this cold and wet mists get on my nerves – it seems to gather on the marshes with the sole purpose of making straight for where I am. When can we make for Italy? I need bright vistas, then I'll be happy again.'

'My dear Estelle. That is what I should enjoy most in all the world, but I shall have to consult Papa with regard to a loan...' Estelle's tinkling laughter broke his earnest expression.

'You can be *so* sweet at times. You can't have forgotten so soon that I now have enough money for both of us?'

'Estelle,' faltered Alexander, 'how could I, in all pride, allow you to subsidise my pleasure? Why, for all I know, you might even think my attendance on you has some ulterior motive...'

'You amuse me sometimes, my dear. I know you too well ever to believe that. Besides, you're not exactly a pauper yourself – anyone would think you'd been cast penniless into a ditch. How funny you can be sometimes, Alexander.'

'I should be mortified if I thought people would talk adversely about us...'

'Let them!' Estelle drew herself up. 'That is one of the penalties of our position. People like us must expect to be the centre of attention and comment. Just think – if it were otherwise we would be of no value.' A servant announced that Mr Matthew Pocket waited in the hall to see Miss Havisham, please. 'Come with me, Alexander – let's see what my poor relation wants. Ah, Cousin Matthew! What an unexpected pleasure. And so soon after the funeral. Did you leave something behind?'

'Cousin Estelle,' acknowledged Matthew, barely nodding at Mr Compeyson. 'I make no apologies for disturbing you this evening, but what I have to say is better said sooner than later. I am here on behalf of others who can't rightly stand up for themselves. May we go somewhere private?' He followed them into the library.

'I requested privacy,' Matthew reminded her.

'I have no secrets from Mr Compeyson,' his cousin also reminded him. 'He needs to understand our family and all its petty annoyances.'

'Very well then, but what I have to say may be considered too truthful for some tastes.'

'You won't take a glass of wine, will you, before you amaze us with the truth,' she observed, not seating herself. 'I commend these others you speak of for sending such a worthy representative – dear Cousin Sarah, always ready to point her sharp features into anything she can complain about – quite unlike dear Camilla who can barely drag herself off her couch should the house be burning about her ailments.'

'I would agree,' said Matthew unexpectedly. 'Sarah cares only about herself – Camilla was born middle-aged. But they are not a-party to this visit. I come only as my father's representative, knowing you are ashamed of us because we are far from affluent.'

'Learned your pompous way of speaking from those dull proceedings in Parliament you report,' said Estelle, unprepared for his honest assault.

'It is of Mr and Mrs Comfrey I wish to speak,' continued Matthew, not to be intimidated.

'They left of their own free choice. Their return is impossible now, if you've come to plead their case.'

'Most certainly I have not. There is no case to plead. And to return is the last thing in the world they wish to do. No – you were unkind to Mrs Comfrey, Estelle, and not a little uncharitable. You have made light of a lifetime's devotion she's given to the Pockets and the Havishams. For that, Uncle Augustus at least saw fit to remember her – and her husband. His consideration will wisely be used to establish their well-earned independence.'

'You came all the way from Chelsea on top of a coach in a five-shilling seat to lecture me about equality?'

'I came because I dare. I've tried to like you, Cousin Estelle, even when we were children. I've tried for Papa's sake as he always put forward your good qualities – he believed you had a certain softness which made you approachable. But you've become cold – cold and hard like your money – like the only people who interest you.' He looked pointedly at Mr Compeyson who was on the point of forcibly ejecting him from Estelle's presence before she had an hysterical fit, though he was momentarily unsure of his place in this family exchange. Of his own accord, Matthew moved towards the door, facing his two stunned opponents. 'I am so glad to have learned, through Papa, what a true gentleman is, for as I understand it, if he's not one at heart he's not one in manner. No varnish, says Papa, can hide the true grain of any wood – the more you add the more the grain shows. The same goes for a true lady…'

'I've heard enough!' Estelle's anger caused even Alexander to flinch. 'The whole house would stand by and let this nonentity harp on with his insults. How *dare* you come trespassing here when you've nothing to offer but jealous enmity and frustrated expectations. You are forbidden this house in future. If you attempt it again, I shall have the garrison on you as well as the dogs.'

Matthew had already swung back the front door and was striding the forecourt on his way back to The Blue Boar – he would be back at Chelsea tomorrow. Somewhat upset by the unpleasantness but pleased that his self-imposed penance was over, he declined supper and went to his room, wondering if he had spoken a little too forcefully. All his achievement amounted to, if any had been intended, was banishment from a place whose tainted fabric he had no intention further of visiting. He meant to have spoken of Arthur, too, had he not lost the chance; and had he been in the tap-room later, instead of in bed, he would have been able to speak with Arthur direct when he emerged like the creature of the night he had become, to drink with his usual companions.

Estelle sought to dismiss Matthew's onslaught from her memory, aided by Alexander's attentions. He encouraged her to calm herself and concentrate on preparations for more important immediate matters, the chief being the projected Italian caprice which he made plain he was happy enough to organise and manage. He suggested that as soon as could be arranged, Mr Adolphus Fawn, a gentleman known to him through London contacts, would escort her and Zilla by sea to Marseilles, thence by road to Como, near Milan in Northern Italy. As companion, they would take with them Mrs Bracegirdle, a stout woman of daunting capability obtained through Mr Brand. She would remain at Como when Mr Fawn returned to London from safely establishing them to await Alexander's arrival. He would not leave for Italy until completion of the brewery sale, the reallocation of Arthur, the settling-in of Mrs Ferry, the promotion of Mr Brand to official brewery manager and a visit to his parents at Rookwell.

Mrs Ferry arrived from Brentford in one of the house gigs, sent on Alexander's instructions, to collect her from The Cross Keys, Cheapside. He introduced her to her new employer who took time off from her breathless preparations to conduct her round the house, concluding with the domestic quarters and Mrs Comfrey's old sitting room. Though surprised by Sally's apparent lack of years, she trusted Alexander's judgement, reading again the character handed her by Alexander from a certain Sir Reynard Fox-Huntingden of High Ravenscarsdale Hall, in far off Yorkshire, extolling her diligent efficiency and honest demeanour.

Estelle, on the afternoon previous to her departure, slipped out to the stables in the knowledge that on her return to Satis, her life and expectations would have matured into everything her father had hoped for and prophesied. She had, however, one last bond with her old life to break – a nostalgic affection for her early appreciation of male attraction made her still vulnerable enough to acknowledge it one last time. Hugh had been discreet – loyal – a welcome *divertisment* in times of stress or plain fancy, the secrecy of their *liason* adding heightened colour.

'As you know, Hugh,' she began, wrapping a twist of hay about her fingers, aware of his power still to affect her, 'much has happened here lately – your Master's death, the Comfreys' departure, changes of property... I don't need to enumerate all that to you... and I've – well – not been in the best of health through it. But Mr Compeyson has arranged for me to go abroad for a while – to recuperate. The house won't exactly be shut up, but a few of the servants are being taken on elsewhere for the duration as you know, and Mrs Ferry is in charge – Mr Compeyson has seen to every detail. You will remain... and I shall think of you often. When I return there will be a new Master of Satis – life will begin again. But our secret is safe. Especially from him. I know I can rely on your permanent discretion in return for your employment – you quite understand?'

'Look to me, Miss, not to let you down,' said Hugh, with an intonation Estelle hoped was not suggestive of guilt. To prove she had nothing to reproach herself for, she slipped a reminding hand across his breeches front beneath his short coat whilst placing a strangely clumsy kiss on his cheek before letting him go.

As she returned to the house, a watchful Alexander remained in the shadows, perfectly at home amongst other people's secrets as well as his own.

* * *

Feeling very much like the fourteen-year-old departing for Versailles, Estelle at last was ready to enter the post-chaise which would take her to London in order to make some last minute purchases. In a second vehicle, with the luggage, sat an excited Zilla and a Mrs Bracegirdle looking unlikely to be excited by anything. Adolphus, who had organised the passports and a good deal else on Alexander's behalf since their recent cardless meeting at The Bargee Joe, had instructions to escort them to Tower Dock in order to join the small group of passengers boarding the *Commodore,* a brigantine of 127 tons. Once free of Gravesend, where they would drop the river pilot and be cleared by customs, they could all then relax – weather permitting – as the south coast receded in anticipation of a warmer south waking earlier to spring. As the post-boy directed his horse between Satis's gates, Estelle glanced back at Alexander standing squarely on the step. She smiled, blowing him a kiss as she anticipated their reunion in sunshine over Lake Como. He considered her going with a lightness of heart which increased with every turn of the wheels. By the time she was out of sight he had re-entered the hall, closing the front door as if it were already his own.

'Inform Mrs Ferry I wish to speak to her in here please,' he asked one of the servants in Estelle's boudoir engaged in trying to tidy the remnants of departure. Sally, when she entered, had recovered some of her former confidence tempered by her initiation into domestic duties.

'Alexander, what a place, eh?' she blurted enthusiastically, once they were alone. 'What a house – look at this pretty room – what a dressing table.' She fingered the draped muslin.

'Mrs Ferry!' came the reprimand. 'You forget yourself.' He pulled her away from the table into his arms. 'I will dictate our familiarity – this is neither the place nor time.'

'You're asking me to go against my feelings,' said Sally. 'I don't know if I can.'

'Remember what I said to you.' He gripped her shoulders. 'Harden yourself.'

'Like you?'

He smiled. 'The north winds gives way to the south on occasions.' He allowed her to nestle against him as his arms closed her in. 'I have to be away from Satis for some time – a business transaction with Miss Havisham abroad – so your duties here will not be too onerous. Remain dependable but aloof. All you have to do is your best and await instruction from me. You have agreed to my word. Have a care. Believe me, our lives depend on it. Now then – I wish to show you something Miss Havisham did not.'

He led the way across to Arthur's rooms. Despite the best efforts of those servants in the know, particularly Zilla, their air hung stale and closely heavy with depression.

'This is Miss Havisham's half-brother Arthur,' he said softly, so as not to wake him. 'I am working on his behalf too. As you can see, he relies on what I do for him – he is lost without it, so let that be a warning'.

'Poor mite,' said Sally. 'What's wrong with him? How long's he been like this? I *thought* the servants were keeping some mystery from me'

'Long enough to become a habit. He's half-crazed with his own genius – something I may be able to help him realise. I've organised that he will shortly be going to London to start a new life amongst new people. When he is gone, Miss Havisham wishes these rooms to be dismantled and thoroughly cleaned as she will have them redecorated when she returns. She would like you to see to that as soon as is practical.'

'He could be good-looking if he was in good health.'

'I remember him before he was ill – at school – a sort of second cousin to the fair Adonis. He's still my friend and I'm fond of him.' Arthur stirred amongst his bedding, opening his eyes. 'Now then, old fellow. How are you feeling? This is Mrs Ferry come to see you. She'll look after you as well as Mrs Comfrey did. You're soon to be given a new lease of life, so just rest and I'll be back again soon.'

'Will that involve the White Queen?'
'The White Queen's gone. You've nothing more to fear.'
'White Queen?' whispered Sally in puzzlement.
'I shall explain,' said Alexander, leading her from the room.

* * *

Within the next two days, Old Jaggers's letter arrived requesting Arthur's attendance at Little Britain in order that the conveyance of the brewery may be affected. It was the moment Alexander had been waiting for. He hastened to Arthur's room at six o'clock the following morning and with Sally's help, cobbled him together in his well-worn garments.

'Have you come to put me in a shroud?' he asked drowsily, as they tried to smooth out some of the worst creases in his coat.

'We're off to London, Arthur, you and me. You're going to friends. I'll explain it all on the way.' Clutching such folders of drawings and scant possessions as could be found, Alexander helped him downstairs and out to where Estelle's speediest gig waited in the forecourt. Conscious of his passenger's proneness to coughing, he settled him comfortably and well-blanketed beside the driver's seat, his bundles safely at his feet. After some final instructions to Sally they were away into a steady canter. The crisp, rushing air brushing his face revived Arthur's spirits, flushing his features with a colour for once not encouraged by alcohol. By the time the two young men confronted Old Jaggers before he repaired to The Magpie and Stump for lunch, Arthur had acquired some semblance of bonny youth first encountered at school.

Though he attended to the transactions, he allowed his friend to guide and advise him – *he* seemed capable of producing just the right word at just the right moment, the mellifluous phrase, the apposite expression – an informed and elegant gentleman of the world able to converse on equal terms with the legal fraternity; how Old Jaggers regarded his performance never occurred to Arthur. But, as had been so carefully explained, Alexander acted as Miss Havisham's appointed and approved agent, for which he expected to receive no remuneration; as Old Jaggers had said of his own duties, 'I am paid to do the bidding of others, not to ask questions.'

And afterwards, couched by the smoke-room fire of The Bell, Greyfriar's Passage, a jorum of hot brandy and water between the two friends to spirit away the bleary, early twilight, he knew his money would be safe in Alexander's bank account until his own was set up, another service his friend promised to provide.

'Drink with me,' invited Alexander. 'To a new life – *your* life. You're free of Satis now. You and Estelle have no further claim on one another. You must promise never to return – on any pretext whatever. Do you promise?'

'Of course I promise,' said Arthur, almost laughing. 'Satis was my grave.'

'Then I have brought you back to life. The London air is in your nostrils. We will make your promise legal and binding in due course, when we open your banking account.'

Arthur, relishing the alcohol's warm suffusion, placed an appealing hand on Alexander's arm. 'I can never repay you for your kindness to me. With you to help and guide me like this I feel I can achieve anything.'

'To see you well again is payment enough, my aspiring friend,' said Alexander, 'and to take charge of your capital – not actually yours, you'll doubtless agree.'

Arthur looked puzzled. 'I've just sold the brewery.'

'And I've paid your outstanding debts, Arthur. The brewery sale, you must have realised, stood as surety otherwise I'd never have been so rash. It's not sufficient, mind, what with the interest, but because we're friends I'm prepared to waive the difference. That seems fair. I'm also prepared to fund the minimum required to open your new account at the bank.'

Arthur gaped at him in gratitude – incredulity – disbelief – Alexander could not tell which.

'What is more to the point is this: do you remember your promissory note for £400? Well, here it is. See – I tear it up… throw it on the fire… watch it burn. There. That obligation to me is null and void. You can start again with a clean slate. You look bemused, dear boy.'

'I thought I'd have money,' said Arthur in a lost voice. 'How can it have gone?'

'It went *before* you had it – while you were in London prior to returning to Satis. Remember? Your creditors looked to me knowing I would see them right. And there were a number of them. Recall the stranger who appeared the day of your father's funeral, for instance? A sticky customer *he* was, but I managed to deal with him to his satisfaction. You have known me a long time – when have I ever let you down?'

'I *have* known you a long time,' agreed Arthur, with some heat, 'but I still feel I *don't* know you – not completely. When I *think* I know you, you seem to become someone else.'

'And am about to again.' Alexander looked Arthur straight in the eyes. 'Part of your debt to me is loyalty – obedience – silence. Forget that at your peril.'

'Where are you leading me, Alexander?'

'I'm leading you to another who has my features – my voice – my looks – another gentleman. He is well known to you but you have yet to make his acquaintance. He is harder – more exacting – than Alexander *Compeyson*, your friend. He is Alexander *Fleece*, your friend. Mark him well, I warn you. Respect his wishes, do his bidding and he will have every cause to favour you as I do. It is he who will *seal* your freedom from Estelle and Satis's oppression.'

Whether or not it was the effects of the brandy, Arthur was experiencing a certain confusion of mind; though not yet seeing double, he certainly believed he was hearing double.

'I am two people, Arthur, with two lives. You have to *know* this – you have to *accept* this – unconditionally – unquestioningly. I am not altogether the person you *think* I am. It makes *no* difference to our friendship or my loyalty to you. My continued affection is to be *depended* upon. *Trust* me. Arthur, as I trust *you*.'

Alexander sat back, a little breathless, his heart battering its cage. Arthur was in the know at last; and, by knowing, sworn into the circle at The Bargee Joe, as he would soon discover.

Eager, now, with nervous energy, he led Arthur back to the gig and drove him across to Humphrey's in New Bond Street, where Mr Gillray was sent for to meet Mr Fleece and his expected *protégé*. He leafed through Arthur's folios, impressed by his style and imagination, agreeing to take him for a trial period. 'Engraving,' he impressed upon his visitors, 'is an exacting art relying on a clear eye and steady hand. We'll see if you've got what it takes, my lad. Be here at eight on Monday morning, and good luck.'

Alexander next directed the gig to Holborn where, in his capacity as Mr Fleece, he called on his own lawyer. Not for him the prosperous firm piling up business in a brisk new development north of Gray's Inn as patronised by the Compeysons; he preferred the anonymity of Cramp's Twist Court, barely nudging Fleet Lane; a shady, retiring covey of clusters, huddled as if picking over the remnants of half-forgotten mysteries. With Arthur beside him, he strode to the peeling door up steps unlevel enough to trip the unwary. Arthur tripped. Mr Sharps, with nose like a bill-file on which drops from his nostrils were impaled, shuffled to attend him personally, perhaps hoping to charm from his enigmatic client the outstanding account.

'Two small matters,' said Alexander, ill-disposed towards Mr Sharps's hard wooden chairs and sparse lighting. 'I have to be abroad shortly – for an unspecified period. I shall keep you informed of my whereabouts as and when I choose. If it should be longer than a twelvemonth, I wish you to undertake payment from my bank of the rental on my property at Brentford. It can be done through my landlord's lawyer, Mr Chiplock of Lincoln's Inn – my methods are quite agreeable to my landlord, you will find. If you will also be so good as to supply me with a writing implement and scrap of your worthy legal paper – thank you so much – I will supply a note of authorisation for you to present at the bank who I shall also notify…' He strung out the ink across the surface, dried and sealed it. 'The other matter concerns my companion here, for which I require a second sheet of…ah, many thanks.'

During the ensuing silence, marked by the uneven tick of Mr Sharps's lop-sided wall-clock, Arthur watched as Alexander's quill made slower work than of the previous document:

I, Arthur Havisham, do hereby disassociate myself from my half-sister, Estelle Havisham of Satis House, Rochester, in the county of Kent, and all she represents in a personal, monetary and property capacity.

I also appoint my loyal friend and mentor, Alexander Fleece, of Tudor Cottage, Brentford, in the county of Middlesex, to be advisor and enabler in my business affairs, trusting to his superior understanding of such matters, until any time as I may declare otherwise.

'This is your legal ticket freeing you from your past,' commented, Alexander, emphasising its significance by almost stabbing in the full-stop.

'What does it mean *monetary and property capacity?*'

'It means that neither of you have any claim on the other. All you need to do is sign it, then you're your own man.' He handed him the quill. 'Don't dally – time presses. Mr Sharps will act as witness.'

A thread of confusion again knotted Arthur's mind as he formed his name, followed by Alexander, witnessed and dated with a sniff by Mr Sharps from whom plopped a large blot forming a watermark. Wiping the threat of a second with his finger, he rolled the papers, tied them with pink ribbon and locked them in a fusty cupboard.

'I am indebted to you,' said Mr Fleece, rising thankfully from his inhospitable seating. 'Have copies made, authenticated and sent to me. When I return to England I shall be in a position to settle what I believe to be your trifling account. Until then, Sir, I wish you good day.'

He conducted Arthur back to the gig almost embalmed in twilight. 'To a bank now, my fine buck, then we shall be in a fit state to be sociable.' He drove to Tolland's in Bullion Row, careful to avoid association with the area round his own in Threadneedle Street. Stumping up £100 with which to open an account, he oversaw Arthur's transaction, satisfying himself that credit would be forthcoming by the next working week's end.

'Now,' said Alexander, once back in the gig, 'you're an independent man of some worth – a man in employment – a man in need of a home. If all this excitement isn't too much for you, we'll repair to a cosy place I know and meet with friends who await your arrival.' He drove down to The Golden Cross opposite the lion-topped frontage of Northumberland House, Charing Cross, paying for the gig to be temporarily housed in a corner of its coaching yard. On foot, with Arthur dutifully beside him, he made for the slop and shingle of Old Hungerford Stairs where the oozing lights of The Bargee Joe clotted on the sticky walks and treads. Mr Fleece, true to his prior arrangements, ushered his companion through to the cell-like room where he saw Mr Abel. Arthur faltered.

'I believe you two *have* met,' began Mr Fleece as The Cap'n entered with liquid refreshment. 'Arthur – there's no need to be alarmed – this gentleman is now here to help you – trust him as you trust me.'

'May me heart an' liver be tore out if you can't,' said Mr Abel amiably, 'roast an' ate in the bargin.'

'I don't doubt,' observed Mr Fleece, mildly. 'In the meantime, Arthur, Mr Abel and the Captain here will be your guardians, so to speak. When Mr Adolphus returns from Italy he will take you under his wing and add a little... what shall we say? – *grooming* – to your new life here. You will know Mr Adolphus when you see him, but remember him as Fawn – our companion on many a jaunt in our academic days. He, like me, has more than one personality, but less ability; as in your case, he looks to mine with a clear eye when his runs short. The Captain, on the other hand, looks with that bloodshot specimen most likely poached from some reeking slaughterhouse.'

'Well, the cow weren't wantin' it,' he growled, sleeving liquor from his slack lips. 'What th' 'ell, as long as it's good enough to see the colour o' your money any bright day.'

'I need to know of Mr Arthur's accommodation. What have you found for him?'

'A nice room, like you sez,' put forward Mr Abel, 'wi' glass in the windows an' boards on the floor – a lock on the door as well, against them wot'd come pinching and stealing.'

'Rental?'

'Twenty pound a year – first instalment paid – coals an' candles extra.'

'Situation?'

'Maiden Lane, Covent Garden – above a pawn-broker's – a safe gent wi' two eyes but three balls.'

'My time is short,' said Mr Fleece, with the vestige of a snigger, 'and my temper shorter, if you're ill-advised enough to try it. I entrust Mr Arthur to your care – secure him no shortage of diversion and fellowship and no short measures in noggin or magnum. You will not let me down – not you, not Peg-leg, not Croak.'

'Come, Sir, 'ave we ever now?' reassured The Cap'n. ''Ave an 'art.'

'I'll have yours – *and* your liver – and I'll use Mr Abel's recipe. If I *am* let down, I shall know – even though abroad.'

'Abroad?' Arthur seemed dazed.

'Business, unfortunately, calls me away. My talents are needed elsewhere, otherwise nothing would have given me greater pleasure, or saved me more money, than to see you settled in your new life instead of having to farm it out to others.'

'I *will* see you again?' Arthur swallowed hard, coughing a little.

'Of course, dear boy – probably when you least expect it. Alexander Fleece never abandons a trusting and trusted friend. A toast, gentlemen – *To Arthur and his Great Expectations.*'

Later that evening, after sampling The Golden Cross's best dinner, Alexander relaxed before its welcome smoke-room chimneypiece and wide hearth, his feet almost stroking the firedogs. Though bolstered by a four-shilling plate of poached carp savoured with liberal measures of an acceptable old hock, he could not completely erase Arthur's haunting voice sounding his departure from The Bargee Joe. *'When will I see you again? Where can I find you?'* still resonated in the echoing galleries of his mind, making him uneasy. He felt uneasy, too, about travelling to Rookwell just now in answer to a letter he had received from his father asking to see him; Mr Compeyson also registered surprise at his son informing him by writing of his impending visit to Italy as Miss Havisham's escort. His concern centred on the continuing European situation in the aftermath of the Revolution in France, not least the rise of military dictatorship under the dynamic Corsican, Napoleon Bonaparte, who seemed to have his sights set on Italy. Was it a wise place to go, knowing of possible danger? Had Mr Compeyson appreciated that his son thrived on danger, he would not have noted down his fears so readily.

Eventually blotting them from his consciousness with another glass, Alexander decided to see his parents on his return, when ever that would be, preferring to anticipate an innocent night's sleep before returning, albeit temporarily, to Satis and its new housekeeper.

TABLEAU VIII
1796 – 1800

The Mistress of Satis saw no reason to set a limit on the time she and her retinue remained abroad. The knowledge that her estate and affairs were being managed by those paid to do so became enhanced by her belief in Alexander's all-round professional and thorough capabilities. She preferred to leave decisions to him, including the duration and destinations of their time away from home. Adolphus, too, could be relied upon to provide efficient service, as proven by their safe passage to Italy and establishment at their first small villa near Genoa overlooking the Ligurian coast towards Levanto and La Spezia. She also felt no compunction about writing back – indeed, she could not think of a single person in England, other than Alexander, who would wish to hear from her nor cared, particularly, where she was; nor was she inclined to write to Alexander either, believing he would be with her before he received it.

She did, however, hurry off a note to the Boulevard du Temple, though unsure of whether Marie Grosholtz had survived the Revolution; she wrote that if she was able to come to Paris, she would dearly like to see her again, if only to show Alexander to her – perhaps commission his portrait head. A similar note went to Uncle Emil in Versailles, but though she left a forwarding address to *L'Albergo Perdita* on the shores of Lake Como, nothing from them awaited her arrival from Genoa. She took charge eagerly of the single communication to her inscribed in Alexander's elegant copperplate; other considerations dispersing like morning mist from the *lago* as she read of his intended day of arrival, freed at last from the delaying clutches of his family at Rookwell Park which had detained him, alas, longer than he had anticipated, by which he was mortified. It would have been nearer the truth to explain that he had, in fact, written the family a letter, even as he left England, stating how mortified he was at not possessing the time to visit them before pressures dictated he leave immediately.

The reunion of Estelle and her Apollo took place on the terrace of her suite commanding the polish of blue waters reflecting hills and snow-peaked mountains radiating in leaps and swoops on all sides. He saw how the drawn, careworn stresses she had left England with had disintegrated, restoring her features to their customary serenity. Her enthusiasm at holding him again – hugging him to her – feeling his substance within her embrace – reinforced his appreciation of his own worth. They kissed often, saying little of any consequence at first. Gradually, Alexander learned of her voyage from London to Marseilles, the boat across the Ligurian Sea to Genoa and thence her progress to Como – the people, the places, the value for money; the success of Zilla's attentions and delight in changing scenery, Adolphus's refined efficiency and Mrs Bracegirdle's monstrous seriousness. They agreed, with much hilarity, that she could be dispensed with at the earliest opportunity.

His conversation inevitably revolved round the well-being of Satis, its estate and business. He reported on the reliability of Mrs Ferry, Mr Brand as new manager of the brewery – its sale also. He initiated her into the relative costs of the transaction, assuring that legal fees and any other small considerations here and there had been taken out of was due to the recipient.

'And what of Arthur?' Alexander detected the first frown in Italy to knit her brow.

'You are free, rest assured. Old Jaggers pointed out to him the advisability of his signing a document promising to disclaim any further monetary and property rights, making him legally independent now from you and all you represent. There's no need for you ever to mention any of this to Old Jaggers – you know how gruff he can be. Would you be wishing, I wonder, to know what might have happened to Arthur?'

'No. Yes – no… yes, I need to know.'

'I have set him up with friends of mine in London and found him somewhere to live. I've also found him employment in a drawing and printing capacity. Who knows – we may soon see his work in print shops and The Academy – where he might earn a knighthood!'

'Don't you think London a little near Satis? Couldn't you have got him to Edinburgh or back to Paris?'

'He won't trouble you again, my dear, even in London. He's sealed his name to his word. I shall ensure he keeps it. Shall you object if I see him again? It *might* be necessary.'

'I shan't want to know,' said Estelle, quite categorically. 'I can't stop you seeing him – he's an old school friend. Of course, I'd rather you didn't, but that's not realistic. As far as I'm concerned, he's simply another beneficiary of your cleverness and generosity. For me he does *not* exist – until he gets his knighthood.'

On Estelle's instruction, Adolphus, Zilla and Mrs Bracegirdle were asked to remain downstairs all evening; on the terrace above the lake, servants laid for *una cena romantica*, spear-straight candle flames in the purple air enrobing the best damask, silver and crystal *L'Albergo Perdita* could provide; beyond the urn-clumped balustrade, Cernobbio, Moltrasio and Urio along the coast speckled the shoreline like glow-worms which had rolled down the hillsides and stopped at the water's edge for fear of drowning.

Once the servants had been dismissed at the end of the meal, Estelle, enhanced by the glowing pink gown fashioned from Alexander's bolt and wearing his Italian pendant, placed her hand on his frothily-cuffed wrist.

'My very dear friend... I can't believe we are really here – together – you and me alone – after so much has happened.'

'It must seem like a dream,' suggested Alexander, sipping the heady wine beading his goblet.

'A dream? I think you're right. And you are part of it. But I want my dream to become a reality. Alexander... I want you to make love to me.'

'I make love in all I do for you...'

'No.' Her breathing became shorter. 'I mean *really* make love – in the fullest sense of the word. I want to *feel* you making love.' She watched Alexander swallow rather hard, as if unsure of how to respond. 'I've wanted to say that for a long time, my love. But I was hoping, perhaps, *you* would say it first... there are those who'd disapprove of us speaking in this way, but what do they know? I say what I think. Tell me what *you* think, my dear.'

'I think you're very beautiful.'

'Anything else?'

'I think you're very bold.'

'Anything else?'

'I think I should like to make love to you more than anything in the world. As a gentleman you would never expect me to force my true feelings on you – that would degrade us both.'

'But you must know I love you, Alexander? If you love me you'll do as I ask. I want to know you properly – I still think there are times when you can be as distant as those lights out there.'

'But a child,' warned Alexander. 'Surely...'

'I don't want a child – not yet I mean. I want to enjoy my freedom – enjoy *you*. That's what I love about you, Alexander – you're so capable yet so unassuming. Besides... there are ways... of... *not* having a child – I have heard it referred to as *armour* – I can't believe you don't know what I mean...'

'I *do* know,' he replied. 'I can't believe *you* do.'

'I've made it my business to know. But I don't know how to find it. Do you?'

Alexander knew perfectly well, of course; he and Adolphus had armoured themselves first in Venice, then kept themselves well stocked against the *ragazze* and *prostitute* on a tour which had been grand in ways beyond their most ardent wishes. 'The anatomist Gabriello Fallopio,' he said, seriously, 'described such devices as early as 1564, and the great Italian lover, Casanova, is known to have armoured himself at times, I believe...'

'Alexander, dear,' pointed out Estelle patiently, 'I'm not asking for a history lesson – I'm asking if you have access to some.'

'I have armour,' he replied, brazenly, 'and you have *amour*. Come with me.' He leaves the table and half scooping her into the room, takes her out across the landing to his own softly cushioned suite where he unlocks a small drawer in his dressing case... 'I'll use what Adolphus asked me to procure for him.' He turns whilst Estelle begins divesting him of his coat and cravat, her colour, like his ardour, risen to compliment the pink sheen of her gown as she clutches his arms whilst sinking back on the crimson bed covers. He almost topples over her like a statue from its pedestal – but a statue active enough to work the fastenings of her dress, imagining her to be a loose-busted Neapolitan *puttana*, his nostrils suffused with her vapours and fumed by local wine, his loins heavy with a dragging ground-swell as she releases him from his flore-flap. Once armoured, he unintentionally causes her an expression of initial pain as she clings to his all too swift release – his euphoria enhanced by recollecting a serving wench picked up at midnight in Cockspur Street, not many weeks before, and pleasured beside the King's Mews at the top of Whitehall. Estelle is calling his name, kissing his lips, holding on to him as if drowning, the eventual remnants of her voice murmuring, 'I love you... I love you...'

They lay together *en desordre* until their flushed skins began cooling in the naked air. For Estelle, her return to the conscious world brought an extreme emotional response, the tears of which at first alarmed her partner until she was able to explain that his display of love meant more to her than anything she could remember. Despite her entreaties, he begged to be allowed to spend the night alone, putting forward a certain fatigue due to such an amount of travelling. He wished her a lingering and grateful *bon nuit* as she returned to her suite. Satiated with calm pleasure, she remained awake after putting herself to bed without Zilla's irrelevant and potentially embarrassing attendance. A languid voluptuousness suffused her drowsy contentment like incense. To feel his arousal against her was reminiscent of Hugh's – poor perplexed Hugh. Had she been unkind to him? – a little selfish, perhaps? But now she realised her thankfulness at not having let herself succumb when it would have been so easy not to save herself for Alexander.

Once beneath the canopy of his half-tester, Alexander smiled to think of the ease with which he had been able to unpen Estelle's happiness and gratification – auguring well for a future of idolatry on her part, drawing from him enough physical expression to keep her amenable and pliant. He drifted into what he considered a well-earned sleep, but not before revisiting, in his mind's eye, one particular night of Venetian pleasure with Adolphus back in that sultry high chamber they had shared near the *Campo San Stefano;* the gusto with which his school friend responded to the services offered by Giovanna and her full-blooded *gondoliere.* It had not only threatened to split the room at its seams but would have offended Estelle's sensibilities – particularly after Alexander's eventual participation.

The following morning, arrangements were put in hand to let Mrs Bracegirdle return to England, thus freeing the party of her awesome humourlessness. Adolphus, too, was requested to escort her back, but not before Alexander had been able to talk over with him the details of Arthur's life in London, outlining the arrangements made and how he wished Arthur to be taken care of – as far as possible. 'Don't be tempted to lend him money, though,' he warned, 'unless you don't mind not seeing it again. He is your responsibility while I'm here – I shall catch up with you both when I return. Until then I wish to know nothing.'

Within the week, as if to salute their freedom, Alexander and Estelle arranged to hire a small sailing boat to take them along the coast to Tremezzo, then across to the promontory of Bellagio before returning to Como by way of Nessa and Torno. Beautiful as Alexander appeared in the limpid morning air freshening their embarkation, Estelle did not remain impervious to the two delicious dark-haired sailors stacking the food hampers and wine baskets, manning the deck, unfurling the sail – their faces and forearms testament to last year's high summer, their lithe young bodies feeding her heightened state; she attempted to contemplate the coastline sharpening on either hand as the daylight strengthened – the greening hills, thickening with spring, clustering up in mounts and chasms to snow-slaked peaks slanting with sun and shadow against a downy sky.

Midday drifted ranges of bells from each lakeside town's *campanile* as if in celebration of morning mists clearing to release the full jubilance of sunlight on lapping ripples; on water-fronted villas stepped in ochres and terracottas, their terraced gardens punctuated by fountains and statues, conferences of dark cypresses silhouetting their prominence. At one of these – on a whim because the sailor lads told them it was temporarily uninhabited – Estelle and Alexander decided playfully to alight at its water-gate. Like a couple of errant schoolchildren, they ran hand in hand up the steps of the *Villa Cherubini* laughing and joking, to become absorbed in highlights and shade from pines, palms and pergolas streaked across green swards bisected by gravel paths. They tumbled breathlessly into the *Villa's* Ionic portico pillared from the garden and blue waters below. Its shuttered windows turned blind eyes on their presence – also on the only other inhabitant under the richly decorated ceiling – the *Apollo Belvedere,* whose polished marble perfectly expressed his antique nudity poised in elegant authority on his plinth.

'Look, Alexander, no fig leaf,' giggled Estelle, comparing her new interest with recollections of the last few days.

'Nor have I,' said Alexander, approaching her from behind. 'How do I compare?'

Estelle glanced round to see her god approaching, revealed many times larger, indeed, than the great Apollo, a shaft of sunlight emphasising his classic proportion as he pressed her back against the statue's plinth, its feet and shapely ankles at the back of her head. Alexander's attentions soon moulded her into his kisses – his protestations of love – so that by the time she greedily took him, their upright union might have dislodged a lesser giant than the mighty Apollo, whose gaze remained diplomatically fixed on the horizon to his left. Their vociferous expressions echoed unheard into the bird-loud air, floating over *parterres* and temple-dotted groves to be lost once caught by the first thermals of coming summer over the aquamarine lake.

To Estelle, her bosom heaving with emotion, her legs reluctant to support her, there was no distinction between Apollo and Alexander – their beauty and perfection were equal. The only difference – one in which she rejoiced – was that Alexander did not possess a heart of stone.

On their return to the boat, warm though controlled, the sailor lads' exchange of knowing smiles, as they cast off, hinted that their passengers' secret might not remain intact once back at their local *taverna* with other saucy shipmates. But what did their passengers care? With strong appetites and healthy thirsts they turned their attention to finding a picturesque picnic venue across at Bellagio.

That evening, whilst Zilla attended to her mistress's preparations for bed, she would have to have been remarkably insensitive not to notice the change in her appearance and demeanour, bordering occasionally on the downright frivolous. She attributed the developing good humour to Mr Compeyson's presence and influence, but knew her place well enough not to put forward so bold an observation.

'Zilla,' said Miss Havisham at last, with a glint in her voice, 'I simply *HAVE* to tell you – to tell *someone*... it's all so marvellous... do you mind?'

'No, Miss, I don't think I do,' said Zilla tamely, almost choked with suppressed excitement.

'Do you remember a conversation we had at Satis before Christmas... about love... about how it's done?'

'Yes, Miss, I think I rightly do, but I haven't remembered since, though...'

'Zilla, it doesn't matter if you have – what *does* matter is that you were right – it *is* nothing to be afraid of, if you love somebody. *Nothing* else matters – it *is* enough!'

'Oh, Miss, right pleased I am to hear you say such things...'

'And this "armour" you told me of... how lucky he has some with him for a friend – it takes away all fear.'

'I did say so, Miss, but it's as well to find out – proper like.'

'I'm finding out a great deal *proper like*,' she agreed, 'and how considerate Mr Compeyson is... efficient... loving... he will make a superb Master of Satis – the envy of the aristocracy.'

'And he's so handsome, Miss, isn't he?' thoughtlessly enthused Zilla on a personal note, tidying clothes. 'Like Hugh. It must make it easier.'

'That, Zilla, is an impertinence – altogether too familiar.' She watched her maid colour with embarrassment. 'But you're right, of course. I couldn't love someone who isn't beautiful. But I've never *loved* Hugh – not in *that* way – and I'll thank you never to repeat, allude or consider what you may think ever again, you bad girl. That was then. I needed to know so many things... I doubt my Mama would have helped me. It doesn't seem fair – men find out about everything, but how do we women?'

'Will I be turning your bed down Miss?' said Zilla, returning to the safety of mundanaties.

'If you wish. But whether I'll use it I haven't yet decided.'

'Right you are then Miss. If that's all, then goodnight and pleasant... dreams.'

* * *

The months in Como provided Estelle with happiness beyond any dream; stability, too, her tensions drained by Alexander's reliability. She felt at one with his appearance, his presence, his word; she revelled in his competence: the hiring of carriages, (she resolved that on returning to Satis she would have her own travelling chariot built), the paying of drivers and cads, the dealing with currency. She accorded him complete control, never questioning the rate of exchange or how he disposed of it on her behalf. Had she known, that from time to time, he withheld discretionary sums, sending them to Mr Sharps in London with directions to pay them into Mr Fleece's bank, she might not have rested so soundly as became her habit in the heavy summer afternoons. Being fashionable was exhausting, even abroad – expensive too, according to Alexander, who liked to blame Bonaparte for the rise in prices and costly bribing tourists needed to undertake in order to secure their wants and rights of passage.

The year had reasonably advanced when the travellers reluctantly left Como, continuing their progress to Milan, Venice, then west to Bologna, Lucca, Pisa, Florence; after a period at the delightful and romantic *La Casa del Mulino*, on the shores of *Lago Trasimeno* near Cortona, they headed for Rome; crossing to Brindisi they took a boat to Greece and its islands.

Alexander let no opportunity escape of stunning her with facts – geographical, historical, classical – the language, the customs, the cuisine. But however attentive she tried to be in such-and-such a range of crumbling pillars or limbless statuary, she was more attracted by the living – whether they were English, what they wore and for how long they could afford to be on tour at this expensive time.

Towards the close of a further summer, having wintered within sight of the Acropolis, they left Athens for the waters of the Aegean which daily flashed their latest dream-palace overlooking the bay of Smyrna – one of a number of gracious houses belonging to rich Greek merchants thriving on city trade with the west. The prosperous, cultured atmosphere of Smyrna appealed; its lush bounty of exotic fruits and flowers; luxuriant fragrances from jasmine, mimosa and oleander; its fertile vineyards and tobacco fields; its fashionable residences ornamented with trellised balconies; its cheery white villas behind stately entrance gates; its stone seats where families gather to talk and watch the sinking sun burnish the bay in floods of molten gold; its strains of zither, mandolin and guitar jangling from early nightlife stirring in clubs and taverns.

Alexander soon discovered the Smyrnean addiction to card games and gambling, proving himself no novice in communication nor currency. As he would say, with his captivating smile, 'in cards and love the language is the same;' and as if to prove it, he frequently returned proudly to present Estelle with a heavy purse. What he did *not* present, though his pride was no less, were details of his involvement with Emilia, a notably ripe beauty sporting eyes as black as the ace of spades, with whom he found himself compelled to gamble in an almond grove, amongst other places, but without the use of cards.

The night before he left with Estelle and Zilla to return to Italy, his attentions were deflated in the olive grove by the tearful news that she was with child. True or false he could not argue, nor as to whether he was the father, careful as he had been. He could only give her money, prompted not by pity but a need to prevent her turning up at the house and causing a scene before he had managed to slip away.

A chartered boat with good cabins from Chios took days to reach the Straits of Messina and from thence the bay of Naples, curving like half a coliseum impressively enough to cause even Estelle to draw breath and stare in wonder. She surprised herself at being only slightly perturbed to learn that Vesuvius had last erupted three years previously, devastating an area of five thousand acres, the crater widening to two miles; indeed, she relished all the more her visit to Pompeii because of it.

During one of their explorations on the island of Ischia, she and Alexander discovered a villa of lightweight charm perched amongst ilex and tamarisks on rocks overlooking the bay. The elevated site, lush in Mediterranean somnolence, had once housed a Roman signal station, some of whose foundations still scarred the gardens of the *Villa Romana*. Its delights increased on discovering, from the guide, that the owner had directed it to be let to suitable tenants during his absence.

Once settled there to his satisfaction, Alexander's increasing concerns about Arthur's current London situation began dominating his mind. Though he had written several times to Adolphus Fawn, his enquiries had prompted no replies, his worry over lack of facts causing his imagination to work to extremes. Facts might, however, be obtainable from one reliable source – those moist nostrils of Cramp's Twist Court; Mr Sharps would be most adept at sniffing anonymously about The Bargee Joe in order to send a report in confidence – not to the *Villa Romana*, but, say, the Packet Office in Naples. Resolved, he composed his letter dispatching it personally on the next packet boat. In due course, the reply he had grown impatient for revealed itself in writing as scratched and pointed as his lawyer's nose:

Your kind instructions received have been acted upon to our best standards in the secretive circumstances you requested. The Bargee Joe keeps itself bottled up, you understand, with a suppression worthy of its inmates when it comes to concealment and other screening cover.

There is one there who stows his own counsel under the name of The Captain – a knowing old cove who would not have lurked in the background, I dare say, had he been priced up in spirits. But secrecy being your cipher and ours to obey, I can only report what was gleaned by unsuspicious methods.

The young gentleman of whom you wrote has not been seen at The Bargee Joe for some time. There are those to whom sums are outstanding, not least in line being his landlady in Maiden Lane, Covent Garden. Discreet enquiries at his place of industry, too, revealed nothing more than that he had remained there but a shortish time, some kind of periodic affliction marring his long-term employment.

Do you wish us further to pursue? I feel it incumbent upon me to indicate that should this be so, then certain monetary considerations due to us at this present time, enabling the clearance of an uncompleted account, would not be looked unfavourably upon by those who, as ever Sir, are pleased and honoured to await your further instructions.

Septimus Sharps

Alexander chose not to further his enquiries – he questioned their purpose and expense, knowing he had no intention of following up his former life until his return. He had, at one time, considered punctuating his continual wanderings by making a healthy reacquaintance with Porridge Island and its *coterie*; had Estelle's reliance on him not been so insistent, as well as his on her funds, he might have taken leave of absence on the pretext of a pressing request from Rookwell Park – a possibility not so far from the truth as an early letter to him at Como had indicated that his Mama was not well. He had replied that he was sorry at the news and hoped she would soon make a complete recovery. Since then, his wish to be free of parental surveillance had occasioned dutiful letters about what he knew the family would expect to hear from his assorted destinations.

The other bite at his conscience concerned Estelle's expectations of him as a man. Since the early heady days of embracing the universe together, she had made no secret of her desires and demands; he knew as a *fait accompli* that she expected him to become her husband – would have taken him to the riotously gilded altar of any *chiesa* surrounding Lake Como and elsewhere, had he not stalled her with the advisability of being in England for such a wondrously significant and momentous occasion. He managed to persuade her not to be perplexed by his not having yet proposed but that he intended to when settlements had been reached with his family. Besides, were they not as good as married? What difference, for the duration, would the absence of a legal document make to their current idyllic nomadic life bereft of responsibilities?

In private, he admitted to himself that though their union was now to be somehow inevitable – and with it the transference of Estelle's property legally to him – he would feel more at ease being back in England with his own finger on the pulse of Porridge Island, not least on matters concerning Arthur and his whereabouts...

As the old century wintered into the new, Estelle began to talk of her increasing readiness to return; she had become such an agreeable companion that on the one hand, Alexander was reluctant to see her reinstated on home ground for fear of a return to her old oppressions. After much discussion, a sea route from Anzio was decided upon, thanks to Bonaparte's continuing presence and influence in reshaping Europe, making land-travel, particularly through France, more problematic. Alexander had wanted to take Estelle to the Bayonne district of France in order to meet some of his more influential relations – if they had survived or returned after The Terror; she, in turn, was keen to seek out Marie and Uncle Emil up in Paris and Versailles. But they were well aware that the Revolution had depleted stocks, rather – those who had escaped would come back to find a Republic determined to cancel its past – to start anew; even its calendar had not escaped, its months redesignated under such fanciful and evocative names as *Vendemiaire, Nivose, Germinal* and *Thermidor*. Better to revisit in a more stable future.

The first letter Estelle wrote to England since leaving almost forty-eight months previously was to her housekeeper, whom she hardly remembered; she set down her intentions regarding the journey back, intimating that it would be a leisurely progress from Anzio, calling at any coastal town or picturesque port of call that caught their fancy; that they would arrive back in London sometime during the early summer when, after a likely stay of an unspecified duration, they would repair to Satis.

With not a little regret they looked back from the departing boat at the *Villa Romana,* only too aware of the agent officially closing over the shutters, as if barring them suddenly any further freedom and independence in such Arcadian surroundings. Not to be denied so easily and irrevocably, the travellers employed their hired boat and small crew to cruise the dramatic and often mysterious coastline of the *Riviera di Levente* and *Riviera di Ponente,* arriving, after many stops and excursions, at Marseilles. As coincidence would have it, they were to embark on the same *Commodore* as conveyed them there in 1796.

Once in London, not wishing the commitment of using either Brook Street or Hanover Street, they prolonged their sense of carefree anonymity by taking rooms at de Boissiere's Hotel in South Audley Street – an establishment newly opened by a French *émigré* and already extending successfully into its adjoining property. From there she wrote again to Mrs Ferry that their arrival was imminent, directing that fires be lit in principal rooms, bedding aired, flowers and evergreens cascade urns and vases – everything, in fact, to which any self-respecting housekeeper would attend as a matter of course.

Mementos had already arrived – from Carrara a marble copy, with fig leaf, of Apollo Belvedere for the garden, a pair of gilt-framed canvases from Perugia glowing with Claudian romance, an assortment of blown glass from Murano, a variety of trinkets and wearing apparel, including several bolts of swan-white silk, satin and Valenciennes lace, destined for short-term storage in a lavender-sweet trunk.

Alexander complimented Mrs Ferry on Satis's immaculate state during his visit to her room in the small hours.

'Five years as nearly,' she complained, between embraces. 'How could you be away for so long? Let's have a good look at you – my, you've filled out a bit and what a good colour you are. I've missed you that much I thought I'd go mad, honestly I did. I've worked well for you, have I? – you're pleased with me?'

'Is it not obvious by my actions?' said Alexander, pulling her closer. 'When I'm pleased I don't disguise it. I'm proud of you – keep up the good work just a while longer.'

'Did you bring me anything back from your travels?'

'Myself. Judging by your obvious intent to eat me where I stand I'd have thought that sufficient. What are you hoping for?'

'Oh, I don't know – a little something to show I'd not been forgotten. I've been here on my own and you've not written once and me not knowing where you were. I could be very angry.'

'But you won't because you'll find out what I've got for you in a moment, and you'll like it. First, though, I need to know if there have been any callers asking for me – any strangers?'

'None as I know of.'

'Not Arthur Havisham – the man I showed you when you arrived?'

'Not him – not a word. Were you expecting something?'

'Nothing at all. You're absolutely certain?'

'I'd tell you if I weren't,' complained Sally, frowning. 'No strangers been here seeking you.'

'And you? How many strangers have sought *you* out?'

'Believe me, none. You've *got* to believe me, Alexander. I wouldn't do it – not now – not in this house and everything.'

'You'll have to prove it to me then,' said Alexander, rubbing his chin in mock doubt. 'If I'm satisfied I *might* believe you. Now, my dear, you'd better come here and get your present – I've been looking after it for you. It's larger than when I entered your room...'

As Estelle settled into a routine made rusty by so long an absence, she took Alexander's advice by being seen to be familiarising herself with her birthright – talking to managers, gardeners and all branches of staff – making an effort to ask questions, to look intelligently over accounts and audits as intelligible as the majority of dialects she had been amongst recently; in no time, columns of figures swam before her eyes like yeast bubbles frothing the surface of brewery vats now hers. Alexander's authoritative presence helped promote her cause – a presence not entirely lacking in self-motivation as he understood only too well a thinly disguised enthusiasm she tried to underplay for visiting the stables at the earliest opportunity. He, too, was curious to see how the passage of time had affected Hugh; as with Estelle, he noted the groom's maturity with approbation, but unlike her was able to appear outwardly impassive – not for him the less sure pitch of the voice nor even the merest tell-tale twitch of the eye. Glad to have familiarised himself with the current situation concerning what he considered to be his competition, he talked with her about his need to go back to London – not for pleasure now, but to catch up on business: see his lawyer, see his banker; he would stay at de Boissiere's Hotel rather than Hanover Street before going on to Rookwell to discuss further business with his father. He let her talk to him about the wedding and its complicated preparation; her most original stroke was to declare that she wished it to take place on her next birthday – January 31st, 1801. He made no objection, delighting in her prospect of a double celebration.

Some days later, as he approached The Bargee Joe's fitful October lights, Hungerford Market's familiar territory reminded him of Neapolitan slums. His first sight, in The Cap'n's back room, was of Peg-leg's wooden appendage strapped firmly to its stump, projecting obliquely from his chair to upset the unwary as he sat at cards with Croak the schoolmaster, a few less teeth ranged inquisitively over his bottom lip before his well-thumbed flush. With conspiratorial intensity, The Cap'n and a fourth squared off the table.

'I apologise for being late, gentlemen,' announced Mr Fleece, making himself at home with wine. 'I trust the stakes are high. It'd be a shame for such talent to be wasted on trivia.'

'*Achilles absent was Achilles still,* as Homer said,' croaked the schoolmaster, looking up. 'Having plundered the land and ploughed the sea he returns victorious to his comrades.'

The Cap'n swung his singular eye into the harbour of Mr Fleece's vision. 'Welcome aboard, Sir. I take it all is ship-shape an' Bris'ol fashion to your 'onour's likin'?'

'That awaits the outcome of our speaking together,' replied Mr Fleece, darkly, 'though it makes my heart bleed to disrupt such edifying proceedings. I'll wager for a start that Peg-leg has an ace snuggling under that meaty backside of his.' Before guilt or innocence could be proved, Mr Fleece took The Cap'n out to a candlelit table between two high-backed settles in a private corner of the public room.

'You can guess my mission, no doubt.' Mr Fleece opened one of his little ready bags. 'A certain young gentleman from Kent... he's not here?'

'Nor 'e 'aint,' replied The Cap'n, his good eye charmed by the coins his interrogator lined along a crack on the board before him. "'E's beyond the reach of sich as I.'

'Dead?'

'Might be. As I reckon, the Fleet's no place for the livin'.'

So. Arthur had got himself in debtors' prison. Mr Fleece pushed the money slowly forward. 'Information,' he hissed. 'Begin at the beginning. I brought him here…'

'Like you did, Sir, an' no mistake. A young gen'leman if ever there wos one. You'd 'ardly been gone a whistle's squeak afore 'e 'ad some sort o' fit – coffin' 'e were an' all at sea, askin' fur a Mister Cumpissn or sitchlike, who we'd never 'eard of. "*Alexander, Alexander,*" 'e sez again an' again, like a babby wot's lost its chew, but we takes no notice on account of 'is confusions, like, as wot you sez 'e wos strange an' to pay no 'eed. That 'is 'ead wos aching somethin' chronic he sez so we doses 'im up wi' brandy an' 'e's sick… wot a time we 'ave wi' 'im. An' at night too, 'is landlord sez, in Maiden Lane – near woke the dead with 'is shriekin' an' a'ollerin' an' a-wailin' as if 'e were goin' off through 'ell an' 'igh water.'

'Had a woman all in white come to put a shroud on him?'

'The same exact. Next night 'e wos in 'ere pointin' 'er out so's we could see, only we coul'n't, or the blood neither. I tell you 'onest – it were the colour o' your 'onour's money wot kept us with 'im – but for that 'e would soonest be in Bedlam and the neighbour'ood the peacefuller for it.'

'I left you well paid for your hospitality, let me remind you,' said Mr Fleece, 'and your silence, which I'm glad to know you kept. I am happy to recompense you for any damage to your nerves. What do you know of his employment?'

"E's 'ad that,' resumed The Cap'n, wreathing his narrative in tobacco smoke which threatened to suffocate the candle. 'Work for this printer, 'e did – drawin' an' the like – estirical cartoons for laughin' at – them wot understands 'em. Paid 'is rent reg'lar as the night watch – never a complaint on passin' over 'is shiners. Nor for a bottle or two when th' mood were on 'im, which wos of'en. Then 'e took to lodgin' in Little Windmill Street along 'is friend Mr Abel. They got into scrapes, as I 'eard, durin' sober moments, by which time your young gent wos out of 'is job and soon in the Fleet. But not afore Mr Abel wos tenantin' Newgate agin along wi' Filcher Nick an' Swift Ned whose neck strained the rope a bit back, to the delight of 'is adorin' public.'

'I was not aware Mr Abel and the young gentleman were at all acquainted,' lied Mr Fleece. 'What was their game?'

'A good crib is The Bargee Joe – it 'as a 'appy way of bringin' souls together – nice an' friendly like. They takes to each other, y'might say, in a money-making matter, meanin' to set up a *pardnership* they calls it, before they wos casted away from eyes o'man 'n' beast.'

'Moneymaking? How? Investment? Lending?'

'Drawin', I suppose. You draws y'money, then y'spends it – if it looks real enough. They made a deal o'work together, them two, 'im bein' good at drawin'.'

'Forgery, you mean?'

'In a word, morelike. Only they 'aint time to forge as much as they owed. Mr Abel –'e jest 'elps 'iself to wot 'e fancies, but you woul'n't get your young gent doin' the same...'

Mr Fleece's eyes narrowed. *Arthur and Magwitch. A partnership? And both careless enough to get themselves into prison.* His first inclination was to let Arthur remain – he was well out of the way, even if not actually dead. But what of Magwitch on his release? It would be only a matter of time before he came looking for his partner – asking Mr Fleece why he had not effected his release; his anger could well get the better of him – as unpredictable a character as Magwitch ought not to be underestimated.

'Mr Arthur's debt,' he resumed. 'I don't doubt you know its value, and to whom?'

The Cap'n picked at his nose. 'Funny y'should mention that as I *do* 'appen to know 'is landlady's a bit on the pressin' side o'eleven shillin', not menshunin' a schooly individu'l not a yardarm from 'ere as might be grateful for to get 'is winnin's eventual in 'is edicated paw, though it weren't 'im as got Mister Arthur to the Fleet.'

'Croak's feeling the pinch, is he?' said Mr Fleece. 'I can see I must transact a little business with him. As to the remaining sum – eleven shillings you say? – I suggest you supply it to the right quarter from the coinage you've so eagerly just taken charge of. At the same time, be good enough to arrange for Mr Arthur's release and for him to be brought to the following address in, say, four day's time.' In the candle flame he blackened a cork from a nearby wine bottle and printed on the table top: TUDOR COTTAGE, BRENTFORD.

''Appy to oblige you further,' said The Cap'n, running his eye along the sooty information. 'Felt sorry for the young gent, I did, seein' 'as 'e wos not right in the 'ead. If I ever sees a body with the 'orrors on 'im, then that's it an' no mistake.'

'Most regrettable, indeed,' Mr Fleece tutted, wiping the table clean with a swift hand. 'There is simply no saving some souls in this world. One can only hope that providence will take care of them in the next. Now – to Mr Adolphus. I have business with him. When can he be expected?'

'Why, Lor' bless y'Worship, y'won't be knowin' 'ow it is with *that* young gent. It could be said 'e's lost 'is 'eart.'

'To a lady?'

'To a pistol ball – waddin' an' all. Shot through, it wos, on 'Ampstead 'Eath, just as the sun come up.'

'You mean a duel?'

'Aye a jewel – near the Vale of 'Ealth, only 'e lost 'is.'

'Come on, man, tell me straight.'

'It wos a gent like 'iself – not one of our crew – one 'e got across at Covent Garden Theatre, over money. Mister Adolphus – 'e were blacked in front of a full 'ouse so chose to make a stand for 'is 'onour, only 'e fell. It were a shame as 'e were a treat to Mister Arthur when 'e come back from across the sea – the only one of us wot could 'andle 'im when 'e got screwy, like.'

Alexander's eyes misted. He had been anticipating sharing his amorous adventures with his old comrade-in-arms, an equal since early days; he had also wanted to relive with him their own Grand Tour – Adolphus had always been liberal in his attitude and broad-minded to Alexander's sometimes more individual attentions; he would be missed.

'I'll see Croak,' said Alexander, quietly. 'Send him here.'

Anticipating repayment, the worthy schoolmaster soon appeared, writhing one sinewy hand expectantly in the other; he seated himself, raising his portcullis of teeth to send forth an appropriate quotation.

'I have one for you,' interposed Mr Fleece, with a gesture. *'It's the scrawniest hen that soonest feels the fox's teeth on its bones.* Do you know who composed that? I did. Your neck looks none too plump to me.'

'Then again, good sir,' said Croak, with a smug grin, 'the scrawniest hen would surely be beneath the fox's contempt.'

Mr Fleece smiled sourly. 'I advise you not to attempt being over-clever with me, for all your knowledge. I am a scholar also, I would remind you. And – what is more – a Gentleman. It's about another Gentleman I wish to consult you. I understand he has become indebted to you?'

'Would I could deny it,' said Croak, placing his hand effectively on his greasy coat-front. 'Alas, life's golden apples are few and far between to pluck – one needs to keep one's hand prepared in case of any chance journey to the Garden of the Hesperides.'

'I suggest it will be Tartarus for you, more-like, if you continue to covet this particular apple once I've plucked it for you – I'll find it no trouble to arrange for every serpent and dragon you ever imagined to join up with Ladon in defending the bounteous tree. I shall provide you with your apple on Mr Arthur's behalf – will these two silver snuff boxes now enable you to abandon the tree?'

The schoolmaster grasped the trinkets, turning them again and again in his fingers as a spider winds silk about its prey. 'Superior quality,' he reflected, letting them gleam in his eyes.

'For a superior intellect. I've no doubt Heracles would have agreed that no one with your wisdom ought to refuse. That is settled then. I now propose that those apples also purchase information concerning our mutual friend.'

'Heracles or Atlas? Or do I jest out of turn?'

'Mr Arthur and yes you do. I'm anxious to know what was in his mind regarding his appraisal of a certain Mr Compeyson who delivered him here into his new life in London. I cannot imagine that he was not discussed over your evenings cheating one another round the card tables of the underworld.'

'He spoke warmly of Mr Compeyson and of his help and friendship in many matters he'd not understood; but he appeared confused and didn't seem to know Mr Fleece at all. Would you be surprised to learn,' said Croak, lowering his voice, 'that our mutual friends Mr Compeyson and Mr Fleece are spoken of in the same breath? And that certain factors pertaining to both cause certain interest in certain quarters?'

'But not for certain outside these trusted walls, I trust?'

'Walls have ears, you can trust to that,' warned Croak, clanging the snuff-boxes in his pocket together like an alarm. 'Perhaps you will decide to inform Mr Compeyson, when next he chooses to reveal himself, that his *and* Mr Fleece's secrets are safe at The Bargee Joe – and for the want of continued apples, always will be. I know I speak on behalf of The Cap'n.'

'And so eloquently. Mr Compeyson will, indeed, be mightily relieved to know he can trust to your confidences,' said Mr Fleece, preparing to leave, 'as I also am. You will find neither ungenerous to those who continue to turn a blind eye. Emulate our worthy Captain is my advice. A very good night.'

Once alone, Croak shifted to Mr Fleece's side of the table and tried in vain to decipher the three sooty words irredeemably disfigured by his late associate's trusty hand.

At Tudor Cottage, four days later, a whiskered being, thin and as grey as November fog, sat beside the parlour fireplace. Though he did not sleep his eyes were closed, as if the dark rings beneath them hung too heavily on their mechanism. Mr Fleece could not prevent his own eyes from returning over again to the sight before him, lately delivered from Farringdon Street by The Cap'n's men in a hired carriage.

'Bad off 'e is, Sir,' one of them informed him during payment. 'Warders sed as 'ow 'e's bin wus of late an' a disturbin' influ'nce in the 'appy 'ome – turnkey fair pushed 'im owt sayin' wot gladness to 'ave 'im goin' from where 'e should never've bin put in fust place.'

Mr Fleece said that the gentleman would now be taken care of, and would have been sooner had not an enforced absence on his own part have not detained him abroad. With a message to The Cap'n that he would soon attend upon him, he ushered the men out. Pulling up a chair he sat opposite Arthur, encouraging him to converse, patting his hands, saying his name as he opened his eyes.

'I'm glad to see you again, Alexander. Why have you left me so long?'

'It was necessary, Arthur. But I'm back now and won't see you left again.' Throughout the evening, he learned, by degrees, that he had not been ill-treated, nor confined to his room on the double-chambered gallery known as the Third Flight. The noise of his nocturnal fears had dealt him a kindly hand by ensuring that for the majority of his three-year internment, no inmate had been anxious to share with him or put up with his cough when he became agitated.

Those times when feeling well and not hounded by migraine, had provided opportunities to observe life around him; those inmates vaguely mooching the lengthy galleries and staircases; those crammed six to a room and three to a bed; those permanently immersed in sickly yellow tallow light rearing large families; those permanently fighting over hands of cards and littering every ungenerous corner with brawling and blood. Then there had been those outdoors, working off their energies with low-flung force against impassive nine-pins or on the gravelled racquets court footing the towering spike-topped wall over which crept, like escaping prisoners, sounds from an uncertain world outside.

Before he had become compelled to sell first his drawings, then pencils, then drawing books, for the price of liquor, Arthur had committed all he saw to line, light and shade, trying with his waning powers to capture the very essence of activity and inactivity around him: groans of the drunken and beaten, restless comings and goings, bangings of endless doors, shoutings, cryings, moanings...

'You abandoned me,' he said suddenly. 'I trusted you and you betrayed me when I needed you.'

'You were not abandoned, Arthur – simply left to find yourself, and I don't mean find yourself in goal.'

'Magwitch said you paid my debt by giving him the salver at Satis. But you blamed me for stealing it.'

'You're absolutely right, but you have to understand that it was all part of a plan to protect you from him and to convince Estelle she was justified in wanting you gone by buying you out. Your freedom was part of the plan...'

'You're always talking about plans. Everything involves plans. Do you ever do anything that *isn't* part of a plan? They said at The Bargee Joe you're to be feared – that you stop at nothing to get your own way – Magwitch too. I didn't want to believe them because you were the friend I've always known and trusted. But then I suddenly didn't know who my friend was any more – Compeyson or Fleece? Fleece or Compeyson?'

'You are fortunate – you know them both and both will serve you well, if you let them. Only Fleece is known at The Bargee Joe – it harbours raw fellows used to life's basic ways and happy to make a quick shilling. You and I can do that, if you put your mind to it and let me help you.'

'You being Fleece or Compeyson?'

'Alexander, dear boy. That's who. Like old times. You and me. Not you and Magwitch – he's far too rough for you. And he's a criminal. Listen. You learned to engrave with Gillray – work a press – print a plate?'

'Of course,' said Arthur,' and I was getting better but didn't know where my money went...'

'That doesn't matter now. And you did some work with Magwitch?'

'He stole me some printing equipment and talked about a partnership but I became ill again...' Arthur settled back in his chair, accepting the drink he was offered. 'We were going to make money – lots of it.'

'What happened to the equipment?' asked Alexander, after a pause.

'I don't know. I went to the Fleet and now I'm here.'

'And here you shall stay,' said Alexander. 'I'll come and go but you'll be safe. Eventually we shall decide what's to be done. What I can *promise* you is that I shan't let you go a second time.'

As a further week progressed at Tudor Cottage, Alexander came to realise, by careful attention to Arthur's unstable state, that any sort of partnership with him would be a positive hazard, particularly where the art and craft of foolproof forgery was concerned. In the meantime, he had enlisted, through the Cap'n's services, a well-worn but suitable Mrs Wormold, lately an attendant in the Foundling Hospital, Coram Fields, to live-in and look after Arthur. She commenced her duties the day Alexander departed after persuading Arthur not to fret, assuring him that he would return. He left instructions with her that she address any written communication she may need to make to the care of his lawyer, Mr Sharps in Holborn.

As he rode to London on a horse hired from The Ferry and Flood, he pondered on Arthur's state. The week had not been easy, the patient comfortable but proving difficult at times, at others, affectionate and trusting, quite like the old days. Alexander had even felt encouraged enough to buy him paper and pencils which were soon put to good use, with an occasional return of former skill. But the more he approached the working metropolis's concentrated seriousness, the more he doubted any long-term or sustained ability on his would-be partner's part, that could make him a viable proposition in any plan aspiring to success; Alexander found it increasingly easy to view him, in fact, as a liability – even a threat; he acknowledged, with sadness in his heart, how this philosophy had dug into his subconscious early in their friendship, no matter how he had tried to evade it. But now it seemed to be proving itself well founded. Within a few weeks, then, he would know if his promise of not letting him go a second time would have to be kept.

Stabling his horse at The Golden Cross, he hired a gig, making straight for his sharp-nosed lawyer whom he instructed to redirect any communications from Brentford for Mr Fleece not to The Blue Boar but a more distant public house, The Three Jolly Bargemen, situated in one of the marsh villages some safer distance from Satis House, from where they would be collected. On his return to de Boissiere's, he found that during his absence at Tudor Cottage, a terse note from his father had been delivered, asking him to call at Hanover Street on immediate receipt of receiving it. His mind racing, his heart pounding, he crossed Grosvenor Square, passed Estelle's house in Brook Street and entered Hanover Square. He and his father had not met for nigh on five years; at the threshold he apprehensively greeted Pritchard, the steward, who informed him that Mr Compeyson was at work in the back study. As his father turned from his paper-littered desk, he was quick to see that the once familiar healthy complexion reflecting his love of break-neck gallops about Hampshire had vacated his features; shaded rings puffing his eyes, evidence of lack of sleep, over-compensated for the sense of unexpected submission loitering in the air. He stared momentarily at his son as if he were an apparition from the grave.

'Hello, Papa. How are you? I was about to set off for Rookwell when I received your note.'

Mr Compeyson held his shoulders. 'My boy... I hardly recognised you. You're a stranger to me.' He hugged him close. 'It's good to see you again. I called at Satis on the way here – Estelle said you were at de Boissiere's. Were you on your way to Rookwell for money?'

'To see *you,* Papa, and Mama and the girls. Are they here?'

'Your Mama is at Rookwell, Alexander, the girls married. Mama is unwell – I am unwell – all is unwell.'

'I don't understand.'

'No, how could you? You have not been in touch for a long time.'

'Talk to me, Papa, for heaven's sake – come to the fire and talk'

'Not for *heaven's* sake,' said Mr Compeyson, slumping wearily. 'For *your* sake, surely? Everything I have tried to do has been for your sake, your Mama's and sisters'. You knew something, I believe, of the problems when you went away. I have been extravagant, Alexander – made unwise investments – lent too freely – trusted too liberally – borrowed too emphatically... even gambled once in a while. I have let your mother down with my mismanagement. I supplied monies for her family... the Revolution did the economy no favours and I love your mother...' He covered his face with his hands. Awkwardly, Alexander drew his chair to his father's, putting his hands on his. 'The girls have been taken care of – I saw they brought respectable sums to their marriages. But your Mama is not well and I have been to blame.'

'How can I help?'

'You could have written – come to see us – let me discuss matters with you as my only son – by not spending our money abroad.'

'It *wasn't* your money – it was Estelle's.'

'Exactly. It wasn't *yours*.'

'You give me my allowance.'

'And what do you do to earn it? I blame myself for being soft with you. You have never done anything in this life you haven't wanted to do; you've never listened to anything you haven't wanted to hear. You succeed, and always will, by personable looks, charm, a glib tongue and self-importance. It's not entirely your fault – I can see that... your Mama spoiled you and your sisters flattered you. And I... what did I do? Indulge you, along with the rest. But... despite all this... you *are* my son... and I love you...'

Alexander poured them both a large glass of port wine, putting one in his father's shaking hand and steadying it for him.

'Never fear,' he continued, after a sip or two. 'My creditors will be paid off, if it's the last thing I do. I'm in town to discuss matters with our lawyers... our secrets are theirs at last.'

'Secrets, Papa?'

'That it is largely your Mama's money which is involved. Well may you look surprised – you were not to know, but now you must. When I was courting your Mama I was not in love with her – I was in love with her capital. I had none to speak of, nor was I sophisticated, though I think I was passing fair enough to turn a pretty head my way. It was you Mama's generosity which bought Rookwell, the horses, the friends. I wanted money to work for us and at first it did. But then it seemed to get out of hand but I always thought I could win it back. My management – or should I say *mis*management – inevitably brought us to this low point. But it isn't impossible to surmount the problems... the lease on this house and St James's Square is sold – I'm hoping to get a good price for Rookwell, its acreage and stock.'

'Where will you live?' asked Alexander, swallowing hard. 'In London?'

'Too expensive. Your Mama is perfectly content with a small attractive property we've engaged in Winchester – Little Minster Street, overlooking the Cathedral and Close – most pleasant and snug, where we shall be able to save on servants. She's looking forward to giving up Rookwell's damp and draughts I think.'

Alexander tried to sound detached and businesslike. 'Would it be feasible to retain Rookwell but let it for a good rental on the open market?'

'You *mind* the Estate going, don't you, my lad? Quite a symbol of your status in life, I imagine. Very well – *you* pay for the re-roofing of the east wing – the rot in the servants' attics – the upkeep of the tenants' cottages. I would welcome it.'

Alexander stared into the fire, the only comfort at this bleak moment. 'You say you went down to Satis?' he ventured, after an uncomfortable silence. 'Did you see Estelle?'

'I saw Estelle. She looked as well as you. You are obviously good for one another.'

'Does she know anything of this?'

'Don't you mean that if she did, she might withdraw her favour? You can't pretend with me, Alexander – I know you too well – you have your share of Compeyson weakness too, don't forget. She will never know because you will never tell her. Am I right, or are these the ramblings of a demented old fool?'

'Papa, I intend to marry Estelle.'

'Then I suggest you do it sooner rather than later – before she finds out. Believe me, women have a nose for these things. Be warned.'

'She wants it to be on her birthday next January. Will you come?'

'Of course. I won't ask if you love her.'

'Oh yes,' Alexander replied, rather too emphatically. 'And her me.'

'Then you're a lucky man – love *and* money in one catch. She will save you from destitution in a way we can't.' Mr Compeyson stood up with open arms. 'Now come to your stupid, weak Papa and give him a hug – tell him he's forgiven.'

As sobs welled in Alexander's chest, he sank his face into his father's coat, clinging to him like the prodigal son. He smelled of Rookwell, its comforts, its nostalgia, its kindness. He heard his father say, 'go and see your Mama – she'd be so comforted – she deserves your consideration more than I.'

'Of course,' murmured Alexander, crying like a five-year-old...

He spent three days at Rookwell before returning to Satis. As anticipated, the visit was not without emotion on both sides. Though older and more careworn, his Mama retained a wistful stoic beauty, reminiscent of the Park's late autumn leaves, as he watched their dying glory enrich their fall.

Estelle fairly flew down the staircase to meet him as he set foot inside Satis House. She hurried him into the library, barely allowing him time to pass through the door before shutting it. 'Your Papa came here on his way to London,' she said. breathlessly. 'It was lovely seeing him again but he looked ill, I thought. He wanted to talk to you – I said you were already there on business. Did you meet up?'

'We've been together in Hanover Street.'

'You look worried, my dear. Is anything amiss? Your Papa seemed not himself.'

'Everything is perfectly fine, only Mama is not well. I've just visited her at Rookwell – I shall have to see her again before too long. I expect he was as worried as I am, that's all.'

'I'm so sorry. Such a lovely lady. Of course you must see her. I'm sorry to add to your worries, but I have a little matter you must sort out for me. Such goings-on here whilst you've been gone. I can't run the house, what with her poorly.'

'Estelle. Sit down. Tell me calmly. Who is poorly?'

'Mrs Ferry. She went off to bed after the business with the scissors and hasn't got up since and won't see Dr. Sawley. That was days ago!'

'Business with *what* scissors?' said Alexander despairingly.

'My fruit scissors. I don't know if you remember them but they used to live in the dining room – silver – beautifully designed out of vine leaves and grapes – very expensive. It was one of our valuables that went missing before we went to Italy. Remember?'

'Go on.' said Alexander, the hairs on the back of his beautiful neck beginning to bristle.

'Well, I found her with them while you were away. I had to go in her room one morning because she'd been sick and I saw them on her table – I knew them instantly because one of the points was slightly blunt where Arthur had…'

'Estelle…'

'I said, *what are you doing with my scissors, Mrs Ferry? Excuse me, Madam, they're mine,* she says, not too poorly to argue, *they were a present.* I said, *they belong to me,* to make it plainer, *and match the epergne in the dining room. We thought they'd been stolen.* She said, *I don't know anything about them being stolen – they were a present. Present from whom?* I persisted, but she wouldn't tell me – was just sick again, all over the carpet, and it was a good one. Naturally I took the scissors and she's been in bed ever since. The servants are coping remarkably well at the moment.'

'Let me see her,' suggested Alexander, forcing a dry swallow. *What a foolish blunder; but how was she to know?* 'You probably frightened her without meaning to, Estelle – woman to woman like that. I'm sure if they *are* the same – and it seems incredible they could be – she's probably found them somewhere. She certainly didn't steal them, take my word for it.'

Sally was not asleep when he entered. She had heard his return and waited hopefully.

'I've been that frightened,' she wept. 'You've got to help me. Where did those scissors come from? She thinks *I stole them.* I've done nothing wrong.'

'Sally, Sally,' soothed Alexander. 'I've told Miss Havisham you're not a thief and she believes it. You're quite safe'

'It was you. I knew it – that's why I didn't let on. Why did you get me a job in the place you took them from? That wasn't very bright.'

'Don't criticise me,' Alexander hissed through clenched teeth, momentarily nonplussed but improvising wildly. 'I shall say one of the servants who left here gave you the trinket when she came to work at your previous situation.'

'With Sir Reynard Fox-Huntingden.'

'In far off Yorkshire, yes. She'll believe me and soon dismiss the whole affair, so get up, there's a good girl, and go about your work as if nothing had happened.'

'I can get up,' said Sally, drying her tears, 'but I can't go about as if nothing had happened.'

'Why ever not,' Alexander said, sternly. 'You're only drawing attention to yourself lying here.'

'Alexander... I think I'm with child.'

She's wrong, of course, he thought. *She's been wrong in the past. The doctor told her she couldn't have children.*

'I'm not wrong this time,' she pleaded, 'I know it. It feels different.'

'Is it the ferry boy from Brentford?' he said, at a loss, 'or Hugh the groom, perhaps?'

'I swear on my mother's grave...'

'Be thankful you're not swearing on yours.' Alexander became calmer. 'How long?'

'Since your first night back. Please hold me – you'd have been pleased once.'

'Let me think... let me think what is to be done... you'll have to go back to Brentford... get rid of it... there's a housekeeper there at present looking after Mr Arthur... you three can look after each other. Yes, that's it – I'll organise something – Mrs Wormold will help – and you must do as I say without question. You must allow the doctor to examine you – pronounce your condition. Miss Havisham will have to accept your resignation.'

'But how will you explain about the father?' said Sally, drying her tears a second time.

'Leave the father to me.'

'I must be looked after, Alexander. I've been on my own too long...'

As Alexander expected, Dr. Sawley's diagnosis could not have caused Estelle more surprise had he discovered her waxen head. 'A child?' she repeated, as if it were customary for women to expect octopuses. 'You're sure?'

'I should estimate about two months gone,' said the doctor. 'She's young and hardy, but one can never be absolutely certain.'

Once he had departed, Alexander was able to say, 'I have the full story from Mrs Ferry. I hesitate to impart it to you because of the pain I think it'll cause you.'

'Why in the world should it? I'm sorry for her, naturally – was it one of the servants?'

'I suppose you could call him that. They have been seeing rather a lot of one another – in more ways than one – as is now evident. It seems you are not the only person attracted by... what shall we call it... a certain beauty of face and limb? I was not, you understand, completely impervious to your appreciation of Italian *ragazzi,* I think.'

'Alexander, what *are* you trying to tell me? Yes, I appreciate beauty, which is why I appreciate you.'

'You would agree that Hugh is beautiful?'

'Hugh? Out in the stables?' She paused. 'Oh...! no... you can't mean...'

'I thought it might cause you pain, my dear, and I'm sorry. He's a lovely man, that's true. You're not alone in thinking so.'

Estelle put her hands to her burning cheeks. 'He's been here since we were children,' she whispered. 'His father's dead now. I've known him all my life...'

'And admired him all your life?'

'You're not jealous, are you, Alexander?'

'Far from it – and please don't stint yourself of feelings on my account, Estelle. I know why this upsets you so and I understand. I could be disposed to feel the same, if I was similarly attached.'

'But,' she pleaded, 'I've never *loved* Hugh – not as I love you. He may be pleasant to look at – to be with – but that's all. How can you think such things of me, my love?'

'Then it's good you've been able to resist his advances; but that's what I'd expect of you, my Bright Star – poor Mrs Ferry was not so lucky.'

Bright Star. Estelle wept at hearing again her father's name for her, spoken by her *fiancé* at such an emotional moment. He told her that with her permission, Hugh would have to be dealt with as he saw fit. Mrs Ferry also, would be taken care of – with his many contacts a replacement housekeeper could soon be found.

Sad at heart as Estelle felt that evening, it was fortunate she decided to retire to bed earlier than usual; through pondering, with conflicting emotions, the image of the gentle groom whose physicality had helped open windows on herself as a woman, she was spared knowledge of his immediate eviction at the personal hands of her future husband. How Hugh was hustled from his room into the yard at gun-point, his few possessions flung after him, and told that thanks to Miss Havisham's Christian nature, he would be spared what fate rightfully awaited him. Furthermore, that if he dared return on any pretext, he would be torn to shreds by the dogs. Distraught, almost incoherent, the lantern illuminating a handsome face now disfigured enough with pain to satisfy his persecutor, he begged the opportunity to protest his innocence to Miss Havisham. But Alexander forced him into the lane, throwing him down in the mire. He slammed shut the gate against him, but not before leaving him squirming in agony as he booted his rival a personal comment between the legs.

* * *

Mr Fleece, having instructed Mr Sharps to withdraw some of his accruing capital, presented the Mistress of Satis seventy of her own pounds, telling her that it represented the remainder of Hugh's business transactions over purloined snuff-boxes and other valuables, including the gold and enamel *etui*. He further requested Mr Sharps to arrange for a well-sprung carriage to be sent to Satis House on the following Monday at ten o'clock in the morning, to convey a lady in a delicate condition to Brentford. He also wrote a letter of explanation to Mrs Wormold which he required Sally to deliver on arrival.

As far as her replacement was concerned, Estelle, when consulted, was in agreement with Alexander enquiring of Old Jaggers; an immediately efficient reply recommended the sister of the housekeeper he and his son employed at their house in Gerrard Street, Soho. Within the week, Mrs Hall arrived – a dedicated, bustly sort of individual intent on working diligently towards middle-age; she brought an uncanny aura of industry, evoking in Alexander's mind, multifarious windings of activity in and around Little Britain's many shuffly ginnels.

As December brought the first light pepperings of snow and salty winds hustling in from the east, Alexander informed his *fiancée* he felt duty-bound to spend his last Christmas as a single man at Rookwell out of courtesy to his sick Mama, pleading her malady as an excuse for not including Estelle. Though not enamoured of the idea, she accepted Alexander's dedication as further proof of his sterling character. One evening, enjoying the library fire, they fell to talking over the forthcoming wedding, the guests who had been invited, the bride cake being created to a French recipe in their own bakehouse; Mrs Hall's efficiency in interpreting her mistress's wishes and instructions.

Arthur's old rooms opposite Estelle's boudoir had been redecorated most handsomely, her dislike of the dining room downstairs encouraging her to use the larger as the banquet room for the wedding breakfast. Her dress, already cut and loosely stitched by Mrs Needler from the marble-white silks and satins brought from Italy adorned a dummy in the sewing room – a guarded secret from Alexander until the *moment just*. She talked through the new *trousseau* she intended acquiring in the latest fashion during their imminent visit to London – she wished to be worthy of Queen Antoinette herself; the return visits to *La Casa del Mulino* and *Villa Romana*; the improvements to be made at Brook Street... Alexander could only agree and continue to offer his help and support whilst engaged in some quick thinking. He told her that St James's Square and Hanover Street were out of commission due to renovation... oh dear, there seemed so much to cocoon her from until after the wedding, not least the rumours circulating amongst the staff regarding the manner of Hugh's dismissal. Some diversion in town could be an advantage.

'If only my Papa could have been spared to see me escorted by my husband back from the church,' said Estelle sadly. 'It would have been the moment of his life. Look at the clock, Alexander – twenty minutes to nine – it will always have special significance for me, reminding me of talking here, in this room, with the one I love, about our future together... and with so much happiness and success to look forward to. Oh, how I'd like to stop time at this one moment and enjoy it for as long as I want! Do you ever feel the same, my dear?'

'I'd rather keep time on the move – I like change – it makes for more freedom.'

For part of their time in London, during which Estelle descended on every shop of fashion, and as many people and places as possible, Alexander dutifully accompanied her hither and thither. He fully appreciated her patronage and never, for one moment, appeared as anything but the fine-looking possession she so proudly and lovingly displayed. They had taken rooms at de Boissiere's again, rather than having cheerless Brook Street specially opened up and staffed so late in the year when there was such an amount to do at Satis. It was easier in South Audley Street's more neutral surroundings for him to insist that he, also, had matters of importance to attend to and that she did not question his possibly erratic hours. Good at her word, she made no attempt to pry into what he did not choose to tell her.

A few days before Christmas, Estelle reluctantly but bravely bade her young Apollo *adieu* in the festive yard of The Cross Keys, Cheapside, as she boarded the four horse stagecoach eager to be off at the horn's barking wail. Wishing him a happy time with his family in Hampshire and exchanging sentiments of love and contentment, she spent the journey anticipating the jostle of boxes and packages which, thanks to Alexander's efficiency, had been delivered to Satis and awaited her – new trunks and *portmanteaux* also. Time would be of no consequence as she strutted before her mirrors reviewing her finery, directing Zilla and Mrs Needler just to straighten a stitch here or tighten a tuck there. Nothing, from the most puffed turban bestraddled with pearl chains and ostrich plumes to the merest lace-bordered handkerchief monogrammed in crimson silk, would edge out of her attention. Estelle Havisham... Estelle Havisham... her name's rhythm beat out in her thoughts, lulling her asleep as it transformed itself into Estelle Havisham - Compeyson... Estelle Compeyson... Estelle de Bayonne - Compeyson...

* * *

Left to himself at last, Mr Fleece headed straight for the snug of The Cross Keys, where he ordered a shilling mutton steak and enough liquor to lubricate the machinations of his mind. He found it impossible not to be somewhat gratified by knowing that he continued to make a favourable impression – he who graced the drawing rooms of society as naturally as he did the gaming rooms of Covent Garden or the fetid 'rookeries' of St. Giles. His versatility acquired an added *frisson* when he took into account what he had achieved whilst in Estelle's innocent company: a visit to Dame Clap's four-postered shrine to Eros in Lisle Street, hard by Leicester Fields; the casual involvement in the shadows of Temple Bar one night, with a willing young fellow fresh to London ways, but as personable as Hugh, who would not have missed his money bag until needing to pay for a late supper at Clifton's Chop House in The Strand; a call at Henry Wadell's Rat Pit at Clerkenwell, to bet and cheer as the terrified vermin, streaking across the planking or piled in frenzied mountains at each inescapable corner, fell in bleeding numbers to prize terriers with prices on their teeth.

But now that Mr Fleece was his own master again, he removed himself from de Boissiere's, renting a pair of rooms in Shug Lane off Piccadilly, from where he hastened to The Bargee Joe that evening to see The Cap'n who, astute as ever, greeted him with, 'does 'im wi' one eye who knows a gent wi' two take on board trouble below decks?'

Taking the drink offered, Alexander welcomed his rough but reliable kind of concern — all that was available now Mr Adolphus had become lost to him. 'Mr Fleece is troubled by an acquaintance of his — a Mr Compeyson — another gentleman like himself. He is to be married.'

''Earty congratulations to the 'appy bridegroom — or do I spy it as not bein' a time for double rations all round?'

'You may as well know the truth of it, Captain. Mr Fleece feels he is drowning on Mr Compeyson's behalf — he feels cornered, like Wadell's rats. Mr Compeyson stands to gain handsomely by his union but is finding it a strain trying to time events as he wishes — too many cannon balls in the firing line at once, you understand; his Mama is ill, his family undergoing hardship, his complex plans a burden because his bride-to-be must remain in ignorance of so much, quite apart. Mr Fleece must intervene and sort things out.'

'But Mr Fleece — 'e always sorts things out — never one to balk at plans and plots as'll be right for th' place or person.'

'With your assistance, Captain, as Mr Fleece relies on your counsel. One stumbling block in Mr Compeyson's matters concerns Mr Arthur. What is to be done with him?'

'A lost soul if ever I clapped mi good eye on one. But there's those, beggin' your 'onour's pardon, who *would* 'ave 'im rescued, instead of leavin' 'im to nat'ral causes in The Fleet.'

'His rescue was necessary. Mr Abel needed placating, having been his one-time associate and partner. I also anticipated, wrongly as it has subsequently transpired, that Mr Arthur might have made *me* a suitable partner... what shall we call it... artistic money matters? But in the light of this forthcoming marriage, such a partnership is now totally redundant.'

The Cap'n nodded, puffing at his stumpy clay pipe.

'Mr Fleece's *protégé*,' said Alexander, 'and Mr Compeyson's bride are related, you see.'

'As are Mr Fleece an' Mr Cumpissn.'

'Precisely. Each one is being played off against the other with the idea of making money – and it may yet be achieved – but Mr Arthur remains as the weakness – he is too unpredictable to be safe.'

Moving closer, The Cap'n said, 'let me get mi ear within firin' range. Does Mr Fleece an' Mr Cumpissn see Mister Arthur as wot'd be termed a *threat* – like this Frenchie Boneypart?'

'Not a threat – not even a hindrance – *if extreme care to remove him is taken*. Fleece and Compeyson now agree on that.'

The Cap'n nodded, knowingly. ''Indrances 'ave a way of bein' washed out to sea, though... specially if they can't swim.'

'And talking of hindrances... there is another who might wish Fleece and Compeyson washed out to sea if he found Mr Arthur was in deep water with anchors round his feet.'

''Im as took 'im for a pardner – 'im as might be termed Abel-bodied?'

'Exactly. He must be kept sweet at *all costs*. Take my word for it – there's a ruthless streak in him best left untried. I mean, do *you* want your heart and liver tore out, roast and ate? Neither do I – or Fleece and Compeyson.'

'When 'as The Cap'n ever let either of 'em down? Instructions given is instructions acted upon. Will it be Puddle Creek or the Specific Ocean?'

'Neither at present. I shall be absent over Christmas but here again in the New Year. When matters are clearer you will be instructed – and no doubt presented with an acceptable Christmas box.'

'*No* doubt.'

Glimmering solutions to some of his quandaries guided his thoughts as he journeyed to Brentford, Sally's pregnancy amongst them. On alighting from the coach at The Ferry and Flood, he reserved a room from Mrs Barklea for an unspecified period, knowing both bedrooms and garret at Tudor Cottage would be occupied by Sally, Mrs Wormold and Arthur – it would provide a retreat if so required. As he let himself into the cottage, he relaxed somewhat to see the parlour clean and inviting, everything placed, polished and pleasing.

'Thank heavens you're back, Sir,' welcomed Mrs Wormold, drying her hands, 'Sally's been asking for you... it's my opinion she's fretting over something but won't tell me what. The doctor says there's nothing wrong as far as he can see, only she shouldn't be stressed, not in her condition – and Mister Arthur doesn't help matters.'

'He's worse?' said Alexander, ascending the stairs.

'He's no better, if that's what you mean. A terrible time I've had keeping him off the drink, but he would get it, and what with not sleeping nights...'

'Is that you, Alexander?' came a thin voice from Sally's bedroom. Alexander lifted the latch as she sat up in bed. 'I've missed you that much.'

'I told you I had things to see to – I have a great deal on my mind at present. You look none too bad to me – Mrs Wormold and the doctor are looking after you well enough?'

'Yes, but it's not the same as you. What's to be done about the baby?'

'Don't pressure me, Sally,' he said, sitting beside her. 'I have yet to talk with Mrs Wormold on that issue. You either *have* it – and it goes to the Foundling Hospital, or... she arranges for you *not* to have it. Now, dry your eyes and trust to my judgement. Mrs Wormold says Arthur's still drinking. Where's he obtaining the money?'

Sally shook her head. 'I don't know. His leg hurts sometimes, and his head, but he never complains, even about his cough. He *mumbles* sometimes – says he's got secrets.'

'What sort of secrets?'

'He doesn't say – only that he'll be *wrapped in a shroud* if he tells them.'

'They sound like the ramblings of a madman,' said Alexander, concerned nevertheless. 'Has he told *you* any of his secrets?'

'Not really. They seem to confuse him and he's confused enough.' She lay back on her pillows blinking away a glisten of tears. 'He could do with a bit of love, that lad, but I wouldn't disobey you, Alexander… I *did* promise and I've kept it.'

'In both your states I don't suppose you'd get up to much,' smiled Alexander, as though amused. 'Better to leave him to his secrets.'

Mrs Wormold knocked and entered with a tray. 'Downstairs there's a nourishing broth, Sir. Come and have some while it's fresh and hot.'

'Thank you, I'll just see the other invalid first,' said Alexander, getting up.

'Mr Arthur's out at present – he usually is at this time.'

'Where?'

'The Ferry and Flood, mostlike. I know they look after him there… as they do at The Old Northumberland.'

'Mrs Wormold,' said Alexander, his voice rising, 'I pay you extremely well to keep Mr Arthur under close surveillance…'

'With respect, Sir, I think we should be discussing this downstairs…'

'Then follow me!' snapped Alexander, clattering down to the parlour. 'I need Mr Arthur to keep a clear head – he is my business partner and friend. *I* will say when his weaknesses can befuddle him.'

'But you don't know what times we have with him – it's his fits that are worsest – you never told me of his fits, though the doctor's treatments have dealt with them for the most part.'

'Treatments?'

'Laudanum generally, I think. Then he sleeps sound as a lamb and we all get some peace. I don't half earn my money here, I don't mind telling you.'

'Keep that broth hot,' commanded Alexander and he left the cottage. In a sequestered corner of The Old Northumberland Arms, he eventually recognised Arthur's gaunt features ruddy with liquor and firelight. He sat beside him, holding his thin hands as his one-time school companion made little sign of recognition.

'You've come back,' he observed, in a matter-of-fact tone, as if he had been expecting him. 'Have you come from Estelle?'

'There's lovely broth at the cottage, Arthur. I'm here to help you. We need to talk.' Still holding his hand, he led him from the building along the High Street as if he were a pet donkey. Once in his parlour chair he slurped his broth with the poise of old men in the poor house.

'Believe me,' regretted Mrs Wormold, surveying his pasty countenance, 'I've done all I can. Some days he's better than this – really friendly – likes helping about the house. I haven't wanted to lock him in for fear of the damage he'd do. I'm ready to go, Sir, if I haven't given satisfaction.'

'Of course you've given satisfaction, Mrs Wormold – no question of it. I need your services... how can *I* cope with pregnant women and lunatics?'

The following day, after a troubled night at The Ferry and Flood, he sought an interview at the imposing house with a clipped yew hedge opposite. Dr. Gravely relaxed in his chair.

'Her chief complaint is a depressed state of mind, Mr Fleece,' he said sombrely, as though thinking aloud. 'It's unfortunate that business forces you to be away so much. But she will get over it, with God's assistance.'

'And ours,' reminded Alexander, with a polite smile. 'But it is Mr Arthur's condition I came to speak of. He is totally outside my experience.'

'I was about to mention him. Is it imperative he stays under the same roof? His disturbances are most undesirable for an expectant mother. I would think of having him committed where he'll be suitably looked after...'

'*Absolutely* imperative – for the moment. There are reasons. He is an old friend of mine. In order to help him at present, it is essential I know the true state of his condition.'

'Poor young man, and such a nice nature, too,' sighed Dr. Gravely. 'He will die, Mr Fleece. That is the plain truth. His system is poisoned. His cough, too. is taking hold. I don't really know how he's lasted *this* long – he has the consumption. The only constructive action is to alleviate his sufferings as much as possible. Mother Nature will take her course... we call it *marasmus* – wasting-away.'

'You treat him, I believe.'

'I cannot cure him, please understand. He should never have been left in Mrs Wormold's charge alone, capable as she is.'

'What treatments?'

'He is asthmatic. He is in pain. He suffers headaches. He is prone to fits and he doesn't sleep well. Of *course* I treat him, though he treats himself better with alcohol. I have tried to substitute it for more controlled preparations but it's probably kinder to allow him his refuge, I would say.'

'He takes laudanum?'

'Between twelve and thirty drops, depending on his condition – our most valuable medicine for most ailments. But he has morbid irritability, Mr Fleece, which I think undermines his wish for life. Even *with* proof spirit of opium, he will certainly be in no fit state to attend his sister's wedding in January.'

The bones in Alexander's hands almost broke through his skin as he clutched the arms of his chair.

'My dear Sir,' said Dr. Gravely, in surprise, 'are you quite well? You've gone as white as a winding sheet.'

'I... was not aware his sister... was to be married. He has not told me.'

'Nor me – my old friend and one-time colleague Edward Sawley it was. He has a practice in Kent – been attending the Havishams for years. It appears Mr Havisham's sister – or half sister rather – is to marry a rich gentleman from Hampshire. A fine-looking man too, I'm told. Sawley has been invited to the wedding breakfast, fortunate fellow, though there has been some trouble with the estate since Miss Havisham's father died – I think her half-brother sold her the business... Sawley doesn't know many details. Seems ironical, does it not, to sell your brewery when you like your drink. But it's believed that her future husband – Grumpyson, or some such name – put her up to it in order to further her fortune and turn her brother out of the house. Incredible, don't you think? People do the strangest things!'

'Mr Havisham has talked to you of this, has he?'

'No, not directly. What little I know has come from Sawley. In one of Mr Havisham's more lucid moments – he does have them from time to time – I did mention Sawley as being a mutual acquaintance... it was something to talk about. He didn't seem to understand what I meant when I expressed my good wishes for his sister's future happiness. He pressed me to tell him what I knew. It's strange, but I remember that when I said she was to marry this Mr Grumpyson – he made me repeat the name several times – he became most distraught and needed a sedative. I gather your old friend has always been disappointed in life at the hands of his sister and this man, but as he seemed very confused, I don't know how much truth there is in all this. Do you know either of these people?'

'I don't know the man. The sister I know slightly – she appeared to me self-centred and proud.'

'Her father's money made her so, they say.'

'As Arthur's oldest friend, how could I turn him from my home when his sister turned him from his? Do you know whether or not *he* has been invited to the wedding?'

'That I don't know for certain. Though if I read the situation correctly, he would not attend under any circumstances, other than to shoot this man Grumpyson on sight.'

'Arthur said that?'

'His actual words were, if I remember correctly, that he would shoot them *both* on sight. Take my advice – if you value your friend, see that he is taken care of sooner rather than later. If he is drunk, or *non compos mentis,* or both – he won't be responsible for his actions.'

'Oh,' assured Alexander, rising, 'I can promise you he's going to be taken care of.'

'A most Christian spirit, if I may say so. And in one so young. What a delightful chat – don't hesitate to send for me should the need occur. Good morning, Mr Fleece, and peace be with you this Christmas.'

Mrs Wormold's absence shopping gave him some time to think of Arthur. *Non compos mentis* he may be, but a threat to shoot is a threat to shoot and the germ of an idea is as good as the deed. After ascertaining that Sally slept, he tip-toed up to Arthur's garret and shook him gently awake beneath the dismal light slumping down from one scant skylight.

'Arthur. You know me?'

'Alexander... my friend...' He seemed ready to doze again.

'Alexander who? Who is Alexander? Compeyson or Fleece?'

'Alexander is clever... both of them. They should be introduced... they'd get on well together...' He chuckled to himself in a private, silly way. Then he became serious. 'Which one is going to marry Estelle? I need to know which to shoot.'

'Who said either of them is?' replied Alexander, coolly.

'Dr. Gravely did. He was told by Dr. Sawley because they're friends.'

'As *we* are, Arthur, which is why I have always told *you* things. We shall remain firm friends for ever.'

'That's what you said when you used to get into my bed at school.'

'And haven't I kept my promise? I want to make us rich, you and me. Just a few weeks more, and it can be done. Trust your old friend and partner.'

'Partner in what?'

'It was to be business, Arthur. I told you when I rescued you from the Fleet. But you are ill. And that you can't help. It has altered some of the plans I had for us – you and me – but it doesn't alter my attachment to you, for old time's sake. That's why I need to explain. Do you understand what I'm saying?' Arthur nodded. 'Then listen carefully. You are not going to shoot anyone. That is murder. You may be a keeper of secrets, Arthur, but you're *not* a murderer. Get that clear in your brain. Get what I'm now going to explain clear too... when I first met Estelle – through you – and discovered she was an heiress of some reckoning, I was naturally open to future possibilities. I was *not* responsible for the rift between you both, but as it was there, it would have been a bad business move not to have let it aid the cause by playing you off against each other. In wining her dependence I am within striking distance of my objective.'

'As Compeyson or Fleece?'

'Compeyson – you know that well enough. Fleece was born some years later out of necessity in London, until Compeyson's inheritance fell into his hands.'

'But what I *don't* understand,' said Arthur, frowning, 'is which of them intends marrying my half-sister. I don't want to congratulate the wrong friend, you see, because one of them is already married.'

Horrified, Alexander stared at him. 'Arthur! Don't be idiotic. You're insane!'

'So I may be, but that's the truth. I know it's true because it's secret.'

'You're out of your head – you don't know what you're saying. Be quiet now!'

'I *do* know what I'm saying – Mrs Fleece is downstairs going to have a baby. She wouldn't tell me lies – only secrets. She's lonely and she loves me but she's married to Mr Fleece.'

'Damn you, Arthur Havisham! *Forget Fleece*, will you? He was blackmailed into marriage. He doesn't exist therefore the marriage doesn't exist. Get that through your thick skull! That marriage is an encumbrance, even without the wretched baby – it's of no consequence, do you hear? *No consequence!* What's of *more* consequence is that Alexander's father... Alexander *Compeyson's* father... is bankrupt – Alexander will get nothing, or virtually nothing, compared with what he ought to get. There's even greater reason to marry an heiress or else everything he's worked for will be wasted.'

'You don't love Sally, then?' said Arthur, reasonably.

'Don't be a fool. Marriage was the only solution to keeping her quiet about her first husband's death. The Cap'n did for him because he cheated on me. A bad lot the pair of them. You don't think I'd choose someone like her of my own free will, do you? You obviously consider me as demented as you.'

'So you love Estelle?'

'I *loathe* Estelle! Apart from her fortune. Are you not pleased? Why else do you think I've been pursuing her all these years? Estelle cheated you, Arthur – you've said so often enough. She's thrived on cheating you, let me tell you. So through me, don't you see, you'll get back some of what's rightfully yours – because we're friends. Haven't I always told you I am working for us and that you must trust me?'

'But the law says you can't marry two people at once.'

'If everyone minds their own business, the law won't have a leg to stand on. When you get what's coming to you, dear boy, you'll see things from your friend's point of view and not the law's.'

'I'll see it from his point of view if he promises to give me *all* Estelle's money. I was the son of the house and have more right to it than him. If he doesn't, I'll tell Estelle about Sally and Sally about Estelle and the law about everyone else.'

Alexander fought to remain in charge of the situation, a dizzying nausea loading his apprehension as he prepared to ask him who he thought would listen to, let alone believe, the gibberish of a consumptive bedlamite in *delirium tremens?* The garret door opened – Sally leaned against the doorpost.

'What do you want?' shouted Alexander. 'Get back to bed.'

'I didn't want to listen... what you said...'

'Said? *What* was said? What *of* it?'

'Through the ceiling... I heard you...' Her voice fainted away as Alexander leaped across Arthur's bed towards her while her body slipped limply sideways. He lunged at her as she slid off the top step and banged to the bare boards at the bottom of the stairs, ending up on her back. Alexander jumped down beside her, patting her cheeks.

'Help me,' he commanded Arthur, peering over the top step like an inquisitive rooster. Together they lifted her onto the bed where she groaned as he roughly sponged her face with cold water from the ewer.

'I saw you push her,' announced Arthur, from the other side of the bed. 'It's because you're cross at being thwarted.'

'That's absurd. She fainted. You saw her.'

'I saw her faint and you push her because you want to marry the White Queen,' Arthur continued, with simple conviction. Sally's groaning increased, her hand pressing instinctively over her stomach, her face contorted. Arthur caught sight of a spreading stain crimsoning her white nightgown from beneath. He gripped Alexander's arm.

'Look,' he pointed, his eyes dilating with ready fear, 'look there – I've seen that colour before – I know what bright red means...'

'She's only cut her shin,' said Alexander, folding back her nightdress enough to see it was more serious. 'Here's the bowl of water – sponge away the gore while I get the doctor.'

'No, no,' begged Arthur, following him down to the parlour, 'don't leave me here alone...' Unheeding, Alexander ran to Dr. Gravely's, only to be told he was out attending a patient.

'*You* must come then, Mrs Gravely,' he commanded. 'I think my wife's having trouble with the baby and I don't know what to do...'

Tudor Cottage rang with Sally's cries as they hastened through the parlour and up the stairs; Arthur, cowering at the door, hands in mouth stifling coughs, watched the figure writhing like an animal ensnared by the bed; they crunched over littered shards of shattered ewer, its livid contents seeping into the floorboards – to Arthur, scaffold-planking in the *Place de la Revolution*.

'Hot water.' Mrs Gravely spoke efficiently. 'Towels. Quickly.' Alexander pulled Arthur with him, closing the door.

'The blood,' he kept repeating, following Alexander into the kitchen. 'So much blood. We'll never get rid of it all.'

'Have some sense,' Alexander said, impatiently. 'Blood's gone to your head, that's your trouble.' Mrs Wormold returned with her shopping basket, took stock of the situation and immediately relieved Alexander of his uncertain activities at the range. Water soon went up with her, down came Mrs Gravely and away, the doctor shortly taking her place.

Alexander mopped up what liquid had percolated through the ceiling floorboards, giving him time to think again. He sat beside Arthur. 'I'm sorry I became so heated earlier over the money. We must remain on good terms, you and I, particularly since Sally's accident. To that end, I feel duty bound to put you right regarding your alleged claim on Estelle's money – to remind you of a past transaction…' He reached for the wallet of personal documents he invariably carried. 'I *think* I have it here – ah, yes. I obtained a copy from Mr Sharps – see, this is his signature of authentication. Do you wish to read it for yourself or shall I assist? Look, it says: *I, Arthur Havisham, do hereby disassociate myself from my half-sister, Estelle Havisham… and all she represents in a personal, monetary and property capacity. I also appoint my loyal friend and mentor, Alexander Fleece… advisor and enabler in my business affairs, trusting…* need I continue? You can't back out of a legal document, Arthur – you of all people, being so particular about the letter of the law.'

'I wasn't well at the time… I wasn't sure what I was doing… you advised me.'

'So I did – in order to free you into your own life. It was what you agreed to.'

'I don't care what I agreed. All I know is that if *I* can't have Estelle's money, then neither can *you*. If you marry Estelle the money and everything else you gain must come to me. If not, Dr. Gravely shall know your secrets – how you had Sally's husband killed and wanted to kill Sally so you could get rich by Estelle. I'll tell him when he comes down.' He appeared almost triumphant as he sat back in his chair.

'Arthur, I'm proud of you.' Alexander poked the fire rather noisily. 'What a scheme. I fear I've taught you too expertly. Very well. I can see that you're too clever for me in the long run. I shall *not* marry Estelle. There. It's easily said. That makes us both equally penniless but inside your precious law. In fact you become the victor, knowing that your dear half-sister will be brought low by desertion – and she will be brought *very* low indeed, as she worships me for the many qualities I possess.'

'I want my money – my inheritance.'

'You can have it – only through me. I'm still willing to do a deal with you. And furthermore, I'll throw in an extra five hundred pounds for your secrets and silence.'

'Write it down.'

'What?'

'Write down your deal, like you once made me do at Satis and again at Mr Sharps's. I want your written agreement or there is no deal. Here's a page from a sketchbook and quill and some bistre. You know what to put – you have a way with words. Then sign it. Pretend you're writing it for me.'

'Very well, my friend, and you shall do your last one for me – that will place us on an equal footing. This is what I'm writing:

I promise to forgo any claim to the hand of Miss Estelle Havisham, of Satis House, Kent, her assets, property or revenues, considering that under the name of Alexander Fleece (who is one and the same with the below signed), I have already married Sally Blacker, widow; (though it was of necessity and not free will). Being mindful of the consequences should I break this contract.

He signed it *Alexander Compeyson* then made Arthur sit at the table and sign what he wrote to his dictation:

I promise, on receipt of £500, to guard for all time all known secrets relating to Alexander Fleece-Compeyson as if they were my own and my life depended on them, being mindful of the consequences should I break this contract.

After dating them December 19th, 1800, Alexander slipped them into his documents wallet along with his lawyer's other. 'These I shall take to Mr Sharps who will have them copied, authenticated, one for each of us. I shall deliver yours back to you personally. Let us drink to our transaction. Forgive me mentioning it, dear partner, but I think we can now safely assume I did *not* push my wife downstairs.'

Throughout their business, though the occasional sound emanated from upstairs, Alexander considered it a stroke of luck that they had not been disturbed. He decided to wait until sent for, content to turn matters over in his mind whilst letting Arthur help himself as he wished from the bottle.

The doctor's countenance left Alexander in little doubt as to the outcome of his attendance. 'Sometimes, Mr Fleece, nature takes its own course. It has to be viewed as for the better, I'm always inclined to believe – I'm afraid there won't be a baby. I understand your wife had a fall?'

'She slipped on the loft steps,' interposed Arthur. 'Alexander and I did all we could...'

'Most unfortunate. She'll recover, of course, but there'll always be a delicacy to consider – I warn you of that now. She needs peace and rest over Christmas – Mrs Wormold is a good woman – highly efficient.'

When Alexander finally was allowed to see Sally, he found her the centre of Mrs Wormold's ministrations, propped up on extra pillows as crumpled as her unhappy face.

'What have you done?' she breathed softly, 'what have I done? Don't leave me...'

'Pay no heed, Sir,' reassured Mrs Wormold, 'her mind's still wandering, poor dear. She's kept on about it... she blames herself for losing the baby... afraid you're going to abandon her because of it...'

'Mrs Wormold, perhaps you could go downstairs and put together something for us to eat?' Once she had departed, he leaned over Sally and said firmly, 'can you hear me? I shan't leave you. Do you understand that? I shan't leave you if you dismiss from your mind what you think you heard. What Arthur and I discussed has confused your mind. Expel it as you did the foetus.'

'I didn't want to, Alexander...' Sally swallowed dryly. 'Marry Miss Havisham... I don't remember much...'

'So leave it that way. I am married to you – nothing can be otherwise – you're muddled. Soon you'll forget – then you'll feel safe.'

'Safe...' she repeated sleepily.

* * *

Within the first three or four days of the New Year, Alexander left Brentford for The Golden Cross, Charing Cross, with assurances of his return, before long, to collect Arthur for a last piece of business he had in mind which would be to mutual advantage. Once in the squeezed funnel of Cramp's Twist Court, and having negotiated Mr Sharps's tricky steps, he continued to humour Arthur by having their two documents copied by his lawyer, his nose as constant as a thawing pump – but a drop in the ocean compared with his prompt service and gratitude for at least *some* payment of his client's outstanding account.

Mr Fleece returned to The Golden Cross with his duplicates, sending a lad down to The Bargee Joe to request The Cap'n attend on him in The Cross's private snug for some seasonal glasses of smoking bishop. The Cap'n found him basking before a volcanic fire, the circular tripod table at his side almost buckling under wine and port bottles and cut oranges pricked with cloves.

'Ah, The Captain brings the tang of salt and tar to the flowing bowl,' observed Alexander, stirring the contents of a skillet almost a-boil in the grate. As The Cap'n closed the door, he transferred the ruby liquid to a capacious earthenware dish, spooning in sugar and spiced fruit.

'Compliments o' th' season, mi Lord,' The Cap'n wheezed, as Mr Fleece ladled him a goblet full. 'To wot does we owe the 'onour o' this jovial festivity? Someone snuffed it?'

'Not yet,' said Mr Fleece, raising his glass in salutation, 'but with your connivance, we've not long to wait. Recall our meeting before Christmas.'

'You 'as mi full attenshun.' The Cap'n scraped his chair nearer. 'Would the candidate, by any chance, be the 'indrance afore mentioned at that time?'

'Your memory does you credit. And as you once observed, I think, hindrances can be washed out to sea.'

'The best place for 'em... aye, keep toppin' up mi glass, I thank'ee... easy as fallin' out th' crow's nest. Let's be 'avin the plan so's I can chart a course.'

'An instance has arisen necessitating Mr Arthur's removal rather sooner than I'd anticipated – *the end of this month*. Father Thames *could* be his grave but I need surer anonymity – he has an uneasy habit of offering up his secrets at low tide. I have a better solution... it will be done on the Kentish marshes and the body disposed of there. You need to find me a man who is a crack shot. And I mean *crack*. Anything less won't do. You shall be furnished with the final details nearer the time. Here is one of the Christmas Boxes I promised you.' He placed one of his welcome little money bags with a cold smile amongst the clutter of smoking bishops.

'May I make so bold,' said The Cap'n, warm alcohol and financial gain suffusing his loquacity, 'as to refer to a certain varmint wot eats roasted 'earts an' livers who be out o' Newgate an' on the loose... in the Joe yesterday an' today an askin' after Mister Fleece an' Mister Arthur...'

'How convenient – you shall contrive our meeting later. What are you attempting to tell me through your alcoholic cloud?'

''Ow'll 'e take to 'is one-time partner snuffin' it?'

'I shall deal with Mr Abel in my own way,' asserted Alexander. 'Get word to meet me under your hospitable roof at nine tonight. Take a room for him covering the last week of this month at Mistress Farrow's lodging house across in Tooley Street – south of the river will suit better for what I have in mind for him. I will organise *that* with you at our next meeting. Now, away with you – do as you're bid under oath of strictest secrecy.'

'Let me be sowed up in mi own 'ammock with a stitch through mi nose an' throwed to the sharks if I don't – I swear it on Davy Jones's locker.'

Alexander remained where he was to enjoy a substantial supper and doze until the appointed time drew him out to bend his head to the icy blasts whipping The Strand from the east, reaching The Bargee Joe as the half-hunter repeater he had found in one of Mr Havisham's bureau drawers tinged nine o'clock in his greatcoat pocket.

His card-sharp friends, reliable as fully wound clockwork, knotted their familiar smoke-hazed corner of the room, Mr Abel's thick-set appearance instantly recognisable. Mellow as was Mr Fleece's attitude since his beneficial supper, he was in no mood for banter, preferring to bypass Peg-leg Jem, Croak – even The Cap'n – with a seasonal greeting. Mr Abel he gathered up and as the small back room was occupied by a conclave of seemingly equal privacy, walled him in a snug between two high backed settles.

'I will come straight to the point, Magwitch. You and I are about to become partners – I shall have a job for you before this month's out – not in London – but important, nevertheless – it could be rich pickings all round if it goes well – it will depend on your expertise. I can see by your eyes you're not averse to this plan. You will receive your instructions through The Captain and also, as a place of cover away from here, a temporary address in the Borough, where you'll go a week before the job. All you have to do before then is keep out of Newgate, much as I appreciate your attachment to your second home. I have your unquestioning agreement in all matters concerning?'

'A mere varmint here is right glad to shake a young gent's hand again, specially if it's lined with gold. You always was a true gent, Mr Fleece, as sticks by them who buys his per-rogative.'

'My prerogative knows no bounds to those who respect it, Magwitch,' reminded Alexander. 'Never let that be underestimated. As long as you and I understand that, there will be no contention between us if we work together again.'

Visibly more relaxed as the familiar Mr Fleece back in control, Alexander joined his cornered cronies in The Bargee Joe's claustrophobic environment, condescending to affable but inconsequential conversation before returning to The Golden Cross's more salubrious amenities. What was it Croak had edged into the conversation prior to departure? Another sliver of Latin superiority: *vincit qui patitur*. Well, Alexander said to himself as he drank his negus, how apposite – if only that sebaceous scholar knew *how* I intend to put *He Who Endeavours Conquers* to the test.

As sure as he could be of his forthcoming strategy, he rewarded himself with the comforts of the hotel's bed, board and Barbara.

TABLEAU IX
1801

Estelle had been far from idle during her *fiancé's* absence. When he returned at the start of the second week in January, she lost no time bustling him up to Arthur's old sitting room opposite her boudoir, the hefty dining table from downstairs, its long surface tight with extra leaves, lining the centre like a royal dais.

'Here – in the middle of it,' she explained, indicating a height roughly level with the top of her head, 'will stand the great cake – my bride-cake! It's in several tiers, like the spire of St Bride's, Fleet Street – it's the latest fashion to have them modelled in its style, I'm told. You'll have to imagine it because I'm not letting you see it until after we're wedded. This is my position at the banquet – and here, beside me, is yours. Oh, Alexander, it's too exciting. Why do you look so glum?'

'My Mama,' he reminded her, quietly. 'I can't help thinking about her white face on the pillows. She looked so small and frail. Christmas wasn't the same as usual. I only hope she's well enough to attend. I have to return to her before the wedding, my dearest – I do hope you'll understand. But it'll be the *last* time I leave you – I promise.'

'If you must do,' sighed Estelle, 'then you must. Your poor Mama – I'm so sorry. But because I love you I'm prepared to make this last sacrifice before we marry. Then we'll be able to visit Rookwell together – such a dear place – I loved being there and shall again.'

'And because I love you,' said Alexander, taking her arm through his, 'I'm happy to appreciate your sacrifice. I'm looking forward to our time back at the *Villa Romana* – I've arranged for us to have it for three months, then the *Casa del Mulino* for another three.'

As they walked later through the hoary garden where Apollo Belvedere's classic nudity braved the Kentish cold, Estelle stopped, wishing she had chosen the model without fig leaf.

'He's still as lovely as you, Alexander. Do you remember the *Villa Cherubini* and how we loved each other at his feet in sunshine? I'd give anything to return and do it again by moonlight, with the nightingales singing... but please try to get rid of those dark rings under your eyes, though – you must be in your full beauty when everyone sees us together as man and wife.'

'I'm not sleeping well at present,' he explained, tentatively. 'Mama, you see...'

The morning of his departure, Alexander asked to talk to her in the library, her curiosity awakened by the solemn nature of his request. She sat by the fire as he stood with his back to the chimneypiece.

'I have some news,' he began, 'which I've been saving for fear of spoiling our time together, because I'm uncertain as to how you'll receive it. It concerns Arthur.'

'I have no concerns about Arthur. Thanks to you he is a thing of the past, like the Revolution.'

'But do you wish to know of him?'

'Do you think I should?'

'Yes. I think you should know he is dead.'

Estelle held her breath. She left her chair and walked a few paces. 'Dead? Arthur?' she whispered, holding her chair back. 'It can't be so, surely? That boy had nine lives at least, just to be awkward.'

'The prospect of a further eight obviously proved the final straw,' said Alexander, grimly humouring. 'The Marshalsea it was – after a couple of years' dissipation and ruin. At least he was spared admittance to the Bethlehem Hospital. He's buried in a pauper's grave – it happened while we were abroad.'

'It doesn't seem possible,' said Estelle, incredulously. 'There's always been an Arthur for as long as it's mattered. I knew he'd come to a bad end. What a very silly boy he's been – all his life – what a waste, and after all you did for him. He could have been a great artist if he'd been different. How have you found out?'

'Through my business contacts in London. One of them knew of him so I had him traced to the prison – he was in debt to the tune of some hundreds, of course, mostly gambling. He'd had a turn in King's Bench for theft and arson I believe – the Fleet also – but never quite made Newgate.'

'He never quite made anything. How can we be sure he's made death?' She brushed away some confused tears.

'Are those of relief or regret, my dear? Now he's gone do you wish him back?'

'Please, I don't want reminding of that Whelp ever again. I feel strangely free, now, as though his death has put a seal on the old life. We seem more able to go forward into the new.'

'And going forward means making a start for Rookwell – my parents will start worrying about me.' He told her that before he took the Winchester coach from London, he needed to see his lawyer about his new will, attend to copious other matters, as well as purchase his own new clothes and luggage. He would next see her on the day of his new life, having accompanied his Mama and Papa down the previous day when they would all be staying the night at The Blue Boar. He asked her not to call and see them, as it would spoil the excitement of the following day's wedding.

* * *

On his arrival at Tudor Cottage, Mrs Wormold was pleased to report favourably on Sally's progress; that she enjoyed making bread in the kitchen and helping with the cooking but still needed to rest a good deal; Mr Arthur, too, seemed calmer in his mind, but needed to rest even more.

'Very shortly I shall be taking him into London to be with some friends of my lawyer. Look after Sally until I return – Arthur may remain in town for much longer.'

'Very good, Sir. It'll do him good to get away... change of scene and company always does the trick.'

That evening, his arm round Arthur's shoulder, he took him to his room at The Ferry and Flood, having ordered a fire to be lit and supper table laid before its amplitude. He filled Arthur's glass and clinked his against it, as he said how good it was to see him again and know he was so much improved. 'I promised you I would return soon and so I have, complete with copies of our agreements legalised by my lawyer.'

'When can I have my copy?'

'Before very long, Arthur. There is still just one remaining piece of business to transact – when its over, you shall receive your final dues.'

'You are not married to Estelle?'

'I am not married to Estelle. I have returned to you in order that Nemesis maybe honoured.'

'Nemesis? Is he another of your aliases?'

'Really, Arthur, what's happened to your education? The Goddess of Revenge, dear partner – you can't have forgotten your life-long ambition? Here I am to enable your dearest wishes from the time we first met. So – yes, I suppose in a way I *am* your Nemesis for the moment. You'll be coming to London with me tomorrow where we shall work on the finer details – we haven't too much time left.'

Despite Sally's entreaties, but reassuring her of his return, he drove Arthur in the gig to The Golden Cross where, after a fruitless search in streets and courts north of the King's Mews and St Martin's Workhouse, he set on housing him in the hotel where he could be more closely controlled.

Keen to see The Cap'n without delay, he sent word to The Bargee Joe for him to meet Mr Fleece at the more anonymous but nonetheless crooked Neptune Inn on the south bank, isolated among obscure fields and market gardens between the Patent Shot Factory on the shoreline and Halfpenny Hatch west of Great Surrey Street and Blackfriar's Bridge. Over as good a dinner for two as could be expected in such circumstances for under three shillings, Mr Fleece enlarged on his directions, commencing with Mr Abel, at present residing just south of London Bridge.

'I want him out of commission for a few months as from this last week of January. I want him back in Newgate where he can't complicate my intentions. Get him to Hampshire without delay – to a country house called Rookwell Park. I am familiar with it – I happen to know it's newly bought, with rich pickings to be had. Let Filcher Nick go with him to sort out strategy. But you *must* ensure Mr Abel is apprehended – caught in the act. Inform a Magistrate – the garrison – do what you have to, only he must be *taken*. Is that *absolutely* clear?'

'Clear as St Elmo's fire,' asserted The Cap'n, draining his tankard of porter. "E'll be took red-'anded, an' Nick alongside, unless warned.'

'What ever your strategy, Mr Abel must suspect *nothing*. It'll be your heart and liver if he does.'

'Roast an' ate, as sure as eggs is eggs. It shall be done as you command, Sir, an'a first-rate job it'll be.' He leaned closer to Mr Fleece. 'There be *two* matters relatin' I 'ears you a-mention as dinner wos ordered, for which I thanks your 'onour. Would the second, by any stretch o' th' mizzen shroud, be evolvin' round Mister Arthur?' He understood Mr Fleece to indicate that he follow him outside. Only scattered glints of illumination from distant habitations tampered with the tight, cold oppressive darkness surrounding and absorbing Mr Fleece's incisive whisper.

'Early on the morning of the thirty-first of this month, he will be visiting a fine house in Kent on my behalf with a *most important letter*. I shall drive him to The Three Jolly Bargemen in Cooling, six miles distant and wait there as he drives himself to Satis House along the marsh road. Before he reaches the house – it must be *before* he reaches it – he is to be picked off. You already have the men to do it – see that they drive their trap to the area the night before. No one will hear a pistol shot in that God-abandoned wilderness – there's nothing around for miles – it's even more desolate than this place. His death must be *quick* and must be *clean*. His body is to be taken to the disused old lime kiln then the trap returned to The Three Jolly Bargemen to collect me. He will have that letter on him which it is *vital* I retrieve *at all costs*. I personally must destroy it. I cannot *stress* this *sufficiently*. We will then dispose of the body on site. You have lined me a reliable gun?'

'I were a crack shot myself wi' two eyes, but if it's to be done once an' neat wi' no mess, Jake's th' man, wi' Sol for ballast, ready to set sail.'

'Remember – it has to be done on his way *to* the house – afterwards is too late. *That letter must not be delivered.* Now, in with us – it's perishing out here.'

'Not wishin' to appear inquisitive,' said The Cap'n, readjusting to the slight increase of warmth, 'but 'as 'is Lordship considered doin' the job 'iself – in the gig as 'e bools along – all cosy an' friendly like?'

'It'll come as no surprise to know that he had, but prefers it *this* way – there are personal reasons which he is not prepared to divulge. Has he made his intentions *absolutely* plain?'

'Plain as a yard o' oakum,' assured The Cap'n, 'an' a pleasure to do business on sitch an 'efty scale – wi' an 'efty reward on top, no doubt?'

'*No* doubt.'

Alexander had engaged for Arthur a south-facing room at the front, looking down on le Seur's equestrian statue of King Charles 1st riding towards the Westminster which claimed his head. The view delighted Arthur, particularly the squint to the left allowing him to catch the stone lion above the central parapet of Northumberland House facing his way in defensive stance, as if guarding the stratagems he and Alexander currently considered. Indeed, the two of them appeared to have restored some of their one-time *camaraderie,* talking and laughing over the old days, drinking in the evenings, walking the Strand to the City or into St James's Park with its oblong canal, flat like a long sheet of frosted mirror obscuring their reflections. Had Arthur been well, thought Alexander as he eyed the Ladies of the Town, what strapping times they might have enjoyed together – to compare, even, with those heady episodes in Venice and Naples with Adolphus. But Arthur was Arthur – and here for a different purpose. A certain need for neutrality also led Alexander to keep him away from The Bargee Joe, though his intake of alcohol had in no way abated nor his occasional need for laudanum – for which Alexander made certain he could be relied upon.

'For the first time in my life,' said Arthur, 'I feel I almost know what's in your mind. You've always been too crafty for me – too wily. You're like a labyrinth and I became lost trying to find my way.'

'Crafty, wily, cold and heartless,' replied Alexander, with a shrug. 'Those are my qualities. Only true friends and partners know them, so consider yourself privileged. Estelle will be the first outsider.'

'I hope they kill her.'

'No, Arthur – *that* she does *not* deserve – I think you must be even more heartless than I! It will be painful enough if they kill her *spirit.* You should allow for that and be content.'

'And the waxen head. Are you going to tell her it's been in the cellar all this time, under her very nose?'.

'I think not. Let it remain where it is – someone in the future may find it and wonder about its story.'

'What will you do if she hounds you for breaking your promise of marriage? She can be vicious when things don't go her way.'

'I don't know that I ever *did* promise – I think she *assumed* we would marry – as if it was required. I was a necessary part of her expectations. If she did hound me, I think Mr Fleece would be required to spread his black cloak round Mr Compeyson a little longer... make it into bat's wings to fly him abroad...'

'To France! We could go to Paris... find Citizen David. He praised my work...'

'Once upon a time,' reminded Alexander. 'That fairytale is over now.' He raised the piece of paper he had intermittently jotted on for the last hour or so. 'I wonder what he would make of *this* work of art.'

'Is it the view from the window? Let me see. I can help you with the perspective'

'You're right – it *is* a view, but not *this* one. It's a view of our freedom: my letter of resignation to Estelle. And I have everything *perfectly* in perspective.'

'When will you send it?'

'I *shan't* send it.'

'Deliver it, then?'

'I shan't *deliver* it. *You* will. On the morning of her wedding. In person.'

Arthur hardly found voice. 'In *person*?'

'Then you'll come away and tell me all about it and what she said and did.'

Arthur stared out over the fuming chimney pots of Charing Cross dropping their soot flakes like so many dark souls, each intent on blacking each other out.

'Now,' said Alexander, 'don't disturb me. I need to draw up the fair copy – my *magnum opus*. Then you shall see what sort of an artist I am.'

Palazzo Campanello, Canale Grande, Venezia.

La mia stella brillante,

It is with the saddest and heaviest of hearts that I pen these inadequate lines to you, laden as they perforce must be with such painful tidings at this your life's most brilliant moment. I have directed my lawyer in London to pass this epistle to the bearer, my business representative in England, who once again graces his old home – and you – before he joins me and my wife as Chief Steward here in Venice, and then in southern climes where you and I enjoyed such intimacies.

Yes, dearest Estelle. It grieves me to say that though I shall eternally love you (and from now on, externally), I have received it as my Christian Obligation to accept the responsibilities providence has thrust upon me in the form of an unfortunate widow – a rich Countess – desperately seeking a sound union to benefit her sadly fatherless children – as well as the child she so graciously bore me a little while ago. He is a dear son who, for reasons I needn't explain, I have named Arthur.

Having thus placed Duty before all other material considerations, I simply desire that not only shall I prove a worthy husband to the rich Countess, but also be deserving of your understanding and forgiveness. Had time not been so short whilst in England recently, the Countess and I would surely have been delighted to favour you with a personal visit and invitation to our wedding – a splendid affair in Santa Maria della Salute; Venice was particularly opulent in decorations for the occasion. By the time you read this my wife will be on her way south with her retinue, whilst I

...in at our Palazzo against the arrival of my steward, Arthur — trusted friend and confidante — before we follow suit.

I am mortified at having to inform you of such tidings in such a manner; but better this way than leaving you to cope unprepared and single-handedly with my absence at the altar, what with you all in your finery and the guests looking on. I'm sure they will be a great comfort.

If you search hard enough, you are certain to find another willing slave to save you from yourself. I send my Daphne greetings, good wishes and many happy returns of her birthday, assuring her of a constant presence in the mind and memory of her idol without figleaf.

Apollo.

* * *

The unguarded wind fleeing from the sea across the lone, level marshes pushed the damp dawn ahead. From the slow snakes of cloud ribbing the eastern horizon, it blustered every shiver of cattle-cluster, gate, dyke, grass and insect foolhardy enough to expect leniency; it fussed the corners of the Havisham church where, later, the Havisham living were expected to gather in witness near the bones of the Havisham dead; it infuriated the scatter of marsh villages; it fiddled the peeling weatherboarding of an isolated blacksmith's forge and cottage; it harried the sagging boards of the disused sluice-house next to the old lime kiln, its lame door no barrier to frantic gusts thudding and hissing all ways at once.

Two horses hidden in the overgrown quarry behind cropped what sparse grass they could between the abandoned workings' weedy rocks and boulders, grumpy blasts wrestling with their manes and tails and blowing in their nostrils; two men huddled shiftily with flintlock pistols by the fractured window, their watery eyes concentrating on the rough causeway ahead...

At The Three Jolly Bargemen, after a fortifying early breakfast, Alexander had bid Arthur a more than usually affectionate *adieu* and *bon chance* as he packed him in the hired trap for Satis. He ensured, yet again, the safe banking of Estelle's letter in the vault of Arthur's inside coat pocket, for fear the wind would snatch it in its desire to acquaint itself with such bleak contents.

'Be certain to return and tell me of your adventures,' he called, as he watched him drive slowly out of the yard – out of his life. He returned to the Smoke Room fireside; but, on-edge and unable to wait patiently for The Cap'n's men, he decided to take a turn about the neighbourhood. Wrapping warmly, he made for the empty marshes with no sight of the trap or its driver along the causeway he trod in the direction of the blacksmith's forge. Other than the wind's boom and bump, the only sound to accost his ears clinked from clanking rattles of chains flung this way and that on a solitary gibbet, as though it were lashing its tentacles in the wild hope of catching a felon or pirate – or murderer – to keep it company.

The forge, when he reached it, was all closed up; in front of the wooden cottage to which it was attached, a lad upwards of fifteen or sixteen, fair flaxen curls billowing like a field of golden rod about his features, knelt on a pad of cloths. With an assortment of stones and pebbles, he filled in some of the larger potholes in the path leading to the forge from the front. His blue eyes turned to the muffled stranger pausing at the gate.

'Good morning, boy,' said Alexander taken by the gentle face reminiscent of how Arthur's used to be. 'You're about your work early. Is this your home?'

'Aye, Sir,' the lad replied shyly, continuing working.

'Blacksmith's boy, eh?'

'Blacksmith's 'prentice, Sir.'

a boy no longer – a man of iron – a veritable Hercules, to be sure.' The lad made no reply. He had not heard much anyway, what with the labouring wind. 'And what is the name of this 'prentice Hercules?'

''Tis Joe, Sir.'

'Jo, is it? Jo for Joshua? Jo for Josiah? For Jonah, perhaps?'

'Joseph, Sir. Joseph Gargery's my father too.'

'Joseph. An honest name. And I don't doubt an honest heart to go with it, Joe Gargery, son of Joseph.' The lad continued with his occupation. 'Stick to your stones and horseshoes, Joe – they will *keep* you honest...'

Suddenly, Alexander straightened. An icy shiver streaked his back and neck. Could that sudden sound the cracking air had thrown him have been a pistol shot? His ears strained as if for confirmation – the relentless wind kept its own counsel – Joe seemed oblivious of anything unusual. Convinced he was far from mistaken, Alexander turned back in the direction of the village.

Joe watched the stranger make off across the marshes beneath a gun-metal sky...

* * *

Hardly able to sleep, Estelle had awakened almost as early as the servants. Before commencing dressing at eight-fifteen, she had toured the house to see for herself that every arrangement was of the highest order: the shining apartments, wedding and birthday presents displayed in the old dining room, the humour of leaping fires on well-swept hearths, the brushed stonework, sleek woodwork, even the scoured intricacies of handles on drawers and keys in locks.

The banquet chamber thrilled her most particularly, for there, centring the swan-white lawn of damask-draped table and surrounded by jostles of ruby goblets, decanters, plates, dishes, finger bowls, silverware, candelabra, rose the white-pillared pride of confectionery art encrusted with marble-white sugary swags and topped with star white flowers, sweet and brittle. The room's panelling and decorative features glistered with polish and *panache,* the velvety crispness of their carvings as finely buffed and glowing as good pie crusts glazed and baked; here stood lead-lined cisterns encased in brass-bound mahogany, protecting nests of ice from which protruded necks of dumpy green wine bottles as if they were songbirds ready to pour forth liquid music into clusters of fine-stemmed glassware; there ranged *buffets* beneath mirrors steadying themselves beneath responsibilities of foods and fruits of all shapes and sizes, colours, consistencies; everywhere, wreaths and swags of such winter flowers and foliage as could be worked, garlanded to soften the harder edges of a wondrous space which, to Estelle's dazzled eye, equalled the magnificence of the *Galerie des Glaces* at Versailles. She stood amongst it all as if contemplating a potential challenge to her own forthcoming glory.

She crossed to her boudoir where Zilla, as excited as her Mistress, waited by the dressing table to assist with extra care and not a little shake of the hands. Estelle sat before her glass, absorbing its candid reflection; she thought of Alexander, wondering if he would be wearing his bottle green or royal blue coat – but hoping he would engage everyone with his fawn buckskin breeches fitting like a second skin; she thought of her Papa – if only he could have seen his Bright Star shine. As Zilla began dressing her hair, she fingered the collection of jewels laid out for her, deriving some consolation from their crisp, cold sparkle – some steadiness from the gentle feel of scented white lace handkerchief, soft vellum-bound prayer book, white embroidered gloves and gold watch and chain – one of many of Papa's presents... he was not to be entirely absent after all.

Zilla and Mrs Needler assisted her into her gown; a classic cut of full but sleek high-waisted folds from a white embossed

, modelled close and marked low in order to show off a ...ay of diamonds; miniature puffed sleeves frothed down in graded sizes to lace-cuffed wrists. Before she picked up some lavendered lace for her bosom, she viewed herself with a hem-brushing turn before the *cheval* mirror.

'*Est ce que n'est pas magnifique, Zilla? Tres convenable pour une Reine,*' she enthused in over-excited, uncomfortable French. 'I shall want all the servants to assemble in the hall to see me when I go. Quickly now, arrange my veil and the flowers in my hair. Just imagine! This is how Queen Antoinette must have felt when she married the *Dauphin*. It's almost twenty minutes to nine, Zilla – go down and instruct Mrs Hall to have everybody gathered. I shall finish my veil – I just want to pin some jewels to the flowers...' As she concentrated on her reflection, another loomed behind her – a cloaked and hatted figure with white face and faded eyes. She turned in her chair – the door continued to open back on itself – Zilla continued to stare, her hands stifling her mouth – inquiring servants peered cautiously from the threshold. Somehow, Estelle managed to get to her feet.

'Good morning, Your Majesty.' The apparition bowed low, sweeping his hat in a courtly way. 'The Whelp conveys his greetings in abundance on today of all days.'

Arthur is dead, a voice repeated in her mind. When she opened her mouth, no sound reached it.

'This is the shroud I have come to put on *you*, sister dear.' He pushes forward, stabbing a sealed letter in her unresponsive hand. He smiles to see her eyes register confused fear. 'Do you remember the shroud you wanted to put on *me?*' He attempts to spin-out his moment of triumph – there is so much he has prepared to say. But seeing her again at last – still beautiful, still imperious, still fearsome, though with a face drained to the whiteness of her finery – words dry in his throat, choking him like a blocked flue. A pale trunk of faintness inexorably uproots his stability as she drops the letter, addressee downwards, his hazed attention caught by the single circle of red sealing wax glistening like a spot of fresh blood. His surroundings merge into a vortex of white and crimson, crimson and white... stains on Sally's nightgown, the Versailles staircase bleeding massacred victims, rolling drums, cheering crowds, the White Queen on the scaffold, the severed, dripping head... As Zilla picks up the letter and hands it to Estelle, he staggers round almost tumbling from the room, alarmed servants sidling back to let him pass, no one assisting as he shambles down the decorated staircase before she finishes reading. Out he stumbles to the waiting gig setting it clumsily in motion with a lacerating whip, the horse's clatter through the gate, however, not preventing his catching Estelle's hysteria screeching through the scarified air. Her shrieks inflame him like triumphant clarions: *La Revolution! Vive la Republique! La Reine est mort...*

* * *

Impatient and apprehensive as Alexander was, he waited impassively by the smoke-room fire back at Three Jolly Bargemen for The Captain's men to report. With an urgent sense of clearing his way through the last obstacles Arthur had thrown in his path, he rapidly consigned Mr Sharps's incriminating documents to the flames. His conscience, impervious to any retribution Arthur's ghost might bring upon his, he turned his attention to a rather out-dated copy of *The True Briton,* intrigued and chastened by a lengthy front page advertisement for Dr. Brodum's Botanical Syrup and Restorative Nervous Cordial – the leading alternative to mercury for venereal complaints. He had just reached a section in the case account of a certain Lieutenant N – of Hull, whose throat and nose had been eaten away by the complaint, when his fascination became distracted by the shadowy presence of a young man with rather watery eyes which blinked as if they troubled him.

..r Fleece? I'm The Cap'n's man, Jake.'

'At last,' he sighed, folding up Lieutenant N – .'You took your time. Let's get off to the lime kiln.'

''Old 'ard a minute, sir,' said Jake, rubbing an eye. 'It's not as it should be. We did our best, but it's the weather… the wind swishes mighty strong in these parts… we was conspired against.'

Barely believing what he heard, Mr Fleece commanded the ruffian to sit, regain his breath, tell him straight.

'We was there, Sol an' me, last night, smooth as you like – all ready in the sluice-house; pistols, powder, shot. We've 'ad our eyes on the causeway since first light, no 'itches. Then we sees 'im through the window – no mistake – just as The Cap'n described 'im. 'E trots up in 'is trap – gets in perfect range. So I fires more-or-less 'ead-on – would 'ave got 'im lovely through the 'eart. Flint strikes a flash in the pan but went dead – no report – don't ask why… powder's dry an' clean as a whistle – 'appens sometimes. I tried with the other as 'e come on, still in range, but a swill of wind blows the powder clean in my face – nearly blinds me it did, so by the time I sees again 'e's out of range. Sol made for the door an' fires off *'is* piece – a great shot – but it missed. 'E ran after 'im but the trap was at a faster trot an' was gone before Sol got second aim.'

For the first time in his life, Mr Fleece found himself lost for words. With his head in his hands he stared at the floor, knowing he should have been at the limekiln himself to finish Arthur off. These bungling idiots had allowed delivery of the letter and cost him his one last, late chance of success.

'And on the way back?' he barely whispered. 'Did you get him on the way back?'

'Nothin' was said about the way back,' ventured Jake. 'The Cap'n, 'e says be sure 'e gets picked off *before* 'e reaches the 'ouse – 'e even said after would be too late. That was our instructions. Do you *still* want us to pick 'im off, Sir – somewhere less windy?'

'Don't be ridiculous,' snapped Mr Fleece. 'The damage has been done, you simpleton. He'll be returning here very soon – yes, why *not* do it out there in public? – it would make about as much sense! Hook it, dunderheads. I'll even with you back at Hungerford...'

Only too relieved, Jake retreated hastily, but not without a deferential nod. Outside he joined Sol who, having won the toss as to which one of them would go in to break the news, held the horses. They leaped to their saddles as a mud-splattered trap bolted like Jehu's chariot into the yard, frightening their steeds. Recognising their late target they dug in their heels without delay and clattered off towards the marshes. The trap struck a mounting block which smashed a wheel, toppling its driver onto the cobbles as it skidded into a corner with a broken axle and confused horse. Alexander ran to assist in retrieving Arthur from the splinters, finding him remarkably in one piece with no broken bones or cracked skull. Taking him inside for a couple of brandies to steady his nerves, he hired a bed chamber for the day, insisting he lie and rest. Relieved that The Three Jolly Bargemen was too inconsequential and obscure for the wedding guests of Estelle's calibre to entertain patronising, he endured no pressure in wanting to leave for London, letting Arthur sleep until mid afternoon when he ordered a lunch tray to be sent up for them both. Though he appeared more rested, signs of a highly charged state were not difficult to detect. His agitation seemed to centre on some form of attempt on his life.

'...I'm sure it *was* the crack of a pistol as I passed the old sluice-house, because when I turned round I saw a man in a doorway levelling one at me so I whipped up the horse...'

'Arthur – it's cheering to realise you've not lost your vivid imagination. But these are the Kentish marshes, dear friend, not the streets of Versailles or Paris.'

'He was there, I tell you, pointing a pistol at me – I didn't *imagine* that – I *saw* him...'

, you see the phantasms and ghouls of your dreams! They _ in your mind I'm afraid, old partner, and have been for years, due to all you've been through. They don't actually exist, though you see them everywhere. This must have been a trick of the light – the weather... who can say?'

'But my trip to Satis wasn't a trick.'

How, Alexander asked himself, *can I tell you it was intended as a trick? That I was banking on your death and retrieval of that letter to leave me free to marry Estelle's fortune then magically dissolve into thin air?* 'No, Arthur, your trip to Satis was real. I wish to know what took place. Can you tell me? – slowly, now... have some more brandy...'

'I somehow didn't want to go in... all the old feelings overpowered me – Papa, the cupboard, the cellars. But Satis looked different – more cheerful – lots of activity – not so deadly. I recognised some of the servants and they me because they whispered to each other as if I was a secret.

'I asked to see her in a good voice but was told she was dressing so went up on my own despite them not wanting me to. Her Majesty's door was closed but mine was open so I went in. It was prepared for The Tribunal – lots of chairs round a long white table full of knives and glasses red with blood...'

'Miss Havisham. Did you see *her?*'

'I crossed to her boudoir. She sat at her dressing table preening, just as she used to. I wanted to bring in the wax head from the cellar – present her with it on a plate as if it were Salome's and I John the Baptist. She gaped at me as if I didn't exist – she looked like wax herself about to be incarcerated in the half-packed trunks and boxes littering the room.'

'She spoke to you?'

'I said, *Greetings, Your Majesty!* That's what I said. *I am the Messenger from the Tribunal of Life which is meeting in the other room to decide on warranting your arrest and execution. You'll be put in a dung-cart and taken to the guillotine on the marshes.* She said, *I am willing to go with you if it's the will of the people. Let me read the warrant.*'

'Arthur...'

'As I slid it into her hand, the sharp edge of the paper sliced into her finger, letting blood gush onto her white dress. Again and again the drums thundered the Marble Court beneath the King's bedroom window as The White Queen showed the soaking crowds the shroud she held for me... I had to escape... I didn't want to die in the cellar along with her head...'

Alexander tried slapping his face but it was difficult with him writhing on the bed, shivering and gasping as he had done the night of his return to Satis from France. He dosed him with laudanum and covered him with blankets; the sooner he could be transported back to Tudor Cottage the better. He realised that if he took the stagecoach from The Blue Boar he might run the risk of encountering those wedding guests not yet recovered from their shock, including his parents. He settled on hiring a post chaise, trusting, with satisfactory changes of horses, to make the journey in less than five hours.

The following morning, after an early breakfast, he bundled Arthur's incapacity beside him, directing the driver to join the main route west, a good distance the other side of the town and Satis. On reaching Southwark, one of the horse changes took place at the hostelry of St George's turnpike, where Alexander encouraged his passenger indoors for a warming drink. Arthur, his back to the window, remained oblivious of what caught Alexander's vigilant attention through the glass – the enviable physique of Hugh the groom working in the traces. As his industry reminded him of earlier, friendlier associations, a certain inexplicable relief suffused Alexander's appraisal, for with the removal of Estelle from his affairs, he found a defused jealousy allowing him a certain gladness, for Hugh's sake, that he had sought salvation from Mrs Comfrey enabling him to resume the only work to which he had always been devoted. As a result, her of how things were done at Satis would have doubtless ..k even further into the corporate mire of disapproval, invoking fire and brimstone and every damnation of hell on the fraudulent head of that black-hearted wolf in sheep's clothing, Compeyson – adventurer, trickster, humbug!

With this recognition of his true qualities chastening his mind as effectively as winter frosts visiting spring, he appreciated the value of leaving the area before being recognised. He virtually smuggled Arthur, his hat pulled low over his face, back to the chaise on the last stretch to Kew where they left it at The Hog's Hole before taking the ferry across to Brentford. Arthur had contributed little to the tedium of the journey, nor had Alexander demanded of him. His sole aim now was to enshroud him to the last with Tudor Cottage's benevolence.

Mrs Wormold's surprise at seeing him back so soon turned quickly to concern as she beheld his spectral state; Sally said he resembled the shade she first encountered as housekeeper at Satis.

'He's had a bad time, poor little cat's paw, and it hasn't exactly been a pleasure outing for me neither,' said Alexander. 'Let's get him up to bed.'

Over the first few days of February, he saw to it that Arthur remained in his darkened garret, for the most part dosed into stupefaction or crying out that the White Queen drifted towards him carrying his shroud. Alexander requested that Dr. Gravely should not be sent for as it would surely mean committal to Bedlam and less loving attention unworthy of their affection.

On the evening of the fifth day, during which Arthur's horrors had become more pronounced, Alexander asked Mrs Wormold to take a respite from her duties by spending some time with her friend Mrs Barklea at The Ferry and Flood, which she gratefully accepted. He and Sally then sat in discussion by the parlour fire, aware of Arthur's restlessness above; as the half-consumed logs collapsed in a crackle of springing sparks, a commotion descending the stairs heralded his appearance, his white face lacerated with fear, his hair and nightshirt strung with sweat.

'Sally! Alexander! Help me for the love of God! She really *is* upstairs and I can't get rid of her – all in white – white veil – white madness... and a shroud over her arm she says she will put me in at five in the morning... stop the clocks at twenty to nine... I don't want to go in the trumbril – it's a cold white journey and it's raining...'

Alexander took him comfortingly in his arms. 'She can't be there, Arthur, without coming in at the door or window. We've been here all the time and not seen her pass up the stairs.'

'But she's in the corner by the foot of the bed and she's mad – dreadful mad. She wails, *my heart's broken – he's broken my heart – my heart bleeds through my bridal gown... see – here where my heart is. Broken! And white flowers that now are red.*' A choking spasm convulsed him, saliva threading his lips and unshaven chin. Forbidding Sally to yet alert Dr. Gravely, and herself not to come up, Alexander managed Arthur back to his bed where he clung to his arm.

'Don't you see her? Look – she shakes the shroud at me still. Tell her to take it away – I don't want it on the scaffold... is that her head bleeding on a pike?'

'Hush now,' Alexander soothed, fingering back strands of wet hair. 'She won't be harming you ever again.'

'Lock her in the cupboard, bad animal – she may try to escape with the King.'

'Sleep, Arthur. Close your eyes. I'm here. You're safe. I'll stay with you and watch. I won't let Estelle affect either of us.' He dried Arthur's brow of scalding perspiration.

Arthur closed his eyes and sighed. 'Keep watch... that's right... we need that shroud for *her*... she'll get it on *me* if she can... hold me safe...' He reached out, his face a carnage of pain, his body as if withstanding an unseen force. Coughing clamping

, he stared straight into Alexander's eyes. *'You have... ...en... my... heart...'*

The candle's flaccid flame slumped low in its socket juggling exhausted shadows about Arthur's troubled form. After some minutes, during which his breathing settled in awkward rhythm, Alexander slowly arose without averting his eyes from the prone body. He paused, swallowing hard as an unbidden mist clouded his vision. Imperceptibly, he lifted Arthur's head, carefully sliding a pillow from beneath. With infinite grace, as if lying a baby in its cradle, he placed it over his upturned face, holding and pressing gently but firmly, his heart almost rent in two as he encountered some faint resistance. He pushed down further, long after resistance subsided. He halted his own breathing a moment, then, to ascertain that Arthur's was stilled.

After replacing the pillow with dignity, he sat for a while holding one of Arthur's clammy hands – his drawing hand; the hand which might have drawn a fortune, legally or illegally, had no human frailty cut short two such potentially lucrative careers; he studied his face too, liberated now of strain or hardship – a fair face once again, reminiscent of lighter earlier days. Bending as if in homage, he kissed him softly on the mouth, whispering, 'sleep in peace, my dear,' as had been his custom in those easy, boundless days at school. Arthur's dead mask suddenly caught at what vestige of human feeling still glimmered in the shadowy crypt of Alexander's personality. Arthur's pain had melted into an almost wax-like calm; in its place glowed once again an innocence symbolising for Alexander his own lost youth – one as yet unchallenged by the need to establish identity and power – the need to remain also, the dominant force over one's actions, own destiny, and those of others.

Opening the garret door, he descended unhurriedly the two floors to the parlour where his wife tried to occupy her mind with some darning. She stopped, wool taut in her needle, as her husband stood before her.

'He's calm now, Sal. You'd better go for Dr. Gravely.'

For a moment they shared a conciliatory hug as Sally murmured, 'he's well out of it, poor tortured soul. It's a service you've done him, Alexander, and no mistake, God forgive you.'

'It was the least I could do,' he replied, straightening his back, 'before his sister put a shroud on us both.'

TABLEAU X
1803

A short, neat, middle-aged lady, determinedly clutching her reticule, peered through the locked gates of Satis House. With eyes as piercing and dark as those of twittering birds flitting about the untidy, wind-blown premises collecting nesting materials, she surveyed the rank forecourt, the numerous iron-barred windows, the two chains linking forces across the once proud entrance; the communication gate to the brewery over the narrow side lane swung on its strained hinges as though exercising to keep itself warm. The mansion's abject appearance came as no surprise – she had been warned that nobody arrived, nobody departed; that each year another few slates slipped and smashed on the yard-stones, another foot or two of ivy strangled casements and sashes, human life within indicated only by incessant smoke meandering from certain chimney pots summer and winter, heat wave and freeze.

Gathering her shawl tighter about her slight shoulders, the lady tugged at the bell-pull. A woman, appearing from a side-door, crossed to her with a bunch of keys.

'Are you the lady who wrote respecting a visit to Miss Havisham?' she asked, politely. 'I suppose you know Miss Havisham sees virtually no one.'

'I am told of this at The Blue Boar,' replied the lady, with a foreign accent. 'Is it Madame Hall I am addressing?'

'Indeed,' she said, unlocking the gate. 'Please come if you will, Madam.'

Carefully locking up behind her, she led her visitor into the airless house and down a long corridor to a compact sitting room cheered by hospitable hearth; it drained even further the emaciated view of leafless tangle through the stone mullions framed with heavily fringed burgundy curtains.

'Yes, Madam, the garden too is a wasteland,' said Mrs Hall, as though reading her visitor's thoughts. 'Please sit – here, by the fire. You'll be something mystified by appearances, I dare say?'

Madame perched on the edge of her chair, her hands folded just-so over her reticule, her eyes seeming to assess every detail of her surroundings as if they possessed some deeper significance. 'I was wishing to visit long before I came to England at this time, but was not understanding of my letters being unanswered.'

'Miss Havisham has been extremely ill,' said Mrs Hall, sitting opposite. 'For months, Dr. Sawley despaired of her life, but she recovered, contrary to expectations. From then until now she's seen no one except me... and her lawyers... received no letters, no outside contact for two years. You know her story, do you?'

'I learned it at The Blue Boar – how her *fiancé* abandoned her...'

'Since twenty-minutes-to-nine on her wedding morning,' said Mrs Hall, warming to the tale, 'time and daylight have ceased for her. Now she's a shade of her former self. She lives upstairs, I live down. The house was full of presents, you see – guests waited at the church, the bridegroom's parents amongst them – the wedding breakfast was laid. It was the worst day of my life, Madam, as you can imagine... having to deal with upset guests – angry, some of them. As if it was *her* fault! The groom's parents were so humiliated – I could have wept for them as they returned to Winchester, and all that food going to waste and this house looking so lovely. You're better not wanting to see her – I urge you not to press it, for I don't want to forfeit my character.'

'I shall see my friend,' confirmed Madame, 'and you shall not lose your position in this house.' She opened her reticule, and withdrawing a piece of paper, unfolded it. 'Be so good as to place

Madmoiselle Havisham. I shall remain here until you ⌐nce me.'

Mrs Hall had only to appreciate Madame's penetrating eyes and set mouth to realise that here waited a possible match for her mistress. She smiled, taking the paper out of the room. Madame waited by the window, depressed at so much inexplicable disarray. Apollo Belvedere, green with slime and fallen backwards in the grass, continued optimistically to hail the environment…

'I am afraid it is as I say,' said Mrs Hall, on her return, 'Miss Havisham wishes to see nobody. She wouldn't even let me tell her your name – I'm very sorry.' She returned Madame her folded paper. 'She is not herself any more, you realise.'

'Who else is living here? Cooks? Servants? The house is of some size.'

'I was housekeeper here when her catastrophe befell – we had a large staff then but I alone remain – Miss Havisham's requirements are neglible… I've yet to see her eat anything, even… I know she wanders about at the dead of night with her candle foraging for what she can get. All you hear is the swish of her silks along the floor and a low moan – either her or the wind through the cracks – sometimes both.'

'It is true she remains in her bridal attire? Such is the rumour of the town.'

'It's no rumour, Madame. She was dressing for her wedding when it happened. There was a letter – brought by her half-brother. That was shock enough because we'd all been told he was dead – died in prison some time before – and there he was looking so like the living dead no one dare approach him. Nobody saw what was in the letter for she pitched it on the fire after reading it while screaming the place down… she had a collapse of the mind and when she recovered, she dressed herself exactly as she had been at the time the letter arrived, closed all the curtains, had all the clocks stopped at twenty-to-nine, instructed her lawyers to close the brewery, dismiss the staff, lay the place waste. Even the breakfast feast remains on the table, with the cake all rotting in the middle. She just mopes about all day and night in her upstairs rooms thinking about I don't know what. She has property round about and in London but nothing matters to her any more and her business in not my business. Her money certainly brings her no joy now. Never had any Havisham scandal, and there'd been a few, Madame, attracted such attention and so many heads shaken so readily for the fall of so many hopes.'

'And her *fiancé*? What manner of person was he to have caused so much damage?'

'Between ourselves, Madame, woman-to-woman, I can admit to his attractive appearance being something you're not likely to forget in a hurry – she bought that statue out there because it looked like him – and his manner and voice were all any mother could want for a son. It was easy to follow Miss Havisham's infatuation with him – I believe they'd met some years previous when she'd set her sights on him then. But he was a fake – a charlatan. He deceived her as cheats, swindlers and hypocrites do. There was no manner of skulduggery he wouldn't stoop to. It was thought he'd skipped off to Italy before the wedding – they'd spent a lot of time there – but the last I heard was he'd got himself found out over some piece of malpractice he'd organised in Hampshire and was in a London goal – it was in our newspaper a while back... and that's where he's best off, in my opinion, where he can't infect innocent folk with his charm and poison. But obsessed with him she was – and still is, if you ask me – possessed more like... as if she's inhabited by an absent ghost, if you understand my meaning.' She arose. 'I'm sorry, Madame, your visit has been fruitless. May I offer you some tea before you go?'

'Fruitless it has not been, I assure you,' returned Madame, 'and I do not require tea, *merci*. Nor, indeed, am I intending to leave without achieving what I came to do. I shortly will be

...dinburgh with my work and do not know when I may ... to England. I have waited many years to see my friend again and *I will do it.* If you'd be kind enough to show me the way I shall announce myself.'

'Madame, I dare not. I hear the last person to go against her wishes – a male cousin I think – was forbidden to come here ever again.'

'She shall not forbid *me,*' replied Madame, going to the door with a flourish. *'Mon dieu,* I am not to be beaten.'

Mrs Hall saw she had no option but to light a separate candle and make her way across the sullen hall, beetles and spiders scampering back from their unaccustomed disturbance. With silent misgivings, she ascended the cavernous staircase and indicated Miss Havisham's boudoir. She retreated, leaving the candle on a side table as Madame turned the door handle without knocking and slipped inside the room.

Miss Havisham, clad in her bridal weeds, sat like a weary doll in her armchair beside the fire, her back to the door. The room's half-packed trunks, untidy furniture, tightly pulled curtains, emerged in candlelit prisms of rainbow colours glancing from chandelier lustres and scattered jewels scintillating amongst her dressing table's dusty clutter. She did not look round as Madame took in the scene at a glance. Softly, Madame placed the unfolded paper on the white lap, its paleness intensifying the printing's block-blackness.

LATELY ARRIVED FROM THE CONTINENT
THE GRAND EUROPEAN
CABINET OF FIGURES
MODELLED FROM LIFE. AND NOW

EXHIBITING AT THE LYCEUM, STRAND, LONDON.

MADAME TUSSAUD, ARTIST,
Respectfully informs the Gentry and Public of the
Great Metropolis, that her Unrivalled Collection
has just arrived here.

The full-length PORTRAIT MODELS of their most
Gracious Majesties
King George III & Queen Charlotte
and entire Royal Family
and notables
of England.

'I told you not to bother me,' said Miss Havisham flatly, not looking up. 'Tell who ever it is to begone.'

'Estelle,' said Madame, gently, pointing further down the handbill, 'don't you remember?'

UNIQUE Exhibition also contains Portrait
..acters, as large as life, in full-dress, correctly executed:

The Late Royal Family of France, viz:
King, Queen, Madame Elisabeth, Princess Royal and
Dauphin.

Also: Princess de Lamballe, murdered in Paris by the Mob.
Madame du Barri, Mistress of Louis XV, guillotined in Paris.
Count de Lorga after his release from the Bastille.
Heads of Robespierre, Danton, Fouquier de Thionville, etc.
as they appeared after the guillotine.

ALSO CURIOUS AND INTERESTING RELICS.

'Versailles, Estelle? Petit Trianon? Uncle Emil?'

'Dead! All of them. Particularly Estelle.'

'You are as alive as I am, Estelle. I have come from Paris to visit you – to talk over the good days.' She knelt beside the unresponsive figure, touching her thin arm.

Miss Havisham continued staring into the fire. 'Have you also come back from the dead to taunt me? Arthur did.'

'I am not dead, Estelle. I am very much alive and you should be with me. I shall be going to Scotland at the end of April – if I put you in my exhibition of waxworks, who would know the difference? This is not like you, dear friend? It is springtime outside...'

'Don't speak to me of place or time. I am done with them all as they are done with me.' She fingered her veil as if to conceal her existence. 'I trusted the world and it broke my heart.' She turned her empty gaze on her visitor. 'Are you the same Marie from years ago? The face is the same. So is the voice. But not the name.'

'I married after the Revolution.'

'Married. I see.'

'Joseph is a good man – a Civil Engineer – but, *quel dommage,* so careless about money! I am not. When Uncle-Papa became ill and died during The Terror, he willed everything to me, including his debts. If I wished to retain the Boulevard du Temple, it meant work – I have always been used to work. Within seven years I'd cleared the debts and was free to travel abroad with my collection if I wished. I've been in London for...'

'I don't wish to know of where, or how, or why. They mean nothing to me.'

'Do *I* mean nothing to you, Estelle? I alone remain of our youthful days. I have reconstructed my life with a new heart.'

'If your heart had been damaged like mine, you would not talk so. If you only knew my story.'

'I *do* know your story, *ma cherie,* and it grieves me deeply. But life cannot fall like a balloon at one tiny rent...'

'A broken heart one tiny rent!'

'*My* heart is broken too, Estelle, many times over, let me tell you. Many times it is broken, like my models, but I mend it, as I do them. And the more the mends the easier it is to do. I have never let my heart rule my head, *comprends-toi?*'

'*Your* heart? *How* broken?'

'To explain would mean involving the whens, whys and wheres you profess to have done with.'

'*How* broken? You seem in remarkably good condition for a broken heart.'

'My heart was broken when Uncle-Papa obliged me to leave Madame Elisabeth and Versailles. Do you remember? My heart broke again when three of my soldier-brothers in the Swiss Guard at the Tuilleries were slaughtered in the September Massacres as they defended our King from the citizen mob, their heads hacked off, gutter-snipes playing ball with them in streets running with blood – people washing in it – drinking it – flesh and entrails being eaten raw and roasted... Paris was wild and as butchered. I vowed I would never speak of this ...stelle – it is too painful still.'

'I wish to know. I loved him, you know – my Alexander – I adored him with my whole heart.'

'Do you think I adored my King and Queen any the less – and my Royal Mistress? They were as good as my family. Their crime? – Being Who They Were. *Vive la Nation,* the King had said – *the Nation has no better friend than I.* The Queen listened to the poor and needy –visited workplaces and hospitals, but it was too late – *la Revolution* was in the hands of the people, not the monarchy. If only their escape in that ridiculous German coach had not failed at Varennes! They were arrested and executed like common criminals – my Queen they sent in a common dung-cart – at least they'd had the decency to provide a covered *caleche* to keep the rain off my King. The little *Dauphin* they left in prison to cruelty, neglect and merciful death. ' Marie paused, mastering her tears.

'For my love of them I was imprisoned in La Force,' she continued, after a moment, 'and there *I* nearly died. But it was industry – my work – which kept me alive. I learned to keep my fingers busy and my tongue still and not be particular as to what the Tribunal required of me, however distasteful. Hurrah for Citizen David – Danton – Robespierre. Ugh! – but I barely escaped the scaffold for my pains. The days and days I spent in the *Cimetiere de la Madeleine* taking casts of death-heads. The Tribunal intended to punish me with overwork as it was doing *la guillotine,* newly designated a Saint! Can you credit? The Princess de Lamballe was raped, slaughtered in the street and her head paraded on a pike before I was obliged to accept it at my melting pot. The King they brought me in a barrow, his head stuck between his legs like a cabbage; and my lovely Queen – Madame Elisabeth – your Uncle Emil – friends all, loved and loving – brave – serene. I preserved their serenity, but at each my heart broke anew.'

Miss Havisham had remained impassive, except for watching some molten candle-grease overspill a sconce high on the mantelpiece and dribble over in petrified spears, like blood drained of life.

'Then the work was brought to my cell after my loved ones were deep in their pits of quicklime. There seemed no end to my labour until Robespierre and his *confreres* passed under my hands – and soon the bloodiest of them all: Fouquier de Thionville... how fearful I'd always been of his mean, bloodless lips – nor did they model well. It was all over. By some miracle I had been spared and was soon released. I reopened the *Cabinet de Cire*, mine now under the terms of Uncle-Papa's will. I would not see it squandered on his creditors – the Phoenix rose out of the mayhem but a Phoenix alone – I, a woman in a man's world, can fight as well as any of them!'

'I was Queen Antoinette,' said Miss Havisham in a wandering sort of way, 'but she was fortunate enough to enjoy a *real* death. I tried when I was ill but the Havishams are notorious for their resistance. I know my half-brother would have liked me to join her on the scaffold. He saw her die, you know. How would you have cared to cast *my* death-head, Marie?'

'But I modelled you in life, Estelle. That counts for more. Come. Let me see it again. I have a fancy to recall *happy* days now. Where do you keep it? I don't see it in here, though I am a little short-sighted as you know.'

'It has been missing many years,' Miss Havisham sighed. 'For all I'm aware, it is *also* broken.'

'Time is a potential mould for healing,' said Marie, 'if you give it chance to fill. Do you think I felt nothing at leaving my husband and two-year-old son at home with Mama? Yes, my heart is toughened, but not quite numb. Business is business and I have my eldest boy with me in London – a true comfort.'

'How old is your boy?'

is four. He has his father's name but not, I am sure, his weak business head.'

'Bring me your boy, Madame, and I will teach him how to break a girl's heart. Bring me a girl and I will teach her how to break a boy's. And yet... I would wish to save them both from a fate like mine.'

'I consider ignorance a worse fate than a broken heart, and I would be ignorant myself if I did not face my need for finance in order to aid what I am doing – helping those who can't read or have little education. I want them to benefit and learn from what I set before them – picture-language is the oldest in the world. I know my work is good – it informs – it entertains – it has survived the Terror and I don't intend to waste it now. As my beloved Queen wrote not long before she died, *tribulation first makes you realise who you are.*'

'You are very sure,' said Miss Havisham, bitterly. '*I* was sure... now look at the difference between us. I, too, appreciate the value of ignorance, so am thinking of taking in a companion – a youngster – whom I can educate against developing such a heart as I used to have. As you say, the mould of time has the potential for healing, even if a generation too late. Young Jaggers will find me what I require – his father is retiring, but no matter, he'll do just as well – I have jewellery here a girl would be pleased to play with.'

Marie had got the measure of Miss Havisham well enough to hold her own counsel as to the wisdom of such a proposition.

'What is money, anyway?' Miss Havisham drummed her fingers on her chair arm. 'Due to my father, I once thought it represented power, and that's what I wanted, like him. But I see now it's worth only what someone wants you for. You were kind to me when we were young, Marie. I have never forgotten. Your visit is kindly meant, and I thank you for it. I should like to be kind to you in return – to give you some money to help with your business here. Will you accept such a gift from one who has no further use for it?'

'*Ma cherie* Estelle, how I appreciate your generosity,' she replied, taking hold of her sinewy hands. 'I am shrewd enough to know the value of your offer. But... I feel bound to say I can accept only if I earn it – if I can persuade you to abandon this prison – this tomb – to come out into the vibrant world – live again – join me in my business, even – then should I feel justified. Forgive me – that is how I feel.'

Miss Havisham nodded silently to herself. 'Then there is no more to be done,' she said awkwardly. 'Come with me.' She left her chair, the handbill slipping off her lap onto the hot hearth; she stalked across the room with the first show of purpose Marie had recognised. Following in her rustling wake, she crossed the passage to where she flung open the door of the room opposite, also lit by candles. Like a catafalque down its centre, the celebration table bore the components of its feast like a corpse beneath its funeral veil of cobwebs – the silver black with neglect, the crystal dull with abandonment, the springy white damask yellow with fatigue.

'This is my other sanctum,' said Miss Havisham, almost glaring round the lavish decay. 'When I grow sick of sitting in *there* I come and grow sick of sitting in *here*. But I have my rats and mice and spiders for company This is *my* place – *here* in the centre, where the cake is. And this is *Alexander's*, next to me; and *this* Cousin Sarah's...'

Marie considered that though she had witnessed many bizarre events, none could compare with this time-stopped *tableau* with its untasted cake rising like a mouldering watchtower over the field of defeat.

'My heart is as broken as that vase down there.' Miss Havisham pointed to the shattered glass remnants of a fluted urn-shaped container amidst a pile of rotten flowers on the floor. 'Alexander brought me it from his first visit abroad – from

...ity, like his love, built on water. Oh, Marie, what a ... was... so handsome... so *dangerously* handsome. He ...oke my heart so I broke his vase. Oh, *why* did he make me fall in love with him? Why did he let me lose control of my feelings? He used me, Marie, and I didn't realise. Now I feel humiliated and ashamed. That is what my love has cost me – that's the price I've had to pay, and it's left me the poorer. I *so* wanted to be loved – to *rely* on being loved... for ever... That is why I have stopped time – in order that we may stay together, he and I. When you return to London, or Paris, or wherever, make a model of my wedding feast, Marie. Make an effigy of me and place me amongst it. *That* should educate your audiences – perhaps even entertain them – who can tell? You could do worse than to warn them of expectations like mine.'

'This *tableau?* What should I call it? *The Price of Vanity?*'

'Call it *The Price of Love*. It's a price I have paid in full. He was my Apollo, and I his Daphne. He said he hoped I wouldn't change, but I have – the laurel is all dried up. My father's bright star fell from her heaven.' She sat on the carpet in front of the fire, her arm resting on the seat of a throne-like arm chair. 'Alexander caught me in his snare and I cannot find my way out. I am ensnared for life and so I shall remain. Thank you for coming. Now I am tired.'

Marie stood her ground, her natural inclination to drag the musty curtains from blocking the daylight; to dash the rubbish from the table revealing the polish beneath; to lead Miss Havisham out into the garden to receive the clamour of Spring on her timid flesh.

'Estelle... my dear...'

'I want no pity. The choice is mine. I know what I have done. It is enough.' Miss Havisham cushioned her head on her arms, hiding her face. 'Satis.'

Marie could do nothing but respect her wishes and withdraw. Reluctantly, she closed the door, and collecting her candle, made her way downstairs to where Mrs Hall came to meet her.

'You saw her then, Madame? I'm so glad. Enough to make a body shudder, don't you think? And what a waste of a fine house...' She led Marie back along the passage, passing the door to the cellars. 'She'll never change now I don't suppose. Still, better to be caged up here than in the madhouse I reckon.'

'Please take care of her,' said Marie, at the gates. 'I doubt I shall visit again.'

'You can be sure of that,' said Mrs Hall, 'though she looks after herself, you might say, and I looks after me. I mean, you have to in this life, haven't you?' She let Madame out then locked up securely.

When, a little later, she went to check on Miss Havisham, she found the boudoir empty; the scorched remains of Madame's handbill curled like a dead leaf on the cooling hearth. After tidying the embers and rekindling the blaze, she placed the fragment in the centre, watching as the springing flames consumed the last characters of a legend:

CURIOUS AND INTERESTING RELICS.

LOUIS XAVIER'S POSTSCRIPT
1882

Eighty years have passed since Miss Havisham and Madame Tussaud met for the last time. Miss Havisham has been dead these fifty-two, Madame Tussaud nearer thirty.

Having just read through the foregoing chronicle, I must confess to viewing myself also as something of a curious relic – whether *interesting* or not I shall leave others to decide. I certainly find no difficulty in reliving the emotions I had to combat back in 1861, when Mr Dickens declined to publish. I took his rejection very much to heart, coming, as it did, so soon after Mrs Eldon's and the death of my Mama – a rejection of a sort.

Through working all those months at so frantic a pace, both physically and mentally, it was not surprising that when it ended and Mrs Eldon possessed my book, I suffered from a type of nervous exhaustion. My convalescence provided me with ample opportunity to consider my future. With impetuousness typical of youth, I decided I would be unable to continue visiting Mrs Eldon impassively – that I would, in fact, rather not see her at all. Nothing, therefore, prevailed to keep me in London – or England, for that matter. I resolved to take what talent I had and try my luck elsewhere. The financial consideration I had received from Mrs Eldon for my labour encouraged me to contemplate a sweeping horizon; by the end of the year I found myself justifying by post to her that my move to Australia would benefit my career, whilst regretting that preparation for my departure absorbed my time to the full, allowing me no opportunity to say farewell personally. Did she understand, I wonder, the true reason why I dared not trust myself finally to confront her before leaving the land we both shared?

We exchanged letters occasionally throughout the ensuing years; but one event I never divulged. It occurred on that outward journey. I took with me all my possessions, of course, including the waxen head. During some particularly ferocious weather, our ship struggled to ride it out, with two of the crew washed overboard and I, not least amongst the passengers, ill for days. The luggage, when we got it disentangled, had taken a pounding – the band-box, splintered like shards of some cadaverous pot. It revealed a smashed mess barely recognisable as the model – all that was left to me of the driving force behind threads of events unwound when I was eleven and leading to my place now aboard a ship set for the other side of the world. I could not help wondering if its wreckage signified my punishment for contemplating marriage with Miss Havisham's adopted daughter – a woman of fifty-four! Or did it emanate from Miss Havisham herself, for having delved too deeply into the melting pot of her desire to break men's hearts? If that was the case, then her posthumous intent had succeeded.

But how ever many miles I imagined I could distance between Mrs Eldon and me, I could not distance her influence; time and time again I regretted not having her likeness with me, though it never ceased focusing as positively as a *daguerreotype* on the clear plate of my mind.

So, until April, 1880, I had to remain content for correspondence to be my only physical contact with her. It remained, for my part, on a superficial level, its crust of gentility protecting my vulnerability as efficiently as a mould protects its cast. For all I could deduce, Mrs Eldon followed my example; in 1870, she informed me of Mr Dickens's death, at the early age of 58, from overwork – even uncharacteristically hinting at morbid humour by saying that having died whilst engaged on his new novel, *The Mystery of Edwin Drood,* the rest of the mystery would now be designated a space beneath the floor of Westminster Abbey. I learned, too, of how her various philanthropic causes progressed; of her recovery from a bout of rheumatism; of cultural matters she thought would interest me, such as the construction, further west along Kensington Road from her house, of the Royal Albert Hall of Arts and Sciences on a site almost opposite where the Crystal Palace had signified our first meeting in the summer of 1851.

I was able to keep her informed of my journalistic abilities, my posts of sub-editor, then editor, of a Melbourne newspaper and eventual ownership of a pleasant modern villa in a leafy suburb. After my father and brother Charles died, my brother Henri and his new wife also emigrated. They established themselves not far from me, where with immense pleasure and not a little envy, I watched their family increase and thrive.

I derived much satisfaction from giving Mrs Eldon notice of my return to England. I found a letter awaiting my arrival at Ketteridge's Hotel in South Audley Street (as coincidence would have it, developed on the site of de Boissiere's). It requested me to call upon her as soon as convenient. I had deliberately provided her with no reason for my return – I assumed she regarded it as a well-earned holiday.

Nothing at the Kensington house had changed, except the maid who ushered me in; it was as if it were time-stopped Satis, and I not Louis the forger of words but Pip the forger of metal. There was Mrs Eldon, ready to greet me at the top of the staircase. Dressed in dark green silk, her bustle and bows the height of fashion, she stretched her arms to me as I almost took the stairs two at a time.

'Louis, my dear...' We embraced with silent, unashamed emotion, tears streaming down my face whilst I hugged her as though my life depended on it. Her beauty had softened with the years, though her voice and deportment retained their customary dignity. An adolescent heart pounded once again in my breast as she conducted me into the drawing room to resume my place, after such an age, in those familiar surroundings: Mr Dickens's arm chair; the maid bringing in tea; the red and gold china; Mrs Eldon before me on her *chaise-longue*, emeralds as lambent as spring in Hyde Park.

Our conversation covered a range of subjects; she inquired about my life abroad, showing particular interest, as I expected, in social concerns and active work. Inevitably, we returned to our past literary association. It set me thinking again of all the information which had fallen outside my work undertaken for Mrs Eldon: Cousin Camilla's energetically pursued hypochondria foiled to perfection by Raymond's humouring; Matthew Pocket's successful marriage to the only daughter of a Knight of the Realm and the birth of their eldest son, Herbert; of the sour Sarah's eventual installation, at twenty-five pounds *per annum*, as housekeeper at Satis – some compensation for her jealous and unmarried state; Abel Magwitch's marriage to wild young Molly and the birth of their daughter; Alexander Compeyson's abandonment of Sally on perfecting his life of crime with Magwitch – their eventual apprehension would have provided for fascinating writing. Mr Dickens however, had alluded to these in his work.

I also regretted not having had the opportunity to enlarge on how young Mr Jaggers brought Miss Havisham a two-year-old girl to adopt and call Estella; nor on Pip, Joe Gargery's young brother-in-law, whose infatuation with Estella began when invited to Satis to play one day... but then – all this had been dealt with so thoroughly powerfully by Mr Dickens. What, I wondered, would he have made of Estella's and my story!

'It was unfortunate,' said Mrs Eldon, at length. 'that circumstances were against the publication of your work. I had nothing to do with that I assure you – Mr Dickens knew my history quite independently of what you were told. He published with my full cooperation. I was glad of it, as it dispelled many of my fears. If you can tell the truth, no one can have further hold on you.'

'I think you were extremely brave allowing Mr Dickens to fashion *Great Expectations*,' I said with a certain awe. "If I had been a person of your standing in Society, I don't know how easy I'd have found it to advertise that I was the true adopted daughter of an unbalanced recluse. I think it would've broken my spirit, if not my heart.'

'I was often accused of not *having* a heart,' replied Estella ruefully. 'Miss Havisham's one ambition was to ensure its suppression. But I have proved her wrong. Charles Dickens and you made it easy for me. I believe he was also aware of two similar cases to Miss Havisham's. There is still nothing wrong with my memory, Louis, for I remember him reporting the first in *Household Narrative,* a supplement to *Household Words.* I recall quite clearly, in the first issue for January, 1850, an account of the death of a girl called Martha Joachim, of twenty-seven, York Buildings, Marylebone. She lost her reason when her suitor blew out his brains with a pistol whilst sitting next to her on a sofa. Like Miss Havisham's, her dress was white, and though covered with blood, she wore it until she died – unlike Miss Havisham, she was not burned to death where she sat but died in her bed from bronchitis. The other tale, which Mr Dickens himself told me, concerned an educated eighteenth century gentleman called Nathaniel Bentley, who lived in Leadenhall Street. He went insane when his bride-to-be died on their wedding day. He closed up the room where the wedding feast was set out – let everything go to rack and ruin – in complete contrast to his former elegance. I expect all these factors, including mine, came together in Mr Dickens's mind when he had to make that sudden move to win back readers to *Household Words* after Lever's *A Hard Day's Ride* failed so dismally. When *Great Expectations* was concluded, we never spoke of such strange goings-on again and I lived at peace with myself. He had your manuscript still, I think, but you were gone.'

'His was the greater creation,' I said. 'I was happy enough simply to have known him.'

'He is sadly missed,' said Mrs Eldon, wistfully. 'We see his like only once a generation – if we are lucky.'

I thought for a moment she was about to cry – a phenomenon which alarmed and upset me, for never had I known her let slip her mask of composure; concerned, I took the place beside her to hold her hands letting her speak on.

'Louis, my dear... it must seem strange for you to be back in this room after all these years. It is so good to have you here – your presence enhances it. It compensates for the hurt I felt at your going – without a word – until you were out of reach, but I accept I may have deserved it though I never intended to hurt you. You have never married. That is sad.'

'It would have been sadder to marry someone I didn't love.'

'Have I something to do with your not marrying? Be honest.'

'You taught me honesty,' I replied, a lump in my throat. 'As you once told me: *we can't alter the truth without being untruthful to ourselves.* Because I have preferred to preserve the truth of my love for you, I have found no one to live up to it. Many years ago you once said you loved me as the son you'd never had – loved my character and honest determination. I'm proud to have meant those things to you and am content if I still do.'

She arose and walked slowly to the window. 'Most certainly you do, my dear. Your honesty gives me courage – Wordsworth was right when he said that the child is father of the man. I am an old woman, Louis. I have endured much suffering in my life. I understand how you suffered, just as Pip before you must have done. But I suffered with you, though I believe my decision for us to remain friends apart, as Pip and I did, was correct. I have had to find more courage than ever before to ask you here today.

I was terrified you might not want to come, though I had to speak with you – see you – put my mind at rest – even ask your pardon for any disservice I may have done you...'

She used the word *terrified* in connection with *me?* 'Please don't,' I implored, going to her. 'There's nothing *to* pardon, and how can you speak of disservice? Have you done me a disservice by making it easy to love you? – to recognise what love is? I loved you then and I love you now. I always *will* love you. You may pardon me *that,* if you wish, but I shall never pardon myself. And you certainly needn't be terrified I shall make another embarrassing proposal – my only ambition is to be allowed to continue loving you until I leave this world – I value you too highly to want you as nurse to a dying man.'

'Oh, Louis... it can't be so...' The break in Estella's voice affected mine.

'This is my other reason for coming back – coming home. I have a cancer the doctors say will kill me. At first I was afraid. Not any more, because I've seen you again – you are still the ideal I have found nowhere else in the world. That's what matters more to me. Your courage in facing the realities which is at the root of *Great Expectations* only reinforces my feelings. I love you as much now as I did when a boy of seventeen, Estella, and, believe me, my dear, that is sufficient.'

Our arms enfolded one another as we remained quietly together for a lengthy time in the stillness of that hushed room...

* * *

So. I am brought full circle – back to the present – back to me – here – now. Mr Dickens, my youth's glorious beacon of life and enthusiasm, passed away twelve years ago; Mrs Eldon at Christmas. She had offered me one of her properties in Hyde Park Gate but, grateful as I was, I preferred to remain – for that period anyway – in the less obligatory surroundings of

Ketteridge's Hotel. Under the terms of her will, however, the Kensington house became mine, complete with contents and an annuity. It is here, at her desk, that I have spent my last Spring composing the Prologue and Postscript to her story.

From her executors, I also received the blue-bound copy I had prepared for her of *Expectations Of A Great Lady* – a story of dishonesty – which I have lately been rereading. Attached to the fly-leaf is a letter addressed to me, written at this very desk I presume, dated before I took up residence at Kensington.

My darling boy,

Should I be the first to die, I wish you to know that I do not consider myself the perfect individual you are always kind enough to credit me with being. Had my character been as blameless, I would have spoken to you personally of the matter contained herein. But it is my courage alone which fails me in this, not my honesty.

You will recall, from the pages of Great Expectations, that in 1821, Miss Havisham sent me to be educated abroad. You will appreciate her connections with your family in France from the time her own father sent her there at the age of fourteen. It became known to her, long after the Revolution, that her Uncle Emil's children had escaped The Terror and were still alive – I believe, though I don't remember seeing them, that they attempted to visit Miss Havisham at Satis, in the same way Marie Tussaud had. This provided her with the opportunity, through Mr Jaggers, of sending me to France to tread in her footsteps, so to speak.

Whilst there, and distanced from Miss Havisham's influence, I fell in love. He was a young man of your family – one of Emil's Grandsons. He was little more than a youth, as you had been. It was then, for the first time, that I discovered the power of immediate love and something of what Miss Havisham had gone through.

Etienne, like Miss Havisham's Alexander, was beautiful and I found myself unequipped to manage myself. I was not at liberty to seek help, nor did I know how to – expected as I was to play my role in Miss Havisham's scheme. Diamonds and other riches awaited me at Satis – I was never allowed to forget. I caused Etienne as much hurt as I did you – even as I hurt Pip the blacksmith's boy from the moment we met at Miss Havisham's rusty gates. You were entrusted with Miss Havisham's story, Mr Dickens with mine. That double burden is now removed – the slate is clean.

The only way I could see to expiate my conduct was to record some explanation and place the blame, if blame it be, at Miss Havisham's door. We were both victims of our upbringings. My expectations, like Miss Havisham's, like Pip's – even like yours, dearest Louis – can be said to have been blighted from their outset. Though I know you do not think I have made use of you towards my own ends, I would ask that you try and attribute the entire business, my dear, to the harmless whim of an inward and rather lonely old woman who nevertheless loved you, in her way, for more than twenty-five years.

Your Estella Eldon

I was familiar with the reputation of Etienne du Monde; he had been my father's elder brother – clever, handsome, gifted in the arts. He died seventeen years before my birth, the general belief being that his suicide was the result of a secret but hopeless *affaire de coeur*.

For my part I shall take no secret love to my tomb. Though I am, by nature, an expressive person, I have spent all my life expressing the thoughts of others without ever expressing myself. But now, once and for all, I am being self-indulgent – selfish even; I think I have earned it. I look back from these days of my so-called maturity and set down my heart at last. And the beauty is that when other eyes than mine see into it – other tongues than mine dissect and moralise – my heart will be impervious to other hearts' values; achievement will be my last word; silence my victory. That is my destiny – one moulded by time, for worse for better, for poorer for richer, in health and in sickness.

All that remains for me to do now is combine my two narratives – to discard the blue cover, the colour of restraint, and bind them both together – Estella and me – in red, the colour of passion. I shall leave it here, on the desk, at the end, with such surviving letters and Arthur's drawings as she gave me. Then I shall be ready to slip out of a time which moulded us as certainly as the mould which formed the waxen head of my formative years.

As I moulder into oblivion, I take with me not only my experience of love – but in addition, its timeless expectations.

Finis

BATTLE OF Largs

BY
TODD FERGUSON

WITH ILLUSTRATIONS BY VICKY PATCHETT

'The magic gale blew o'er the host
On board the sea-steeds closely manned,
And that restless bane of earth
The sea, drove warlike crews ashore
On Scottish land, their warshields bearing,
Eager to combat for their king.'
Sturla Tordsson (1264/5)

ISBN: 978-1-7385397-0-3

TOWER RIDGE PUBLISHING LIMITED
Printed by LPC Design + Print, Largs - www.lpcprint.co.uk

The Battle of Largs 1263
Norse Account

CHAPTER ONE
SETTING THE SCENE

The following account will provide the reader with an introduction to the Battle of Largs in October 1263.

A discussion, held at the Glasgow Archaeological Society in 1911, provides part of the inspiration for the commentary in the chapters that follow.

To locals and visitors alike, the events of early October in 1263, and particularly the enigmatic Vikings, are usually what people associate with Largs in North Ayrshire, on the west coast of mainland Scotland.

If the reader is in any doubt, they only need to look at the world-renowned Viking Festival, the giant 'Magnus the Viking' memorial on the promenade, the Pencil Monument, the Viking fish and chip shop, and the sign on the road from Glasgow signifying that you are now entering 'Largs: the Viking Town.'

However, visitors might be entirely unaware, of the reasons behind this fascination with the Vikings in a small town on the west coast of Scotland.

Hopefully, this little booklet will help to explain the history, and look behind the myths which have endured.

It is a story full of wonder and it seeks to transport the reader back to a wild and stormy couple of days in early October 1263.

The Battle of Largs is one of those episodes which is often, misunderstood. From the size of the conflict to the decline of centuries of the Norse associations with Scotland.

A good place to start, is to explain that the historical accounts recording the events cover centuries. They have evolved during that time to take on gargantuan proportions and significance.

In the second section of the book, we will cover the Scottish historical sources and illustrate how the story has changed through time.

In the first section the source we are using is the Norse Saga, called the 'Hakonar Saga Hakonarsonar,' which dates to a contemporary timeline.

Historians date it to circa 1265, although theories suggest that the medieval author commenced his magnificent work in the spring of 1264, only a year after the Battle of Largs had occurred.

Its author was a historian named Sturla the Lawman, great name. He was the nephew of an eminent Norse historian by the name of Snorri who had been responsible for the seminal work called 'The Heimskringla' which is regarded as the best known of the Old Norse kings' sagas.

Therefore, Sturla was probably an accurate, and a reliable source for the events.

Furthermore, two additional medieval chronicles survive which are similar to the Norse version of events, the 'Chronicle of Melrose' and the 'Chronicle of Mann.'

Finally, and perhaps more troubling, the first full and detailed account which recorded the events of 1263 from a truly Scottish perspective were not composed until much, much later.

Andrew Wyntoun compiled an account about 150 years after the Battle of Largs. While Walter Bower did so about 180 years later.

Historically, this is problematic, as we will see in the second section.

Following the events of 1263 some historians like to describe the Battle of Largs as the final nail in the coffin for Norse influence here in Scotland.

However, as we will find out in the pages that follow this is not as easy an argument to make as it first might appear to be so.

Following the expedition to Largs the Norwegian king, Haakon IV, sailed back up to Orkney. The sources clearly explain that he was on his way back to Norway with the purpose of raising a new force so that he could resume campaigning the following year.

When Haakon died, his son Magnus VI succeeded him, and he was far less interested in continuing the military campaigns against Scotland. Therefore, he began negotiations with the Scottish king to agree a financial settlement for selling the Western Isles.

The result of these discussions was the Treaty of Perth in 1266. The treaty stipulated that the Scots would pay Magnus four thousand marks, and that every year following a further one hundred marks would be paid to cede the Hebrides and the Isle of Man to Alexander III and the Scottish crown.

The treaty further stipulated that Alexander, and the Scots would recognise Norwegian claims to Orkney and Shetland, which remained under Scandinavian influence until they were annexed by the Scottish crown in 1472.

CHAPTER TWO
BACKGROUND INFORMATION

he distinct historical advantage of the Norse version of events is that the author relied upon eyewitness accounts from people who had personally accompanied the 1263 expedition.

As mentioned previously, the saga was written by Sturla the Lawman, around 1264/5. It is probably the most accurate version of events available.

Nonetheless, as with all historical sources there are caveats. Whenever using historical sources, it is always important to investigate if there is a patron, or sponsor, for the work. This is crucial, as it allows for a better understanding as to the motivations of the author for writing an account.

In this case, the history of king Haakon IV of Norway, was commissioned by his son Magnus VI. Therefore, it is important to consider that Sturla could have been trying to impress the new king when writing his version of events.

However, when you read the Norse saga closely, it is evident that Sturla has tried hard to present a balanced version of events.

Now, let us look at the Norse saga in more detail.

An entry for the year 1262 describes how the Scottish earl of Ross, William I, and Kjarnack Machamal's son went with a force of Scots to raid in Skye. It says that they:

'...burned farms and churches and slew a host of men and women. And they said this that the Scots had taken small bairns and spitted them on their spear-points and shaken them till they fell down on their hands and cast them dead from off them.'

Gruesome stuff indeed. It is also quite different from later Scottish accounts of these events. In the second part of this booklet, we will look at what those changes were in more detail.

The Saga explains that the news of these attacks by the Scots travelled quickly. Several 'kings,' who were living in the Western Isles, sent letters asking for assistance from king Haakon who was then in Bergen, Norway.

When the letters finally reached king Haakon, the Saga recorded that the news:

'...touched him with great care.'

Sturla claimed that the attack on Skye, by the Scots, was the catalyst for gathering a mighty host that would set sail from Norway to the Western Isles.

CHAPTER THREE
THE ADVENTURE BEGINS

fter king Haakon received the letters from the 'kings' of the Western Isles that described the atrocities committed by the Scots in Skye, Haakon set about rallying his forces in Norway.

The saga tells us that Haakon's son, Magnus, the future king of Norway, had offered to go on the voyage, one can assume in place of his father. However, Haakon declined the offer with warm words and instructed Magnus to oversee the kingdom during his absence.

By the standards of the mid thirteenth century, Haakon was an old man having reached almost sixty years of age. Magnus, on the other hand, was a man of twenty-five. So, why did Haakon want to personally go on campaign instead of his son.

The saga explains that Haakon refused Magnus because he personally knew the Western Isles. Furthermore, it states that he understood the politics, and so preferred to lead it himself. The entry provides an interesting insight into how medieval authority was undertaken in practice, personalities played a part and understanding the political complexities made Haakon the best man for the job.

There is a wonderful description of the preparations which tells us that Haakon:

'...had fitted out that big ship which he made them build in Bergen, and which he had designed for his own crossing ship. It had thirty-seven benches and was big besides and built of oak alone.'

Pretty cool huh. Well, it gets better still, it continues:

'That ship was made with a splendid Dragon head, all plated with gold; and so too the beaks fitted in the same fashion.'

Remember this description of Haakon's ship, it will be relevant to a later chapter.

Haakon sent several people in advance to Shetland and Orkney before he himself left Norway. The reason being that they needed to find 'pilots' for their ships. A practice still employed today whenever captains are not familiar with the local seafaring conditions.

Having arrived in the Northern Isles they met one of the Western Isles 'kings,' Dubghghall mac Ruaidhri (MacRuari), a descendant of the great twelfth century Norse-Gaelic lord Somerled. The mac Ruaidhri family would become one of the main Gaelic medieval kindreds of the Western Isles alongside the mac Dughghaill (MacDougall), mac Suibhne (McSween), and mac Domhnaill (MacDonald).

As this is primarily a booklet about Largs, I will not go into too much detail about the procession of Haakon's fleet amongst the Northern and Western Isles of Scotland.

The saga provides some wonderful verse explaining that behind this advance force came Haakon with the main fleet and it was said:

'Valkyrie lanterns (shields)
To bulwarks made fast,
Smote the bright heavens
With gleam of red gold;
The host of the king
As it skimmed o'er the main
Was like unto lightening
That springs from the sea.'

The names of some of those who went on the expedition were also recorded. The following were part of the handpicked crew of Haakon's ship:

Thorlief abbot of Holm	Sigbert Bodvar's son
sirra Askatin	Hoskuld Odd's son
Four priests	John easy
Aslak gush – the king's marshal	Arni skilful
Andrew of Thissis-isle	Sigurd son of Ivar tail
Andrew Harvard's son	Helgi son of Ivar of Loflo
Guthorm Gilli's son and his brother Thorstein	Erlend blackleg
Eric shot Gaul's son	Dag of Sudrheim
Aslak Dag's son	Brynjolf John's son
Steiner tough	Gudleik snack
Clement the long	Erlend the red
Andrew mocker	Ogmund crow-dance
Eirikr the son of king Dubhghall	Andrew clubfoot (kings' treasurer)
Einar Lombard	Eric quarrelsome
Arnbjorn stifler	Thorfinn Sigvald's son
	Kari Eindrid's son
	Gudmund John's son

The account contains many more names which are not listed here. The reader will no doubt agree that there are some fantastically colourful and descriptive names listed.

According to Sturla many famous captains accompanied Haakon on this campaign. This was a gathering of the absolute best in late thirteenth century Norse circles.

CHAPTER FOUR
HAAKON ARRIVES OFF LARGS TO PARLEY WITH ALEXANDER III

In the interests of time, I have condensed events. The saga contains detailed descriptions as Haakon sailed down the west coast collecting men, securing oaths of fealty, and harrying certain islands into submission.

What is clear is that many agreed to come out in support of Haakon. Men such as Ruadhri who laid claim to ownership over the Isle of Bute. Alexander III king of Scots had outlawed him, and it suggests why he would swear allegiance to Haakon. It is from Ruadhri's Isle that we apparently get the modern name of Rothesay.

However, there were also those who did not support Haakon such as Eoghan MacDubhgaill of Argyll. The paternal second cousin of Dubhghall mac Ruaidhri mentioned in Chapter Three.

Moving down the coast Haakon arrived with his force off the Island of Arran. Messengers came from Alexander III to try and secure peace.

During the discussions Haakon agreed to send messengers to meet with the king of Scots at Novar (New Ayr).

According to the Norse account these discussions went quite well. Haakon's messengers named all the Western Isles that belonged to the king of Norway.

However, as part of the negotiations the king of Scots said he wanted Bute, Arran and the Cumbraes. Haakon could not agree to give these islands up and because of this refusal peace could not be secured.

During the negotiations, the Norse saga says that the Scots:

'spun out matters more and more...'

because,

'...summer was then passing away, and the weather took to getting worse.'

The Norse saga noted that these delaying tactics were a ruse so that the king of Scots could gather more forces from up the country. It claimed that those with Haakon pleaded with him to ignore the truce and to begin harrying the surrounding countryside as they were, at that time, running noticeably short of supplies.

Haakon did not pay these concerns any heed and while the negotiations were ongoing, he moved his entire force in between the two Islands of the Cumbraes and the Scottish mainland, near Largs.

Haakon sent the king of Scots an emissary, Kolbein the knight, in a final attempt to resolve the diplomatic stalemate. He offered the king of Scots two options. Meet Haakon to discuss peace or meet him to fight it out and let God decide who would be victorious.

The king of Scots declined to meet Haakon marking the official end of the truce.

Things were about to get serious.

CHAPTER FIVE
THE OTHER EXPEDITION TO LOCH LONG AND THE STORM ARRIVES WITH A VENGEANCE

fter the truce negotiations had fallen through, and the Scots had delayed long enough to push the date further in to Autumn, Haakon had finally had enough of talking.

He sent sixty ships, almost half of his fleet, further up the Clyde towards Loch Long, with Arrochar at its head.

The expedition never really gets much airtime in the story of 1263. However, it is important because the force was comprised of the Norse-Gaels from the Western Isles.

The Western Isles force was led by Magnus king of Man (Isle of Man), king Dubhghall mac Ruaidhri mentioned previously, his brother Ailean mac Ruaidhri, and two other high-profile Western Isles magnates called Murchadh Mac Suibhne and Aonghus Mor mac Dohmhnaill.

These are names that we would recognise today as some of the biggest Gaelic families, and they had sided with Haakon and the Norse. Furthermore, during this raid they enthusiastically took part in the despoliation of lands on the Scottish mainland.

The Norse part of the fleet was commanded by Vigleik priest's son and Ivar Holm.

It was on this expedition that one of the most amazing feats occurred. Sailing down Loch Long they landed in Arrochar and were confronted by a natural barrier. Instead of turning back, they instead carried their longships over the hills and down into Loch Lomond so that they could continue raiding.

They wasted the lands belonging to the earl of Lennox with fire and sword, all around and the islands themselves in Loch Lomond. The land was 'well tilled;' that is, given over to agriculture.

The saga tells us that Ailean mac Ruaidhri:

'...went almost across Scotland slew many a man. He took many hundred neat and did much ravage.'

It was while on the way back from these raids that the fleet ran headfirst into a massive storm and ten ships were destroyed. Ivar Holm became sick and died.

At the same time as the Loch Long raid was taking place, back up off Largs, on Saturday the 29th of September, Haakon was still laying up in front of the Cumbraes.

Reading the account it is clear that they remained in their boats, not on land. Awnings were erected on the boats to provide shelter, under which they slept.

Unbeknownst, to Haakon all hell was about to be unleashed on the unsuspecting fleet bobbing about in the Clyde.

Sturla recorded that on Monday night, the 1st of October 1263:

'...came a violent storm with hail and tempest.'

Then on Tuesday the 2nd of October, early in the morning just before daybreak, while it was still dark, those on the boats:

'...called out who kept watch at the moorings of the kings ship that a bark was driving on the cables forward.'

Now, cast your mind back to the description of the figurehead made of gold on Haakon's beautiful ship. The 'bark' had broken free from its anchor and the saga says that it struck the figurehead of the king's ship where it carried away the beaks.

So, here we have a primary source account describing a violent collision amongst the fleet. It is quite possible that lying somewhere in the watery depths, between the Cumbraes and Largs, are parts of king Haakon's own ship which are no doubt still covered in gold. What a wonderful find that would be for the archaeological record.

Also, you will recall that during the negotiations with the king of Scots that Haakon's men had been concerned about their supplies running low. A bark was a ship in the fleet that carried all the supplies needed for a successful military campaign. Therefore, the bark becomes an important centre piece to events that would play out on the Largs shingle.

According to Sturla's account, during the ferocity of the storm, the bark had become tangled in Haakon's ship and in attempts to save the boats the anchors were cut away.

It could be that it became stuck as the tide went out and were driven onto Great Cumbrae during the night. This still catches modern vessels unaware even today. However, by morning the bark had drifted upon the Scottish coast during the high tide.

We are told that Haakon left his ship, and his crew rowed him onto Great Cumbrae where it is said that he had a mass sung for him.

To try and combat the wild weather the saga explains that the Norse attached eight anchors to Haakon's ship. Even with all the additional supports in place his boat still drove on into the sound, and towards the Scottish mainland.

In all, the saga describes that five boats were driven upon the shore near Largs. The account is quite specific saying that of the five mentioned, three of them were altogether driven onshore and were now in trouble.

Furthermore, the Norse believed that witchcraft was at play in conjuring the storm against them, and there are two wonderful verses:

'The careful king
Met witchcrafts many
From the wizard lord
Of Scottish land;
The rolling surf
By black-arts driven,
Looses many a ship
Of canvas bright,
From moorings stout
Made fast on shore.'

And:

'The magic gale blew o'er the host
On board the sea-steeds closely manned,
And that restless bane of earth
The sea, drove warlike crews ashore
On Scottish land, their warshields bearing,
Eager to combat for their king.'

CHAPTER SIX
THE FORCES MEET ON THE SHINGLE AND THE FIRST ENCOUNTERS

uring the huge storm, ships from Haakon's fleet had been pushed onto the shore of the Scottish mainland and crucially one of these ships was the bark, the main supply ship.

The saga tells us that on Tuesday the 2nd of October the Scots force witnessed the stricken ships on the beach and decided to attack them by shooting at them.

One can only assume that arrows, spears, and stones were hurled at those on the shore. Sturla is clear that aerial missiles were used during the beginning of the fray which undoubtedly allowed the Scots to keep their distance from the Norse below.

While under this aerial bombardment the Norse took shelter behind the bark and defended themselves. Imagine colourful shields being raised above heads to protect them from the missiles that were raining down upon them.

In the account the commencement of battle is hardly representative of the glamorous depiction of a grand chivalric battle between the two combatants which are often recreated in romantic Victorian representations depicting the Battle of Largs.

Nonetheless, the saga tells us that although the numbers of those killed were small, there were many wounded.

Haakon watched this unfold and decided to act by taking a cutter out to his own ship. The saga is not clear, but it seems as though Haakon was still on the Isle of Great Cumbrae while all of this was going on.

He took with him Thorlaug the hot, probably named for his temper rather than his looks, and once they landed on the shore:

> '...the Scots fled up country...'

And so ended day one of the Battle of Largs.

What is striking is that it was hardly the massive, pitched battle that we think of once the Norse hit the shore. The saga tells us that the Norse stayed on the beach all night and on Wednesday morning they went into the buss, given the name unsurprisingly a transport ship, and headed back out to the king's ship.

This is where the information and importance of the bark (supply ship) comes into play. To sustain a military operation, you need adequate supplies to support your army. Keep in mind that it was coming into early winter so there would not have been much supply in the surrounding countryside for foraging either.

It could be argued that the purpose of the second expedition which went to Loch Lomond was a strategic decision taken by Haakon to go raiding for additional supplies.

Remember, that the Scots had previously employed delaying tactics during the negotiations whereby the saga explained that the Norse were already worried about their declining supplies.

This was a severe problem. If the bark (supply ship) had not been one of the vessels to beach itself on the shore, then it is entirely possible that the Battle of Largs would never have happened at all. At the very least it would not have been the uncoordinated mess that it had become.

On Wednesday, according to the saga, the Norse armed themselves and rowed back to the shore because it says:

> 'the Scots had come to the bark and taken such of the goods as they could get at.'

Unmistakable evidence that the Scots also saw the advantages of a boat laden with supplies just waiting to be carried off. At this time Haakon landed on the shore and he:

> '...made them strip the bark and bear her cargo into boats and carry it out to the ships.'

This is a point that is often overlooked by those writing about the events of 1263. It is sound military tactics to protect your supplies and resources. That is why Haakon had no option but to land after the initial mayhem caused by the arrival of the sudden storm.

Furthermore, it is unbelievable that later Scottish sources talk about the size of the opposing forces being 15,000 mad Vikings who were facing up to 1,500 Scots knights on the shore. The dubious figures of the Vikings are obviously massively inflated, while the number of Scots is small. This is discussed at length in the second section in this booklet.

Unsurprisingly, the Norse saga provides a completely different view as to the balance of the two forces.

'When the bark was all but cleared, the host of Scots was seen, and most thought the king of Scots himself must be with them, for the host seemed great.'

As this force approached the men pleaded with Haakon to return to the ships and send more men to help them.

He offered to stay, as most kings would, and any good saga author would include for the son of the said king, but eventually he was put onto a boat and taken back out to the main fleet.

The saga provides us with figures as well, and while they were substantial, they were certainly not into the multiple thousands as recorded in Scottish sources.

'By the reckoning of most men there were in all eight or nine hundred men on land.'

It is important to remember that these were eyewitness accounts. To ensure accuracy, like any good historian, Sturla claims to have spoken to as many diverse sources as he could to get confirmation for the record.

He says that of these:

'two hundred men were with Ogmund crow-dance up on a hillock, but the other force stood down on the shingle.'

There has been a lot of debate as to the precise location of the Battle of Largs. Some suggest it is Largs, others Skelmorlie, and some further down the coast towards Hunterston.

It may prove difficult to locate the actual site as the landscape has changed over the centuries. However, the saga does offer some tantalising environmental clues to look out for and a hillock capable of accommodating two hundred men, close to a shingle beach, would be the perfect place to start looking for answers.

CHAPTER SEVEN
THE MAIN BATTLE OF LARGS ENSUES

 s the previous chapter confirms the Norse saga explains that the Scots force assembled against them was:

'...a very great host.'

Sturla, interviewing his eyewitnesses in 1264/5, explained that some had believed there were five hundred knights, and others that there were less than this. Furthermore, they recalled that they were very well armed and had:

'...mail-clad horses, and many Spanish steeds all covered with armour.'

As well as the force of mounted knights it says that there were:

'...a great host of footmen, but that force was badly equipped as to weapons. They most had bows, and Irish bills.'

The Norse, on top of the hillock, were advised to come down onto the shingle alongside the remaining force, which was duly accomplished saying that they were:

'...not to hurry like runaways.'

Seizing on the initiative, the Scots attacked quickly and showered them with stones and other missiles which rained down on the Norse. Under this onslaught they fell back facing the enemy with shields to protect themselves from the missiles which were raining down on them from an elevated position.

However, as some of the retreating Norse reached the brow of the hill, they picked up the pace trying to be faster than the others to get back to the beach. The saga says that most of the Norse coming off the hillock:

'...took to running.'

This must have looked like they were fleeing from the Scots and in turn caused a panic amongst those who were on the shingle. They started to run for the boats, which quickly disembarked. Most of these boats sank and some men were lost.

The saga explains that some of the force stayed on the beach and took shelter around the bark (supply ship).

Someone, the saga does not say who, shouted for them to stand their ground and not to run away. Hearing this command some stopped and turned back, but the saga says that it was only a 'few.'

It was at this point that Haakon's personal bodyguard Haco of Stein was killed, and the saga bewails:

'Then the Northmen (Norse) still ran away.'

This mayhem hardly seems to fit with the traditional image of an orchestrated battle and the Norse, those who were still on the shingle, were scattered all along the shoreline.

It is due to these types of entries that the Norse version does not appear to be a particularly biased account of the events. Sturla seemed quite content to write about his own Norse compatriots panicking and running away.

However, this could also have been deliberate to please Magnus VI, for whom the saga was written.

Eventually, the Norse managed to regroup into a more cohesive unit and:

'...then there was a hard battle...'

The saga certainly says that the Scots had the ascendency claiming that the fight was a:

'...very unequal one, for there must have been ten Scots to one Northman.'

It will be interesting to compare this to the Scottish sources from one hundred and fifty years later to see what they say about the numbers involved.

A champion of the Scots is mentioned at this point. The saga calls him Perus, and he is apparently Sir Piers de Curry.

He makes such a valiant impression on the Norse that they singled him out because:

> '...he rode more boldly than any other knight.'

He was struck down by the Norse as the following poem by Sturla explains:

> 'Our brave men laid low,
> In the tussle of war,
> The foes chosen champion,
> That valourous knight;
> The vultures were sated,
> With flesh from the life-lorn,
> O Perus proud horseman,
> Who shall thee revenge.'

There is another version about Sir Piers which reads:

> 'He wore a helmet plated with gold and set with precious stones; and the rest of his armour was of a piece with it. He rode gallantly up to the Norwegians, but no other ventured. He galloped frequently along the Norwegian line, and then back to his own followers. Andrew Nicholson had now reached the Scottish van (vanguard). He encountered this illustrious knight and struck at his thigh with such force that he cut it off, through the armour, with his sword which penetrated to the saddle. The Norwegians stripped him of his beautiful belt. The hardest conflict then commenced.'

The saga states that:

> 'Many fell on both sides, but mainly Scots.'

CHAPTER EIGHT
THE END GAME AND SOME ANOMALIES

hile the Battle of Largs raged on the shingle another fierce storm began blowing which prevented Haakon from being able to land more of his men on the shore.

It is said that even despite these challenges Rognvald and Eilif of Nautadale had attempted to land in support of their colleagues.

Rognvald was driven back, but Eilif was able to land with some men:

'...and behaved very daringly...'

The tide of battle began to turn and the Norse advanced, with the Scots retreating up the hillock. There followed a lingering fight with missiles of shot and stone.

Nearing the end of that day the saga says that the Norse:

'...made an onslaught on the Scots up on the hillock and there fell on them most boldly.'

The Ravens song captures the moment:

> *'The chosen barons of the king,*
> *Chief-justice of North-Maeren folk,*
> *With war-songs hailed their sturdy foes,*
> *What time the hill at Largs they scaled.*
> *The valiant henchmen of the king,*
> *Who keeps his throne in awful state,*
> *Marched iron-hooded, cased in steel,*
> *Against the foe in sword-stirred fray.*
> *Brown brand bit the rebels sharply,*
> *At the mail-moot (battle) on the hill;*
> *Up the 'How' the red shields mounted,*
> *Till their bearers reached the top.*
> *Then the Scottish brand-gale cloudmen,*
> *Took to flight with terror stricken,*
> *Turned their heels those doughty soldiers,*
> *From the champions of the king.*

The description is interesting because often discussions of the Battle of Largs only describe the fight on the beach. Many accounts do not explain the ebb and flow of battle as it shifted across the landscape as is evident from the Norse saga.

The saga concludes by telling us that the:

'...Scots fled away from the hillock as fast as each man could to the fells.'

On witnessing the withdrawal, the Norse headed back to the boats and reembarked. They rowed back out to the ships with some difficulty due to the continuing storm.

Many of the accounts about the Battle of Largs describe the events as a single battle which ended with defeat for the Norse and describes them sailing away for Norway never to be seen or heard of again.

However, that is not what happened, at least according to the Norse saga. It explains that on Thursday the 4th of October the Norse sailed back to Largs seeking the bodies of their fallen comrades.

This is hardly in keeping with the actions of a soundly defeated enemy who had been sent home with their tails between their legs.

The saga provides the names of some of those who had fallen in battle:

> Hacon of Stein and Thorgils silly - of king Haakon's bodyguard
> Carlshead - a good freeman from Drontheim (Trondheim)
> Halkell - another freeman from the Firths (Shetland and Orkney)
> Thorstein boat, John ballhead, and Halvard bunjard, all pages

The saga does not record how many Scots fell because they had gathered their fallen and carried them back into the woods.

Haakon then ordered that his men be borne to the church, probably the old church of Largs which is known to have been standing at the time of the battle.

So, according to the saga, not only could the so-called 'vanquished' Norse land their boats on the beaches of Largs the day after the battle, but they were able to gather up their dead and carry them to the local church for burial.

The saga then says that:

> *'the Thursday after (i.e., the day following the battle) he let the anchors be weighed and his ship be moved under the isle (of Cumbrae).'*

It was around this time that the second force which had been sent to Loch Long, Arrochar, and Loch Lomond re-joined the fleet.

On Friday the 5th of October the storm had slackened and:

> *'...the king sent on land his guests (possibly meaning Dubhgall, Ailean, Aonghas, Murchadh) to burn those ships which had driven on shore.'*

It was not until late Friday that Haakon finally sailed away from Cumbrae and stayed a few nights at Lamlash, Arran.

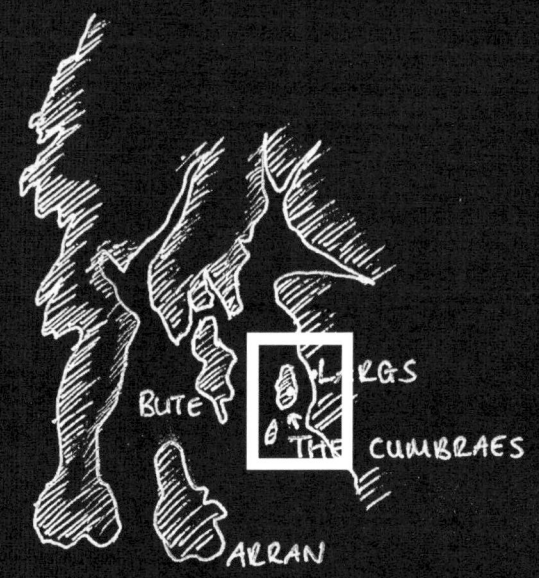
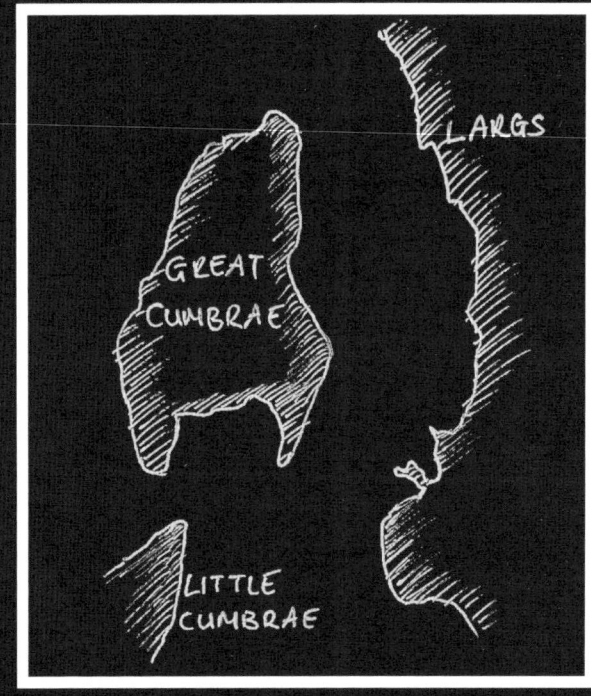

CHAPTER NINE
Beyond Largs 1263

arlier in the saga, before setting out towards Largs, Haakon had been contacted by Irishmen (Hiberno-Norse) who had asked for help to:

'...free them from the sway of the Englishmen.'

Following the battle the saga explained that after the arrival of Irishman at his camp, while he was in Arran, Haakon was:

'...much inclined to sail to Ireland...'

However, his men were not remotely interested and as a result Haakon said that they could sail for home once the weather improved because:

'...the host had fallen short of victuals.'

This confirms that the loss of the bark (supply ship) on the shores of Largs had huge consequences for being able to continue the campaign.

Ivar holm, who had died of disease on the Loch Lomond campaign, would be transported to Bute where he was summarily buried.

Haakon and his force then began to weave their way slowly back up the western seaboard of Scotland towards Orkney.

On the way Haakon laid a fine on Islay. Some of that had to be paid in meal and cheese, another indication of how desperate things had become for his force.

Sailing onto Kerrera between the 24th and 26th of October they hit another storm and scarcely a ship in the fleet managed to retain their sails.

While here Haakon sent emissaries to Eoghan MacDubhghaill, who had not joined him due to having previously sworn allegiance to Alexander III, but nothing came out of this meeting.

The supply issues are evident again as the saga tells us that while in Mull:

> 'Haakon heard that his men had slaughtered many cattle on the shore of Mull and some men of the Mull-dwellers were slain, and two or three Northmen as well.'

Sailing himself to the Calf of Mull he parted company with Dubhgall and Ailean. He gave them the lands that had previously belonged to Eoghan. Again, further evidence that Haakon certainly did not think that he had lost anything at Largs.

King Magnus of the Isle of Man, and other southern islanders, parted company here also.

He gifted Ruadhri, the Isle of Bute, Murchadh, the Isle of Arran, and Dubhgall, Kintyre Castle. Interestingly he gave nothing to Aonghas.

Haakon met up with more of his followers along the way and ran into yet more dangerous weather trying to reach Orkney. As a result, the fleet had to put in at Loch Snizort in Skye where he again levied a fine for supplies.

Sailing past Cape Wrath, they put in at Durness where his men captured some Scots who promised to bring him cattle. Haakon gave them peace to do so, keeping one as a hostage.

A bizarre episode is described here which is worth retelling from the saga:

> '...eleven men of the ship of Andrew kuzi went on land in a boat to fetch water. A little after it was heard that they called out. Then men rowed to them from the ships; and there two of them were taken up swimming much wounded, but none were found on land all slain. And the Scots had come down on them, but they all ran to the boat, and it was high and dry, and they were all weapon less, and there was no defence. But as soon as the Scots saw that the boats were rowing up, they ran to the woods, but the Northmen took the bodies with them.'

Haakon still had the hostage, but the saga says that he let him go in peace the following day.

More drama ensued with the weather and seas on the way to Orkney where some ships were lost. One boat having a near miss with '...the Swelchie...' or whirlpool which explains why the Pentland Firth is still considered to be one of the most dangerous stretches of water in the world today for mariners.

Faring to Orkney Haakon let some of his fleet sail home to Norway while he decided to winter in Orkney, because the weather had hardened. Keep in mind that he was sixty years old by this stage.

While in Orkney Haakon became unwell. Perhaps knowing that he was dying he decided upon gifts of land for those who had accompanied him westwards on his campaign and instructed Andrew clubfoot, his treasurer, to arrange payment.

Haakon improved slightly and was able to walk to St Magnus' Church in Kirkwall and around the shrine to earl Magnus that the church is named after.

The saga says that he:

'...allowed a bath to be run for him and let himself be shaved.'

Following this he became very unwell and after first instructing that Latin books should be read to him, he soon switched to the old Norse sagas and stories of the kings from Halfdan the black onwards.

He began dividing up his possessions amongst his bodyguard, guests, dish-swains, and the rest of his serving men.

He wrote letters to his son Magnus and others. He was attended by bishops from Norway and Orkney.

Intriguingly, the Norse saga records that he was asked by his trustiest men if he had any son other than Magnus to which Haakon strongly confirmed that:

'...he had no son to succeed him but king Magnus...'

A few days later, on the 15th of December 1263, just after midnight, the mighty king Haakon IV died:

'He was buried in the choir of Magnus' Church (Dec 17th).'

His faithful bodyguard kept watch over his body all winter and a huge feast was provided by Andrew clubfoot in honour of the king. It was at this feast that wages were given to all his men.

Haakon had prearranged that in the event of his death that his body was to be moved to Norway when it was possible to do so. His body was exhumed on the 5th of March 1264, for this reason. After the journey across the sea, he would finally be reinterred at the church in Bergan, Norway, to rest alongside his ancestors three days before Lady's Day (March 22nd).

The following poem was sung by Sturla, the author of the saga, at the burial of Haakon:

'Woden's companion
To Bergen came
Three nights before
He was buried in Church
There stood many thanes
Not lively with wet lids
Very sad o'er his grave
It tried the heart hard.'

That brings us to the end of the journey explaining the Battle of Largs from the Norse saga as Sturla Lawman wrote it.

In the next section I will provide the reader with an understanding of these events from a Scottish perspective.

It will illustrate the ways in which history has been embellished over time.

CHAPTER TEN
THE LANERCOST CHRONICLE

The Lanercost Chronicle is a northern English source that was compiled during the reign of Edward I, king of England between 1272-1307.

The account is believed to have been a continuation of an older source covering events between 1201-1346. Historians suggest that the older source was written first by Franciscan monks, before being further added to by Augustinian monks at Lanercost Priory, Cumbria. It is a contemporary source for the Battle of Largs.

However, there are inaccuracies within the account, as we shall see.

The first issue is the date. It is given as 1266, instead of 1263.

The chronicle records that the writer had attended the burial of Nicholas de Moffat, the Bishop Elect of Glasgow, at Tyninghame, Lothian, in 1270.

In the chronicle, there are other examples where the writer is either an eyewitness or had spoken to eyewitnesses in relation to major events. Some of the entries involved the family of Alexander III, demonstrating a close association with the royal house of Scotland.

Given this close personal connection with the writer, it is plausible that he was present at the Treaty of Perth in 1266, when the western isles of Scotland were sold by the Norwegian king to the king of Scots.

It is exciting that Scottish sources record that two of those who were designated as messengers of the new king of Norway at The Treaty of Perth, Sir Askatin and

Andrew Nicholson, accompanied Haakon as mentioned in earlier chapters.

Another plausible explanation is that the writer could have discussed the events with someone at Tyninghame in 1270 and made a mistake in terms of the chronological sequence of the events.

There is no firm evidence to support these claims, but human error in other sources is a regular occurrence, so it is entirely plausible in this case as well.

A second error is that the record mistakes Haakon for Magnus. This could be explained due to Haakon being buried on the feast of St Magnus, in St Magnus' Church Kirkwall, Orkney, he was succeeded by his son Magnus, and the king of Man was also called Magnus. It would be easy to be confused.

However, the mistaken identity, between Haakon and Magnus, could explain why the year recorded for the Battle of Largs was done so incorrectly, after all it was Magnus who had secured the Treaty of Perth in 1266.

Nonetheless, the English chronicle was not kind to the Norse 'invaders' when recording the events.

It is important to keep in mind that the authors of the Lanercost Chronicle were not particularly benevolent to the Scots in later sections, and it is the primary source for recorded events during the Wars of Independence, so it is interesting to see the cross-border connections that predate those events.

The entry describes that 'Magnus', as mentioned an error in the source, the leader and prince of the invading Norse:

> '...through his own infirmity died at the extreme limits of the kingdom. They landed, however, at Largs with a great fleet and arms; but on the day of battle, their king being absent, those who were set in array to do battle in his stead, abandoning their lines before the advance had begun, bestowed the glory of victory upon a few prudent men and upon themselves a brand of shame; for the foreigners, who had more of the art of fishing than of fighting, not so much by blows as by billows, perished among their boats.'

It is quite noticeably a different account to the Norse version of events in 1263.

Firstly, it is exceptionally short on detail, and with some glaring errors. Naturally, for historians the question is why?

It could be that the author is relying on second-hand information, from someone who had heard of the event and was recalling it years later.

Given the scarcity of information it could be argued that the account is not using eyewitness testimony at all.

Remember, the Norse saga specifically states that Sturla spoke to people who were eyewitnesses.

The additional confusion in relation to '...their king being absent...' could be relating to Magnus king of Man, who had led the campaign up Loch Long and into Loch Lomond.

Alternatively, if the writer had spoken to Sir Askatin or Andrew Nicholson at the Treaty of Perth in 1266, about the events, they may well have confirmed that their king Magnus was not at the Battle of Largs, which is factually correct according to the Norse saga (see Chapter Three). This could in turn explain the errors in the chronicle.

A decisive point of note is the intriguing reference to the 'foreigners' being '...more versed in the art of fishing than of fighting...' and points to a changing Scandinavian society.

It is often forgotten, that while popular culture likes to remember these warriors romantically as the thunderous Vikings of yore, terrorising monasteries, and coastal communities across Europe, by the middle of the thirteenth century the actual 'Viking Age' had been over for almost two hundred years.

Modern Scandinavian historians claim that the Viking era ended in 1066. Although, here on the west coast of Scotland we would dispute that finding.

The Battle of Largs 1263
Scots Account

CHAPTER ELEVEN
THE CHRONICLE OF MELROSE c1270 AND THE CHRONICLES OF MANN c1261-2

he Chronicle of Melrose is a Scottish medieval manuscript covering the period between 731-1275.

It is thought that the record referring to Largs are contemporary with the events of 1263. The record was kept by Cistercian monks housed at Melrose Abbey, in the Scottish Borders.

Its historical accuracy can be ascertained as it is one of the earliest surviving sources which describes the agreement reached between king John and the barons, the famous Magna Carta of 1215.

The Largs entry is here recorded in full:

> 'Haco [Haakon] King of Norway with an enormous multitude of ships, came across the western sea to overthrow the king of Scotland. But in truth, as H. himself admitted, he was repelled not by human strength but by the divine power, which wrecked his ships and sent death into his host and further, by means of the helpers of their native country, overthrew, and destroyed those who had convened for battle the third day after Saint Michael's

Mass. For which cause they were compelled to seek again their ships along with their wounded and dead, and to turn homeward more shamefully than they had come.'

This is an interesting passage.

The version of Haakon coming from Norway to avenge the attacks on Skye, which were recorded in the Norse saga, have been replaced by a version that Haakon was coming to '...overthrow the king of Scotland.'

The Norse saga, from a few chapters back, described in detail the many reasons Haakon set sail. The letters from magnates in the Western Isles following the attack on Skye, the parley between the two parties trying to find an agreement, and then the eventual clash once the boats had been stranded following the storm. At no stage does the account mention that Haakon ever sought to remove the king of Scotland from power.

Furthermore, the author is using a source that was close to king Haakon, '...as H. himself admitted...'

If we can agree that 'H' is referring to Haakon, then it is unlikely that the author had spoken with Haakon previously. His death in Orkney not long after the events would have made it difficult to get Haakon's personal views on why they had been defeated. However, it is an unusual phrase for the chronicler to have used and it speaks of a personal connection between the author and Haakon, or at the very least with those within his close inner circle. Otherwise, how would the author have known what Haakon had personally admitted was the reason for failure?

Two more points worth consideration; The Chronicle of Melrose was compiled by churchman from Melrose Abbey and given their ecclesiastical devotion can explain the reference to '...divine power...' as being the instrument of the destruction of the fleet. This is divine intervention in the guise of the storm.

Intriguingly, the account is quite explicit to record that it was not the Scots forces that had defeated Haakon '...not by human strength...,' this is in part like the Norse saga.

If you recall, the Norse saga had blamed witchcraft and wizardry for conjuring the storm. It is a crucial point to highlight that the ancestors of the pagan Viking raiders of previous centuries had for a long time been Christianised.

Therefore, by 1263, Christian imagery in the Norse saga is evident with several references to ecclesiastical practices, from worship to burial. The author of the

Chronicle of Melrose, by mentioning 'divine power,' is stating that God had favoured the Scots, and what is more is that it explains that this 'divine retribution' was freely admitted by H. [Haakon] as the reason for his defeat.

A last point of note is that the Chronicle of Melrose says Haakon's defeat was brought about '...by means of the helpers from their native country...' is the chronicler providing evidence that the Scots were ably assisted by people from Haakon's own country? If so, were they from Scandinavia, or the Western/Northern Isles of Scotland?

Haakon is best known for putting an end to the Norse civil wars and brought Greenland and Iceland under his control around 1262. It is possible that some opponents from these conflicts assisted the Scots, although the historical evidence for this is tentative at best.

The second source from this period is the Chronicles of Mann, which is brief to say the least.

The key point here is that Magnus Olafsson was king of Man and the Isles (1254 – 1265). Magnus supported Haakon having led the campaign into Loch Lomond.

Therefore, the entry was composed under the watchful eye of a Norse-Gael cultural community in Man. Although ceded to the Scots kingdom, in the 1266 Treaty of Perth, the Isle of Man was not fully incorporated until the defeat of the last king of Man, Godred Magnusson, at the battle of Ronaldsway in 1275.

The Chronicles of Mann was completed in 1376 and started its record of events from 1017. It is thought that the author responsible for the Haakon entry was writing contemporary to the battle of 1263. It is claimed that Cistercian monks from the Abbey of Rushen, on the island, were responsible for the chronicle and that the main parts were composed and written 1261-62.

It says:

> 'Haco, King of Norway came to the territories of Scotland and, effecting nothing, returned to the Orkneys, and died there at Kyrkewal (Kirkwall). In the following spring he was carried to Norway and buried in the church of the Holy Trinity at Bergen.'

Concise, to say the least.

CHAPTER TWELVE
THE SCOTICHRONICON
THE ACCOUNT OF JOHN OF FORDUN c1384
FORDUN CONTINUATOR c1441

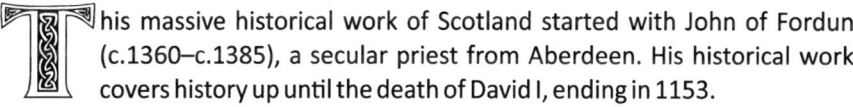his massive historical work of Scotland started with John of Fordun (c.1360–c.1385), a secular priest from Aberdeen. His historical work covers history up until the death of David I, ending in 1153.

This means, that even though John of Fordun was writing his account one hundred and twenty odd years after the Battle of Largs, circa 1380s, the portion of the chronicle which relates to events in Largs were written by someone that historians refer to as Fordun's continuator.

Historians believe that the continuator was Walter Bower (c.1385 – 1449), Abbot of Inchcolm Abbey in the Firth of Forth.

It is important to note that, if Bower is the continuator, he did not write about the events at Largs until approximately one hundred and eighty years after the events, roughly 1447.

The Scotichronicon is undoubtedly a hugely important chronicle for Scottish history. However, Bower's work has been regarded as a poor substitute for that of Fordun, and historians have claimed that there are many inaccuracies contained within the work.

When considering the entry for Largs there are some noticeable swings away from the Norse Saga, and from the subsequent entries mentioned in the other contemporary medieval chronicles we have discussed in previous chapters.

The key issues seem to be with dating the event, and the enormous number of people who are said to have accompanied Haakon.

To put the challenges of Bower into some perspective, historically speaking recording these events one hundred and eighty years after they had happened would be like asking someone today to write an account of the First Afghan War (1838 – 1842), without the aid of Google or any surviving eyewitness testimony. That would be quite the challenge.

Below is the entry in full and the reader can make up their own mind as to the accuracy of the events recorded.

> 'About the Feast of the blessed Peter (Lammas falls on the 1st of August, see note below), which is called ad vincula, in the year 1263, Hako, king of Norway, came to the new castle of Ayr, with eight score warships, having on board 20,000 fighting men; for he said that all the Scottish islands lying between Ireland and Scotland were his by right of inheritance. So, he took the castles of Bothe (Bute) and Man (unusual, as Magnus, king of Man, had accompanied Haakon on the campaign as discussed in the previous chapter) and sacked the churches along the seaboard (this is also a new narrative. Remember that the Norse saga had claimed the despoilation of churches in Skye by the Scots as part of the reason for Haakon launching his campaign). Whereupon, at God's command, on the very day that both the kings had appointed for battle, there arose, at sea, a very violent storm, which dashed the ships together; and a great part of the fleet dragged their anchors, and were roughly cast on shore, whether they would or not. Then the king's army (Alexander III) came against them, and swept down many, both nobles and serfs; and a Norican (Norwegian), king Hako's nephew, a man of great might and vigour was killed. On account of this, the king of the Noricans (Norwegians) himself, sorrowing deeply, hurried back, in no little dismay, to Orkney; and while wintering there, awaiting a stronger force (20,000 men as quoted earlier is an absolutely huge army, so I am not sure how much stronger Bower thought the force should be) to fight it out with the Scots, he died.'

These rhymes have been made about him:

'Hako, that bold and mighty lord,
Of lamblike gentleness
Holds o'er the unjust his threat'ning sword,
But does the just caress.'

He was succeeded by his son, named Magnus, a man of great wisdom and sense (is this because he ceded the islands to Alexander III in 1266?) and renowned for his love of letters.

The following was made up about him in like manner:

'I rule the Noric coast;
Magnus the name I boast.'

Note: The date of Lammas is an error in the text of the Scotichronicon. It is possible to prove this as Haakon was still in Rognvaldsvoe, Orkney, on the 5th of August 1263. We know this as it is recorded in the Norse saga that:

'...a great darkness came over the sun, so that a little ring was bright round it on the outside, and that lasted a while of the day.'

Using modern dating techniques, it has been proven that there was an annular eclipse of the sun.

This has allowed modern historians to accurately place the events in early August of the year 1263.

Thus, providing evidence that Haakon was still in Orkney and confirming that the Scotchicronicon entry is inaccurate.

CHAPTER THIRTEEN
THE ORYGYNALE CRONYKIL OF SCOTLAND
ANDREW OF WYNTOUN c1420

The Orygynale Cronykil of Scotland was compiled by Andrew of Wyntoun (c.1350 – c.1425), prior of St Serfs Inch, Loch Leven and, later, a canon of St Andrews.

Writing in a poetically stylistic way Wyntoun was a contemporary of John of Fordun and Walter Bower, who are discussed in Chapter Twelve.

The account is produced in Scots verse, which can be tricky to read in parts, although there are some historians who claim it was written in northern English and Wyntoun himself refers to his language 'Ynglys.'

What is unusual is that although writing at the same period, about the same topics, these early ecclesiastical historians (Wyntoun, Fordun, and Bower) apparently did not know each other or use each other's work as references. That is hard to believe. Nonetheless, it is what some contemporary historians have argued.

Before going on to describe Wyntoun's version of events in Largs there are two astonishing facts in relation to his work.

Firstly, Wyntoun's work contains one of the earliest references to Robin Hood, there are some who argue that the inspiration for the character is none other than the great Scottish hero William Wallace and co:

> 'Litil Iohun and Robert Hude
> Waythmen war commendit gud;
> In Ingilwode and Bernnysdaile
> Thai oyssit al this tyme thar trawale.'

Translation:

> 'Little John and Robert Hude
> Forest outlaws were praised;
> In Inglewood (near Carlisle) and Barnsdale (West Riding Yorkshire)
> They practised all this time their labour.'

The other exciting fact is that it is from Wyntoun's account that we get information relating to Macbeth and the witches which William Shakespeare used to profound effect in later years.

Now, back to Largs and 1263.

Below is the entire verse that relates to the events. While the reader should be able to follow most of it, a tip is to try and speak it aloud in a phonetic style, a translation can be found in the appendix at the back of this booklet should the reader require extra assistance, where any mistakes are entirely my own.

> 'A thowsand two hundyr sexty and thre
> Yheris efftyr the Natyvyte,
> Haco, Kyng than off Norway,
> Come wyth hys ost and great array
> In Scotland on the West Se.
> In Cwnyngame at the Largis he
> Arrywyd wyth a gret multitud
> Off schyppys wyth topcastellys gud.
> And thare be a tempest fell
> Off gret weddyrs scharpe and snell
> Off fors thai behowyd to tak
> Land, and thame for battayle make:
> And offt syne, as thai mycht wyn
> Thare schyppys, thai wald enter in,
> And ordaynd thame wyth dilygens
> In thare schyppys to mak defens.

The Kyng Alysandyre off Scotland
Come on thame than wyth stalwart hand,
And thame assaylyd rycht stowtly:
Thai thame defendyd rycht manlyly.
A Scottis sqwyare off gud fame,
Perys off Curry cald be name.
Amang the rapys wes all to rent
Off tha schyppys in a moment.
And mony wes slayne that ilk tyde
Off Scottis and Norways on Ilke syde.
Thare thai fetchand war sa fast,
The Kyng off Norway at the last
And hys men fer revyd sare,
That evyre thai arrywyd thare:
For off hys schyppys in the se
Ware monydrownyd; and thare menyhe
Ware sa sted in gret peryle.
The Kyng hym-self into that qwhylle
Wytht his nawyn, that sawffyd was,
Wychtly wan owt off the pres,
And tuk the se hamwart the way,
Thare trad haldand till Orknay.
Thare than tuk land Haco thar Kyng,
And in gret seknes mad endyng.
Men sayd, that sum Scottis men,
Off Scotland mychty Lordys then,
Send thare lettrys oblygatore
Till off Norway this Kyng before;
Gyff he wald cum wyth hys powere
In till Scotland to mak were,
Quhare thai mycht wyt hym till arywe,
Thai suld mete hym thare belywe
On thare best wys to gyve cownsale,
And mak hym help and suppowale.
This mowyd the Kyng off Norway
In Scotland to cum, as yhe herd say:
Bot thai held hym noucht cownnadd,
Quhen he come, as ye herd, in Scotland.

> *Tharfore in till Orknay*
> *In till hys dede-ill quhen he lay,*
> *The lettrys sellyd off that cownnand*
> *Till the Kyng Alysawndyr off Scotland*
> *In gret hy he gert be send,*
> *To mak hys mennys dedys kend.*
> *Till Alysawndyre the thyrd oure Kyng beforne*
> *Ane fayre sone that yhere was borne*
> *In till Gedworth. Schyre Gamelyne,*
> *Byschape off Saynctandrewys, syne*
> *Baptyzyde that barne, and Alysawndyre*
> *Hym callyd, as we before hys fadyre.*
> *And quhen off that byrth come tythyng*
> *Till Alysawndyr the thyrd oure Kyng,*
> *It wes tauld hym that ilk day,*
> *That dede the Kyng wes off Norway:*
> *And swa in dowbill blythness*
> *The Kyngis hart all (that) tyme wes.'*

An intriguing little entry and quite different from previous ones in terms of style. It is a wonderful part of Scottish medieval history.

What is fascinating is that Andrew of Wyntoun explained in his account that mighty Scottish Lords invited Haakon to make war in Scotland.

This could be a reference to the letters that were written by the Hebridean kindreds and sent to Haakon following the attacks on Skye.

It is worth noting that by the time Andrew of Wyntoun is writing the Western Isles had been in the Scots domains for over one hundred and sixty years and as far as Wyntoun would be concerned the great Gaelic magnates were indeed mighty Scottish Lords, for example the powerful Lordship of the Isles.

Furthermore, the dynasty of Alexander III had been completely replaced. First by Balliol, then Bruce, and in the time of Andrew of Wyntoun the early decades of the newly founded Stewart dynasty.

The Orygynale Cronykil of Scotland is a fascinating piece of historical source material.

CHAPTER FOURTEEN
LIBER PLUSCARDENSIS c1461
A STUDY IN HOW HISTORICAL SOURCES CAN CHANGE THE TELLING OF A THING

So far, we have looked at several sources from a Scottish narrative which roughly follow information contained in the 1264/5 Norse saga, give or take some rather fanciful and extreme poetic licence on the numbers of Viking invaders that accompanied Haakon's fleet in later Scottish versions.

However, this next source, the Liber Pluscardensis, provides an excellent example of why proper historical analysis should always try and use as many sources as possible to find the best possible understanding of what transpired.

The Liber Pluscardensis was written at Pluscarden Abbey in Elgin, Moray circa 1461 by a secular cleric called Maurice Buchanan.

It was written on behalf of the Abbot of Dunfermline. which was the mother house of Pluscarden. This source relied heavily on the previous sources already discussed. However, the narrative is quite different in many areas.

Firstly, Chapter XXIII, which contains an account of Largs, is called the 'Battle of Largs, and victory through Saint Margaret.'

Interesting, as this is the first version that mentions Saint Margaret and her 'involvement' in the victory of Largs.

For those who may be unaware, Saint Margaret of Scotland is none other than Margaret of Wessex (1045-93). Her brother was Edgar Aetheling, who had inherited the throne after Harold II, king of England, was killed at the Battle of Hastings in 1066.

Edgar was never officially crowned king of England and the reader will no doubt be familiar with the story of the Norman invasion of 1066, Hastings, William the Conqueror etc and requires no re-telling here.

However, what is less known is that the Anglo-Saxon elite sought safety and protection in Scotland. Within four years Margaret would become queen having married Malcolm III, king of Scotland.

Margaret was a very devout Christian, and she established ferry crossings, at Queensferry and North Berwick, across the Firth of Forth so that pilgrims could easily travel to St Andrews, Fife. She would become the mother of four subsequent Scottish kings.

So, the reader may be asking what any of this has to do with our story at Largs and the Liber Pluscardensis. Well, Margaret founded Dunfermline Abbey circa 1070 along with Benedictines from Canterbury. Therefore, as Dunfermline was the motherhouse, she was venerated by those at Pluscarden and in their history they credited Margaret with bringing about the victory at Largs.

She was canonised, that is made a saint, by pope Innocent IV in 1250 and the author of the Liber Pluscardensis drew on that story to build his narrative.

The Largs story follows the same tact as Fordun et al. and continues the error of earlier editions by saying that the events occurred '…about the feast of Peter ad Vincula…'

As discussed in a previous chapter it is known that Haakon was still in Orkney at Lammas. This is convincing evidence that the author was relying on earlier sources for their own source material.

However, the author must have had additional information from other sources as they correct another error in relation to the islands that Haakon was supposed to have attacked on his way to the Ayrshire coast.

Instead of 'Bute and Man,' as described in an earlier source, this is corrected to 'Bute and Arran,' which follows the description in the Norse saga.

This makes sense because in circa 1461, when the Liber Pluscardensis source was written, the Isle of Man had been firmly within English possession for almost a hundred years. To the author it probably would have made no sense to have

Haakon attacking islands belonging to Scotland (Bute) and England (Man). However, it could similarly be that the author relied on a selection of sources and had access to the Norse saga.

Another error contained in the Liber Plusardensis is that it states that Haakon:

> '...invaded, plundered, and sacked the neighbouring lands of Scotland along the seaboard; nor would this man, (Haakon) out of honour, and reverence to Almighty God, respect the sacredness of the churches, but he cruelly harried and wasted everything with fire and sword.'

This narrative all seems very strange, especially considering that Haakon was a devout Christian according to the Norse saga.

Historically, evidence shows that Haakon had petitioned the papacy for support, offered to go on crusade by vowing to wage war against pagans, and was eventually officially recognised by pope Innocent IV in 1246, the very pope who would canonise Margaret four years later.

Remember this point as there is an interesting theory which will be discussed at the end.

The Liber Pluscardensis records that Haakon:

> 'on the feast of the nativity of the Blessed Virgin Mary, September 8th...gained the land and pitched his tents at a place which is called Largs...'

Where is the violent storm recorded in other versions? In this version Haakon arrived a month early and is now camped on the mainland in tents. This is all new narrative, which has been created out of thin air by the author in Pluscarden Abbey.

It is in this source that a new saviour of the Scots comes into the fray. It is someone the sources have not mentioned up until this account:

> '...Lord Alexander Stewart of Dundonald (1220 – 1282), great grandson of the first Walter Stewart.'

Now, what must be remembered is that the Stewart dynasty had become the royal line of Scotland in 1371 when Robert II became king of Scotland. Is it any surprise that Stewart ancestors have now appeared in the narrative as the primary heroes of Largs?

Further connections are evident as the author of the Liber Pluscardensis,

Maurice Buchanan, had been treasurer to the Princess Margaret Stewart (1424 – 1445) who went onto marry the Dauphin of France. If this is the same Maurice who was son to the 12th Chief of Buchannan then a second connection is that his father's second marriage was to Isobel Stewart (circa 1392 – 1458), daughter of Murdoch Stewart (1362 – 1425), 2nd Duke of Albany who was the grandson of Robert II.

Therefore, it makes sense that the author would write favourably about the Stewart dynasty. He even manages to include a reference in the account stating that Walter Stewart had been married to a daughter of Robert de Brus.

There are further incorrect details in the Liber Plusarcdensis. The narrative places the battle first and then the storm arrives, but only after Haakon has already been defeated for the first time by Alexander Stewart of Dundonald, who it says:

> '...set upon them manfully, overthrew their army and humbled their pride; and through God's vengeance he fought and overcame them and punished their wicked attempt.'

Overall, rivetting stuff and Alexander Stewart of Dundonald, according to this version, did not require the assistance of a maniacal storm to defeat his foe.

Following the storm, the account tells us that another battle ensued, and it says that Haakon's forces:

> '...were overcome and borne down through the grace and miracle of the blessed Queen Margaret of Dunfermline (Saint Margaret)...'

The narrative finishes by sticking pretty much to the narratives contained in other sources with Haakon going back to Orkney to gather a new fleet and dying before his son Magnus takes over who, according to Maurice Buchanan, was:

> '...a man of letters, peaceful and distinguished for kindness and of great wisdom in the eyes of all...'

There is a further chapter in the Liber Pluscardensis that goes into great detail about a vision that Sir John de Wemyss had of Saint Margaret while he was in Dunfermline. The story ends with news of the Battle of Largs arriving at court. For additional information, the Original Cronykil of Scotland, which was discussed in Chapter Thirteen, was apparently written for Sir John de Wemyss.

A final thought, remember the account talking about Haakon despoiling churches and his general behaviour. In 1390 Pluscarden Abbey was burnt. It just so happens that it was burnt by the infamous 'Wolf of Badenoch.' His name,

Alexander Stewart (1343 – 1394), and he was the youngest son of Robert II.

The entry in the Liber Pluscardensis which places Alexander Stewart of Dundonald as the saviour of Scotland from the rampaging Haakon, who is recorded as the maniacal despoiler of churches could be a way to try and square the ledger in favour of the Stewart elites.

This is only a theory, but it is certainly worth considering why the Stewarts suddenly appear in the narrative of Largs in 1263. This is intriguing as they were never mentioned in any of the earlier sources.

It is important to note that the previous hero, Sir Piers de Curry, has completely disappeared from this account, which is something to consider, and an interesting angle for future research.

CHAPTER FIFTEEN
Final Historical Sources
Boece 1465-1536
Holinshead 1529-1580
Buchanan 1506-1582

s we come to our final historical sources in this discussion it is important to recognise that without them, we would be far poorer, historically.

The works have improved our understanding of the world in which they lived, and we should applaud their dedication to committing their views of Scottish history to vellum and parchment so that for all posterity we can enjoy them.

This short series, looking at the Battle of Largs, simply would not have been possible without these sources.

While some of them may have changed over time, that is not a negative appraisal of the content. Rather, it helps explain more about changing influences at different periods of Scottish history.

Understanding and comparing these sources makes it possible to track change through time. To recognise different forms of patronage, changing fashions and styles of writing, and which sources the authors themselves relied upon to create their own works. I hope you agree that they are fantastic.

Nonetheless, what is plainly apparent is that by the sixteenth century when Hector Boece, Raphael Holinshead, and George Buchanan were writing, the narrative relating to Largs 1263 have evolved into an event of mammoth proportions.

The account of Boece, the Historia Gentis Scotorum which was finished circa 1527, is a massive history of Scotland. However, the record that relates to Largs does not bear much resemblance to earlier accounts.

Historians have lamented that the writing of Boece can be overly patriotic and the Historia Gentis Scotorum has many historical inaccuracies. The work had a powerful patron in James IV king of Scotland (1473 – 1513) and Boece follows the tradition by flattering the Stewart ancestors of James IV.

Quickly summarising the differences between other sources Boece tells the reader that Haakon is not only the king of Norway, but also of Denmark. This is interesting as Denmark and Norway had been in union from 1397 – 1523, and again between 1523 – 1814.

Therefore, at the time when Boece was writing it would have been normal to combine the two monarchies, but in 1263 the king of Denmark was Eric V Klipping (1249 – 1286); Boece continues the long persistent error in relation to dates by stating Haakon arrives at Lammastide (that is the incorrect date of the 1st of August); Haakon captures the castle of Ayr after a long siege. This is not mentioned in any of the other sources and where did he get siege engines from; following on from these errors there follows an incredibly detailed account of the two armies, which are huge in this account.

Boece claimed that the Scots army alone had 40,000 troops available! Boece also includes two speeches in his account delivered by Haakon and Alxexander III to their troops. The battle speech of every movie we have ever seen springs to mind here.

However, what it does tell us is that the work of the Roman classic author Tacitus (AD 56 – 120), The Annals, had been rediscovered during the fifteenth century and one thing known about Tacitus is that he loved a good speech for his heroes. In The Annals, Tacitus put a speech into the mouth of the Caledonian champion, Calgacus, who had valiantly fought the Romans at the Battle of Mons Graupius (AD 83).

The inclusion of stirring battlefield speeches demonstrates, to the educated people who would have been the desired audience of Boece's work, that he had read the magnificent work of Tacitus and that it is this inspiration that gives us the two speeches from the opposing kings in his account for Largs.

Another new 'fact' is Boece states Haakon and Alexander fought it out manfully in the front ranks of their own troops. Is it any wonder that later historians such as Robertson and Skene completely discredited Boece as a 'fabulist'!

The following is Boece's account of the final stages of Largs. It has been simplified using modern words so that it is easier to read:

> 'On the morrow, King Haakon fled, with a few number, to the castle of Ayr, which was taken lately by him; and, in the meantime, he got tidings, that his fleet, which contained fifty ships, was perished by unmerciful tempest, and none of them saved except four, besides, the mariners which escaped after the loss of their ships, were all slain by the inhabitants of the country. King Haakon broken in this manner, got their four ships and fled to Orkney.
>
> In this battle were slain 24,000 Danes; and of Scots, 5,000. This battle was fought at Largs, on the third day of August (we know it was October).'

Quite an incredible version. Personally, I love it, fabulist or not, Boece is certainly riveting reading.

Raphael Holinshead basically copies the Boece narrative, although interestingly, considering he is an English chronicler, he adjusts the date of battle to correctly stipulate the '...third day of October...' It would be interesting to find out which sources Holinshead used for his version.

George Buchanan is widely considered as one of, if not thee, preeminent Latin historian Scotland has ever produced.

It is even more impressive to know that this was also how he was seen in his own day and age. Both Buchannan and Boece wrote their histories in Latin.

Here follows his short account in full:

'In the year 1263, on the 1st of August (the error that never ends in the early Scottish histories, proving that one error follows a text through 300 odd years of sources) Haco, king of Norway, arrived at Ayr, a seaport in the coast of Kyle, with a fleet of six hundred sail (huge increase on the original 120 mentioned in the Norse saga) where he landed twenty thousand men. The alleged cause of the war was some islands which he said had been promised by Macbeth to his ancestors, but never delivered up, viz. Bute, Arran, and the two Cumbrays, which although never reckoned among the Aebudae (Hebrides?) yet being islands, was enough to him who sought an occasion for quarrel. Haco took possession of the two largest and reduced their castles before it was possible to oppose him; and, elated with this success, he made descent on Cunningham, that part of the continent which lies opposite to Bute, at a place called Largs. There he was struck almost at once by two disasters - first, he was defeated by Alexander Stewart, grandfather of the first of that name who sat on the Scottish throne, and being nearly surrounded, escaped with difficulty to his ships. Then the fleet being overtaken with a terrible tempest, a very few only were able to reach the Orkneys. In that battle, the Norwegians lost about sixteen thousand, and the Scots five thousand. Some writers assert that Alexander himself commanded in this engagement, but also make honourable mention of Alexander Stewart (Buchanan stating on record that the Stewarts should not be left out of the narrative, mainly because their ancestor does not appear in the earlier sources, as we know).

Haco died of grief for the loss of his army, and a valiant youth, his relation, whose name is not mentioned.'

As the Glasgow archaeological society closed off this discussion so must I.

They said, and I am sure you will agree with them, that:

> 'The history of the story is, like that of so many other stories, the history of a snowball rolling down a slope, accumulating matter and momentum as it goes.'

CHAPTER SIXTEEN
SOME CLOSING THOUGHTS AND FUTURE DEBATES

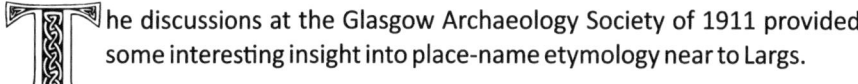he discussions at the Glasgow Archaeology Society of 1911 provided some interesting insight into place-name etymology near to Largs.

Archaeologists use 'place-name' analysis as a means of identifying settlements or farms within certain cultural groups. Some incredible work in this area has been undertaken by Professor Thomas Clancy.

Recently, Professor Clancy's research has been particularly absorbed by work on placenames. He has directed a series of research projects involving placenames and the evidence they can give us for language, society, and religion in medieval Scotland. If the reader would like further information on this, they can easily find details online that will direct them to articles and books on this fascinating area of research.

In terms of Largs, and the surrounding geography, there are a plethora of Norse names to be discovered. According to the work undertaken by the 1911 contributors those locations are: Noddsdale/Noddle (Nautadale), Black Fell, Tourgill, Bessel Moor (Bessa-myrr), Girtley Hill (Grjot-hlio), Langley Hill (Langa-hlio), Wooy (=Quoy in Orkney, Kvi 'sheepfold'), Thortermere (poroar-myrr 'Thord's Moss'), Greeto Water (Grjot-a 'stony stream'), Gogo Burn (Gauk-a, 'cuckoo stream' there is also the prehistoric Gawk Stane in Cumbrae), Gowk Craigs, Haylie (Hey hlio), Swinside (Svein's setr), Fairlie (Fogr-hlio), Skelmorlie (Skalmar-hlio), Meigle Bay (Mjo-gil) amongst others.

The contributors in 1911 identified between 20-30 local names which they believe are of Norse origin.

This is one of the arguments as to why Haakon headed to Largs in the first place. The claim is that further up the Brisbane Glen, between Largs and Greenock, there was once a settlement from the time that Olaf the White, Norse king of Dublin, was in the vicinity.

It was this Olaf who had sacked Dumbarton, the 'Fort of the Britons,' in AD870 after a prolonged siege. These long Norse connections with the local area may have continued from there.

However, there are further arguments that claim that Haakon had wanted to visit the Cumbraes, Arran and Bute because they are specifically named within the Norse saga.

There has been another argument which has always been about the exact location of the Viking burials. The saga is clear that the people who were killed on the Norse side were taken to the church at Largs where they were buried. This church is recorded in a historical document dating from 1265, and the original location of this church is probably where the Skelmorlie Aisle is now. There was for a very long time a suggestion that the bodies were buried in a large mound north of the Gogo Burn.

The belief was that the location was a large mound near to Gallowhill Place. The argument has been been discounted by more excavations, which claim it is a natural feature, rather than a burial mound.

However, if it is a natural feature, and if it is the same place we are talking about, then how would the recent excavations explain that in 1831 a Dr Dillon claimed that:

'the owner of the ground had occasion to dig into this cairn when building an outhouse and found human bones.'

Again in 1873, further excavations were conducted by Dr John S Phene who:

> '...discovered burnt clay and charcoal from oak, interspersed with flakes of bright green, supposed to be copper or bronze, probably 'remnants of armour,' and some substances supposed to be bones - some partly and wholly calcined. Human teeth were also found.'

The local tradition is apparently that these were people who had been executed upon Gallowhill in ancient times.

None of which makes much sense in an archaeological context of our period. More than likely the mound is prehistoric in origin.

Therefore, we can safely argue that most of the archaeological evidence is sketchy at best. If excavations could find any graves in the old Kirk, then that would provide an answer to the part mentioned in the saga and provide evidence of reliability in the narrative.

Furthermore, if someone were to scour the seabed with appropriate archaeological equipment and using modern technology then it may be possible to uncover anchors which may still be in situ from those that were cut away during the storm.

All archaeological links are, at this stage, tenuous and the chances of finding anything directly attributable to the events at Largs remain slim to say the least.

Of course, we all live in hope. And, if the place names, evidence is anything to go on, then there is every possibility we may get lucky and discover another gem of national and international significance sometime in the future.

Appendix
ORIGINAL CHRONICLE OF SCOTLAND (TRANSLATION)

'A thousand two hundred sixty and three
Years after the Nativity,
Haco, King then of Norway,
Come with his host and great army
In Scotland on the West Sea.
In Cunninghame (Ayrshire) the Largs he
Arrived with a great multitude
Of ships with top-castles good.
And there be a tempest fell
Of great weather sharp and snell
Of force they behoved to take
Land, and them for battle make:
And often seen, as they might win
Their ships, they would enter in,
And ordained them with diligence
In their ships to make defence.
The King Alexander of Scotland
Come on them then with stalwart hand,
And them assailed right stoutly:
They then defended right manly.
A Scottish squire of good fame,
Perys of Curry called by name.
Among the ropes was all to rent
Of the ships in a moment.
And many was slain that same tide
Of Scottish and Norways on same side.
There they fetch and were so fast,
The King of Norway at the last
And his men fair received sore,
That everyone arrived there:
For of his ships in the sea
Were many drowned; and there many men
Were seen there and then in great peril.
The King himself into that short time
Without his ships, that saved was,
Courageously won out of the press,

And took the sea homeward the way,
There a course taken hold to Orkney.
There then took land Haco their King,
And in great sickness made ending.
Men said, that sum Scottish men,
Of Scotland mighty Lords then,
Send their letters obligatory
To Norway this King before;
If he would cum with his power
Into Scotland to make war,
Where they might wait him till arrived,
They should meet him there believe
On their best ways to give counsel,
And make him help and aid.
This moved the King of Norway
In Scotland to come, as he heard say:
But they held him nought covenant,
When he come, as you heard, in Scotland.
Therefore until Orkney
Until his dead-ill when he lay,
The letters sold of that covenant
Till the King Alexander of Scotland
In great haste he caused to be sent,
To make his many deeds well known.
Until Alexander the third our King before
One fair son that here was borne.
Until Jeburgh. Sir Gamelin,
Bishop of Saint Andrews, since
Baptised that bairn, and Alexander
Him called, as was before his father.
And when of that birth come tidings
Until Alexander the third our King,
It was told him that same day,
That dead the King was of Norway:
And so in double blitheness
The King's heart all (that) time was.'

hydrodaktulopsychicharmonica

hydrodaktulopsychicharmonica

Matt Merritt

ISBN: 978-0-9565514-4-3

Copyright © Matt Merritt 2010

Cover image: Optic at Portland Bill Lighthouse
© Jane Commane 2010

Author Photograph: © Mark Cureton

All rights reserved. No part of this work may be reproduced, stored or transmitted in any form or by any means, graphic, electronic, recorded or mechanical, without the prior written permission of the publisher.

Matt Merritt has asserted his right under Section 77 of the Copyright, Designs and Patents Act 1988 to be identified as the author of this work.

First published November 2010 by:

Nine Arches Press
Great Central Studios
92 Lower Hillmorton Rd
Rugby
Warwickshire
CV21 3TF

www.ninearchespress.com

Printed in Britain by:
imprintdigital.net
Seychelles Farm,
Upton Pyne,
Exeter
EX5 5HY
www.imprintdigital.net

hydrodaktulopsychicharmonica

Matt Merritt

Nine
Arches
Press

Matt Merritt's second collection is *hydrodaktulopsychicharmonica*. His debut full collection, *Troy Town*, was published by Arrowhead Press in 2008, and a chapbook, *Making The Most Of The Light*, by HappenStance in 2005. He studied history at Newcastle University and counts Anglo-Saxon and medieval Welsh poetry among his influences, as well as the likes of R.S. Thomas, Ted Hughes and John Ash. He was born in Leicester and lives nearby, works as a wildlife journalist, is an editor of Poets On Fire, and blogs at http://polyolbion.blogspot.com.

ACKNOWLEDGEMENTS

Thanks are due to the following publications, in which some of these poems, or versions of them, first appeared:

Anon, BBC Wildlife, Blackbox Manifold, Brittle Star, The Delinquent, Gists & Piths, Horizon Review, Ink, Sweat and Tears, Iota, London Poetry Pearl, New Walk, The New Writer, Ouroboros Review, Peony Moon, Poetry Nottingham, The Reader, The Slab, The Smoking Poet, Tears In The Fence, Umbrella, Under The Radar and *Stripe* (Templar Poetry Anthology 2009).

'Unquiet' was originally written for the book *Vagabond Holes: David McComb and The Triffids* (Fremantle Press, 2009).

For advice, proof-reading and encouragement, many thanks to Tom Bailey, Lizzy Dening, Matthew Stewart and James W. Wood. For constant use of the reference library that is his house, I am grateful to Kirk Parsons. And for their support, patience, editorial expertise and willingness to listen to the same poems at readings again and again, I am greatly indebted to Jane Commane and Matt Nunn.

CONTENTS

Prelude for Glass Harmonica   11

Uchronie

English Literature   17
Unquiet   18
The American version   19
With Immediate Effect   20
Uchronie   21
A Fixer-Upper   22
Farewell, fantastic Venus   23
Halcyon   24
Treaty House   25
Dio Boia   26
Lyonnesse   27
Your Search Also Found   28
Things Left In Hotel Rooms   29
Request Hour At The Numbers Station   30
Stanislav Petrov   31
Truth Or Consequences   32
Worst Case Scenario   33
January   34

Glass   37

Maps & Legends

Dreams From The Anchor Church   43
1984   45
The sea at Ashby de la Zouch   46
The Archaeologist   47
Leland's New Year Gift To The King, 1546   48
Seven Whistlers   49
from Tesserae   50
St Beuno Meets The English   55
Capel-y-Ffin   56
Drinking With Godberd   57
Breedon-on-the-Hill   58
Jubilee   59
Pheasants   60

Gabble Ratchet	61
The Ends Of The Earth	62
Trees	65
Winterbourne	67
The Shortest Night	68
Waiting To Cross	69
Sketches For A New Town	70
West Leicester Lullaby	72
Warning Against Using These Poems As A Map	73
Fantasia for Glass Harmonica	75

Goose Summer

Zugunruhe	81
Poem	82
Pinkfeet	83
Coolidge	84
In St Martin's Square	85
The Old Country	86
Wader Flock, Thornham Harbour	87
Troglodyte	88
Dotterel	89
Kilter	90
Stoat	91
Variations On A Theme By J.A. Baker	92
Yellowhammers	95
The Limits	96
The New Parks School	97
Searching For The North West Passage	98
Pluvialis	99
Live At The Hope & Anchor	101
Birdsong	102
Summer Breeze	103
Swifts	104
Gossamer	107
Happiness	108
Cahoots	109
Nocturne for Glass Harmonica	111

"The harmonica excessively stimulates the nerves, plunges the player into a nagging depression and hence into a dark and melancholy mood that is apt method for slow self-annihilation. If you are suffering from any nervous disorder, you should not play it; if you are not yet ill, you should not play it; if you are feeling melancholy, you should not play it."

Friedrich Rochlitz, *Allgemeine Musikalische Zeitung*

Prelude for Glass Harmonica

You wake late
to hear it, muffled and opaque

in a distant room,
or maybe only dream

that quicksilver music,
feel as much as hear it

playing up and down your spine,
your mind

tuned to a different pitch.
Each day becomes a search

for the frayed ends of what's
just been lost

in that instant between sleep
and consciousness, a melody you keep

twisting, turning, trying to make
new, pristine. Still it takes yesterday's shape.

Uchronie

"Though they [the stars] seem close to us, they are infinitely distant, and so *per consequens*, they are infinite inhabitable worlds: what hinders? Why should not an infinite cause (as God is) produce infinite effects?"

Robert Burton

English Literature

Pens pause one last time,
above the gaping permafrost
of the page

while outside
swifts are scribbling furiously
upon the thinning haze

and summer is swaying us
with the slow, emphatic argument
of the trees.

One chance, you get at this,
he is telling us from the front.
One chance.

Unquiet

Forget the verdict, speculation in the gutter press,
a service for family and close friends, or the tight
clusters of pilgrims round the spot where they found the car
and the condo he left unlocked and lit up like Christmas.

Sometimes, late night, the phone rang
and I answered to find unfinished business
strung silently between us in that heartbeat before the click

and purr. And twice, in later years, I saw him out there.
First, in the migraine-light of mid-morning,
blinking back an evening of cheap local wine
in a town not twenty miles beyond the border.

He was wearing his hair longer, and his face was leaner,
harder, but even as I reached to smooth away inconsistencies
he was gone into the colour and sway of the market. Then

again, in buzzard weather, way out on the flats, when our bus
slowed for some wreck, he was driving an oncoming truck.
And, of course, this time eyes met. His rewrote the story so far
for me, while mine reflected back his original edit.

The American version

of this poem contains several ideas, concepts and tropes
rejected from this, the original draft,
plus a quite different calibre of wit,

designed to explode and flatten on impact.
The packaging is largely the same, but the text
does feature a number of innovations

intended to heighten your reading pleasure
and exclusive extras available nowhere else.
It can be seen as therapy, essential self-expression

or job application. It is bigger, of course, and louder
than anything you are used to, and should
only be read in the appropriate location

using the approved mindset. It is 100 per cent natural
and exclusively tailored to local tastes
although readers should note that it may

contain traces of irony.
People who like it have also liked
this poem. On no account should you conclude

that you can live without one or the other.

With Immediate Effect

If you ever
created an imaginary country as a kid
& elected yourself president for life, in an uncontested

contest, & charted every contour
in dried-out Woolworths felt-tips,
named mountains & towns in your honour,

& wrote & rewrote history to show yourself
founder, victor & visionary, & ruled
with the arbitrary hand of the middle-aged & incurably lazy,

watching suns go down beyond blue woods
from your summer palace in the piedmont;
if, during those balmy salad days

following the gala opening of the first permanent
high-speed link into the interior,
you ever called together

your most trusted confidantes to admit
that the years of plenty & prosperity
were built on shifting sands,

that the hordes were massing on your mountain borders
& a towering wave was poised to drown
the rich alluvial plains, but that

you'd called shotgun on the final seat
in the eccentric inventor's lighter-than-air life's work
– then you'll know exactly how he feels right now.

Uchronie

World broken by countless horizons. No light or sound
flows over them. Swifts scythe rents in the present

momentarily, air crackles and closes in their wake. Wait
while wind harps on wires. Symphonies of electricity

and shadow play behind suburban curtains.
Mirror-fronted new-builds placed face-to-face

make infinity, hollow earth wracked by rumour
of alternate existences. Walls between lives thin

to near nothing. Suspect the survival of stations
never stopped at, dayglo line-workers in on the secret,

while trying to map points of divergence, signposts
to each new reality. Back up on the street,

late arrivals resonate the heart's cage. Still
they keep coming, wiping the dreams from their eyes.

A Fixer-Upper

The cracked quarter-light open all night,
so long before dawn we are woken
by the babble of broken drains and grass-filled gutters,

scent of the cherry trees' blossom litter.
The small room stale with unmade love,
still stacked with alternative versions of past

and future, to pack or unpack being to admit
one or the other. Elsewhere, everywhere, potential,
evidence of an effort we know we ought to make.

Doors to stain, floors to strip, a handful of tiles slipped
from the roof that came unscathed through a century of rain,
pollution, pea-soupers and the Blitz. So this? This is nothing.

Farewell, fantastic Venus

> sister planet in our fondest imaginings,
> closest of kin who yet held herself
> coldly alone in the glare of the sun.

Farewell Earendel, bright son of the morning,
> Phosphorus, Lucifer, fallen from heaven.

Farewell Astarte, Ishtar, Aphrodite
> – all of you long-worshipped girls of the evening.

Farewell faithful muses, metaphorical standbys,
> the slant rhyme we reached for at Earth's every turn.

Farewell easy analog, co-opted to our causes,
> your face made and remade, but always in our image.

Farewell perpetual, cloud-shrouded gloaming,
> the long-dreamed memories of unendurable light.

Farewell you all-in-one, elusive Eden,
> your cloud-shrouded forests and unfading flowers,
> sun-seared deserts and wind-scoured canyons,

> our words now weightless in the face of your strangeness.
> Farewell teasing sibling, farewell unborn twin.

after Brian Aldiss and Harry Harrison

Halcyon

You found the feather and brought it home,
a charm against the longest nights,

but dulled by dust or
washed out under electric light

it lost its lustre,
stubbornly refused to ignite

to that fabled bolt of blue-sky lightning.
I found you there, hefting

it in your open hand,
wondering how such a tiny thing,

weighing as much as a few grains of sand,
could ever have calmed the heaving seas

that leave us cast up on this strand,
the past submerged, the future flown.

Treaty House

Here's the hallway, the ante-room
where blood cooled and settled in the system,
and walk-outs ended with a tear trapped
quickly against the cheek. Like that.

Then the living room (forgive all the gaps –
souvenirs snatched by bit-part players).
Behind these bamboo blinds, prayers
for peace, then covenants and compacts

that satisfied no one. And the rest.
The furniture, what's left, fashionably distressed,
and that spot on the windowless landing
that would stay hot long after the storm broke.

Dio Boia

A curse, literally "executioner god", in some northern Italian dialects

Not that he is one
for anything too public or exemplary;
tumbrils, gallows, gibbets
or a cloud of doctors
around a chair festooned with wires.

Much more the type
to abandon you to the badlands.
Howling emptiness, fierce skies.

Often, you'll forget the sentence
entirely, until you arrive home one day
and unlock the sun-blistered front door
to find the history piled up behind it

and him, patient in the easy chair,
toting the tools of his trade.

Lyonnesse

The usual place, then? A corner café
in a previous life, but now a near-empty
bar, all flat-pack tables, laminate floors,
leather-look sofas. This suburb where

the house sparrow is still holding its own
among the repossessions and buy-to-rents.
And I'm deep in conversation with myself,
finally getting on with my past. Still time

for you to arrive, though, for the old world
to be hauled up intact, fresh and dripping,
the plane trees green and neatly baubled,
the wide streets clean of exactly what drowned it.

Your Search Also Found

Meanwhile, you are walking away
from the rodeo, bruised but still laughing
with all the other clowns,

you are spending your every offline minute
building the car that will revolutionise lives
and save the ailing planet,

you are Angry, of Anchorage,
unable to find words that do justice
to this latest injustice,

you are back on the street by mid-morning,
pale moon a slice in the gin-blue sky,
head full of steam, a few quid short

but with daylight pouring through your eyes
and the neighbours still suspecting you
of knowing something.

Things Left In Hotel Rooms

Smiles and grimaces, of course, stranded on the shelf
in the bathroom, with its skyline of coloured plastic
filtering the sullen strip-light to washes of green
and burnished gold. The shape of troubled sleep, cooling
and hardening in the unmade bed. Half a pair of spectacles.
Three glass eyes. Once, a wooden leg, and all the stories
that go with that. A poetry of pseudonyms. The ghosts
of Saturday night. Scattered like fox-kill across the floor,
the eclipse plumage of the adult female. Unfinished novels
and the best intentions. Clichés, cringing, ashamed
of their redundancy. Threadbare excuses, glad of the company.
A mobile phone, battery flat, and the air charged
beyond its limit. An ever-expanding universe of dust.

Request Hour At The Numbers Station

"For 30 years, intelligence organizations have allegedly broadcast one-way messages to their agents in the field via shortwave, and the transmissions happen to sound weirder than any Stockhausen score or minimalist electronica you've ever heard – a child's voice, or the obviously synthesized intonation on the Lincolnshire Poacher station, named for the folk song accompanying the numbers."
    Salon.com

For those born too late for the romance of radio, the magic of the lighted dial, to huddle under quilt and candlewick listening to Hilversum, or ships anchored off East Anglia.

For those still bound to the old routine – curtains drawn and door double-locked a half-hour ahead of schedule, then trawling the short-wave for her grey, metallic drawl.

For all you sleepers through those long winters of nations, the mad, bad, fêted and forgotten,
left waiting for the word that never came.

For all those out there who know they'll never know, who harbour no delusions about cracking any code, who'd hate to hear the climax of a never-ending story.

For those still lost amid the fizz and jitter, the hiss and twitter of far magnetic fields – *oh 'tis our delight on a shiny night in the season of the year.*

For all those this finds, face-down on the duvet, or dead-eyed in the easy chair. ¡*Atención!* ¡*Atención!*
Of course, we're everything you suppose we are.

Stanislav Petrov

The hardest part? How to stay alive
(inside the bunker, remember,
there are no days or nights)
to a sight you'll see only once,

the screens suddenly flowering
with tendrils of light, taking hold
of the world as we always imagined
they would. For some, perhaps,

the danger is a mind that wanders,
to football, or vodka, or the legs
of Comrade Ivanovna.
For me, only a waking dream

of days awaiting autumn in Fryazino,
and my wife asking, *what did you do today
Yevgrafovich?* Answering her
as I always do. Nothing. I did nothing.

Truth Or Consequences

Down from the high ground at last. Motels full
of film crews and photographers
who misread the signs
and expected a drive-through metaphor. Fight

the urge. Gun her the length of the
blinkandyou'llmissit
strip. Take your time.
Take your pick. Leave the desert

as a tidemark in the hot tub, and ask yourself this –
Exactly how long was I in there?
Meanwhile, out on the abstract plain,
no mothership over the mesa

but an answer with your name on it
heading for the hole in your head.
One road in. One road out.
Good to be back on the level again.

Worst Case Scenario

for Janette

to never tire of
           telling of
the many battles lost   the small victories

the freedom in here
or its cost without   we're left a life

too small for irony,
inhibition or the easy imposition
of meaning   I mean

to waken one night

      to that tiny, fugitive truth
slipping back like a runaway
hungry for home comforts
believing you're not around

to wait   not frightened but curious

to never think you'd see the day

January

Back on our black hill. Day's first spark
still an hour below the Beacon. Past the usual
joggers and dog-walkers, fluent in the unlearned argot
of raised eyebrows, nods and grunts. A tinnitus of distant
guessed-at lives. Quarries, slab-sided industrial estates,
the motorway already almost in full spate. And so

close to the stars. The chill of their long-dead light
unseaming your aching spine, already bowed
by their terrible weight. Look both ways into the dark;
to watch for them falling away from you, so slowly
as to seem unchanging, or walk down into
familiar constellations, remade with your every step.

Glass

"A word is not a crystal, transparent and unchanged; it is the skin of a living thought…"
    Oliver Wendell Holmes Jr

And yet, most days, crystal's exactly what they seem.
Frosted, smoked, stained, caught in a beam
for an instant, they collect, then separate, light.
Turned another way, they disappear from sight.

Every flaw and bubble
holds the glass-blower's breath, their every joy and trouble.
So a skin, yes, but fragile, thin. Even here,
polished in the vain hope they start to sing,
they're always on the point of breaking.
That much is clear.

Maps & Legends

"...when in the long course of time the story seems to belong to a rather distant past, I am afraid that I shall be regarded as a mere teller of fairy tales or listed among the tragic poets."

Procopius, *The Secret History*

"Well, what would we do if we found ourselves, anyway?"

Lee Harwood

Dreams From The Anchor Church

"There, beside the former course of the Trent near Ingleby, is a cave carved out of the low cliffs. Local tradition has it as an anchorite's cell, the abode of one of the more obscure Anglo-Saxon solitaries, and it still bears the colloquial name Anker Church."
      Rev Richard Kirke, *A Derbyshire Itinerary* **(1778)**

"Hope is the dream of the waking man."
      French proverb

After teetering long on the edge of the leap
    I made my home in the mean cell beneath.
Behind me rose the bluff of chances missed
    and plantings failed of their promise.
A thin pallet of leaves and moss for a bed,
    and the rising waters, close about my head,
I fell asleep with the full moon in my eyes,
    nursing a child's desire to hide

    and saw every *cape, baye, creke and pere,*
river, breche, washe, lake and mere,
woode, cytic, castel and monasterye,
fenn, mountayn, valley, more and hethe,

    and played both sides at Brunanburh
for the sake of the perfect elegy,

    and made light of what's most prized,
waged war on the terror of knowledge,

    and watched the grass fall and rise like the tide,
or the slow, deep breathing of a sleeping god,

    and struck out with my face to the future
to find myself walking through the past,

    and started out a man of no great means
but ended up weighted by wealth,

    and served my apprenticeship of silence,
learned the skill of leaving no trace,

    exhausted the childish desire to hide,
and am finally ready to talk.

1984

but we were stuck in 2000AD,
dystopia being no more
than a half-mark in Friday's spelling test.

Half the Met were camped behind the chapel
at Battleflat, their riot shields and batons
scattered on the scorched grass,

waiting for flying pickets who never showed,
while the Dirty Thirty settled for awkward silence
and the vindication of history,

but we were talking Judge Dredd
and future shocks. The coming apocalypse
was inevitable, but not without its attractions.

If we were scared, it was by what
Malcolm Marshall could do to an unprotected skull
on a late season flyer. If we had questions,

they were about hosepipe bans, average rainfall,
the type of temperatures you'll never see again.
About what Frankie said, and why the girls cared.

The sea at Ashby de la Zouch

is every artist's dream. The muted blues
of distant Charnwood are (just ask
Sir Walter Scott) as nothing

to its azure depths, the mescaline
textures of its shifting surface a gift
to all who ever flirted with the muse.

Civic-minded townsfolk work to maintain
the beached hulk of the castle
as a serviceable metaphor, while the littoral

is a rich seam of inspiration, where present
and future mingle to lap against
the petrified forests of the past.

Along the front the pubs are full
and in The Lamb two youths
beat themselves up over the words to the old song

but draw only a glance from the landlord,
a character, who spent his best years
working the treacherous coast of Bohemia

and still can't believe he ran aground here.

The Archaeologist

He arrived by National Express, though
the railway remained a sporadic
possibility. Or disappointment.
Delete as appropriate.

He showed us maps and legends,
histories to explain how
we'd happened. The decades fell away
like hard black dust under the shower

as we took him from one tumulus
to the next. He took photos,
made endless notes and sketches,
and remarked upon the remarkable

uniformity of their construction,
products of a society that didn't exist.
The suspiciously rounded, regular contours
crowned by new conifers, nature trails

and picnic areas, the distribution hubs
and technology parks sprawled just beyond.
When he asked us straight we told him
in words of one syllable

and pointed him back to the war memorial
from where he caught a return service
no one could quite recall. He left one neat
back-filled trench, about where No.1 shaft was.

Leland's New Year Gift To The King, 1546

Nothing less than the past.

The past presented in fifty volumes,
or as many more as it might take to complete the task.

The past newly freed from its fetters
of idolatry and rude superstition.

The past captured,
and sealed off for safety's sake.

The past made strange
behind the mask of the Middle Ages.

The past thrown from its pedestal.

The past that's not so hard to write
(the labour's in divining what to leave out).

The matter of Britain and the past recast
as the drama of the man who destroyed it.

The past multiplied into infinite recess
as fast as he could reach out to grasp

what left him, fallen, beside his wits.

Seven Whistlers

"Seven birds, flying by night, whose cries forebode disaster, variously identified as curlews, whimbrels, golden plovers, wigeons and, in Leicestershire, swifts. In some areas, it was held that six called to a lost companion - finding him would herald doomsday."
        Green Willoughby, *Folklore of Leicestershire*

As if
all six had swallowed whole
a sky long swollen with rain

and pouring themselves
into the night
might make them seven again,

with only the silence
of the wild places, loud in the gap
between each call;

as if
to never find what's lost
wouldn't be the end of the world.

from Tesserae

"The city is also lives we do not lead."
Jeremy Hooker, *City Walking*

I

Having rewritten the past
a dozen times this morning,
I find myself at the museum
next to the Wall.
              I haven't been
since I was 10, but it's still the
case that everything
happened a very long time ago.

II

Reconstruction of a life from the flimsiest evidence –

pottery (fragments)
        bone combs   coins   belt buckles
certain items of jewellery suggesting contacts
rippling way beyond
                      this small pond.

Love is no object.

Reconstruction of a face from forensic analysis of the skull
the painstaking process
     of building up   layer by layer.

Reconstruction of a face from memory

the painstaking process.

III

Some cities show walls, baths,
a forum. The whole circus.
Us? We misplaced our past
under factories, railway arches,
a 1960s Holiday Inn,

adrift in the tidal race
of the ring road. Left this
crumbling remnant, dimpled
with footprints of dogs
who chased across still-wet wares
in the tiler's workshop.

The walls came down. The world
poured in. Stones washed up
in every church for thirty miles around.
All run aground on their ridges,
with whatever they thought to carry abroad
long since gone. Still,
sometimes you'll catch the eye
of one who fled the wreck.

A man hurries past, hauled
towards Castle Gardens by his wolfhound.
Good morning, we agree,
then I'm dragged back to High Street
by an unholy lust for curry.

IV

A city's slow migration. Find the focus,
close to where the Romans left it, between Rackhams
and the Handmade Burger Co. Retrace its trail, glacial detritus,
all the way down High Street into Cheapside, the medieval market
opening out before you. Cut back, through Victorian arcades,
then a 1980s idea of the past.

My city's shifting centre. *Omphalos*.

Gallowtree Gate, Christmas lights and the Lewis's tower. Later,
all the way out to Filbert Street. For years, The Charlotte,
sweat forming stalactites from the ceiling, ears bunged
with the sound of the suburbs. Five years at a desk,
an autumn at the Infirmary, and a bar on Braunstone Gate,
its name changing every eighteen months.

V

Not yet six. Behind every counter, someone
prays for window-shoppers to think again, walk on,
come back Monday. In the Market Place, rails of shirts, jeans
and a dozen Nehru suits make their own way
towards white vans, their 12-year-old shepherd
hidden between ranks of half-price anoraks.

The bright green snout of the street-sweeper
pushes between benches, brushes snuffling. A breeze
noses bin bags, empty fruit boxes, ruffles the fur
of a dog fox which, finding its work half-done,
hurries up Cank Street towards St Martin's,
pathetically grateful for a recent outbreak of café culture.

Rain-shiver faces of early evening
lights coming on
        an unfinished sky.

VI

History, the drinker's curriculum.

The High Cross is all
Anglo-Saxon attitudes,
with Harold at the corner table,
nursing the same stale
grudge all night, like Grendel's mother
in the deep cave of his misery.

In The Last Plantaganet,
kingdoms are being promised
for the price of a pint of wife-beater
and a microwaved burger and chips,

while in the Queen of Bradgate, of course,
someone is losing their head.

VII

Reasons why –

a fat Kia-Ora sun
squatting on Danehills,

a westbound plane,
flying into the light,

turning the corner into Churchgate,
followed by the curious moon

and the growl and hiss
of the last bus

or walking home,
wearing summer's silk.

Waking late,
in a house full of people.

St Beuno Meets The English

The day still clean and chill,
willow-meads soft and slow,
drowsing beneath webs spun
            by slant sun and dew.
The mist has boiled down to this.
Hillsides blinking in the light,
paws stretched out before them,
stray clouds grazing the furthest fields

and beyond Afon Hafren, a man
playing out a chain of low, jangling gutturals
to haul his hounds back in from the limit,

but already they strain to my scent.
Tomorrow we will rise in a grey dawn
and hurry west for as far as this land allows

until the gulls' keening thrills
the cloak of darkness, and rain and wind
howl indifference. There will be a space
that is almost silence, then the distant
plainsong of the tide's advance.

Capel-y-Ffin

So
thread the gap between
the brown folds of hillside, or slip

below
the grey weight of sky. Before you,
a vision:

the deep cleft of the valley
kept in perpetual shadow.
At this pass, a word

is all it would take to send us
striking out for the light
we suppose

lies somewhere below, like some
outlaw band of legend
bound to beg forgiveness

and restoration of the rightful order
from their one true king
returning from the long struggle.

Drinking With Godberd

"Roger Godberd, of Swannington, Leicestershire, now looks even more convincing as a contributor in some way to the tale of Robin and the knight. Roger was the leader of an outlaw gang; he was pursued by a posse; he was protected by a knight whose estates were scattered between the verges of Sherwood and the neighbourhood of Barnsdale…"
    J.C. Holt, *Robin Hood*

Last night I went drinking with Roger Godberd.
On his own ground again, home
after the fettered and fugitive years.
We started at The Station

where he sipped in the differences
slowly, then turned and told me nothing had changed.
By the time we reached The Fountain
though, he was really hitting his stride

and spent a good hour rebuilding a reputation
with the arrows. After a third consecutive
bullseye finish, some bum-fluffed youth joked
that he was better than the big lad from Sherwood

but Godberd silenced him with two well-placed barbs.
We finished up at the Robin Hood, where he
took a particular shine to the homemade
venison casserole, and the bitter irony of it all.

Breedon-on-the-Hill

For 'bree', read hill.
For 'dun', read hill.
For 'on the hill',
read a straggle of houses
beneath the quarried cliff,

as if the shock
of its appearance
here among much
easier slopes demanded
something more.

From the top
the world recedes. The stone
frieze. Curious beasts.
A blessing. How
many words are enough?

Jubilee

You see the fields of summer waving,
mountains purpling in the haze
and a distant flowering of smoke or steam
that must be the London train.

You suppose the day is warm to stifling
despite the high-buttoned collars and cuffs,
the neckties and waistcoats, tweeds and Norfolks.
You wonder at the awkward, upright postures

of bodies fretting to be away, to return to where
the evening has only just begun.
When you look closely at the solemn, frozen faces
you hear lovers' voices in the lanes,

low and urgent, and the tune the band is playing
as they waltz into the future.

Pheasants

Even distant thunder is enough to set them off
like car alarms brushed by the touch of lightning,
each rasp saved from monotony
by a note of surprised indignation.

A story we've heard in umpteen versions.
How all the birds of Norfolk
relayed first rumour of the Battle of Jutland.
Or the pheasants of Hampshire heralding the daytime Blitz,
and London was a long way then.

Now their chorus of hacking coughs
is taken up along the drowsing margins.
The evening heavy with the old debate
of safety-catch versus hair-trigger,
then a sudden wind, and the crackle of conjecture.

Gabble Ratchet

Corpse hounds, he calls them,
each one the soul of a child
taken too soon to be baptised,

or gabble ratchets, with all that suggests
of infernal machines, devices

of a consciousness that bedevils
our gentle swoop into sleep, dying only
in the first confusion of new light.

The Ends Of The Earth

for S.M.

I

At first sight

        a ruin, a menhir, a town, a harbour.
Arrive behind the grey tide of dusk,
pale local stone still softly luminous
with the heat and glare of the day,
this whole scene almost monochrome
but the scent a vivid green, guttering streetlamps
igniting moths on their way to the moon.

II

Woken at four by the singing
of unfamiliar birds, or the farm dogs startled
by the passing of some solitary creature,

hunting or hunted.

III

Everything moves by night. Up and out
before the lark   before anything
with the sky only just thinning and coloring

a slow warming
like a black and white TV set

the hillsides almost bare   but look
they're spackled with pebbles

a scatter of sparrows here
and there   two wheatears
listening for what

(I don't know what)

still   a ring ouzel
struggling to swallow
a crescent of daylight moon.

IV

Eight miles out before the sun
fizzes above the rim. Each smudge of colour
trails its own festoon of gulls. Others spiral higher,
higher, until the sky heals over them, and you
screw your eyes up against the spray
and dazzle of it all.

V

ophiussa
   promontorium sacrum
      finisterre
       land's end

         a life beyond words

VI

New-minted day behind us,
        plunged towards the quench
                of the unmapped ocean
showering terns everywhere.

Everything still unsaid.

Trees

for Mark Cocker

Bluebell Wood, Coton, February

Hanging on below the ridge, only
about as wide and long
as one robin's song.

The beeches at the centre
stand tall and straight,
while those at the edges

grow to the shape
of the struggle to grow.
The sky's blue drains to a pale grey,

ebbs away into leaf litter
lying rich and deep,
to wait for the thaw and flood

of the year's frozen flow,
to pool beneath our feet.

Scaddows Oak, near Foremark

scaddows (noun): enclosure or boundary (Old Norse)

You fall asleep
beneath the waning moon
and wake under searing sun.
The single oak
that stood in silhouette
has split the sky in two,

opened it like a door
between worlds. Its shadow
deepens, inches nearer,
outstretched fingers
of a hand that makes
as if to pull you through.

Winterbourne

Where summer daubed a broken promise
in every yellow, brown and green,
storm and season have thinned the trees
to a glint of running water
where no stream has been for years.
It is pooling across the lowest meadow
and forcing the sheep to the furthest corner,
bringing gulls down out of nowhere.
It is making a nonsense of our certainties,
making good on all the old maps,
explaining the fields, the hedges, the villages,
the line of the road, the meanders of this path.
They'd have you believe it rises only
in time of war and trouble, or else to herald
great good fortune, but today it means nothing
beyond the turn and turnabout of seasons,
the muddy ubiquity of water
and all its small insurgencies.

The Shortest Night

…and she was singing as she slipped away,
amazed to find she could navigate it from instinct,
finesse the dial like a safe-cracker, counting the hours
down in weather reports, scanning faded fingerposts
for each small shift in the language of backroads.
Gate. Drove. Drift. All in the time it took her to fade
from one station into another, to decide whether
the rain was to blame for the way she felt, or
if her mood was responsible for the weather.
For a bloodshot sky to resolve to try again…

Waiting To Cross

Sun-squashed or salt-flayed
on a flat-earther's worst nightmare.
Furious baptism by storm and squall,
every north-easter a crisis of faith
then the wait

for the world to re-emerge
from thin air. Take the tide tables
to heart. Any distinction
between sea and sky
is merely a question
of density. Or walk on

to where the glistening strand
is a glib reminder of fresh starts
and the pilgrims' path an elision
of memory and GPS. The causeway's
a pale splinter
refusing to work its way
back to a tender surface.

Sketches For A New Town

for James W. Wood

I woke still walking through streets
wide with wonder, pennypacket parks
green with promise, the clean suburbs
speaking of a certain simplicity,
the protective geometry of straight lines
giving on to the fields of our future.

* * * * * * * *

I have centred my designs
upon the highest point in our compass.
Not because the top
opens out some brave new vista;

instead it's how the climb
leaves no choice but to fill your eyes
with one patch of sky
and all its changes.

* * * * * * * *

I have tried to envisage the scenes
in which the inhabitants might make
much of the raw materials of their days,

in which families arriving from
the overcrowded cities might raise
more than a little dust,

in which any man or woman
might leave their mind open
to the ice-blue lens of the evening air.

* * * * * * * *

High ceilings, deep windows
and judicious use
of the pale local ironstone.
This is how we plan to hang on
to every precious grain of light.

* * * * * * * *

You will notice we have framed her
between two north-south straights
that neither diverge nor draw together

      oblivious parallels

although projective geometry and the curvature
of planes says that, followed far enough,
they meet at the point known as a singularity.

* * * * * * * *

Seen from here, the clean lines, the mirror-image squares,
the smooth crescents and the whole easy symmetry
might be supposed to represent a world in microcosm,
or else the symbol, or device, of our progress.

Consider *this* prospect, though. From this lower,
closer vantage, all that can be said for certain
is that one way opens onto another, at a point
somewhere just beyond our comprehension.

West Leicester Lullaby

This window is open to everything,
that's true. Tonight, a gusting that threatens
to loosen the first frail hangings of spring,
the slurred siren song of the happy hour,

the receding screams of the devil birds
circling high at the edge of sleep.
So, soft now. Let me tell you instead that
the sullen sky is no more than a blanket,

that the wind is wings to keep us
from falling straight back to earth, that swifts
will sometimes disappear for days
to boomerang behind an approaching storm front,

feed in the roil and churn of its wake
and surf home on the warm, rising air.

Warning Against Using These Poems As A Map

No scale is provided.
You are being left
to guess the exact distance

between what's said
and what was,
between a mere projection

onto the flat page
and a curved plane,
constantly in motion,

spinning through nothingness.
You are your own key.
Assign the appropriate value

to each symbol, and allow
the wide white spaces
to fill up with invisibles,

bloom with the language
of implication. Wait
for the words to accumulate

the sediment of meaning.

Fantasia for Glass Harmonica

In the warm, loose embrace of a slow summer
twilight, the wine-puddled drowse
through some winter afternoon, the crystal flutes

of the city's skyline fill to brimming
with a pale, living gold. Now and then
a breeze searches out openings, blows gently

as seraphim to produce the few pure notes
that slur gentle yearning into endless promise.
But in the hours after hours, light dies within

and birds break upon the blackened surface,
while the wind only deigns to run a careless hand
across the empty vessels, to summon that elusive

whine and glide, down your longest, darkest incline.
Not so much the descending motif you remember
from way back when, as slivers unseen

beneath the skin, keen as the touch of all your fears.

Goose Summer

"…Each day now
I leave the house as if I'll never return."

Richard Caddel, *Against Numerology*

Zugunruhe

A shiver of moon
casts its baleful eye

from the August afternoon's
sky. Autumn upon us

before we notice
anything changed

but we hear them, nights,
call to each other above us

and look up to know them
already gone. Hopeless

creatures of habit
bound to the same great circuit,

tracing memories they didn't know
they had until the moment

they started to relive them.

Poem

The curtains blowing back into the room,
thin yellow curtains that paint every morning
in the sun-washed shades of our dreams, even when
the syncopation of fat, warm rain on parched leaves
tells a different story. And close
                                  so close we haven't
touched. Outside, a woodpecker laughs at his own joke
beyond the subsong of a city stirring, and our thin slice
of sky and roofscape colours and hardens. August.
Sunday. Early morning. Late night, we used to call it.

Pinkfeet

Heading south, but still four hours out,
I was pretending I knew how the saints felt
there on their island, shrinking the world
to a stone's throw with every other turn of the tide.

Threading a border between belief and bereft,
between the short day slipped away,
beyond, and an ice-blink sunset to come.
All gleaning done, geese flew down off the bare hills,

calling; not lost squadrons straggling back to base,
a doubtful gaggle of pilgrims, or an arrow storm
thinned by the wind, but tired runners
urging each other on, in a race where everyone must win.

Coolidge

All is translation. A prolix version
of the language we dream in, think in,

gasp a lover's name in. So what
of the morning we wake to discover

these words all wasted on trifling things,
the moment pressing but nothing saved

against just such an occasion? No.
I think this divided republic of my self

demands a solemn ass. *I think
I will give it what it wants.*

In St Martin's Square

Most remember it only days, weeks
later, their deep-shadowed peace
fractured by its unbearable tenderness,
the cold hour afterwards
spent searching for the blanket of sleep.
They murmur a name
familiar from popular song
and picture it, serenading the last ghosts of sunset
or describing the slow parabola
of the moon's surprise.

    Others wander
their waking hours unquestioning,
supposing it the soundtrack
of half-grasped dreams
they're not sure
they want to retrieve intact.

    A few carry it about their day
like something they're terrified to spill,
as if the will to spring clear
still lives somewhere within it.

    None see the big black eye
drinking in light to fire and flare
upon the trembling chest. Unblinking,
not fooled by false dawns, while he pours out
his distillation of the dark.
               I exist. I sing
               so I still exist.

The Old Country

It's this I miss, he tells them, twelve hours away
from choked-back tears in Departures, then waking
to second thoughts at the wide, white summit
of the great circle. It's knowing how one man's line
writes the next for someone else, how any story
told enough times grows flesh for its bare bones.
Casual telepathy. Temptations of a tidy narrative.
          Here there are no children, no women.
They have their own countries, far distant
and bordering on the fantastic. Here
he is the hero, always bathed in the glow
of history, weighing his fame against what waits for him
over on the other side. Plots full of holes.
Jokes without punchlines. Sentences he doesn't know
how to finish, yet.
          Here? Here it was always like this,
wasn't it? The pleasures of repetition,
deceptions of a tidy narrative?

Wader Flock, Thornham Harbour

Grounded, they give themselves up reluctantly,
bleached to first-glance uniformity
by the brilliant, cold sun. But when they fly,

they separate by species. First the redshanks,
flutters of raw nerve, skimmed inland by the wind.
Curlews, tailing away down the deep curves
of their calls. Godwits, oystercatchers, dunlin,
gone, until all that's left is a scatter of grey plovers.

Cranky old bachelors, almost content with their own
reflections, finally trying to outfly their shadows,
mourning themselves in a thin diminuendo.

Troglodyte

On the first day, I interrogate myself at length,
in my favoured style – TV guide hagiography –
then give the whole of the next afternoon
to reciting the corpus of our mythology

but the discovery of fire is no help. Its tongues
speak the secret language of colour
and point up the bare, empty corners,
paint them a warmer shade than they deserve.

Instead, the hour before dawn, third morning,
finds me huddled deep within, listing
the procession of stars from memory. Fourth day,
I lift my voice in a litany of bird-Latin,

Gavia stellata to *Emberiza hortulana*.
Day five, hunger briefly draws me out
beyond the laager of lamplight, but I am
headed off by an army of doubts.

By today, hope has become habit, or ritual,
and imagination will no longer reach
as far as your return with the blessings of news,
cheap wine, the unadorned gift of speech.

Dotterel

Morning found me out. An alloy sun picked out flints
spackling the heavy clay. Braille of worm-casts
and rune text of the first birds' wanderings.
My eye, tight to the lens,
                met hers, and I was persuaded
we were about the same business, that spiteful hour,
divining something stirring beyond the vague horizon.
Her wings were a promise, her eyes a mirror, the purr
of her song invocation, or incantation. The hour passed,
I blinked first, and when I looked again
she was gone.
               I saw her once more, later that stillborn day,
the weather closing in at last. She hurried past,
never lifting her head from her strange passion
and vanished into the low, thickening sky. Her voice
was dulled, her wings weighted with the wet, her eyes
a poem in which I was a metaphor for rain.

Kilter

Sky white and three days swollen,
memory akin to the consequence.
Whiteness that contains every colour.

Mind outruns body until meetings are
casual, contingent. Muscle-memory. Coasting.
Don't fight the flight response.
When the world goes missing, wait

for it to return, recalcitrant and willing
to make amends. Don't let distance
or time tame the respect.

Silly to still be writing the same thing
years on, yet room, surely,
to hazard a different ending? Not happier,
maybe, but briefer and with better dialogue.

Read every book starting from the back,
or work both ways towards the centre.
Be surprised by twists of plot or character,

innovative use of unreliable narrators.
Live side by side with worse surprises.
Imagine a darkness that contains every colour.
Not everything that happens to you is fascinating.

Stoat

eight days   white-sky stone-crack cold
he explodes from a petrified forest
of sedge   half in

ermine   spills like mercury
along the well-worn path
of his hunger   furious

at the intrusion
and his own heedlessness

we freeze

a minute   no more
then he emerges from
frost-furred grass
and we watch   helplessly curious

instinct   memory   fear
circling one another

unknown
unknowing harbingers

Variations On A Theme By J.A. Baker

I

walk from east to west
by hidden ways

sun at your back

looking for the places
they might be

pause at the corner
of time and space
and expect
no/any thing

II

two possibles mid-morning
then fuck all
all day

III

fire-eyed owls
cling to contours
afraid to let go of the earth

but test yourself
against the wind

first select
the correct
density of air

perfect angle
of attack and hang

then notice how every
incline smoothes away

and all foreshortening
is undone

IV

so many times
he has described this indistinct
perimeter

knowing all the gaps

the rough margins
and secret places

the points at which
it is as well to go on
as turn back

he has mapped the shape
and compass of lives
traced
the heavy progress of days

beaten the bounds
of possibility
wearing his divinity
lightly

v

prey to your imaginings
in the owl-song hours

a long low murmur
slow beneath the skin
thrills the thicket of sleep
sends you out

beyond sound and sight
bare tops of trees
knotted with life
    untied
by first fingers of light

a tether pulled tight
    tight
then sprung

as some wild hope
puts up another
heart in hiding
and clear-eyed
races it home

Yellowhammers

Snow brings them in off the fields. That's all.
Impatient for the lifting of its veil,
see two, gaudy as canaries in the rowan

with winter's first fall untrodden on the lawn.
Not since, maybe, four Christmases ago,
when one flew full tilt into the kitchen window

but in minutes picked itself up and was gone
before the sleeping cats could catch on,
have they… but no. No, that's a lie.

Not since the day you died,
in fact, and that sudden buoyant swarm
appeared from nowhere to warm

next door's leylandii. No pretence
or grand goodbyes, and even then no change of tense
as we talked on and on, while they – little tongues of fire –

flickered against the dank green spires,
impatient for the lifting of the veil.
Snow brings them in off the fields. That's all.

The Limits

Thursday, early, you reach them. Sometime
between seven and eight. Somewhere between
earth and sky, the one becoming the other
a hundred yards further on, the whole scene
a sculpture in ice, and you feel it slide away
from under you. Not the way you're led to imagine,
an abrupt stop in the motion of the world, or time,
the sped-through showreel of memory, a feeling
of unconditional love and a glimpse of the light
at the far end of everything. The opposite, in fact.
They both roll on without you while you wait –
wheel loose and useless in both hands,
headlights eyeing you greedily up ahead – for the bite
of traction, for the cold earth to catch
and hold you again, then you're speeding away
from what you'll barely recall six months from now,
while the next time lies beyond a thin white line,
where snow is already folding upon snow.

The New Parks School

I was calling myself a writer by then,
you were calling me for hours every night,
Michael had me pegged as one of those

northern anecdotalists; all attitude but nothing much to say,
he'd say, and a terrible fear of using language.
I was prepared to admit a tendency towards

saloon bar narrative and a weakness for joke endings,
but I had to put him right and explain
the north doesn't start until Nottingham at least.

Searching For The North West Passage

Strapped until next Wednesday, and in the back
there's a damp patch the shape of Greenland.
In defiance of global warming, it is inching across Baffin Bay
towards a framed photo of her graduation, and south-east to Iceland,
or the clock as she prefers to call it. At breakfast
between bills and fliers for loan offers
                                    interest-free
she thinks of the tongue-tied Eskimo
watching the distance whiten
as he trawls his mind for another word for snow
but knows it's a myth that Inuits
have a hundred ways of describing
the one thing they have lots of. Similarly, it's not true
that Greek is better equipped to express the idea of love.
That night she's still wondering
if that half-pot of undercoat might hide the worst
when Billy calls on his way to the Crowns
and they walk there past the garage and its cash machine
which may make a charge for some cards
while she tells him four times
she's strapped until next Wednesday.

Pluvialis

Lovers lounge, oblivious.
                A fisherman casts
his frayed patience
upon the afternoon. Beyond them

a last flock of waders, at the end
of their strange alchemy, drab of winter
swapped for waistcoats in full-dress black,

gold-leaf mantles worn lightly. Clockwork toys,
they whirr and
                stutter on,
and here and there one leapfrogs the loose huddle,
the lead changing constantly.

They shape to startle
with each shadow overhead, each slam
of a distant car door, each soft explosion
of the courting couple's laughter; and birds lift into the air

but just fail to carry off the rest of the flock, drop
back to earth, false starts only serving to defer
                                    the inevitable,
the muted percussion of the first drops
then the hard drench, and a moment's intense

silence   before they are gone,

gone as one, air dense with the stretched iambs
of their calls, flickering across the cloudbank

like pain or pleasure across your grey eyes

until finally   at distance
a thin strand unties

                        then unites again,
all of them rising in slow, wide circles
like smoke from a sacrifice,
each bird dissolving into the storm
or each drop of rain carried away
on the wings of the plovers.

Live At The Hope & Anchor

Spud is warming to his usual audience. The little fella.
The one who once asked if you were a film star.
Whatever doesn't kill you makes you stronger.
They drink it in, and nod, and drink

and he says it again louder, and slower.
Repetition is truth. And we're all psychiatrists,
sitting on couches, back seats, bar stools, but really,
it doesn't, you know? It leaves tiny flaws, hidden scars,

a mosaic of hairline cracks that will only open up
years from now when something hits you hard enough.
God! Spare us from saloon-bar philosophers!
Walk with me now, outside, to where the moon remains

amazed by everything, and the old painted sign
is rattling in the wind. Two things worth having.
Somewhere to be going. Something to catch
and hold you, keep you from drifting for ever.

Birdsong

This evening, a call I don't know,
and will never know, perhaps, drowning
the lisp and whisper of goldcrests
at the edge of the new plantation.

Something hard, metallic, insistent,
but quite distinct from the blackbird,
hammering chinks of light from the dusk
to ward off darkness at this time each night.

Across the street, somebody is yelling
you don't listen. You never listen,
a door's half-heartedly slammed,
and a car radio plays to no one,

but still the unseen bird sings on,
that urgency pitched above
and beyond the background clutter.
Its only sense is now. Is this. Is gone.

Summer Breeze

i.m. G.S. Birdi

We found Phil sitting on his doorstep
watching the pigeons on the aerials
across the street. He told us they had
finally got their love thing together.
It was the first day that really felt like summer,
the first the sun warmed the front rooms enough
that the plane trees' evening shadow
came as a relief. We walked down to The Hind
to stand with our pints, talking too loud
over the jukebox, drinking too fast, repeating
ourselves by the time we'd had three. Phil said stay

but we had to plead an early start and leave.
The sky was so clear that even the city's halo
couldn't erase every star, or a tiny cross of light
that must have been a jumbo still catching
the vanished sun. And there is no easy metaphor
or symbol, and none of this is anything to do
with you, except that somewhere in all that –
hearing that Isley Brothers song again,
and outside the smell of blossoms piling up
by the drain, or just that clear embrace of sky –
I remembered. I thought you'd want to know.

Swifts

I

a tiny rip in the fabric
of our reality

      and another
           and another

then suddenly they're everywhere
tearing up the sky

II

all mouth
and hot air

until they run their invisible labyrinth
without once missing a turn

III

summer's supreme realists

slow to show
then gone again
while autumn's still only an instinct

hard-wired into the space
behind that gape

IV

the dark matter of their days

each a tiny black hole
hurtling on a random orbit

until memory's gravity takes hold
and hauls them in to the centre
of any one of thousands

of red-brick universes

V

my neighbour tells me
about the nest he found
              a loose tangle of dry strands
hidden behind the gable-end

how he'll miss their constant
wow and flutter
but

VI

a bow   unstrung
its arrow   unfletched
but still flying true
down the slipstream of a scream

VII

shuriken hurled by alien gods
emissaries from that other place
or a hell of a summer

anchors weighed
from out of the blue beyond
that never quite snag
on earthbound lives

VIII

only at home
in their loose tangle of flyways

on still nights we hear them
recede above us
flinging themselves together
then apart

sometimes
this is how we sleep

rising
on memories of heat

flickering in and out of dreams
of falling from a great height

Gossamer

While you sleep, they've been running themselves
    to this silk,
thinning themselves to a fine mesh of filament
    visible only
under a low sun, yet with all the tensile strength
    of steel.
They've been smoothing away the sharp edges
    and putting
their soft focus spin on the night just gone.

Some have already climbed to kite the breeze
    that must
be moving despite the seeming calm, have already
    unlearned
the knack of gravity, are ballooning beyond sight
    to where
the unforgiving glare threatens to dissolve them
    and strands
snag like draglines on all that's to come.

Happiness

Not the sparrowhawk's dash
to catch it, unwary,
and snatch it from
out of the everyday

or the cormorant's
relentless pursuit of what flashes
gleaming and silvered
somewhere in the murk

but the sparrow, oblivious,
caught up in the business
of being. Only
the smallest troubling

of the fugged, flickering air
between two doors leading
to one idea
of the dark.

Cahoots

Tonight you find me, drinking on an empty
head again, surrounded by a handful of words
I will never use in a poem.
Tortiloquy. Liminal. Susurrate. Cahoots.
How late it seems, the evening star
fading into the furthest suburb
of its sprawling city of stars, a jaundiced moon
rising in its place, and you watching, one foot
growing cold in a puddle of lamplight,
the other already out of the door. Come closer.
Listen to the wind, catching its breath
among the huddled trees. Watch us
reflected in the darkened glass,
conspirators putting their heads together,
uncertain just what the night is insinuating.

Nocturne for Glass Harmonica

The glasses all standing
empty, or abandoned
a little before the end,

or filled for a last time
against our best instincts
because someone offered

and we couldn't say no.
Time to see them off again.
A final glissando

on the brushed rims
that follows and skitters us
all the way home, down streets

brittle with the frozen light
of countless spent stars.

The Jackaroo
Outback Tales of a £10 Pom
By Roger Coote

© Copyright Roger Coote 2016. ISBN 978-1-326-74329-1
All rights reserved. No part of this publication may be reproduced, stored in a retrieval system, or transmitted, in any form or by any means, electronic, mechanical photocopying, recording, or otherwise, without the written prior permission of author.
Character names and places in tales have been changed in
This book is printed by LULU (on demand printing).
Contact for any enquiries to author.
Roger Coote 21 Heighton Road, Denton. Newhaven. East Sussex. BN9 0RB. Tel. 01273 515373

CONTENTS

FOREWORD **Letters from Australia**		1
Synopsis		2
Widening Horizons		3
Early Days		5
The £10 Voyage		9
Mount Barlas Station		13
	Mount Barlas Developments	15
	Sheep Handling Yards	15
Gundooee Station		17
	Working Day	21
	Australia's wildlife	22
Sue's Pep-Talk		25
The Role of The Jackaroo		26
The Health Hazards of The Jackaroo		28
Currawong Station		31
The Fate of Australia's Kangaroo Population		34
	Questions – Answers	35
Northern Adventure		37

		Coober Pedy	38
		Kulgera	38
		Alice Springs	39
		Ayres Rock/Uluru	41
		Darwin	41
		Mount Isa Mines	41
		Bundaberg	42
		Magnetic Island	42
		Summary	43
Milo Station			44
Return to Australia			52
Back Country Boys			54
A Mess of Pottage			55
Royal Flying Doctor Service			57
The Crystal Highway			59
Three Short Stories		Three fictional stories based on the author's experience in Australia	
		The Adavale Dance	63
		Boxing Day In The Bush	67

	Ringers' Revenge	77
Epilogue		85
Gallery		
	MV Fairsea	87
	MV Fairstar	87
	Roger on the Coorong in 1960	88
	Northern Adventure route map	89
	Milo Map	90
Acknowledgements		91

FOREWORD

Letters from Australia

My reasons for writing this book are that throughout my six years in Australia and particularly after the death of my father, I tried to self-impose the discipline of writing a weekly letter to my mother and brothers at home. These were all acknowledged at the time and a regular correspondence established.

Years later, when sorting papers following my mother's death, I came across a large brown paper envelope containing every letter that I had written to her in the form of aerogrammes from MV Fairsea in 1959 and from the MV Fairstar in 1965 (page 86). They have taken a lot of sorting into chronological order, but present the best record I have of my travels and are all written by myself!

As the airmail letters contain my most detailed observations at the time, and as it all took place some 55 years ago, I felt it was worth recording, together with my personal impressions, both at the time, and to date.

My decision to offer for publication was reinforced by the discovery of the map of Milo Station (page 89).

My six years in Australia was facilitated by the Australian Government's Assisted Passage Scheme that gave an immigrant a discount of £100 on the £110 fare thus the '£10 pom' epithet was born.

Synopsis

This is a personal story which all took place over fifty years ago. It tells the tale of a grammar school boy who was a farmer's son who studied agriculture at college, followed by a year in Kent as a farm management assistant. It tells of his experiences in a strange new country and of the hospitality and friendship he was shown by hard working people, mainly graziers, living on outback properties.

The author's interest in land reclamation and pasture development is explored and put to good use as a plant operator on a big project on the Coorong, South Australia, before working as a 'ringer' on a mustering camp at Milo Station, Queensland.

Because this was all over 50 years ago, values and costs of production have been deliberately avoided. The writer's experiences have, however, been summarised in a number of 'short-story' illustrations relating to life in the Australian Outback with some amusing anecdotes which show sympathetic understanding of the current problems relating to wildlife conservation and the treatment of aboriginals in the modern world and competitive financial climate.

It is not intended as a technical book, but, rather as a good yarn with some poignant recollections on an interesting life.

Widening Horizons

Having passed out at the top of my entry at Seale-Hayne College, I obtained a position as Farm Management Assistant with a group of farming companies in Kent. The farms were owned between Sir Edward Hardy (Bart) and R.M. Older Esq, who were responsible for the overall farm management and which involved three businesses:

(i) Sir Edward Hardy's Farms Ltd. Boughton Court,
(ii) Penstock Farms Ltd. R. M. Older Esq,
(iii) Romney Marsh Farms Ltd., a partnership between R. M. Older and Sir Edward Hardy.

Before the days of computerised farm accounting, the provision of reliable management and personal taxation information involved a great deal of repetitive clerical and accounting work, including the completion of double entry accountancy ledgers which became very tedious.

I enjoyed the opportunities to work with sheep under an excellent shepherd Hylton Roberts from Cumbria and also learnt to drive a combine harvester and operated cultivation machinery at harvest and busy times.

During the winter I played rugby football for Ashford and also I joined Kent Gliding Club where I was able to continue as a solo pilot after my training with Southdown G.C. at Firle Beacon.

I still had my Morris car, I had digs in Wye High Street and all my meals at Wye Hill Café and found staying at Wye very comfortable. At weekends, I returned to Littledown farm with my parents and brothers, and my time was spent on Sundays gliding but then needed to return to the office in Kent by 9 am on the Monday morning.

It was a good job. Prospects were good and I got on well with both Reg Older and Sir Edward, who was the absolute epitome of an English country gentleman.

But I slowly realised that it held no future for me. I needed a bit more excitement. I needed to get my hands dirty again. I had already decided to hand in my notice before receiving Ann Brookman's letter from Mount Barlas Station so I was able to accept her invitation to see Australia for myself.

I left the job in Kent and parted company with some regrets on both sides, but horizons were widening again and I felt justified in my decision. It turned out to be one of the best decisions I have ever made.

Early Days

In order to provide some background information, I summarise my training and education at that time. My brothers and I all followed the same schooling and general education. We all attended Lewes Grammar School. This was privately run by an eccentric clergyman, where we learned some latin and a traditional syllabus, but no science and precious little English Literature.

From the age of eleven, on passing our 11+ examinations we attended the County Grammar School at Lewes. That opened up many new areas including rugby football and choral music.

We also had the opportunity to join the school's Young Farmers' Club and also the local Senior Young Farmers' Club where we learned livestock judging and appraisal, match ploughing, and public speaking. We all enjoyed these ex-curricular activities and although perhaps I should not say so, we did rather well at them.

We all three left school at the age of 16 and moved on to more practical farm training. I went home to the farm at Littledown and my brothers to neighbouring farms which were good examples and exceptionally well run.

In response to advice from my headmaster I applied to and was awarded a place to study agriculture for two years at Seale-Hayne Agricultural College in Devon which was reputed to be the best agricultural college in the country. The County Council produced a Scholarship to cover all my fees and expenses and I was fully independent.

My friend Colin was also at Lewes and had been

accepted for Seale-Hayne. Very recently, on a visit to Cornwall, I met up with Colin and his wife Kaye who reminded me it was now sixty years since he and I first made the journey to Seale-Hayne.

We travelled together in my little Morris 8 (cost £67) and safely made the long way to Kingsteighton, a village near Newton Abbot, where we took up lodgings and became even more independent.

This created one of the most enjoyable periods of my life, the memories of which shall remain ever-precious. Seale-Hayne College opened up even more horizons and opportunities. Indeed, they were halcyon days. Looking back, one's childhood and school days are bound to change in perspective after sixty years.

However much we criticised the politicians of the time, we have to give credit to Clem Attlee the first Labour Prime Minister after the war for establishing the Grammar School system and advancing education where working class children of sufficient ability had a clear route ahead to University and beyond.

Small farming families such as ours had to struggle with a deep-set tradition in dealing with their problems. Fortunately, both I and my brothers had the benefit of a free Grammar School education, we came from a very traditional small farm, Littledown Farm, Lewes.

The Coote family had farmed at Church Farm, Climping, West Sussex for four generations (200 years) by the time my father was born. Between them, my grandfather and his generation got into financial difficulties and had to sell the farm business to settle debts, keep the old folks solvent and to provide a pension.

My father was the junior partner with my grandfather. They farmed at Littledown with a hundred acres of chalk downland and carried 30 dairy cows, pigs and poultry and generally struggled to survive.

Grandfather had volunteered in his youth for the Hampshire Yeomanry and together with many other farmers' sons had gone to war with 'Johnny Boer' in South Africa. Father joined the Sussex Yeomanry, but never saw active service as family and farm had to come first. Snobbery was a powerful attitude. Neither my father nor my Grandfather would consider himself 'working class' but neither would be backward in coming forward when hard work had to be done.

They were 'gentlemen farmers', hardworking but hard up. My father ran the poultry enterprise which supplemented our income, and Grandfather struggled with his pigs and market gardening where he lost money.

Nevertheless, there was always friction between father and son. I recently heard a story which illustrates their entirely different characters and viewpoints.

Grandfather, en route to feed his pigs one morning, came across an elderly man carrying a full basket of mushrooms. "Where did you find those?" he asked and the chap gestured toward the cow pasture.

The old man's temper gave way "they're mine!" he said. "You hand them over to me!"

Grandfather grabbed the basket and made off to Dad's cottage. In his blustering manner, he told how he got them and made out that he had settled a great social injustice in claiming ownership of the mushrooms.

Dad grabbed the basket and immediately intercepted the bus to Brighton where he identified the man and handed him back the mushrooms.

"These belong to you," he said. "Take them and enjoy them, they are wild and belong to whoever picks them!"

Grandfather's blustering shouting match that followed with Dad was typical of many that were the background to our lives when we were little boys. Grandpa was a self-centred old cuss, although, to be fair, he was always very kind to me.

He would take me shooting rabbits and pigeons and make me responsible for various jobs on the farm. I was really quite fond of him. Together, we would attend cricket matches at Hove to watch Sussex play and we would also go to agricultural sales, markets and ploughing matches and various other rural demonstrations.

He was a difficult man to get on with and gave my father a very hard time. However, his volunteering as a young man to fight in South Africa needs to be recognised but I think, even so, his treatment of my father was still unreasonable and unfair.

The £10 Voyage

It all started in 1958 when I read an article by Ann Brookman in the 'Seale-Haynian'. Ann had been a student at Seale-Hayne College some ten years previously and had met and married Nigel Brookman who had bought a small grazing property at Meningie in South Australia.

The income from wool produced by 2,000 ewes was pretty marginal but the property contained several thousand acres of poor quality grassland which the Brookmans recognised as having potential for improvement.

Ann's article told how they had set up a programme of pasture improvement based on ploughing and re-seeding to more productive specialised grasses and clovers, coupled with improved fencing and watering for the flock.

I had always been interested in land reclamation and pasture improvement, having observed neighbours' attempts to increase pasture grazing capacities and stocking densities on the South Downs in Sussex, and having read Arthur Hosier and A G Street's writings on the subject.

I followed up the invitation contained in Ann's article and wrote to her at Meningie. She was quick to reply, explaining a number of technicalities which I had questioned her about and an invitation to come and stay with them and see for myself. I quickly accepted.

That was the era of the '£10 Poms' (Australian Assisted Passage Scheme), and I rapidly applied and was given a place on the Sitmar Line's MV Fairsea, sailing from Southampton to Melbourne, Victoria in November of that year.

What a wonderful holiday that was! We saw how the 'other half' lived and thoroughly enjoyed our five weeks at sea with stops at Port Said and Freemantle. This was like a free cruise!

Port Said was for most of us the first glimpse of Africa. We enjoyed being on shore again and were suitably pestered by the inevitable 'gully-gully' men in their cement bags and turbans.

Perth provided an air of quality, if not opulence and will always be remembered as a shining example of hospitality and generosity for which Australia is regarded, worldwide.

As I stepped out from the gang-plank, a couple came forward and greeted me. They were complete strangers to me but introduced themselves as 'Aunty Marge' and 'Uncle Harry', distant relations on my mother's side of the family and determined to give me a welcome to Australia.

They took me in their car to Perth where we spent a most enjoyable afternoon together. We saw all the tourist sights and went back to their house for tea (Australia's universal term for the evening meal). I never saw them again but that effort on their part and their charming company will always place my introduction and welcome to Australia as a very special memory.

On the last leg of our journey on board, we all got pretty drunk but that was traditional.

We crossed the Great Australian Bight and docked at Port Melbourne. The coastline showed very little sign of habitation until we reached Geelong, where the landscape was as described in Nevil Shute's book 'On The Beach'.

We docked at Melbourne without incident. My cabin mates and I exchanged farewells, best wishes and addresses and I have never seen any of them again. I made my way by taxi to the youth hostel where I had already booked a bed and spent the rest of the day exploring the city of Melbourne which I toured by taxi.

I found Melbourne to be a very civilised and gracious place, well designed, clean and well cared for.

The next morning I was up early and made my way by taxi and bought a ticket at the interstate Bus Station to Coonalpyn, South Australia - not one of their more popular destinations!

We travelled well on good dual-carriage highways through Geelong and then turned inland for Adelaide.

The road was also the route for power and telephone lines, carried on knobbly looking poles, never quite straight and cut from the original gum trees. Tin-roofed bungalows, in wide, bright gardens sped by as we traversed the suburbs. Purple bougainvillea, electric blue jacarandas and the occasional banana and pau-pau trees lined the road.

The magnificent blue gums and flowering trees were an indication of the different rainfalls and soils in the area. The bus continued westwards and the land improved. The better land was growing crops, mainly wheat, and the remainder was devoted to grazing of variable quality.

The further west we went, the shorter the scrub became and the bigger the paddocks. In the enclosed areas were sheep, predominantly Merinos, as the principal livestock.

Little townships became fewer and further between but we were not yet in the notorious Australian bush. Much more of that to come!

Windmills created a frequent punctuation of the horizon. Most of these were for pumping bore water for livestock and the land was mainly flat. We crossed the state border at Horsham and headed via Keith and Tintinara for Coonalpyn where I disembarked.

By that time it was dark and a solitary jeep was parked outside the Coonalpyn Hotel, with Ann Brookman at the wheel. She greeted me enthusiastically, and apologised that Nigel had been crutching sheep all day and was too tired to accompany her so we set off across the 90 mile desert for Mount Barlas Station.

Our journey was frequently interrupted by kangaroos which bounded across the track in front of us, otherwise all was quiet.

On arrival at their homestead, I made my way to bed at the earliest opportunity and enjoyed a heavy night's sleep.

Mount Barlas Station

I was awakened after daybreak by a knocking at the door and the entrance of a little girl in a very pretty pink nightdress "Hello Mr Coote," she said. "Mummy says would you like some breakfast?"

That, and the days that followed at Mount Barlas are amongst the most precious of my memories of Australian Station life.

The Brookmans had no permanent employees and all the station and stock work had to be handled by Ann and Nigel with contractors dealing with such matters as cultivations, fertiliser spreading, seeding, and of course, shearing and crutching.

Everything was closed down ready for Christmas and provided that the water troughs stayed full and the boreholes continued working reliably, then this was the time to enjoy some of Australia's outside activities.

So much depended on the water supply. Stocking capacities are governed primarily by this factor. Everything else is secondary to a reliable supply of safe drinking water. One of the main risks is 'creeping' salinity which causes scouring in the sheep and will generally lead to the water supply being rejected by cattle. The water supply is the lifeblood of the Australian grazing business and if it fails then the land rapidly reverts to desert and businesses go bankrupt.

Recent piped water schemes and developments supplied and financed by the Australian Government, have enormously increased stocking capacities.

At Mount Barlas, bore water covered much of the drinking water supply for the stock, otherwise as a last resort, rainwater (stored in huge galvanised iron tanks) would be pressed into service. A damaged water tank or piping could spell disaster for livestock at Mount Barlas, and the risk of running dry was extremely high. A leaking water pipe is equal to an offence in that part of Australia.

So, Nigel had to carry out the daily inspection, both of the livestock and their water supply with immediate priority being given to threatened water supplies. Thus, I was invited to accompany Nigel to go round the livestock and check the waters every morning before the heat (100 degrees Fahrenheit in December) became excessive and unbearable. Then and only then, could we enjoy a day off.

They kept a small motor boat at Meningie and we spent several happy days enjoying Christmas, Australian style, while water skiing on Lake Albert and Lake Alexandrina and on the Coorong, that reef-like 60 mile strip of lagoons which runs from Salt Creek to the mouth of the Murray River.

Apart from going round the sheep with him in the mornings Nigel found other jobs for me to do, such as bits of fencing to repair and vehicles to service. In addition, Nigel fitted in time to give me a few riding lessons which I thoroughly enjoyed. He also instructed me on how to kill and butcher a sheep for our weekly meat requirement, after first servicing and cleaning the kerosene powered refrigerator.

Similarly, there was no main's electricity at Mount Barlas but they had an electricity generator for the homestead, powered by a stationary diesel engine which was a vital piece of kit.

Mount Barlas Developments

Mount Barlas Station buildings were constructed at minimal cost and provided little in the way of luxury.

The house or homestead dwelling was a timber framed two roomed Housing Association style bungalow. It was both roofed and clad with corrugated iron sheeting.

In addition, the house had a veranda on the shady side. This was built of timber and could double-up as an extra bedroom when necessary. The windows and open spaces all had fly screens because the flies were a particular problem during the hot weather in summer. These provided some protection to the oven dry heat which is felt in December and January, although it could occur at other times of the year as well.

The 'little tin boxes' were the usual accommodation on the 90 mile desert and on the Younghusband Peninsular and the Coorong District. They were very basic in every way and did not present a very attractive prospect for station families or for new settlers (immigrants like me). They tended to be uncomfortably cold in winter and uncomfortably hot in summer.

Sheep Handling Yards

These backed onto the main shearing shed which was accommodating a shearing board large enough for six shearers to operate concurrently and a wool classing table with supporting wool bins for the various grades of wool.

A system of races connected to the holding and drafting yards (outside) to the catching pens (inside) via a drafting race, enabled the overseer to hold uniform types of sheep separate and subsequently the level of fleeces being baled. These were packed in hessian wool packs for short term storage and then transferred by the Stock and Station Agents who marketed the wool and held frequent summer auction sales at Murray Bridge and Adelaide.

All this was explained to me by Nigel as we went round the property together on our morning inspections of the sheep and the water supplies.

A couple of days later, Nigel announced at breakfast that he had invited some neighbours to dinner as he thought I would be interested to meet them and that the feeling might be mutual.

Gundooee Station

Rob and Sue Hodge had bought a property of some 4,000 acres on the Coonalpyn Downs some 25 miles to the South East of Mount Barlas. The two properties were separated by some very poor grazing land and the 90 mile desert. They held similar numbers of sheep of similar breeding to those at Mount Barlas.

The Hodges were in their thirties and had a two year old daughter called Faerlie at home.

Later that evening, Rob asked me if I would be interested in a job at Gundooee. This was entirely unexpected and he invited me to come across for a few days once the Christmas holidays were over. Nigel offered me the use of his jeep for the day and having prepared directions and a rough map, I set off the next morning for Gundooee Station.

The ninety-mile desert was mainly mallee scrub country consisting of short and sparse eucalyptus plus yaccas which were a form of course rough grass with a large seed head. The land was also stocked with sheep where there was enough grass. The grazing land was occasionally sub-divided with breaks of trees either of conifers or eucalyptus.

Lone kangaroos and up to forty emus appeared from time to time, but the general appearance was pretty desolate and my principal concerns were that I might get lost by mistaking the correct track through the desert. However, everything worked according to my amateur navigation and I finally arrived at the Gundooee homestead.

Rob and Sue welcomed me to Gundooee (aboriginal for 'one emu') and after a quick cup of coffee we set off in his Land Rover to view the property.

Rob and Sue carried 4,000 ewes which were a hybrid of British breeds (mainly Border Leicester and Swaledale) and Merino sires from the East Bungaree Merino Stud. They were all in very good order and condition and Rob concluded that he had made a fortunate choice in his selection of breeds which was reflected in the wool cheque he had received.

1,200 acres had been reseeded to grassland that spring and was now germinating and showing, along with tree breaks of blue gum and conifers which were clearly thriving.

The greatest risk on this land was failure or lack of drinking water supplies and services had been carefully tested against salinity. It was essential to carry out testing in order to determine that a safe level of supply might be obtained. Stocking density was entirely dependent on the water supply which in turn was subject to the risk of creeping salinity.

If the salt was too high this could cause unacceptable saline levels and samples needed to be taken regularly and tested under a wide range of conditions. If the ground water remained satisfactory then the cost of the land improvements could be justified, however if the ground water or bore water were to fail the cost of carrying out the pasture development could lead to bankruptcy.

Rob was under some stress having taken out a mortgage to buy Gundooee and he was now borrowing more money to carry out his pasture improvement programme. With no cash to spare, times were hard.

Rob also had health problems but had tended to push himself too hard and set about his routine work at a brisk trot if not at full gallop. However, he had a good sense of humour, although he did not suffer fools gladly.

Rob and Sue explained that tighter stocking and grazing could cause livestock complaints such as parasitic nematodes, so this was a constant threat which required a programme of regular drenching and vaccination.

Much of the work required two men of which Sue was, of necessity, the second man. They had recently employed a jackaroo, a family member from Scotland but he had quite recently moved on and his place was vacant. It could be mine if I wanted it. I gladly accepted their offer on the understanding that I wanted to continue my travels, but if I stayed initially for six months we could re-negotiate the position so that I could either stay or move on.

Terms were agreed. I was to have all my meals at the homestead and with the family, and I was allocated a very pleasant stone built cottage for accommodation for which I was to be responsible.

Both Sue and Rob came from grazier families. Rob's father (Heck) had a sheep farm in Victoria. Sue's father (Rollo Hawkes) had a property in South Australia and was an expert and a much respected grazier.

The Hawkes family were derived from a branch of the highland aristocracy The Featherstonehaughs. Tim Featherstonehaugh was the jackaroo that had recently left.

I found the Hawkes to be delightful people and I owed a great deal to them for their help.

They had a son named Bob, who had recently returned from military service in Korea. He lived at Moorara on the Victoria border which he managed with his father, Rollo. Bob and his wife Colleen had two little girls, Kate and Jo who lived on the Moorara property.

At Gundooee, I got myself organised in my little stone house and tried not to let it become too much of a pigsty. Housework has never been a strong point with me but I usually get by.

My first job every morning was to milk the house cows. There were two cows each suckling a calf. The calves had to be shut into their own pens overnight during which time their dams would accumulate a few pints of milk which I would strip away by hand in the morning.

As a dairy farmer's son, milking cows was nothing new. Before we installed milking machines at Littledown Farm in 1952, the whole herd had to be milked by hand twice a day and that was a little job I learnt to do the hard way. At Gundooee I would take the milk over to the house in time for breakfast at 6.45 am, ready to start work at 7.30 am.

The first job was to inspect the sheep and most importantly, to check water supplies. This was a critical time with temperatures running at least 100 degrees Fahrenheit or more. At this time of the year water supplies were under severe pressure. Gundooee's water was mainly from slow soakage bores. A low point would be selected and a hole of some 20 feet deep by three feet diameter would be dug by hand.

A tripod would be erected and buckets of soil and rock would be raised to the surface by means of a rope and pulley with the trusty Land Rover providing power.

That was gut-tearing hard work but if we had got the assessment right the water would slowly accumulate in a precast concrete liner that would be set at the bottom of the hole. If the water did not accumulate satisfactorily another test hole would be dug elsewhere. If it did accumulate satisfactorily it would need to be very slowly pumped for a start otherwise the salinity would increase. Satisfactory accumulations of water would be pumped into a holding tank and filled by a windmill driven pump.

The secret now was not to draw off too much water too quickly otherwise the water would run salty, the sheep would get the scours and the cattle would reject the supply completely. If the water ran salty the bore had to be abandoned, and the machinery would have to be dismantled and the whole back-breaking process started elsewhere.

Drinking troughs were coupled to the holding tank by plastic pipe and the supply would be run in to the troughs by gravity via a float-valve floating in the trough itself.

Working Day

The Australian working day was generally adhered to.

Start at 7.30 am then two hours hard yacca. Stop for a smoko at 9.30 am.

Smoko involved a mug of tea (usually made in a billycan) a fag and a few precious lazy minutes before returning to the work. Then lunch (dinner) for an hour as it was important to have further sessions of rest to punctuate the hard working day.

Smoko again at 3 o'clock (afternoon smoko) then get the cows in, separate out calves from the cows, check the water supply for the night. Then back to the stone cottage, a quick shower, put on some clean (or cleaner) clothes, then up to the big house for tea. There being no television in those days, we listened to the 7 pm News from Australian

Broadcasting Corporation and then read for an hour or so by which time we were ready for bed.

That was the working day for a working man and generally accepted and observed by visiting contractors, shearers, crutchers, fencers and the like. It provided in the smoko breaks a much needed rest and a certain amount of social intercourse (not to be confused) and usually finished up with the whole gang in a heated argument about some silly subject and mainly addressing one another by such terms of endearment as "you daft bugger" or more commonly "you galah".

Smoko was also an opportunity to see something of the wildlife on the Station.

Australia's wildlife

Australia's wildlife is both complicated and unique.

Apart from species introduced by early settlers, such as the rabbit (food) and the fox (hunting), the remaining wildlife has been unique to the Antipodes for 150 million years. They breed true and there is no hybridisation between species.

The native animals are all mammals and can be separated into three categories

(1) Marsupials having a pouch in which the babies are suckled and reared.

(2) Placentals having an afterbirth which is destroyed at parturition.

(3) Egg Layers

The wildlife seen at Gundooee, Currawong and Milo could be categorised as follows:-

Marsupials	-	Kangaroo
		Wallaby
		Wombat
		Bandicoot
		Opossum
Placentals	-	Dingo
		Fox
Egg Layers	-	Echidna (Spiny anteater)
		Sleepy Lizard
		Snakes (Viviparous)
		Goanna

The Duckbilled Platypus is an exception to all the rules! It is an egg-laying marsupial which suckles its young and incubates its eggs in termite mounds of rotting vegetation.

Kangaroos were common and little groups of females carrying 'joeys' in their pouches were often to be seen along with the grazing sheep.

Emus tended to congregate in bigger groups and went for crops and grain which the kangaroos did not. The dry grain crops were more at risk from the flocks of galahs, the pearl grey, pink faced wild parrots, which kept up a continuous chatter throughout the daylight hours.

At times, according to the weather and conditions in the Southern Ocean, on the Coorong there would be visiting flocks of female sea birds. Not only gulls but also pelicans, flamingos, and a wide variety of geese and black swans and brolgas.

Foxes and the occasional wombat could be seen and there were rabbits, that much regretted importation from the Old Country, everywhere.

A charming, if not exactly common resident of big old gum trees was the kookaburra or laughing jackass who provided melodious chortles and derisive laughter to the background of our working day.

Another indefatigable and amorous warbler was the Australian magpie which has a soft and truly melodious call which it happily demonstrates the whole year long.

We also regularly saw many parrots in a wide range of colours from pink through yellow to green; corellas, lorikeets, cockatoos and apostle birds (usually seen in groups of twelve or so).

Around the homestead there were also myriads of little brown birds and black and white birds (sparrows, finches, larks, robins and willy-wagtails).

Apart from Antarctic visitors and emus, the largest birds we saw were the wedge-tailed eagles and the currawong (or bell magpie), that member of the crow family, after which Currawong Station was named. Sadly, the currawong is now almost extinct according to a recent survey.

When gliding at Murray Bridge, the 'wedgies' were the best and most accurate of thermal indicators. Circling, usually in pairs, opposite one another immediately below the clouds producing the strongest lift, whilst searching the ground below for carrion or signs of a kill.

Sue's Pep-Talk

After three months at Gundooee, I began to feel that I had settled in very well. There was a lot of stockwork to do:-

Drenching against parasitic nematodes (e.g. barber's pole worm).

Crutching.

Vaccinating against pulpy kidney and lamb dysentery disease.

Dipping against fly strike and wool infections.

Rob and I were handling good numbers every day and worked well together. We had also worked well together at Moorara where Rob, the two Hawkes and I dipped and vaccinated 800 sheep in one day.

But, one evening, Rob was away at a meeting, Faerlie was in bed and Sue and I were left to have 'tea' together.

Tea consisting of ram stag mutton chops with boiled potatoes and tinned peas, followed by the usual tinned pineapple and condensed milk (my favourite, jolly good grub!)

After tea, when we had washed up and put away, Sue asked me how I thought I was doing. I replied that I enjoyed the job and thought I was doing alright.

"Well, you're too slow and it's annoying Rob" said Sue. "Wake up!" she demanded. "If you can't work any faster we won't be able to keep you on". Fortunately, I took heed of Sue's remarks and a year later I was still working there.

The Role of the Jackaroo

Jackarooing is the traditional means by which young men are trained to take responsible positions in the Australian Pastoral industry. When I was a jackaroo, the role was not officially recognised, either in terms of a salary scale or of special privileges.

Those managers or owners who did the job well, tried to give the jackaroo some experience of all the stock management tasks and also to back up with a wide range of station duties e.g. water supplies, fencing, building repairs, maintenance, bookkeeping etc.

If a proper curriculum, ideally structured to that of an apprenticeship is followed, the jackaroo would usually progress to the next standard (e.g. overseer) within 3 years. It follows that the better the schooling and standard of education, the better his career in the pastoral industries. Most successful managers have been jackaroos at some stage in their careers. Nevertheless, the system is frequently abused and it is often regarded during the early period, as a recreational opportunity for the wealthy.

The alternative is better expressed by this little ditty which always crops up whenever this subject is discussed.

> ……I'm just a homestead jackaroo
> Despised by ringers good and true,
> Instead of branding calves and foals
> I'm all day digging shithouse holes……
>
>   Anon.

The same applies to the female of the species, the Jillaroo, which is generally less numerous and is less easily co-opted into the workforce on a large sheep or cattle station.

Jackarooing, as it is currently practiced, does not fit in too well with Australia's vision of a 'classless society'. It needs to be formalised along the lines of a recognised apprenticeship.

Many still regard the practice of jackarooing as the relic of a hierarchy based upon class distinction.

Whether or not that is the case, it has certainly been of great personal value to me and I doubt if I could have held some of my more recent positions without it.

Health Hazards of the Jackaroo

Jackarooing is intrinsically dangerous and appropriate precautions are necessary at all times. With sensible management, the Jackaroo's health will respond positively and the health of the team will respond to the hard physical nature of the work and to the open-air nature of the accommodation. Diet needs to be as varied as possible – not too many tins!

KEEP CLEAN !! BOIL DRINKING WATER.

The areas where precautions are advisable are as follows:-

(1) Allergies e.g. harvest and crop dust can seriously affect breathing. Carry some antihistamine tablets prescribed by a doctor.

(2) Boils. The result of infection from livestock or from dirty clothes. Carry prescribed antibiotic and ensure dosage taken on time.

(3) Sleepiness/drowsiness. Query excess medication or lack of sleep. Take a break. Seek medical advice.

(4) Diarrhoea. Scrupulous cleanliness required. Avoid fruit. Carry a shovel!

(5) Deteriorating eyesight. Protect eyes from very strong sunshine. Use dark glasses and wide-brimmed hat.

(6) Back pain/slipped disc/scoliosis. Causes – lifting heavy weights, riding horses, motor bikes and trucks etc. Physiotherapy or chiropractic massage.

(7) Brain damage e.g. trauma or concussion. First Aid/Hospital treatment.

(8) Mental disorders e.g. depression. Visit to General Practitioner or neurologist.

(9) Riding and shoeing accidents. Watch out for puncture wounds which can lead to general sepsis. Seek professional advice re: Septicaemia treatment.

(10) Intoxication and fighting. Rum & Whisky banned from Milo. Still a popular spectator sport. Avoid!

(11) Loss of body weight. Beneficial if not in excess. Otherwise check bowels for infection.

(12) Skin disease. Main danger is skin cancer and Keratosis. Infection carried by dust & flies and dirt. For mosquito bites apply mosquito repellent to diminish risk.
Visit doctor for prescription and further treatment.

(13) Snake and Spider bites. Of the 12 most venomous snakes in the world, ten are native to Australia.

- Red Bellied Black Snake
- Western Tiger Snake
- Brown Snake
- Eastern Brown Snake
- King Brown (Mulga) Snake
- Western Brown Snake
- Coastal Taipan
- Inland Taipan (Fierce)
- Common Death Adder
- Common Copperhead
- NB: Funnel Web Spider can also be fatal.

Snakes thrive in rubbish. Check boots, socks and clothes before putting them on and keep the camp clean!

Be aware of latest First Aid treatment.
DON'T TAKE RISKS!

Assume all snake bites are venomous

The Royal Flying Doctor Service operates a General Practitioner Service for outback areas. Contact your district hospital for a flying visit.

Currawong Station

The Hawkes family had for many years been interested in selling Moorara Station and investing in a much bigger property with potential for development. Their agents contacted them with details of a property at Salt Creek, on the Coorong. The property had very little development work carried out at that time but carried a wool shed and a station homestead built along the usual Housing Association lines.

The principal advantage of the property was that it contained some 2,500 acres of fresh water lakes and so the stock water requirement could be safely assured. The lakes area was well bordered by native blue gums and also a few ghost gums, thus providing adequate quantities of shade.

The Hawkes family also bought a brand new Caterpillar D7 Crawler Tractor, two x 8 furrow disc ploughs, a roller made up of ex-railway truck wheels and axles on a heavy steel frame. They were well equipped to start ploughing straight away on completion of his purchase, with a view to seeding some 15,000 acres for short term grazing, using Australian subterranean clover, at 2 lbs per acre and South African Veldt grass at 1 lb per acre, plus a dressing or super phosphate at 170 lbs per acre.

The super phosphate was applied by aerial contractor as was the grass and clover mixture. Before seeding, the land was ploughed twice and thoroughly rolled with the railway truck rollers. The roller did a marvellous job of levelling the rough ploughed surface and was able to squash rocks and mallee and yacca roots and leave the surface level and firm, ready for the seeds to germinate quickly, following rain. The roller was also used to create temporary air strips following ploughing.

In order to achieve the target of 15,000 acres it was necessary to keep the plant going 24 hours a day. Bill Helyer was appointed as head operator and Johnny Taylor and I were employed as drivers

The working shifts were (1) Midnight to 8 am
(2) 8 am to 4 pm
(3) 4 pm to midnight.

We had an old Land Rover for transport both to service the plant and for our own personal use (e.g. Salt Creek Café or Meningie). In the event of one of the team not being available, the remaining two would have to work a 12 hour shift.

We were very much in demand! After having my breakfast and getting ready for a quiet kip, Bob would appear "Come on Rog. I would like some more water skiing practice. Will you drive the speed boat for a couple of hours?" This was great fun but a bit wearying, especially when one had been working all night.

Between them, the Hawkes and the Hodges had bought the fibre glass speed boat and were determined to get the maximum use from it.

The grass seeds mixture had already proved superior and very successful at Gundooee. It is vigorous, germinates quickly and produces good quality herbage. I have since successfully advised its use for a pasture improvement project in The Sudan on which I acted as consultant.

Ploughing continued 24 hours a day until by May the target of 15,000 acres had been finished. Rolling was yet to follow and the aerial seeding contract i.e. super phosphate spreading, could be done from hastily constructed airstrips made ready for use by the giant roller built up of railway wheels. The ploughed land would then be worked down ready for seeding.

When Rollo Hawkes completed his section of land clearing and re-seeding, the Hawkes family decided to name each of the 5,000 acre paddocks after one of us. So the Hawkes family described the whole 5,000 acre paddocks as follows:-

    1. Helyer's Paddock
    2. Taylor's Paddock
    3. Coote's Paddock

Thus, we gained recognition for our many hours work and can feel that we have something to leave to posterity, even if only the name. It is one which we will always remember with pride!

Rollo also indicated his thanks by writing to his friend, Macilroy and recommended me for a job on a cattle station, near Charleville, Queensland. Macilroy was a good contact. He spoke to Milo Pastoral Company who offered me a job as jackaroo to start in six months' time on Milo Station, a sheep and cattle property extending to over a million acres in far west Queensland.

This holiday break was welcome as it enabled me to do some more travelling which is the next part of my story.

The Fate of Australia's Kangaroo Population

One of the saddest moments during my tour of the Northern Territory was witnessing the skinning and butchering of the freshly shot kangaroos. I have been similarly disturbed by coming across a kangaroo shooter's butchering site, miles out in the scrub, where heads, thoraxes, paws, legs and feet, all severed with an axe were littered over a wide radius by dingoes, foxes and predatory birds such as wedge-tailed eagles.

My opinion, to date, has been that the practice reflects badly on Australia's environmental ambitions and, perhaps also, on it's treatment of aborigines who are frequently involved.

The kangaroo is able to withstand long periods of drought and can digest and utilise poor quality herbage for example mulga, or gidyea leaves.

It has already been demonstrated that the kangaroo is mechanically efficient and that it has a good and alert brain (10% of a kangaroos live weight is in his brain), compared with 3% in the sleepy and somewhat drowsy koala bear. It is also a beautiful animal with fine skin, exceptional muscle development and a serene expression when observed in its wild state.

There are a number of points that need to be settled before any conclusions can be drawn or recommendations made. This is best indicated by a question and answer procedure, as follows:-

Questions – Answers

1. Do kangaroos endanger pasture land?
Occasionally, in sensitive areas and according to season.

2. Do they carry disease organisms e.g. TB or cattle plague?
No.

3. Do they contribute to spread of parasites or diseases e.g. barber's pole worm?
No.

4. What is the value of meat and skins?
Increasingly commercial, especially skins.

5. Is there a tourist demand for kangaroo shooting?
Yes.

6. Should kangaroos be formally classified as vermin?
No.

7. What is the stockman's opinion?
Variable, but frequently favour negative approach and uphold classification as vermin.

8. Are kangaroos formally regarded as vermin?
Yes, it depends on seasons and sensitive areas.

9. Is the kangaroo population of Australia known?
No fluctuates with seasons.

So they are a bit of a mixed blessing! They are subject to seasonal changes but apart from the occasional fence damage, do little harm and do not spread diseases or parasites to sheep or cattle. The greater problem is the professional 'roo' shooters, especially when tourists are involved.

I conclude that this requires further research and development. Local authorities should issue licences, only the carriers of which can shoot 'roos'. Butchering and skin sites should be cleaned up immediately or that licence will be revoked.

Long term views of environmental experts should be sought to provide local authority guidance. Not a police issue.

Kangaroos, being mainly nocturnal in their habits, we often disturbed large groups of night – grazing kangaroos, when going out before daybreak as we often did! Several hundred 'roos' would all set off at a relaxed bounding pace, giving the impression that the whole paddock was bounding and heaving in unison.

As kangaroos are all marsupials with many genetically based characteristics, it has been suggested that a process of selection over the generations might produce an animal which is much more efficient in its ability to survive and to produce meat and skins on a diet of poor quality herbage (mulga-gidyea-tussock grass).

No hybrid has been proposed. If they could breed together with wombats, it would surely have already happened after 150 million years. Nor can the kangaroo or wombat be persuaded to produce wool. So the idea is probably not a starter.

Northern Adventure

Not having any transport of my own at that stage, I planned the whole trip from Salt Creek to Milo Station, using public transport and seeing as much as I could of inland Australia by the tourist route.

My route was:-

Departure	Destination	Form of Transport
Salt Creek	Gundooee	Land Rover
Gundooee	Adelaide	Car
Adelaide	Alice Springs	Bus
Alice Springs	Ayes Rock	Bus
Ayres Rock/Uluru	Alice Springs	Bus
Alice Springs	Darwin	Bus
Darwin	Mount Isa	Aeroplane(Super Viscount)
Mount Isa	Bundaberg	Rail
Bundaberg	Magnetic island	Rail
Magnetic island	Townsville	Boat
Townsville	Brisbane	Rail
Brisbane	Roma	Rail
Roma	Charleville	Rail
Charleville	Adavale	Bus
Adavale	Milo Station	Land Rover/Mail truck/Weekly mail run

Adelaide to Darwin is probably one of the loneliest roads in the world, being two thousand miles with no towns of any significance. Darwin was certainly the thirstiest town with a beer consumption of 69 gallons per head per year.

Coober Pedy

We missed out on Coober Pedy as heavy rainfall was expected. Although it is the principal Opal Mine in Australia, impending rain forced a short stay and also there was little of tourist significance on that route.

We needed more time but storms were building in the west and heavy rain was forecast as the local event known as 'THE WET' in central Australia.

Kulgera

A little 'one horse' town in the Simpson Desert straddling the Stuart Highway. As this is not a normal stopping place there is nothing much at Kulgera to stop for but there was heavy rain ahead and the bus driver, very wisely, decided to pull up and make alternative arrangements for his passengers.

The Kulgera roadhouse was able to accommodate all the white passengers and the aborigines were catered for at the 'blacks camp' further away from the highway.

The Kulgera residents were exceptionally hospitable! Realising that the 'WET' could delay us for some time, they organised a visitors' dance, a party, tourist games and a kangaroo shoot, all in our honour. Although saddened by the kangaroo shoot, I was glad to have seen it and the interest it created.

My later years with the Duke of Norfolk have put me off shooting forever – but that's another story. The bus passengers included a group of 10 aborigines who were being transported from a mission in South Australia to a working site somewhere in the Northern Territory.

They all wore identical 'army surplus' type of uniforms and were segregated to their own section at the back of the bus.

They were well enough behaved and caused no trouble. At meal times, the whites were accommodated in the hotel, the coffee bar and restaurant, while the blacks were relegated to the back yard. Here they organised themselves on whatever seating was available or squatted native fashion on their heels on the wood heap or in the dust. They were served beef soup in a billy can together with sliced bread, which they obviously and noisily enjoyed.

That was my first experience of Aborigines and my opinion is still that it did not reflect well either upon the Mission or on the Australian community. Two generations on, with racial conflict in so many countries, I wonder if attitudes are any better towards the 'abos'?

Alice Springs

Everyone wants to see Alice Springs if they have read Nevil Shute's book 'A Town like Alice'. Consequently, it is one of the major tourist attractions of the Northern Territory and of Northern Australia. It is located amid huge deserts and the vastness of the country is tremendously impressive.

The magnificence of the surrounding soil with sands and rock has already placed Alice Springs at the top of that particular ladder. The town has a charm of its own and has been a prosperous tourist centre for many years. Further interest in The Alice has been achieved by books such as 'A Town like Alice' by Nevil Shute and 'Fair Dinkum' by Douglas Lockwood.

On top of all this, the discovery of oil in the Tanami Desert has increased interest and the income of Alice Springs and the style of the new buildings is a great improvement on the old ones. But Alice itself has a special quality derived from its own character and history.

Frequently when travelling along in the back country we would come across a single or small group of horsemen. They were on their way out to pick up cattle and drive them back to sale centres or for slaughter. Small groups are often seen miles away from anywhere travelling parallel to the 'The Bitumen' which is the main road from Adelaide to Darwin.

The stockmen are a special feature of Alice Springs and should be regarded with interest because of the work that they do and the life that they lead. The back country stockmen have a great deal of style, doing fast and dangerous work, risking their lives in following desert tracks for many days at a time to find wandering cattle out in the unfenced country to bring them home

The aboriginal stockmen are suitably clothed which benefits their work. Broad-brimmed felt hats providing shelter from the sun, and brightly coloured shirts, that will show up in timber or thick scrubland. Skin-tight moleskin trousers and elastic-sided, high heeled leather boots that will not go through a stirrup on the saddle of a bucking horse. A wide, heavy leather belt constructed to use as hobbles, if necessary, at night. A quart pot or billy-can, either carried in its own holster or attached to the saddle straps and very strongly built.

The water is not safe to drink and boiling plus a good handful of billy tea helps to keep the men clear of infection and 'Jimmy Brits.'

It would seem that the poor and often derided black fellow, squatting on his heels by the wood-heap, becomes a proud and stylish artisan the moment he gets into the saddle.

Ayres Rock/Uluru

Located in the Macdonald ranges to the west of Alice Springs, the rocks are best seen at sunset or sunrise when atmospheric wave creates colour bars across the sky and up to 25,000 to 40,000 feet or so. Colour contrasts are outstanding due to rock formation and to laterite dust in the atmosphere. Colours change from red, through to gold, offset by the white bark of the ghost gum and yellow spinifex. A photographer's paradise!

Darwin

I travelled on by bus on the State Highway. It was cloudy with increasingly warm conditions. Darwin is interesting as the major port and trading centre along the North Australian coast. I would not want to live there due to the stifling heat.

Mount Isa Mines

I flew on from Darwin to Mount Isa by Australian Airways on the Viscount. Doctor Jose in Adelaide had given me an introduction to his son-in-law, Peter Hill, who was in charge of ventilation at Mount Isa Mines which deal with copper and lead.

The mine shafts went down to 2,800 feet and thus ventilation was clearly a priority and a considerable responsibility. Peter dressed me up in mining gear with overalls, gloves, boots and Davy Safety Lamp and gave me a tour of the mines followed by a night at his house with his family and wife P'Anne.

Once again, I was impressed by the exceptional hospitality that I was shown and enjoyed my stay with my new friends.

Bundaberg

Another contact that I made was a friend of my mother's, Mrs. Baldwin, who had emigrated to Queensland several years previously. I travelled down the coast by train and spent a happy couple of nights at South Kolan before travelling on to Townsville and Magnetic Island.

Magnetic Island

Brilliant sunshine, coloured contrast between sea, sky, beaches, sand, rocks and masses of tropical foliage made this another photographer's paradise.

One of the best bits of Queensland so far in my view. The land was well used with vineyards and tropical crops and the poorer land was given over to grazing cattle.

I spent the night in Townsville before taking the train via Brisbane, Toowoomba, Roma to Charleville where I took the bus to Adavale and made my final arrangements to reach Milo Station.

Summary

A good trip. It opened my eyes and enhanced my admiration of Australia. Now I was ready for work and whatever Milo might hold for me.

Milo Station

My trip over, I travelled to Milo Station on the weekly mail run, and I met the Manager, Peter Young and his wife Marion who lived in the 'Big House' or Station Homestead. Milo is now the biggest sheep station in Australia and is sometimes referred to as 'The Milo Million'. At that time, 1961, Thylungra in Queensland held that distinction, but it has since been subdivided and the leases re-allocated. In the year I was at Milo, we shore 39,000 sheep and carried 2,000 cattle and 120 horses.

Mainly unfenced country supported the cattle and fenced country supported the sheep.

The fenced country is surrounded by a dog-proof fence protecting the sheep from predation by wild dogs or dingoes.

Shearing time was the peak of activity when a full gang of contractors was employed and that included their accommodation and meals.

The actual team at the Milo woolshed comprised:-

Shearers	13
Rouseabouts and wool pressers	2
Wool classer/expert	1
Cook and Slushy	2
Yard Men/Rouseabouts	3
Total	21

Station staff had to ensure that all machinery, electricity generators and diesel engines were in first class order before starting the shearing contract. The essential point also was that they were all safe. Also, that fencing, gates and yard equipment were all in good working order. The workforce, before shearing started, was thus extremely busy and all long term repairs had to be completed in good time before the full operational work.

Most of the planning was the full responsibility of the Manager and the day to day work fell to the overseer, and fitter or mechanic.

Milo had a permanent staff of about 12 men with additional men coming in locally as and when needed on a part time basis. Most of the stockwork was carried out from outside camps, or outstations set apart from the main homestead.

1) These were designated by their distance from the homestead or woolshed and consisted of Hay Paddock (12 miles) Trousers Outstation (10 miles), Dowlings Outstation (24 miles/cattle only), Shearing Shed (3 miles), Ambathalla (20 miles).

Each of these camps had a bunkhouse, showers, loos, kitchen, veranda and all the very basic requirements for a working team.

One man (a boundary rider) was usually accommodated full time at each camp, contactable by telephone (lines strung out along fences) or short wave radio. Flying doctor radio was also needed and was vital in the case of emergencies, three of which occurred during my year at Milo.

The staffing was extremely flexible, but under normal conditions was as follows:-

Station Staff	Homestead	Outstations	Camps
Manager	1	Ron Rudd	1
Overseer	1	Simon Tracey	1
Fitter/Mechanic	1	Max	1
Cook/Slushy	2	Dougal	1
Housemaid	1	Christy Collins	1
Bookkeeper	1	Johnny Jones	1
Jackaroo	1	Jim Jones	1
Boundary Riders	1	George West	1
Casual/Stockworker Ringer	1		
Sub Total	10		8
		TOTAL	18

Old customs and attitudes die hard. Milo had no fewer than three dining rooms - one for bosses, one for jackaroos and one for station hands. This was the relic of an old custom, based upon snobbery, where 'blacks' ate outside only.

The overall organisation for livestock management on a station of the size of Milo was daunting and Pete Young at Milo and Ray Richardson at Ambathalla had a heavy workload with which they coped extremely competently. Mustering, droving and handling 39,000 sheep was a major task in itself and required good planning and overseeing plus a willing staff.

My first job at Milo was as homestead jackaroo doing much the same work as at Gundooee. I milked the Station cows, killed and butchered sheep for rations, attended to the mail and generally shackled about as the lowest form of life employed on a station. I also had to stand-in as relief bookkeeper and camp cook which marginally improved my status.

After a couple of weeks, I was promoted to the 15 Mile stock camp. The team there comprised:-

Boundary rider (Overseer)	Ron Rudd
3 Jackaroos	Simon Tracey
	Mac
	Big Douglas
3 Stockmen (Ringers)	Christy Collins
	Johnny Jones
	Jim Jones
1 Cook	Roy Ferris

Each man carried his personal gear in a canvas bedroll or swag which could be chucked into the back of a truck or strapped to the saddle of a horse when it became necessary to shift camp to another site. Usually another boundary rider's hut.

The teams required another 20 or so horses for seven stockmen ringers which all had to be kept in feed and duly rested. Each man required a fresh horse to ride on the day and another three on spell. The work horses also had to be shod regularly and that was another skill that I managed to acquire.

Roy had the camp cooking organised and did an excellent job. He had been on the station for about a year and was beginning to feel it was time to take a break from the post.

An advertisement for a camp cook had been placed in the local Times and we received a telephone call from Charleville from a man applying for the job. The overseer at the shearing shed took time to drive to Adavale to meet him.

Greg Hoddle the overseer took time to interview him. He returned with the most extraordinary little man. He was about 5ft tall, had a toothy grin, a huge beer barrel of a belly, little skinny legs and wore shorts and sandals. He stuck out his hand "G'day mate," he said, "Old George Keel's me name".

And so we got, in a country of characters, one more extraordinary member to our team. But he was a good cook and that's what mattered, instead of the usual grub of fried mutton and tinned vegetables had extended his menu to include pies, steaks, curries, lasagne and all sorts of other dishes. Barbeques where laid on in the evenings and we all lived royally for a while.

I returned to the campsite one working day to find breakfast cereal scattered out in the yard and old George hiding round the corner with a .410 shotgun over his knees. Two freshly shot top-knot pigeons lay at his side. Old George liked to cook his own personal feed and was using cornflakes as bait and he was able to shoot enough pigeons to make a special pigeon pie which he kept for his own lunch, twice a week. I didn't let on. It kept Old George happy and stopped him getting lonely when men were out working all day. After all, good cooks are worth looking after.

And so we continued. Shearing finished, fresh mobs of sheep drafted up and returned to the outside paddocks, marking and branding completed on calves and foals, plenty of grass, plenty of good stock water and it was time for a bit of a spell off and away from the Station.

Having taken my Northern trip, I was content to remain at Milo where Peter Young always had jobs for me to cover. With the bookkeeper on holiday, I was given the job of working out and paying the men's wages each week which was tedious but a change from the 'dust and flies and dirt' routine at the mustering camp. I was becoming used to the property and to the staff.

On Christmas Eve all the outside staff came into the homestead and Old George had laid on a splendid barbeque to which everyone was invited. Enough cans of beer were brought in from The Adavale Pub and the evening became progressively rowdy as the big day approached but we made a reasonable job of clearing up when it was all over.

When we got up on Christmas morning there was no cook to be found and no breakfast. A search was then started and Old George was discovered in bed with the housemaid. Thus on Christmas day we had a housemaid in tears and Old George certainly was not a happy man. Old George was tight as a tic and wanted to fight anyone who came near. There was no one to cook for the staff or serve Christmas luncheon.

So that became another little job for me to do and accepting that it was a little late in coming to the table we served a reasonable feed and it didn't turn out too badly.

Before I became completely over cooked, or over-burdened with bookkeeping routine I was transferred to the mustering team together with four horses to the Trousers Outstation which was the home of the solitary boundary rider, name of 'Shorty'.

He was another reliable, sensible and practical man and well respected by all. We spent the time in moving mobs of sheep into the yards for crutching and on yard work, drafting and culling the ewe flock in preparation for tupping – again using broad wool Merino rams from The East Bungaree Stud which I had visited with Rob and Sue Hodge while working at Gundooee.

The cattle herds were mainly outside the dog fence and Trousers Outstation was just inside so it was all sheep work with no significant amount of cattle handling to do.

We also carried out some branding of foals and calves and this was a tricky job which had to be done extremely carefully, the temperature of the branding irons had to be absolutely right. If the branding irons were too hot they could cause serious wounding, whereas if they were not sufficiently hot the brand would not hold throughout the life of the beast.

We were fairly self-contained at Trousers which had a good display of wildlife. Not only kangaroos and emus which were common but also wombats, rabbits but no camels. There were also a lot of coloured parrots and galahs, while at night the chorus of frogs and crickets was enough to keep any tired man awake.

When we had finished mustering for the day and taking sheep back to the main camp, Shorty would ride up alongside me and say "How about you trot on home and start getting some tea ready." So then I would trot on ahead so that by the time the men arrived we had hot steak, chips and peas ready for dinner followed by tinned apricots and condensed milk.

On one of these occasions when we were trotting home for tea I asked Ruddy who was riding with me.

"When are you going to retire?"

He replied "I am not, unless I win the Melbourne Cup. When I can't work anymore, all I ask is to come off a good 'orse going fast. And mark you it's got to be a bloody good 'orse not one of these yang-yang fucking bastards you got on this camp!"

We worked well together and with Shorty as overseer our team covered a lot of work and handled a lot of sheep.

One evening, the Manager Peter Young turned up as we were sitting down to supper

"Is Roger about?" he asked.

"He's here, just turning his horse out" replied Shorty.

"I've just received an urgent telegram for him, his father's died."

The telegram read: "Father dead – love Mother."

That was a real bombshell. I had no idea that his condition was so weak or so fragile. He had never been a strong man, but had only reached the age of 56. His father was still alive and was now living with my mother. That was untenable. I needed to go home as quickly as possible.

Australian Airways and my bank sorted things out for me and obtained a seat for me on a Boeing, leaving for London in 48 hours. Three days later I was met at Heathrow Airport by my mother and my brother Joe.

The sense of death and depression was palpable, there was a great deal of sorting out to be done. It took us nearly a year before I could return to Australia. But that's another story!

Return to Australia

There were a number of items which could not be finished. These included some of the farm land, sale of orchard cottage, my parents' home and the completion of various leases and grazing licences.

My brother Joe and fellow executor, undertook to keep an eye on things at home. As soon as I could, I bought a ticket for the SS Stratheden heading for Melbourne in September 1963.

I had the choice of two jobs. Rob and Sue's offer of the management at Gundooee and Milo Pastoral Company's offer of a place at Ambathalla, as overseer. Peter Young, the Milo manager said that the job could be started straight away, but that he was prepared to give me six months longer in which to make up my mind.

I accepted the Gundooee offer first, to see how it worked out. Rob was extremely busy. The Currawong re-seeds were coming through and we had plenty of routine stock work to keep us both more than fully employed. I bought a second-hand Volkswagon and thus became even more independent. I was able to go to town and go gliding at Murray Bridge and at Gawler (Adelaide).

After the six months were up, I decided to take up the challenge of the overseer's job at Ambathalla and to drive up the Crystal Highway as soon as Rob could let me go.

The Ambathalla job went well. I liked working with the manager, Ray Richardson and his wife Hazel. The homestead was unusual as it was two storeys high and had a most attractive garden with tropical shrubs and orange and lemon trees which gave out a delightful scent.

Just as my job at Milo had been curtailed by my father's sudden death, problems arose here when I was struck down by a bout of acute sciatica. Two weeks of intensive treatment in Charleville hospital failed to cure it. I was strongly advised by doctors to give up earning my living on horseback. I was very disappointed that I couldn't continue at Ambathalla which was enjoyable, but involved a lot of work in the saddle.

After this set back, I decided to return to the UK and try for a job in research or management. So, my planned stay in The Outback was reduced to six years and that is covered in my story.

Throughout my working life, I devoted as much time as I could spare to my beloved sport of gliding and was a qualified instructor for forty years. I had numerous magical flights along the South Downs as well as in Wales, Scotland and overseas. I eventually became Development Officer for the British Gliding Association.

Back Country Boys

Johnny and Jimmy had lived in Adavale all their lives. Johnny was 27 and Jimmy was 25. If not in Adavale, they were working for Milo Pastoral Company and were living at an outstation or in a boundary rider's hut. Johnny was the quieter of the two and had dreadful buck teeth while Jimmy was the taller and better looking and often became a bit of a 'skite', tending to 'blow his bags', especially at meal times.

Between them, they had never been further from Milo than Toowoomba, on the train route to Brisbane. Neither had ever been to the coast and although they were living within a day's train ride of some of Australia's best beaches, they had no wish to see them or to visit the sea.

"You're missing out ," I said to Johnny.

"She'll be right, mate," he said. "I see too much bloody sunshine out here. What we want is some shade!"

Each unto his own!

He was happy. He did no-one any harm. I believe he was shy of becoming involved in an unfamiliar environment and felt insecure and apprehensive of strange and new surroundings.

These country boys were the 'salt of the earth'.

What we need is more boys like Johnny and Jimmy, not less.

A Mess of Pottage

It was one of those days when nothing goes right.

The team were camped at 'Trousers' Outstation.

A mob of sheep had accidentally got 'boxed' and needed re-drafting so they were taken to 'Trousers' where they were quickly sorted.

Then the utility truck ran out of petrol and a small can had to be sent out by horseback as nothing else was available. It all wasted time on a blistering hot day.

In the afternoon, we were drafting and re-paddocking the 2-tooth ewes, ready for joining them with the Merino rams.

As was our usual practice, two of us then trotted home to get some tea going for the team. I decided that we would use the shearing board as a table. The yards had seen many overnight holdings of sheep and the pens had built up a deposit of some 6" deep, hard, sun-dried pellets of dung.

I had all the ingredients for a 'ram-stag' mutton stew. We had some carrots and some red onions which would make a good mix and we also had a jar of curry power which would liven it up a little more.

Once they got home and turned their horses out, the mustering team were bringing up their tin bowls at the ready.

"Bloody good tucker!" said Christie. "Any more going?"

"Help yourself." I said and soon several more wanted another helping. Big Mac came up beside me and took my shoulder

"What the bloody hell's going on?" He said quietly.

"This stew is full of sheep shit".

Someone had lifted the lid off the stewing pot and had put it down on the deeply pelleted yard. The pellets of sheep muck had stuck to the underside of the lid which was wet and steamy and had then fallen off into the stew. There was a thick skin of sheep dung pellets floating on top of the stew.

"Quick, give me the ladle for a bit" said Mac I handed the ladle to Mac who gave the remaining contents of the cooking pot a vigorous stir.

"Jeez," I said, "they can't eat that!".

"No-one will ever notice", he said. "What the eye doesn't see, the stomach doesn't grieve for!" And they didn't.

So we all went to our swags full as 'googs' and happily content.

And no-one was late for breakfast next morning.

* Mess of Pottage - Source 'The Holy Bible' Genesis 11. Esau sold his inheritance for a pot of lentil soup.

Royal Flying Doctor Service

No reference to the outback is complete without recognition of this 'major' aerial medical service.

Cattle work on horseback is notoriously dangerous and there is a long history of accidents, many fatal on the big cattle stations in the North of Australia.

During my time at Milo Station, there were three accidents which, if it had not been for the RFDS would have been fatal.

Henry Geiger a stockman of German descent was riding hard to head off the lead of a mob of cattle which was breaking away. He did not see the remains of an old rusty broken fence line until it was too late. He hit the barbed wire entanglement at full gallop and both he and his horse hit the ground hard. The horse limped away but Henry was out cold and so he remained for the next eight days.

He would never have survived but for the skills of the Flying Doctor from Charleville who navigated his Cessna aircraft and found the site in thick mulga and then applied medical aid and nursing care to keep him alive until they reached Charleville Hospital.

Henry did survive and was back in the saddle some six months or so, later.

Another stock accident was Big MacDougal known as Doug who was badly gored in the cattle yards by a charging bull. Doug had severe internal injuries but RFDS were with him within an hour and attended to his wounds. Then they had him back at Charleville Hospital in double quick time.

The third accident concerned a Milo jackaroo, one Simon Tracey who was preparing a cattle truck for road train use when he dropped a heavy steel cattle crate on his leg and broke it in several places. The aircraft arrived at the station in double quick time and Simon had lost a lot of blood and was in a very weak state. Nevertheless, once again, the RFDS saved his life although he took rather longer to recover than either Henry or Doug.

In addition to this aerial accident emergency service, the RFDS also runs a special GP Medical Service for outback stations

The Crystal Highway

I was driving my Volkswagon 'Beetle' from Gundooee in South Australia to Milo Station in Queensland, accompanied by my Kelpie sheep dog puppy, Tippy, on one of my recent visits to Australia. We left at 5.30 am and made good progress to Hay on the New South Wales border. We were headed via Forbes-Parkes-Dubbo-Charleville on the Cobb Highway, through the Darling Downs.

A road train, containing several trucks loaded with cattle, was approaching so in order to avoid driving in the dust and in limited visibility, I pulled over to the left hand side. Then, 'CRACK!' A shower of stones had hit my windscreen and shattered the offside. I pulled up but nothing could be done, other than to give my sheep dog a drink. I then removed as much as I could of the broken windscreen making it temporarily safe before I carried on.

About five miles up the track, I saw a utility truck parked on the road side with a notice on the roof, headed 'WINDSCREENS FIXED TWENTY POUNDS'.

Within an hour, I was on my way again with a brand new windscreen. "Thanks Mate" said the fitter as I handed over my £20. He also said "Have a cup of coffee on the house!"

Before I got to Dubbo, I passed another three utility trucks, all loaded up with a variety of replacement windscreens and obviously very busy.

Good luck to them! It was a good day for business and an acute need was being met with skill and good humour.

Lucky for me, it was!

Short Stories

Three fictional stories based on the author's experience in Australia

The Adavale Dance

The camp cook stood in the firelight. A good meal had been served, the clearing and washing-up, all done.

"Looks like another Saturday night in the bush" he said.

"Youse blokes going to the dance tonight?"

"Too right we are!" said Jack

"Oh my word!" said Jimmy

"Bloody oath!" said Christie

"Who's coming back here tonight?"

"Depends on our luck!" said Christie

"OK. Breakfast at nine o'clock. Give the poor old cook a blow"

The boys all met up in the Adavale pub, where they stayed for the first hour or so. Eventually, they headed mob-handed, for the Town Hall. A small band had been hired from Charleville and with a saxophone, a double bass and two guitars provided some very acceptable music and the Master of Ceremonies from Charleville was doing a good job.

The blokes all tended to congregate just inside the door where a good bit of chyiking and good natured taunting went on.

Sheilas were, as usual, in short supply and tended to stay chattering together in little groups, hoping to be asked for a dance. Three couples were already waltzing, albeit a little stiffly, in the middle of the dance floor and one of these was recognised as Charlene, the girl from the pub, who was quite a looker.

The next dance was announced as a 'general excuse me' quick-step and the number of dancers doubled immediately. The tempo increased and so did the number of dancing couples, when a gaggle of housewives and several elderly men joined the throng.

Things were warming up nicely when a couple started to jive. This was clearly popular and within minutes the whole gathering was having fun.

Suddenly, a rough looking character appeared on the dance floor and demanded that Charlene should jive with him. She was dancing at the time with Johnny who refused the demand. The stranger's response was to take a swing at Johnny which, unfortunately connected and dropped him to the floor.

Greg, the Milo overseer witnessed all this. "No more of that," he said. "Come outside."

"No, bugger you!" he replied.

Just then, a large utility truck drove up to the hall with lights rotating, siren blaring and Police Sergeant McGhee at the wheel.

"You two," he hollered, "up to the Station. You are under arrest!"

"You can stay in the cooler tonight till 7 am. If there is no more trouble you can go home, otherwise you will stay 'on remand' until the Chief of Police decides what to do with you".

After that, the dance continued rather despondently, but it soon ground to a halt. The evening was spoilt and everyone went home.

All except one, that is.

Charlene surveyed the scene from Johnny's ute.

"How's about we go back to my place?" she said.

"That's the best thing I've heard all evening" said Johnny.

Boxing Day in the Bush

Meekafara in the late 1940's was not everyone's idea of a place to settle. The little frontier town stood at the railway junction in the middle of a mulga and salt bush plain where sheep farmers just eked out a living on the edge of the fenced country. Beyond the dog fence, cattle and dingoes competed in a dusty and lonely landscape. Dusty, that is, until Christmas and the coming of the rains.

Let the new Storekeeper tell his story of the Festive Season:-

Christmas Day had been a quiet affair but just before midnight, I woke to a heavy banging on the door of the General Stores. Pulling on a pair of shorts and thongs I padded on to the verandah.

A Stockman stood there, his dark countenance grey with dust and fatigue. His bony stock horse with its high poly saddle stood splay footed and lethargic under the old pepperina tree in the main street.

The greeting was unexpected.

"You the undertaker?"

"No – sorry mate."

"Well you just bought the General Stores, aint ya?"

"Sure."

"Well, you're the bloody undertaker then."

In a back country town in Australia, the storekeeper automatically assumes a number of roles. He is postmaster, newsagent, casket agent, saddler, draper, baker, grocer, in fact together with the stock agent and the publican, he performs most of the public services in the township. Almost all. Chuck in the minister and the barmaid and you've got the lot.

Having just invested my Returned Serviceman's gratuity in the Store, I was still learning my duties day by day. This last request, however, was something for which I was completely unprepared.

"The camp cook's died out Mullanganna and the Boss want him buried proper. He says come tonight."

Mullanganna Station was a big spread owned by one of the national stock and station agents. It was a valuable source of business for my store. We made a weekly mall run out there by truck and provided all the basic stores from petrol to pumpkins.

The homestead was about 40 miles along a dirt track to the North West and lay on the far side of a tributary of the Murchisson River.

I had been out there on a mall run a couple of weeks ago and recalled meeting Quinn, the manager, a hardened grazier of the old school who had a reputation as a hard man on his staff but a wonderful man with cattle. In keeping with so many of his origin, he was a devout Catholic and I began to understand his anxiety to ensure a decent burial for his unfortunate late employee.

The night was hot and sultry. For the last couple of weeks, the long awaited summer rains had been brewing up but never quite managing to materialise. Heavy storm clouds had formed in the late afternoon and by nightfall rain had once again seemed imminent.

Christmas was a quiet time on the stations, most of the young men having taken advantage of the holiday for a spell at the coast, but I was still puzzled.

"Why didn't Quinn send the 'ute'?" I asked.

"12 mile creek coming up."

"You've had some rain then?"

"Too right!"

Storms were notoriously sporadic and localised in December, yet there must have been some heavy rain further out. Either that or Quinn was not trusting his utility truck to the old stockman who would probably succumb to the temptations of Mulligan's Bar, once his grizzly message had been delivered.

Clearly, this was not a mission to be attempted single-handed. Mick normally drove the mall truck and I decided to enrol his assistance. He would not be too pleased at being called on Christmas night, but I could count on Mick. Fortunately, I was also the town's telephone exchange.

Mick brought the truck round half an hour later.

"What are ya going to put 'im in?"

"Buggered if I know."

"We used the last of the coffins for old Mrs. O'Sullivan just before you took over. Better get one sent up on the train."

Messages were duly left and with a large softwood packing case labelled 'Union Carbide' slung on the back of the truck, we duly departed.

Mick knew the track like the back of his hand and I was soon nodding off in the passenger seat beside him. The truck droned on and apart from the red eyes of an occasional 'roo in the headlights, we saw nothing. Behind us, a great plume of laterite dust – fine as talcum powder – rose into the night air.

The horizon ahead was continually being illuminated by flashes of summer lightning. Someone was getting welcome rain! We conjectured as to whom the lucky station might be and then fell silent again as the dusty track wore on.

I opened the first of the paddock gates at the 12 mile and was surprised to find that the creek, dry as a bone when we last crossed it, was now flowing strongly.

Downstream, the creek divided into numerous gulleys and tributaries which opened up into an area of brigalow, belah and channel country where lakes of water dried out to produce lakes of grass for a short period following a good flood.

The area was broken by short Coolabah and ghost gum trees and opened out into a wide plain before eventually joining the watershed of the Murchisson.

The 12 mile crossing had been well reinforced with stones and the truck ground through comfortably in 2 feet of fast flowing, yellow water.

By the time we reached the Station we had driven into the rain, intermittent at first, but now settling to a steady downpour as the lightning and accompanying thunder became more frequent.

Quinn was waiting for us at the homestead.

"Good of youse to come so soon." he said. "Better get loaded and away quick as you can or you won't get back across the 12 mile."

The Cook was laid out in the workshop.

"We shifted him down here this afternoon," Quinn explained. "Blokes reckoned they could smell him up in the quarters."

We certainly could. He had not been properly laid out and was becoming bloated and greenish in colour and was beginning to ooze onto the rough bench where he lay covered by a grey blanket.

He was a big man. Mick and I looked at each other.

"How we going to get him in the box?" He asked.

Quinn led us back into the slightly fresher atmosphere of the store and from a locked chest in the corner produced a bottle of rum and a couple of tin pannikins.

"Git yourselves a drink." He said and disappeared.

We had a couple of snorts and were grateful but before we had time for a third, Quinn had returned, a butchers knife and steel in his hand.

"O.K. youse blokes come and give us a hand."

We gently lifted the body into the packing case. With his head hard up against one end, his legs hung out by half a yard at the other.

"Grab his foot," said Quinn.

As I held the foot up Quinn picked up the butchers knife. The tip of the razor-sharp knife found the joint behind the knee cap and with a few deft stokes, I stood holding a severed leg.

"Lay it alongside him in the box," grunted Quinn as he sought for the knee joint in the other leg.

When both severed legs were lying alongside the corpse in the packing case, Quinn stood back and with surprising reverence, crossed himself.

"Sorry Pat, old fella," he said. "The Lord have mercy on ya."

Quickly, we nailed down the lid and between us carried the box outside and loaded it onto the back of the truck.

"Another one for the road!" said Quinn, as he filled the pannikins, joining us this time. The rain was now settling to a steady beat on the tin roof and large puddles were forming on the track.

Quinn handed me the rum bottle. "Take it with you. You might need it. Now for Christ's sake get moving if you're going to get home tonight."

The road quickly cut up and we left deep ruts as we set off from the homestead. The track had been well graded and little water lay on the surface. For the next half-hour we made good progress.

"If we can get across the 12 mile we should make it," said Mick, as the stony gibber plain and mulga began to give way to the black soil and Mitchell grass through which the 12 mile creek slowly meandered.

We pulled up short of the crossing at the 12 mile hut. The creek was now twice the width it had been a couple of hours earlier and the stoned crossing was no longer as clearly marked.

Mick was an old hand and after wading in to discover the course of the crossing, he unstrapped his bedding roll from behind the seat. Quickly lifting the bonnet, he disconnected the fan belt and laid the heavy canvas swag-cover across the top of the engine and well down in front of the radiator.

"If we can keep pushing a bow wave we shall get across without wetting the engine." he explained. "You wade ahead to mark the crossing and I'll follow."

Gingerly I waded out into the yellow water. I could feel the firm stones of the crossing underfoot, but the water was up to my waist and the pull of the current was strong.

Mick could still see me in his headlights as I started to clamber into the shallow water on the far side. He gunned the engine and eased her gently into the creek. With the engine revving and clutch slipping in bottom gear he steadily sank deeper into the water. The bow wave built in front and on she came.

For a dreadful moment in mid-stream the headlights disappeared beneath the yellow torrent and the engine began to splutter but Mick knew his business and slowly but surely she clambered up to the track on my side.

We removed the tarpaulin from the engine block but kept her running to help dry out her saturated electrical system.

Then we finished the bottle of rum.

It was breaking daylight when I got out to open the dog netting gate and the rain had eased to a steady drizzle. As Mick drove through, my fuddled brain realised that something was wrong.

The back of the truck was empty. The packing case with its grizzly contents must have floated off and we had been too stupid to realise.

That afternoon, a coffin was gently laid to rest in the town cemetery. The Shire Clerk and the old stockman were the only witnesses apart from Mick and myself who acted as pall bearers.

The coffin was quickly covered up. Bodies cannot be left for long in inland Australia and some builders' rubble and a bin of offal from the slaughter house made a sufficiently convincing substitute for the late lamented cook. Fortunately, no-one had requested to see the body.

As soon as the rains stopped, Mick and I returned to search the 12 mile creek and its many channels. We spent several days out there but we never found him.

A headstone now stands in the cemetery, donated by Quinn and his staff and a few distant relatives from the Old Country.

That all happened 30 years ago. Since then I have officiated at many funerals in the town. Some have been tragic, some riotous, but none stands as clearly in my memory as that occasion when I first became the town's undertaker.

Ringers' Revenge

I slept badly again last night. Alright at first, but woke in the early hours in a cold sweat having been troubled again by the dream that has recurred many times over the past twenty years.

That dreams can be a premonition of fate has always worried me. Last night's dream was no exception.

Lying wakeful and disturbed throughout the early hours, I again tried to reason. Were we not justified? Would not a clever lawyer put up a good case for us? Why should anyone know? Surely after twenty years….

It had been a particularly heavy day. Shearing time in West Queensland was no sinecure even in a good year, but shearing in a drought was murder. The sheep had not the strength to walk for more than three or four miles a day and following months without rain, there was no feed to hold them close to the shearing shed.

We had been constantly moving sheep for the past two months. Weak bedraggled woollies were droved in gentle stages to the sheds and poor bony shorn sheep already stained red ochre by the laterite dust returned to be drafted, sorted into lots and paddocked out for the summer and hopefully, the rains.

My little gang of musterers and drovers were camped together with our team of horses, our dogs and our cook at the 12 mile hut. Twelve miles, that is, up the droving route from the great shearing shed where twenty shearers battled for six weeks to secure our only cash income, the wool cheque.

For most of the year, six of us coped with all the stock work on the place. There were John and Jimmy, from the local town. Brought up in the bush, neither had ever seen the sea.

They were wonderful horsemen with a genuine love for their work. John, the elder, was tall and spindly with dreadful buck teeth. He looked awful on a horse but in the years that I knew him, I never saw him come off one.

Jimmy, on the other hand, was the 'skite' of the camp. Big, rough and good looking, Jimmy would have a go at anything but there were times when his loud and raucous ways became a bit of a strain on the rest of the gang.

Old Jim was the only other white man on the team. Nearly 70 years old and after many years of saving, old Jim had been unable to settle in his little bungalow near the coast and the lure of the bush life had brought him back to the work that he knew best. The other two were of aboriginal stock.

Westie was a full blood, quiet, gentle and the best man I have ever seen at quietening a young horse. 'Munger Jack', so called because a buck jumping horse had once torn most of one ear off on a tree, was a quarter-blood but by this time of the summer, he was almost as black as old Westie.

We had worked together for long enough to develop a degree of mutual tolerance. For most of the year, the 12 mile hut was our home. We camped there, did our horse breaking and shoeing there and used it as a nursing home for any sick or lame horses.

Extra members of the team were always regarded with some suspicion. We had seen too many come and go. I suppose we expected them to earn their place in our team. Mick was one such newcomer. He had come out from

Charleville the previous week, driving his own utility truck. At such a busy time, help would have been welcome. But Mick was precious little use.

"Typical bloody Queen Street Ringer," said Jimmy resentfully after Mick's first day's effort at mustering.

Jim was subtler in his appraisal. "Like a boarding house cup of tea," he said. "Big and bloody weak; but this one's vicious with it."

Our camp horses, after weeks of mustering and droving work in the drought and heat, were getting poor. They were leg-weary and needed to be nursed along, otherwise they would get sore backs or go lame.

Mick had no regard for the horses. Admittedly, he could ride but he was flash and whatever mounts I gave him, he knocked them about unmercifully. He even wore spurs which the rest of us normally reserved for fast work on cattle. Because he had already given one of the horses a sore back, I had allowed him to ride a little roan mare of mine called Tassie.

She was a fiery little animal and I had plans to train her as a camp drafter for Rodeo work but Mick had no respect for her and as the day wore on my temper grew steadily worse. He whaled into her with a stick, he spurred her on, and galloped the little mare mercilessly and quite unnecessarily up and down the flank of the mob of tired old wethers that we were taking back to one of the far paddocks.

Finally, I could stand it no longer. "For Christ's sake give it a go will you," I shouted at him. "Take it easy or you'll ruin her, the same as you did your last horse. You can't expect me to keep giving horses up to you at this rate. Best thing you can do is roll your swag and get off the bloody place."

I thought there was going to be a fight. He said that he was a cattle man, wasn't going to spend a day longer on sheep work and that he would pull his time straightaway. His last remark upset me.

"If I can't have this mare," he shouted. "I'll see no-one else gets her." With that, he turned, and to our collective fury galloped off back towards camp in a cloud of dust.

Two hours later, the last wether stumbled painfully through the paddock gate and joined his mates at the long water trough. At last we could go home. No galloping for us though; our horses were tired and we too weary. At a steady walk we were back at camp by nightfall two hours later.

Mick's truck was gone. He had driven to the homestead, drawn his cheque and left the same evening. We hosed the sweat off our tired horses' backs and let them go. Dejectedly they stumbled off to the creek for a welcome drink before returning to fill their empty bellies on the sparse herbage.

It was then that I noticed Tassie. The little roan mare stood alone under a group of Gidyea trees by the creek. She was plastered in sweat, her flanks were white with drying foam and flecked with blood from repeated spurring. As I walked closer, the full horror of her condition became apparent. She had been deliberately blinded. Blood and fluid had streamed from her empty eye sockets and congealed down each side of her cheeks.

I have been mad on occasions but I don't believe I have ever known such bitter anger as welled up within me at that pitiful sight. The others had by that time joined me. Jim and Jack stood in open-mouthed disbelief. Westie and the brothers unashamedly wept.

"He's not getting away with this," choked Jim, expressing the anger we all felt. "If I ever catch up with that bastard again, I'll crucify him."

Never had I seen my lads so angry. Bitter resentment at such wanton cruelty overcame our own fatigue and exhaustion and we decided upon a plan of campaign.

I gave the Jones boys the job of destroying Tassie. They led her away to a patch of heavy scrub outside the horse paddock and shot her with a .22 rifle. They both loved horses and I knew that I could rely on them to do the job as humanely as possible.

After grabbing a quick supper, I filled up the truck with petrol. Then old Jim, Munger Jack and I set off for Adavale.

I was banking on the assumption that with a cheque in his pocket, he would not pass the first pub. Sure enough, Mick's utility truck was parked outside the Adavale Hotel. We blundered straight into the Bar, still in our working clothes. He gave us little trouble being almost too far gone. We bundled him into his truck which Munger drove.

About 5 miles out of town he started getting awkward so we dumped his utility amongst some scrub away from the main track and Jim and Munger Jack sat on him, none too gently, in the back of the station truck.

We got back to the 12 mile about midnight, by which time Mick had sobered up enough to realise what was happening to him. Screaming abuse, Mick was manhandled to the horse yard where we lashed his outstretched arms to the top rail.

We were determined to teach him a lesson. Jimmy Jones was ready with his stock whip.

"Just let me get at the bastard!" he screamed as he brought his stock whip down across the bewildered ringer's back.

We took turns to lay into him. Even the cook demanded to be given a go. I do not know how long we continued. Blind fury and the pleasure of sweet revenge took command. In the moonlight, it was hard to see how much damage we were doing and we carried on long after his demented screaming had stopped.

Feeling slightly nauseated, I called them off. I filled a bucket of water from the horse trough and slung it over the spread eagled shape on the stock yard rails. There was no movement. With the aid of a carbide lamp, we examined our handiwork. His back was raw and he had lost a lot of blood. I felt for his pulse, gripped by a chill feeling in the pit of my stomach. No pulse. We had gone too far. Mick was dead.

It was a very different group that sat down by the light of the carbide lamps in the camp kitchen. The faces, that half an hour ago had been flushed and excited, were now ashen grey.

The cook seemed to know what to do.

"We are all in this together," he said. "No one need ever know."

Together, that night we made a pact. Then we set to work again. We loaded Mick's body into the station truck and dumped him down the shaft of an old opal mine, long since disused. We then retrieved his utility truck and drove it 70 miles into Charleville where we left it, complete with all Mick's gear behind the town's notorious 'Cattle Camp' Hotel.

We locked the door but carefully left the side window ajar. In the morning, we reported to the Station Manager that the mare had broken her leg in a paddy-melon hole and had to be shot. Then, slightly later than usual, we carried on with our usual work.

My dream was not without meaning. A letter, forwarded by my bank, arrived at breakfast time. It was from the publican in Adavale and contained a clumsy attempt at blackmail. A series of lurid newspaper cuttings provided the story. Old Jim had died in a Brisbane hospital. He had been delirious during his last few days and the whole story had come to light.

One of the patients had reported his suspicions to the Police. An enquiry had been held, the body discovered and as a result, the only surviving members, John and Jimmy had admitted their complicity and were now in a Brisbane jail, pending an appeal.

They had honoured our pact to the last, but the cunning little Publican had gone one better. He suspected that I had been involved and although he knew my story was safe with the brothers he would need a little present of some $5,000 to keep his mouth shut.

I have pondered over the contents of his letter all day and now my mind is made up. The full story must be told. With the right legal aid, the brothers' appeal should be upheld. Otherwise, well, we were all in it together. Now that the story has been told, I feel confident that I can obtain the brothers' release.

Then, I shall deal with that snivelling little publican.

Epilogue

The reader may well ask "What have you been doing for the last fifty years?" The answer to this is Farming and Gliding. The first job on my return to the U.K. was as lecturer in animal husbandry at Plumpton Agricultural College near Lewes in Sussex. I stayed there for four years, during which time I married Jenny, my Australian wife.

Next, I wanted once again, to do something more practical and applied for the assistant farm manager's job on the Duke of Norfolk's farms at Arundel, West Sussex.

Later, when the manager was promoted, I was appointed in his place. During this time, the Old Duke (Bernard Marmaduke) died and I could not get on with the new management. So after this, I became General Manager of 23 farms in Bedfordshire. Bedfordia Farms Ltd was a family farming company near Sharnbrook where I was able to buy my own house once again, which was preferable to being in another tied farmhouse.

A further six years and a lot of back pain later, I obtained a position as farming partner and Consultant for a national firm of Land Agents based in my home town of Lewes.

Gallery

MV Fairsea
Sitmar Lines postcard

MV Fairstar
Sitmar Lines postcard

Roger on the Coorong in 1960

Northern Adventure route map

Milo Map

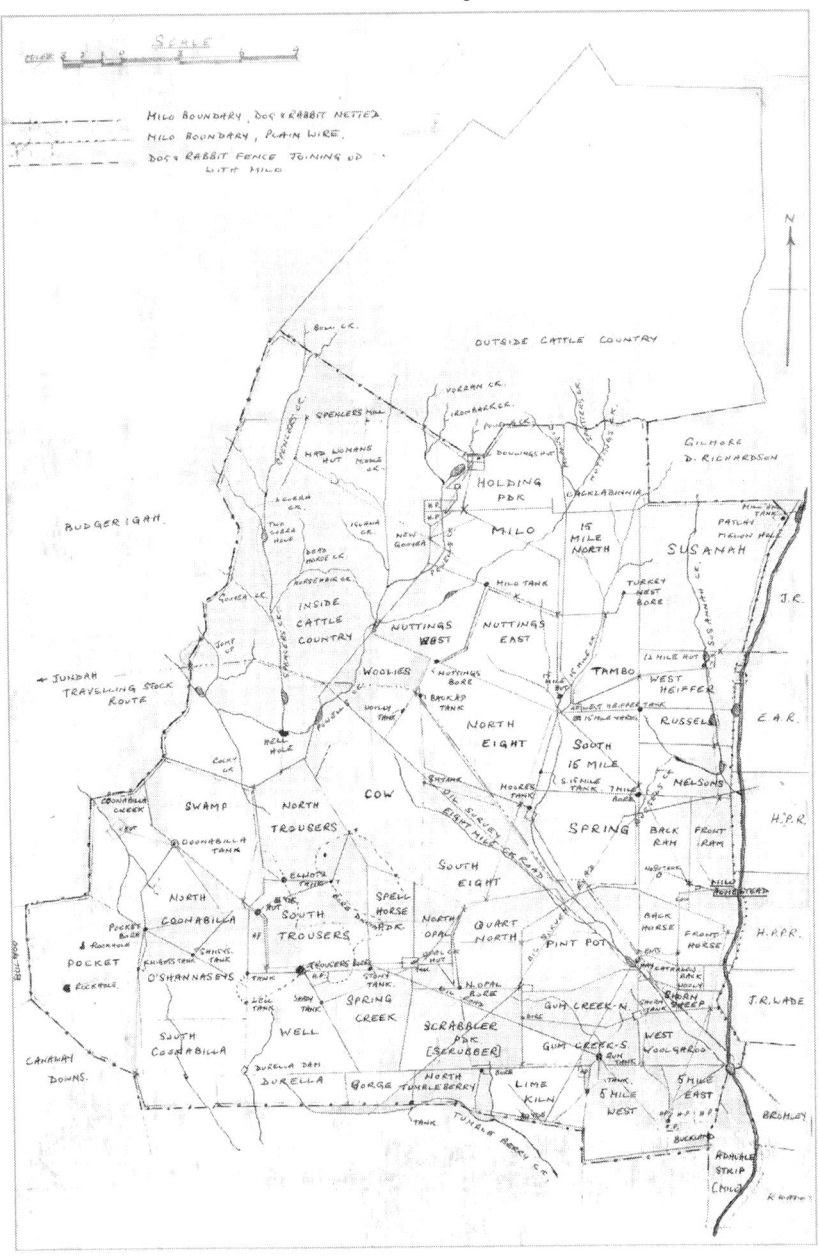

Acknowledgements

My hosts-all those who welcomed me into their homes and showed me such great hospitality.

Diane Lonnon who typed the script and gave me invaluable support.

Susan Hill who designed the cover and formatted the pages ready for printing.

My Australian wife, Jenny, who sorted out all the computer problems and acted as my project manager.

My employers	Rob & Sue Hodge Bob & Coleen Hawkes Mr. & Mrs Rollo Hawkes Milo Pastoral Company Limited
Book References	Arthur Hosier, Hosier's Farming Systems A G Street, Harvest by Lamp Light, Farmers' Glory, Christmas Eve, 1872 Neville Shute, A Town like Alice, On the Beach, Banjo Patterson The man from Snowy River Douglas Lockwood. Fair Dinkum
Seale-Hayne College	and The Seale-Haynian Club
Ann & Nigel Brookman	who wrote to The Seale-Haynian and started it all.

Lynda Vicars was born in inner city Liverpool, raised and educated in Kirkby, on the outskirts of the city. After attending Liverpool University and completing her teacher training, she volunteered to teach in Nigeria, and travelled throughout that country and other parts of West Africa. On her return from volunteering, she taught in schools in Northern England, with a three-year interlude teaching in Papua New Guinea in the company of her husband and young family. Whilst starting as a teacher of English and history she latterly qualified and specialised in Special Needs teaching. Now retired, she and her husband live on the Beara Peninsula, South West Ireland.

To Andrew, for his constant support and encouragement for my writing, for my children, Michael and Rachel, and my grandchildren.

To the members of my writing group in Castletownbere, Beara. Your recalling of your lives, interests and experiences were invaluable insights for me. Your critiques of our works were selfless and instilled confidence in us all.

Lynda Vicars

MAGNUS, MORGAN AND MYRA

AUSTIN MACAULEY PUBLISHERS
LONDON · CAMBRIDGE · NEW YORK · SHARJAH

Copyright © Lynda Vicars 2025

The right of Lynda Vicars to be identified as author of this work has been asserted by the author in accordance with sections 77 and 78 of the Copyright, Designs and Patents Act 1988.

All rights reserved. No part of this publication may be reproduced, stored in a retrieval system, or transmitted in any form or by any means, electronic, mechanical, photocopying, recording, or otherwise, without the prior permission of the publishers.

Any person who commits any unauthorised act in relation to this publication may be liable to criminal prosecution and civil claims for damages.

This is a work of fiction. Names, characters, businesses, places, events, locales, and incidents are either the products of the author's imagination or used in a fictitious manner. Any resemblance to actual persons, living or dead, or actual events is purely coincidental.

A CIP catalogue record for this title is available from the British Library.

ISBN 9781035887262 (Paperback)
ISBN 9781035887279 (ePub e-book)

www.austinmacauley.com

First Published 2025
Austin Macauley Publishers Ltd®
1 Canada Square
Canary Wharf
London
E14 5AA

Table of Contents

Magnus	**9**
1 An Odd Name for an Odd Boy	*9*
2 In Grandad's Company	*13*
3 Mr Wallace	*16*
4 The Library	*20*
5 The Funeral	*24*
6 Magnus and the Funeral Tea	*28*
7 Cross Words Explained	*32*
Morgan	**37**
Myra	**62**

Magnus

1 An Odd Name for an Odd Boy

Magnus. An odd name for an odd boy. Not an odd name, if you were a farmer living on the side of Eskjellfjiord in Iceland. Not an odd name if you captained a ferry in Copenhagen harbour. Not an odd name, if you were the man from the telly your grandad told you about, the one who used to ask the questions on Mastermind. But an odd name for an undernourished-looking twelve-year-old boy who lived in a New Town on the outskirts of a Northern city.

Pale, slight, with indiscriminate dark hair. Not odd with protruding ears, teeth, ginger hair, and an abundance of freckles, or the misfortune to have to wear NHS glasses, the very qualities likely to put you firmly in the sights of the playground bullies. Not odd for any physical characteristics or medical limitations.

Not odd for being the only Child of mature Parents who had resigned themselves to being a family of two. Not odd for seeking the company of the older members of his extended family, Grandparents, great Uncles, and Aunts, to sit, listen, and observe. Not too odd for his rumbustious cousins, who always included him in their games and exploits like hide and seek or daylong picnics that were just far enough beyond the control and clear sight of adults. They were never unkind to him. They no longer questioned his name, not his choice after all. They were sure he would rather be called Billy, Harry, Alfie, or Todd. But although he followed in their footsteps and carried his fair share of sandwiches, Penguin bars, and pop bottles, he never really, well, looked as if he was enjoying himself. The cousins would shrug their shoulders at each other and silently agree, "That's our Magnus for you." And the cousins were not backward in coming forward to warn off potential tormentors. This was an unspoken code of honour mysteriously instilled in them by Grandad.

Not odd, but a bit of a worry for Grandma Pat, his father's mum. He would sometimes catch her stealing a glance at him and he would return it with the biggest grin he could manage. It was best to do this, or Gran would start with those questions again. "School okay, Magnus? Is something worrying you? You can always tell your Gran, y'know. Nothing shocks me. Would you like a piece of toast?" Grandma Pat would rack her brains to think who in their family he could take after. It must be Julie's family.

But Nana Joan, his mother's mum, would be thinking exactly the same thing. Uncle Bobby, Julie's brother, would arrive in any sitting room, bright and breezy. "Now then, our Magnus, get your nose out of that book and get yourself outside in the fresh air." Magnus never knew if this was out of concern for his health or Bob's discovery of an unwanted companion in the sitting room, which he tended to monopolise for the watching of football on the telly.

Magnus liked books and did not like football. Never played it, never watched it. But he could tell you the name of every playing ground in the country ("the whole world" Todd once revealed in hushed reverence), describe the colours of each league club, and identify the flags of each competing nation in the last World Cup. "I need you in my pub quiz team." Uncle Tony had laughed. "A pity you're too young to drink."

Magnus would smile. It was not a big thing to him. Football strips, flags, planets, dinosaurs, fjords – they were just there, in his head. No big deal.

The smile. Now that was a big deal. Magnus had not always smiled, had not known how. He had overheard his parents whispering one night when they had thought he had gone to bed. "He's alright, John. He's just quiet and likes his own company."

"Well, that's as maybe, but maybe his teachers were right. He does not smile, or cry for that matter. She thinks we should let the school have someone have a look at him." Magnus did not hang around to hear the rest. He had crept up to his bedroom, and by the light on the landing, stood in front of the mirror. Where to start? He tried a lip-only smile. He tried a lips and teeth smile. He smiled a variation of smiles until his cheeks ached. If the only way to stop someone having a look at him was to smile, then he would smile. Not all the time, like some crazy cartoon character, but at the appropriate times, like when Grandma Pat looked worried about him, or when complying with uncle Bobby's request to vacate the sitting room.

Crying. That was going to prove more difficult. What had gone unnoticed by his parents and his teacher (the one who had thought that someone should have a look at him), was that there had been many occasions when Magnus had felt the rising lump in his throat. Had willed the welling tears to go back from where they came. Had held a cushion to his face to avoid letting his mother and father see his distress. Many incidents had made him want to cry. Watching a film about baby geese being taught to fly by a man in an aeroplane because their mother had died. Reading the bit about David Copperfield's mother dying. The trick was not to let anybody else see you cry or being upset.

Weakness. Girlish. Softie. Big boys don't cry.

So Magnus had retreated into his world of books and films to feel the emotions engendered by them, skilfully not demonstrating the signs that showed he was moved by them.

2 In Grandad's Company

Magnus found himself in the company of his grandad one weekend when Mother and Father had gone out for the day. Magnus was a regular visitor to his grandparents' house. Once a week, when both his mother and father had to work late, he would go to his grandparents' house after school, do his homework, and have his tea with them. Magnus liked being with his grandad and was not fussed about Morecambe or its bracing air. "Done your homework, Magnus? Good. That's the ticket." Magnus had not had any homework and had not had the time to tell Grandad this. Grandad had dutifully asked the question his daughter-in-law had posed and was not the slightest bit interested in any reply Magnus may have had, so he left the room to fetch his coat.

Magnus waited in his grandparents' front room. He counted the roses on the wallpaper. Same number as last time. His eyes followed the spiral from the middle of the rug to its outer edges, where, between the edge and the fireplace something white stuck out.

Magnus teased it out of its hiding place. A photograph. A black-and-white photograph, of a young man, dressed in funny clothes. The young man was smiling shyly, a lip-only smile. He sat astride a motorbike, which Magnus did not recognise. The rider's legs were obscuring the make and model. *Very old,* he thought. That explains the funny clothes. He had not heard his grandad re-enter the room and was first aware of his presence when Grandad's fingers shared one edge of the photo. "Ee, Magnus, where did you find this?" His grandson sensed that the older man, again, was not interested in a reply.

Grandad sighed. Magnus stood close to his grandad but he was far away. The boy studied the older man's face. First the smile. Then the smile dropped away. Next, the eyes, more watery than usual. Finally, the contortion of teeth biting a lower lip. Magnus felt something move inside himself. What and where, he could not tell. He tried to categorise it and attach it to a list. While he tried to make sense of it, Grandad came back, abruptly, cheerfully. "Righto, Magnus, let's get moving." He placed the photo face down on top of the television. Not the time to ask about the man in the photo. "I thought we would go and see a man about a dog." This was one of Grandad's favourite expressions, which covered anything from a visit to the bathroom to sneaking off for a quick pint to the King's Arms.

Saturday afternoon. Magnus and his grandad walked to the east end of town, beyond the railway station, under the bridge and onto the allotments. They walked between the neat rows of vegetables, chicken wire, and water butts. They stopped outside a shed, the door of which held a neatly painted sign: Chez Fred. Fred himself emerged from the opening door.

Magnus sat down on an upturned bucket while Grandad and Fred admired the cabbages, exchanged allotment gossip, that week's obituaries and the price of bread. They were interrupted by sounds of squealing and yelping coming from inside the shed. "Let's get down to business," said Fred, indicating that they should follow him into the shed. In one corner, inside a large cardboard box with its top cut off, lay Fred's dog, Lassie, tenderly licking three puppies. "Take your pick," said Fred as he picked up two of the puppies, one in each hand.

"What do you think, Magnus? Which one should I pick?" asked Grandad. Magnus did not answer. He leaned over Lassie who did not seem to mind when he picked up the third pup.

Fred looked surprised. "You don't want him, lad. He's no spark in him. Don't you think he looks odd? I call him E.T."

Magnus considered this statement while studying the pup that was watching him, with his oversized eyes, furrowed brow and trembling limbs. "Not odd, just different," said Magnus to grandad and Fred. "And I would call him Elliot." Magnus smiled. A secret smile. A smile to allay the fears of his parents, his grandmas, and his teacher. A smile that brought comfort to Magnus because he felt contentment. He did not know why, or what it was, and he did not possess the hindsight of his older self that would look back on that afternoon and make some sense of Magnus, the not-so-odd boy with the odd name.

3 Mr Wallace

Magnus finished the last problem of his maths homework. He propped his head on his hands, elbows resting on the carpet, his legs parallel to the fireplace. He squinted at the page, narrowing his eyes and contemplating his finished work. He was sure he had correctly solved all the problems and had remembered to show all of his workings. The need to do this bemused Magnus but it was something his teacher got quite het up about.

He listened beyond the silence. The clock ticked on the mantelpiece and Grandma Pat could be heard rattling pans and turning taps in the kitchen as she prepared tea for Magnus and his grandad, who would be home from work soon. Magnus looked at the time. Four fifty-four. There was nothing on children's television to interest him and he would not be allowed to walk Eliot until Grandad could accompany him, and that would not be until his tea had gone down.

Magnus raised his body off the floor, wriggled his toes to stop them tingling and stepped over to the television. The old and faded black-and-white photo of the man and the motorbike still lay on the top where Grandad had left it some weeks before. It surprised him that Grandma Pat had not put it away, as she hated mess. He picked up the photo. No dust underneath, so Grandma must have replaced it after her weekly topping out of the room. He replaced it and wondered when it would be a good time to ask Grandad about the man.

A shadow passed the window. Magnus was drawn to investigate what had made the shadow. Mr Wallace, his grandparents' neighbour. He was not swaying. His large, over-coated, and flat-capped figure, opened and closed his garden gate and walked up the path to the front door. Magnus could hear the keys turn in the lock and the door close quietly. Mr Wallace was famous for things in his immediate neighbourhood. One, his first and last names were the same. Wallace Wallace. Two, he was known to sway quite a bit as he made his way home from work, but not before stopping off at The Magpie.

The third thing for which Mr Wallace was famous was the one that Magnus found most amazing. A work colleague of Grandad's had been interested to find out that Wally Wallace lived next door. "Very clever man, Wally. Distinguished war service. Speaks fluent Japanese. Worked on submarines in the Pacific, intercepting Japanese radio messages."

Grandad had related this information to Magnus one afternoon when they walked a discreet distance behind the swaying figure of Mr Wallace. Grandad had remonstrated with a group of boys who were jeering at his inebriated neighbour. Magnus was having a hard time imagining this old man in his oil-stained coat and grimy flat cap with that of his younger self, dressed in Royal Navy uniform, headphones in place, assiduously writing down Japanese secrets. Grandad had noticed his look of disbelief and uttered one of his grandadisms, "You can't always judge a book by its cover, Magnus." Magnus was still in the bowels of that Pacific submarine to give any thought to converting Grandad's pronouncement to something he could understand and store for his future social skills.

The following day, this amazing piece of information instigated one of the many trips Magnus made to the reference library. Mrs Cadwalladr, the chief librarian, had formed one of her rare smiles when Magnus approached the desk. Magnus was her kind of child library user. Quiet, polite and absolutely no bother. "What can I do for you, young man?" It is fair to say, that of the many unusual requests Magnus had made, this was up there. "An English-Japanese dictionary, you say? Take a seat, Magnus. I'll see what I can find."

Mrs Cadwalladr had no luck, but she asked Magnus to write down what he wished to know and instructed him to return to the library on Monday afternoon. Magnus had the weekend to wait. He busied himself as usual but the return to the library was never far from his mind.

He left the library on Monday afternoon clutching a piece of paper. He had thanked the librarian in his usual understated manner, but she knew him well enough not to take offence. Magnus hurried home and acknowledged his mother's greeting. "Tea in twenty, Magnus." Then raced up the stairs and closed his bedroom door behind him. He practised before tea, after tea, and every spare moment he had before his next visit to his grandparents.

Two days later, Magnus stood outside his grandparents' garden gate. He looked up the road in the direction of the bus stop. He tapped his foot in anticipation. He looked over his shoulder at the window. Grandma Pat was peeking out from behind the curtains, looking puzzled. Magnus raised his hand to wave, but Grandma had disappeared, no doubt shaking her head and tutting about the mystery that was her grandson. Magnus heard the engine of the bus as it pulled up at the stop further down the road. The familiar figure of Mr Wallace disembarked tentatively and hesitated as to which foot should lead his walk home. He found his rhythm and tottered down the road. Magnus estimated the number of steps Mr Wallace would have to make to draw level with him and mentally practised his greeting.

Mr Wallace stopped abruptly when the boy stood in his way. "Konnichiwa. Anata wa genki desu ka?"

The man looked confused. He scrutinised the boy and before he had time to consider, the words came tumbling out, "Okagesama de, genki desu."

Man and boy stood confronting one another, neither knowing what to do next. Magnus held his breath. Mr Wallace smiled and nodded. He sidestepped Magnus, who watched his every move, opening and closing the gate, shuffling up to his front door, and putting the key in its lock. Before he stepped inside and closed the door, he turned, and bowed his head to Magnus, "Sayonara".

"Sayonara," the boy replied and smiled with relief.

4 The Library

Magnus tried to keep up with his father's steps as the two made their way through the shopping precinct. Magnus was struggling with two tasks. Carrying an armful of library books and trying not to step outside the black lines of the pavements. He had not failed yet. "You should have put those books into a bag, Magnus. See you in an hour," said his father as he disappeared around the corner out of view. This was a regular trip for Magnus and his father. Magnus would spend the hour in the library while his father scoured the shops and market stalls for his bits and pieces. His father was never very clear about those bits and pieces and sometimes he returned home empty-handed.

Magnus had grown bored shopping with his father, perusing bargains in the DIY stall or testing fishing rods for weight. He had once enjoyed wandering Joe's Lines and Tackle but ever since Joe got rid of his tropical fish tank it had lost its magic for him.

The library retained its magic. Its exterior blended in with its neighbouring shops. Concrete and glass. But once you pushed your way through its revolving doors, you left behind the graffiti and wind-blown litter to find yourself on the threshold of a mirror lake. The highly polished floors reflected the wide-spaced library shelves and the floor-to-wall windows let in light and formed shadows. Sometimes Magnus imagined he was walking on water and beneath him, swirled cloudy sea creatures of all shapes and sizes. The main library was to the left and the children's library was to the right. The public and private areas were demarcated by an open tread staircase, which led to a gallery of reservable private rooms and library offices and to the front of the staircase, a large circular librarians station, which would not have looked out of place on '*the Starship Enterprise*'. Mrs Cadwalladr, in her librarian's uniform of tweed skirt, twin set, pearls, and sensible brogues, was no substitute for '*Lieutenant Uhuru*', Grandad had once sniggered. Magnus frowned at the memory. Grandad could be very silly at times. Uhuru was black and Mrs Cadwalladr was white. Parallel to the children's library, bordered by the back wall of the library building was a similar-sized space for the reference library. Here, it was usual to find a collection of retired men, some reading daily newspapers or the '*Racing Times*', some snoozing in the padded chairs and some using the library's heat and space to offset their own heating bills and sense of loneliness.

For all its majesty, the library was under used nowadays. Magnus's mother had told him of the library's first weeks of opening when people queued for hours and had to be allowed in and out in shifts. The majority of the townspeople may have ceased to include the library in their weekly social engagements but they were still incredibly proud of its existence and that it stood there, atop its concrete steps like a beacon proclaiming that were worthy of its treasures and promises of betterment.

Magnus was able to take advantage of this social and educational neglect. The librarians, under orders from Mrs Cadwalladr, allowed Magnus to roam the adult library. He bent his head at a 45-degree angle until his neck ached and his eyes lost focus, to read the titles and their authors. He touched the leather-bound volumes and pretended he was reading braille as his fingers traced the inlaid gold lettering. He breathed in the wax odours of the heavily polished and reflective floors. He listened to the squeak of footsteps as they made their way from desks to shelves and back again, and to the occasional suppressed cough of one of the newspaper-reading old men.

Magnus deposited his returned books on the librarian's desk with effortless silence. "My goodness, Magnus, you gave me a fright," said Mrs Cadwalladr as she replaced the top of her fountain pen. "You go off to choose your books while I deal with these returns. I'll put your card under the desk till you are ready."

Magnus made straight for the Reference Library. He read the headings; Cookery, DIY, Hobbies and read on until he reached the category that he wanted; Transport. He craned his neck and squinted at the titles on the uppermost shelves. He found the sub category but alas still out of his reach. He turned to look over towards the librarians' station. Mrs Cadwalladr was talking to a young woman and a child. He took a few steps back and looked over a set of half shelves to a corner of the children's section. A young female librarian was replacing books. Magnus raised his hand and was successful in getting her attention. She seemed to skate over the polished floor to him, graceful and smiling.

Magnus sat, the only occupant of a solid wooden table, with a Pictorial History of British Motorcycles before him. He never knew there were so many different types of motorbikes. He tried to remember the bike in the old photo that stood on his grandparents' mantelpiece but the image he retrieved could be one of many. He looked at the wall clock. One twenty-seven. Time to meet his father. He closed the book and left it on the table as instructed. The elder and younger librarians were talking in hushed tones as Magnus went to collect his card. "Did you find what you wanted?" asked the younger woman. Magnus shook his head. "It's Eddie's Saturday off today," she started but corrected herself when she met the older woman's disapproving stare. "It's Mr Markham's Saturday off today. He knows a lot about motorbikes. Why not come back next Saturday? I am sure he can help you."

Magnus decided that was a good plan. He said goodbye to the two women and set off to meet his father. Perhaps next Saturday he should bring the old photo. That would involve asking Grandad if he could borrow it. But that might mean that Grandad would know what type of motorcycle it was. If he knew that, then he wouldn't have to ask Mr Markham, the young librarian.

5 The Funeral

The day of Grandma's funeral had arrived. She hadn't been ill as far as Magnus knew, she just died. The warm, sunny, July day was incongruous both with how Magnus was feeling and with the arrival of the black hearse and cars. The sight of the hearse and coffin filled Magnus with an anxiety he had never felt before. The calm and business-like attitudes of Grandad, Father, aunty Shelagh, and uncle David of the preceding days were instantly undone. There was mild panic to be seen by the searching for keys, wallets, tissues, the rummaging through handbags and the patting of pockets. Delaying tactics. Magnus and his cousins, Billy, Alfie, and Harry, but no Todd, who had a summer cold and was at home being looked after by his mother. The cousins sat quietly and impatiently, not altogether sure what was expected of them. "It is just like Gwen," hissed Aunty Shelagh to his father but out of earshot of uncle David. "Making an excuse of a silly summer cold." His father gave Aunt Shelagh a reproachful shake of the head that meant, "Not now, Shelagh".

Magnus bit his lip as he sat down in the car, averting his eyes from the figures of sympathetic neighbours standing at their garden gates. There was a delay. Magnus raised and turned his head to see who or what was causing the hold-up and in doing so his eyes locked on to those of Mr Wallace who was standing self-consciously in that awkward space between the half-open door and its step. He gave the briefest of smiles and a nod of the head to Magnus who shyly raised and waved his hand in a return gesture.

The cortege moved slowly down the road that now threw up speed bumps that had not been needed thirty years ago, his father said to no one in particular. The hearse slowed down to preserve its dignity. It turned left at the first corner into a road that disappeared into the distance with yet more speed bumps. Magnus sat on the right-hand side of the car and took in razed, the unkempt ground where once had stood maisonettes, "They would have been the same age as my parents' house," his father said. He tried to remember the names of families that had lived in them. One former schoolmate came to his mind.

Two boys were playing football close to the road's edge, *'Shouldn't they be at school?'* Magnus heard his grandma's moral tone and before he could finish the thought, *'the two stood upright to attention, the taller cradling the ball in one arm and saluting with the other.'* His smaller, impressionable friend copied his action, his eyes diverting from the funeral procession back to his elder to check that he was keeping in time and actions. Magnus suppressed a smile but then his attention turned to an older youth crossing another piece of litter-filled derelict land. He appeared too thin and had a look of meanness to match, the sort Magnus was instructed to keep well clear of. The youth turned his head, noticing the slow-moving cars. He removed the baseball cap, an item of clothing Magnus's grandma had disapproved of, and kept it in his hand until the coffin turned out of his view. *'He must have family values,'* Magnus thought. A grandmother must have instilled in him this last showing of respect. Magnus spoke silently to his grandma. *See, not all young lads in this area are bad through and through.*

The cars ran out of speed bumps but they did not appear to be moving any faster. Magnus had not thought the journey would take so long. The crematorium was a short distance out of town, not far from the allotments that were a short walk from Grandma and Grandad's house. A lump rose in his throat. He would not be able to call it that any more. It would just be Grandad's house. Magnus's world felt a little emptier.

The cars turned right into a long sweeping drive that was the approach to the crematorium. The cars pulled up behind the hearse under the cover of the chapel porch. The mourners got out of their cars and Magnus was struck at how quietly the doors closed behind them, a repetition of velvet thuds. Magnus's father, uncle David, along with other men he did not know, raised the coffin onto their shoulders and shuffled into the chapel. Grandad, arm in arm with Aunty Shelagh, were next to enter followed by his daughter-in-law and grandsons, then by remaining family and friends.

Magnus could not follow everything the vicar said and did not recognise any of the hymns and other music. Grandma Pat was a woman renowned for her cakes and biscuits not for a young woman who had danced the night away. An old school friend of Grandma's reminisced about the time they both attended Baggot Street Primary and the day they glued their desk lids together. Magnus was having a hard enough time imagining his grandma as a ten-year-old never mind as a naughty ten-year-old.

The time came for the coffin to glide away behind the closing curtains. His grandad bowed his head and Aunty

Shelagh clutched his arm as she sobbed silently into her handkerchief. Magnus felt his father trembling and he turned to see him swaying slightly. His mother took hold of her husband's right hand and Magnus took his left. He winced at the tightness of this father's grip.

The funeral director gestured for them to leave and they exited the chapel in the same order as they had entered. People broke ranks and mingled once they breathed in the fresh air. The cousins stood with their fathers who were determined that their children preserve dignity for a little while longer and not resort to kicking up the gravel or pinching each another until one relented and pierced the silent solemnity with a cry of pain.

The funeral director ushered them to the waiting cars with the information that the next funeral would be arriving shortly and that they needed to make space.

The cars covered the return journey with greater speed. *A little too quickly*, thought Magnus. *Was it really necessary?* After all, they would be returning Grandad to a home without the presence of his wife.

6 Magnus and the Funeral Tea

Magnus had never seen so many people crammed into such a small house. They sat in chairs, in the front room, in the back room, and around the kitchen table. They were standing in the middle of floors, obscuring the views of those sitting down and disjointing the conversations trying to be had with those sitting on opposite sides. They were standing in the hallway and outside in both the front and back gardens. His cousins were playing in the back garden, relieved of their black ties, the top buttons of their crisp white shirts undone, attempting to play a quiet game of football, each kick being harder and the running commentary getting louder. Magnus wandered around the house unnoticed.

In the kitchen, Nana Joan, his mother's mum, was orchestrating the funeral tea, giving instructions to her small platoon of neighbour helpers. Along one length of the kitchen, door to door, the countertops were filled with plates of meat, cheese, sandwiches, pork pies, sausage rolls, bowls of salad, pickled onions, piccalilli, beetroot and a plate of what looked like to Magnus, pastry bombs, some topped with prawns, and some topped with cream cheese. He stared at them. "Those are vol au vents, Magnus. You buy them frozen and plain, defrost them, and put on whatever toppings you fancy. Very quick and mess-free," said Nana Joan, as she was busy in the kitchen.

One of Grandad's neighbours whispered to her companion, "Pat will be turning in her grave. Frozen pastry indeed." Her companion, another neighbour, nudged her in the ribs when she noticed Magnus who was confused by the notion of turning in a grave. Grandma was to be cremated and her ashes scattered in some of her favourite places. His mother had explained it all to him.

Magnus wandered back to the front room. He was surprised to see Mr Wallace sitting on a chair in front of the window, talking to another man. He looked cleaner and shinier than normal. He was balancing a cup and saucer on his knee and at the same time reaching behind him to the window ledge where he had placed his plate that contained items of the funeral tea. His father was standing talking to his aunt. Grandma's sister and his mother were going backwards and forward to the kitchen carrying full plates, empty plates, cups of tea, glasses of beer and sherry.

His grandad sat in his chair, courted by an endless procession of men and women offering their condolences and keeping him informed of their own family births, marriages, and deaths.

He desperately needed to talk to his grandad about that awful day, two weeks ago. Since he was told about Grandma's death, Magnus had been troubled and unable to sleep imagining that he was somehow responsible for it. He had not been able to eat properly and could not concentrate enough to read. His mother and father thought he was missing his grandma. He was, but he could not tell them the real reason for his unhappiness. The only times he had felt this black cloud around him disperse a little was when he kept Eliot company.

Eliot was not here today. Fred had collected him this morning and taken him to his allotment out of the way of all the expected mourners. "He'll be happier with Lassie and me. Your Grandad does not have to worry about feeding him and taking him for a walk, today of all days." Eliot had trotted at Fred's heels, happy to sniff the pavements and bushes whilst pulling on his lead and slowing down Fred's receding figure.

Magnus sat on the middle step of the stairs, peering through the spindles at the traffic below him. Here, with doors wedged wide open, he had a good view of both living rooms and one side of the kitchen, where now the opening dishes of the funeral tea had been replaced by cakes, trifle, jelly, cream, and biscuits. Magnus smiled as he noticed the defrosted Arctic Roll, another in Nana Joan's culinary repertoire. He wondered what the neighbours had to say about that. *'He watched people walk below him. Bald heads, permed heads, people with no feet visible beneath their widened waistlines and one lady with an elaborate hairstyle who was transporting a bit of food in it.'*

People were beginning to leave, in ones, twos, and family groups. The women of the family began to clear and wash dishes in the kitchen while Magnus and his cousins were called to help their fathers rearrange the furniture and return it to a facsimile of its former self. A gentle knock at the door interrupted them. Fred and Eliot stood on the threshold. Eliot was nervous, shivering with his tail between his legs, unsure if he was to be allowed back in. The four cousins, in unison, called his name, and he bounded in, grateful for their welcome and soon basking in their petting and affection. Fred followed apologetically. "No problem, Fred. You and Eliot come in here," said Grandad and shepherded his dog and his friend into the front room. The boys were ordered to get back to work but Magnus lingered by pretending to inspect a chair for faults. Grandad fetched Fred a glass of whisky and then sat in his armchair. Eliot sat at Grandad's side, looking up at his master, enjoying this unaccustomed privilege of sitting on a carpet in a room beyond the kitchen and feeling the weight of the man's hand as he patted his head. Magnus was hoping that they would be the last to leave so that he would have an opportunity to talk to his grandad. Fred refused a third whisky and took his leave.

Grandad took Eliot into the garden and placed him in his run. Eliot did not seem to mind and immediately went inside his kennel to take a nap. Group by group, the family left for their own homes. "Are you sure you don't want one of us to stay the night?" asked Shelagh. His grandad declined the offer, and Shelagh gathered her family to depart.

That left Magnus and his parents to gather their belongings before their departure.

"*Come on, Magnus, Grandad needs a rest.*" Magnus hesitated and his grandad read the trouble in his frown.

"I'm done in, Magnus. My right arm is aching from shaking all those hands and I'm sure my cheeks are smeared with every colour of lipstick under the sun." Magnus shook his head gravely. Grandad drew him closer by holding both of his shoulders and whispered into his left ear. "You and me will have a chat next week." He released his grandson's shoulders, gave him a conspiratorial wink, and watched the family walk down the path.

7 Cross Words Explained

Magnus was trying to give his full concentration to what his grandfather was telling him. He had looked forward with trepidation to his first time alone with Grandad since his grandma's funeral. He had fretted for weeks. Firstly, about the upset he had caused about the photograph. Secondly, the news about his grandma's illness. Thirdly, the unexpected night time phone call from the hospital informing them of Grandma's death. To Magnus, all three events were obviously linked.

Now Grandad was trying his best to put Magnus at ease, absolve him of any responsibility for cross words, illness, and death. Grandad shifted in his chair, absentmindedly patting Eliot on the head and rubbing behind his ears, as the dog took his unaccustomed position in front of the fireplace. So far, Magnus had understood that Grandma had suffered a weak heart since she had had rheumatic fever as a Child. He tried to think of occasions when Grandma had been ill but nothing came to him. He could not remember her ever complaining of being unwell. She was Grandma, making his tea, asking him about his day at school or deriding his grandad for the many misdemeanours Grandads make.

According to Grandad, bits of your body weaken, as you get older. With Grandma, it had been her heart. With Grandad, it was his back and knees. Every morning it took him longer to get out of bed. Magnus had shot him a worried look. "I expect I need a new mattress on my bed and to eat more greens," he said reassuringly.

Magnus relived to his grandad about the photograph and the cross words he heard that day.

That day, Magnus had let himself into his grandparents' house. He overheard voices coming from the living room, unusually cross. "Why have you put that photo away again?"

"I haven't touched it."

"I left it on top of the television. That's where I left it."

"It must have blown off and got kicked under without us noticing it."

"After all these years, you still can't bear to look at it."

"That's not true. I was just surprised to see it in Magnus' hands. I left it on the television, I tell you."

Magnus stood in the hallway, still clutching his coat and bag, as Grandma came through the door.

"Hungry, Magnus? I'll get you your tea," her face looked pinched as she closed the kitchen door behind her.

A feeling of panic came over Magnus. The photograph, he had borrowed it to take it to the library. Mr Markham, the librarian, said it would be useful to identify the year and make of the motorbike. The pair of them, librarian and boy, had scanned the reference book, comparing the photo with pictures of motorbikes. "It looks pre-Second World War to me," said the librarian as he flicked the pages of the book backwards and forwards. "Ah, I think this might be it," he said as he lined up the photo next to a Royal Enfield D model 250. "Mystery solved, Magnus?" Then the telephone rang rudely on the reception desk and he went off to answer it, leaving

Magnus to write down notes about the bike's details. He returned to his grandparents' house.

He stood in the hall. He searched through his school bag. He should have the photo in there. No. Had he left it inside the reference book? He would have to go to the library to look. The library was closed now. He would have to call after school tomorrow. He went uneasily to join his grandad, who smiled and nodded in welcome as he flicked through a newspaper. Magnus slithered into an armchair, desperately wanting Grandad to begin his volley of questions to ease the tension in the small room.

The following afternoon, Magnus had dashed out of school leaving his cousin, Todd, puzzled at his unusually hasty retreat. Magnus was usually last out the gates. He arrived at the library out of breath. Mrs Cadwalladr was sitting behind the reception desk as Magnus pushed his way in through the revolving doors. She beckoned Magnus, holding a brown envelope in her other hand. "Does this photo belong to you, young man? Mr Markham realised you had left it on the desk in the reference library. He kept it under the counter for safekeeping." A relieved Magnus whispered his thanks, carefully placed the envelope in his bag and left the library behind to make his way to his grandparents.

A surprised Grandma opened the door. "Why Magnus, it's Friday. What are you doing here?" Her flustered grandson tried to talk and retrieve the envelope from his bag at the same time as she stepped back to let him in. She got the words "borrowed" "sorry" "photo" "library" "left behind" and "my fault" as he thrust the envelope into her hands. She stared at her grandson. Her eyes moistened. She was lost for something to say.

Magnus had never uttered so many words in one go before and she saw from his agitated expression what it must have cost him to open up and volunteer this information. She embraced him gently, her arms reassuring him that whatever it was that caused the cross words between Grandad and herself, was now forgotten. She found her voice. "Nothing but a storm in a teacup, Magnus." In his relief, Magnus decided not to dissect those words, which he would routinely do but enjoyed those brief seconds of intimacy and forgiveness. That was the last time he would see and speak to his grandma.

Grandad's voice brought Magnus back to the present. Magnus did his best to focus on his grandad's face and to appear mature, as Grandad informed him that it was not easy to tell such a young boy these family details, and histories. His mother and father knew, his aunt and uncle knew, but the cousins did not. Grandad was asking Magnus to keep this information from his cousins. They would be told later when they were a bit older if they were interested.

The man in the photo was Grandad's older brother, Graham. The photo had been taken in 1939. Graham and his bike were called up to join the army. At the time, Grandma was Graham's sweetheart. Magnus frowned and rubbed his neck, uncomfortable at the reference to romance. Grandad continued the conversation. They were going to get engaged on his next leave but that leave kept getting postponed. They wrote each other letters. Magnus was grateful Grandad left out the word love. Eventually, he was allowed home for a few days, spending most of his time with Grandma. A few weeks after his return to the army, the family got the terrible news that Graham had been killed. Grandad paused, coughed, and slowly put the kind words around the secret. He had always liked Grandma and had always been a bit jealous of Graham. One evening after the terrible news, Grandma had come to visit the family. Grandad was in the house on his own. Grandma had her own news and if she did not tell someone, she thought she would go mad. Grandma was going to have Graham's baby.

Now Grandad's story became littered with such expressions as "in those days" "the shame" "harsh words" and "nasty gossip". Grandad asked Grandma to marry him. She had not been sure, but he had. They had married, Aunty Shelagh had been born, and they became a family. They had two more children, Magnus' father, and uncle John. It became harder to talk about Graham and the photo was the only one they had of him.

Every so often, Grandad would go through the old photos and remember his brother. And unbeknown to him, Grandma had done the same. But they could not look at the photo together. Grandad was not sure why. Regret? Remorse? Grief? Best to leave things unsaid.

Grandad, head down, stared into the nothingness of his clasped hands. Magnus left his chair, perched on the arm of his grandad's chair and tentatively laid his hand on Grandad's shoulder. He combed his thoughts for something to say. It had to be appropriate, fitting, something to show his grandad he was mature and had understood all that he had been told. "It was a kind thing to do, Grandad."

The older man looked into the face of his grandson as if to protest something. But he smiled. "Maybe, Magnus, maybe. Now how about something to eat? Sausage rolls do you?"

Morgan

In a ramshackle collection of assorted one-storey buildings of a school located in the Middle Belt of Nigeria, the teaching staff, office workers, the cooks, and the driver, all stood around two sides of the courtyard veranda. The students mingled in the courtyard itself, some with kulfis on their heads distinguishing the Muslims among them. The evening air lacked the intention to cool and sustain the scent of the frangipani that lined two sides of the open space. Dusk descended, and the whispers of those assembled trailed into polite coughs, then silence.

Mrs Shima led the proceedings. Unusually, she was not wearing her colourful iro and geleh, but an outfit entirely subdued in colour and extravagance. She held seniority over the other teachers, male, female, black, and white. The white teachers stood, self-consciously, in the shadows of the staffroom, taking no part in the hastily arranged ceremony, but their attendance illustrated their respect.

Morgan stood furthest back, her heart pounding, her ears ringing and her composure shredding. She fixed her hands to cover her ears. When would this stop? The rise and fall of the ululating women brought her no comfort. It was the second student death of the week, and the public grieving ceremony of the first seemed to have carried on seamlessly to the next. She hoped, rather selfishly, that this was the end of them.

Why this community show of grief? Why this outpouring of lamentation for a child most people present, outside of his clan, did not know or probably had never acknowledged? Brief words had been spoken against the background of the women's death song. Feet shuffled around her. The Tilley lamps and torches began to disperse, leaving the moths churning the air with the choices of light sources on offer. She was indignant. Tomorrow everyone would have forgotten the death of this child. His male relatives and his Imam would collect his body and take it back to the village and the teaching of the timetable would continue.

She did not wait for an escort. She hurried back to her house, neglecting the rules of safety. With the sound of ululation receding, and closed the door loudly, it's reverberating rattle informing her colleagues to leave her alone.

She lit the candle and it's flickering brought areas of the small room to her attention. Her eyes settled on the single photograph she had displayed on her meagre sideboard. Her brother, Eddie, smiled at her. *'Lighten up, sis'.*

Unbeknown to Morgan, as she had stood in the shadows and later, as she made her way to her house, another troubled fugitive had observed her from his own self-imposed exclusion in that wavering place. He stood back, half hidden, leaning against the corner of the dormitory. In the distance, he could make out the figure of Madam Shima, even though she was not wearing her colourful clothes. Her voice stood out amongst the other women, like a cock crowing.

Madam Shima frightened him. In her lessons, she switched languages from Tiv to Ibo to English then back again to Tiv. But she spoke no Hausa. He thought that she must despise the Muslim boys. He could not learn well. He got confused and when she called on him to answer a question, he mumbled and so she shouted louder. Another reason for his classmates to laugh at him.

Among the boys crowded into the small courtyard, he made out the tall figure of his brother Isa. He was wearing his Kulfi, the one their father gave him. His father was proud of Isa, but not so proud of his younger son. His father wanted to beat out his 'wicked behaviour' and with the absence of his parent, Isa was the surrogate. He had been hiding from Isa all day and had only come out of hiding because he knew that Isa and his friends wanted to be at the front of the crowd.

He looked towards the veranda outside the staffroom. *The white teachers are hiding like me,* he thought. The thought gave him some comfort. Mr Murry was whispering to Mr Tanaka. Mr Tanaka was not pleased. He put a finger to his lips, the way you do when you want someone to be quiet. At the back of them, stood Madam Morgan. He could tell it was her by her golden hair. She was a kind teacher who spoke softly and only in English. Why was she covering her ears with her hands?

The prayer ceremony was over. A small group of men followed the shrouded body as it was taken to a disused classroom. The boys began to move. He should hide again. He saw Miss Morgan leave the other teachers, and head for the staff houses. He was concerned. She should not walk by herself. She had no lamp, no torch, to guide her way. He followed her, keeping to the shadows of the buildings, bushes and the cars that were parked outside the houses, darting quickly between them. He was proud of his tracking skills. His mother used to say that he was the best tracker in the family, in the village even. They used to laugh together. His chest had tightened and his throat constricted at this happy memory, making him feel bereft. The sound of a door slamming brought his thoughts back to the present. Miss Morgan was safe inside her house.

As he turned to go, to the refuge of his hiding place, a hand grabbed his shoulder. He went weak with relief. It was not Isa.

She had slept fitfully. It was the dry season and even though the morning was chilly, the heat of her thoughts meant that she rose early, and dressed before the sun rose above the horizon. She was not hungry but she ate the carefully dissected orange segments that John, her houseboy, had prepared. She did not look at the photograph as she passed the sideboard on her way out of the house. The morning's teaching did not start for another hour but she was restless and her house had no distractions for her.

The school was a short distance from the teachers' housing compound. She noticed a very young kitten mesmerised by a chicken scratching at the ground. But then her attention became internal and her feet automatically carried her towards the school, ignoring any other visual interruptions. The air was sharp and cool and the draining dark made way for an orange sun, which bounced slowly on the dissipating clouds and the infant heat haze.

She shoved the staffroom door open, turned on the ceiling fan, opened the louvres, and stood before the hot water urn. One of the cooks would have turned it on earlier that morning.

She made herself a black tea, a newly acquired taste. The lack of fresh milk and the use of sweetened tinned milk had, she thought wryly, been her biggest cultural and culinary hurdles to overcome, until the events that had begun the previous week. These events had overwhelmed her and rekindled her own questions about death and grief. She settled into a chair, and no matter how hard she tried, her mind kept returning to the proceedings of the previous evening and the photograph on the sideboard.

The silence was interrupted by the entrance of Mrs Okorafor. On other occasions, with her beautiful face and elaborate hairstyle, her presence should have lifted Morgan's spirits and she would have enquired about the new baby and the rest of her children. But that morning, Mrs Okorafor's features were cross and she tutted. She helped herself to a cup of tea and emptied half a tin of milk into the steaming black liquid until it became almost paler than Morgan's skin. "The baby kept me awake. That Canadian does not know how to construct a timetable. He only gives me two breast feeding breaks this morning."

Morgan felt waves of disdain at the woman's grumblings. The two colleagues offered no comfort to each other. Morgan would have usually enquired about the frequency of the breastfeeding breaks for the day and the older woman would have asked the younger, "What is troubling you, Child?"

The staffroom slowly filled up with bodies and lively chatter. She took no part in the conviviality. She felt very alone, physically and emotionally. There was no reference to the dead child until the entrance of the headteacher cut the chat and he reminded the staff of the time for the removal of the dead body. Morgan mentally sneered, business as usual.

The students were beginning to shuffle through the laterite, their unshod feet kicked up the red dust as they made their way from the refectory to the classrooms. Some rubbed their heads in an effort to shake off their sleepy stupor. No kulfis were worn that morning. The boys were one.

As the teachers trooped out to their classrooms, they saw the colours of Mrs Shima approaching the building before Mrs Shima's entity itself. Bright blues and greens, held together by a crimson sash. "Business as usual, again," Morgan murmured indistinctly.

It was a week after the funerals. The end of term approached. Morgan had to travel to Jos, four hours away, in order to go to the bank, obtain visas and finalise her travel plans. She had been offered a lift by Mr Jackson, a Sri Lankan, and a science teacher, in his new car and this would save her time and the hassles of public transport. She also had to post a letter to her parents. The reply was overdue. It did not answer their questions and she had ignored their pleas for her to return home, if only for a short holiday. She made no excuses and had been vague about her immediate future plans. But she reassured them she was well.

She was walking on the only pavement in Jos. The trip with Mr Johnson had been unremarkable. He was a safe driver and had wanted only to talk about his forthcoming trip to London. He was excited, giving her potted histories of London landmarks. He did not ask personal questions and for this, she was grateful. They agreed on a time and a meeting place for their return journey and she set off on her errands.

She was halfway between the bank and the post office when a familiar face stepped in front of her. It was Mr Hassan, a colleague, a history teacher at the school. He broke into a shy smile and she strained to hear him above the groaning of the passing lorries. Unexpectedly, he invited her to join him for a cold drink. Her mood had not improved in the preceding week and she continued to want only her own company. Mr Johnson had stayed within his self-absorbed boundaries but Mr Hassan was a kind and gentle man whom she respected and she did not want to cause him offence and embarrassment. She returned his smile and nodded with acceptance.

He escorted her to a cafe down a small street, one which she would never have ventured down alone. They went to sit inside. Mr Hassan, in Hausa, called into the back room, and a small darting child delivered an almost clean cloth with which her colleague gallantly wiped the seat of her chair. He gestured to her to sit. Mr Hassan ordered a Maltex for himself and a Fanta for Morgan. He opened the conversation. "How have enjoyed your first year with us? Are you returning next year?"

"I have enjoyed it very much, and yes, I will be returning next year. I would like to see my examination class through to the end." He nodded in appreciation.

"That is good. It is always nice when overseas colleagues feel that they can commit to another year. It is better for the boys' education."

They continued to bat their questions and answers back and forth until Morgan lost the advantage.

"And will you return to England this holiday to visit your family?" The question unnerved her. She was irritated and that made her fluster.

With an emphatic negative, she replied, "I want to see a bit more of West Africa."

"But they must miss you very much." Mr Hassan's eyes fixed her to her chair.

"No," she lied. She compounded the lie. "They understand." She hurriedly turned the conversation from about herself. "You, Mr Hassan? What will you do with your holidays?"

Mr Hassan considered his reply, "I will travel north. I have not visited my brother's widow since his death. I was unable to attend my brother's funeral and I want to find out if there is anything I can do for his widow and children."

Morgan was caught unawares. "Oh, I see." Mr Hassan's concern for his bereaved relatives seemed contrary to her perception of the African attitude to the dead after the two recent funerals she had witnessed.

It was Mr Hassan's turn to be confused. "Forgive me, but you sound surprised. What else should I be doing with my holidays?"

"I…" She was embarrassed that her reaction had been that transparent.

"Now that we are talking about funerals, please permit me to ask another question. How do people in England treat death in a family? Do they stay in mourning clothes for a certain period of time?" Mr Hassan was one of the first Nigerian-educated graduates of history and a keen, continuing student of British cultural life.

"Well, I cannot really say. Different people treat death differently."

"Because they have different religions?"

"Not just because of that. Different members of a family can also grieve in different ways. Sometimes members of the same family cannot agree on the best way to grieve," and her voice tailed off.

"That it is to be expected but not always easy to understand, I think," he paused. "The deaths of our pupils this term troubled you greatly?"

"No. No more than the other teachers." She sounded defensive.

"With respect, Miss Morgan. I think it did." Mr Hassan's face displayed not only curiosity but also concern.

Morgan struggled to find the words to express the discomfort and disbelief she had experienced at the feverish pitch of the wailing lamentation of the assembled mourners. The public outpouring of grief was repugnant to her. She was the detached foreigner, whose cultural and religious background differed to that of the unassuming man who sat opposite.

Why she was not expecting his next question later puzzled her.

"Have you recently experienced the death of someone in your family?"

The bee sting of the question made her shoulders drop and the air escape from her lungs. She sat with her shoulders hunched over the table, fighting back her tears. Mr Hassan absorbed her account of the circumstances she had left behind in England, the death of a close relative, and the remorse and recriminations of a grieving family. She omitted what she had considered the most important details. Mr Hassan once again took control of the conversation. "We have to look after one another. Why, on the evening of the second funeral I apprehended a student who was watching you approach your house. He was concerned that you were walking home alone and without any light to guide you. We both waited until you were safely inside. A most unfortunate boy…" Mr Hassan's voice tailed off and paused a few seconds and then rather abruptly said. "Well, I must detain you no longer. We both have business to attend. Good afternoon, Miss Morgan." After paying the cafe boy, he waited for her to exit the premises and watched as she returned the way they had come until she rejoined the main street. When she turned to wave goodbye, he was already out of sight. Perhaps Mr Hassan had been embarrassed to think that he had been watching Morgan that night and had wanted a chance to explain in case she had been aware of the situation. A collision on the pavement between a cyclist and a market stall interrupted her thoughts as she sidestepped the mayhem of crushed tomatoes, the gesticulations, and the quarrelling of the cyclist and the stall owner.

Two weeks later, she found herself in another shared taxi in another marketplace on the Nigerian-Cameroon border, in the town of Ikom. Hi-Life was booming out of a plethora of cheaply made speakers that were attached to the shop and stall fronts, adding even more tinny resonance to the music. Different artists were competing to assail her ears. People mingled young, old, able-bodied, and crippled Nigerians and Cameroonians made up the mingled multitude. She hoped that the taxi driver would be able to find enough passengers to make it to the end of her journey for the day, a Government rest house in Mamfe on the Cameroonian side of the border, before dark.

A young man tapped her on the arm. "Madam, Madam, you do not want this taxi. It is very bad. Look at his wheels. See how the doors are held in place," he said, pointing to a variety of straps running from one side of the luggage rack, down over the door, under the chassis and back up to meet itself on the other side. She had a passing moment of anxiety, and with a lack of foresight of her age, banished any lingering fatalism, because this was the only vehicle heading to where she wanted to be next.

The driver appeared clutching a wheel brace, screaming in the face of the youth. The young man tutted, then shrugged his shoulders and walked away nonchalantly, now indifferent to Morgan's fate.

'Very safe, very safe, Madam. No mind stupid boy.' Morgan had become used to such exchanges, the Nigerian version of conflict resolution. No one usually got hurt. Morgan accepted that she would survive, or not survive because this was her only offer of transport. Wraith-like, out of the miasma of the market, her fellow passengers slowly assembled. The usual travelling salesmen, two in number. A market Mama, one of the many industrious and astute businesswomen who plied their wares across the length and breadth of West Africa by the trusty Peugeot 504. Or maybe not so trusty, this journey. The woman tried to haggle with the driver to accept the carriage of an extra basket, 'at a good price'. Travelling with this impressive woman was a younger, slimmer, apprentice Market Mama, perhaps her daughter. An elderly man and his wife, each of them cradling a hypnotised chicken in each arm, were another two of her fellow passengers. The last of their party, a sullen young man, disguised behind a pair of sunglasses, the lenses of which still displayed the make (fake) and the price. The driver invited Morgan to sit in between himself and his assistant, a boy of indeterminate teenage years. The other passengers vied for the highly prized window seats. The VIP in the front seat was glad that the chickens and their protective guardians were assigned to the back, furthest away from her.

The taxi limped its way out of the cacophony of the marketplace, which camouflaged the vehicle's coughing exhaust, and surprised everyone, within and without its rusting body, when it joined the main highway. Itinerant roadside stalls flashed by, displaying their wares of tin utensils, recycled goods from old tyres (flip-flops, mats, straps) and vying for the best position with hawkers carrying baskets selling fried fish, fried plantain, peppe chicken and ten kobo loaves. The stalls and vendors petered out as the taxi approached the line of trees at the edge of the rainforest. The driver turned to smile, indicating the direction in which they were travelling, nodding with delight. '*Good taxi, good taxi, get there in good time.*' Morgan wondered if the repeated phrase was more of an incantation of prayer than a statement of fact. It was to prove the former. Not an hour into the journey, the taxi spluttered to a stop. The assistant exited the vehicle through the windowless door. All the passengers climbed out, some the way of the assistant, others through the one remaining functioning door. A few passengers crowded around the boy who was tapping away at the engine, no doubt offering mechanical advice. Morgan sat at the roadside under the shade of the towering jungle trees.

With an enormous roar from both, passengers and engine sprang into action. The driver beckoned to his VIP, the frantic waving of his hands indicating her need to hurry before the engine failed again.

The taxi climbed and curled its way further into the trees. Trees seemed an inadequate word for the Goliaths of the forest. Passing through small villages, children carrying bamboo panniers of sliced pineapple shouted to them to 'Stop and Buy. Good for thirst' but the driver paid no heed. His hands grabbed the wheel and his eyes peered at the road ahead. They bounced and jolted, avoided potholes, skirted the rims of potholes and eventually came to a dead stop in the bowels of an enormous one just before an army checkpoint. Morgan's fellow passengers began shrieking, berating the driver. From a small, thatched hut, a tall, athletic soldier emerged, tucking his shirt inside his trousers with one hand and carrying a rifle in the other. At the same time, behind him, Morgan noticed a young girl scurrying out of the hut from which the soldier had just emerged. She was clutching her lap-lap to her chest with one hand and a bright pink bra in the other and disappeared behind the hut.

The soldier approached, taking in the scene before him. As he drew nearer, talking to the driver in French, his eyes and mouth were smiling. He was among the complaining passengers when he could contain his mirth no longer. He circled the taxi, prodding the tyres. Still laughing, he spoke to the driver. Morgan heard the word 'imbecile'. The young man who was seriously attached to his sunglasses translated for Morgan. 'I should lock you up', 'The taxi is not fit', 'You will have to stay here for the night'. For the first time during her travels, Morgan's recently acquired independent spirit and laissez-faire attitude to the potential threats and hazards to be encountered on these public transport journeys through West Africa began to drain away. Where would she sleep? There were no primitive toilets even. The soldier looked at Morgan, perhaps seeing the concern in her features. As he began to speak to her, he was interrupted by the sound of an approaching engine. A white, estate car. The passengers were about to throng around it when the soldier roared. They stopped in their tracks. The soldier authoritatively marched up to the car in a manner that underlined his military training. He put his head inside the driver's window, indicated in the direction of where the passengers were stood and called Morgan over. 'Madam, English, come here please'.

After formal introductions had been made and appreciation expressed on her behalf to both the soldier and the car's occupants, Morgan was relieved to be continuing her journey. She was even more relieved to find that the couple in the white estate car delved no further into her reasons for travelling alone in the jungles of Cameroon in particular, a holiday, and here in West Africa generally, other than she was a volunteer teacher halfway through her tour and using the school holidays to travel and explore. She politely enquired about their reasons for this day of travel. The couple, both in their forties, were publishers based in Lagos, on their way to visit a friend based in Cameroon. They looked at this short visit as a bit of R&R in the cool highlands, an escape from the traffic and pollution of the big city.

Morgan had sat back and enjoyed the comfort of the well-maintained car and the experience of not having to share cramped seats with complete strangers, with or without baskets of chicks or boxes of dried fish. She stared out the window. They were still climbing but the canopy of trees grew no thinner and the shafts of light penetrating the boughs and leaves gave no indication of the colour of the sky above them. She wound down the window. There was no air, just the smell of decay and moisture, combined with distant hints of fires.

"Regeneration of the forest floors," her driver had told her. Rustling in the trees was evidence of wildlife, monkeys most likely, but she only heard their shrieking and their calls to one another. *One sound was not unlike the ululation of the women at the school,* she thought.

Just on the cusp of darkness, the car ascended its final climb of the night and pulled into a clearing of trees in front of an old, colonial Government Rest house. "I am sure there will be room for you. Shall we meet for dinner about seven thirty?" said Mrs Purves, as her husband unloaded their luggage and Morgan's backpack from the car. Morgan smiled and nodded.

The remainder of Morgan's tour of West Africa continued in the same manner, with new experiences and fleeting acquaintances. Long waits in taxi parks, riding in Peugeot 504s of various ages, colours, and states of roadworthiness. She overnighted in a variety of hotels, Government Rest Houses and possibly brothels. One bar owner had rented her a room. He had handed her a bucket and proceeded to lock her room door behind him, telling her no matter what she heard, she was to stay inside the room until the morning. A few minutes later he had returned ahead of schedule, tapping quietly on her door, identified himself, unlocked the door to the room, and on its threshold, handed her a warm bottle of Coke and two bananas. She did not sleep that night. The thumping of the disco, the angry voices, and the scuffles that sometimes spilt out of the bar made it impossible.

Once she broke the cardinal rule for European travel in West Africa. She travelled overnight, and in doing so, had submitted herself to the inconvenience of military roadblocks. Her fellow passengers invariably tried to charm the soldiers with obsequies and flattery in the hope that they would not demand too big a 'dash'. At one such roadblock, a young woman travelling in that taxi intervened on Morgan's behalf when a soldier indicated that Morgan should step out. She accompanied Morgan to the barricade where the soldiers had made a fire to stave off the cold. One produced a piece of paper. "He want you for pen pal," her guardian angel smirked, safe in the knowledge that the soldier could not speak or understand English as well as her. But that was not his reason.

"You British?" he asked of Morgan, nodding on her behalf. "You choose football teams for me," he said as he thrust a Football Pool coupon before her face. She looked back at the imploring faces of her fellow passengers, all listening intently to the soldier's demands.

"Two, fifteen, twenty-three, thirty, thirty-eight," she gabbled hurriedly. The soldier ticked his coupon as quickly as Morgan volleyed the numbers at him.

The soldier beamed and slapped his thighs, saying, "Yes! I think so!" He gestured for Morgan and the guardian angel to return to the taxi while his companion lifted the barricade and waved the taxi through. The relief of her fellow passengers was palpable and vocal, singing together in a language common to them all. Morgan hummed the tune to indulge in the camaraderie.

Mr Hassan had been correct. We do have to look after one another, she thought. It was these moments that she would cherish and remember, a week later back in her schoolhouse, as she lay on her bed in the relative comfort of her room. Not the dangers, not the near misses. Not the dead bodies, casualties of traffic accidents that had sometimes happened only minutes before she had arrived on the scene, as cars, taxis, and Mammy wagons hurtled down highways. She believed she better understood why her fellow travellers had become impervious and hardened to the covered casualties of the roadsides.

She now accepted why her colleagues could quickly go about their business following the death of two pupils. The country had suffered thousands of casualties incurred during the recent civil war. People had suffered loss and grief, some at younger ages than herself, and others on a much larger scale. Things were not always as they had seemed to her in Africa – Nigeria. She resolved to be more open-minded, less critical, and more positive for the remainder of her time at the school and in the country.

She had returned to the school a week before the term began. The return had enveloped her in familiarity and this feeling brought her comfort and put her in a positive frame of mind. Her house, the furniture, the whirring of the fan and the noise of John adjusting his belongings in his small Boys' Quarters. "Welcome back, Madam," he had beamed as he carried her rucksack into the house. There were very few teaching staff around but some of the students had also returned. If they lived in very remote areas at greater distances, they had to time their returns to coincide with the weekly or monthly lorries journeying from the village to the towns.

Back at school early, for amusement and to pass the time, they kicked a ball around a dusty field, walked down to the neighbouring girls' college hoping to practise their chat up lines, or volunteered for care-taking duties around the school in return for the extra week's board and lodging.

On the first morning of her return, she had risen early, drank a coffee and made her way to her classroom. As she passed Mrs Okorafor's staff quarters, she heard the babble of small children and the admonishing voice of their mother. Then laughter, all of them contributing to that very particular form of music. A happy house, despite the scoldings and wailing of young children. As she crossed the courtyard, she saw the approaching figure of Mr Hassan, who waved in greeting while continuing his way towards the boys' dormitories. Mr Hassan lived off-site. Morgan considered his presence and acknowledged that he must be working additional days of the holiday as a Boarding Master. She reminded herself that she must enquire about his sister-in-law and her family.

She made herself busy in the classroom, shifting tables and chairs, cleaning the blackboard and dusting the six weeks' worth of red sand that had accumulated on the bookshelves. The books had been placed in the Stores for the duration of the holidays. The Stores would be locked so she collected the key that was hanging in the Staffroom and crossed the dusty courtyard. As she placed the key in the lock, she caught sight of a leg poking from the side of the store. *One of the assistant storekeepers*, she thought. The key was jammed in the lock, and as she teased it to turn, she noticed that the leg moved slightly and at the same time she heard a low groan. *He is drunk,* she thought. But then she froze, willing herself not to investigate. She was pushed forward by a recurrence of a feeling, something which she thought she had successfully buried.

On the ground, cradled in the imprint of his body in the sand, lay a student. She recognised him. She also recognised the meaning of the red necklace around his throat as it dispensed its small beads of liquid into the brown earth. She dropped to her knees and instinctively tore at the sleeve of her shirt, to place the fabric against the wound to stem the flow of blood. She did not hear her own voice as she was screaming for help. She was not aware of the scurries of bodies approaching her from all directions. Mr Hassan, Mrs Okorafor and the students, perspiring and gasping from the interrupted football game. She screamed, again and again, "Eddie, no, no, Eddie!"

Someone, Mrs Okorafor perhaps, had wrapped her in her arms and led her to the staffroom, and had held her still until the screams subsided. Another figure, a student, passed her a cup, and the soft voice of her colleague implored her to drink. The liquid was hot and bitter. Her teeth chattered and her body shook. "You saw a ghost, my Child?" asked the older woman.

Morgan nodded. "My brother, Eddie. I could do nothing to save him." Her eyes searched the room, agitated, beseeching. Mr Hassan tip-toed into the room. "Musa will live. The cut was not very deep. A cry for attention, I think."

She wailed, "But Eddie, he cried for help and we did not hear him, I did not hear him. He died."

She remembered nothing after her staffroom confessional. Not being carried back to her house, not being laid on her bed. Not the doctor's visit, nor the bedside vigil of Mrs Okorafor and sister Rose, the young nun, a teacher at the girls' school.

She awoke the following morning, her head heavy, and her eyes stinging from the shining sun penetrating the curtains. She heard noises in the kitchen, pans, cups rattling and the murmur of voices. The door opened, and in walked Mrs Okorafor, carrying a bowl of orange segments and a cup of coffee. "I told your boy to go to work and not to worry. I will look after you until sister Rose returns. She had to attend prayers at the convent."

Morgan whispered thank you but could say no more. Mrs Okorafor filled the silence with details of the previous day's events she imagined that Morgan would want to hear. The student, Musa, was recovering. He was being looked after by a cousin who lived in the town. The boy was confused about his life. He thought he loved another student, a boy. Other boys teased him and his older brother beat him. He was afraid to return home. He hid himself away, among the bushes, inside the stores, scavenging for food at night. Morgan did not challenge Mrs Okorafor's accounts. She listened at the same time as she reconstructed her own memories of another boy, older, in another culture, in another country, one as unforgiving and as alienating as Musa was experiencing in the present.

A voice called out beyond the bedroom door. Mrs Okorafor went to see who it was. She returned. "I will have to leave you. My youngest needs feeding. sister Rose will be here soon."

"I will be fine, thank you. I think I should get up and dress."

Morgan closed the door of her bedroom and crossed the inner courtyard of her house. She met sister Rose as she walked into the kitchen. The young nun smiled shyly and enquired if she wanted a drink. Morgan returned her smile. "Yes please." She went to sit down in the living room. She looked out through the open doors, across the scrub of land that separated the staff quarters from the school, and beyond that, more scrubby land that would eventually yield into the

Sahara. Out of the growing heat haze emerged Mr Hassan. He stood apprehensively at the open door. Morgan beckoned him into the house and indicated he should sit down. He sat with his back to the sideboard and Eddie's face appeared to sit on the man's shoulder.

They exchanged pleasantries, Mr Hassan accepted the offer of a glass of water from sister Rose who then quietly took a dining chair into the shade of the courtyard and left the two teachers alone.

"You saw a ghost yesterday?" Morgan was not surprised at the question and did not find it intrusive. She was calm.

"Not a ghost exactly, but bad memories filled my mind." Morgan stared intently over Mr Hassan's right shoulder.

He turned his head to follow her gaze. "This is Eddie?"

"Yes, Eddie, my brother." Morgan heaved a sigh that not only expired her lungs but was the starting point for her release of grief, something which she had contained within herself for too long. It had been a poison to her, rendering her incapable of reforming her relationship with her parents, her elder sister and her remaining brother, and preventing her from experiencing new, meaningful relationships. At their chance meeting in Jos months before, Morgan had told Mr Hassan only of a death in her family. Now she found herself recounting the reasons and circumstances of her brother's suicide, her anger at him for leaving her, anger at herself for not understanding his torment and remorse, for not being able to stand at his side to fight his demons, to help him become stronger.

How much Mr Hassan understood of what he was privileged to learn about Morgan's past, she could not gauge, but this kind man sat and nodded and let her talk without interruption.

She stopped talking and in that awkward silence, Mr Hassan rose to hand her a box of tissues. Morgan had been unaware of the quiet tears dropping onto her lap.

Mr Hassan cleared his throat and began to speak, hesitantly, "Perhaps your ghost has been good for you." She did feel better now, but what of tonight, tomorrow, years to come?

Mr Hassan continued his story. The Crisis, as she heard Nigerians refer to the recent Civil War, left the once-warring factions living with their ghosts. The ghosts had to be accepted but sometimes ignored for the sake of the haunted who needed to continue with their lives. He illustrated his account with the experiences of the school staff, Christian and Muslim, but it was Mrs Okorafor's story that caused her most discomfort.

During the war, Mrs Okorafor had returned to her village following the heavy fighting that had delayed her journey home. Her village had been destroyed and in the smoking ruins of her house, she discovered the bodies of her mother and her own three young children, their throats cut.

Mrs Okorafor's grief was overwhelming, her desire to live but the knowledge of a new life inside her helped her to talk to her ghosts and eventually, their appearances became less frequent as she and her husband rebuilt their lives with a new family and in a new town. "Did she see ghosts yesterday?" Morgan contemplated the awful scene Mrs Okorafor had come upon as she was out walking with her children.

"Perhaps," replied Mr Hassan. "But she recognised that realisation within you, that the present can sometimes reawaken bad memories."

The sensible, matter-of-fact, sometimes grumbling bereaved mother and teacher, had come to Morgan's aide despite her own ghosts and bad memories. Morgan was nurturing her understanding of her misconceptions of her fellow teachers' attitudes to dying and death.

They had experienced normal and grotesque abnormal events in abnormal times, and so much of it in a relatively short period. The shrieking of sorrow was necessary however, one's environment and culture determined one's responses.

Mr Hassan left and walked back into the fiercer heat haze of the afternoon. Morgan reassured a reluctant sister Rose that she could return to the convent and that Morgan was able to look after herself. She promised sister Rose she would send for help if she felt overwhelmed by her sadness and sorrow.

When she had the house to herself, Morgan assembled her afternoon's work at the dining table. A glass of water, a writing pad and pen, and the photograph of Eddie. Before she wrote the letter to her parents, she rehearsed what she wanted to write in conversation with her brother.

The new term began with the customary three-hour staff meeting. The headmaster's voice droned on in the overcrowded room punctuated regularly by the swish of the ceiling fan. Some staff had endured fighting shuffles to occupy the back row of chairs where they could fall asleep. Unluckily, Morgan found herself on the curving front row directly opposite Mrs Okorafor who acknowledged her by raising one eyebrow, which seemed to say, "How are you today?" Morgan nodded and smiled. Mrs Okorafor's reply was to nod slowly with a satisfied grin. Then retaining Morgan's attention, she raised both eyebrows while rolling her eyes in the direction of the headmaster. "What is this foolish man going on about?" Morgan smiled into her lap, hoping nobody noticed her shoulders laughing.

As the Headmaster left the room, there was a scurry among the staff to join the queue in front of the hot water urn. Mrs Okorafor had Larry Tanaka cornered against a wall, demanding to know how many breastfeeding breaks she had in the new timetable. Mr Hassan was talking to a colleague about the new line-up of the latest Military Government. He broke off when he saw that Morgan was standing alone.

"Are you ready to face the challenges of teaching Romeo and Juliet to your new fifth-form class, Miss Morgan?"

"Yes, I am Mr Hassan. I have applied for a British Council touring theatre company to perform some of the play here in the school."

"Excellent! Excellent! Miss Morgan."

They were interrupted by another volunteer inviting Morgan to join him and some other teachers for a drink at a bar in town. She did not hesitate in accepting and after his disappearance, she continued telling Mr Hassan her news.

"I have written to my parents to tell them I will visit them for Christmas. But I will be back in January," she emphasised.

Mr Hassan's eyes were smiling as she left the staffroom to make her way to the classrooms. Outside the Headmaster's office, she noticed an older student leaning against the railings. He stood up to his full height as she passed. "Isa? It is Isa? How is Musa?"

The youth looked embarrassed and his eyes searched the vicinity for eavesdroppers before he met her eyes and whispered his reply, "He is very well, Madam. You are very kind to ask."

Morgan knew that this conversation was at an end but as she walked away, she called back to Isa, "When you see him, tell him to come to see me so that we can set up extra lessons." If Isa did reply, she did not hear him, as the bell for the students' lunch rang out across the campus.

Myra

A promise of a breeze passed over her face as she lay dressed on top of her bed. She held her breath in anticipation but the curtains at the window defied her and remained as stiff and as formal as two sentries at their posts. The air was thick and muggy, heavy with the scent of frangipani. Distant thunder rolls collaborated with the absent breeze to endorse her discomfort. She reached for the glass of water at her bedside table and took a long gulp.

She listened to the rustle of the palms, envious of their grace and sway while she felt trapped and suffocating on top of the bed. She peered through the curtains which acted as a filter for the sunlight and subdued the colours of the flowers standing proud in the garden. Her daughter had called them "her jewels" and had often threaded them into a necklace to wear around her neck. Myra missed her daughter at that age. Her smile, her laughter, and her sunny nature.

What would Myra be doing now back in England? Working in the dress department of BHS or operating a till at a Co-op supermarket checkout? She had forsaken that life, as ordinary and as menial as it was, to travel thousands of miles to accompany her husband to the land of his birth and childhood when he inherited his mother's house and land.

"Just wait, Myra. The sun shines here all day and there is no sitting in front of a coal fire to keep warm." She smiled at the memory of that day when his eyes shone and he smiled, the truest of smiles his features had displayed in a long time.

She felt that she had owed it to him and their young children, to move away from everything she had known, the grand buildings, the river, the parks, so that they may leave behind the bullying and prejudice that was creeping increasingly into their lives. Her husband, then, was a good man who worked hard to provide for their family. Myra had been ostracised by her family for marrying a man of colour (not their chosen words) and they could not and would not look behind the colour of his skin to see his even character and his many other qualities. The week before they had left England to start their new lives in the Caribbean, she had gone to the home of her parents to say goodbye. Her father had stood in the doorway blocking her entrance to the house and her tearful mother was silhouetted against the backlighting of the long inner hallway. She felt her cheeks dampen at that last image of her mother. That was over thirty years ago. She had lived in this house, on this island, longer than she had lived in England.

Why hadn't she asked Leonard, her husband, more questions about the move? When he spoke of the town, she expected an English-sized town, not some loose settlement of houses spread over two square miles. When he spoke of neighbours, she imagined chatting to them over a fence, not having to walk half a mile to the nearest house. She soon found out that the neighbours were distant not only in miles but also in attitude and slow to offer friendship or display compassion. They did not want to talk to the English woman.

They could not understand her accent and asked others, irritably, why didn't she sound like the Queen?

She heard a clucking outside on the veranda. One of the chickens had ventured beyond the yard in search of a tasty morsel. She was proud of her chickens. Round and plump, free of lice. Not like the chickens she had found when she had first arrived at the property. As she stepped out of the taxi and took in her surroundings, her body shuddered with fear and disgust. Leonard and the children had busied themselves removing suitcases and packing cases from the roof and trunk of the two taxis which had hauled them and their belongings along the rutted, red laterite roads from the distant port. She was transfixed at the sight of scrawny, bald chickens pecking at a heap of household rubbish. The smell of putrid, decaying vegetation was never to leave her. Not even the array of scents from the variety of flowers and bushes around the garden could wholly insulate her from the dominant smell of the jungle. For that was where Leonard had brought her, to an old wooden house with a tin roof that sat in the midst of an overgrown garden fashioned out of the jungle.

In time, she, Leonard, and the children, and sometimes help from her husband's extended family, cut back the grass with machetes. Their hard, blistering work revealed avocado, lemon, and grapefruit trees. She learnt to appreciate the fruit and the shade of the mango trees. The butterflies and birds were cheerful spectacles. But she had never learnt to appreciate the house. The wood stove occupied a corner of the main room. She struggled to cook meals on it. Water was drawn from an outside pump and the privy was housed in a wooden hut some way from the main house. At first, she and the children went to relieve themselves as a group, taking turns to use the toilet while the others stood outside patrolling the walls of the hut to shoo away cockroaches, beetles, and geckos in order to give the nervous occupant a modicum of calm and relaxation. What passed for the kitchen sink and in a small room off the inner corridor, the bathtub, was dirty with years of accumulated soap suds and grime. Her hands had become sore trying to erase the tide marks. She had given up in despair.

In those first days, weeks and months, Leonard had been sensitive to the problems she struggled to overcome in her alien surroundings. He promised changes for the property. He would have power brought to the house and she could have an electric stove and a small refrigerator. He would build an extra bedroom for them so their sons and daughter would not have to share as they got older. The toilet would stay outside because it was more hygienic but he would improve it, and build an outside shower. This turned out as a cubicle, with three sides of wood and one side shower curtain, the water fed from a metal bucket hung from a pole, with holes drilled into the bottom and a separate floor-standing bucket with a ladle. In the beginning, the children had thought this was fun but as they got older; they canvassed their father for an inside bathroom. By this time, Leonard had grown tired of his family's demands for home improvements. Money seemed to become in short supply and Leonard began to stay away from home for increasingly longer periods, sometimes a night, sometimes for days, looking for extra work or spending time with friends and family at the grog shop. Myra had not the time to feel sorry for herself or ruminate on her situation. She just did. Did the cooking. Did the washing. Did the gardening. Helped the children with their homework, and looked after the chickens. Once the youngest child had matriculated and left home, she often found herself alone with the chickens, considering her past and future lives.

The memory of all that hard work to stand still, making no progress out of their meagre existence, had exhausted Myra and she dozed off. When she woke again, the sun had passed over the veranda and the room was in welcome shade. But still no breeze. The distant sound of an engine labouring up a hill told her that school had finished for the day and the babble of children's voices carried to her as they made their way from the school bus to their scattered houses. She wondered, '*if her grandchildren had finished at their school for the day. None of them lived locally, their parents having migrated to the proper town or to the bigger island, a four-hour ferry journey away.*'

She heard movement in the house. It was a neighbour, and relative of her husband, Beatrice. The recent arrival of a young pastor in the parish had re-energised some of his parishioners. He espoused good works as a way to recompense for former sins. Beatrice had been persuaded to look in daily on her relative's wife who was now ill. She made tea, washed pots and did the laundry, or anything else she saw fit. She was not one for much conversation but her manner towards Myra had improved and she rattled off her gossip about people Myra did not know. She was like a newsreader, imparting information and not expecting a reply. Myra became accustomed to her presence.

The soft slap of Beatrice's shuffle down the corridor competed with the noise of grinding gears of a car on its way up to the house.

"It be her. You want I make tea?" Myra nodded in assent and pulled herself up to rest against the pillows. She noticed the small suitcase behind the door. It came back to her how this day was to end.

She could hear greetings being exchanged between Beatrice and her visitor. Mrs Williams, a retired teacher, returned from living in England after thirty years. She had sought Myra out when she had heard about a poor English woman, mostly alone and languishing in poverty, up in the hills. Myra had discovered Mrs Williams had arrived and lived in the city that had been her home about the same time she had left it. They exchanged reminiscences of the areas they both knew and the most recent returnee described the changes she had witnessed during her life there.

It had been Mrs Williams who had first shown alarm at Myra's weight loss when she had not seen her after an interval of a month. Leonard hardly acknowledged her even when he was at home. It was Mrs Williams who had arranged her doctor's appointment and accompanied her to the subsequent hospital appointments. She would not hear of Myra travelling in discomfort on the unreliable and overcrowded public buses. Who wants to share a seat with a crate of chickens on their way to market, she had protested. Myra had not made many trips to the town during all her years on the island. As a family, they had rarely made the journey. The fares were too much of an expense. Leonard often upgraded his succession of second and third-hand motorbikes but had never been able to save enough money for a truck or a car. But the journeys to the hospital became too much for her and with the intervention of Mrs Williams and the pastor, a place had been arranged for her at a local hospice. "Respite care," they had said.

"Are you ready, Myra?" Mrs Williams asked quietly as she picked up the suitcase. Myra swung her legs to the side of the bed and planted both feet on the wooden floor. She made faltering steps to the door and along the corridor. Beatrice hovered by the sink in the process of washing the teacups.

"The Lord be with you, Myra," she said, and in a moment of unexpected emotion, dabbed her eyes with a corner of her apron.

Mrs Williams helped her down the steps. She sat in the front passenger seat and as Mrs Williams put the case into the trunk, Myra turned to look at the house, perhaps for the last time. She should feel more than this tiredness. The house had never felt like her home. It was a place of chores and sleep. She need not worry about her chickens. In time, their ownership would transfer to Beatrice, or another neighbour eager to add to their flocks.

Mrs Williams drove slowly, taking care to avoid the large ruts and potholes, all the while remonstrating her fellow road users for bad driving and lack of courtesy. The windows were down but the breeze was warm and it brought no comfort to the car's occupants. Trees distant houses, and plantations gave way to the better-grade roads of the port. The car turned into the grounds of the Cathedral, and they drove down the side of it and parked in front of a large lawned area. The group of low white buildings occupied a slight rise at the far side of the lawn. As well as a hospice, the buildings housed a day centre and an old people's home.

Myra and Mrs Williams were greeted by a young nurse who showed them to a room, a single bed, and a bedside cupboard on which there was a lamp. On the wall facing the bed was a cork board and pinned on to it were three postcards depicting scenes of Myra's real home, Liverpool. By this time, Myra was too tired and beyond conversation to express her thanks to Mrs Williams, because it was she who would have pinned them there. She smiled weakly, first sat, then lay on top of the bed. The curtains at the window billowed in a breeze blowing onshore and Myra felt it caress her body, first over her feet, travelling up and finally over her face. She inhaled deeply. Her mind cleared and she relaxed but willed herself to stay awake so that she might enjoy the unfamiliar cool of the late afternoon.